A TRILOGY OF DESIRES
ROGER & LEONIE PARTS I-III

STEELE INTERNATIONAL, INC. A BILLIONAIRES ROMANCE SERIES BOOKS 3-5

CHARMAINE LOUISE SHELTON

CONTENTS

Free Book   vii
Also By Charmaine Louise Shelton   ix
About STEELE International, Inc. A Billionaires
Romance Series   xi

IGNITE MY DESIRES ROGER & LEONIE PART I

About Ignite My Desires Roger & Leonie Part I   5
1. Prologue   7
2. Roger   14
3. Leonie   24
4. Roger   33
5. Leonie   42
6. Roger   50
7. Roger   59
8. Leonie   71
9. Leonie   78
10. Roger   87
11. Roger   94
12. Leonie   100
13. Leonie   107
14. Roger   118
15. Leonie   129
16. Roger   135
17. Roger   144
18. Leonie   153
19. Roger   162
20. Leonie   169
21. Leonie   175
22. Roger   184
23. Roger   189

24. Leonie 199
25. Leonie 211
26. Roger 221
27. Leonie 228
28. Roger 243

STOKE MY DESIRES ROGER & LEONIE PART II

About Stoke My Desires Roger & Leonie
Part II 261
1. Leonie 263
2. Roger 275
3. Roger 282
4. Leonie 291
5. Roger 299
6. Leonie 311
7. Roger 319
8. Roger 330
9. Leonie 340
10. Leonie 350
11. Roger 364
12. Roger 374
13. Leonie 386
14. Roger 393
15. Leonie 399
16. Leonie 409
17. Leonie 415
18. Roger 428
19. Leonie 434
20. Roger 446
21. Roger 451
22. Leonie 460
23. Roger 472
24. Leonie 480
25. Roger 489
26. Leonie 498

27. Roger   506
28. Leonie   518

JUSTIFY MY DESIRES ROGER & LEONIE PART III

About Justify My Desires Roger & Leonie
Part III   529
1. Roger   531
2. Leonie   542
3. Roger   549
4. Roger   555
5. Leonie   564
6. Roger   573
7. Leonie   582
8. Roger   592
9. Roger   601
10. Leonie   613
11. Leonie   627
12. Roger   636
13. Leonie   644
14. Roger   659
15. Leonie   665
16. Leonie   672
17. Roger   682
18. Leonie   690
19. Roger   697
20. Leonie   705
21. Roger   717
22. Leonie   725
23. Leonie   732
24. Roger   746
25. Leonie   756
26. Roger   765
27. Leonie   775
28. Roger   786
The STEELE Family   795

Note From Charmaine Louise   797

Coming Next: A Trilogy of Desires Malcolm &
Starr Parts I-III   799

The Series Continues…   809

Welcome to CharmaineLouise — The Sensual
Lifestyle   811

FREE BOOK

Get the start of the STEELE International, Inc. A Billionaires Romance Series with *Discover My Desires Sebastian & Lola Prequel* FREE!

Click Cover Below or visit **bit.ly/CLBooksNewsletter** to subscribe to my newsletter for latest news and launches, books from my author friends, and sizzling reads in book promotions. Plus, start reading the steamy billionaire romance *Series Prequel* of Sebastian Steele and Lola Lewis.

Their stories. Their discovery of unknown desires...

FREE BOOK!

EXCLUSIVE FOR SUBSCRIBERS!

ALSO BY CHARMAINE LOUISE SHELTON

STEELE INTERNATIONAL, INC.
A BILLIONAIRES ROMANCE SERIES

Discover My Desires Sebastian & Lola Prequel
(Available Exclusively to Subscribers)

Fulfill My Desires Sebastian & Lola Part I

Heighten My Desires Sebastian & Lola Part II

Ignite My Desires Roger & Leonie Part I

Stoke My Desires Roger & Leonie Part II

Justify My Desires Roger & Leonie Part III

Deepen My Desires Sebastian & Lola Part III

Capture My Desires Malcolm & Starr Part I

Embrace My Desires Malcolm & Starr Part II

Cherish My Desires Malcolm & Starr Part III

A Trilogy of Desires Sebastian & Lola Parts I-III

A Trilogy of Desires Roger & Leonie Parts I-III

A Trilogy of Desires Malcolm & Starr Parts I-III

Series Extras

Series Playlist

STEELE INTERNATIONAL, INC. - JACKSON CORPORATION
A BILLIONAIRES ROMANCE SERIES CROSSOVER

Tempt My Desires Lachlan & Haley Part I

Tease My Desires Lachlan & Haley Part II

Grant My Desires Lachlan & Haley Part III

Intrigue My Desires Harris & Kat Part I

Decode My Desires Harris & Kat Part II

Honor My Desires Harris & Kat Patt III

A Trilogy of Desires Lachlan & Haley Parts I-III

A Trilogy of Desires Harris & Kat Parts I-III

Series Extras

Series Playlist

ABOUT STEELE INTERNATIONAL, INC. A BILLIONAIRES ROMANCE SERIES

Welcome to the titillating world of the multibillion-dollar global company and the love affairs of the family that controls it.

STEELE International, Inc. is a series of interconnecting Billionaire romance. Follow the Steele family as they fly around the world chasing the women they love and their happily ever afters. Get ready for glitz, glamour, and steamy romance books. What's better than that? The Jet-set Lifestyle has never been hotter...

The Desires Series is not for the tea set; it's for the top-shelf vodka straight up in a pretty crystal glass coterie!

Don't miss any of the sizzling romance books in the STEELE International, Inc. A Billionaires Romance Series:

Discover My Desires Sebastian & Lola Prequel

(Available Exclusively to Subscribers)

Fulfill My Desires Sebastian & Lola Part I

Heighten My Desires Sebastian & Lola Part II

Ignite My Desires Roger & Leonie Part I

Stoke My Desires Roger & Leonie Part II

Justify My Desires Roger & Leonie Part III

Deepen My Desires Sebastian & Lola Part III

Capture My Desires Malcolm & Starr Part I

Embrace My Desires Malcolm & Starr Part II

Cherish My Desires Malcolm & Starr Part III

A Trilogy of Desires Sebastian & Lola Parts I-III

A Trilogy of Desires Roger & Leonie Parts I-III

A Trilogy of Desires Malcolm & Starr Parts I-III

Series Extras

Series Playlist

Ignite my
DESIRES

ROGER & LEONIE PART I

Charmaine Louise Shelton

I dedicate this novel to never giving up on coupe de foudre and second chances.

Fulfill Your Desires.

xoxo
Charmaine Louise

ABOUT IGNITE MY DESIRES
ROGER & LEONIE PART I

Leonie The Lion Beaulieu stunning supermodel based in Paris; who's fun loving, confident, easygoing with a budding career in residential interior design. Every man wants her. But her heart's broken once.

Roger The Responsible Steele president of his family's luxury real estate empire's residential properties division; intense, focused control freak meets bubbly supermodel who upends his structured world. He let her get away once... Not this time.

Can they reignite their coup de foudre? Or won't lightning strike twice?

Roger and Leonie's second chance billionaire romance story takes you on their journey around the globe—Cabo San Lucas, Nice, Paris, New York...

Their love story is a standalone second chance romance trilogy in the series. Get a glimpse of their dynamism in other books.

Anthem: "Vogue" Madonna
https://www.youtube.com/watch?v=GuJQSAiODqI

Playlist:
https://www.youtube.com/playlist?list=
PLXwYvn0e218Bx18MlEj1svXS-8-NachjU

Visit CharmaineLouiseBooks.com

PROLOGUE

ROGER

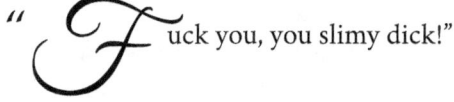

"**F**uck you, you slimy dick!"

CRASH!

All I saw was red as that bastard Giovanni Mattei slid his hand up the dress of the blonde who'd been eyeing him for the past hour. We're at my future sister-in-law's opening night party for her luxury lingerie company, Lola's Coterie Dubai. The entire Steele clan is present to support her latest endeavor in her global expansion goal. Lola opened the flagship in Paris five years ago, followed by a location in London three years later.

Her initial goal to open boutiques in the United States

started with New York and Las Vegas. But since meeting with STEELE Intentional, Inc. and my eldest brother Sebastian, the President of the Retail Properties Division, Lola's expansion now includes Abu Dhabi, Dubai, and Beverly Hills. Lola's Coterie Abu Dhabi opened last week, tonight is Dubai, and in a month another boutique will open in STEELE Galleria Rodeo Drive.

That fateful meeting a year ago between the two companies started a chain reaction. Sebastian and Lola dated within the week. Even moving in together. He surprised everyone since he was a notorious playboy.

Then, the spark hit me to fall for Leonie *The Lion* Beaulieu, the stunning supermodel, muse for Lola's Coterie, and Lola's best friend. Or as she calls it, *un coupe de foudre* —stroke of lightning, love at first sight. So we thought...

All I want to do right now is strike Mattei.

For the past year I've had to look at his smug face as he paraded around Monte Carlo, Las Vegas, Paris, the fucking globe with my woman on his arm.

Or at least she was for a brief two months.

The wildest two months of my life. I never knew what to expect with Leonie. One minute passionately wrapped in each other's arms, her long legs around my neck, my dick buried deep in her tight core. The next arguing about her not finishing reading assignments for her interior design degree from the Paris American Academy. The next, her feline amber eyes gazing lovingly at me to only narrow in anger when I reprimanded her lack of focus. My head aches as much as my dick just from thinking about Leonie.

What a fucking rollercoaster. We held on as long as we could before an argument went further than normal. Yeah, we had smaller disagreements. Bu nothing too major. The last one, though. No cuddles and coos of apology or incredible makeup sex could bridge the chasm we created. Words said, struck a chord and there was no going back. At least not at the time.

I let her get away from me once—well, I contributed hugely to her dumping me—and I won't let it happen again. First, I have to deal with the asshole she keeps going back to, fucking Mattei. He's always waiting in the wings to capture her with his charm. Only now she's distracted with the opening, as it's a work event for her representing Lola's Coterie. Mattei takes advantage of her lack of attention to *God's Gift* and shoves his hand up another woman's dress. Asshole.

Blondie wasn't the only one who couldn't keep her eyes or hands off the Italian playboy. Add the billionaire and nobleman status and he's irresistible to certain women. And any woman is irresistible to him... Without fail he flirted right back—a wink, a sly pinch on their rump, an unnecessary brush of his groin against their ass as he passed by them. Ridiculous.

Now observing Mattei and his shenanigans pisses me off. The self-proclaimed *God Has Shown Favor* shows only disrespect for Leonie. I would hate for his stupidity to upset her on such an important night. She deserves so much more. So I can't stop myself from telling him just that.

"You could at least have enough respect for the woman you're here with, then to feel up another woman within eyesight of her."

The sleaze turns his gaze towards me. His eyes take me in from head to toe as if assessing my seriousness.

Yeah, ass, I'm serious as fuck. If she's with him, he needs to act like a man and not a randy teenager who can't control himself. It's the middle child in me that demands balance and loyalty. I want Leonie for myself, but until she's fully mine again, he will respect her.

"What I do is of no concern of yours, Steele."

I'm surprised he knows who I am since we've never spoken. He must recognize my shock as his smirk widens.

"Oh, I know who you are, Steele," he starts. "You're the loser who can't keep Leonie satisfied. So she keeps coming back to me. You see..."

He leans closer for dramatically to pseudo-whisper. But loud enough so the blonde can hear his words.

"I know how to make her cum so hard on my big dick screaming my name, she forgets all about your sorry ass."

Fuck Roger *The Responsible* who knows better than to act crazy in public. This asshole just sent me over the edge with a vision of him pounding into my woman. No... Fucking... Way.

"Fuck you, you slimy dick!"

CRASH!

In a blind rage, my fist connects with Mattei's jaw and he falls back into mannequins. As they topple to the floor, he recovers and clips me with a punch to the chest. Damn, I didn't expect the pretty boy to know how to fight. We're even at six feet, three inches. I have ten pounds of muscle on him, though. Plus, I spar regularly. I use both size and skill to my advantage.

We exchange only a few blows before my brothers Malcolm and Harris grab Mattei. Luc Montaigne, Lola's mentor, and Sebastian grab me. Security stands by, ready to step in to take over.

Still pissed, I struggle against their hold as does Mattei, who tries to shrug my brothers off. Unmatched by their combined strength, Mattei and I can only glare at each other. Itching to square off again. I give two fucks as the crowd stares on in silence. I want to finish this shit once and for all.

Until the figure of my father Morgan, the Steele Patriarch and Alpha Dom, storms over with such a wrathful look that Mattei and I stand stock-still.

Fuck. My father is pissed.

"You will cease this outrageous, infantile behavior at once and apologize to Ms. Lewis and her guests. Then leave. Do… you… understand?" Morgan issues his edict.

All eyes turn to him, including that dickhead Mattei. Morgan's Dom stare knocks us down several notches. In fact, we're below ground by the time he finishes his chastisement of us. Everyone else stands in silent awe of his power.

Morgan's words reset my out-of-control brain. I shake my head to dispel the angry red haze. Sure, Mattei was disrespectful to Leonie and said some stupid ass shit. But I never should have allowed it to get to me. It sent me on a downward spiral of jealousy, driven by an intense need to flatten him for having what is mine.

No matter the circumstances, I should have maintained command of the situation. Particularly at a highly public event held by STEELE. Before Leonie, this would never have happened. It goes against every cell in my physiology.

I gain control before Mattei and turn to seek Lola out in the crowd gathered around. I hope she's not as upset as I imagine. I spot her standing between my mother and Leonie. My younger sister Haley and Lola's assistants Blair and Billie stand near them. All have shocked expressions on their faces. Damn.

I notice Mattei tries to walk to them. But Malcolm puts his hand on his chest to stop him since he recognizes that I headed their way already. Mattei has the sense to back down.

"Lola, I apologize for my poor behavior. Please forgive me," I beseech her.

With grace, she nods her head and accepts my outstretched hand. Her eyes meet mine before she searches for Sebastian, to whom she nods, too.

I turn my attention to the other women who stare at me, surprised by my unusual outburst.

"Mother, Leonie, I ask for your forgiveness, too," I say to both of them, but my eyes lock on Leonie whose amber gaze shies away.

My shoulders rise and fall on a disappointed sigh in response to her reaction. Not wishing to prolong the situation and knowing now is not the time to address Leonie's dismissal, I turn to the guests and apologize to them. Then excuse myself from the event.

As I pass Sebastian, he squeezes my shoulder to offer me support. I nod without breaking my stride. I don't even wait to hear Mattei's apology. I have to get out of here. Try to save some face from my lack of decorum.

Minutes after I exit the boutique, I feel my mobile vibrate in my trousers' pocket. I know who it is without even checking the name on the display. I answer on the first ring.

"Sorry. That was a shitshow Lola did not deserve. Does she really forgive me? Are you going to kick my ass?"

Of course it's Sebastian. I'm sure our father told him to call me or he would. I'd rather deal with my eldest brother than the elder Steele…

I must sound like a wreck since Sebastian doesn't go in on me, as would be his right. It's his woman's event for our family's company. He's the heir apparent to CEO and

Chairman of the Board. So besides being the oldest who leads his siblings, he's the future leader of our multibillion-dollar business at which each of us leads divisions. I'm thankful when Sebastian doesn't add to my ill ease.

"Yes, and no. Dad gave the guests gift cards. What the fuck happened?" He asks.

I clue him in on the details. He tells me he understands. Baz is an Alpha male like me, although he's a Dom, too. So he understands protecting my woman's honor and my irrational possessive behavior. But he reminds me to keep my shit together in the future. Then teases me about not being responsible.

I grouse over the gibe. Then we hang up with a reminder about breakfast.

FUCK!

In my rage, I punch the wall. The plaster clatters to the floor, leaving a hole and splatters of blood. Too pissed to feel the pain, I stalk around the living room of my Rulers' Suite at STEELE Dubai I.

This shit is crazy. How can I allow myself to get so out of control that I make an ass of myself at a STEELE business function? So out of character for me—Roger *The Responsible*.

I roll my eyes in disgust at myself for letting Leonie upend my structured world. But I can't help myself. I call her mobile.

Leonie doesn't answer. What else is new…

I have no other choice than to leave a voicemail. How many will this one be? After twelve months, I've lost count. I just hope she'll listen to it and respond to me this time.

"How did we get here? Baby, I miss you. I'm so sorry. Tell me what to do. Please tell me, baby. Please…"

ROGER

12 MONTHS AGO — NEW YORK CITY

"*H*ey, when did you get in?"

I lift my head to see my eldest brother, Sebastian. His gray eyes and ebony hair are just like mine, Steele family traits. Baz wears his hair slicked back, accentuating his firm jaw covered with a 5 o'clock shadow. My hair is slightly long, cut to skim my ears and neck. I keep my face clean shaven over my cleft chin. Although my olive skin tone doesn't completely hide the shadow of hair beneath the surface.

I watch him as he strolls up to my desk. He mutters to himself about me and laughs at my intense stare. Unlike my easygoing siblings, I'm the most serious of us. As the middle of five children, I'm the mediator, the one to keep the scales balanced—Roger *The Responsible* Steele. A nickname given to me by my siblings as a child.

Sebastian at thirty-five is our intrepid leader. Both as the eldest and as the heir apparent CEO and Chairman of the Board of our family's multibillion-dollar, luxury real estate development and management corporation. None of us are envious of either of his roles. We're a tight-knit family that loves and respects each other—a fiercely loyal and supportive clan.

Currently, Baz heads our Retail Properties Division of STEELE International, Inc. as the president. Our father, Morgan set to retire next year, also views Baz as the most appropriate choice to take over for our generation. Due more so to his abilities than to his age or last name.

A glance at my watch shows it's still early morning at seven. Sebastian must be on his way to his corner suite of offices. There's no missing me through the glass walls as he passes my suite next to his. I've been here for just over a half an hour, earlier than expected. Although I'm based in our Paris branch, I spend about twenty percent of my time at our headquarters in New York City.

The STEELE Tower is a modern, gray-tinted glass fifty-seven story mixed-use skyscraper on the southwest corner of Fifty-Seventh Street and Fifth Avenue within Billionaires' Row. We're on the twenty-ninth floor for the executive level where my father, second oldest brother Malcolm, Sebastian, and I have offices. Our finance and legal departments along with various conference rooms occupy the remaining space. The other divisions have designated floors below along with my younger siblings', twins Harris and Haley, STEELE Technology and Cyber Security.

As I turn to face him, my eye catches the view through the floor-to-ceiling windows. The city stretches out before me with unobstructed views. Central Park to the north, the Hudson River to the west, the East River opposite, and the rest of Manhattan to the south from Midtown to Battery

Park. On a beautiful, cloudless day like this morning, the panoramas are riveting.

The interior reflects the metal our name represents. The decor—as sleek as the exterior—features platinum silk wall treatments, ebony wood floors, dove gray and white leather furniture, crystal light fixtures, Lucite tables, steel accents, and original artwork. The reception area has a spacious desk. Three attractive receptionists with headsets in their ears and custom-tailored light gray dress suits and skin-tone heels that serve as uniforms sit behind it.

The majesty of our power awes all who enter SI's offices.

I ease my stare with a smile, happy to see my brother.

"Late last night. The investors canceled our meeting because of an ill associate, so I flew out earlier than planned."

I reply as I rise from my chair and stride around the desk to give Baz a bro hug and slap on the back. My focus has been on our European projects these past few months. So I've spent less time here than usual. Baz is just as happy to see me as I am to see him.

He settles his substantial frame into the leather guest chair opposite my desk while I lean against it. I cross my long legs clad in custom-tailored trousers at the ankles and rest my hands on the edge. At six feet, four inches, he's an inch taller than me. Both of us are fit with musculature developed from our training—Baz MMA and traditional boxing for me—with former champions.

I catch him up on the happenings with two of the new builds I'm managing in Positano, Italy and Monte Carlo, Monaco. As the president of our Residential Properties Division, I'm responsible for the global development, sales, and management of villas, estates, gated communities with clubhouses and other amenities. I have a passion for architecture, interior design, and overall aesthetic of residential structures.

As we are a multigenerational, privately owned company, each sibling works at STEELE: Malcolm, president of the Entertainment Properties Division; Harris and Haley, fraternal twins, co-founders of the subsidiary STEELE Technology and Cyber Security. Like Baz, we're not just here because of our DNA.

Our mother Michelle, or Shelley as she's known by those close to her, wasn't born into a wealthy family. She's a native New Yorker who came from a middle-class background. Fate had her employed as a shopgirl at a men's store in one of STEELE's retail properties when she met my father. They joke that it was love at first sight. Well, over thirty-six years later, they still behave like young lovers in the honeymoon stage of their relationship.

As a result of her levelheadedness because of her as she says "normal upbringing," we interned every summer and school break at STEELE. The proper way to learn our family's business from the mailroom on the lower level to the twenty-ninth floor. Both of our parents insisted upon the best education possible. We attended private schools and received our Harvard undergraduate and MBA degrees, the family legacy school. Each of us earned the right to sit in our C-suite offices.

Sebastian fills me in on his division's meeting with Lola's Coterie that he's having with his business development team in a few hours.

"Actually, I'd appreciate you sitting in on the meeting," he says as he snaps his finger enlightened by the idea. "I could use your opinion. It's always useful to have your perspective."

He pauses and adds with a smirk, "That is if you don't mind, Roger *The Responsible*..."

"Obviously, you could use my insight after that Rockett Construction blunder..." I rib him back, referencing the sour deal he just lost to STEELE's major competitor two months ago.

Sebastian presses his lips together in a thin line. His facial expression switches to his Dom visage.

"Don't get all swole in the chest with me. That Dom shit doesn't work. I'm no sub," I chuckle.

He may be a Dom, but we're all dominant personalities— Alpha males to the core. Only Haley being female lacks that STEELE trait. She's a sweet, shy young woman protected fiercely by her older brothers. Although independent, she doesn't have the innate urge for control like us.

I fold my arms over my massive chest and cock my head to the side. We stare at each other until we crack up at our antics. We don't really need to prove ourselves. It's all in jest.

"Sure thing, bro. I accept your invitation."

Baz's mobile buzzes, interrupting our conversation. He retrieves it from his pants pocket and remarks the time is 8:20 already. Tina Nickles, one of his two assistants, texted to ask if he was running late. He types a quick response that he's in my offices and will be there in ten minutes. Between Tina and Melody Lawson, they keep a tight rein on his schedule because they know how valuable his time is and that he dislikes wasting it.

Baz returns to our conversation for a few more minutes, then says he needs to head to his offices.

"Fine, go take over the world. I have work to do anyway," I say as he strides out the door.

I use the time before the meeting to respond to communications forwarded by Françoise Faucher, my assistant in

Paris. The time difference makes it early afternoon there. I have enough time to wrap up some tasks. Like Baz hates to waste time, so do I. If I can—

"Absolutely, not! I don't mind at all! In fact, while I'm in New York, I'm filming a public service announcement that encourages adolescent girls to follow their dreams!"

"Thank you—"

Her melodic laughter follows in their wake. It captivates me like a siren's song. My eyes track her through the glass wall of my office until she disappears around the corner, headed for the conference rooms.

Damn the most exquisite beauty I've ever seen walks past my office. A STEELE security staff member strides beside her. Her long legs easily keep pace with his steps, and he's well over six feet tall.

She looks so familiar. I rack my brain trying to remember where I've seen her before. It escapes me. Who is she?

The ring of my landline breaks the beauty's spell over me. I blink to clear her silken web wrapped around my mind.

"Roger Steele…"

As I HEAD to the conference room for the meeting, I continue to scroll through my tablet.

Thanks to Google, I now know the mysterious beauty's name—Leonie *The Lion* Beaulieu. Of course she's familiar, duh. She's all over Paris, Europe, the States, the world.

The stunning supermodel stands at five feet, ten inches. With the fuck-me heels she's wearing, no wonder she kept up with the guard. Along with her nickname, her tall, voluptuous frame is her trademark.

The Parisian-born, feline beauty must be here for Sebastian's meeting with Lola's Coterie. As the brand's spokesmodel, Leonie has the perfect body to showcase the luxury lingerie. Her sensuous, statuesque figure harkens to the bombshells of yesteryear and the '90s supermodels, full bust, small waist, shapely. My dick twitches just looking at her photos—covers of *Vogue*, *Cosmopolitan*, *Sports Illustrated*.

Her golden, caramel skin reflects her biracial heritage—her mother Joséphine is Tunisian and her father Guy is French. She's the only child. Leonie means brave as a lion and Beaulieu means lovely place. I'm not a stalker, I like details and Wikipedia is just chock full of interesting tidbits.

Social media and bloggers dedicate themselves to her career and love life... Wherever she goes, men flock to her. Undoubtedly as attracted to her siren's song as I am. I swipe through the posts until I see a regular face parading her around the globe. Some schmo named Giovanni Mattei.

Thanks to Google and Wiki, I learn he's a wealthy nobleman from an aristocratic Italian family dating back to the Middle Ages and her on-again-off-again paramour. An insane urge to knock him out comes over me. The fucker.

Distracted, I walk into the conference room without lifting my eyes from my tablet's screen. The background noise of people talking and laughing suddenly stops as I open the door. I raise my gaze.

Holy... shit...

If this were a cartoon, it would be *Who Framed Roger Rabbit*. My mouth would drop open to hit the floor and my eyes would bug out of my head at the sight of Jessica Rabbit in front of me.

But it's not a cartoon, it's actual life, even if my name is Roger. Instead of a lush cartoon woman, an equally lush lioness stands before me naked save for a scrap of silky material covering her bare mons. My mouth gapes and my eyes widen. Hell, my dick gets hard and presses uncomfortably against the zipper of my trousers. Hot damn!

"They're only breasts, *chéri!*" Leonie laughs, cupping her mouthwatering mounds in her hands as emphasis. "No need to look so stunned!"

Her brown nipples peak between her red manicured fingers, calling me to suckle the plump tips while she writhes beneath me. Unconsciously my tongue sweeps across my lips, wanting a taste of her succulent tits.

"Ahem."

Someone discreetly clears their throat and breaks the spell Leonie has cast her spell on me, again. I feel heat rise even more on my reddened face. I avert my intense stare. Then mumble an apology as I pivot to leave the room. But her siren's call draws my gaze to hers as I glance over my shoulder on my way through the door.

Her amber eyes have darkened and spark golden with interest. The predator senses her prey. Is the Alpha now in another's sight?

A slight smile plays on her full lips. My dick twitches once more when her little pink tongue darts out to moisten her full lips. Leonie must feel the pull just as much as I. Neither of us can escape it.

Damn.

I shake my head. I have to get out of here. I feel my control slipping as thoughts of carrying Leonie over my shoulder back to my office to pummel into her plays in my mind. I have the sudden urge to bury my thick cock balls deep inside of *The Lion's* sweet pussy.

I hasten out the door as her sultry chuckle follows me.

How the hell did I walk into the wrong conference room? I lost my focus thinking about a woman... I shoot

Baz a quick text to ask which one the meeting is in. His response comes immediately. I make my way to the one down the hall.

I beat Sebastian inside the room. So, I nod to members of his team, then stand to the side. It's not my meeting. I'll wait for him to lead it.

Meanwhile, I observe another gorgeous girl who must be Lola Lewis, the eponymous founder of Lola's Coterie. The petite raven-haired beauty's hazel eyes sparkle as she speaks with an older, distinguished Frenchman. Her curvy body is alluring. But doesn't attract me like my sweet Caramel Bonbon.

My gaze shifts to the door when it opens to reveal Sebastian. I notice he falters mid-stride when he enters the room. His eyes widen when he observes the brunette is now in an embrace with the Frenchman. Sebastian's reaction makes me wonder if he knows her.

Oblivious to the sudden tension in the room, Walter Smith, the director of development for the Retail Division, continues with the introductions. I was correct in my assumption; the brunette is Lola.

Lola's hazel eyes widen even more than Baz's and she flushes deeply. She too appears dumbfounded at the sight of my brother. Unconsciously, her hand moves to cover her bottom. Interesting...

Finally catching on to the lull in the room, Sebastian draws his attention from Lola to his team who watch him with curiosity in their eyes. He also notices me staring between Lola and him. His expression confirms he knows I know something is up with the two of them. Yup, my intense gaze never misses a thing. Obviously, I would catch the tension between Lola and him.

Sebastian quickly recovers and continues to stride over

to Lola and Luc Montaigne the Frenchman to shake their hands. Lola starts the meeting and I join Sebastian at the table. My thoughts still distracted by Leonie and her delectable body, I barely pay any attention to the presentation. Lola and Montaigne take turns. My attention only piques when Lola announces the commencement of the fashion show.

My dick and I sit up straight at full attention.

Leonie sashays in through the door, looking like a goddess. Her hair is curled in ringlets, cascading around her face and down her back. The shiny mahogany shines beneath the lights. Her makeup is soft with a touch of nude gloss on her lips. The cups of the chemise barely contain her breasts, a hint of the dark nipples peek through. Her toned torso framed by the sheer core of the chemise, while the dainty embroidered hem grazes the tops of her thighs. A slight glimmer of gold body makeup adds sparkle to her caramel skin. As she pads around the conference room, Leonie is the epitome of feline feminine grace and lusciousness. My dick weeps for her.

Her captivating amber eyes flick to mine as she prances on the temporary catwalk. Each time she models pieces from the collections, I can't help my intense stare. My gaze follows her every move. I'm caught in The Lion's sights.

For the first time in my life, I'm not the one in control.

LEONIE

"Oh *Chérie*, I understand. Go, go have fun with your lover, the gray-eyed wolf! Have some fun for me! Don't worry. Shoo!"

Lola hesitates in the foyer of the Presidential Suite at the St. Regis Hotel New York where we're staying for our week of business in the city.

Suite is an understatement for what's more like *une belle maisonette*. It features a large foyer that leads to the formal dining room, living room, exquisite wood-paneled library, three bedrooms, four bathrooms, powder room, and a complete kitchen. The floor-to-ceiling windows open onto large balconies with spectacular views of Central Park, Fifth Avenue, and Fifty-fifth Street. A personal butler is on call to oversee our every need. With a five-figure per night rate, it has every luxury imaginable for a home away from home. It's our preferred residence whenever either of us are in New York.

"Are you sure? We had planned to spend some nights at the latest clubs and restaurants. I feel terrible—"

"*Non*! Go! Let that Alpha Dom of yours tie you up or spank your booty or whatever you get into," I laugh, waggling my eyebrows suggestively.

For a moment, Lola's face flushes red and her hazel eyes widen at my references to her newfound sub kink. Her last lover—of over a year ago, I might add—was a Dom who spanked her before they had sex. She finally admitted it to me and how much she enjoyed his play. Not only "the release was incredible." But the punishment drove away her nerves. Good for her!

Now, I give my BFF a hug and gently push her towards the suite's front door. Lola is off for another night with the enigmatic, sexy Mr. Sebastian Steele. The billionaire playboy appears taken with her. In fact, she's just as taken with him!

"Well... If you insist!" Lola's tinkling laughter floats behind her as she heads out the door for her rendezvous.

She deserves some fun. She's so focused on growing her company these past six years we've known each other, Lola rarely takes time to enjoy herself. All day, she works in her Parisian atelier on new designs, collection themes, and plans.

Only in the last three years has she turned over the minor business affairs to her marketing and sales teams and to her assistant Blair Thomas. Lola relinquished some duties after Luc, her mentor and major investor, rationalized she focuses on the creative end of business and let others handle the rest with her final approval. Lola's Coterie has come far in the six years since she launched it.

I remember Luc insisted I meet a new lingerie designer, and I thought, *mon Dieu*, really?

At twenty-five, I was at the height of my modeling career with well-established designers pleading with my agents to book me to open and close for their shows. Global cosmetics companies clamoring for me to represent them with exclusive, multimillion-dollar, multiyear contracts. The face of *The Lion* graced hundreds of billboards and magazine covers.

So, an up-and-coming designer like Lola was far from my radar. Luckily for her, Luc knew me through mutual acquaintances and insisted that I meet with Lola. I chuckle to myself as I remember how persistent Luc was for me to give her a chance to discuss me being the spokesmodel for Lola's Coterie. The very handsome and sexy nobleman— or *Le Renard Argenté*, the Silver Fox Lola and I nicknamed Luc—can be very persuasive. How could I say, no? But really, I knew that if he said she was worth it, she must be special.

Over time, as Luc and I became more acquainted and not just people who saw each other at society functions, our friendship developed into him being my top advisor. His recommendations are purely in my best interest since he doesn't gain financially from any deals he assists me with. Luc is the personal eye whereas my agents have a commission tied to their suggestions. They strike the perfect balance.

Luc draws his knowledge from being the CEO & Chairman of the Board of his family's multigenerational banking empire, Banque Montaigne headquartered in Paris. It has branches worldwide with New York as the United States headquarters. The banker in him added the role of financial manager to his advisor status. His wise investments turned my fifteen-year modeling career income into a multimillion-dollar fortune.

My coffers don't compare to Luc's billionaire wealth. Not only does he run his private banking empire, he's a

French nobleman. A wealthy aristocrat raised in the French nobility, he's the last *duc* in his family's line.

Sadly, he became a widow when his wife Carole died in childbirth with his only son Lucas seven years prior to meeting Lola and me. He was still grieving, and Lola's Coterie became a distraction from his sorrows. It was a project different from the banking industry. So it took his mind off of his losses. Fortunately, Luc is in a better place now. Particularly since he appears to be interested in Blair and his head flight attendant Daphne Fontaine. A sweet young thing for the fifty-year-old *Renard Argenté*!

A smile plays on my face as I pad around the living room gathering the things I dropped off when I arrived back from my busy day. The meeting with STEELE International was the impetus for my trip. But I added other activities: rounds at New York's most prestigious design houses; a visit to the New York office of my modeling agency; an interview at *Vogue*; prep work for the PSA commercial I film tomorrow during which I share my dream of becoming a model and switching to residential interior design as encouragement for young girls to go for their goals. It's best to take advantage of the transatlantic trip since I'm based in Paris.

I'm thankful for the extensive travels my modeling has provided me. The fascinating cities of Singapore, Rio, St. Petersburg; the hidden gems of Koh Yao Noi, Bequia, Udaipur; the unique locations of Alta, Taranaki, Salta. I've stayed in breathtaking five-diamond hotels and resorts, spectacular multimillion-dollar villas and flats, and beautiful native accommodations immersed in the local culture. Posing for the camera has allowed me to experience various forms of residences and added to my love of design developed from childhood.

My father, Guy, is from a prominent Parisian family of

merchants who date back to the Merchant Court of the eighteenth-century. From the French royal court to the grand bazaars of the Mediterranean Sea, they traveled seeking antiques, antiquities, and fabrics.

It was during one of his excursions that my father met my mother Joséphine in a souk of Tunis. She was bringing lunch to her father, who was a craftsman of ceramics intricately painted by hand. They fell in love on sight. It was a true *coupe de foudre*. Their love struck in the middle of a busy, vibrant, North African bazaar. Sounds like a romantic movie!

So my blood and DNA dictated my penchant for beautiful, extraordinary, aesthetically pleasing surroundings. As much as I've enjoyed modeling, I look forward to completing my Bachelor of Arts in interior design from the Paris American Academy. The three-year program is taking me longer to complete due to my hectic schedule. I don't mind since I love them both. I don't let it stress me or put pressure on me. Besides, the professors and faculty understand my situation—being famous definitely has its benefits.

I have one ultimate project to present this year where I must design an entire house. *Architectural Digest* wrote a cover feature on my Parisian duplex and Monte Carlo penthouse. I did the interior design for both. They impressed AD. The editor praises my eye for detail and the combination of high-end and low-end pieces to create sumptuous, luxurious abodes reflective of the cities. The issue was their top-selling book of the year.

So despite my nerves about my project, I'm sure someone will trust me to redo their home. I'll take inspiration from my journeys and family ties.

As I walk in my bedroom of the suite, I spot my textbooks on the desk. Well, since I don't have any hot-happening plans for tonight, I might as well get some reading done. Lola teases I'm a bookworm now. Especially since I wear reading glasses.

Just as I sit on a chaise on one balcony with a glass of Réserve Jean de Lillet Blanc, my favorite aperitif, my mobile chirps with a text message.

LEVELS New York Masquerade Night Text YES to RSVP Text NO to Deline

Interesting...

Lola did gift me a seven-day guest pass to the global, luxury, members-only BDSM/dance clubs' flagship in Manhattan's Meatpacking District. We went the first night we arrived. It was a blast! The sensual atmosphere, the writhing bodies, the pulse of the seductive music. *Incroyable!*

I chose a black enamel bracelet and Lola picked a red one. The different colored bracelets display the wearer's status to other members and guests: partnered subs wear collars given to them by their Dom; partnered Doms wear gold bracelets; available subs wear red; unattached Doms wear white; voyeurs wear black. She met her Dom Sebastian that night.

Hhhmmm.

I might as well make good use of her generosity, I laugh to myself. As I rise from my chaise, I reply YES to RSVP. With a mask on and my hair in a messy bun on top of my head, I can be incognito. Even though I didn't wear a mask the first night, I don't want people to think I make a habit of patronizing a sex club.

Plus, I garner enough attention from men regularly. I don't need them to approach me when I'm alone at this kind of club. Albeit a very safe one with applications for membership that include an initial background check with periodic random ones throughout the year, among other safety measures. However, it's usually Lola who fights off the unwanted suitors. She may be petite, but she's a feisty firecracker who uses her native New Yorker attitude to tell them to scram. Without her there, I'll stick to the shadows as a voyeur.

I'm not on the hunt for a partner at the moment. I'm taking a break from dating. Giovanni Mattei, my on-again-off-again paramour, is on the outs. He's well-built, six feet, three inches tall with lustrous curly brown hair that falls into his chocolate brown eyes adding to his rakish gorgeous look. Women flock to him in droves.

Well, I've had just about enough of his philandering playboy antics. Although he invited me to watch him race at the Grand Prix next month in Monte Carlo. I'm still undecided.

Mr. Thinks He's God Gift to Women is on my shit list. Gio is a wealthy Italian nobleman from an aristocratic family as old as the Middle Ages. Two weeks ago, he sent an oil painting from his Paris gallery that I had my eye on. I promptly returned it. Last week it was a beautiful pair of yellow diamond earrings with a note: "They remind me of your eyes right after you cum screaming on my cock." Returned to sender.

I'll give it to him, Gio—that handsome devil—definitely has the confidence of a man used to getting whatever he wants in life. He doesn't give a damn about how others view his arrogance. We've dated for two years. But I'm not tying my heart to his unfaithful one. He's not ready to settle down, and I'm not ready to settle.

For now, I'll enjoy LEVELS and select a black voyeur bracelet again to just observe. I'll live vicariously through others' hedonistic trysts tonight.

With a decisive nod, I put my textbook back on the desk. Tomorrow is another day!

I stride to the walk-in closet to select a piece of lingerie from Lola's latest collection in anticipation of her New York boutique opening. I pull out the skimpiest bit of lingerie. A delicate cream lace teddy that skims the tops of my thighs and matching barely there thong is perfect. Since a half mask will cover my face, I'll just add a touch of shiny, nude gloss to my full lips. My look completed with a sexy bed-head updo and five-inch marabou mules.

Next, a soak in the oversize bathtub to pamper my work-weary muscles with essential oils. I wash and style my hair. Then slip into the lingerie set, shoes, and a Burberry trench coat. I leave a note for Lola on her pillow to let her know where I went for the evening. Not that I expect her to return tonight since she hasn't the other nights. She'll see it in the morning before she heads to her temporary office at Banque Montaigne United States headquarters in Midtown on Park Avenue.

My heels click on the hotel lobby's marble floors as I strut from the elevators to the front doors. I pass well-dressed guests on their way to dinner or to one of the city's happening night spots. Since I don't have on my mask yet, several guests do a double take when they recognize me. Accustomed to seeing my visage graces magazine covers on the newsstands and on the billboards in Times Square, I impress even the most jaded New Yorkers. With my signature predatory smile on my face, amber eyes twinkling, I prance past the gawkers and nod at the doorman as he smiles sheepishly at me. I glide down the stairs and sweep into the chauffeured Bentley Bentayga that Leonie hired for our seven-day stay.

"Good evening, Ms. Beaulieu," the driver greets me as I

settle into the plush leather seats. "Where would you like to go tonight?"

"Good evening, Stan. Please take me to LEVELS, thank you," I reply with a smile.

Stan drove Lola and me to LEVELS that first night, and I know he's driven her there to meet Sebastian. So, his face remains neutral. As the quintessential professional, he doesn't allow a judgmental expression to cross his face. I'm sure he knows LEVELS is a hedonistic establishment. Instead, he responds, "Yes, Ms. Beaulieu, right away."

ROGER

$\mathcal{M}$y dick can't take another tug from my fist as I fantasize about driving my thick length between Leonie's luscious tits slicked with warming oil. I can't get her out of my mind. The vision of her standing naked, holding her bountiful breasts in her hands has kept me hard for days. Her ripe nipples calling for me to lave and suckle them as an act of devotion for hours. Her melodious laugh transforming into a throaty moan. Her luminous amber eyes rolling back as she bows her body, feeding her breasts deeper into my greedy mouth...

Fuck!

I need a more substantial release than my hand allows. A night at LEVELS New York offers the solution my body craves. Undoubtedly I'll find a woman who's more than willing to have a one-night tryst with one of the STEELE Quaternity, as the media has labeled my brothers and me. They've dubbed us the most sought-after of the world's eligible billionaires. Our near-limitless wealth, power, and good looks attract women like bees to honey. They clamor for a taste, even one night.

We're all guilty of not having longstanding relationships. Our work to increase STEELE International's success as the next generation takes most of our time. All of us, including our sister Haley, commit at least ten hours a day on business. In Sebastian's case, it's fourteen hours. We put pressure on ourselves, but he does it even more. I'm not far behind with twelve. We're not left with enough time a relationship requires.

Fortunately, Malcolm and our cousin Lucien Jackson opened LEVELS New York five years ago that provides just what we need. We're Global All Access Members. Other than Haley, who we forbid membership.

While completing his hospitality and culinary training at the prestigious Le Cordon Bleu in Paris, Lucien thought of a BDSM/dance club. He figured the club would fill the void for safe, uninhibited sexual activities amongst the world's wealthiest and most influential people. They convinced Sebastian a global, luxury, members-only entertainment venue focused on hedonism would add to STEELE's bottom line. Baz, the net-net guy, saw the potential and gave them the green light.

Their venture with a high profit margin proved it's bigger than "a titty bar" as Baz originally called LEVELS. Malcolm and Lucien opened additional locations in Paris and London. An idea Lucien, who's now referred to as *The Sexy Chef*, literally cooked up is worth millions.

LEVELS is one of many business partnerships that STEELE has with Jackson Corporation. World-renown for their award-winning eateries, choice cigars, and distinguished liquors and wines, their products pair well within

STEELE's casinos, hotels, resorts, and residential and retail properties.

On the personal side, our mother Shelley is best friends with Lucie, the Jackson matriarch. They spent most of their adult lives together forming a closer bond than they have with their blood siblings and relatives. Not sharing DNA doesn't keep our families from being a close-knit group and Lydie, Lachlan, Lucien, and Laurent as our cousins. Connor their Patriarch has become a close friend of our father Morgan.

As my driver Eric Vogler cruises from The STEELE Tower on Fifth Avenue and Fifty-Seventh Street where I was at my penthouse to the Meatpacking District, I chuckle. Lucien and Malcolm's deliberate choice for the location adds to its allure. They selected a multilevel brick ware-house in the historic Manhattan neighborhood as a play on the area's name. Put a club where men pack their meat into willing women, and willing men allow women to pack them with their toys.

The historic reference continues with the decor. The lobby is minimal and industrial. The fixtures and furniture that appear well worn are high-end, modern replicas used to add authenticity without the grime of old pieces. The two sides have coordinating greeter stations that allow access to the separate Dine & Dance levels and the BDSM levels.

All Access members can choose from any of the seven levels. While the Dine/Dance members only have access to the party levels—Sky Lounge, Dance Club, and Level 4 Restaurant. For consistency and members' comfort, locations share the same layout with varying views:

Seven levels: 7th Sky Lounge that offers for the Meatpacking location a stunning, 360-degree view of Manhattan and across the Hudson River to New Jersey's shoreline, a bar, restaurant by day dance club by night, a coverable pool that's open during the warmer months, and a glass-retractable roof; 6th and 5th multilevel dance club with two bars and a lounge for food and drinks; 4th Level 4 Restaurant and bar open for breakfast, lunch, and dinner; 3rd has twelve private suites for members to continue their pleasure apart from the BDSM levels; 2nd Peepshow for BDSM with seating alcoves, primary stage, mini-stages, performance rooms, and a bar that serves non-alcoholic mocktails; below ground the Cellar a BDSM dungeon with mocktails bar.

Impatient to get inside, I don't wait for Eric to open my door. I hop out and stride past the queue that extends around the corner of people in expensive attire patiently await admittance to the club. Not surprising given LEVELS is for the über-wealthy and influential, too refined to behave boorishly. The hopeful patrons are not rambunctious as one would ordinarily see waiting outside a Manhattan nightclub.

I nod at the two members of the security team in custom-tailored black suits who stand outside the front doors.

"Good evening, Mr. Steele."

"Good evening," I respond as I make my way into the renovated warehouse.

I incline my head at the two stunning greeters as I step into the lobby. Their eyes gleam as brightly as their smiles when they recognize me. I don't break stride. A hard limit—no fraternizing with the staff. Instead, I press for the BDSM elevator. Once inside, I place my keycard against the panel to select the second level for Peepshow.

I stop at a greeter station in front of the doors. Another

attractive staff member holds enamel bracelets. I listen as she explains the differences in the colors to two males who must be new members or guests of members: partnered subs wear collars given to them by their Dom; partnered Doms wear gold bracelets; available subs wear red; unattached Doms wear white; voyeurs wear black.

Their excitement is palpable. Interestingly, the shorter of the two selects the gold bracelet. Then attaches a silver metal chain to the black leather studded collar around the neck of his taller, more muscular partner. The Dom strides through the doors leading his sub who trails behind him.

"Good evening, Mr. Steele," smiles the greeter. "Would you like to choose a mask or do you have one of your own for Masquerade Night, Sir?"

I don't miss her emphasis on the word Sir as a sub innuendo. The rule of us not engaging with employees is not the only deterrent to dealings with her. Unlike Baz and Malcolm, Harris and I are not Doms. We're Alpha males who like control. But don't dabble as far into a D/s relationship as our older brothers. Hell, I think our father may be a Dom, which would make our mother a sub. Not the visual I need right now. I have to resolve one of my own.

"Yes, I'll take the black one, thank you," I respond in an even tone, purposefully ignoring the downward cast of her brown eyes.

I opt out of a bracelet since I will select who I want, not someone selecting me as a partner. I need not show my availability; I need to know their status. Since everyone signs a contract that includes a consensual clause, I know everyone here is open to a connection. The bracelet determines at what level.

Once my mask is in place, I walk through the doors. A cursory glance around the room already has my body relaxing in anticipation of release. With the smile of a hunter on the prowl, I enter the world of Peepshow.

Not ready to pick my willing prey for the night, I stride pass seating alcoves filled with members in various stages of sex. A main stage and several smaller platforms showcase demonstrations in bondage and edging. I continue through performance rooms with viewing windows where members watch others live their fantasies. I stop to get a drink at the bar that only serves non-alcoholic mocktails to keep everyone's minds clear.

The atmosphere is all about bacchanalia, with the melodic thrum of sensual music and the moans and groans of men and women as the backdrop to intense sexual play. The air is heavy with the scent of perfume, cologne, and sex.

As I tip my glass to my lips, my gaze lands on doors where a statuesque woman stands with a mask covering the top half of her face. Backlit by the crystal chandelier in the entry, her curvy body is on display beneath a skimpy cream-colored lingerie set. The hem of her teddy barely brushes her toned caramel thighs. The sky-high mules stress her legs for days. Her mahogany hair piled atop her head makes me want to pull the pins out to watch her glossy strands cascade down her back.

Leonie.

If she thinks wearing a mask and pulling her mane of hair in a bun can disguise her, she's mistaken. My keen eyesight detects who she is as soon as I see her. My cock comes to life in an instant, harder than it's ever been. Her siren's song calls to me once again.

As she steps onto the floor, my eyes travel to her right wrist. A black bracelet adorns it. Hhhmmm. My feline beauty is a voyeur... For now.

I observe Leonie. Determine her intentions. Is she on the

hunt like me, or does she truly want to watch others in their play? I slip into the shadows, eyes trained on her every movement.

Even hidden partially by a simple black mask, *The Lion* commands attention. As she prowls around the room, several pairs of lust-filled eyes including those of a few women track my beauty as she stalks past them. Sadly for them, I have her in my sights. I will allow no one to partake of my Caramel Bonbon.

"Hello, I don't see you with anyone and your sleeve covers your wrist. Are you interested in doing a bondage and punishment scene?"

For a moment, I glance down to see a woman with waist-length blonde hair and light blue eyes staring up at me. A soft smile plays on her pouty lips. When she notices my gaze on her mouth, she darts her tongue to moisten her bottom lip suggestively. A filmy slip clings to her voluptuous figure. Taut rosy nipples press against the thin fabric.

Encouraged by my stare, she places a small hand on my broad chest. She rises to her tiptoes as she presses her lips to my ear to whisper illicit promises of pleasure.

Ordinarily I would claim her, and we'd head up to a private suite. But not tonight. Not when I have the woman whose image taunted me day and night within reach. I shake my head I'm not available at the blonde vixen. Then, stride towards Leonie who's surrounded by three men.

Not happening.

Unable to control myself, I slip my hand around her waist to rest on her flat lower belly. In a possessive hold, I angle my body directly behind hers, aligning my front to her back. A surprised gasp escapes her lips as she swings her head around to stare over her shoulder at me.

Her fuck-me heels bring her mouth on a level with mine.

I feel the warmth of her breath as the gasp slips out of her mouth. I ignore her wannabe suitors and brush my lips over hers before I bring them to the delicate shell of her ear.

"Ms. Beaulieu, what are you doing here alone?" I ask in a guttural growl.

She trembles against me. Responsive to the demanding tone of my voice, as her eyes widen in surprise. Her amber orbs search my gray ones for a sign of recognition. Subconsciously, her hand comes on top of mine, unsure of pushing me away or pulling me closer. Without a doubt, she can feel my enormous erection pressing into the crease of her firm ass.

"Wh... Wh... Who are you?" She stutters softly.

"Roger Steele," I respond, pushing my groin into her bottom on Steele, my dick as hard as the metal.

Leonie bites her plump bottom lip, and her feline eyes narrow.

Before she can respond, I move her away from the others. Leaving them to gawk after us. Leonie keeps pace with me as I stride to a corner alcove for privacy. She must want some anonymity since she wears a mask. So I will respect her wishes. As always, the woman's needs surpass my own. One of my kinks.

Seated on the semicircular red velvet banquette, our long legs touch, shooting jolts of electricity between our bodies. Leonie watches me in silence. The Queen of the Savannah analyzes her prey, waiting patiently for me to make the wrong move. I give her a moment to wonder at my behavior before I speak. In the dim light, I remove my mask.

"You haven't answered my question," I state.

Leonie's gaze sweeps across my face. She cocks her head to the side and arches her elegant eyebrow.

"What makes you think I have to answer to you, Monsieur Steele?"

Taking her challenge, I grasp her chin between my thumb and index finger to hold her face still as I bring my lips within a hair's distance of hers.

"Parce que je vous avais posé la question, et parce que je peux te donner ce que tu désires," I murmur huskily.

Once again, her eyes widen shocked by my fluency of her native tongue.

"Bof!" Leonie scoffs, shrugging her shoulders.

I can give her what she wants. Arrogant? Yes, but factual. I've never not satisfied a woman. And the way my body burns for hers, I will delight in her immensely.

"Oui mon Bonbon au Caramel, je parle couramment français," I smirk.

A seductive smile sparks across Leonie's gorgeous face, lighting her amber eyes from within. On a purr she responds, *"Est-ce un fait, Monsieur Steele?"*

"En effet, ma beauté. En effet."

When I want something, I make it mine. Methodical and determined go hand-in-hand with my intense nature.

And I want Leonie *The Lion* Beaulieu.

LEONIE

"*M*mmmmm..."

I raise my arms overhead and bow my back, pressing my hips into the mattress, thighs trembling, toes curling. My eyes close tight as a satisfied smile spreads across my face.

"Aaahhhh…"

I flop back onto the bed and open my eyes. Sunlight streams in through the windows, illuminating my bedroom at the St. Regis Hotel. With a contented sigh, I snuggle into the luxurious sheets and pull the blanket up to my chin. My mind wanders to the night Roger absconded with me at LEVELS New York a few days ago.

"Well, that sounds very interesting, monsieur. But I will have to pa—"

My words get snatched from my mouth, replaced by a startled gasp as the large hand of a man slips around my waist to rest on my lower belly. Its heat sends a zing to my core. He places his substantial body directly behind mine, aligning my back to his front.

And what a front! His chest is massive and firm. My derriere rests against his groin where his large cock stands at attention. His thick thighs press against the backs of my legs. He's so tall, we match body part to body part. His heady cologne is a sensual blend of Bulgarian rose, clary sage, and patchouli. His posture is so possessive.

I nearly swoon.

Instead, I get a grip on my raging hormones and whip my head around to stare over my shoulder at the brute. What is up with these cavemen at LEVELS? First Sebastian growls at Taylor, the head of membership, when he was giving Lola and me a tour. Now, this giant has me in his tight embrace.

Baise moi!

My five-inch mules bring our mouths so close were merely a breath apart. As though he and I are the only ones in the room, the mysterious stranger brushes his lips over mine. Then brings them to whisper in my ear.

"Ms. Beaulieu, what are you doing here alone?"

I tremble against him at his guttural growl. My body fights my mind for control as it responds to the demanding tone of his voice. Another gasp escapes as my eyes widen in surprise. Then search the gray orbs for a sign of recognition of the man behind the mask. Of its on accord, my hand comes on top of his. Do I want him to let go? Do I want to give in to his possessive behavior? My mind and body struggle to decide, unsure of pushing him away or pulling him closer. His enormous erection pressing into the crease of my ass makes the decision even harder...

"Wh... Wh... Who are you?" I whisper.

"Roger Steele," he responds, pushing his groin into my derriere on Steele.

And steel it is. Roger's dick is just like the hard metal. I allow his turgid rod to distract for a moment. I bite my lower lip trying to decide the proper action to take faced with the brother of Sebas-

tian who's completing a deal with the company I'm the spokesmodel. Thoughts of ruining the deal for my best friend Lola with a fling with Roger swings in favor of my mind's logic and not my body's lust. A decisive mais non, Monsieur Steele!

I narrow my eyes at him to tell him just that.

Before I can open my mouth, he moves me away from the three men I was in the middle of speaking with prior to his arrival. They continue to stand in shock, watching us. Roger leads me to a corner alcove that's more private than the middle of the floor at Peepshow. He must realize I want to remain anonymous. Dieu merci pour cela!

Seated on the semicircular red velvet banquette, our long legs touch, shooting jolts of electricity between our bodies. I watch Roger in silence. The first to speak loses the advantage. I wait. In the dim light, he removes his mask.

"You haven't answered my question," he states.

My gaze sweeps across his gorgeous face. Roger Steele could be a male supermodel. His sultry gray eyes, angular cheekbones, cleft chin that begs for me to lick it. Hhhmmm... I cock my head to the side and arches my eyebrow. I can't give in to his seduction. But I can flirt.

"What makes you think I have to answer to you, Monsieur Steele?"

Roger takes my challenge. He grasps my chin between his thumb and index finger to hold my face still as he brings his lips within a hair's distance of mine.

"Parce que je vous avais posé la question, et parce que je peux te donner ce que tu désires," he murmurs huskily.

Once again, my eyes widen shocked by his fluency of my native tongue and his arrogance. He can give me what I want.

"Bof," I scoff with a Gallic shrug.

However, his confident smirk leads me to believe he is being truthful. Roger Steele knows how to satisfy a woman. My body vibrates with need. I feel my pussy moisten and clench, aching for his massive member. I shift uncomfortably on the banquette.

"*Oui mon Bonbon au Caramel, je parle couramment français,*" he continues with his smirk.

Intrigued, a seductive smile sparks across my face as my body and mind come to an agreement. Lola's Coterie won't suffer if Roger and I have a little tryst...

"*Est-ce un fait, Monsieur Steele?*" *I purr.*

"*En effet, ma beauté. En effet.*"

Although we moved from the Peepshow banquette to one of the private suites, our tryst turned into an evening of sharing our lives and goals. A release of our souls to the other. I've never felt so connected to a man as I do with Roger.

The connection deepened when he told me how his passion for architecture, interior design, and overall aesthetic of residential structures lead him to president of Residential Properties at STEELE. I impressed him with my decision to move into interior design after my years as a top model rather than do nothing once I retire. He told me with focus and determination, I could make a successful transition.

Not only does he have an intense stare, Roger is an intense man. Twelve hours devoted to STEELE every day drives his work ethic. Boxing sessions release the tension. He's rigid with his need for order and balance. But I'm sure there's a fun-loving man inside. There's an exceptional dominant lover present.

I squeeze my thighs together as I remember Roger's dark head nestled between them while his hooded eyes pierced mine last night. His talented tongue tuned my pussy, then played it like a fine instrument for over an hour. He had me naked, bound by silken cords, spread eagle on the bed in a suite at LEVELS. Unable to move, I could only feel my body spasm as wave after wave of orgasms rolled over me. He was relentless.

By the time Roger sat back on his haunches—like a statue chiseled by the hands of Michelangelo—I was a quivering mess lying in a puddle of my juices. His nose, mouth, and chin were wet from my climaxes. I scanned his strong shoulders, hard chest, and eight-pack abs with a happy trail that led to his massive ribbed cock. The bulbous red head leaked pre-cum. I licked my lips, wanting to taste his creamy essence.

Instead, he rose onto his knees and straddled my torso. With his thick length fisted in his hand, he tugged on it as he groaned my name. Rope after rope after rope of his seed spewed forth to cover my heaving breasts. He collapsed over me, then suckled and laved my nipples as his still hard dick bobbed against my pussy entrance.

I writhed beneath Roger, aching for him to drive his staff deep inside of my core. But no.

Since I told him I only had two lovers and just ended it with the last, Roger told me we had to take it slowly. He didn't want me to rush into sex with him, then regret it. However, he promised to take care of my needs without the penetration of his glorious cock.

So, my pleas of *bais moi, bais moi maintenant* were met with his lips, tongue, and fingers.

Merde!

I roll over and scream into the downy pillow. Frustrated, I opened my big mouth about not giving in easily to suitors. Also, I fear I shared too much with my desire for genuine love like both of our parents experienced—*coup de foudre*. Roger, being the man he is, takes me at my word and refuses to go further for now.

So despite the pleasure he gave to me. I... want... more! *Je n'aurai aucun regret!*

* * *

OUR WEEK in New York City ends where we started. Gathered in the conference room at The STEELE Tower with the same cast of characters as our first meeting.

This time, Dom Pérignon Rosé Vintage 2005—somehow Baz knows Lola's favorite champagne—flows as they sign the contracts for Lola's Coterie and STEELE International, Inc.'s multiyear, multimillion-dollar partnership.

I'm happy for my best friend. She's worked hard for her success. We're so thrilled that we do our merry dance around the table while Luc and Sebastian laugh. Roger stares, his gaze as intense as ever. Or it could be because of the sleek knit mini dress with satin stiletto boots, the tops of which rest just below my hemline. Today, I taunt him with my curves and long legs that wrapped around his head. Tonight, the wait is over.

"I'm so excited for you, *Chérie!*" I squeal and hug Lola close. "Your dreams are coming true!"

"I know!" She exclaims. "It's so awesome! We have so much to do! I can't wait to get started."

She continues and as she hugs me back.

"*Oui, petite chérie,* but no need to think of it all at this very moment," Luc interrupts as he joins us and pulls Lola in for a warm embrace. "*Jouissance du présent!* Let's have dinner tonight at Per Se, your favorite New York restaurant, to celebrate."

"Lola and I already have plans for this evening," Sebastian cuts into the conversation, staring challengingly at Luc while placing a possessive hand on Lola's lower back.

After a tense moment where they eye each other, she ends the standoff with a compromise for dinner with us at eight and desert with Baz. Perfect for what I have planned for Roger.

Lola and I are the last to arrive at the restaurant. I spy Roger immediately. Seated at the bar, I study his handsome profile as he laughs at something Luc said. I notice the women near them circle like hawks attracted to two powerful, obviously wealthy Alpha males.

Well, Roger has my name written all over him. At least I expect my scent still fills his nostrils. I giggle at the thought even as my core clenches.

As if sensing my presence, Roger turns to face us. His pupils dilate as he takes in my attire for the evening.

The white one-shoulder velvet-trimmed sequined chiffon mini dress covered in scores of iridescent sequins sparkles so brilliantly under lights. Made from chiffon, it's cut to skim my figure and has a '70s-style one-shoulder silhouette. My narrow waist defined by the velvet belt. Strappy sandals lengthen my exposed legs provocatively. A smirk curls my lips as I toss my hair, blown straight over my shoulder where it brushes the middle of my back.

As Lola and I near them, Roger stands to offer his seat to me while Blair and Luc greet us with double-cheek kisses. I turn to Roger and brush my lips against the corner of his mouth when I repeat the kiss with him.

His hands rest at the top of my derriere in an embrace. But I slip out of it to sit. A little tease never hurt. I take a sip of his drink, eyeing him with my predatory stare over the rim. His nostrils flare.

"Where's Sebastian?"

I switch my attention to Lola, who's scanning the area. Roger shifts uncomfortably next to me and looks past Lola.

We follow his gaze and see Sebastian off to the side in an animated conversation with a gorgeous blonde woman who has her hand on his chest. *L'idiot!* She's the Finnish model Bridget Heimonen.

"Le playboy occupé à une autre tâche à ce moment," I spit out while I glare at him.

Fortunately, Luc takes control and we head to the private room he reserved for Lola's celebratory dinner. No one pays Sebastian attention when he finally joins us. We laugh and toast, enjoying the evening. When he follows Lola to the bathroom and they don't return, I know they worked it out. I gaze across the table at Luc, who's in deep conversation with Blair. Okay, so *Le Renard Argenté* appears set, too. Now it's my turn.

Again, as though emotionally attuned to me, Roger places his hand on my upper thigh as he inclines his head to mine.

"Time for dessert," he states in a deep voice filled with desire.

Hidden by the tablecloth, his fingers slip beneath my dress and slide along my inner thighs to nudge at my silk covered seam.

I shiver, but hold firm. Placing my palm on top of his significant bulge, I murmur my response against his ear.

"Only if you give me all of you."

Roger's thick cock twitches in my hand as his breath quickens. Gruffly, he answers.

"Comme tu le désires, mon Caramel Bonbon."

ROGER

"Take your dress off. I want you bare to me."

A low growl of appreciation rumbles from deep within my chest as Leonie unties the velvet belt from her narrow waist. All night my mouth watered for her puckered nipples that poked against the fabric of her little white dress. I guessed she was braless since it draped off one shoulder, revealing more of her delectable caramel skin.

When she and Lola walked up to the bar at Per Se, I wanted to drag Leonie off to my den to have my way with her. The inane idea I had of taking it slow to keep her from regretting fucking me so soon after her break up nearly killed me.

Sure, I feasted on Leonie's luscious body almost every night and tugged my junk over her naked body. But those acts do not compare to being buried balls deep inside of her delicious pussy. The little sleep that I garnered filled with fantasies of me pounding inside of her channel until I fill her with my seed.

Damn.

I'm losing my shit. Not a very responsible thought to have about sex with a relative stranger. Never have I considered unprotected intercourse with the women I've slept with in my life. There's just something about Leonie that makes my rigid stance on life bend to her whims.

Over the last few days, I let myself get caught up in her playfulness and blowing with the wind carefree attitude. She's so opposite to me. And I find my attraction to her increasing. Again, as though beyond my control.

And right now her painstakingly slow striptease has me on the edge of the precipice. Leonie's amber eyes twinkle in the ambient lighting of the bedroom in my penthouse on the fifty-second floor of THE STEELE Tower. Another against protocol move.

No woman besides my mother and sister has been to my home. My dalliances happen at LEVELS New York and Paris. Or if I'm in London at that location. Tonight, instead of going to the Meatpacking District, I instructed my driver to take us here. Leonie looked at me in surprise. But I didn't comment further. She must sense I'm not the guy to bring women to my private space. I'm not even sure why I brought her here. Except I know it feels right.

As I sit at the foot of my bed, my intense gaze slides from her hands down her torso to her long legs. As Leonie lifts the hem of her dress, a mischievous smile plays on her full lips. With a deliberate languid pace, she reveals her thighs inch by inch.

Grrrr!

In one unexpected move, I leap to my feet and lunge towards her. My hands grasp her by the waist, and I lift her from the floor. Deftly, I drop her onto the bed. She lands splayed before me. Without giving her a chance to react, I lengthen my body over hers.

One pull and the front of her dress rips open to expose her more than a handful C-cup breasts. Her brown nipples tighten in the cool air. I drop to my forearms to engulf her tit with my mouth. Forceful sucking has Leonie writhing beneath me in moments. I alternate nipping and laving her peaks, eliciting guttural mews from deep in her throat.

"Aaahhhh... Roger... Mmmmmmm..."

I stroke her belly as my fingers trail to her silk-covered mound. I slip my middle finger under the elastic, and palm her bare mons with my large hand. My finger slips between her wet labia to tease her clit. The sensitive bundle of nerves swells from my artful ministrations. A quick pinch and a nip cause Leonie to bow off the bed, screaming my name as her body rocks with a powerful climax.

I continue to caress her breasts with my hungry mouth as two more fingers join the first inside of her core. Leonie is so fucking tight. Her pussy walls squeeze my digits. I need her loose enough to take the invasion of my thick, ten-inch dick.

"Are you sure you want all of me, Bonbon?" I croon in her ear as I slide my fingers in and out of her slippery pussy.

"Mmmmmm... *Oui... Oui... Plai*—"

Her words cut short by my insistent finger fucking. Her tight walls stretch around the invasion and pulse with her impending orgasm. I plant open-mouth kisses on her long, delicate neck, aching to mark her as mine. Claim *The Lion*.

"Rogeeerrr..."

As Leonie wails, I rise from the bed and quickly strip out of my custom-tailored suit and shirt. I toss it all to the floor, toeing my shoes and socks off my feet. Ripping my black silk boxer briefs down my muscular thighs, my hooded eyes never leave Leonie's squirming body as I roll a condom on.

Her feline eyes narrow in on her prey as they crawl over

my body. Until they alight on my colossal cock. Then they widen, and her little pink tongue darts out to moisten her bottom lip. Her chest heaves on an inhalation, making her tits bounce. She widens her thighs as she lifts her arms to welcome me.

"*Mon Chéri, viens à moi,*" she purrs seductively.

My dick thumps against my stomach, pre-cum dripping from the slit.

I blaze a trail of scorching open-mouth kisses from the arch of her foot up her inner thighs to the hollow between her breasts. Goosebumps dot her smooth skin as she shivers despite the heat of her moist body.

Pressure from my hips between her thighs urge Leonie to open wider to accommodate my much larger frame. I settle my groin against hers, and I kiss her passionately. Her soft mewls make my member thicken and lengthen more between us. Gripping the base, I feed the broad head of my cock slowly into her core. Although she's sopping wet, I'm met by resistance.

"Open up and let me in, baby," I croon against her neck. "I need to feel your tight pussy wrapped around me."

I swipe the tip inside her folds to collect her juices for natural lube. I press forward again. Fuck... Her wet heat feels so good. Groans escape from between my lips brushing her throat.

"Ooohhh... Roger... Aaahhh, *Amoureux... Donne moi tout de toi.*"

I give her what she asks for—all of me—as I drive my dick balls deep inside until I hit her cervix. Her squeal a combination of pleasure and pain. Her hot pussy walls pulsate around my dick with each thrust that sends her sliding up the bed. She grips my biceps and holds on for the wild ride.

We've waited so long. Now, we lose each other in our rhythm. Connected as one as we ride waves of rapture.

"So, good, baby... So fucking good," I rasp against her damp neck.

The slick sounds of our bodies joining fill the room as the headboard hits the wall. Too far gone to care, I pummel into Leonie like a lust-driven fiend.

At... fucking... last.

* * *

THE ELEVATOR ARRIVES WITH A PING.

Leonie and I fall through the doors, too engrossed in a passionate kiss with our arms wrapped around each other, to notice that we're not alone. As I hike Leonie's long, shapely leg around my hip, thrusting at her pussy, I hear a cough.

"Good morning!"

I nearly drop Leonie in my haste to find the source of the unexpected greeting. She squawks, flailing her arms out to find purchase on the wall of the elevator. I lift my head to see Lola smiling, her eyes twinkling in merriment.

I swing my gaze to find Sebastian beside her with his jaw hanging open in shock. Undoubtedly since I'm *Roger The Responsible* and not prone to one-night stands nor to overt public displays of affection.

However, I'm equally surprised. It's my turn to pick my jaw up from the floor at seeing Baz with a woman coming from his penthouse two floors above mine. His cheeks flush from his attempt to suppress his laugh until Lola bursts out giggling.

Leonie joins in, her amber eyes dance in delight. She and Lola crack up and converse in French about how funny the whole situation is and how they can't believe they're so busted.

Meanwhile, Baz peers over their heads at me. I try my best to remain stoic while I study the floor indicator to avoid his inquisitive stare.

"So, what's up, man? Good night?" He ribs.

Now a flush creeps up my neck from beneath my shirt collar as I ignore his question and their gaiety.

Pressing on, he adds, "I take it the dessert was more than satisfying? A bit of sweet passion fruit filled with lots of seeds? *Succulente, n'est pas?*"

At that, Lola and Leonie's laughter increases, filling the elevator with their unrestrained guffaws and snorts. Fortunately for me, the doors open, and I grab a still laughing Leonie by the hand to drag her out of the elevator. I stalk through the lobby to the sidewalk where our cars and drivers await.

"Seriously, where are you headed?" Baz asks, looking between Leonie and me. "Lola and I plan to get her things from the hotel and bring them back here."

Leonie bugs her eyes out at Lola and starts speaking rapidly to her in French, gesturing animatedly with her hands. With a glance at Baz, Lola pulls Leonie to the side, murmuring a response. Leonie's eyes filled with concern dart to his, then back to Lola before speaking rapidly, again. I hear Luc's name mentioned with not going to be happy and too fast. Finally, I pose a question of my own to Sebastian.

"Better question, what's up with you? I've never seen you bring a woman to your home before and definitely never move them in if that's what you meant by bringing Lola's things back here."

I consider his answers. But let it go. He's a grown man and can decide for himself.

"I'm taking Leonie back to the St. Regis for her to pack while I do some work at the office before we fly back to Paris this afternoon. I'm giving her a lift since Lola and Luc are staying for the meetings."

Sebastian smirks, and like me, he lets it go. For now.

"*MERCI.*"

Leonie graces my pilot and flight crew with a dazzling, million-dollar smile as we board my Gulfstream G650 bound for Paris. Clifford stutters a response. So taken by the beauty. I drop my head to hide a smile of my own. She is breathtaking.

Even dressed casually in an Adidas tracksuit-style maxi dress and sneakers, Leonie strikes a pose. Supermodel through and through, she's flawless.

I place my hand on her lower back to guide her to the middle of the private jet for two extra-large, leather club chairs. Situated across from the burl wood console with the built-in television and entertainment center. It's my favorite spot, aside from the bedroom. We'll explore it later.

Leonie makes herself comfortable in the plush seat. Then sips Evian water from the Baccarat Crystal goblet. She notices my stare and smiles at me over the rim of the glass.

"You know the American saying, 'take a picture, it lasts longer,'" she giggles.

"I don't know if it's 'American.' But I know you've got jokes," I smirk.

Laughter bubbles up, then turns into a snort as the water tickles her nose. Her amber eyes glow with mirth.

I lean over and kiss the tip of her nose. Then on second

thought slant my mouth over hers, sucking her cool tongue into my mouth. She tastes divine.

"Mmmmmm, Roger," Leonie purrs.

My dick hardens as our kiss deepens. I can't get enough of her. Our tongues parry and I slip my hand into the vee-neck of her dress to cup her bountiful breast. Just as I pinch her nipple, another slight cough intrudes. We break apart, panting.

"Pardon me, Mr. Steele," Stacey my head flight attendant says with her eyes averted. "The captain has cleared us for takeoff. So I need to collect your glasses if you don't mind, sir."

I nod, handing my tumbler to her. Leonie passes hers over, too. Once Stacey makes her way to the crew area, I press the alert button for privacy. No more unwanted interruptions for the rest of the flight. I have almost eight hours with Leonie and I don't plan on any disruptions.

I reach across her lap to secure her seatbelt. She smiles at me and kisses my cheek.

"So thoughtful of you, *Chéri. Merci.*"

During the flight we share more stories of our childhood, dreams, and challenges. Even though it's only been a week, the connection I feel for Leonie is strong, unlike with any other female.

She's a warm, loving, smart woman. I tell her again I believe her transition to interior design will be a success. She just has to stay focused and get her work done in her last year. Her lighthearted laughter fills the cabin as she slips her arms around my neck.

"Oh, *Chéri*, loosen up! You can't go through life so rigid. *Joie de vivre!*"

I smile at her and nod. A little laxity won't kill me, I

suppose. Well, only a little. I join in her laughter as I pull her from her seat to lead her to the bedroom.

"Let's see how loose I can stretch your tight, little pussy, *Chérie...*"

Her laughter cuts off as a tremble runs through her body to our joined hands like a spark of lightning. Her amber eyes turn black as her pupils dilate with lust. Her breath quickens, and she nibbles on her bottom lip as she peers at me. Yeah, Leonie doesn't mind my control in the bedroom.

And I'm not about to give it up. Ever.

ROGER

"*M*r. Steele, what do you expect in a relationship? I mean in a business partner-ship with an interior designer."

The women in the lecture hall titter as the brunette in the front row asks her sixth question with a misspoken work, innuendo, or blatant flirtation. An American named Delia something or the other.

I sigh inwardly and glance at my Vacheron Constantin Patrimony Traditionnelle. The watch may have a lot of complications. But it easily shows another twenty minutes remain in the class.

Wonderful...

I lift my gaze to Leonie, who's barely containing her glee. Those enchanting amber eyes shine as she holds her fingers over her mouth. I cock my eyebrow at her and flex my fingers—the sign my palm itches to connect with her round bottom.

She guffaws out loud. Then pretends to cough. A male student seated beside her rubs her back and whispers in her ear. The entire class session he's used excuses to engage with her—giving her a tissue, picking up her pen, offering her a piece of candy.

Fucker.

My eyes narrow at him. This time, my fingers curl into a fist. I want to smash him.

Mine!

These past few weeks Leonie and I have been inseparable when she's in town. I've even scheduled my Positano and Monte Carlo projects' site visits for when she's off shooting in some tropical or urban locale. I'd rather spend time with her. It's worked out well. That is mostly.

We've had some disagreements about her work ethic for her studies. She uses the excuse of her modeling schedule for not completing her assignments on time. I told her just because the faculty allows her tardiness doesn't mean she should continue to miss deadlines. She accuses me of being controlling—that is, outside the bedroom.

Just the other night she went to a party instead of writing her paper due the next afternoon. She worked on it that day and submitted it last minute. But she could have finished it earlier and not rushed. Leonie doesn't see it that way. The light laughter and teasing me about my rigidness morphs into pouts and rebukes.

The upside is the incredible makeup sex. We can't go long angry with one another. So when we get back together, sparks fly. There's no holding back. Just like our first time together. Our passion ignites us.

Not everything revolves around sex in our relationship. And it is a relationship at this point. Two months is the longest I've been with the same woman. As Sebastian was so shocked to see me with Leonie since I don't do one-night stands, I'm also never with a woman longer than a couple of weeks. I'm doing a lot of firsts with Leonie.

Like now, I'm doing her a favor. I'm her show and tell—guest lecturer, she laughed—for one of her business courses at the Paris American Academy. They're discussing career paths. The pros and cons of working independently, for a firm, or at a large corporation. STEELE International is renowned. So Leonie figured she'd score cool points or "chilly points" with the professor if I did a class takeover. She pointed out the opportunity for me to meet potential new hires. Her negotiation tactics along with exuberant kisses convinced me.

The concept was good. But the women flirting with me in hopes to score a billionaire combined with the overly helpful jerk outweighs the benefits. I have to wrap this up. Before I answer the brunette's inane question, I pinpoint my gaze on Leonie and the fucker.

One glance at my expression and my balled fists, Leonie shifts away from the guy. She attempts to mollify me with a charming smile and nod of acknowledgment. The guy finally picks up she's mine when his gaze follows hers to me. I glare at him with my lip curled in a snarl and he hastens to move away from her.

Smart move, loser. I give zero fucks about what anyone may think about my possessive behavior.

I glance at my watch once more. Fifteen minutes. Then turn my attention to the eager student to answer her question. The countdown begins.

"MONSIEUR STEELE, *qu'attendez-vous dans une relation? Je veux dire dans un partenariat d'affaires avec un architecte d'intérieur,"* Leonie mimics the woman from earlier.

Leonie's purr zings my balls as she stands before me. She's dressed in a white round-collared, cap-sleeved blouse, navy pleated micro-mini skirt sans panties, red knee-high socks, and black patent leather, high-heel Mary Jane shoes. Her long mane pulled into a high ponytail with a red bow. Reading glasses perch on her nose.

I'm still fully clothed in my bespoke three-piece suit and A. Testoni Oxford shoes. Instead of standing at the lectern, I'm sitting at a desk in one of the Peepshow performance rooms at LEVELS Paris with the curtains drawn for privacy. No one sees Leonie in the throes of ecstasy except for me.

This LEVELS in the 7th Arrondissement Palais-Bourbon Le Faubourg inhabits the former Parisian home of a pampered courtesan to a French king. The magnificent *maison* on a tree-lined street sits behind duplicates of the original double carriage doors and features a spacious interior courtyard. They host grand soirees during the warm-weather months under the stars and strings of fairy lights.

The layout—the same as the other two locations—spreads across seven levels. As with each club, the Sky Lounge offers a view of a nearby landmark. With Paris, it's the grand Eiffel Tower resplendent in lights at night. The beauty and history of the property makes this location my favorite.

"*Oui, petite étudiante. Je fais beaucoup,*" I respond.

I plant my feet further apart to widen the space. Then pat my legs to beckon Leonie to me. She arches her elegant eyebrow and tilts her head, regarding me with her sharp, cat-like eyes.

"Come here, Caramel Bonbon, and I will answer your question," I say as I pat my thighs again.

Leonie licks her lips, then sashays towards me. The hem of her minuscule skirt sways with each movement of her hips. Her long legs close the gap between us. She pauses before me and waits for my next command.

I slip my hands around her hips to cup her firm ass. I squeeze each cheek in my palms, pulling them apart slightly. More than a handful. Perfect.

Leonie bites her plump lower lip on a moan and sways in my grip. She places her hands on my broad shoulders, leaning into me.

The curve of her full breasts peek from behind her blouse. The top buttons undone afford me a glimpse and I nuzzle my face between her mounds. I suck on her skin enough to leave a red mark. It stands in contrast to her honey-color complexion.

Mine!

My dick throbs as it presses painfully against the zipper of my trousers. I shift uncomfortably on the chair. The ache unbearable. I have to get inside of her. Now.

Wedged between my thighs, I tip my face up to hers.

"Open your blouse for me, baby."

Immediately Leonie complies. Her tits bounce free in my face. My mouth closes on her fully aroused nipple, suckling hard on the distended tip. Delectable.

"Oooh, Roger, *Amoureux*," she murmurs with her head thrown back.

I slip my index finger into her mouth and she sucks on it like a lollipop. I remove the wet digit and place it against her back entrance.

She stills, then presses her hands on my shoulders to move away.

I grip her tighter and growl against her breast. Not giving her the chance to avoid my touch. I massage the tip of my finger against her puckered hole.

"Roger…"

"Yes, baby?" I croon as I hum on her heated skin.

"I... I've never... um... I've never had anal sex," she whispers.

"Mmm mmm mmm," I purr in delight.

Yes, another first! No other man will ever have the claim of her ass.

"I'll make it so good, baby. Trust me?" I ask.

Leonie considers my words. Her hesitation is only for a moment. Yet it feels like an eternity. I would never force a woman to do anything she doesn't want to do. But I will push their limits enough for them to decide if they want to continue or stop.

"*Oui, Amoureux,*" she replies confidently with a nod of her gorgeous head.

A breath I didn't realize I was holding expels from my mouth to blow warm air against her nipple. It pebbles even more. I kiss the tip softly. Then stand.

In her lower heeled shoes, I tower over Leonie. She tips her head back to search my face. I keep my expression open to ease any doubt she may have. She finds none. Able to relax fully, she smiles at me. Heat simmers in her amber eyes.

I take that as my cue to move us to the large four-poster bed with a trellis canopy. Like the rest of the clubs, Paris is just as sumptuous with high-end period furnishings, fixtures, and accents. This performance room features a school theme. Except for the armoire full of toys and the St. Andrew's Cross built into a wall, one wouldn't know they were in a BDSM club.

I play with certain elements. But tonight I'll keep it simple for Leonie's first time. My girth and ten inches are more than enough.

I sit on the bed and stand her between my thighs again.

She slips her fingers into my hair, twirling the strands around them. A tug sends a jolt from my scalp to my dick as she stares at me with hooded eyes.

I draw the soft flesh on the underside of her breast into my mouth to add my second mark. She growls softly. The vibration pulses against my lips, and my cock twitches in response to her primal call.

Her clothes have to go. Now.

First, I unzip the skirt and it falls to the floor in a puddle. Holding her hand, I help her step out of the circle of fabric. Then lift her leg to drape her thigh over my shoulder. I press my nose to her pussy to inhale her sweet arousal deeply. In one long swipe of the flat of my tongue, I lave the juices collected on her lips. Delicious.

As I make a meal of her pussy, Leonie mewls and rides my face. When her inner walls quiver around my probing tongue, I pull back and swat her ass. No cumming until I give permission. The jiggle of her flesh makes my dick weep, eager to dive deep.

"Off," I growl, as I tug at her blouse.

Leonie scrambles to remove the offending garment. Her wide eyes stare at me, surprised by my aggressiveness.

Fuck.

She drives me wild. I want to claim her and fuck her like a wild beast until I wreck her pussy as she writhes beneath me. The thought urges my hand to unzip my trousers and free my turgid dick from the confines of my boxer briefs. With a groan, it springs out and thumps against my shirt-covered abs.

Leonie shivers.

I bite her inner thigh.

She squeals, folding her torso over my head, yanking my hair hard.

I take the opportunity to partake of her succulent core again. Her legs tremble from the exertion of holding back her orgasm. So, as I push my thumb into her bottom hole, I draw her engorged clit into my mouth and suck it hard.

The pleasurable pressure from the duo sensations sends her over the edge. Her body convulses as she screams my name mixed in with French curses. Satisfied, I swallow her sweet honey as my mouth floods with her release.

Soft cries come from Leonie as she pants while her body reacclimates. I slip her limp form to the mattress. Then stand to undress. Her eyes are closed as she unconsciously plays with her nipples. A smile spreads across my face, proud that I put her in a state of bliss.

As I stand there stroking my cock, Leonie's eyes flutter open. Their feline shape narrows as she assesses me. Pleased with my naked form, she draws her lower lip in her mouth with her teeth. She stretches contentedly and purrs.

"Roger, *Mon Chéri*, you're too far away. *Viens à moi maintenant.*"

With a low growl of my own, I crawl up the bed then sit back on my haunches. Her gaze drops to my bobbing cock as I stroke it once again.

"Hands and knees, Kitten," I tell her as I give my dick a last tug.

Slowly, Leonie flips over. When she's in position, I press my palm between her shoulder blades. The slight pressure is enough for her to lower to her forearms. She peeks at me over her shoulder when I wrap her ponytail around my fist and tug.

Her body bows. Beautiful.

"You look so beautiful, Pretty Kitty," I growl against the delicate shell of her ear.

Leonie mews and lifts her hips upward to brush against my groin.

I swat her ass with my free hand. She growls, wiggling her lush ass. I lower my torso over her back as I wrap my arm around her waist to pull her bottom and thighs flush to me. My thick dick slips between her cheeks.

"So good, Pretty Kitty, I promise," rumbles from my chest to her ear.

I reach into the nightstand for the lube. Then apply a generous amount to my cock and her puckered hole. As I slip my index finger in to the first knuckle, Leonie whimpers, but doesn't move away. Fuck, yes! My dick grows impossibly hard knowing she's so responsive and trusts me.

Once she's suitably prepared, I pepper her back and neck with open-mouth kisses. She calms, and I grip my member to feed it into her body slowly. Her rear muscles push back against the invasion. So I slide my hand around her hip to caress her clit. Distracted, she allows her muscles to loosen and I slip another inch inside.

"Fuck, baby... You're so tight," I groan into her neck.

She whimpers softly, but tilts her head to give me better access to the column of her throat. I plant more kisses on her skin, humming with pleasure.

"Aaahhh... Ummm," Leonie moans as the discomfort transforms into rapture.

With one last thrust of my hips, I seat myself inside of her fully. My balls slap her distended clit as I finger fuck her pussy. She's so wet, squelching sounds spill from her core. As I stay still to allow her rear channel to adjust to my size, I continue to plunge my fingers in her pussy. The feeling of my dick in her ass drives me crazy. I don't stop until she squirts in my hand and collapses to the bed.

I grip her hips with both hands, withdraw my dick to the

tip, then thrust into her hole. Leonie cries out in wild abandon, tossing her head and bowing her back.

"That's it, Pretty Kitty. Take... every... inch," I piston with each word.

Leonie shakes as her muscles clench around my dick painfully.

With a whoop, I jackhammer my diamond hard dick into her.

"Whose is it? Who does it belong to?" I snarl, caught in her vise grip.

"Oh. Oh. Oh. Oh."

"Words, Pretty Kitty. I'll have your words!" I demand.

Leonie mewls as I feel her pussy tighten around air aroused from the pleasure she's receiving in her rear.

"*Oh, mon Dieu! Le vôtre ... Le vôtre ... Ooohhh,*" Leonie screams as her body quakes from the force of her climax.

Sweat glistens on her flushed skin. I lick the condensation feverishly, wanting to capture every bit of her essence. I lean over to press my front against her back possessively. Then return one hand to her pussy.

She's not done, yet. I'll wring a few more orgasms from her before I seek my release. My balls protest as they fill with my seed. But I hold on.

"Cum for me, baby. Cum hard on my fingers. I want to feel it all the way to my dick!"

Leonie keens as another climax claims her. Two more follow on the tail of the one before. The vibrations jolt my cock, and I roar from the intensity of them.

"FUCK!!!"

"ROGER... PLEASE..."

Leonie's had enough, and I won't push her past her limit as I promised. With both hands on her hips to hold her up, I pump in and out of her tight bottom hole. My lower back tingles at the base of my spine, then shoots to my balls. My dick swells and I roar my release, digging my fingers into her soft flesh. I lose all control.

My strokes become erratic. The rhythm gone. My hips work of their own accord to guarantee every drop of my jizz empties into Leonie. Blinded and brain numbed by the sheer intensity of the euphoria, I'm rocked to my very soul.

I collapse to my side, holding Leonie close to me, still connected as one. My body doesn't want to part from her warm embrace.

She moans softly as she murmurs my name.

My fingertips stroke her flank and lower stomach to soothe her as I croon words of comfort. We settle, and my spent dick slips from her rear hole. She snuggles into me with a contented sigh.

I wrap her in my arms and nuzzle my face into her neck. Then take a deep inhale of our combined scents and the smell of our sex. Nothing is better. I fall into a peaceful sleep knowing no one will disturb us.

SOMETIME LATER, I awaken unsure of where I am until it rushes back to me. Damn. Leonie is incredible. I glance down at her now wrapped in my arms with her head and hand on my chest as I lie on my back. Idly, I trace circles on the soft skin of her back.

She murmurs something indecipherable in French and cuddles closer to me.

I think back on our time together over the last two months. The thoughts we've shared, the fun we've had, and how much she makes me happy replay in my mind. The good times transcend the disagreements.

My wish is for Leonie to be a little more serious. I've

been more zany than rigid. Well, at least in my opinion. Leonie may argue not enough. I realize that I harp on her a bit—it's my nature. I just want her to succeed.

One thing's for sure, it's been the most interesting of my life. Leonie is full of surprises and I enjoy every second.

"Mmm mmm, *Chéri?*"

"*Oui, bébé?*"

"*Chéri*, stop thinking so hard! I can feel how tense you are—"

I flip us over and press her smaller body into the mattress with my larger frame. My hips spread her thighs for her to cradle me close. My burgeoning erection wedged between us. She gasps from the unexpected move and touch. I put my lips close to hers as I murmur.

"Well, then... What are you going to do about it?"

Leonie giggles and wraps her arms around my neck, gripping the hair at nape. She pulls my head down to slant her mouth to mine. Her passionate kiss sends tingles shooting through every cell of me.

Could this be our *coupe de foudre,* like our parents?

As she lifts her long legs to lock around my hips, my mind and body are in agreement.

I hope so.

LEONIE

"*Bon sang!*"

I cannot believe Roger! This is absolutely the worst thing he's ever done to make me feel less than. I want to hit him on the back of his head with my Judith Leiber minaud!

How dare he!

I glare at the mirror as though it's his reflection. As I fume in the bathroom lounge, another guest at the end-of-the-semester reception enters. One glimpse at me and she scurries back out. My face is flushed red with anger and my eyes shoot daggers. I hate that my irritation with Roger kept her from her task.

Merde!

Frustrated, I dab my face with a cool damp cloth and practice calming breaths. I lift my hair to press the soft cotton to the nape of my neck. With a sigh, I toss it into the bin, then return my gaze to the mirror. My eyes, no longer lit with anger, stare back in defeat.

I thought we were doing so well.

. . .

"Hi, baby, I missed you. I'm sure you're tired. But I'd like to see you. Have dinner with me?"

I hug my mobile to my bosom, so happy to hear his baritone voice over the speaker. It's been four days since we last saw each other. Roger had to visit Positano and the Harper's Bazaar cover photoshoot took me to Mustique. Over the last six weeks, we rarely spend more than three days apart.

So although jet lag has me in bed at eight in the evening, I lift the mobile back to my lips with an affirmative answer.

"Never too tired for you, Mon Chéri," I purr seductively.

"Mmm mmm... Delighted to know," he croons in response. "I'll pick you up in half an hour."

Only moments later, we're wrapped in each other's arms standing in the foyer of my duplex. An overwhelming need to be one with the other zings through us. Roger's thickness presses against my lower belly. Moans slip from my mouth as I sway my hips to rub my mons on his burgeoning erection. His hands cup my ass to hold me in place while he grinds his pelvis into mine.

"Fuck, Bonbon. If we don't stop now, we won't leave," he growls against my lips as he steps back reluctantly.

I pout. But he only chuckles and kisses the tip of my nose.

"Later, I promise."

I clap my hands joyously when we arrive at Septime. The one Michelin star restaurant is the city's most difficult to reserve. The attraction because of its scrumptious seasonal menu and its respect for the heritage of French cuisine while moving on from traditional and more formal fine dining.

It's a favorite of mine I mentioned to Roger weeks ago. I can't believe he remembered. He's so thoughtful!

My glee dampens when as soon as we walk through the door a beautiful, raven-haired woman rushes over to pull Roger into her *embrace. Her ice-blue eyes devour him as though he's the entrée du jour. And as though I cease to exist.*

"Roger, Mon Amour comment vas-tu?"

He extricates himself from her clutches. But she continues to hold on to his biceps. I notice his expression glazes over like it does when he's attempting to remain civil and distant. Fortunately, he's never used that look on me.

"Hello, Anouska," he responds in French. "You appear well. Give my regards to your family."

Not deterred, she steps with him as he moves around her. With a flirtatious giggle, she responds.

"Oh, what formality, mon amour! I will not have it! Come! Tell them for yourself. We're just over here."

She slips her palm down his arm to grasp his hand, leading him into the dining room.

Que se passe-t-il!

Roger must sense my ire because his intense gray eyes turn to me, and he shakes his head.

"Anouska. Enough. I am not alone as you can see," he says, as he pulls back, dropping her hand and extending his for me to hold. "Leonie Beaulieu, this is Anouska Albert. Anouska's family does business with STEELE. Anouska, Leonie and I are dating. Say hello to your family for me. Now, if you'd excuse us."

He strides past her with me in tow. He doesn't even offer a backwards glance.

Meanwhile, I'm beyond thrilled by his declaration. I cannot wait for Roger to make good on his earlier promise of later. My body tingles in anticipation.

Later, the tingles turn to jolts of electricity as our bodies become one. While he moves deep inside of my core, he cradles my head and stares down at me intensely.

"Only you, Leonie... Mmmm mmm... baby, only you."

· · ·

I was mistaken.

Tonight, instead of supporting me, Roger lectured me in front of the faculty and some of my classmates. All because I dared to joke about handing in my final term paper three days late. I had a legitimate excuse. Work on the other side of the world in Chile with no internet access can thwart attempts at digital submissions.

Merde!

I close my eyes and inhale deeply. I will not let Roger ruin my evening. On the exhale, I lift my chin high and strut out of the bathroom. I'm *The Lion*. A successful, independent woman who doesn't take shit from anyone. Not now, never. *Non!*

"Leonie, are you all right?"

I glance to my right to find my seat mate Antonio Vasquez beside the door to the bathroom. He must have been waiting for me. How sweet of him. I smile and nod.

"Well, that was a dick move by him," he continues as he stands to his full height of six feet two inches in front of me.

Antonio's concerned eyes search my face. Then he tucks a strand of my hair behind my ear, caressing the side of my face. He cups my chin in his large hand as his eyes drop to my mouth.

"I would never disrespect you, Leonie. You are precious," he murmurs.

Surprised, I stand transfixed by his luminous emerald stare. My lips part to respond, but he brushes his mouth against mine. I lift my hands to his chest to push him away gently. Abruptly, he's snatched away from me. I stagger from the loss of balance.

My eyes widen when I see a red-faced Roger gripping Antonio's shoulder. Then my mouth drops open when Roger punches him in the face. He reels backwards, hitting the wall. Then lunges forward. They grapple. But Roger who's a trained boxer has the advantage. His cool demeanor never waivers. His focus laser sharp. Coming out of my stupor, I call his name.

"Roger! Enough!"

He turns to pin me with his intense stare. Antonio sees an opening and hits him in the stomach. Roger doubles over from the impact.

"Fuck you, asshole! If you don't know how to treat Leonie well, then I will!"

Antonio makes to knee Roger in the head. Quickly, I push him.

"Enough I said! Both of you!"

I glare at the two Alpha Males. Antonio rubs his swollen jaw and mumbles as he heads to the men's room. Roger gives me that damnable blank stare. I close my eyes and count for ten breaths. When I open them, he's gone.

Merde!

* * *

THREE DAYS LATER, and I refuse to take Roger's calls or answer his text messages. The hurt and embarrassment too much to bear. I haven't left my duplex. Instead, assignments take priority. Whether or not it's to prove Roger wrong, I dive into my studies. In no time, I'm caught up.

Perhaps he's right. If I apply myself more, I can finish faster. I should call him—

Non!

He disrespected me in front of my instructors, peers, and the world. Thanks to camera phones, videos of my chastisement and his subsequent brawl appeared all over social and mainstream media. The Billionaire and the Bombshell splashed everywhere. The saying all publicity is good publicity may be true. But my private affairs remain just that... private. Ugh!

With a groan, I rise from the desk in my home office and stretch my arms overhead. I roll my neck in circles and my shoulders back. I rid my body of the stiffness from sitting for so long.

I need some fresh air. A walk to the café will do me a world of good. I trade my Lola's Coterie romper for a Missoni sweater, Alaïa jeans, and Chanel ballet flats. I leave my hair in a messy bun and cover my eyes with classic Ray-Ban aviators. I toss my mobile, wallet, and keys into my 2.55 handbag and head out.

It's a beautiful afternoon. A sunny, clear blue sky and cool breeze greet me as I stroll out past my doorman. A few blocks over takes me to the hidden gem. It's only locals. No one asks me for my autograph or a photo here. Grateful for the peace, I sit at one of the outdoor tables on the quiet street. The server takes my order for a pot of green tea and a light salad.

My mobile entices me to listen and read Roger's messages. I slip it out of my handbag and turn it on. As I scroll through, my heart aches.

What the fuck, Leonie?

Mouth locked with that guy,,, Really?!?!?!

Not cool, Leonie

The tone changed with more recent text.

We need to talk

I shouldn't have spoken to you like that...

If you don't answer, I'm coming over there...

Hellooo

Similar words spoken in his voicemails. Only his tone of voice changes from angry to remorseful to demanding.

I put the mobile down with a sigh. Then stare into space as I sip my tea. I miss him. But he constantly harps on me. This time it's too much. I'm not sure it's worth his pendulous behavior.

I wish I could speak to my best friend. But Lola's busy with the New York boutique's opening and working on the Las Vegas site. Besides, Roger is Sebastian's brother, and I don't want to cause any drama.

The vibration and chirp of a text cuts into my reverie. I flip it over and see a familiar name on the screen—Gio Mattei.

Bellissima, I haven't heard from you in forever! You didn't answer my text to come watch me race at the Grand Prix next month in Monte Carlo. You know you're my good luck charm! I'll send the jet for you. Baci, amore mio. Ciao!

Obviously I could use the distraction. Not that I'll sleep with him. *Non.* But I haven't been to my Monte Carlo penthouse in a few months... *Non!*

I have to put on my big girl panties and speak with Roger.

Another chirp, this time a text from Sebastian about surprising Lola in Las Vegas... tonight. He writes how Roger has been trying to reach me all day so we can fly over together and asks if I can make it. I respond yes right away.

A shadow looms over me just as I hit send. Odd since the rest of the area is sunny. With a frown, I glance over my shoulder to see Roger standing behind me. He looks deliciously rumpled with his thick jet black hair tousled about his head, eyes a flinty gray, and a five o'clock shadow on his normally clean-shaven jaw—gorgeous.

"Baby, I'm sorry. Please forgive me. I want to make it right."

Merde...

LEONIE

"*Y*ou must understand how you hurt me deeply, Roger. If not, let me be clear."

I turn to face him seated on the banquette of his private jet.

"You reprimanded me as though I were a simple child and not an adult woman. You humiliated me in front of my teachers, faculty, and classmates. People I have to interact with regularly and who judge my competency. Now, they may think less of me. Why? How could you?"

We have a ten-hour flight ahead of us. I won't sit in silence or pretend nothing is wrong. It's very wrong. I stare at him expectantly.

Roger squirms. Hi eyes dart from mine to the floor.

At least he appears contrite. But he has to tell me what he was thinking to treat me in such a manner. It hurts more since he's teased me about being flighty.

I hate the stereotypical misperceptions and expectations of models: dumb; only clothes hangers; just stand there and pose prettily, not think. I serve as a mentor for girls and teens. My entire career I've fought against those beliefs and urged others to to do the same—models, designers, photographers.

Now to hear it from someone I've grown closer to than any other man...

"I apologize, Leonie. I was out of line. There's no excuse."

He takes my hands in his and stares at me intently.

"I met with the faculty and your professors. I made a public apology at each of your classes. My Human Resources team set up an annual paid internship program for two students awarded in perpetuity."

My eyes mist with tears. I turn away, ashamed to show any weakness.

Roger refuses my denial. He cups my face in his large hand. Automatically, my gaze meets his intense stare. He's so open I perceive no artifice in their gray depths. Only his sincerity and remorse shows.

"Please forgive me, baby," he murmurs.

I nod. But remember, he didn't address his other gaffe.

"Thank you for all that you've done to rectify your behavior—"

Roger leans forward to kiss me, but I put my fingers to his lips. He lifts his eyebrow in question.

"What about Antonio?" I raise my eyebrow in return and tilt my head.

His eyes darken to a steely gray, then close off. He sits back and folds his muscular arms across his broad chest. He looks like a petulant man-child.

But I already miss the warmth of his touch. However, I will not speak first. He has to answer for his egregious conduct. Antonio's face was already swelling like a balloon!

It's a tense few minutes before Roger responds angrily.

"What about him? He was mooning all over you when I

guest lectured your class. I warned him then with a glare. Next he's kissing... No correction... The two of you are kissing while you're with me—"

I cut him off, but he stops me.

"How would you have felt if Anouska flirted with me in front of you one day and later you come across us with our lips locked in a passionate kiss?"

He looks at me sharply. A dare for me to lie and say I wouldn't have behaved like he did. But I can't. Anger wouldn't describe the intensity of my reaction. I can only nod.

"You're right and wrong. I would not be happy to find you with Anouska, or anyone for that matter. But I was not kissing him—"

"You had your mouth on his and your hands on his chest. What do you call that?" Roger growls, eyes in slits.

His possessiveness makes my pussy clench. He's like a caveman claiming his mate. Crazy, but it turns me on. He must sense the electric charge in the air or my arousal because he cocks his head to the side, scanning my face. I bite the corner of my bottom lip. His nostrils flair. My pussy pulses.

Merde...

As though internally deciding, Roger takes a deep inhale. Then closes his eyes and presses his forehead to mine. He slips his hands around my waist to clasp them at my lower back.

My fingertips trace the prickly stubble along his chin to caress his powerful jaw. As I slide them into his thick hair that brushes his shirt collar, his exhale escapes as a soft sigh from his full lips. In the stillness, our breath carries like a whisper on the wind, mingling with the drone of the jet's engines.

Lulled by the rhythm, we allow our bodies and minds to reconnect. The past days dissipate with each exhale. A new start grows as we inhale. Rekindled, I slant my mouth over his. Without hesitation, Roger opens to me. Our reconnection deepens as our tongues dance.

Roger shifts on the banquette and scoops me onto his lap. My long legs bend on either side of his muscular thighs. Never breaking apart. He takes control of our kiss as he will not deny his desire. His dominance reclaims me.

"No one else gets your kisses, Leonie," he growls against my swollen lips. "They are mine and mine alone... As are you, Kitten."

I whimper and slide my heated seam along his thighs. On a groan, he slides down in the seat to notch his bulge with my pussy. Hampered by our clothing, we can only rub against fabric. The friction increases as my clit strikes his cock. The fire builds. I want more. I need more.

But no.

"I forgive you, but we can't rush into—"

Roger groans and tightens his grip on my ass to lock me in place.

Gently, I press against his chest to stand. Then straighten my clothes.

He throws his head back against the top of the banquette, his eyes squeezed shut. Long calming breaths cause his chest to rise and fall. He drags his fingers through his hair. Then leans forward and presses his forehead against my belly.

"Oh, baby," he groans as he cups my ass. "What's wrong?"

Now it's my turn to close my eyes tight. I have to be strong and not give in, as tempting as he may be. With my hands on either side of his face, I tilt it up to me. My heart bleeds when his entreating silvery eyes stare into mine.

"As much as I burn for you right now, we can't. Let's take some time off this trip. Okay, *Mon Chéri*??"

I stroke his cheek and smile encouragingly.

Roger groans as he buries his face under my sweater, nuzzling the sensitive skin. He plants a trail of open mouth kisses from my navel to between my breasts. Then blows warm air against my flesh, heating it up even more. He pulls his head out. Then stares at me intently before nodding and pulling me to sit across his lap.

I can't help but squirm as his prominent bulge rests against my ass. In response, Roger pulls me tight to his firm chest and zerbets my neck.

The tickling sensation increases my movement as laughter bubbles from my lips. He hooks his thigh over mine. It prevents me from jumping off his lap to evade his probing fingers as they add to the tickling of his mouth.

Breathless, I squeal, "Stoppp… Rooggeerrr…"

His booming laughter joins mine as he wrestles me to the floor of the jet where he straddles me. His handsome face looms over mine. His hair falling into his sparkling eyes. He continues his onslaught with no care for my yips and yowls.

"You little temptress," he mumbles against my throat. "You rub one out on my dick, then decide we need to 'take… some… time?' Really, Kitten?"

Each poke of his fingers causes tears to spill from the corners of my eyes. They slide down my face to pool in my ears. I take a quick breath, then wheeze out a stuttered response.

"Roger, please! I can't take anymore!"

His chuckle blows more warm air onto my skin, setting me on fire even more. He sits on his heels as he smirks down at me.

"Fine. As you wish, Kitten."

Effortlessly, he rolls to the balls of his feet, then stands to hold his hand out to me. I clasp it and he lifts me up. But to emphasize his desire, he pulls my torso flush with his. I feel his still hard cock throbbing against my lower belly. Just as eager as my pussy and as denied.

"If you behave, perhaps I'll reward you," I tease, waggling my eyebrows.

On a groan, Roger buries his face in my neck for one last zerbet.

My laughter rings around the cabin.

"Is this it? Is this the space for Lola's Coterie?"

Lola asks Sebastian as she bounces on the balls of her feet, holding her beaded clutch to her chest.

Roger and I along with Luc, Blair, Tina Nickles, Walter Smith, Malcolm Steele, and Lydie Jackson gather inside of the large retail space. Tina and Walter are Sebastian's personal assistant and head of development, respectively. Lydie is a family friend of theirs who's in Vegas to meet with Malcolm.

Recently vacated by the former anchor tenant in STEELE Las Vegas' luxury mall, it's the perfect spot for Lola's Coterie. They set the mall between their two five-diamond resort and casino properties in the middle of the action of the Las Vegas Strip.

Roger and I are staying in his Bridge Penthouse, one of the twelve on the top six floors designed to attract high rollers and the über-wealthy clientele. The penthouses act as a bridge to connect the two resort properties with the mall between them from the ground level to the third floor.

Sebastian just punched in the code for the door lock. As he steps back, he gestures for Lola to enter ahead of him.

We hide in the darkened interior since the lights are off. The paper-covered windows and doors block the inside from passersby's view. So she sidesteps to the right to let him guide the way and claps her hands in delight.

"Maybe," he teases her with a Cheshire Cat grin.

"Don't tease me."—THWACK—"My heart can't take it." She says as she hits Sebastian on the chest with her clutch.

"Okay… Okay. Wait there while I turn on the lights," he tells her and walks further into the interior towards where we stand.

It's our cue to flash the lights flash on and yell surprise. Our screams echo throughout the vast space.

Lola screeches and jumps back as we and the servers wave, clap, and stomp our feet. Sebastian joins in and swoops Lola up in the air, then carries her over to the table set for dinner. As he put her down, she fists his hair and brings his face to hers for a passionate kiss. Reluctantly, he lets her go when I grab her arm to pull her in for a hug.

"*Félicitations!*" I exclaim, beaming with my amber eyes aglow.

Luc comes over next and kisses Lola's cheeks before pulling her into an embrace. "*C'est une excellente nouvelle pour* Lola's Coterie, *petite chérie!*" He extols, hugging her, again.

Sebastian drags Lola away to introduce her to Malcolm and Lydie. I giggle at his jealousy of Luc. My skin tingles as I sense Roger's eyes on me. After spending the rest of the flight working—me with my studies and Roger with his project plans—our amorous encounter took a back seat.

When we arrived at the penthouse, we had less than thirty minutes to change and get to the store before Sebastian brought Lola here. In our haste, we didn't have an opportunity to rekindle the flame. Although surreptitious glimpses kept the embers lit.

Now, however, Roger's eyes simmer blatantly with unquenched ardor. Sparked by our gazes meeting, he saunters over to me. His stare scorches my skin as he takes me in from head to toe.

I can't blame him since I look ravishing in my black mini dress. It's artfully ruched to create a wrap-effect skirt with long sleeves that have structured shoulder pads. The stretch-jersey gives it a close fit and is complete with an open front split that points to my core. My long legs go on forever with black point-toe pumps. The strings wrap around my ankles like a present.

Just before he reaches me, out of the corner of my eye, I see Lola hurrying in my direction. I love her outfit of a black cutout, fringed stretch-cotton and mesh, sleeveless maxi dress with matching black briefs peek out from under the sheer skirt. The plunging neckline, wispy fringe, plus delicate ties that crisscross the open back add to the sexiness. It falls demurely to a billowy, ruffled, asymmetric hem where her high strappy heels lengthen her legs.

"Malcolm's invited us to one of the resort's nightclub!" Lola gushes. "I'd love to go dancing! What a marvelous way to continue the celebration!"

She squeezes my hands between hers and we wiggle our hips, mimicking dance moves.

"I'd love to go, too!" I respond, equally excited.

"Dancing? After dinner you mean?" Roger asks with a disappointed expression on his freshly shaven face.

"Yes! We can't wait!" Lola replies, unaware of the sexual tension pinging between Roger and me.

He peers at me over her head. Then parts his lips to respond.

However, Sebastian calls everyone to the table. With a smirk, I dodge Roger's answer and loop arms with Lola. We strut to the table and take our seats. A grumpy Roger lowers himself in the chair on my other side.

Dinner is fun with Lola and I regaling everyone with stories of our exploits in growing Lola's Coterie's brand image to the fashion set. Luc chimes in with his tales. Only Roger and Sebastian appear glum.

Now in one of the resort's nightclubs, Lola and I dance in the middle of the floor. Carefree and loving life as the young, successful, and wealthy can. As always, the two of us attract the attention of every man in proximity.

Apparently the brothers had enough of Lola, me, and our admirers.

No longer sitting in our VIP area sipping glass after glass of the Jackson Special Blend Scotch, moping for the rest of the night, they stalk over to us. The other men scatter like prey, sensing the hunters.

"Okay, Dancing Queen. It's my turn," Roger growls in my ear as he slides his hands around my waist.

"Whatever do you mean, *Amoureux*?" I ask, staring up at him as I flutter my eyelashes coyly.

He spins me around so my back presses to his front as he bends his knees to grind his pelvis into my ass. His lips trail kisses along the side of my neck as I shiver in delight. His hands slide along my flanks to grip my hips possessively. Locked in his embrace, there's no doubt I belong to him.

"Mine, Pretty Kitty. All mine!"

ROGER

"*Oh, Mon Chéri!* This is just what I needed! A lovely break from the monotony of work, work, work, work, work as Rihanna says! Thank you!"

Leonie and I left Las Vegas for STEELE Cabo San Lucas at the spur of the moment. Might as well take advantage of being on this side of the world for a beachside rendezvous with the current year's *Sports Illustrated Swimsuit Issue* cover girl. One of many for my hot supermodel girlfriend.

She looks as tantalizing now as she does on the cover. Her long hair hangs sleek down her back from the warm ocean water. Pulled from her face, her sculpted cheekbones and swan-like neck emphasize her beauty. The itty bitty, white bikini barely contains her ample breasts and makes me want to bite her generous ass. Every man on Palmilla Beach stares mesmerized by her as Leonie frolics in the waves.

The beach features a one-mile-long stretch of gorgeous, soft white sands and blue-green swimmable waters. The five-diamond SCSL is the only resort with direct access. It's nestled near the southern tip of Palmilla Beach and commands stunning views over the turquoise water. Guests enjoy complimentary activities including snorkeling, stand-up paddleboarding, and kayaking at SCSL's very own Pelican Beach.

"Chéri! Come join me!"

I can't resist her siren's call. As I stride over to her, Leonie's feline eyes eat me alive. Memories of our love-making these last two days stir my cock. If I don't get into the water soon, everyone along the mile will see how much my Kitten excites me. As though sensing my thoughts, Leonie grins and pointedly stares at my rapidly expanding bulge.

"Happy to see me, *Amoureux*?" She teases as I dip into the water in front of her.

Beneath the waves, I cup her mons and smirk, "It's not only the ocean that has you wet, Caramel Bonbon."

She blushes at my reference to how sweet her pussy tastes. Then hisses when my thick finger slides between her folds to stroke her inner walls. I add a second to increase her fullness. Leonie rides my digits. A pinch of her clit sends her spiraling towards her climax. So caught in the throes of ecstasy, she disregards the other beachgoers.

I cover her mouth with mine to muffle the sounds of her pleasure from those around us. No one is the wiser of her release. As Leonie comes down, I nuzzle her neck, planting kisses along her feverish skin.

A hiss escapes my lips as she takes my engorged dick into her hand.

Her insistent tugs bring my release on quickly. My thighs shake as my cum spews into the water. I laugh at the thought of impregnating fish with my copious amount of seed. Leonie cocks her head questioningly. But I shake my own at the absurdity of it.

As we continue to stand in the waves, I pull her to me and she buries her face in my neck. The feel of her heart racing with mine reminds me of how close we've become over these two months. And so fast. This is the happiest I've been in a relationship with a woman in my life. Only her lack of focus mars my keenness of her.

"I don't want to leave tomorrow," Leonie whispers against my skin.

"You have your exam the next day," I murmur, rubbing her back in circles to soothe her as I think here we go. "You can't miss it."

She groans. But perks up, peeking at me.

"I could always tell my professor I had an unexpected assignment…"

What the hell? Didn't we talk about her not shirking her responsibilities? Leonie has to be more serious with her program. How can she expect to make a career out of being an interior designer if she uses flimsy excuses to not complete her assignments and coursework? I shake my head, disappointed with her behavior.

"What? Why do you have such an angry expression on your face, Roger?" She demands, pulling out of my arms.

The Lion stands fiercely akimbo in front of me. Her amber eyes no longer shine with satiety. Rather, they burn with indignation.

Too bad.

"Leonie, are you serious with me right now?" I ask, not bothering to hide my irritation.

She stares at me in defiance. Her chin tips up and her eyes narrow. With a snarl, she responds vehemently.

"I am very serious right now, Roger. Why do you stare at me in disappointment?"

Although we only got over the argument about my treatment of her at the end-of-the-semester reception, I won't back down. This is different. It's only us—no one else. Plus, she should know better than to ditch her exam. It's enough already.

"Leonie, the better question is why do you so readily, and so easily I might add, skip out on your schooling? To what end?" I query, folding my arms across my chest, as ready as she is to battle this out.

For a moment, I think her head will explode. The honey color of her face mottling with red. Followed by her eyes widening in shock. Without realizing it, I'm holding my breath. Fuck it. On an exhale, I continue.

"Right. You don't have a plausible reason. We leave as planned."

I stride back to our double chaise to gather my things. A silent Leonie appears opposite me and picks up her towel and straw bag. I can't get a read on her emotional state. For once, she's the one with the stoic expression, not me.

Without a glance in my direction, she marches back to our beachfront villa next to the resort.

I can't help but appreciate the sway of her hips. Her long, toned legs easily carry her away from me.

Fuck!

Leonie

I'm so upset with Roger. Only by sheer force of will do I keep the tears from falling. I have to get back to the villa, pack, and get the hell out of here.

His words play over and over in my mind. The sour

expression on his handsome face burned a hole in my chest. Not again... Not again.

Fortunately, I make it to the front door and key in the code. I don't bother to check whether Roger is behind me. I hope not. I need to leave without further hurtful words between us. They will only make it worse. And honestly, it can't get any worse than this.

The door clicking shut behind me lets me know Roger is not with me. Was he ever?

I thank the packing gods for teaching me more is less. So, in no time, my Bottega Veneta duffle and garment bag sit on the bed waiting for me as I shower. When I walk into the bedroom wrapped in a towel, Roger is sitting beside my luggage.

We stare at one another soundlessly. I refuse to speak first. But I wait to see what he'll say. Maybe, just maybe, he'll apologize and we can move on. When he only continues to sit and stare at me intently with those gray eyes, I rouse myself.

Not caring that he'll see me naked—nothing unusual in my profession—I drop my towel. Then don the lingerie and clothes that I left on the bed. My skin tingles with his stare. But I ignore him. As I reach for my mobile to call for one of the resort's drivers, Roger breaks the tense standoff.

"Leonie, so you're going to leave? Just like that?"

I swing to face him, skewering him with my glare.

"Are you kidding me, Roger? After all you said, you think I'll stay here with you? *Bof*!"

He frowns, his response, "No, I'm not."

I raise both of my hands palms up and shrug my shoulders while I shake my head. That's it? That's his response? Fuck it.

I turn back to my mobile and punch the numbers on the

screen angrily. As I mutter to myself in French, Roger stands and takes my mobile out of my hands, disconnecting the call. Furious, I glare up at him.

"How dare you! Give it back to me... Now, Roger!" I yell.

His response shakes me to my core.

"Leonie, you were 'clear' with me on the jet. Now let me be clear with you. I want a serious-minded partner and not a wayward woman who cannot stay focused for over five minutes. You consistently flit around and avoid your studies. Coming up with excuse after lame excuse. You want people to respect you. But you cannot respect yourself."

He pauses, then continues, "It is my responsibility to return you to Paris since I brought you here. If you insist upon leaving, give me a moment and I will have the jet prepared. We can leave shortly."

With that, he hands my mobile back and pulls his out of the pocket of his swim trunks. So pompous, he doesn't even bother to look at me. He continues with his task. Roger *The Fucking Responsible* Steele to the very end.

My mouth gapes as tears spring to my eyes. This cannot be happening. Roger of all people wouldn't throw my concerns into my face so cavalierly. I clutch my chest, the pain too strong to bear.

I choke back a sob. Then take a deep breath.

"You promised me, Roger. You promised you'd never judge me or make me feel bad about myself again. You broke your promise and my heart. I can't... I won't anymore."

He turns his steely, stoic stare to regard me.

When his expression doesn't change—the one he used with Anushka and others—I know we're done. I swallow my tears and exert my Independent Woman.

"I am not some woebegone, needy woman who has to

depend upon a man. I can take care of myself. Thank you very much!"

I yank my bags from the bed and storm out of the villa. Once I'm in the driveway, I call for a driver to take me to Los Cabos International Airport. While I wait for the Mercedes-Benz G-Wagen, I pull up my private jet charter app and schedule a flight within the hour. By the time I arrive at the airport, I can board.

I use the twenty-minute drive to return emails and text messages. I'm determined not to dwell on the painful events before I can reflect on them in private. So absorbed in my tasks, I startle when the driver opens my door.

Once we're airborne, I request do not disturb. The flight attendant looks concerned for a moment before her professional demeanor falls back in place. I shake my head when she asks if I would like meal and beverage service. My stomach, too knotted to eat, gurgles in protest at the thought. She leaves me in peace.

Finally, I allow the unshed tears to fall.

My heart breaks. This is not *un coupe de foudre*.

ROGER

"*M*attei! Mattei! Mattei!"

The crowd chants. Their loud cheers erupt from the lower terrace and the deejay stops the music to announce the winning team.

Giovanni Fucking Mattei. Damn.

I watch as he grins, keeping his arm around Leonie as they pose for the cameras at the Grand Prix after party here in Monte Carlo. I barely notice Lola, who's opposite them with her arm looped through some guy on Mattei's professional racing team. Great. It's bound to piss Sebastian off.

Unbeknownst to Leonie, the party is being held at one of my new spec sites. It's a hillside villa used as the venue to showcase the property and to encourage buyers. My team expects the entire community of ten villas and a mini clubhouse to generate over a quarter billion dollars in revenue. The same project Leonie was privy to when we were together. Now she'll see it in person. But on the arm of another man.

Mattei, that slimy bastard. The one who always cheats

on her is the one with whom she now parades around my fucking villa. She ran back into his arms three weeks after the Cabo fiasco.

Fine. Fuck it.

Below me, Sebastian weaves through the guests as he rushes over to the terrace wall seeking Lola. He flew in panicking after pictures of her and Leonie traipsing around Monte Carlo surfaced on the Internet.

I don't blame him. Leonie in tiny bikinis, mini dresses, fitted capris sashaying all over the place. Followed by the paparazzi. Smiling for the cameras. Never once mournful.

Another glance finds Lola laughing with Leonie, who's still glued to Mattei whose tongue is down her throat. Sebastian looks on, too. He's probably not pleased to see Lola with some other guy. I know I'm pissed with Leonie.

Again. Fine. Fuck it.

Finally, Lola's gaze sweeps around the villa and lands on the terrace where Sebastian stands glowering down at her. She does a double take when she recognizes him; her eyes widening in surprise. He merely stares at her. Even I can sense from this distance her astonishment at seeing him here. She whispers something in Leonie's ear.

She promptly lifts her shocked gaze to Sebastian. Her eyes dart around. Perhaps she's connecting the dots with Monte Carlo, Sebastian, a villa... my project. And wonders if I'm here, too.

In my periphery, I notice Sebastian catch sight of me as I stare from a distance at Leonie and Mattei. I'm sure Sebastian can distinguish my facial expression, which may be indecipherable to a stranger. However, since I'm his brother, he can tell by the stiffness around my mouth that I'm struggling to keep a straight face and my emotions under control.

The couple I was speaking with is oblivious even as my

eyes shift from them to Leonie, who's the center of attention sipping champagne amongst the jubilant racers. When the peals of her laughter rise above the music and other voices, I visibly vibrate with white heat.

"Monsieur Steele, this villa is spectacular! When do you expect the completion of construction for the other properties?"

The woman's question pulls me from my musings. I blink and return my attention to the couple. Focus, Steele! Get your head in the game! I loosen my neck to drain some pent-up tension before I respond.

"As you saw during the tour, this model villa is ready for occupancy. Of the nine other villas, three are in construction, four are in contract, and two are in the bidding process. Each property estimates three months to complete, two for an expedited surcharge."

Her husband, the founder of a Silicon Valley software company, nods as he adds, "We don't want to wait. We offer twenty million cash for this villa to close in two days. Enough time to clean up from this party—"

"And for us to enjoy before we fly back to San Jose at the end of this week." His wife interrupts as she nods emphatically.

"My team will make the arrangements tonight," I turn to my lead sales rep who then coordinates with the couple.

No sooner do I shake their hands do I feel a small palm rest on the middle of my back. I glance over my shoulder to see Verónica Casal. Another stunningly beautiful, well-known supermodel with whom I've been involved.

It's been since Leonie that I've had sex, so my dick thumps to life at the memory of Verónica's ardent fucking. Well… Hello there. No point in being a monk for someone who couldn't care less.

"*Hola guapo*," Verónica purrs seductively as she strokes my back. "It's been a while, no?"

Her chestnut eyes glint with mischief in the light. Her full red lips glisten as she licks her tongue across them. My eyes can't help but follow its trail remembering how it felt wrapped around my thick dick.

Yeah. Good plan.

"*Hola preciosa*, too long, yes," I reply with a cocky grin. "You look as delicious as ever."

Verónica preens while I take her hand to twirl her in a circle, admiring her lush curves in the form-fitting white dress she wears. Damn, her round ass is a playground. My neglected cock presses painfully against the zipper of my leather pants.

When she faces me once again, the sight of Leonie with Mattei in tow moving towards Sebastian and Lola distracts me momentarily. She appears anxious as she looks around the bustling terrace. Perhaps she is wondering if I'm here.

"Tell me, *amante*, I saw you with Leonie... But she is here with gorgeous Gio, her on-again-off-again lover. She's parading him around in front of you. So, are Leonie and you together or no?"

Irritation shoots through me like a live wire. The last shred of my desire for Leonie seared away. Roger *The Responsible* takes a back seat. Emboldened, I lean down to whisper in Verónica's ear.

"Would it stop you if we were, *preciosa?*"

"Absolutely not!" Her peal of laughter carries over the sound of the music and guests' chatter.

Out of the corner of my eye, I can tell Leonie heard Verónica and now sees us together. Leonie's cat-like gaze flashes wide with hurt. Then narrows to angry slits that send sparks in my direction. Meanwhile, I continue to whisper passionate promises in Verónica's ear. Too damn bad.

Leonie continues to glare at us until I raise my head. Then pin her with my signature intense stoic stare. Blank as fuck.

We continue to glower at each other until that jerk Mattei glides up behind Leonie. He slips his arms around her waist, burying his face in her neck. Lustily whispering in her ear.

I throw the couple a scornful look, strong enough to make even Dom Sebastian flinch. In response, Leonie lifts her chin defiantly and takes Mattei by the hand, only stopping briefly to speak to Lola. With a wistful smile, Lola shakes her head, then pins me with a scathing glare.

Sebastian says something to Leonie. She replies, attempting to keep her smile in place. I watch as she walks away with Mattei's arm wrapped around her waist tightly. It's apparent to everyone they are a couple.

I feel no remorse as I return my gaze to Verónica, who I find watching me with interest to gauge my reaction. Not to come across as a lovesick wuss, I pull her close to me letting my hard dick answer her unspoken question.

I sense Sebastian's stare. But I pretend my conversation with Verónica captivates me. I'm sure he can tell that I'm agitated by the set of my shoulders. I cannot belie my genuine emotions to my eldest brother. He knows me far too well.

"Do you have to stay any longer or can we catch up?"

I glimpse down at Verónica's upturned, heart-shaped face. Her thick inky black hair falls in waves like a frame. She is a beautiful woman. Not Leonie beautiful, but in her own right an attractive woman. I ponder whether I can escape within her voluptuous body. My cock begs me, but my mind hesitates.

"Come, *amante*, let's lose ourselves in a night of passion," her heavy-lidded eyes beckon me.

One last glance in Leonie's direction and her retreating back with Mattei possessively holding her eases my conscious.

Decision made, I make a mental note to send a text message to my team. They must replace the mattress and bedding in the primary bedroom. I'm not so far gone that I lose sight of pleasing my clients.

LEONIE

"*S*helley is wonderful! You're lucky to have such a nice mother-in-law, *Chérie.*"
I exclaim as I clink my flute to Lola's.

We parted from Shelley and Haley, her future sister-in-law, with hugs and kisses a few hours ago. Now, we're ensconced on a terrace at Lola's STEELE Tower penthouse she shares with Sebastian sipping more Dom Pérignon Rosé Vintage 2005 Champagne—her favorite. Hell, we're more than sipping, we've finished two bottles.

Lola wanted me to stay with her. But I declined, preferring to stay at her Sutton Place penthouse. I offered the excuse that being in her penthouse—I'm doing the interior design for—will allow me to get a true understanding for the space. I get she doesn't believe me. I want to avoid being in the same building as Roger.

It's been eight months since we broke up in Cabo San

Lucas and almost seven since we last caught one another in Monte Carlo. It's still too raw for me. I haven't even told Lola the entire sad story. Thankfully, being the best friend that she is to me, she hasn't pressured me into discussing it.

After she told me Roger is in Paris, I agreed to spend time here after the wedding prep session. As her maid of honor, I'm a vital part of the plans, and I love it! I'm so happy for her and Sebastian. Genuine love!

So, once I realized the coast was clear, my expression went from guarded to relieved. Now, it's blissfully happy from the delectable bubbly. Yum!

"How are you and Giovanni?" Lola asks.

And like that, my stomach flips. I realize she's curious since I haven't mentioned him after she extended my plus one to him. She wants me to be happy, even on her big day when her brother-in-law will be in attendance. She deserves the truth.

I take a moment to stare beyond the glass surround at the city view for a moment. Their duplex is on the fifty-fifth and fifty-fourth floors while Roger's penthouse is on the fifty-second. Once I've gathered my thoughts, I shift in my chaise to face Lola.

"Oh, *Chérie*, I just don't know if I want to—"

Merde… Roger!

Abruptly, I sit up and swing my feet to the floor as I stare with wide eyes over Lola's shoulder at him. Surprised by my reaction, she turns to figure out the cause for my concern.

He's striding over to us with that intense gray-eyed gaze of his pinned on me. I suck in a quick inhalation of breath, startled by my body's innate reaction to him. Lola turns to face me. My normally golden-caramel complexion now ashen with my mouth opened in shock spurs her on. My petite defender as always comes to my defense.

Lola jumps to block Roger's path to me. He towers over her five-feet-five-inch frame.

"Stop!"

She puts her hands up and glares at Roger and at Sebastian, who I notice stands behind him.

"Leonie doesn't want to see you. So, please go," she tells him. Then forcefully she adds, "Now, Roger!"

He blinks away from me. His eyes cut to Lola's red-faced glare. She doesn't waiver before him. Instead, she meets his stare with her hazel eyes blazing.

"Roger, bro, you need to slow down," Baz tells him, putting his hand on Roger's shoulder to pull him back. "You're freaking them out. Not cool, man."

The air is tense. I've got to get out of here. I put my shoes back on and gather my things. I'm a bit wobbly from the champagne, but determined to leave.

"Lola, I have to go. I'll call you later," I whisper in French.

She knows I'm upset because I rarely call her Lola. Her eyes widen.

"No!"

We jump around to stare at Roger who has his hands palms forward, raised in surrender. His stare less intense, but still focused on me.

"Please, Leonie, I just want to speak with you. Just for a moment... Please," he beseeches in a voice rough with emotion.

Collectively, they hold their breath for my response. I sigh again, but nod my head in acceptance. Lola speaks, but I shake my head. She must sense I'm trying to control my emotions, so she gives me the space I request.

The glare she gives Roger would set him on fire. Sebastian turns to me and asks if I'm comfortable speaking with Roger. How kind of him to place my comfort above his brother's. I nod, again. They leave Roger and me on the terrace and head to the living room.

On the chaise Lola vacated, Roger sits forward with his elbows resting on his knees, his hands clasped together. I return to my chaise, perched on its edge with my hands folded in my lap. I don't know what to expect, so I wait for him to speak. At first we stare at each other, apparently waiting for one of us to start. Roger breaks the silence.

ROGER

"Leonie... I don't mean to upset you. I asked Sebastian if I could come over because I needed to make things right with you before their wedding. You weren't answering my calls or text messages. I had no other choice."

I catch a breath and rake my fingers through my already mussed hair. Leonie continues to stare at me. I hope that I'm getting through to her. I need to get through to her. These past few months have been hell.

No matter what I do, I cannot stop thinking about Leonie. Missing what we had. Hating myself for fucking it up with my stupid control-freak ways. She's a grown woman who was doing fine before me.

Who am I to judge her? No one. I was wrong. I take a deep breath and press on with my plea.

"Leonie, I fucked up... Badly. I realize now I was afraid of losing control because I fell in love with you so quickly. It's never happened to me before. From the moment I looked at you outside of my office at STEELE, it was like a thunderbolt jump-started my heart for you. Only you."

Despite my dick's initial bravado to fuck Verónica, it withered and refused to stand tall at its ten inches. When I opened my eyes and saw her face instead of Leonie's, I couldn't pretend. Her scent, her voice, her touch were not those of my lover's. No one's were. My fist and visions of Leonie give me a modicum of relief.

Leonie's response to my lengthy utterance has her hands moving rapidly in agitation.

"*Non*! Not only me! You... You've been with dozens of women... from Verónica Casal to some heiress to actresses. Just stop it, Roger!"

I shake my head in denial, speaking again.

"What you observed and what happened is not what you think. True, I tried with Verónica. But only because you were with Mattei. I couldn't... We didn't have sex. As for the others, we were only together in photographs."

Leonie relaxes a bit. Her hands settle back in her lap and the unshed tears stay in place. My heart breaks. I want to pull her into my arms and never let her go. Instinctively, I perceive it's too soon. So I continue.

"If you don't want to give us a second chance, know that I am so very, very sorry. I should never have judged you and made you seem less than. You are perfect to me. Just as you are. I was the one who was wrong. Every day, I'm reminded of my loss."

I give her time to absorb my words.

"Please Leonie. For the sake of Lola and Sebastian, let's set our situation aside. Put their minds at ease about how we'll behave at their wedding. I promise I will not bother you. Okay?"

Leonie nods and stands, a sign she's ended our conversation.

I rise to stand before her, much as Lola blocked me earlier. Unable to resist, I cup Leonie's face in my hands, then tip it up towards mine. Leonie's body shudders in response when I slant my mouth over hers in a scorching kiss. The intensity of her passion makes me ache for more.

She clutches the front of my shirt in her hands as she swoons from my embrace. My mouth moves to trail kisses along her jaw and throat as I murmur words of love to her.

She trembles, then pulls away, shaking her head. Her hands no longer hold me. Rather, they push me away.

Startled by her abrupt reaction, I lose my grasp on her. Leonie spins around, scoops up her belongings, and rushes to the door, swiping tears from her face.

"Leonie!" I call to her as I stride through the open door.

I pause when I notice Sebastian and Lola watching us. Embarrassed, I wipe a hand over my face. Then attempt to adjust my pants from the not so discreet enormous bulge at my crotch.

"Fuck," I mutter.

No one moves until Leonie tells Lola she's leaving as she hastens to the front foyer. Lola follows her. They discuss going to Lola's Sutton Place penthouse. Decision made, Lola glances back at Sebastian. He nods in understanding. I shake my head dejectedly as I watch Leonie leave.

"What happened?" Sebastian asks as soon as the elevator door closes.

I walk back inside, straight to the liquor cabinet. I pour two tumblers of Jackson Special Blend Scotch neat. I hand one to Sebastian; we sit on the sofa. I toss back the entire glass and rise for a refill. Then on second thought carry the Waterford Crystal decanter to the coffee table.

Sebastian chuckles, "That bad, huh?"

"Yeah…"

I fill him in on every detail. Thankfully, he sits quietly as I spill my guts. Once I'm done, the relief lifts the pent-up anxiety from my chest. On a sigh, I lean back against the cushions and close my eyes. The liquor holds good in my system.

After a while, Sebastian speaks up, "Call her."

One eye pops open to stare at him. Is he serious?

"Yeah, I'm serious. You better let her know you're sorry, even if you said it already. Trust me."

His sage advice has me calling and sending text messages repeatedly since she refuses to answer. Until my last voicemail when I threaten to come over to see her in five minutes. Leonie promptly calls me back.

I apologize for upsetting her. And reinforce my agreement not to pressure her and to give her space. For the sake of peace at the wedding and out of respect for Sebastian and Lola, we hold off on any further conversations.

Sebastian was right. It made Leonie feel better. So, it made me feel better.

I played my hand. Now, we can only let it unfold.

LEONIE

I need a break after my run in with Roger. He has my head swimming. His conviction touched me more deeply than I realized.

So instead of returning to Paris as I originally planned, I continue on with Lola to Beverly Hills earlier than expected. The two of us plus Blair and Billie scheduled some much-needed girls' time before our business meetings start. They're in town for her Lola's Coterie site selection. My agents put a photo shoot and some interviews on my agenda. Haley joined us for the getaway.

The night I spoke with Roger on the terrace, Lola and I escaped to her Sutton Place penthouse. I needed time to wrap my head around what had happened. It was so out of the blue for him to be there. I know he tried to reach me multiple times in the past two months. But I wasn't at a point where I could withstand his pleas. Even now, I'm still weak for him.

Merde!

When Lola asked me if I wanted to talk about it, I finally

gave in. Until then, I hadn't told her the full story, only that he was too uptight.

I spent an hour going over every detail from the meeting at STEELE to our Cabo San Lucas trip. At last, I admitted I still love him, even to myself. I can't help it, he makes my heart soar. And I guess sore, too. That's the problem... I'm afraid of being hurt... again.

Lola was concerned Roger may have acted like a brute since she saw me crying. I assured her he had said nothing untoward. It overwhelmed me.

While we drank shots of tequila, Roger called and sent text messages I refused to answer. Until his last voicemail when he threatened to come over to see me in five minutes. I promptly called him back.

He apologized for upsetting me. His agreement not to pressure me and to give me space went a long way to lessening my angst. For the sake of peace at the wedding and out of respect for Sebastian and Lola, we decided to hold off on any further conversations.

Lola told me she's fine with Giovanni being my plus one for her wedding. I wonder at Roger's reaction when I arrive with Giovanni. Two Alpha Males, one lioness...

"Leonie... Hello there... Leonie?"

Starr's gentle voice pulls my mind from rampant thoughts distracting me from my meditation session.

Focus, Leonie! Now is not the time to think about my messed-up love life! I'm here for some rest and rejuvenation. I can figure out my relationship status with Roger and Giovanni at a later date. Anytime but now. Well, at least I hope so.

I shake my head to clear my ruminations. Then open my eyes to see not only Starr's angelic face, but Lola, Haley,

Blair, and Billie peeping at me. My cheeks redden as I laugh in embarrassment.

"No judgement...!" Starr's dimples appear as she joins in.

The first stop to jumpstart our girls' time was to Starr Light Fitness & Wellness Beverly Hills for yoga and meditation classes. Lola met Starr when she hosted her first international fitness retreat on Fijian Laucala Island. Lola raved about her experience and how cool Starr is as an instructor and friend. So it's a no brainer to come to her center while we're here.

The concentration vinyasa requires prevented my mind from wandering. Instead, I tuned into my breath and the sequence of challenging asanas Starr used in the flow. The vigorous physical and mental workout was just what I needed as opposed to the slower pace of a Hatha class. Starr's dynamic teaching style made it fun.

After a few minutes in the steam room and a quick shower, we head to lunch at nearby Crustacean Beverly Hills. The modern Vietnamese fare specialties include delicious seafood that's the perfect light meal after yoga.

We settle on the gray suede seats at a banquette near the Walk on Water. The path runs from the front door through the restaurant between tables. Interspersed with wood and weight-bearing glass, the water below appears to offer a glimpse of the ocean's depths. Aside from the cuisine, the path is the eatery's highlight.

When the server arrives, we order An Sum—Crustacean's version of dim sum—to share and salads for our meals.

"Have you spoken to Malcolm Steele, yet?" Lola asks Starr.

"No, we keep playing phone tag. Right now he's it!" She laughs. "I was unreachable in India, then traveled a few more weeks. He was away on business, followed by a holiday in Italy."

Lola explains how Starr wants to expand her business to include regular fitness retreats at five-diamond resorts around the world, preferably in unique locales. Fiji was just the start. Malcolm as head of STEELE's Entertainment Properties Division oversees their hotels and resorts. He could help Starr with a partnership.

"So at some point, I'd love to get on his calendar. Ha! Or on my mat! Give him a taste of what he's missing."

I laugh so hard that I snort.

Starr gazes at me, befuddled. And turns to Lola, who also looks confused.

Okay, not the best way to start out when first meeting someone. I clear my throat and smile.

"What you said about getting him on your mat and showing him what he's missing sounds like a double entendre. Especially when the Steele men are involved!"

Lola cracks up and can't stop. Even Starr laughs, now clear on the cause of my hysteria.

"Yes," Haley starts. "My brothers can be a bit much, I must admit. Trust me, growing up with them and observing the hordes of women falling all over them was sickening!"

We laugh some more until the server swaps our appetizers for our main dishes. Silence descends on the table as we replenish our stores after our workout.

"*D'accord*, where do we go for our Girls' Not Out?" Leonie asks.

"The latest hot club to open is the Remy West Hollywood," Billie who knows all the West Coast happenings responds. "Their It thing is dancers bound by ropes Shibari style suspended from the ceiling. It has a BDSM vibe if you know what I mean."

She giggles and lifts her eyebrows up and down.

Lola and I glance at each other, then snort. If only she knew we're All Access Global members of LEVELS. But then I remember Lola mentioned Patrick Rockett is AAG, too. So Billie's probably been there plenty of times with him.

Merde! We're a kinky bunch! I laugh uncontrollably.

"What did I say?" Billie asks, confused.

"Oh, Billie, nothing! It's aah... How do you say... graphic!" I giggle. "Let's meet at eleven in the lobby. *Oui?*"

Billie nods, accepting my save.

"What are you wearing?" Haley asks. "I have a black mini dress or a light blue sequin romper."

Fortunately, the conversation switches to a safer topic. Blair chimes in on how well the light blue would contrast with Haley's gray eyes and ebony hair. Meanwhile, Lola's eyes still twinkle with glee.

* * *

My girls and I sit in the VIP area of the Remy West Hollywood. Billie was right. This is a hot spot. The Shibari tied dancers hover inches above the crowd. The colorful silken cords artfully swathe their long, toned limbs. They blindfolded some. While others stare boldly at the revelers. The dungeon-like atmosphere adds to the BDSM theme. It's a nice attempt at a sex club. But it doesn't compare to the LEVELS locations.

Since visiting LEVELS New York, I've gone to the Paris and London locations when they have Masquerade Night. Not that I'm ashamed of my voyeurism kink, but because I prefer to remain anonymous. Besides, it adds to the thrill.

I think back to my last visit in Paris.

The feather on the mask tickles my cheek as it brushes against the side of my face with each step I take as I head deeper into Peepshow. My destination tonight is one of the performance rooms.

My erotic energy in on the floor presses against me. The sight of men and women in various throes of passion ignites my own. I'll have what they're having, I laugh as I think of the popular movie scene set in a diner in New York City. Except I won't fake my orgasm. I'll get off for real. And I cannot wait.

As I approach the selection of rooms, I slow down to inspect which has the action that I want to view tonight. The first features two men and a woman. She hangs from the ceiling by red ropes tied into a swing. Her legs spread wide and her torso angled to allow access to both her pussy and her ass. The men push her between them, impaling her on their enormous cocks. Her cries of carnal pleasure ring out over the speakers. My pussy clenches.

They're near the end, and I need a full scene to ease my ache. I move on.

I pass three other rooms also in the midst of action. A light shines above the far set of doors to a double-sided room. I quicken my pace, eager to get to the room before anyone else. Just as I arrive at the viewer's door, a man steps up to it.

He smiles at me as his bright blue eyes darken behind his mask.

"Would you like some company?" He asks in a gravelly voice.

I shake my head no and reach for the knob. He steps back to allow me entry. I return his smile as I step inside. The lock clicks and I sigh in relief.

The viewing room has a red leather sofa and a chaise to choose for seating. Along the wall an array of toys, floggers, and cords offer the viewer the opportunity to join in the activity. My fingers trial over the assortment of dildos and vibrators, each still in its sterile packaging, onetime use only. I select a clit stimulator and peel away the packaging as I stride to the chaise. I want plenty of room to stretch out and enjoy the performance.

Once settled, I press the button and the light in the playroom on the other side of the one-way window turns on. It's arranged like a bedroom in a luxury flat. A mahogany hand-carved bed with sumptuous bedding dominates the space. The sturdy four posters and lattice canopy provide various rings for attaching cords for bondage. An armoire undoubtedly contains implements for the play. A St. Andrew's Cross stands in one corner and a pommel horse in the other.

A woman walks in. She's lean and tall with long ebony hair and tawny colored eyes. The only covering on her body is a sheer white slip.

She sits on the edge of the bed and waits. A man saunters in. He's six feet and brawny with brown hair buzzed short. His coal-black eyes rake over the woman, the heat in his gaze makes her shiver visibly.

Without a word, he kneels before her and pushes her thighs apart. His mouth lowers to her pussy. She cries out and leans back on her elbows as he devours her, issuing grunts of his own. The slurping of him feasting on her juices makes mine flow.

I too lean back on one elbow. My eyes never leave the scene before me as I part my thighs and allow the cool air to hit my pussy only covered by a silk thong. My breasts grow heavy in the tight corset as my nipples press against the silk overlay.

As I continue to watch her writhe from his ministrations, my fingers pinch my puckered peaks. I refuse to give relief to my dripping pussy. It's too soon. I want the passion to build.

When she arches her back screaming through her orgasm, my eyes narrow to slits as I lift my hips and gyrate against the empty air. Sadly, I have no lover to hold me down and force me to be still in the pleasure.

The man stands open, strips his jeans off. His massive dick stands proud against his six-pack abs. He strokes it as he watches her intently. She licks her lips and beckons him to join her. He withdraws a condom from the night table beside the bed. As he returns to face her, he rolls it over his thick length.

She scoots up the bed and widens her thighs in invitation. He climbs over her and grips her hips. One back-breaking thrust and he fully seats himself deep within her pussy. Her mouth is open in a silent scream, too shocked by his brutal entry.

As he thrusts in and out of her channel, the shock morphs into a state of sheer euphoria. Wildly, she matches his movements as she bucks beneath him. His passionate dominance drives her mad.

I'm caught in a sexual thrall, riveted to the scene before me. No longer willing to hold back, I pull my thong to the side and place the stimulator on my clit. Set to the lowest level, I increase the vibrations, wanting to reach my climax as she reaches hers.

We're not too far apart as my denial only served to bring me close to the edge. A few more pumps and a few more zings, and I blast over the brink. Only then do I lose focus on them as my eyes roll back and I jackknife off of the chaise. We cry out in wild abandon as one. Then fall back as our bodies spasm from the aftershocks of mind-numbing climaxes.

My pants taper off into even breaths. I open my eyes and witness the lovers wrapped in one another's arms, snuggled close beneath the silk sheets. He strokes her face as he croons to her. She smiles at him languidly.

I blush, their connection is too intimate even for a voyeur like me. Then turn the light out to give them privacy. Their room dims to a soft ambient glow.

"Time to get our groove on one more time, Ladies!" Blair announces as she pulls Billie to her feet. "Let's go. No time to decorate the banquette!"

My reverie fades, and the Remy replaces Peepshow. I shake my head to push the vestiges away.

She's right. We've been dancing and drinking for the past three and a half hours. Girls' Night Out is fun. We enjoy each other's company and our drinks. I finish the last of my cocktail and join my friends on the dance floor. I'm going to make the most out of our GNO, too.

The DJ's music and callouts have everyone bouncing to the beat. I throw my hands up and shimmy in my black silk-satin mini dress. It's cut in a classic slip silhouette and has two shoulder straps at one side and is ruched above the thigh slit. It's one of Lola's latest designs for the evening wear collection she's creating.

"The DJ plays the best music!" Blair says as she bumps her hip against mine.

She flips her chestnut brown hair over her shoulder as she twirls on the dance floor. Catching the attention of a few guys who make their way over to us.

"Hello there, gorgeous," one of them says as he bends down to my ear. "You look familiar. Have we met?"

I peer up to get a good look at his face. He's handsome in a surfer boy type of way—sun-bleached blond hair, chocolate brown eyes, lean build. I shake my head and he cocks his head to the side, studying me for a moment.

Not interested in being dissected even by a hottie, I spin away from him and continue my dance solo. His husky laugh follows me.

He slips his hand around my waist, turning me to face him. I glance up into his smirking face.

"Not so fast, gorgeous," he smirks. "If you think you can get away from me that easily, think again."

He pulls me close and places both hands on my waist.

I just want to dance and have a good time. So I let the handsome stranger move us to the beat. After a while, he twirls me around and with bent knees; he grinds his pelvis into mine. The sensation of his hard dick against my ass breaks goosebumps across my skin.

Already keyed up from my LEVELS Paris memory, I squeeze my thighs together. The ache is strong.

We move as one for a few songs, glued back to front. His lips graze my neck and I tilt my head to allow him more access. My hands rest on top of his on my hips. His hands clutch me possessively. As the next tune begins, he whispers in my ear.

"Let's get out of here. Go make our own music, gorgeous."

Just then, I notice Sebastian grinding with Lola. I hadn't seen him arrive. They look so good together, like they belong with no one else. Lost in their own world.

That's what I want. Not some random guy. Roger's words pop into my head. Giovanni's laughter fills my ears. I may not be sure of those two who I want. But I know for certain it's not surfer boy. Not tonight, not ever.

With a sigh, I shake my head and slip from his grip.

"Come on, gorgeous," he persists.

I step away and tell him no firmly. He nods disappointedly and walks away. I turn and make my way to Billie, Blair, and Haley. They're dancing not too far from Lola and Sebastian. The girls cheer when I reach them.

Moments later, Sebastian strides away from Lola. He leaves her standing with her mouth hanging open. She glances from him to us, apparently torn between her man and her friends. She hesitates.

"Go! Be with your boo!" Billie laughs and shoos her hands at her.

Haley, Blair, and I nod, giving Lola the thumbs up as we continue to dance.

She only hesitates a moment. Blows kisses to us. Then

rushes after her man, pushing her way through the pulsating crowd.

Hell, I don't blame her. I'd do the very same thing. In fact, all of us would opt for our sexy fiancé if given the chance. Girls' Night Out is fun. Being with your friends is fun. But it doesn't compare to a night in with your more than fun lover!

"What's so funny?" Haley asks over the pulse of the music.

"Girls' Night Out or Lover Night In?" I ask, raising and lowering my hands like a scale.

Haley giggles, "That's a straightforward decision… Girl's Night Out!"

My eyes widen in surprise as I stare at her.

She giggles some more and claps her hands.

"Gotcha! Lover takes all every time!"

Billie and Blair ask what's the joke, and Haley fills them in. They laugh and high five with us in agreement. Then we dance some more, getting lost in the beat and a fun night.

ROGER

"*L*ola!"

The flashbulbs of the paparazzi's cameras light up the dark sky like fireworks. The photogs are out in full force for the opening night of Lola's Coterie Abu Dhabi. In addition to the pomp of the event, the press dubbed Sebastian and Lola *Couple of the Century* since their engagement announcement. As the first of the STEELE Quaternity to pop the question combined with Lola's fame as the top lingerie designer, their pairing makes headlines.

Add Leonie's megastardom as the brand's spokesmodel and the night couldn't get any hotter. The cool desert air can't compete with their sizzle. I watch her as stalks the red carpet towards the happy couple.

The Lion commands the crowds' attention without even glancing their way. Their shouts of her name only elicit a brief smile as she's determined to reach her best friend.

As always, Leonie's stunning beauty draws the lenses to her. She captivates in a burnt-orange sequined one-sleeve, fitted gown that reaches one knee then flares at the other like a mermaid's tail to angle down to the top of her foot. Her long legs make quick work of the red carpet in open-toe stilettos. Each sway of her hips reflects the light of the incessant flashbulbs. Her signature mane piled in a bedhead tousled style.

I notice a flicker of irritation shoot across Sebastian's face. My gaze follows his to spot fucking Mattei who must accompany Leonie. Sebastian glances around, more than likely seeking me out to give me a head's up.

No matter. I promised not to pressure her. I'm pissed he's here after all I told her about us. Briefly, I close my eyes and take a deep breath. A hand on my shoulder brings me back.

"Hey, bro, you okay?"

Malcolm just as protective of his younger siblings as Sebastian stares at me with a worried expression. He's the splitting image of Baz, except Malcolm's hair stays permanently tousled while Baz slicks his back. Both sport five o'clock shadows. Although Malcolm shaves his at times.

"Yeah, I'm good," I respond with a nod for emphasis.

"Lola! *Chérie!* How marvelous you look!"

Leonie's exclamation draws my focus back to her. She's like a magnet to my steel. I cannot resist her.

The BFFs hug and the paparazzi start their blitz again. Now that she's caught up to her friend, Leonie affords the press her full attention. She and Lola pose together and apart, ensuring their best angles.

Meanwhile, Mattei and Sebastian stand to the side. My mobile vibrates with a text message.

Listen, Mattei is here. Keep your cool, bro! It's Lola's night, don't fuck it up or else...

I type a quick response to accept his request and my promise to behave even though I'm pissed. Then I glance back up at them. I train every day with my boxing coach. So I'm at maximum strength and performance. However, Mattei is no chump, so it could get ugly real fast. And Baz would kill me. Not worth my brother's ire or upsetting my future sister-in-law.

Lola calls to Sebastian to join her and Leonie for more photos. Fortunately, Mattei keeps his distance and doesn't join them in the shots. As he stands between the two of them, the crowd goes wild. Once he notices me with Malcolm, Harris, and Haley, he calls us over to get in the pictures. The rarity of all the Steele siblings in one frame will make for excellent social media posts and traditional media coverage.

I don't hesitate when I refer to all of us as Steeles, since I won't let Leonie wander much longer. I'm sure Sebastian realizes after my drunken confession to him last month, it's only a matter to time.

As we approach, Leonie stiffens and shifts to move away. My brother won't let her. He tightens his hold on her waist. The professional in her won't cause a scene, so she relaxes at his insistence and beams for the cameras.

I take my cue. I don't hesitate to stand beside Leonie and place my arm around her possessively. I don't even acknowledge Mattei's existence. Now fully assembled, the flashes nearly blind us as the paps go crazy for the best shots.

"Luc!"

Lola calls to her mentor as she waives him over to us. He joins our group to pose for more shots.

"Lola, Leonie, Sebastian, Luc, you have news crews to speak with," Billie Chandler, one of Lola's personal assistants, says as she steps behind us.

As Leonie slips from me, I squeeze her side holding her

to me longer. She glances up at me and bites her full lower lip. I ache to suck it into my mouth. Instead, I smile at her and incline my head.

"You look stunning, Pretty Kitty," I murmur in her ear.

She shivers and I hear her swallow. She's just as affected as I. Good.

I squeeze her side once more, then step back. She sways a bit, her amber eyes darkened to black. As I place my hands on her waist to steady her, she nods and pivots to follow Lola, Sebastian, and Luc. The fucker Mattei moves in. He wraps his arm around her. At first I think Leonie shifts away from him. But when I blink, they're striding away together. Again.

Fuck!

"Come on, lover boy," Malcolm teases as he grips the back of my neck.

"Damn. Am I that obvious?" I ask sheepishly, allowing him to lead me to the boutique's glass doors.

Malcolm's laugh booms around us. The corners of his eyes crinkle in delighted mischief.

"Yeah… I'd say so, little bro. But it's all good. She's a sexy one."

I jab him with my elbow in the ribs, ready to take him out. But he laughs even louder and pretends to wipe tears from his eyes.

"Stop teasing Roger, Malcolm!"

We turn to spot Haley glowering at him. Our sister, the youngest, is the most straight and narrow of the bunch after me. If I'm not the mediator, she steps in. I give her an appreciative smile and loop her arm in mine. We march through the doors leaving Malcolm and Harris laughing on the red carpet.

Half of the night I spend brooding in the corner. My

gaze follows Leonie as she engages with the guests, editors, and admirers. The other half I avoid flirtatious admirers of my own.

With one Steele down, they jockey to catch one of their own. I notice Malcolm and Harris in the same predicament. Only Malcolm flirts shamelessly. Another trait he shares, or rather shared, with Sebastian is his Dom playboy tendencies.

"Lola, you impress me tremendously!"

Her tinkling laughter cuts through my musings. What is this jerk talking about?

"It's the truth! You have the figure for modeling your designs—"

"What did you just say?" Sebastian demands, moving between Lola and the jerk flirting with her.

Oh fuck! It's not me about to ruin Lola's night. I push off the wall and hustle to them. Malcolm apparently heard it, too. He's on his way over.

As we approach, the guy backs up, locking eyes with Sebastian. He's about his height and broad. Not that it matters. Baz will still knock him on his ass.

"You... Come with me," Malcolm demands.

Without waiting for the guy's response, Malcolm takes him by the arm, and I flank him. Quickly, we move him through the clusters of guests.

"Hey, what's this all about?" He struggles against Malcolm's iron grip.

"Respect. You better think long and hard before you disrespect a Steele. Now get out."

Malcolm pushes him in the direction of the two security guards who promptly remove the character from the boutique out the back.

Malcolm wipes his hands on his trousers as he watches

to be sure no drama ensues. We stand shoulder to shoulder. Steele's don't take shit from anyone.

Once he's out of sight, Malcolm turns a questioning gaze towards me. He studies my face and cocks his head to the side.

"Spill."

I run my fingers through my hair and roll my neck. The tension caused by watching Leonie and Mattei all night built knots the size of golf balls. I shake my head at Malcolm.

"Okay. Then I'll tell you what I surmise. You want Leonie back. But she's schmoozing with Racer Boy, even though she's still into you. What the fuck did you do to cause her to dump you in the first place?"

As much as I want to strangle my observant older brother, I love him too much. I shake my head and shrug.

"Okay. Then let me guess... Your control-freak ways drove her away."

When I feel the heat rise on my cheeks, Malcolm chuckles.

"Bingo!"

I glance at him. His gray eyes dance with his mirth. I can't help but to join in his laughter. I feel better already. Nothing like family to make you raise your spirits when you're down.

He claps me on the shoulder and leads us out the back.

"Let's go have a drink. I can't let you knock Mattei's ass on the ground tonight. Sebastian will kill both of us. And we've had enough drama!"

* * *

TAKING MALCOLM'S ADVICE, I left Abu Dhabi the next morning. Instead of staying in the UAE for the week between that boutique opening and the one in Dubai like everyone else, I returned to Paris. Best to remove myself from the situation. Besides, I had work to do.

Now on board my jet for the return trip, I flip through page after page of images on the Internet of Leonie and Mattei. My blood boils.

Leonie at photoshoots in the desert and around the city promoting Lola's Coterie's latest collections. Attending media coverage interviews and in-boutique private parties for the city's wealthiest women. The two of them on dates for dinner at the various restaurants or at nightclubs until the early morning.

Damn. I thought I sensed a spark. Guess not.

By the time I arrive at STEELE Dubai I, I'm wound tight. There are four hours to pass before the party starts. Thankfully Sebastian flew his personal trainer and former MMA champion Borya *The War Defender* Alexeyev to the UAE. I head to the gym to spar with him.

We train occasionally when I'm in New York. My focus can't waiver with the giant Russian. So I know it's all out or get crushed when in the ring. The mood I'm in, I'll be doing the crushing.

"Oh, ho... So the little brother has come out to play, has he?"

I've barely stepped through the ropes and he's taunting me. A grunt is my only response.

"Ah... No words for me, *mal'chik*? Good."—He punches his fists together—"Let's get started, *da*."

"*Da!*"

Borya and I go at it for an hour in the ring. Then another

ninety minutes of strength training and stretching. I leave the gym reinvigorated, with my head back in the game.

Freshly showered, I meet my parents, Malcolm, Harris, and Haley for dinner. Since it's rare that we're all in one place, we take advantage of our time together. Sebastian waited for Lola, who has last-minute tasks before the party, so they can't join us.

"Hi Mom," I say as I bend over to kiss her cheek.

"Hello, honey! How was your flight?" Shelley asks, pulling me in for a hug.

I love my mother to pieces. Both of my parents are great.

"Good. How're things?" I ask as I make my way around the table greeting everyone.

"Oh lovely! Your father and I went into the desert for some dune driving. Hair-raising!" She laughs, mimicking the rollercoaster movements of the SUV.

"Glad you are back, son. How is business?" Morgan questions, always the net-net man.

"Excellent! All projects surpass projections and track on time," I respond, taking my seat beside Harris.

"Nice work, Roger as always," Morgan states. "All of you make your mother and me very proud. We have a big night ahead of us for the soon-to-be Steele. I am positive I do not have to remind you to represent our family and company well…"

His silver-gray eyes pin each of his children, ever the Dominant. We respond in the affirmative and he nods, satisfied.

"Now, let us enjoy our meal," he signals the server.

. . .

"You will cease this outrageous, infantile behavior at once and apologize to Ms. Lewis and her guests. Then leave. Do... you... understand?" Morgan issues his edict.

All eyes turn to him, including that dickhead Mattei. Morgan's Dom stare knocks us down several notches. In fact, we're below ground by the time he finishes his chastisement of us. Everyone else stands in silent awe of his power.

Morgan's words reset my out-of-control brain. I shake my head to dispel the angry red haze. Sure, Mattei was disrespectful to Leonie and said some stupid ass shit. But I never should have allowed it to get to me. It sent me on a downward spiral of jealousy, driven by an intense need to flatten him for having what is mine.

No matter the circumstances, I should have maintained command of the situation. Particularly at a highly public event held by STEELE. Before Leonie, this would never have happened. It goes against every cell in my physiology.

I gain control before Mattei and turn to seek Lola out in the crowd gathered around. I hope she's not as upset as I imagine. I spot her standing between my mother and Leonie. My younger sister Haley and Lola's assistants Blair and Billie stand near them. All have shocked expressions on their faces. Damn.

I notice Mattei tries to walk to them. But Malcolm puts his hand on his chest to stop him since he recognizes that I headed their way already. Mattei has the sense to back down.

"Lola, I apologize for my poor behavior. Please forgive me," I beseech her.

With grace, she nods her head and accepts my outstretched hand. Her eyes meet mine before she searches for Sebastian, to whom she nods, too.

I turn my attention to the other women who stare at me, surprised by my unusual outburst.

"Mother, Leonie, I ask for your forgiveness, too," I say to both of them, but my eyes lock on Leonie whose amber gaze shies away.

My shoulders rise and fall on a disappointed sigh in response to her reaction. Not wishing to prolong the situation and knowing now is not the time to address Leonie's dismissal, I turn to the guests and apologize to them. Then excuse myself from the event.

As I pass Sebastian, he squeezes my shoulder to offer me support. I nod without breaking my stride. I don't even wait to hear Mattei's apology. I have to get out of here. Try to save some face from my lack of decorum.

Minutes after I exit the boutique, I feel my mobile vibrate in my trousers' pocket. I know who it is without even checking the name on the display. I answer on the first ring.

"Sorry. That was a shitshow Lola did not deserve. Does she really forgive me? Are you going to kick my ass?"

Of course it's Sebastian. I'm sure our father told him to call me or he would. I'd rather deal with my eldest brother than the elder Steele…

I must sound like a wreck since Sebastian doesn't go in on me, as would be his right. It's his woman's event for our family's company. He's the heir apparent to CEO and Chairman of the Board. So besides being the oldest who leads his siblings, he's the future leader of our multibillion-dollar business at which each of us leads divisions. I'm thankful when Sebastian doesn't add to my ill ease.

"Yes, and no. Dad gave the guests gift cards. What the fuck happened?" He asks.

I clue him in on the details. He tells me he understands.

Baz is an Alpha male like me, although he's a Dom, too. So he understands protecting my woman's honor and my irrational possessive behavior. But he reminds me to keep my shit together in the future. Then teases me about not being responsible.

I grouse over the gibe. Then we hang up with a reminder about breakfast.

Fuck!

In my rage, I punch the wall. The plaster clatters to the floor, leaving a hole and splatters of blood. Too pissed to feel the pain, I stalk around the living room of my Rulers' Suite at STEELE Dubai I.

This shit is crazy. How can I allow myself to get so out of control that I make an ass of myself at a STEELE business function? So out of character for me—Roger *The Responsible*.

I roll my eyes in disgust at myself for letting Leonie upend my structured world. But I can't help myself. I call her mobile.

Leonie doesn't answer. What else is new…

I have no other choice than to leave a voicemail. How many will this one be? After twelve months, I've lost count. I just hope she'll listen to it and respond to me this time.

"How did we get here? Baby, I miss you. I'm so sorry. Tell me what to do. Please tell me, baby. Please…"

LEONIE

"*H*ow *did we get here? Baby, I miss you. I'm so sorry. Tell me what to do. Please tell me, baby. Please...*"

My heart breaks again. This time not from the pain, but for the ache Roger puts in me. I want him. I want him more than anything in my life. If not for the hurt he caused, I would run to his suite in a heartbeat.

It's the fiftieth time I've listened to his message in the few hours since he left the party. I still cannot believe he fought Gio. And in the middle of the guests. It's so unlike Roger. His rage was palpable. No one has said what happened.

After Roger apologized, Mattei stepped forward. Ever the Italian nobleman, he exuded charm as he bowed to Shelley, Lola, and me, then to the crowd. He increased his accent as he issued his apology. He reminded me of a statesman at the Colosseum.

When he took my hand in his and kissed it with a flourish, I couldn't meet his eyes no more than I could Roger's.

Gio's words of love crooned in my ear made my stomach churn with bile. *Non!* I shook my head. Denied, he pivoted and strutted out of the boutique without a backwards glance.

Typical. He always gets flippant when I don't go along with his wants. Too bad. Not this time.

Not when Roger told me he fell in love with me from the start. I felt the same... I still do.

"How did we get here? Baby, I miss you. I'm so sorry. Tell me what to do. Please tell me, baby. Please..."

I sigh and hug the mobile to my bosom as I roll over onto my back in the empty bed of my Rulers' Suite. How I wish Roger were here with me. Held in his powerful arms, close to his firm chest where his heartbeats the same pulse as mine.

Merde...

I close my eyes and let the mobile slip to the mattress. My fingertips skim across the tops of my full breasts to cup their weight. The turgid, toffee nipples poke against the cool silk sheets. A gasp escapes from between my lips as I pinch and tug them. A zing of electricity shoots to my pussy. I bow off of the bed. My long wavy hair tumbles down my back. Aaahhh...

One hand slides between my mounds to skitter across the soft skin of my flat belly. The destination weeps drops of my essence in anticipation of the pleasurable release. My breath catches as my palm covers my bare mons while one finger slips inside of my throbbing pussy. Ssssss...

One does not compare to Roger's massive girth and length. I... need... more.

A second and a third digit join the first. I jackknife as they stroke my G-spot. Fuuuck...

Relentlessly, I probe my dripping pussy. Shivers rack my

heated body when the juices slide down my butt cheeks to collect beneath me.

"Roger, oh Roger," I moan piteously, my lone cries ring out in the silent room.

My heels dig into the mattress as I lift my hips to meet the thrusts of my fingers. Deeper into my core they drive.

It's not enough!

Frustrated, I flip onto my knees and reach for BOB, the travel version. Not quite Roger, but closer than my slim fingers. My dripping pussy swallows the battery-operated boyfriend. Mmm mmm...

I toss my mane over my shoulder and lower my chest to the mattress, keeping my ass high in the air. The angle pushes the buzzing vibrator deep within my pussy, nearly to my cervix. Rhythmic thrusts match the movement of my hips as I charge towards my climax. My pussy muscles clench as my thighs shake.

"Oh... Oh... Oh... Oooooh..."

I wail as my orgasm pulsates through my core. Subsequent spasms rock me. Once sated, I collapse to the bed. BOB drops from my hand. I lie in a heap. Moments later, I pull the sheets back over my cooling body and curl into a ball.

As my musky scent fills the air, thoughts of Roger fill my dreams.

* * *

"LOLA, darling, you had Sebastian and the boys ready to run to the suite! Sebastian was beside himself! He told me, 'damn tradition!'"

Shelley laughs as we sit in the STEELE Dubai I Spa waiting for our manicures and pedicures to dry. After a full day of beauty treatments, they have pampered us into silky smooth, ultra-relaxed, glammed-up dolls. All to prepare for Lola and Sebastian's wedding. Although all of us knew it was tonight, he surprised Lola.

"Yes! Luc called me hyperventilating!" Chortles Blair Thomas, Lola's other personal assistant. "I thought we'd have to ring for the medic to resuscitate them!"

Shelley, Haley, Billie, and I join in on their laughter. We're loud as our voices echo around the nails room. But it doesn't matter since Sebastian reserved the entire spa just for Lola.

"Pardon me, Ms. Lewis."

One of the spa aestheticians stands at the door. A rose wrapped in white silk held in her outstretched hand.

"How romantic," sighs Billie with a wistful look in her big green eyes. "I'm so happy for you!"

"Shelley, you raised a good man," Blair chimes in.

"Thank you, Blair," Shelley responds and lifts her glass of citrus-infused water in toast. "May you all marry your romantic, good man!"

She smiles and glances at each of us. But she winks at me. I blush and avert my eyes. Does she know about Roger and me?

"Ladies, we hope you enjoyed your spa sessions! You seem sufficiently rejuvenated! The restaurant awaits you!" The manager announces.

"Excellent, right on schedule," Shelley responds. "We'll have your bridesmaids' luncheon. Then Lola, you can rest for two hours before the glam squad arrives."

The five-star treatment continues when we arrive at the restaurant and sit at the best table overlooking the dazzling water. We turn to Lola when she speaks.

"I want to thank all of you for all that you've done to

help me with my wedding and for being such a supportive mother-in-law and friends," she tells everyone "I have special gifts for you. But I didn't know this was happening now. So they're in New York. I promise to give them to you as soon as I return."

"Oh, darling! We knew your wedding would be here all along. So we planned for everything to be in Dubai. Plus, your bridesmaids' gifts!"

"Thank you! Thank you!"

Lola hands out each of our gifts. I tear up when I hold my pair of diamond drop earrings up to sparkle in the light. They're bigger than the others. Instead of one drop, mine has three.

"*Merci, Chérie,*" I whisper as I hug Lola close.

The last gift is for Shelley.

"Lola… This is so thoughtful… Thank you, darling," she says, holding back her tears as she looks at the beautifully framed photograph of Lola and Sebastian. "This will sit in the center of the living room table amongst our photos."

We continue to enjoy ourselves through the rest of the luncheon. Our laughter peals across the room as we trade stories of our love lives. We decline dessert and end with tea.

"Lola, time to rest before getting you ready," Shelley announces with a raised eyebrow, tapping the bezel of her Chopard L.U.C. XP Esprit by Fleurier Peony watch.

"You look so beautiful, Lola!" I gush as I touch a handkerchief under my teary eyes. "*Tu es magnifique, Chérie!*"

"Oh, how absolutely stunning and sexy!" Haley exclaims.

"Simply divine," sighs Blair.

"Sebastian will snatch you away before the ceremony even starts!" Laughs Billie.

We leave Lola to have a moment to herself before she becomes Mrs. Sebastian Steele. Lucky girl...

As I stand outside of the room, my mind drifts to thoughts of my wedding. Would it be just as grand? Will I glow with such pure love and happiness? Will Roger be my groom...

When Lola emerges from the room, I rouse myself and hand her bouquet to her. Then give her air kisses. I adjust her train to flow perfectly behind her sensational gown and fluff the heirloom veil into place.

I love Lola dearly. My sister and best friend has found her genuine love at last. I am beyond excited for them.

As we line up behind the rest of the bridal party, my skin tingles. I lift my gaze to find Roger, who's one of Sebastian's groomsmen, gray eyes focused on me intently. So engrossed, he almost misses his cue to walk down the aisle. Blair has to nudge him to shift his focus from me. When she turns to see what he's captured his attention, I blush and avert my eyes.

I glance over my shoulder at Lola with a smile before I too glide down today's catwalk. Once again, my eyes meet Roger's as the doors shut for Lola's grand entrance.

ROGER

"—*O*ur turn... Roger? Roger, we have to go."

An elbow poked into my side brings my attention from Leonie to my bridal party partner, Blair. Her cerulean blue eyes gaze up at me questioningly. Then she peers over her shoulder to see Leonie blush as she turns to Lola hastily.

A small smile plays on Blairs rosebud lips when she faces front again. Her eyes brighten as though she knows something is going on between Leonie and me. I arch my brow at Blair. But she loops her arm through mine again and proceeds through the doors. We're only slightly off in our timing.

The sight of Sebastian waiting anxiously for his bride makes me think of Leonie. Does she love me? She didn't respond with words of her love for me when I told her I fell in love with her from the first moment. Hell, she was just gallivanting around Abu Dhabi and Dubai with Mattei. So who knows?

Fortunately, Sebastian squashed any chance of that slimy

dick being at their wedding. Sebastian was adamant. No one fucks with his family. He didn't give a damn if Leonie wanted him here. However, Lola assured him Mattei wasn't coming. Thank fuck!

Blair and I take our places at the altar just in time for me to admire Leonie as she glides down the aisle. Her strapless column gown flows around her in a swirl of silk organza layers in various orange and fuchsia hues. Her glossy mahogany hair swept up stresses her long neck. Her amber eyes sparkle more than the ornate diamond earrings. Gorgeous.

I wonder what type of bride she'd make: regal like her namesake; elegant; demure; mine…

Low chuckles from Malcolm and Harris who stand near me makes me realize I spoke mine aloud. Leonie's lips turn up in a smile, but she avoids my gaze. Progress.

Sebastian's sharp intake of air is all the announcement we need to know Lola stands at the top of the aisle. She is breathtaking. My heart swells with joy for my brother. He takes care of all of us. Now he has someone who can take care of him.

I want the same. He may only have eyes for Lola. But only Leonie captures me. Once again our eyes meet. I gaze at her unwaveringly to display my love for her without words. This time, she doesn't shy away. She returns my stare until Lola hands her bouquet to Leonie.

Throughout the ceremony, Leonie and I exchange furtive glances. My jealousy spikes when Malcolm dramatically offers his arm to Leonie before they walk back up the aisle. Although they're best man and maid of honor, it reminds me of someone else being her groom. I don't like it at all.

Mine!

We make it through the wedding party and family photos without a brawl—if not, Morgan and Sebastian would banish me forever. Now at the reception, Leonie stands before Lola and Sebastian like the Queen of the Savannah. She exudes feline grace. Her toast is touching with a story of how she and Lola first met and now are sisters for life. Lola dabs her eyes and blows kisses to her best friend.

Also overwhelmed, Leonie's voice waivers as her eyes brim with tears. I rise from my chair to comfort her. But Malcolm—who's giving his toast next—steps beside Leonie. He pulls her into an embrace as he whispers in her ear.

I freeze. My face must resemble stone. Only my intense stare riveted on Malcolm proves I'm not a statue. Now he's rubbing Leonie's back.

What... the... fuck...

Fortunately, Leonie collects herself and disentangles from Malcolm's arms. She returns to the table. My steely gaze tracks her every move. When she's close, my limbs function for me to stand and help her into her chair. She touches my chest and briefly leans against me with a sigh.

Thank you.

Relief along with the heat from Leonie's body courses through my veins as the stone turns to mush. My baby is back.

Not caring we're in a ballroom full of three hundred guests, I press my forehead against Leonie's.

"I love you, Kitten. I love you so much."

She bites her lower lip to keep the tears from falling. But they spill from the corners. I kiss each one. Her body trembles in my arms.

"I... I love you too, *Amoureux*," she whispers.

My heart leaps. I have to restrain myself from swinging Leonie around and whooping my victory.

She must sense my thoughts because she places her palms on my chest and shakes her head. Her amber eyes twinkle. Then she pulls me down to sit in our chairs.

Malcolm's voice cuts through. He regales us with a fairy tale story of Sebastian's miscreant behavior until the Lovely Lola saved him from imminent doom. Everyone roars with laughter while Sebastian rolls his eyes at the charmer. Malcolm laughs, and the meal continues.

Throughput the night, Leonie helps Lola change clothes and does her maid of honor duties with gusto. We don't have a moment to discuss our exchange. She does glance sideways at me and I stare at her.

When Sebastian whisks Lola off the dance floor hours later, I stride over to Leonie. She's still dancing with Starr Knight, another of Lola's friends. She owns the Beverly Hills-based fitness studio and wellness center Starr Light Fitness & Wellness. Interestingly, Malcolm hasn't been able to keep his hungry eyes off of her. Oh, brother.

I place my hand on Leonie's lower back. She turns around and smiles.

"Lola and Sebastian left. Do you have to stay?" I ask, not wanting to pressure her.

She raises her finger to gesture for a moment. Turning back to Starr, she whispers in her ear. Starr nods and smiles at me. She is a beauty with her flawless chestnut-colored skin and long, curly, dark brown hair with matching brown eyes. Not to mention her killer body. Damn, no wonder Malcolm has her in his sights.

As stunning as Starr may be, I only want Leonie. Thankfully, she places her hand in mine. I smile at Starr. Then lead Leonie out of the ballroom.

She's quiet as we walk through the lobby. When guests approach to offer congratulations for Sebastian and Lola, Leonie charms them with her witty words. Otherwise, she maintains a subdued demeanor. It makes me nervous, and I'm not one who ruffles easily.

Not wanting to spook her, I remain just as silent. But smile encouragingly when I notice her peeking at me surreptitiously. A return smile twitches at the corners of her mouth before she looks away.

Finally alone on the elevator reserved for accessing the Rulers Suites, I slip my arms around Leonie's waist and press my forehead against hers. Thankfully, she allows me to hold her close and even wraps her arms around my neck. We remain locked in place until the elevator doors ping to open on my floor.

Once again I take her hand in mine, clasping our fingers together. She squeezes and smiles up at me. That slight gesture adds a buoyancy to my step and eases the last of my tension.

I pause at my door.

"Are you sure?"

The beatific smile that spreads across Leonie's face zings my heart. But I must hear her verbalize her agreement.

"Words, Pretty Kitty," I request.

"*Oui, Amoureux. Absolument,*" she purrs.

I cup Leonie's face and capture her full lips in a passionate, breathtaking kiss.

She melts against me and tangles my hair in her fingers. Her soft mewls make my cock lengthen and thicken with need. When she feels it press against her belly, she moans and tightens her grip on my hair. Her tugs on my scalp add a touch of pain to the pleasure, and I growl low in my throat. She mewls in deference to my dominance.

Unable to withstand another second, I wind one arm around her waist, locking her to my side as I punch in the passkey code for the door. She's not getting away again. We're all in.

I carry her like she's my bride over the threshold straight to the bedroom. She peppers my face and neck with kisses as she growls impatiently. I chuckle and she growls some more.

"Don't tease me, *Amoureux*! I've missed you so much!" Leonie chides as she giggles.

"I missed you, too, baby. More than you can imagine," I murmur with my lips pressed in her hair.

She tightens her arms around my neck and buries her face as she sighs contentedly. Yeah, she was just as worried as I. No more worries anymore; I vow.

I stride through the bedroom door to the massive bed. As soon as I set Leonie on her feet, she slips her hands inside my classic, bespoke tuxedo to remove it. Eagerly, we strip one another of our garments, laughing as they fall to the floor in a heap around us.

At last, Leonie stands before me, no longer a vision. Her glorious, naked body so real, so mine. As my intense hooded gaze travels over her, my dick hardens painfully. Her exquisite face flush with excitement. Her bountiful breasts heavy, the puckered tips rise and fall with her breaths. The curve of her hips call for my hands to grip them. Long, toned legs tremble. The scent of her arousal carries through the air to ignite my desire.

I tilt my head back, close my eyes, and take a deep inhale. I need a moment to collect myself before I pounce. Slowly, I re-focus on her.

Leonie's feline eyes devour me. My dick twitches from her predatory gaze. She turns and struts to the bed, casting a sidelong stare at me. I watch transfixed as she crawls to the middle. Her round ass high and her head low, *The Lion* on the prowl. She languorously rolls to her back, leans on her elbows, and parts her thighs for me. Her pussy glistens in the soft light from the bedside lamps.

"Roger, *Chéri, Amoureux*," she coos as she beckons me with a crook of her long finger.

Like one of Pavlov's dogs, I salivate and lope over to her.

She laughs, a low, seductive rumble in the back of her throat. Her amber eyes glow.

"Here, Kitty, Kitty, Kitty," I call as I crawl over her lush body.

My lips land on her succulent mouth as my groin notches with her warm, welcoming embrace. We groan in unison as our heated flesh meets. Erotic energy zaps all around us. The air crackles with our frisson of fervency.

"Roger… Please," Leonie implores, eager for more.

I kiss the tip of her nose. Then rise to get a condom.

Leonie places her small hand on my broad chest to stop me. A shake of her head brings me alarm.

"What's wrong?" I ask, concerned by the uncertainty on her face.

She shakes her head, and her hair tumbles from the pins holding it up. I reach over and remove them. Then run my fingers through her glossy tresses, enjoying their silky touch. She peeks at me sheepishly. I lift my eyebrows.

"I… I want to feel you inside of me with nothing between us," she rushes on when my eyes widen. "I took a test a few years ago. And I don't have any STIs. But if you don't want to or can't—"

A test a few years ago isn't enough since she's been with that fucker Mattei. I shake my head and sit back on my haunches.

"I had a test after we broke up and I don't have any either."—I shake my head again when her eyes brighten— "But you haven't had one recently, and Mattei... I don't trust that fucker."

I finish on an angry growl. The nightmare of him inside of Leonie like he boasted before I knocked him on his ass burns my brain cells. I shake my head vehemently to dispel it.

"—had sex with him... Roger?"

Leonie's questioning tone of voice cuts through. I didn't hear a word she said.

"Did you hear me?" She asks as she sits up.

"No," I reply.

She kneels in front of me and cradles my face in both of her hands. A soft smile plays on her lips.

"Roger, *Amoureux*, you are my second lover. I had sex once before you, when I was twenty-one. It's time to do it, I'm a woman, I thought... Disastrous. I have never had sex with Giovanni Mattei."

Stunned, my mouth gapes open. How the hell is that possible? Really? Thinking back, I recall how tight she was around my dick. A shudder runs through me at the memory.

"It's possible," Leonie giggles.

Fuck, I spoke out loud...

"In fact, you nearly split me in two. But you felt so good. So, so good... Mmm mmm," she purrs. "Giovanni and I fooled around, *oui*. But never had intercourse. That's why he was with so many other women. He thought I would get jealous and give in. *Bof*! I used him for some relief and he kept others from pursuing me. I wasn't interested in an actual relationship. My career came first. That is until you, *Chéri*. You changed everything."

Fuck… me! Talk about a boost to a guy's ego! Only once before? That fucker lied! Hell yeah!

I whoop and lift Leonie into my arms, crushing her to my chest as my mouth descends on hers.

Her delighted giggles prevent us from kissing truly. So, I zerbet her face and neck. Her giggles turn into uncontrollable snorts as she squirms on my lap. But I refuse to let her go.

This woman is mine, all mine!

ROGER

"*L*eonie is a special gift of her mother and mine. Madame Beaulieu and I tried for many years to conceive. Many painful miscarriages and the resulting agony finally gave fruit to our *magnifique petite fille*. After she was born, we could not have any more children. She means everything to us."

Monsieur Beaulieu pauses conversing in his native tongue and pins me with a stare so intense it makes mine look like goo-goo eyes. He continues after what feels like hours, but was merely a moment.

"Leonie's mother and I never approved of that Giovanni Mattei character. *Non*! Leonie assured us it was not serious. She never brought him to meet us—no man, in fact. Although unbeknownst to Leonie, I met Mattei one night to tell him what I tell you now."

He leans forward. His obsidian eyes bore into mine.

"Do not fuck my daughter over or you will pay the price."

He rivets me in place for a full minute. Then sits back as

Leonie and her mother return from the restaurant's ladies' room.

Instantly, his demeanor softens as he rises to help his wife into her chair and kisses her cheek lovingly. From behind her, he dings me with another look as I help Leonie into her seat beside me.

Guy Beaulieu is one tough-as-fuck man. Outwardly, he's the impeccable, wealthy businessman from a long line of prominent Parisian merchants who trace their lineage to the eighteenth-century. His brawny frame stands at six feet, four inches, still physically fit for a man in his sixties. Leonie tells me he's studied jujutsu for decades. He's just as comfortable in the French salons as in the back alleys. I hardly want him after me. Damn.

"Roger *chéri*, you appear ill at ease. Did my husband scare you to death with his threats?" Madame Beaulieu laughs, her amber eyes twinkling so like her daughter's.

She's the opposite of her husband. Petite, soft, warm. Her ebony hair cut in a stylish curly bob frames her fawn-colored, oval-shaped face. Pouty lips turn up in a joyful smile. Her daughter is as radiant as she. In her early fifties, she could model as much as *The Lion*.

Leonie gapes at her father, *"Papa, non! Tu as promis!"*

Guy smiles indulgently at his gift, a smile that graces Leonie's face all the time. He shakes his head and holds out his hand for hers. She places her hand in his much larger one and he squeezes it.

"Don't you worry, *Mon Trésor*, if Monsieur Steele cannot handle me... *Bof*... He is not deserving of you!"

"Oh, Papa!" Leonie sighs.

I watch their interaction. It reminds me of my family's loyalty and love. I don't blame her father. He is correct. I would do the same for my daughter. A smile blooms on my face at the thought of having a baby with Leonie. But then I remember what Monsieur Beaulieu said about their difficulties. I pray Leonie and I don't suffer the same heartache. It would kill me.

I ignore those negative thoughts. Then cup Leonie's face and ease her disquiet.

"My love, your father is correct. You deserve a man and not a boy. Trust me when I say I am a man and your happiness is my top priority."

Monsieur Beaulieu sits back in his chair with a grunt. But nods his head in appreciation of my declaration. Madame Beaulieu smiles warmly.

"*Ça c'est bon,*" Leonie murmurs as she leans into my side.

Dinner continues on a lighter note. I guess Monsieur Beaulieu accepts me. I enjoy his company. He's so like my father. I respect his stern countenance. And Leonie adores him. Daddy's Little Girl. I smile again, thinking of our children. She may not realize it yet. But I'm not letting her get away this time. She's mine forever. I'll just give her some time.

"Madame Beaulieu—"

"Don't be silly, Roger, *chéri*! Call me Josy!" She insists.

"*Merci*, Josy," I return her smile. "Leonie tells me you enjoy baking and make the best double-chocolate soufflés."

Josy claps her hands in delight.

"Absolutely! My favorite pastime! You must come to our home for Sunday brunch and I will make them especially for you, Roger. *Oui, Mon Amour?*"

She turns to Guy, and he smiles at her with such unbridled love I have to glance away, afraid of intruding on their private moment. Leonie grasps my hand and grins at me. I kiss her cheek softly. One day, I think to myself.

When the check arrives, guy insists on paying. A dominant move. But I give in to him as he is Leonie's father. I admire him already. Even if he didn't command it.

We depart with hugs and kisses. Promises of Sunday brunch next weekend at their ancestral mansion on the outskirts of Paris confirms his acceptance of me. We shake firmly and he nods. I won't fuck this up.

Eric, my driver, opens the door to my steel-gray Rolls-Royce Corniche. Leonie smiles at him graciously and slips inside. I nod and ask him to take us to my flat. It's a duplex penthouse on the thirty-first and thirty-second floors of The STEELE Tower Paris in the Front de Seine district of Beaugrenelle in the *quinzième*.

The property, like New York City, is mixed-use with commercial and residential space plus the largest mall in Paris. The views of the Seine and of the Eiffel Tower are incredible, especially at night when the spectacular light display flits across the monumental iron structure.

The past month we've alternated nights at her penthouse and mine. Little by little she's left personal items in my bathroom and I made space for her clothes in the dressing room. I've done the same at her place. I'll give her some time. But eventually, she's moving in with me.

"*Amoureux*, dinner was *fantastique!*" Leonie says as she cuddles against my side.

I wrap my arm around her shoulder and she lays her head on my chest, her palm rests on my abs. I kiss her hair and inhale her classic sultry perfume, Dior's Pure Poison. She tells me it makes her feel powerful, like a woman who commands attention. The blend of florals with amber and musk is the perfect balance of femininity and masculinity. It's imprinted on my brain.

"Yes, my love. And your parents remind me of mine."

I put my fingertip to her lips when she sits up with a frown.

"Your father behaved exactly as I would with our daughter's boyfriend," I continue.

Leonie's eyes widen. I cock my head questioningly. Then realize I said, "our daughter." I hold my breath and await her response.

She scans my face. I keep a neutral expression and display no guile. Satisfied, Leonie leans back against me. The remainder of the ride we spend in comfortable silence, each lost in thought. I stare out the window as I rub Leonie's arm, getting as much relaxation from it as she receives.

Eric pulls into the garage and opens the door. Leonie and I head to the private elevator that takes us to my family's floors only. My parents maintain a penthouse on the floor below mine, and a second one below theirs, my siblings use when in Paris. I key in my code, and the lift speeds to our destination.

"Would you like a glass of Réserve Jean de Lillet Blanc?" I ask Leonie.

I added cases of her favorite aperitif to my liquor collection. I prefer the Jackson Special Blend Scotch neat. It's become our habit to relax on the terrace with our drinks in the evenings.

"*Oui, Mon Chéri.* I'm going to change. I'll meet you out there," she says as she walks up the stairs.

I remove my tie and toss it with my suit jacket onto the sofa as I pass. After I pour our selections, I sit on the double chaise and kick off my shoes. The Eiffel Tower is aglow with glittering clear lights. The brilliance reminds me of diamonds sparkling in the inky night sky.

Lost in thought, I don't notice Leonie's return until she

sits beside me and pulls a cashmere blanket over us. She takes a sip of her Lillet as she smiles at me over the rim. Her amber eyes outdazzle the Eiffel Tower.

She places our glasses on the table and crawls onto my lap. Straddling my thighs, she captures my mouth with hers. The taste of passion fruit dances on my tastebuds. As bold in flavor as Leonie's desire for me. I wrap my arms tightly around her waist and loose myself in our rekindled love.

* * *

LE BEAULIEU MANOIR is the family's ancestral home on the westernmost part of the outskirts of Paris in Neuilly-Auteuil-Passy. The majestic property features manicured park-like grounds, stables, tennis court, swimming pool and cabana, and a palatial French Rococo mansion. A part of the 16th arrondissement, it's in the wealthiest neighborhood.

They built the hamlet between the thirteenth and seventeenth centuries. Later, during the reign of Louis XV, it became a fashionable country retreat for French elites. The Beaulieu's twenty acres of land border Bois de Boulogne with parts of the acreage awarded to their ancestors by the monarch.

Even as I glance around and marvel at its beauty, I can't get rid of my concerns.

"Relax, *Mon Chéri*," Leonie says as she squeezes my hand. "My *Maman* adores you and my *Papa*... Well, he doesn't dislike you!"

She giggles and kisses my cheek.

Her joke eases some of my tension. I want her father to at least respect the fact I'm serious about Leonie and not some schmo like Mattei. Guy cannot put me in the same category as that dick.

Leonie and I made good on our acceptance to Sunday brunch Josy extended to us at dinner last week. I'm taking it as an opportunity for her parents to get better acquainted with me and to prove I'm worthy of their *Trésor*.

The large, ornate hand carved door opens. I expected a butler, but Josy rushes out to greet us.

"Bienvenue! Bienvenue!" She exclaims as she pulls Leonie in for a hug and kisses her cheeks.

Josy turns to me and cups my face as she greets me with double kisses, too. She's a gorgeous woman who Leonie will more than likely continue to resemble as she grows older.

"Come, Guy had to take a call. He'll join us shortly," she says as she leads us through the door.

The interior decor is just as impressive as the outside. The furniture, paintings, and sculpture mimic the light elements with curves and natural patterns to form the delicacy and playfulness influenced by Rococo designs.

The Beaulieus as wealthy merchants who traveled the world for the most luxurious items are clear. The mixture of Asian, North African, and Russian influences appears in the tapestries, wall panels, and fabrics. The modern era shows through in accessories, other artwork, and air-conditioning and heating systems. It's extraordinary.

We walk past beautifully appointed salons to an all-glass solarium that overlooks the rear rose garden. They set a table for our brunch and a sideboard arranged for a buffet-style service. The delicious aroma of savory and sweet dishes fills the air. Spices, meats, and baked goods blend to make my mouth water.

"Oh *Maman*! You've outdone yourself today! *Merci*," Leonie says as she hugs her mother.

"You cooked all of this yourself, Josy?" I ask, astonished at the amount and variety of foods.

She smiles and nods, "*Oui!* On Sundays and Mondays, we give the staff the days off. I prefer to cook and bake, anyway. I grew up learning our family's recipes from my *Maman* and *Grand-mère.*"

Josy turns to Leonie and laughs.

"Now this one, she preferred to follow her *Papa* and *Grand-père* around the shops and bazaars!"

I join in her laughter.

"That explains Leonie's not so grand attempts at cooking for us!"

Leonie pouts and mutters under her breath. I kiss her forehead to settle the frown on her face, and she giggles.

"*Bienvenue au manoir Beaulieu!*"

Guy's voice booms in the solarium.

We turn to find him striding into the room, ever the man of the estate. He's impeccably dressed in bespoke blazer, shirt, and trousers with Gucci loafers. He hugs Leonie and gives her kisses. Then faces me.

His obsidian eyes pierce my gray orbs as he takes me in. With a nod, he extends his hand, and I meet him to give a firm shake. He nods again in appreciation and claps me on the back.

"Come, let us eat," he commands.

Guy is so like my father Morgan. I wonder how the two men will get along as I line up at the sideboard.

As expected, the food is delicious. Traditional Tunisian dishes and Continental fare offer more than enough options. I spot deserts, but not Josy's famous double-chocolate soufflés. I hope they're in the oven.

"This is delicious, Josy. Thank you so much," I tell her, meaning every word.

She beams, and Guy rubs her neck.

The intimate touch reminds me of Leonie and me. She

must sense my thoughts as she slips her hand in mine under the table. I smile at her, and she winks at me.

Our meal continues with lively discussions on current events, the arts, and business. Guy asks how Beaulieu Enterprises, SAS can partner with STEELE International, Inc. I tell him Sebastian is on his honeymoon. But I will speak with him when he returns. I assure Guy with his company's goods and STEELE's properties we should be able to come to an agreement. He's satisfied and looks forward to meeting Sebastian.

Later, Leonie and I stroll through the grounds. She points out where she fell from her horse and how she helped her mother plant flowers. She explains although she was an only child, her parents more than made up for her lack of siblings by letting her friends spend time at their estate.

I envision Leonie playing with our children on these ancestral lands, and my heart soars. I pull her close and kiss the top of her head as I stare into our future.

LEONIE

"*A*ntonio?"

I walk into the Human Resources Department at STEELE Paris for my third interview as a part-time junior designer to find my former seat mate in the waiting area. Next to him is the female student who was flirting shamelessly with Roger when he guest lectured my class. I don't remember her name since we never interacted. No matter, I smile pleasantly.

Post the fiasco with Roger, Antonio changed seats. Now, he only offers brief nods to me whenever I greet him. Not that I blame Antonio. His face was a mess. Roger paid for his medical costs and gave him a sum of money in recompense. I guess it goes further with the internships Roger set up. Antonio and the other student must interview for the first slots.

"Bonjour, it's nice to see you. Are you interviewing for the internships?" I ask as I sit across from them in the gray leather Louis XV style chair.

I place my Hermès attaché and portfolio on the floor,

then smooth the skirt of my green Versace suit. The color highlights my coloring and the gold silk shirt makes my amber eyes pop. STEELE is a modern company that fits well with my style and work ethic.

Since Roger and I broke up, I redoubled my efforts to complete my bachelor's degree. I accomplished my coursework and my final project of Lola's Sutton Place penthouse two months ago. My grade average shot up to 3.9. I'll graduate with honors. I missed this years' ceremony. But will take part six months from now in the one at the end of this term.

I haven't given up my modeling career, yet. I plan to transition between now and graduation, starting with a part-time junior designer position. Roger urged me to interview at STEELE after he saw my designs and Lola's place. Suitably impressed, he insisted I was ready for STEELE and would do well. He even teased me about being more responsible than him. I had to laugh since now we're together and he shared his genuine feelings with me; I understand better. And he was right. Once I focused truly, I finished quickly.

C'est la vie!

"Oh, bonjour, Leonie."

Antonio sounds far less enthusiastic about our unexpected meeting than I. He turns back to the other student, but her eyes survey me. I figure since I didn't address her, too. So, I smile and extend my hand.

"Hello, we never formally met. I'm Leonie Beau—"

"Oh, I know who you are... Who doesn't?" She sneers, then turns to Antonio. "If she's interviewing for the internship, we might as well leave. She's dating the president. So of course she'll get it."

So taken aback by her vehement display, my mouth

drops open. My gaze shifts from her to Antonio, who has the decency to redden from embarrassment. He grips her arm and pulls her back to the sofa. Then brings his gaze to mine.

"Leonie, please disregard Delia. She's just nervous. We are here for the internship interviews," he states as he flashes a warning look at her. "Leonie Beaulieu this is Delia Shaw. Delia, Leonie."

I fix my face and re-extend my hand. I try not to let anyone get the better of me. My reputation is my livelihood.

"Hello, Delia. Not that what you assume would happen is correct, I am not interviewing for the internships. I wish you both luck."

I nod at Antonio and sit back in my chair. Just as I reach for my mobile to avoid further conversation, a woman appears at my side.

"Bonjour, Ms. Beaulieu. Please come with me."

I smile at her and gather my bags. As I stand, I glance at Antonio and Delia. He smiles and wishes me good luck. Delia has a pinched expression, but nods when Antonio nudges her. I beam brightly—never let them see you sweat —and follow the assistant.

Suddenly nervous, I touch my hair to be sure every strand remains slicked in the bun at the nape of my neck. The suit is sexy. But it's the combination of my reading glasses and hairstyle that keeps it professional.

Hhhmmm… Perhaps a scene at LEVELS Paris with me as librarian and Roger as naughty schoolboy—

Distracted, I bump into the assistant and apologize profusely. She takes it in stride and opens an office door to usher me inside.

A man in his late fifties rises from behind an Empire era burled-elm desk. As elegant as the piece, the man exudes a confident, dignified persona. Monsieur Bernard Bonnay, the vice president of Human Resources, greets me with a firm handshake.

"Bonjour, Mademoiselle Beaulieu," he starts. "It's a pleasure to meet you. Please have a seat."

"*Enchanté*, Monsieur Bonnay," I respond, gripping his hand with sufficient firmness.

We settle in our seats, him behind his desk and me in a visitor's chair that matches the wood. I cross my legs. The flesh-tone Manolo Blahnik stiletto bounces with my nerves. I shift to cross at my ankles to hide the movement.

Monsieur Bonnay smiles warmly, "No need for nerves, mademoiselle. You've impressed everyone with your designs and ideas. This meeting is merely a formality."

My thoughts drift to Delia's nasty remarks. Did I only make it this far because of Roger? Do they really find my work up to the standards of STEELE? How will others perceive me? The turmoil adds to my nerves.

Merde...

"—about your inspiration. The pairings intrigue me."

I tune in just in time to answer appropriately. Once the conversation moves to my work and love of design, I relax. The interview goes quickly. The end of the hour catches us unaware until Monsieur Bonnay's assistant knocks at his door. His next appointment awaits.

"Well, Mademoiselle Beaulieu, welcome to STEELE! My assistant will help you with the paperwork. You may complete it in one of the conference rooms. We scheduled a lunch to introduce you to the rest of the team on Monday. Please let us know if that date conflicts with your schedule. *Bonne chance!*"

My cheeks hurt from the wide grin. Excitedly, I shake

Monsieur Bonnay's hand when we stop at the door of his office. He and his assistant smile just as broadly.

"Right this way, Mademoiselle Beaulieu," she says, gesturing down the hall with a manilla folder full of papers.

So ecstatic, I practically skip behind her. We enter a glass-walled conference room with a long walnut and brass table styled after the Louis XIV period and brown leather chairs with brass fittings. The decor throughout the offices fits well with Paris and pays homage to its history.

We confirm my workdays as Monday through Wednesday, job description, salary, and benefits. It's so odd for me since I've never had to deal with this onboarding process. I love it!

Once I complete the paperwork, she takes me to the security office for my photo ID. Now, in front of a camera… This is the norm, I giggle to myself. The two burly men become mush when they see me. One asks for a selfie. I oblige happily. My father taught me it's always good to make friends in all areas of a company.

Just as we walk to the elevator—thankfully I don't see Antonio and Delia—my mobile vibrates in my attaché. The assistant leaves me with more words of welcome and good luck. The name on the display increases my grin. Roger, *Mon Amour*.

"Hi," I answer breathlessly.

"Hi, Bonbon. How did it go?" He asks in the deep baritone that makes me shiver.

"Excellent! I got the position and start on Monday!" I exclaim, bouncing on the balls of my feet.

His deep chuckle zips through me.

"Congratulations! We must celebrate with dinner tonight at L'Ambroisie!"

"*Oui, oui! Mon préféré, merci, Mon Amour!*"

The three Michelin star restaurant is my favorite in Paris. The food of the gods bursts with flavor, perfectly executed by Chef Pacaud. It's in a regal townhouse on Place des Vosges in the Marais district.

Roger pauses, triggered. His sexual tension travels through my mobile.

"Take my private elevator on your left up to twenty. I'll send it down. You deserve a full congratulations now, Pretty Kitty," he rumbles.

As I ride up to the executive offices, my heart races and my pussy drips in anticipation of our taboo office tryst. I laugh out loud when I picture Dalia's face. Hater!

The next bubble of laughter gets trapped in my throat when the elevator doors ping open. Roger's dominating figure stands before me. His intense gray eyes peer into me from his gorgeous chiseled face. A smirk plays on his full lips. His collar-length hair begs for me to tug it as I pull his mouth to mine.

The bespoke, navy pinstripe, three-piece suit fits his muscular physique to perfection. Broad chest covered by the custom shirt, vest, and jacket. Long legs encased in the finest Italian wool. Black leather Oxfords adorn his great feet. Big hands, great feet, massive dick…

I rub my thighs together to ease the ache as I step out of the elevator. Roger notices my unmet desire and growls deep in his chest. His eyes darken to slate in an instant. *Mon loup* is on the prowl. My lion bows before him.

Roger takes my hand and leads me past the three receptionists and offices to his in the far corner. We step inside. Immediately, he strides to his desk to press the buttons to turn the transparent glass walls opaque and to lock the double wooden doors.

He lifts me with ease to sit on his desk. Then rucks up my skirt to stand between my thighs. They tremble.

"Congratulations, Leonie, my love," he croons against my open lips as he slides his long fingers along my inner thighs. "You deserve the position."

He nips my lower lip and I yelp. Thankfully, his office is soundproof. The tips of her fingers graze the silk gusset of my already moist panties. He growls in appreciation as he slips two fingers beneath the thin fabric. Hardly a barrier from Roger's determined digits.

"Aaahhh, *Amoureux, merci*," I pant as his fingers plunder my wet pussy, the sound and scent of my arousal clear in the room.

His lips plot a path of open-mouthed kisses along my jaw to my neck where he draws the sensitive skin into his mouth and sucks. He marks me as his. The sharp pain makes me cry out.

I dig my fingers in the back of his neck, unsure if I want to push him away or pull him closer. The pistoning strokes of his thick invasion make me buck against his hand.

When his other hand reaches for the back zipper of my skirt, I open it for him. Roger slips his thumb in my mouth. My cue to suck on it. Then he slips it inside the back of my panties to press against my bottom hole.

I rise from the table. Only to have gravity push his thumb past the rings of muscle into my ass when I land back down.

"Sssss... Ooohhh," I hiss and cry out, even as my body squirms to take him further.

"Will you do your very best, Pretty Kitty?" Roger rasps in my ear. "Or will I have to punish your misbehavior?"

His threat of pleasure mixed with pain sends me over the edge. I keen in response as his fingers continue to pump in and out of my holes. The alternating thrusts coordinated for maximum gratification. He covers my last one with his mouth. He absorbs my screams of ecstasy.

As my body quakes with the aftershocks, Roger doesn't let up. Instead, he adds two more fingers to each hole. I writhe uncontrollably from the onslaught of sensation. Wantonly, I crave more. I meet each of his thrusts with my own. I match his movements and taking him deeper within each part of me.

"So good... So good..." I cry out in French, no longer able to think coherently enough to translate my native tongue.

"You deserve every orgasm, Kitten. Every... single... one..." Roger punctuates each word with a pistoning stroke, purposefully hitting my G-spot.

"*Medre...*"

I wail as the fourth orgasm rocks through my body. My hips undulate of their own accord. Mindlessly, I let my body take over as my damp forehead falls against Roger's broad chest.

"There, there, Pretty Kitten. I have you..." he croons against my hair, no longer neatly slicked back.

I lose count of the number of orgasms he's wrung from my body. My inner thighs press against the sides of his muscular legs, trying to close and prevent any more of his ministrations. I'm done.

"Have I sufficiently shown you how very proud I am of you, Leonie love?" Roger murmurs.

I can only nod. Too spent to make my mouth form words. Fortunately, Roger only chuckles and doesn't demand my "words."

Gently, he extricates his fingers from my body. He places the ones were in my pussy against my lips. Without hesitation, I open for him. Then moan as I taste my sweet essence coating his skin. I lick his fingers clean with relish as our eyes meet above his hand.

His hooded gaze draws another climax from me. I close my eyes and shiver in delight. He chuckles.

Once he's satisfied with my efforts, he pinches my chin between the same fingers and kisses me deeply. Groaning as he savors my flavor, still fresh on my tongue.

"Good girl," he murmurs as he steps back.

Roger's intense gaze takes me in from head to toe. A smirk from witnessing me come undone for him plays on his handsome face, flush from his arousal.

I slide off the desk and drop to my knees to offer him my thanks. But he shakes his head and pulls me to my feet.

Cradling my face in his hands, Roger murmurs, "That was for you, my love. Pleasure for your success. Your satisfaction is all that I desire."

I close my eyes and nuzzle against one of his palm.

I love this man more than words can ever express.

ROGER

"Hello Mr. Steele."

I glance up from the monitor for my laptop to the unknown voice at the door of my office. My eyes must be computer weary. I blink to clear my vision. The daymare doesn't change.

It's the American brunette from Leonie's class. The same one who tweaked my last nerve with her inane questions. Her attempt at flirting with me then, and now her presence in my office makes my hackles raise.

Where in the hell is my assistant Françoise?

Sure, I have an open-door policy. But it's for employees, not an intern. At least I suspect she's one of the two interns Bonnay recently hired.

Please don't let my conciliatory offer turn sour. Too late to retract it. And if she went through the proper process, I have no reason to terminate her internship.

I have to tread lightly. But firmly shut down any notion she has of continuing her flirtatious actions.

A glance at the clock lets me know hours have passed since I started reviewing these documents, and it's Françoise's lunchtime. No wonder she's not at her desk.

Fuck.

The intern saunters into my office like she belongs in my inner sanctum. She stops to stand before my desk. Unfortunately, my hesitancy gave her an opening. Sliding her fingers along the very low cut of her tightly fitted wrap dress, she lets her eyes sweep across my face and upper body.

My skin crawls.

My suit jacket hangs on the valet in the corner, my tie with top button loosened hangs at my throat, and I rolled my sleeves up over my forearms. Sometimes the French cuffs and links prove hindrances when I have a lot to type. I tousled my hair from running my hands through it while deep in thought over these contracts.

Obviously this woman appreciates my unkempt appearance. She pokes the tip of her tongue out to moisten her overly glossy red lips as she fixates on mine.

Inwardly, I groan in annoyance. No way does she appeal to me. I force my eyes to not roll in disgust. I inhale, then exhale to avoid snapping her head off for intruding and flirting, again.

Time to put a stop to her shenanigans. Once and for all. It's enough already. I have work to do. No time for a misguided, delusional intern.

"You seem to need some assistance... I can help ease your load," she says, rounding the corner of my desk.

"That is precisely why Monsieur Steele has a more than capable personal assistant and not a recently hired intern who is out of her depth, Ms. Shaw."

The disapproving voice of Françoise cracks through my office like a whip. The intern stops cold in her tracks. The lash of Françoise's reprimand prevents any forward motion.

A flicker of irritation runs over the intern's face before she fixes her expression into a neutral one. She pivots to face my assistant who has a bag of food in her hand and a scowl on her face.

Françoise has worked for me since I started as president here five years ago. She's in her mid-fifties and takes no shit from anyone—including me. Her work ethic, above reproach, keeps her at the top of my list of the company's best employees. She's an asset. And right now, an invaluable one.

"Let me be crystal clear, Ms. Shaw. You are not to enter Monsieur Steele's offices at any time. In fact, you do not have clearance for the executive floor. We will go to security to correct your ID access immediately. Then proceed to Human Resources for them to brief you on protocol."

Without taking her stern gaze from the intern, Françoise puts the bag on my conference table.

"Monsieur Steele, I brought lunch for you," she says, still pinning the intern with her cold eyes.

"*Merci*, Madame Faucher," I reply and move to the table as far away as possible from the intern.

"Now, right this way, Ms. Shaw," Françoise commands as she blocks her from me and points to the door with her outstretched hand.

From the corner of my eye, I see the intern lift her chin and stride out of my office without glancing at Françoise or me.

My assistant, or rather savior, arches her eyebrow at me before she marches out the door.

Crisis averted.

The sound of my mobile brings my attention back to my desk. A smile dispels the vexation. It's the ringtone I use for Leone.

"Ciao, Kitten," I answer.

"Ciao *Amore Mio*," she purrs.

Another of her attributes I love. She's fluent in French, English, Italian, German, and Spanish. Often we'll converse in French and Italian since I speak those languages fluently, too. We're inspired by one of our favorite movies, *A Fish Called Wanda*. When Leonie purrs any of them seductively in her husky voice, my dick hardens.

Now she sounds breathless and not from our exertions. What is she doing, I wonder?

"If you don't stop seducing me, I'm going to scream in the throes of passion right on this treadmill!" She teases.

Ah yes, the gym. Leonie stays fit through Pilates, yoga, cardio, and strength training. She doesn't take her natural beauty for granted. She enhances it with regular exercise and clean eating. When she swallows my jizz, she laughs and calls it protein.

"What's so funny?" She asks.

"Thinking of your favorite protein," I chuckle.

Leonie roars heartily. I'm sure every man in the vicinity stares at her. Especially with sweat glistening on her skin. Fuckers.

"Are we still on for dinner tonight with your friends?" She asks.

I forgot we're having dinner with Joel Bailey and his long-time girlfriend, Hettie Fuchs. Joel and I met at a business function years ago and hit it off. They've been dating for a few years now. He's an investor in real estate and she's an attorney who specializes in commercial property law. They live in The STEELE Tower a few floors below me.

"Yes. Why?" I ask.

I hear the speed slow down and Leonie swipe a towel over her face.

"I want to be sure I have something to wear," she responds, her voice muffled by the towel.

Now, I chuckle. The clotheshorse wants to be sure she has something to wear? Hysterical! Leonie has taken over three-quarters of my closet in two months. I've had to move some of my out-of-season pieces to one of the guest rooms. I told her she already has her first STEELE design assignment: redo our closets. She laughed and kissed me on the cheek as she put another suit in my hand for removal. Gotta love her.

"Not funny! They're your closest friends outside of your family. I want them to like me!" She says.

I clear my throat. I won't tease her. She's serious. I've had over a year to become acquainted with her closest friends, Luc and of course Lola. We decided to spend time with everyone, so we're comfortable on both sides.

"We're going to Brasserie Lipp. I'm changing into a sport coat, shirt, and trousers with loafers. Does that help?" I ask.

Leonie is quiet and I can tell she's contemplating her outfit, so I give her a moment. The background sound changes to soft music. She must be in the locker room.

"Okay, I'll pick up a dress I had my eye on. I love you! *Caio!*"

And just like that, she's gone. A quick breath of fresh air that my soul needs.

* * *

"LEONIE, I love your dress! The pink pattern is gorgeous!"

I agree.

She's achieved her goal. Joel and Hettie adore her. All throughout drinks and dinner, they exchanged stories and found commonalities in the schools they attended and holiday spots they enjoy. She and Hettie already have plans for lunch and shopping this weekend. Plus skiing in Verbier come winter.

And yes, the airy silk floral-print crepe de chine mini dress is elegant and more than suitable to meet her boyfriend's closest friends. The pussy-bow tied at the high neck and flowy blouson sleeves balance the above the knee hemline. Leonie appears both demure and sexy. I can't wait to unwrap her later.

I glance from the two women to Joel. He wears a smug expression. I raise my eyebrows and cock my head in question. He smirks and leans towards me.

"I'll clear my calendar," he says only loud enough for me to hear.

"Okaaay…" I respond.

Joel hums the Wedding March and wiggles his left ring finger.

"Like I said, I'll clear my calendar. I give you at max five months," he laughs as he clinks his beer goblet to mine.

"I'll toast to that, my friend," I respond with a laugh.

"What are we toasting?" Hettie asks, flitting her gaze from Joel to me and back.

"To the best is yet to come, my dear. The best is yet to come," he responds, winking at me over his glass.

"*Prost! Zum Wohl!*" Leonie chimes in as she clinks her glass of Lillet with Hettie's snifter of brandy and our goblets.

Her laughter rings above the hum of conversations,

music, and utensils on dishes. She glows with jubilance, more intoxicating than the most potent liquor.

I gaze adoringly at the love of my life. Joel is right. It won't be much longer.

And I cannot wait.

LEONIE

"*W*hat the hell, Leonie?!"
Merde...

Roger storms into my new dressing room—I made good on the redesign of our closets—waving my mobile around. His nostrils flare and his eyes narrow to slits. I fear he'll have a coronary as bright red as he appears from the skin exposed by his unbuttoned shirt to his hairline. He yells like a crazy caveman.

When he shoves my mobile towards me, it explains his rage. A text message from Giovanni flashes boldly across the locked screen:

Bellissima amore mia, I can't wait to see you...

Nervously, I swallow. I didn't want Roger to find out in this manner. My plan was to tell him during breakfast, make light of it. Now, it weighs heavily in the tense air between us.

Giovanni has been blowing up my mobile for the past three weeks. Ever since the bloggers and media picked up on my relationship with Roger. They were especially voracious for the story since Roger and Giovanni fought at Lola's Coterie Dubai opening, where I appeared as spokesmodel. The love triangle angle proves irresistible.

Now, I'm once again irresistible to Giovanni…

Too bad. He pissed me off for the last time. It wasn't only the fight. His touching that guest at the party right in front of me was the last straw. We may not have had a monogamous relationship—on his end—but he never dared to throw his sidepieces in my face. To hell with our "understanding."

At first, I ignored his calls and messages. Yesterday, when he showed up at my agents' offices and made a scene, I finally gave in to meet him for lunch. It's over. I plan to disillusion him of any notions of our reuniting. Then inform him to back the fuck off.

I had avoided telling Roger right away since I didn't want to upset him. But I did anyway.

Merde…

"Helloooo… Earth to Leonie!"

Roger continues, irked further by my delayed response.

I close my eyes, take a deep inhale, and slowly let the air out as my gaze meets stormy gray eyes. The tinge of hurt in their depths makes me lose my breath. I will not allow Giovanni to damage my genuine relationship with Roger. *Non!*

"Roger, *Mon Cœur*," I start as I take the mobile with the offensive text message from his hand and place it on the island. "Please forgive me—"

His breath hitches sharply. I swivel my gaze back to him. His gray eyes widened in shock.

Fuck, he must think I'm breaking up with him… again. I shake my head forcefully while I hold his between my hands. His eyes flicker everywhere, but at me. I pull his face closer to mine, making it impossible for him to avoid my gaze. Once his intense glare focuses on me, I continue.

"You misunderstand and it's my fault. I should have told you yesterday. I am sorry."

Roger relaxes a smidgen. But his gaze remains hostile.

I brush my lips over his mouth and sigh as I press my forehead to his. I breathe deeply of his warm breath, letting it soak into me. Strengthen me. Our souls need this connection.

I stand upright and lock eyes with him.

"I agreed to meet with Giovanni because he's been pestering me for over three weeks. I declined his calls and ignored his text messages. Until yesterday. He made a scene at my agents' offices. They were going to press charges. But I told them I would speak with him and tell him to back off since I am with you."

Roger bristles as the words tumble from my mouth. His face deepens in color. He's about to explode.

"What do you mean? That asshole has been harassing you for weeks... Then threatens your agents... And... you... do... not... tell... me?!"

He sputters and wrenches from my hold. He paces the dressing room as he mutters curses and pulls at his hair. Every few steps, Roger faces me and scowls. Then resumes his tirade.

I stand quietly. He needs to bow off the steam. And I really can't blame him. I'd react the same way.

After a good five minutes, Roger pulls his mobile from his trousers pocket and jabs in his code before he jabs the surface again.

"Do it. Do it now!"

I blink in shock. Who is he speaking to? What are they going to do?

Roger takes a deep breath. Puts his mobile back in his pocket. Runs his fingers through his hair. Then turns to me. The storm moved on from his eyes. Instead, they're slate gray and hooded with raw desire. He regards me for a moment. His gaze traveling from my head to my toes, then back to my eyes. Sexual tension replaces the angry vibes.

I shudder under his perusal.

He prowls towards me.

Uh, oh…

Without a word, he yanks the sash on my silk dressing gown and rips it from my naked body. The soft material caresses my skin as it slips down my body to pool at my feet.

My nipples pebble and my pussy floods.

In one swoop of his forearm, Roger clears the island of the accessories and my mobile on top. He grabs my waist and plops me down on the cool marble surface. My heated pussy trembles. From the abrupt change in temperature or in anticipation, I'm unsure. All I know is that I desire this man. A lot.

Roger plants his palms on my inner thighs and pushes them apart. His eyes never leave mine as he lowers his mouth to my dripping seam. One long lick sends a jolt of electricity straight to my core. I lock my ankles behind his head and grip his hair. He thwarts my attempt to pull him closer to my core with three successive spanks to my pussy lips.

"Ooowww!" I yowl.

Holy shit! He's never done that before. A spanking on my ass, *oui*. But my sensitive bits, *mais non*!

A lapping sound replaces the squelching caused by his fingers meeting my wet pussy. Roger devours me. His tongue sweeps in and around my inner channel. I jump when the tip probes the rough texture of my G-spot. Then cry out in wild abandon as I quake with my climax.

Roger's fingers join his tongue. He drives them in and out. Then scissors the digits to stretch me.

My inner walls clench, aware that the strike of his massive cock comes next. I rock my pussy against his palm like a cat in heat. Then throw my head back and scream as another orgasm throws me over the edge.

The sound of the zipper teeth separating and the pressure of his heavy dick against my thigh jerks me back to attention. My gaze falls to the space between us. Roger's enormous dick strains. Every ridge and vein stands out in relief against the velvety soft skin. A drop of pre-cum glistens on the slit of the bulbous head.

My mouth waters.

Still silent, Roger grips the base in his fist and rubs it against my swollen flesh. My juices coat his length in natural lube. He angles the tip at my entrance, braces his other hand at my ass, and plunges his dick inside. The hand at my rear locks me in place as he fills me root to tip.

Roger swallows my scream with a savage kiss. His tongue plunges into my mouth. It sweeps in to conquer. It matches the brutal thrusts of his hips.

I keen from the invasions. But I keep pace with both ends.

Roger's grunts and the slapping of his semen-filled balls against my ass fill the air. I writhe against him, aching for more. I need to feel his possessive punishment. I need to atone for my sin.

My forehead drops to his broad shoulder as my hands gain purchase in his thick hair. His grunts deepen to growls when I pull on his scalp. I know he relishes the pain.

Roger's feral dominance masters my desire. I cum one explosion after the other until I beg for him to stop.

Instead, he lifts me in his arms, widens his stance, and jackhammers up into my core. His muscular arms and thighs hold me aloft easily. I bounce on his thick dick as he chases his release.

With a mighty roar, Roger slams me down on his massive girth one last time. He holds me securely in place. Our bodies locked together. Inseparable.

I feel his cock swell and jerk inside of my depths as his seed fills my womb. Triggered, my pussy clamps repeatedly. It milks every drop of his essence into me. This orgasm wrings the last of my strength from me. Sated, I collapse in his arms.

"You are mine, Leonie. Only mine. I will allow no man to lay claim to you ever again." Roger rasps in my ear.

It's the last thing I hear before darkness pulls me under.

My last thought as my pussy tightens around its mate: *oui, Mon Cœur. Oui.*

LEONIE

*I*t's been a month.

Whomever Roger spoke with on the mobile. Whatever he had done. I haven't heard a peep from Giovanni Mattei. Not a voicemail, text message, smoke signal, nothing. He's disappeared from my life completely. Thank goodness!

Roger still refuses to tell me what happened. Just to trust him and not to worry. I trust him explicitly. So, no worries plague me whatsoever.

We've been back together for three months and it couldn't get better. He's even asked me to move in since we spend most of our time at his penthouse. I go by my duplex to pick up more things to bring back to his!

Mais non.

Billie's adage plays loudly in my mind: why pay for the cow if you can get the milk for free? Her hard-to-get tactic works wonders on her boy toy, Patrick Rockett. Her words of wisdom added to Lola's initial fiasco after moving in with Sebastian keep me from taking that step. Not yet.

I know Roger loves me. But I need more of a commitment. For now, it's all good.

Another bright note is my work at STEELE. The Interior Design Team treats me as being a worthy part of them. They know Roger is my boyfriend. But no one judges me or treats me in a certain kind of way. Every day that they appreciate my contributions proves Delia's snide comments erroneous.

Over the three months, I see her in the office on Wednesdays, one of her two days with Thursday being the other. She's asked me out to lunch a few times. But I don't trust her motives. Roger told me about her incident in his office. Bless Françoise!

Antonio has extended lunch invitations to me, too. I decline them without hesitation. His internship is with the Technical Design Team since he's a computer wiz and specializes in AutoCAD software. Even when our paths cross during the research and sketching process, I maintain my distance. No need to poke the bear named Roger Steele.

As far as my modeling goes, I re-negotiated my exclusive beauty contract with the top cosmetics company in the industry. Since I represented them, their revenue increased by thirty percent over three years.

The extended contract for five more years increases my multimillion-dollar fee over one hundred percent and includes corporate stock valued in the millions. Thanks to Luc and his business acumen, it's a historic deal.

My contract with Lola's Coterie also extended for five more years. She wanted longer. But I told her a fresh face would be good for the brand since I'll be thirty-six by the end of it. Not that ageism plays a role. I'll still be just as fabulous, if not more so! Luc had us compromise with a clause added for a review at the end of the five years.

My agents booked me for the best runway shows for this year's and next year's seasons. My signature feline prowl still rules the catwalk. Younger models try to emulate it or ask for my guidance that I happily provide. I am the acknowledged Queen. RAWR!

Roger and I have a busy social life, too. We've spent a few weekends with my parents, during which my mother fills him with different deserts and pastries. He loves it. Even my father accepts him. They've met at my father's club and he's introduced him to some members. Roger is under consideration for membership.

Other times, we hang out with Joel and Hettie. Either movie or game night at Roger's penthouse or at their half-floor flat. Hettie and I go to the gym and shopping together. She's attended one of my mentorship sessions to discuss her career with the girls.

Our schedules keep us busy.

Now, Lola and Sebastian returned from their two-month-long honeymoon. They're in Paris for a few days. Lola to catch up on work with Luc and her team at her flagship. Sebastian to check in on STEELE Paris as part of his newly appointed CEO and Chairman of the Board positions. Hot Power Couple!

Roger and I plan to have dinner with them, then go to LEVELS Paris for Masquerade Night. Neither man wants others to recognize their women. So, now Roger and I only go when members wear masks, or else we sneak in through the employee entrance and straight to his private suite. Possessive much?

All in all, my world is delightful and I'm thankful for it.

Lola's ringtone blasts through my musings. She's here! Excited, I answer her call.

"Hey, *Chérie*! Are you downstairs?" I ask.

"Hey, Girl! Yes! Sebastian went to Roger's office for some last-minute meeting. I'm on my way up to you," she responds.

I rush to the entry foyer to meet my BFF. As soon as the family's private elevator doors opens, we fall into each other's arms. It's been too long. The most time we've ever been apart and not spoken since becoming friends seven years ago.

"I missed you so much," Lola sniffles as she dabs at her eyes

She lost her parents in a tragic car accident when she was seventeen. With no other relatives, Luc and I were all she had until Sebastian and the Steele clan fifteen months ago. My parents adore Lola and adopted her as a second daughter. But understandably it's not the same as having one's own parents.

"I missed you, too," I sigh, then tease her. "Too busy being spanked and banged by Captain Caveman to think of your BFF, I suppose…"

We look at each other and burst out in loud guffaws that lead into uncontrollable snorts. I grab her arm and pull her through the penthouse's front doors and out to the main terrace. A bottle of Dom P. chills in a champagne bucket.

"*Voilà!*" I wave my hand to present Lola's favorite champagne to her.

She claps and bounds over to pop the cork. As she pours the tasty bubbly, she arches her eyebrow at me and smirks.

"So… Nice place you have here. You seem rather comfy, eh?"

I bite my lower lip to hold back a giggle. She continues to stare after she hands a flute to me. I try to hold out, but fail. A laugh bursts forth and my eyes fill will with joyful tears as I clink glasses with her.

"Ah, yes, here's to the end of the STEELE Quaternity and to the new Steele Duo!" Lola toasts as she joins in my laughter.

The champagne tickles my nose when I take a sip.

"Here, here!" I agree wholeheartedly.

I claim Roger as much as he claims me.

Lola and I fall onto chaises and sip the first glass in silence. Years of camaraderie allow us to enjoy the solitude with no need to rush and fill it with unnecessary words. Lola adds more of the champagne to our flutes. Then shifts on her chaise to face me. I angle myself towards her too.

"So, tell me—"

"How was your—"

We laugh some more for speaking at the same time. Lola inclines her head for me to go on.

"Tell me! How was your honeymoon? Shelley said you went island hopping. How romantic!"

Lola's face beams as she swoons against the back of the chaise. Her hazel eyes glow with an inner flame so heightened by love that she radiates from within. I know how she feels; I smile to myself.

"It was unbelievable! Sebastian arranged the most spectacular trip! One I will never forget."

She recounts the various tropical locales they traveled to over the two months. Her detailed tales of the sunrises, sunsets, private beaches, fresh food with local flavors, take me on a voyeuristic journey. I don't blame her when she says was reluctant to return.

"Now, it's your turn to spill..." Lola says pointedly as she tops off our flutes once again.

I take a slow sip and peer over the rim to tease her. She throws a pillow at me, and I laugh. I recount every iota from the night of her wedding to this morning. Well, I left out the incredible shower sex—TMI!

Sebastian's booming voice interrupts our giggles.

"Oh, so different from the last time you two were on a terrace sipping Dom Pérignon…"

Lola and I glance over at him and Roger, who laughs jovially as he punches his older brother in the arm playfully. They tussle and end with Roger in a headlock, getting a nudgie in the head. He pushes Sebastian off and strides over to give Lola a kiss on the cheek. Then drops onto the chaise next to me, planting a big, wet kiss on my lips.

Sebastian and Lola laugh. He comes over and kisses my cheek before pulling Lola onto his lap on her chaise. His gray eyes hold the same burning light as Lola's as he gazes at her.

I'm so happy for my best friend and Sebastian.

"Well, Sis, how's it going?" Sebastian says as he pierces me with his penetrating stare.

I'm surprised by his choice of descriptive label for me. Does he mean because Lola and I are like sisters? Or is he referring to my relationship with Roger and thus with him? I open my mouth. Then close it, not sure how to answer.

Roger throws the pillow back at Sebastian. But he tucks. He chuckles as he speaks again.

"Well, you and Lola are sisters, *non?*" He asks, his face barely holding onto the neutral expression.

"Ass," Roger mumbles as he takes my flute and drains the glass.

Lola titters and refills it. Roger promptly drinks it down, and Sebastian laughs.

Well, I'm glad they all think it's hilarious. I feel as though I'm missing something from their private joke. I take the fresh glass from Roger and tilt it back. The delicious bubbly fills me. Then glare at each of them in turn. They laugh uproariously.

Roger pulls me onto his lap and kisses the top of my head. I wrap my arms around his waist as I burrow into his chest and sigh. Content with the bliss of my life.

* * *

"TELL me what makes your pussy weep, Pretty Kitty."

Roger rumbles in my ear as I squirm on the seat between his muscular thighs as we sit on the dark red leather banquette. His rock-hard cock presses against the crack of my ass. I squirm some more.

We're at Peepshow in LEVELS Paris. We finished dinner at Arpège and came here with Lola and Sebastian almost an hour ago. Time is hard to track when feeding my voyeur kink.

My eyes framed by an ornate gold half-mask that has peacock's feathers across the top like a headdress widen as I glance around the room. I changed into an ass-skimming, silk georgette negligee. The cream sheer material hides nothing, including my puckered nipples and swollen pussy lips. Gold, six-inch mules adorn my feet.

Roger gifted me a stunning pair of yellow diamond chandelier earrings. They glitter in the low light as my head swivels, taking in the hedonistic sights surrounding us.

The other seating alcoves filled with members in various stages of sex draw my attention first. The lusty sounds of women and men as they climax fills the air. A main stage and several smaller platforms showcase demonstrations in bondage and edging.

The atmosphere is all about bacchanalia with the melodic thrum of sensual music. Somewhere amongst it all or in one of the performance rooms, Lola and Sebastian disappeared.

I yelp when Roger nips the delicate shell of my ear.

"Tell me," he demands on a growl.

My body vibrates with the sensation. I mewl and press further into his firm chest. My nails dig into his thick thighs. His growl deepens. My pussy throbs.

"Th… The man on his knees servicing his Dom… just over there," I pant, pointing my chin towards the left.

A naked man whose eyes blindfolded by a white silk cloth kneels before a giant, muscular man with a crew cut and tight leather pants. His motorcycle boots stand far apart to brace him as he drills his enormous dick down his sub's throat. One hand holds the man's head in place while the other swings a flogger against the man's back. Both men groan in pleasure.

Roger chuckles against my neck. Then sucks some skin into his mouth. Another mark to claim me.

Since being a member at LEVELS, my sexual appetite has expanded to include unthought of desires and things that never intrigued me before. The men case in point.

I look to my right and see a woman dangling from the ceiling caught like a butterfly bound in the web of Shibari rope. Her partner taunts her engorged nipples and pussy lips with hot red wax. The woman shrills as a drop lands on her clit.

Merde…

My pussy winces. Not for me… Yet.

Roger hooks his feet around my ankles and pulls my legs apart.

I squeak in surprise.

Two of his thick fingers crawl across my inner thigh. Then breach my pussy entrance.

I arch my back and raise my hips to give him better access to my achy core.

Roger's other hand presses down on my hip and the top of my thigh to keep me still. He fucks me with his fingers until I break with a toe-curling orgasm.

I toss my head back. My body bucks against his hand as he draws another orgasm from my core. My entire body quivers from the intensity of the ecstasy. My screams join the others to rebound off the walls and ceiling as we reach our climaxes in unison.

"Good, Little Kitty," Roger croons as he pats my plundered pussy lovingly. "Good, Little Kitty."

I purr my pleasure as I lap his fingers clean.

ROGER

"*D*amn, it must be in the water!"

"Hell, as long as it's not in my Jackson Reserve, I'm good. Let those three keep the water!"

"I'll drink to that, bro!"

Everyone laughs at Malcolm's and our cousin Lucien Jackson's banter. They along with Sebastian, Joel, and myself enjoy a Guys' Night Out at Jackson Smoke&Scotch a new lounge Lucien opened last month on Rue Saint-Honoré.

The legendary Place Vendôme/St. Honoré area is the place to see and be seen. Where money is no object for the people it attracts. Old society, fashionistas, and celebrities frequent the nearby high-chic spots to shop, drink, and dine.

It's the latest addition to Jackson Corporation's luxury establishments created by *The Sexy Chef* as legions of his female followers dubbed Lucien. They slated locations in London, New York, and Los Angeles for over the next six months. Another hot property for the Jacksons to add to their list.

"Funny, you were chasing after Starr Knight at my wedding," Sebastian says as he blows out smoke from his Jackson Cuban Cigar.

All heads swing to Malcolm, curious to know who sparked the interest of the Dom playboy enough for him to give chase. It's the reverse—he can't keep women from their pursuit of him. His face flushes and he takes a swig of his Scotch. He mumbles an answer with the snifter at his lips.

"Pardon... Say again? We didn't hear you, Lover Boy, er, playboy..." Sebastian teases him relentlessly as only an older brother can.

Malcolm, now recovered, cradles the Baccarat crystal snifter in his palms as he smirks at Sebastian. His gray eyes flash with devilment.

"I don't know what you're talking about," Malcolm scoffs. "You must have been floating in the clouds, struck by Cupid's arrow."

He makes goo-goo eyes and bats his eyelashes coyly at Sebastian.

We crack up, Baz included. His cheeks even redden with embarrassment. Poor guy. Malcolm's got him down pat.

"Say what you want, Hettie and I have a good thing going... As it is. No signs of marriage on our horizon," Joel states with a decisive nod between puffs of his cigar. "I'm way too young to commit for the rest of my life."

Lucien and Malcolm clink glasses with Joel adding robust cheers and here, here.

I shake my head and chuckle as I sip my Scotch. The burn feels good going down, then settles in my stomach with warmth. But not as warm as I felt buried deep inside of Leonie's lush paradise this morning.

One of the best parts about her spending the night is waking up to bury myself within her body: mouth, pussy, ass. She's a supercharged magnet that pulls me in every time. I shift in my leather club chair as my cock stiffens at the thought of Leonie. Damn.

So far she's denied me the pleasure of moving in with me. Skipping past my many hints and outright requests. As much time as she spends at my penthouse, she might as well just give in. I know she wants to.

Some mornings I pretend I'm still asleep, but I sense Leonie's amber gaze on my face. She traces her fingertips across my cheek or along the cleft in my chin. Her soft murmurs of love in French fills me with such incredible joy. One time I opened my eyes, and she startled, then slipped out of bed without a word. She didn't mention the moment at all. She's not quite there, but she's almost ready.

And I'm a patient man.

"Laugh all you want. I was just like you. Probably worse," Sebastian starts, eyeing each of his hecklers. "It'll happen to you, too. And I'm going to be the one yucking it up."

Malcolm, Lucien, and Joel's eyes widen at Sebastian's proclamation. Then they burst out in hysterical laughter. Lucien wipes his eyes while Joel doubles over. Sebastian and I can't help but to join them.

The conversation progresses to business and sports, typical guy talk. Malcolm and Lucien update us on their latest project Jackson Hole at STEELE. They're high-end, international beach bars with restaurants in jet-set hot spots. The first location at our resort in Monte Carlo opened a few months ago, and the next scheduled for Cannes. It's already popular with reservations and private parties booked months in advance.

I tell them Leonie and I will go to Monte Carlo since we

planned a trip there the following weekend. It's been a while since either of us has visited. We'll stay at her penthouse as it's closer to the action than my hillside villa. We expect a refreshing, fun-filled break.

"No, sir! Paris Saint-Germain will win," exclaims Lucien.

Joel throws his head back and roars with laughter.

"How about a friendly wager? Liverpool FC by one," he responds.

Sebastian rolls his eyes as he leans forward in his seat. They debate the merits of American football and soccer—he taunts them with the very wrong name. Lucien points out American football uses hands with an occasional little kick, so which has the wrong name. Malcolm and I chime in as they parry.

It's good to relax with those closest to me. The familiar companionship combined with the best Scotch and cigars makes it an enjoyable evening.

"Now, that fucker…"

Malcolm gestures to the entrance, and we swivel in our seats.

Fucker is right. It's Mattei with a curvy blonde woman on his arm. He saunters in with his head held high, a smirk on his face as though the emperor has arrived and his loyal subjects should stand and salute. Mattei exudes cockiness.

He hasn't spotted me, yet.

"What's his story with the Steeles?" Lucien asks, already bristling.

"A dick who thinks he's God's gift to women. The wrong one being Leonie," Sebastian sneers as he flexes his fingers.

Malcolm nods and adds, "Well, he better keep it moving. I'm in no mood for his shit tonight."

"No worries, I'll take care of it. This is the last time he'll waltz into a Jackson establishment," Lucien says as he rises to his six feet, three inches. His emerald green eyes blaze.

His movement catches Mattei's attention. His smirk falters and he stops mid-stride as our eyes lock. His lip curls up in a snarl. The woman turns to him in surprise. Then follows his glare to me.

I stand beside Lucien as Sebastian and Malcolm flank us.

At the sight of a pack of four Alpha males, Mattei reconsiders his actions as his eyes shift from each of us.

I step forward, but Lucien holds my arm. He nods at two men in dark suits and they approach Mattei. The baffled woman stands closer to him. Fortunately, he doesn't argue when they escort him from the lounge.

Lucien pulls his mobile from his trousers pocket and says, "No need to let him ruin our evening. What's his full name?"

"Giovanni Mattei," I respond through clenched teeth.

Lucien types on the screen. Then glances up at me.

"I just sent a text to my head of security. He'll alert all of our businesses to deny entry to Mattei."

He claps me on the back and sits back in his chair.

"Time for another round, bros!" Joel chuckles as he pours more Scotch into our snifters.

Yeah, I need to wash the sour taste in my mouth from the encounter with Mattei and end the night on a high note with my boys. Then go home to bury myself in my woman until her body can't take another orgasm and her voice is hoarse from screaming my name.

An even more appealing high note.

ROGER

"*I*t's so beautiful! This was a splendid idea, *Mon Amour!*"

Leonie's smile is brighter than the sun reflecting off the turquoise waters of the Mediterranean Sea shimmering behind her.

We're eating lunch at the restaurant on the terrace of the Château Eza. It sits high above the Jardin d'Eze and lower village. This area is my favorite on the French Riviera. Its borders extend from the Med at Èze-sur-Mer to the hilltop medieval Èze-Village. The villages connect at Saint-Laurent-d'Eze.

Leonie and I arrived in Monte Carlo late last night and went straight to her duplex. Even though it's only over the weekend, we packed a full schedule. Today we drove along the coast and up to Èze. We meandered through the streets, stopping in shops and art galleries.

A beautiful bracelet of gold filigree set with precious stones caught my eye as we passed a window display for antique jewelry. The bold, yet delicate piece in 18-karat yellow gold seemed made for Leonie. I smile as the sun sparks off of the stones when she claps her hands in glee. I need not see her eyes past the giant glamour girl sunglasses she wears to know the gold flecks in the amber orbs shine.

"Come, I want to take a photo with the water behind us," she says as she beckons a server to the table.

"*Oui, madame?*" The besotted server asks as he bows to Leonie.

"*Veuillez avoir la gentillesse de prendre notre photo, merci!*" She asks him flashing her megastar smile.

"*Absolument! S'il vous pla"t!*" He responds.

I hold back a chuckle as he falls all over himself to take her mobile, so awestruck by her beauty. Leonie rises gracefully from her chair as I help her to her sandaled feet. Even in a tiered eyelet gauzy mini dress, no makeup, and her hair piled atop her head, Leonie is breathtaking. The white fabric and freshly painted white nails make her caramel skin glow. I pull her into my arms and kiss her passionately.

Once I let her loose, her tinkling laughter carries through the air. Other patrons clap at my exuberant display of love. Sappy, I'll claim it just as I claim my woman. Mine!

As we turn to pose for the shot, the server smiles and counts to three. He takes two pictures, then shows them to us for approval. Perfection... Nothing can make *The Lion* look bad.

"*Merci, merci beaucoup!*" Leonie tells him as she hugs him.

He bows again and leaves us. Backing away to get one last glimpse at her. Then he turns and rushes to the other servers who slap him on the back. He peeks over his shoulder and blushes when Leonie waves and blows him a kiss. The others clap and whoop.

"More admirers for you, Bonbon," I tease.

"*Peut-être*," she starts as she cups my face. "But you are the only one who matters, *Mon Amour*."

Leonie brushes her lips across mine. A zing tingles from my mouth to my heart down my spine to erupt out the tip of my dick. It weeps at her loving touch. Her soft purr vibrates through me. I close my eyes as I shudder with need.

"Only you, Roger."

"I love you, baby," I murmur, my gaze landing on her gorgeous face.

She smiles and nods, "I know."

We order green salads to start and fresh fish in a crust of peppers and herbs with steamed coconut and Iberian chorizo as our main dish. It's hearty enough after our long walk up the hillside. But won't weigh us down for the return trek. We sip frothy snifters filled with *Rosé à la Piscine*.

"So delicious and refreshing!" Leonie exclaims as she licks a drop of the cocktail from the corner of her mouth.

A low growl rumbles in my chest. I want to bite it.

"*Mon loup* must be hungry, *non?*" She giggles.

Before I can answer, the server places our salads in front of us.

"Bon appétit!" He says with gusto.

"*Merci!*" We respond in unison.

More than the food, I enjoy the contented sounds Leonie makes as she relishes her meal. A woman with a healthy appetite is a turn on. Unenthusiastically picking at a plate of lettuce leaves and lemon juice equates to vanilla sex. What a snoozefest.

"What's the plan for the rest of the day?" Leonie asks as she sips her *Piscine*.

I think a moment as I check my platinum Rolex Day-Date watch. We have a few hours before the sunsets. Plenty of time for a pleasant drive along the coast, especially in my gunmetal gray convertible Aston Martin Vanquish.

"Let's drive west along the coast to Cannes. We can stop at Villefranche-sur-Mer, Beaulieu-sur-Mer, Vieux Nice, and Antibes," I suggest.

"Fantastique!" Leonie claps as she bounces in her chair. "The day is perfect for it! Plus, I feel like Halle Berry as Jinx in *Die Another Day* in your Aston Martin!"

I throw my head back and laugh out loud. I always feel the same way whenever I drive one of them. As a collector of vintage Aston Martin vehicles for the last ten years, I've amassed quite the collection. This one is my favorite. Halle is absolutely stunning, but she doesn't compare to my Leonie. But then no one compares to her.

"We must find you an orange bikini," I wink at her.

"*Oui!*" She purrs.

"Pardon, monsieur, would you care for dessert?" The server appears at the table.

I look to Leonie and she declines. So I ask for the check. We head down through the streets back to my James Bond ride. I open the door for Leonie and she slips in and ties a colorful silk Hermès scarf around her head. She smiles at me as I hop into the driver's seat and rev the engine.

The ride is thrilling with the hairpin turns and narrow lanes. A bus looms in front of us and Leonie squeaks. Then she grabs my arm and buries her face in my shoulder. I kiss the top of her head without taking my eyes off the road. Laughing as I switch gears and the engine roars in response. Passengers on the bus wave as we slip past them. The exhilaration is addictive.

We hop out at Villefranche-sur-Mer. Leonie wobbles on her feet like a newly born cub. I wrap my arm around her slim waist and hoist her to my side. With a tinkling laugh, she drapes her arms around my neck and kisses me silly.

"My super agent! You saved us!" She gushes.

"Always, baby," I croon in her ear.

The village is quaint as we stroll through the streets. We detour to *Église Saint-Michel*. The baroque Italian-style church intrigues our love of architecture and design. We marvel at paintings and sculptures in the cool quiet interior. Hushed we stand and admire its beauty in awe.

After a while, we hit the road for more thrills. We stop in Beaulieu-sur-Mer to visit Villa Kerylos. Again attracted by the architecture, we gaze upon its Ancient Greek style set on the edge of the coast like the kingfisher it's named for. Leonie tells me her ancestors were founders of the village as we make our way back to the car.

A little boy and girl—apparently brother and sister—run up to us with a bouquet of flowers. Leonie lowers herself to their eye level and takes their proffered gift.

"*Pour vous jolie dame!*" They exclaim.

"*Oh, chéris merci beaucoup!*" She responds as she hugs them tight to her chest.

I grab my mobile from the pocket of my shorts and snap a quick photo. Leonie is a natural with the children as she converses with them in French. She stands when their mother hurries over and smiles at her. She explains they're helping her in their flower shop and rushed out to give Leonie the bouquet they just put together.

I hand them some euros. But the mother stops me as the children shake their heads vehemently, insisting the bouquet is a gift. We thank them and get in the car with a wave.

As we drive, I think about children with Leonie. I can't wait. My only worry is for her wellbeing given her mother's experiences. As though sensing the unease rising in me, Leonie puts her arm around my shoulder and strokes the back of my head. The comforting move dispels the negative thoughts.

The beauty of Vieux Nice comes into view. Set on the Mediterranean below the primary area of Nice, the vibrant old town looks like a postcard. Its narrow cobblestone streets and pastel-hued buildings line the coast. We stop in shops to buy Niçoise soaps and Provençal textiles. As we head back to the car, we pick up *socca* crepes from the daily market on Cours Saleya.

We take our time walking to the car as we share the crepes. Leonie licks a few crumbs from the corner of my mouth. I turn my head quickly and nip her lips into my mouth. She moans and melts against me. Our tongues tangle as our kiss deepens.

"*Chéri*," she sighs softly. "You taste delicious... Mmm mmm mmm."

When we come up for air, I kiss the tip of her nose and toss the crepes' wrapper in the trash. Leonie's eyes track my moves like a huntress. When I return to her, I slip my arm around her waist to walk us to the car.

"Next stop... Antibes. All aboard!"

She giggles at my antics as she tightens the knot on her scarf. As we pull away from Vieux Nice, she throws her arms in the air and whoops. I join her, tossing my head back for my own shout of joy. People turn and wave at us. Her excitement is contagious.

When we arrive, we take in the Roman-era architecture and marvels. From the aqueducts and their ingenious arches, to the luxury found in the excavated villas. The history and lore surrounding the area pulls us back in time. After a stroll through the magnificent gardens at Villa

Eilenroc. The scent of olives, lavender, and eucalyptus mingles in the air around us as we walk hand in hand along the paths. We capture the moment with more photos.

The ride to Cannes is just as majestic along the coast. The busy city filled with tourists, celebrities, and the wealthy bustles with a vibrancy unlike any other. We park at the STEELE Cannes and walk along the Promenade de la Croisette. The piers and beaches dotted with colorful umbrellas and chaises encourage sun lovers to stretch out.

As we stand gazing across the sand to the glittering waters of the Med, I glance down at Leonie. She stifles a yawn with the back of her hand. Yeah, it's been a long day. She senses my intense stare and glances up with a bright smile.

"Pardon me!" She laughs. "I'm still wide awake and ready for some more action! Where to next, *Mon Cœur?*"

I pull her into my arms, and she snuggles against my chest. As I brush my lips across the top of her head, an idea comes to me. I tip her face up to mine.

"How about we go find you that orange bikini, grab two chaises, and drink some more *Rosé à la Piscines?* Then change for dinner and stay the night at the hotel?"

Leonie dances and shimmies her hips as she claps her hands—her and Lola's signature merry dance.

"That's a wonderful idea! I wholeheartedly agree!"

I pull out my mobile and dial the general manager. I ask her to book the Joséphine Baker Suite and request the concierge to locate an orange bikini, some evening wear options for dinner, and make a reservation. She assures me they will take care of everything before we return. I thank her and end the call.

"One more photo! I want lots of memories!" Leonie says.

We pose with the sparking water behind us for another

great shot. The walk back is at a slower pace since we know the rest of the afternoon and evening we will spend in the city. Just as we step onto the STEELE Cannes' property, my mobile vibrates with a call. Pulling it from my pocket, I note it's my mother. I answer right away.

"Hi, Mom. What's going on? Everything okay?"

In the background I hear a boat's horn sound as though leaving port. The last I checked, they were touring the Malbec vineyards of Mendoza with Lucie and Connor Jackson. No water for big boats in that area of the world.

"Oh, honey! Everything is fine! Don't worry," She starts. "Your father and I just boarded *Serendipity*. After being at such high altitudes for the past two weeks, we needed the warm weather of the Mediterranean."

I breathe a sigh of relief. Then nod at Leonie to show all is well. The worried expression drops from her face as she asks me to tell them hi for her.

"Oh, good. I hope you had a good time. Leonie says hi," I respond.

There's silence on the other end.

I pull the mobile from my ear to check the call didn't disconnect. It is. Why would my mother get quiet when she finds out Leonie is with me? As I form the words to ask my mother, her voice carries through the line.

"—told me you were in Monte Carlo. So I told your father we should meet up. Spend some time on the yacht tomorrow. Have brunch, sunbathe, catch up on what's happening in your life. Dress up and go to the casino later."

The call must have faded out. But I have to be certain she understands Leonie and I are together. No way will I abandon her.

"Mom, did you hear me when I said Leonie says hi?"

"Of course! And I said that's perfect. Didn't you hear me?" She says.

Thank fuck! I'd hate for them to not get along. Although they seemed fine at Sebastian and Lola's wedding. Especially with the future I have planned for Leonie and me.

"No, Mom. Your mobile cut out," I respond with a sigh of relief.

She tsks, "Your brainiac brother persuaded me to 'upgrade to the best model on the planet.' So now it blanks out... High tech my butt!"

We laugh at her spot-on impersonation of Harris. Not only a gadget geek, he's a coder. We tease him and Haley for being nerds, but they're wizzes at what they do. I can't wait to get him for giving Mom a whacked-out mobile.

"Let me speak to Leonie," she adds.

I pass my mobile to Leonie. A wide smile blooms on her face as she listens to my mother speak. I can't hear what she's saying. But judging by Leonie's expression and giggles, it's all good.

"*Oui, oui,*" she says. "I'd love to! Okay, see you tomorrow. Bonne nuit!"

She hands the mobile back to me after she disconnects the call.

"Eleven tomorrow morning we're to meet the tender at the marina in Monte Carlo," Leonie tells me. "I can't wait to see Shelley again. She's so good to Lola. I told her she's lucky to have such a cool mother-in-law."

At the end, her voice takes on a wistful note.

I slip my arm around her shoulders and pull her to me. I bury my nose in her fragrant hair, inhaling deep of the sultry florals with amber and musk.

Leonie slides her palm along my chest. The tip of her fingernail brushes the skin of my nipple. Then tweaks the tip when she feels a shudder run through me. Her hand continues on its path to cradle the back of my head. She tangles her fingers in my hair and pulls my mouth down to hers. The warm air that escapes her lips as she moans softly against mine makes my dick jump. Her kiss is full of fiery passion that zings through every cell in my body.

"If we don't stop, we'll never get to the beach," I growl as my teeth nip her plump bottom lip.

Leonie purrs seductively, "Who says we need the beach? We can make our own waves, *Amoureux.*"

My dick agrees as pre-cum splashes from the tip.

LEONIE

"*M*mmmm… Mmm mmm… Aaahhh!"

My eyes roll. My head flies back on my neck. My legs snap together against the sides of Roger's head. I jackknife off the bed. It's the third orgasm he's pulled from me since I awoke to his tongue laving my pussy. I'm incoherent at this point. My swollen pussy lips and engorged clit can't take any more of his licks, nips, and probes.

"Ooohh, Rogeerrr!" I wail as my body continues to convulse.

He growls his disapproval and nips my inner thigh. Then he adds two of his thick fingers to the mix. The strumming of my G-spot causes another orgasm to rise from the base of my spine.

I cry out from the unexpected sharp pain and toss my head side to side. My bound wrists struggle against the silk belts attached to the ornate wooden headboard. Not only is Roger *The Responsible*, he's resourceful. He made good use of the sumptuous robes in the suite by repurposing the belts as restraints. I can only move my lower body fully and tug my arms fruitlessly.

"Bad, Kitty," he admonishes as he parts my lower lips to spank my sensitive clit.

The moist sounds of flesh meeting flesh are a trigger for my body to respond with another mind-blowing climax. I mewl as it ignites my body in pure ecstasy.

"Be still or I'll make you cum five more times," Roger threatens.

Ordinarily that may sound like a phenomenal idea. But not after multiple rounds last night and this morning. I hate to admit it, but my body needs a break.

"Rogeerr... Please!" I beg.

Relief floods my system when he crawls up my body, leaving a trail of open mouth kisses on my heated skin. His gray eyes now coal black with lust never leave mine. Hypnotized, I watch his approach. Only when I catch sight of his massive cock in my periphery do my eyes veer from his.

Roger's dick is a sculpturesque piece of art. Hard as steel, covered in velvety soft skin. Veins and ridges stand in relief. The bulbous head reddened with need glistens with a drop of pre-cum on its slit. Its ten-inch length and girth too wide for my fingers to meet. His heavy balls swing at the base like a pendulum. The tantalizing sight makes my mouth water. I lick my lips. He chuckles.

"Hungry for what you see, Pretty Kitty?" He asks as his voice thrums in my ear.

I nod and whimper my response.

He grips the base of his big dick and feeds the tip an inch inside of me.

I groan.

"Open up for me, Kitten. I need to feel your tight pussy

wrapped around me, milking my cock," he says in a voice rough with desire.

Conditioned to respond to her mate, my body drains of the tension to allow him unrestrained entry. We groan together as he breaches my passage. Once fully seated, Roger stills. Entranced by the sensation of my pussy clenching around his pulsating cock, we don't utter a sound. Only the rapid beat of our hearts fills the air.

Not until my hips rise of their own accord demanding movement, does Roger pull out to his tip then piston back inside of me. He wanted to give me the time I needed for my mind to catch up with my body in its appetite for more.

"Oh, baby... You feel so fucking good... So hot and wet..." Roger grunts as his passion builds.

I writhe beneath him. My wrists pull against my restraints, aching to wrap my arms around his neck or grip his biceps for stability. Instead, all I can do is open and close my fists on air. He feels so good. So very good. But I need more.

Roger takes one hand from my hip and places his thumb in my slack mouth. Without hesitation, I suckle it with fervor, pretending it's his dick. Once it's sopping wet, he pops it from my mouth and lifts me up onto his thighs as he sits back on his haunches.

Upright, he has more access to my body. His lips trail down the column of my neck to wrap around my fully aroused nipple. At the same time, he pulls my ass cheek to the side and presses the pad of his wet thumb against my puckered hole. My muscles in my pussy and ass tighten. He grunts from the strength of them on his dick.

"Aaahhh!" I scream as he plunders my bottom hole with his thumb and uses his muscular thighs to pump his cock up into my pussy.

My back arches and I keen with each bottoming out thrust. I seem as though I'll break in two from Roger's power. An orgasm comes upon me with the speed of a freight train going downhill with no breaks. A bolt of lightning strikes me. Blinded with my body on fire, I ride Roger like my life depends upon it.

"Fuuuck... Leoonnieee!" He roars as my climax triggers his release.

Inside of me, his dick swells impossibly larger bumping into my cervix before hot ropes of his seed bathe my womb. Another wave crests over us as we continue to pound fiery flesh against fiery flesh in our frenzy to sate our carnal needs. When the last drop of Roger's essence flows from his body to mine, we collapse breathless on the bed in a state of sheer euphoria.

He brushes his lips against my temple as he murmurs in a voice thick with emotion, "I love you, Leonie Beaulieu."

I find the energy to lift my head from his solid chest where his heart beats in sync with mine to gaze into his eyes. I stroke his cheek and rub my thumb across his full lip.

"I love you, Roger Steele."

He kisses my fingertip and cradles my head back to his chest. We fall into a peaceful slumber.

* * *

"I LOVE YOUR BIKINI! You look great in it. It reminds me of Halle Berry's in that Bond film."

Since Roger and I had more important matters to attend to, I didn't get a chance to wear my new Jinx bikini in Cannes. Lounging on the fourth deck of *Serendipity*, I make good use of it. Lola told me about the boat and how big and beautiful it is, but I never imagined it was this magnificent. And I've been on some of the best in the world.

Morgan gifted it to Shelley for their thirtieth wedding anniversary a few years ago. They keep *Serendipity* in Positano, where their Villa Sogno is located during the season. Then transport her to the Caribbean for the fall and winter months.

Roger told me it's the largest megayacht in the world with a length of six-hundred feet, nine inches. That extra nine just to nudge past the next yacht down. At least for now, *Serendipity* holds the record since everyone competes for the prize of the biggest on the water. There are already rumors that a Russian oligarch contracted a prominent builder specifically to outsize *Serendipity*.

It's definitely a beauty to behold. The all-white, sleek design boasts seven decks. The top for the bridge; the sixth for four palatial suites where his parents, Malcolm, Haley, and Sebastian and Lola stay; the fifth deck for four suites where Roger and Harris and up to four close friends stay, plus our private library, office, family and dining rooms with galley; the remaining decks accommodate twenty-four guests in staterooms, quarters for eighty-eight crew, helicopter pad, submarine and water vehicles and toys garage, swimming pool, spa, gym, barbershop and salon, disco, living and dining areas, and an entertainment deck with a bowling alley, cinema, pool room, cards room, and game room. The open-air decks hold chaises, beds, tables, televisions, and dining spots. *Serendipity* is a floating haven for rest, relaxation, and partying.

I turn on my chaise to smile at Shelley and pat my belly. We just ate the most scrumptious meal and I sip on my favorite aperitif, Lillet.

"Thank you. Even though my belly protrudes over the bottom!" I laugh.

Shelley joins in. But shakes her head.

"Your belly is nonexistent! Flat as a board," she says as she claps her hands together in emphasis.

Roger glances over at us from the sound. I blow him a kiss and he pretends to catch it. Shelley laughs at our hijinks.

"I'm happy that you and Roger are back together. I worried about you two," she says as she peers at me from over the top of her Ray-Ban aviators.

She's a striking woman in her mid-fifties with shoulder-length, wavy black hair and expressive brown eyes. I smile at the Steele Matriarch who I can tell is the boss of the family. As her feisty New Yorker personality affirms.

"My son is set in his ways. But loves fiercely," she says as her gaze drifts to Roger who sits next to Morgan at the table. "He's always been the child who wanted order and for everyone to get along."

She turns back to me with the same intense stare as Roger's—the only difference in their eye color.

"And he loves you. It would please me to no end to see the two of you together for good. He needs a strong and independent woman like you who challenges him out of his comfort zone. Is that possible, Leonie?"

I'm speechless by Shelley's words. I turn to look at Roger. Can I make that commitment to Shelley? To Roger? To us? We're in a good place now and have been for four months. I just worry that he'll nitpick on me again.

I take a deep cleansing breath and return my gaze to Shelley who sits patiently waiting for my response. One last glance at Roger and he faces me with a smile. I'm a goner.

"Yes, it is possible, Shelley," I respond.

"Wonderful! Salute!" She toasts as she clinks her glass of rosé with my Lillet.

THE CARESS OF THE RED, open-back, silk-charmeuse gown makes my skin tingle as the material languidly drapes over my frame, ending in a dramatic mermaid train. The five-inch heels of my matching strappy sandals click on the marble floor. The matching diamond suite of a necklace, bracelets, earrings, and hair brooch sparkle.

The extraordinary gift Roger gave to me took my breath away. I told him no; it was too much. But his intense eyes blazed with indignation. He took the jewelry case from my hands as I stood gaping at the enormous diamonds and put the pieces on me.

"You cannot tell me to not give you a gift, Leonie," he growled.

When he finished adjusting each piece to his satisfaction, he turned me to the full-length mirror. Then put his arms around my waist as he stood behind me.

My gaze went from the diamonds to his eyes, glittering fiercely at me in our reflection.

"*Merci, Mon Cœur,*" I whispered as I touched my palm to his cheek.

He nuzzled into my hand. Then turned to kiss my palm. His hands slipped around to press against my lower belly, possessively locking my ass to his groin.

"You are mine, Leonie. If I want to shower you with presents every day, I will. Do you understand?" He asked gruffly.

"*Oui, Mon Cœur,*" I replied as I turned to face him and kiss his lips just as possessive as he held me a moment before. "And you are mine."

Now the James Bond vibe continues from the Aston Martin to the megayacht to an evening at the French Roulette table in the Casino de Monte-Carlo. Morgan, Shelley, Roger and I stride through the casino's lobby. Once again, I think as though I belong in one of the films: sexy boyfriend looking debonair in a custom Tom Ford tuxedo; being led by the general manager to a room reserved for the most high-profile patrons; to die for diamonds. *Incroyable.*

A squeeze to my hand draws me back from my musings. I peer up at Roger, who's smiling down at me.

"You are the most gorgeous woman in the world, Kitten," he murmurs.

I've been in the most fantastic clothes, primped to perfection, and spoiled immensely. Traveled the globe. Hobnobbed with the most wealthy, intelligent, and successful people on the planet. But nothing compares to the pleasure I get when I hear Roger's words.

The saying about being on cloud nine does not even come close. I am beyond the clouds in the stratosphere with my love for this man. I'm sure we'll get into it now and then about his control-freak ways and my sometimes less than focused ways. But in the end, it's more than worth it to me, to us.

As I squeeze his hand in return, I grace Roger with my most dazzling, megawatt smile that shines brighter than the jewelry he gave to me.

"*Merci, Chéri.*"

The general manager opens the doors to a large room even more elegant than the rest of the casino. Opulent crystal chandeliers hang from the ceiling, adorned with hand-carved woodwork. The walls continue the ornate splendor with even more extensive moldings and reliefs.

Plush wool and silk carpet cover the floors, cushioning our steps as we enter the palatial interior.

Men and women similarly dressed as us for a glamorous evening gather around the gaming tables. We follow the general manager to a center table. Three croupiers and a table manager who plays the role of Master of Ceremonies surround the beautifully crafted table. It's as much a work of art as a gaming table with its fine craftsmanship and quality materials.

We join two couples who sit opposite the four chairs reserved for our party. One couple smiles while the other nods in greeting. The table manager turns from his conversation with one croupier and sees us. He grins and steps down from his high chair.

"*Signore* Steele, it is a pleasure to have you join us this evening! I pray all is well with you!" He says as he shakes Roger's hand enthusiastically.

Roger grins and responds, "Good to see you, Signore Moretti. All is well, thank you. And your family?"

"*Bene Bene, grazie!*" He responds, then glances at the rest of us. "Ah, your family, *s*'?"

Roger smiles and holds his hand out to his parents and introduces them to him. They exchange pleasantries. Then Roger lifts our clasped hands.

"And this is Leonie Beaulieu, my girlfriend," he says with a smile.

Signore Moretti beams as he takes my other hand and kisses it.

"Such a pleasure to meet you, *signorina*," he starts, then turns to Roger. "You are a lucky man, *Signore* Steele!"

He bows, then gestures for us to take our seats at the table. The other couples who now recognize the name Steele are more welcoming. The men engage Roger and

Morgan on business while the women compliment Shelley and me on our gowns.

I laugh to myself at their obsequious behavior. Shelley taps my leg under the table and I know she agrees with me. Such is the life when married to or dating some of the wealthiest men on the planet.

The game begins. The unrivaled accuracy and high-octane thrill of French Roulette captivates us. It's a theatrical performance of sound and movement. As the three croupiers call out enthusiastically, other patrons flock to our table. The onlookers hang on the croupiers' every word.

Roger and Morgan play like professionals while Shelley and I choose numbers at random. When we arrived at the casino, they gave Shelley and me trays of chips worth hundreds of thousands of euros. Again, I attempted to refuse. But Roger pinned me with his no-nonsense stare, and I gave in. Shelley tittered next to me and whispered to just let it go. I did, and now I play with the chips and have a blast.

After an hour passes, I discreetly tell Roger I'm going to the ladies' lounge. Shelley asks where I'm going, and she accompanies me. We excuse ourselves from the table.

Two men ask if they may have our seats. I look to Roger and he asks if I'd like to continue to play. I decline for now. Shelley also opts out. So he allows the men to take our seats.

I kiss Roger's cheek and whisper good luck. His smile melts my heart.

"This is a wonderful night," I remark as we stroll through the doors opened for us by two attendants.

Shelley loops her arm through mine and nods, "Yes, I'm so glad that Morgan and I came. It's given me time to spend with you since we were so busy with Lola and Sebastian's wedding preparation."

She squeezes my arm, and I smile at her.

We walk on in silence. When we reach the ladies' lounge, we part. Once we're back in the anteroom, we continue our conversation as we apply fresh lipstick and fluff our hair.

"I know you are an independent woman and are not interested in my son for his wealth, Leonie," Shelley says as she watches my reflection in the mirror. "Roger knows that as well. When he gifts you with something, you do not have to feel as though you cannot accept it."

She pauses and eyes my jewelry, then continues.

"He's like his father and now Sebastian. They are generous men who willing to give to those they love. And Roger loves you."

Shelley stops to allow me to absorb her words before she goes on.

"I was like you and Lola. Self-sufficient successful," she stops to laugh. "Well, I was a shopgirl and Lola owns shops and you rule the modeling world. But I was making it on my own. So I understand. I too had to get used to Morgan giving me gifts, fancy and simple alike."

She takes my arm and loops hers through it to lead us out the door.

"And now I just go with it. It's their way to express their love and care for you... for us. They don't do it for just anyone. Roger has never done it before. Okay?"

I take a second to reconcile her words. She's right.

"*Oui*, Shelley," I resound as I squeeze her hand in mine.

Her eyes sparkle as she smiles up at me.

When we arrive back at the table, Roger and Morgan stand to offer us their seats. But we decline and stand behind them, preferring to watch. It's even better when not playing since I can see more of what's going on beyond the wheel spinning.

The night goes on with round after round. Roger and Morgan win and lose some. But in the end, we have an incredible time.

Later, after we make love and cuddle in bed in my duplex, I think back on Shelley's words of advice. They remind me of similar ones Lola shared with me about the many gifts Sebastian has bestowed upon her. She too has accepted the situation for what it is—they give to us because they love us.

That's all the explanation I need.

LEONIE

"*O*h, this is just what I needed… Sun, sand, cocktails, and my girls."

Lola says as she sighs and leans back against the chaise lounge. She sips her Tipo Tinto R&R rum and raspberry with a sigh. Her mouth stained red from the iconic Mozambican specialty drink.

Starr, Blair, Haley, Billie, and I laugh at her drama.

"Hold on! You just returned from your two-month long honeymoon full of sun, sand, cocktails, and a sexy as hell husband," I start. "How could you need more two months later?"

Lola swats the pillow away that I tossed at her and sits up.

"Right!" Chorus Blair and Billie.

Starr shakes her head. Her curly, dark brown hair sways along her back as her dimples deepen with her smile.

"Lola, you crack me up! Even I, a staunch believer in self-care, can't imagine why you need a break this soon!"

She throws her pillow and dings Lola on the stomach. She laughs and hugs the pillow to her chest.

"I agree! Give us a break already, Lola!" Haley adds as she rolls her sharp gray eyes behind her glasses.

"Well, so that you know, I've been extremely busy catching up on work I missed while on my honeymoon with my sexy as fuck husband. Now, I need you, Ms. Knight, to work your magic to clear my head and relax me. And boy do you have your work cut out for you, again!"

Lola throws the pillow back and Starr catches it.

"Fine. Challenge accepted, Mrs. Steele!" She replies.

Lola swoons clutching her ginormous engagement ring to her bosom. She's right, it's definitely like her idol Elizabeth Taylor's ice skating rink ring. The nearly 30 carats glimmer in the torchlight.

The ring is a Steele family heirloom Shelley most recently wore. Being Sebastian is the eldest son, he inherited it and will pass it to his eldest son in time.

Lucky girl!

My thoughts turn to Roger. We've been back together for five months, and it's fantastic. Every day proves it was right for us to take a second chance at our relationship. Now, I wonder if we will go further like Lola and Sebastian.

"Leonie… Hello there… Leonie?"

"Girl! Snap out of it!"

"Oh, don't tease her…"

"See, I knew it! He's blown her mind and her back—"

"Okay, okay! I hear you already!" I cut into their chatter with a laugh.

All eyes are on me, varying from expressions of concern to smirks. When Starr called to invite us to her second international fitness retreat, we agreed to make it a Girls'

Getaway, too. Time for us to reconnect with our minds, bodies, and friends. Over the seven days, we plan to do just that.

The retreat is at a luxury beachfront resort on Buenguerra Island off the coast of Mozambique in the channel between the country and the Indian Ocean. The island is a haven known for its pristine, white-sand beaches, peaceful vibe, and five-star resorts.

The property we're staying at is the most exclusive with only three cabanas, ten casinhas, and one large villa scattered across eleven acres of beachfront and lush tropical vegetation. Starr's retreat participants and her staff along with us secured the entire resort. It's our private oasis.

Lola, Billie, Haley, Blair, and I claimed the villa since it features five large bedrooms with sitting areas, living room, dining room, and kitchenette. The outdoor areas include a pool, deck area with thatched-roof cabana and chaises, plus chaises down by the ocean. It's stunning and tranquil.

Starr chose a casinhas since she's working more so than relaxing. She needs more space for her staff to meet and for her one-on-one sessions with guests. It's just through the palm trees on one of the sandy paths that crisscross the property.

"Spill. You've been mighty quiet about Roger and you..." Billie says as her green eyes flash.

"Right! I know I've been away and busy. But even so," Lola starts. "You can always call me. I am your BFF!"

"Oh, don't pressure her!" Blair says concerned.

"No pressure, but... Do tell!" Starr laughs.

I smile at my closest friends. Then take a sip of my Tipo Tinto R&R. When I set it down on the side table, they stare at me expectantly.

"I'm in love with the man of my dreams!" I throw my head back and roar. "He's mine, all mine! And I'm all his!"

They holler and stomp their feet.

"Another brother taken so he can get off my back about my love life! Thank you, Leonie! Hooray!" Shouts Haley pumping her fists into the air as she falls back onto her chaise lounge.

Lola jumps up and grabs my hands to pull me to stand. We do our happy shimmy dance around the chaises.

"Yeah, Girl! Strut your stuff!" Starr calls out as she fans herself.

Billie jumps up and joins our parade. Soon we form a conga line and weave in and out of the furniture. Then we head out to the beach, where we form a circle under the brilliant moonlight and star-filled sky. My girls and I continue to dance around as our laughter carries out over the silent, inky black water.

* * *

"Let us end our practice with three oms together. Inhale through your nose gently, hold it for a heartbeat. Then slowly release your breath back through your nose. Let us begin."

Starr's entrancing voice guides us through the last part of our yoga session. We started with breathwork for five minutes to prep us for a vigorous, forty-five-minute flow sequence. My muscles craved the fast-paced tempo. It allowed my body to focus on the asanas and not wander. The ten-minute meditation grounded me.

"Namaste. The light in me honors the light in you," Starr intones.

We bow to each other with palms pressed together at

our heart centers. We remind ourselves of the good energy and intention we set forth in our practice. As we sit up and open our eyes, Starr's heart-shaped face beams at us. Her love of helping others reach their best mental and physical potential shines from her sorrel brown eyes.

"That was transcendental," Lola breaths out in awe as she sits cross-legged on her mat beside me staring at Starr.

"She's amazing," I whisper in the ensuing silence, just as awestruck.

"I agree," Blair leans over to whisper.

"This is the best I've felt in a while," Haley says softly as she stretches her arms overhead.

"Yes, she's still the best yoga teacher I've ever had a session with," Billie adds as she wipes down her mat.

We follow suit and clean ours, then hang them on the wooden racks inside the beachside, open-air pavilion. Other students gather around Starr to glean more of her sage advice. Two of her assistants offer adjustments for those who want more instruction.

Starr glances up and waves at us. We wave back before we walk down the steps to the sandy shore. Two other assistants offer us frothy shot glasses filled with refreshing juice made from local fruits. The delicious concoctions cool us down and fill us with energy.

"It has ashwagandha in it. An Ayurvedic herb that many studies show increases energy and reduces stress and anxiety," the assistant with a curly afro tells us.

"This is tasty," Blair says.

We nod and thank them for the elixirs as we place the empty glasses on the table. Our next session for Pilates isn't for another two hours. So we stroll along the beach to our villa. The sun glistens on the water between the island and the Mozambique coast. The waves splashing on the sand call to us.

"Hey, I'm going to change into my bikini and go for a swim!" Lola declares.

We agree it's a good idea and a great way to wash away the sweat from our yoga class. The flecks of gold in Billie's moss green eyes glint as she peeks over her shoulder at us. Then she skips ahead.

"Last one in is a rotten egg!" She shouts.

My long legs easily overtake the munchkins Lola and Billie. However, Haley and Blair who are only two and three inches shorter than me at five feet, eight inches and five feet seven inches tall are close on my heels. Their taunts of being number one urge me to increase my speed.

With a triumphant whoop, I yank my sports bra over my head as I race into my room. I ditch the skimpy yoga shorts and rush to the wardrobe. Snatching the first bathing suit I can reach, I step into the bottoms as I head to the door. Then slide them up over my hips. I don't worry about a top since we're on the secluded side of the island—no paparazzi to snap unwanted photos for Roger to go berserk about. I zip out the door, down to the beach, and dive into the first wave.

"Damn supermodel! You're used to quick changes!" Blair says as she splashes me when I come up from the surf.

"*Absolument! Ma chérie!*" I giggle as I sweep my arm through the water to douse her.

Haley who just ran in, tucks to avoid the spatter.

Lola's laughter as she beats Billie into the water by a hair's length, draws our attention to the shore.

"Ha, ha! You lose, Billie!" She shouts. "*Piu*, you stink like a rotten egg!"

Billie laughs and ducks under the water. When she

comes back up, her medium blonde balayage hair cascades down her back in waves. Her pecan-colored skin already browning from the sun glistens.

"Tell her not to worry about it. Patrick thinks you smell divine!" Blair laughs.

The Southern belle from Savannah, Georgia captured the heart of Patrick Rockett, her new Scottish billionaire beau. Sebastian nearly had a fit when he found out Billie was dating the CEO of STEELE International's biggest competitor, Rockett Construction. Lola had to calm him down when she reminded him Billie signed an ironclad nondisclosure agreement and she swore her allegiance to Lola.

"You got that right, honey!" Billie's cheeky reply. "And my brawny babe cannot get enough!"

We crack up as her Southern drawl switches to a Scottish accent flawlessly.

"Your turn, Blair! Leonie and I were on the hot seat last night. Billie fessed up. Do share..." Lola says, splashing Blair.

She splutters as she her face reddens. Her cerulean blue eyes dart everywhere but at us.

"Yes, Ms. Secretive!" I tease. "How are things with *Le Renard Argenté?*"

Blair floats onto her back and closes her eyes before she responds.

"I don't kiss and tell—"

The three of us cover her in a deluge of seawater as we shout at her for being so prim and proper. She flips over and dives under the water, resurfacing a few feet away. She flips her chestnut brown hair over her shoulders, then stands akimbo.

"I won't let you bully me into saying a word!" She declares, but can't hold in her laughter.

After a moment, she wipes her eyes and saunters back over to us.

"You know cheese, wine, leather... They all age well... But not as well as my Silver Fox Luc Montaigne!"

She ends her pronouncement with a two-armed sweep of water aimed at us. We retaliate, and it becomes an all-out, every woman for herself water war. We laugh hysterically while trying not to drown as we jump around splashing in the warm tropical Indian Ocean.

* * *

"HOW DID YOU LIKE THE RETREAT?" Starr asks as we sit at the outdoor dining table surrounded by fragrant torches.

The other participants left yesterday morning. We stayed two extra days to spend some quality time with Starr off of the mats. Yesterday we went for a long hike through the verdant patchwork of forests on the island. Then had a rejuvenating swim in one of the crystal-clear freshwater lakes.

Now, we're eating a delectable dinner of flavorful local favorites prepared by a chef on the outdoor grill and cooktop. The aroma is mouthwatering. I sip my Tipo Tinto R&R and nibble on a flaky chamussa. The appetizer is just enough to keep us sated until he presents the main dishes.

"You did such a superb job, Starr! I can't wait for the next one," Billie answers as she clinks glasses with our hostess.

"Indeed! I thought nothing could top your first one on Fijian Laucala Island last year. That private paradise is surreal," Lola chimes in.

"It was the best I've ever been on! Fantastic!" Haley says as she rises to give Starr a standing ovation.

"Sign me up for all of them! I feel incredible, thank you very much!" I exclaim.

"Me, too!" Blair says as she raises her glass. "A toast... Here's to good friends, good loves, and good times!"

Everyone cheers and clinks glasses. Lola pauses and peers at Starr.

"What's the latest on your conversations with Malcolm?"

No one else notices the tone in Lola's voice but me. I've known her the longest and can understand what she thinks or feels easily. Right now, she's prying because she knows something Starr doesn't or at least Starr hasn't admitted to us yet. As if on cue, Starr avoids Lola's probing gaze. Starr shifts in her chair and pretends to straighten the napkin on her lap.

Lola is relentless.

"Well?" She demands.

Starr clears her throat and returns Lola's gaze. Defiantly Starr lifts her chin as she responds.

"Malcolm Steele is an arrogant, self-focused cretin!"

Blair, Billie, and I gape at Starr's heated reaction. Haley covers her ears not wanting to hear such things about her older brother.

Our normally quiet calm, namaste, om, center your mind friend now flustered completely. Our gazes dart between her and Lola in shock. What the hell did Malcolm do to Starr?

Lola bursts out laughing. Her last sip of Tipo Tinto comes out on a snort. She pulls back from the table, doubling over in glee. The sight is too comical. We can't help but join in—even Starr.

Once Lola gathers herself, wiping tears from the corners of her eyes, she straightens. She lifts her left hand and waggles her fingers. The ice skating rink on full blast.

"That's the same thing I said about his doppelgänger brother, Captain Caveman... Now look at me, my friend!"

Starr looks just as stunned as the rest of us. But Lola just keeps giggling. She definitely knows something Starr is clueless about. When we question her, Lola shakes her head and sips her drink, laughing to herself.

ROGER

"*H*ey man! Where the hell are you today? You're definitely not here in this ring. Get it together real quick, Steele!"

Norman Green, my boxing coach and personal trainer, yells at me when I practically walked right into his sledgehammer left hook. I've never been more thankful for protective headgear and a mouth guard. The former world heavyweight champion nine years straight—eight by knockout—scowls at me as he flexes the muscles in his massive arms.

"Are you ready for this session, Steele? You've been goofy the last few days, man," Norman continues as he eyes me up and down.

He's six feet, five inches, solid two hundred-fifty pounds of muscle who moves with the grace of a gazelle and the speed of a cheetah. Norman has been my trainer for the last four years. I met him in Las Vegas at a party at STEELE LV after his final KO match. He told me he promised his girlfriend, now wife, Anita he would stop with this fight. He was at the top of his game with no more to prove. Norman said it's better to leave on high than get carted away low.

I offered him the opportunity to open his chains of branded gyms through STEELE's Entertainment Properties Division. One for underprivileged youth and another as exclusive elite training facilities for the über-wealthy and star athletes.

Born and raised in Harlem to upper middle-class parents, Norman understands the importance of giving back to the community. A mentor taught him boxing after school and his career took off. Being a celebrity athlete, he understands the need for specialized training and the demands on the body. He didn't hesitate and agreed to the deal. A perk for me is I became his first client.

When I moved to Paris, he and Anita came with me and opened locations in the city, London, and Madrid. The States has several besides the New York City flagship including Las Vegas, Los Angeles, Austin, Chicago, and Miami.

My father, Sebastian, and Malcolm are pleased with the profitable revenue stream. Especially since the membership and assorted fees of the elite facilities pay for the community ones. Norman can continue in the sports world and add even more to his multimillions. It's a win-win business partnership for all.

Anita who is a yoga instructor with a flourishing practice just finished culinary school at Le Cordon Bleu and started a meal plan delivery service. Norman added her customized plans to the paid offerings of the elite facilities and complimentary healthy snacks to the youth. She also took over the food services in both chains. They're a dynamic couple who raise the bar in the fitness industry.

"Well... Shall we proceed or do you prefer to go sit in the

sauna, Steele?" Norman taunts me as he bounces on the balls of his feet and punches his fist together.

I shake the kinks out of my neck and pound my fists. Then do some jumping high knees to get the blood pumping in my legs.

"Nah, Green. I'm ready for you. Let's go. Ding ding!" I respond and hold my gloved fists out to him.

"Now that's more like it, Steele! Ding ding!" He says as he hits his fists on top and below mine. "Let's go, man!"

We spend the next two hours in the ring, and on the mat sparring and doing drills. We end with a bout on the rower to flush out the lactic acid built up in my muscles. Then follow with stretching and foam rolling. The intense workout was just what I needed to get my head on straight.

As we walk to the locker room, Norman gives me the side-eye and cocks his bald head.

"In the end you made up for your subpar start. You're usually more focused than that, Steele. What gives?" He asks.

I run my towel over my head and face to collect some sweat. Then I turn to him.

"My woman's been out of town for over a week on a Girls' Getaway at a fitness retreat on an island off of Mozambique," I start. "It's the longest we've been apart in five months. Leonie in a tiny bikini on a tropical island with a bunch of her stunning friends, including my sister-in-law, has my mind going crazy, man. She's got me all over the place."

Norman nods at my confession as he lets out a wolf whistle, "Leonie *The Lion* Beaulieu... That's one beautiful woman you snagged, Steele—"

I stop cold in my tracks and growl at him, squared up, ready to defend my woman.

Norman also stops and raises his hands. Not in a fighter's stance, but held up in surrender.

"Whoa, man… Anita is my childhood sweetheart. She's the only woman for me, and she's more than I can handle. Not to mention she'd have my balls on a platter if I fucked around with another female. Don't let her little self fool you. She scares the shit out of me when she's pissed. No, sir! I am good! Trust and believe."

I give him the side-eye. But he shakes his head no way and mimics Anita's voice.

"Norman! How dare you!"

We burst out laughing, envisioning her chasing him with a frying pan around their Parisian penthouse. I've seen her when she was less than happy. The petite beauty scares me, too. She's more formidable than her champion husband.

I clap him on the back, and we stride into the locker room.

"You can sit in the sauna now that you redeemed yourself, Steele," he teases. "Oh and don't forget the package of meals Anita made for you. The front desk staff will retrieve it from the refrigerator. The meals include her most recent recipes. She wants your feedback before she rolls them out."

"If they're anything like last week's, they'll be delicious," I respond, patting my stomach.

"Thanks, man. Appreciate it," Norman says as we bump fists.

We part and I take a quick shower to wash the sweat off before I relax in the sauna. Yeah, I definitely deserve it after the grueling workout Norman put me through. I sigh as I lean back and close my eyes. My mind drifts to my "beautiful woman." I did snag a good one, I chuckle to myself. And I can't wait for her to get home…

* * *

"THE PROJECTIONS SHOW an increase in the demand for residential property in the epicenter of the—"

The chirp of a text message to my mobile interrupts my director of research and development's presentation. I slide it across the conference room table to pick it up from beside my laptop. Leonie's name appears on the screen.

"Excuse me. I have to take this," I say as I rise from my chair. "Please continue. I'll review the transcript and contact you with feedback."

I grab up my laptop and hustle out the door to my offices. As I pass by her area, Françoise checks her watch. Then arches her eyebrow questioningly since I left the weekly status meeting an hour early.

"Please hold my calls," I ask her before I shut my door.

Once inside, I lock it and darken the glass walls. Then sit on my sofa. Eager to see the message, I fumble with the passcode. When the Messages app finally pops open, my jaw drops.

Leonie is naked, floating on her back in turquoise water, the sun shining bright above. Her hair floats around her head like a halo, undulating with the waves. Her amber eyes stare boldly into the camera, exuding confidence in her bare form.

The days she's spent in the hot African sun toasted her caramel skin tone. The water glistens across it, making her brown nipples stand erect from her ample breasts. They beg for me to suckle them. Her slim waist highlighted by her hourglass hips that lead to her long, toned legs. Spread wide like a starfish, her arms and legs extend in welcome, reaching out to me from the captivating image. She's a goddess come to Earth to seduce us mere mortals with her gloriousness.

I study every angle. Zoom in and out to see all the minute detail of a woman whose body has become my playground. Not an inch of her am I unfamiliar with. This photo of Leonie in the bright sun laid bare on the ocean waves surpasses Botticelli's *The Birth of Venus*.

Finally dragging my eyes from the image, I read her text message.

Wish you were here, Amoureux. xoxo Your Kitten

Fuck... me...

The only reason I didn't race to my private jet to find out in person who the hell took the picture is the position of Leonie's right arm. It shows she's holding a selfie stick to get the shot. If not... all hell would have broken loose.

My cock, on the other hand, didn't give a damn. It hardened immediately at the perfect vision of its mate. My tongue wishes it were lapping at her pussy like the seawater between her thighs. I flex my fingers, wanting to grip her hips as I shove my hard dick between her wet folds to stake my claim repeatedly.

I growl and unzip my trousers. Relief runs through me when I release my weeping cock from the confines of my black silk boxer briefs. I stroke it from the root to the tip as I open my laptop to AirDrop Leonie's masterpiece to it.

The larger image allows me to appreciate truly the bounty splayed before me. Leonie's lush body beckons me. My hand pumps my dick with fervor as my passion builds. I grunt as I grip it harder to squeeze the shaft, pretending my tight fist is her pussy clamping on me.

As my arousal peaks, I fight to hold it back a little longer, to milk every pleasure out of the sensation. I widen my feet on the rug and scoot down on the cushion. The base of my spine tingles as my balls fill with my seed.

I close my eyes momentarily to force back the impending orgasm. A peek at the laptop screen has my hips thrusting up as my head falls back against the sofa. I close my eyes again, the image of Leonie seared on the backs of my eyelids. I no longer need the photo, I've committed it to memory.

My strokes lose the rhythm as my body prepares for a toe-curling climax. I grip my dick tighter as I use my thumb to smear more of the pre-cum around the tip. One last glimpse at Leonie, and I pinch the bulbous head.

My eyes roll into the back of my head. As I anchor my feet into the floor for leverage, my hips jump up from the leather seat. The pistoning of my hips matches the pumping of my clenched fist. Bright white lights spark behind my closed eyelids. My hearing dulls. A deep passionate roar rips from my mouth as my climax hits me like a careening truck. My jizz shots up like a. geyser, then spills over my hand.

I collapse back onto the sofa, sated and spent. I only want to curl into a fetal position and drift off to sleep. A slumber filled with dreams of my goddess Leonie floating towards me on a wave risen from the depths of the ocean. A spectacular gift only for me.

LEONIE

"*L*eonie, babe. It's time to get up. You have to get to the site on time. Leonie..."

I roll over onto my back toward Roger's voice and peel my eyes open. Instantly, I squeeze them shut with a hiss.

Merde!

The glaring sun streaming through the uncovered floor-to-ceiling windows in Roger's penthouse primary bedroom blinds me. Stars flash behind my heavy eyelids. Why the hell did he open the damn blackout curtains so early? I mutter to myself as I flip over to curl into a ball. With a groan, I pull the covers over my head. Burrowed in the bedding, I try to ignore the persistent buzzing of his nagging voice.

"Listen, Leonie, you have to get up, baby," he drones on. "You slept through your alarm. It's already nine fifteen."

He pulls the comforter and sheets off of my naked body, exposing me to the glare of the light and the cool air.

"Seriously, the team is meeting at the property at ten o'clock—"

I snap my eyes open to, amber eyes shooting darts. I growl at Roger as he looms over me and snatch the bedding from his hand.

He's so shocked by my reaction, it falls with ease from his hand. He scowls at me and shakes his head.

"What the hell, Leonie?" He asks.

I mutter curses as I slip back into my cocoon.

"Enough, Leonie. Don't be irresponsible. This meeting is important, and I don't have time to treat you like a little girl who doesn't want to go to school," Roger says as he pulls all the bedding off from the foot.

The sheets slide from me, and I shoot up to a seated position. We lock eyes as we glare at one another. I break first.

"How do you speak to me that way, Roger! I'm not a child! I'm a grown ass woman!"

He snorts and folds his arms over his chest, feet wide apart ready for a fight. He looks me up and down with a smirk.

"Really? Well, you could have fooled me!" Roger snarls. "You're the one who's lounging in bed past your alarm. I try to wake you and you snap my fucking head off!"

I throw two pillows at him. He ducks his head from one and swats the other away. His pale gray eyes darken to slate as he glares at me.

"Oh, so that's how 'a grown ass woman' behaves?" He shouts. "I don't think so, Leonie!"

"Fuck you, Roger!" Stop always trying to boss me around! You… You control freak!" I scream.

I jump from the bed and storm into the bathroom, slamming the door behind me.

Roger bursts in. I glare at him over my shoulder. Rage contorts his face. His chest heaves as he breathes hard.

"I do not know what the fuck is wrong with you this morning, Leonie. But you are pushing it!" He growls.

He uses his much larger body to crowd me against my vanity. I turn around to face him. Then he cages me in, bending his knees to bring us on eye level.

"I am not a control freak. I came to you to wake you up. Why are you flipping the script?" He demands.

I push ineffectively at his firm chest. He's already fully dressed and his cologne fills my nostrils. It's too much.

"*Bouge toi! Laisse-moi tranquille, Roger!*" I scream, unable to translate my thoughts.

My head is pounding as my heat races. I need air, and I need Roger to give me space. I beat against his chest and shake my head vigorously. Then lower it in defeat. The strength drains from my fatigued body.

"*Très bien, Leonie ... Je vais vous laisser tranquille.*" He whispers, then leaves the bathroom without another word.

The raw pain of hurt in his voice slices into me. But I remain steadfast. I wait until I hear the door click shut before I raise my head. A sigh slips from between my lips. I wrap my arms around my torso and shiver from the cold. Or could it be from the loss of Roger's warmth?

Fuck it...

I shake my head and clap my palms against my arms to boost the circulation. A glance at the clock above the door—leave it to Roger *The Responsible* to have a clock in the bathroom—shows I have half an hour to make it to the meeting on time.

Merde!

Quickly, I walk into the shower and turn on the water. The blast chills, then warms me. Wasting no time, I cleanse myself and don a fluffy cotton towel to dry me. Simple and classic, I think as I choose a crisp white shirt, black pencil skirt, black pumps for my wardrobe.

Selection made, I pin my hair into a bun. Jewelry kept minimal with single pearl earrings and a three-strand necklace. Then I swap the robe for a flesh-tone lace Lola's Coterie bra and panties set. Fully dressed, I grab my pumps and mobile. I run down the stairs only stopping to pick up my handbag and attaché still backed from yesterday.

When I open the front door, I find Eric standing by the elevator. I skid to a halt.

"Bonjour, Mademoiselle Beaulieu," he nods. "Monsieur Steele asked me to drive you to your meeting."

Eric takes my attaché from my hand and rings for the elevator, and it opens immediately.

I'm gobsmacked by what he just told me. Despite our nasty argument, Roger still thought to have his driver take me to the site visit. He must have figured I would have a hell of a time getting a hired car or cab at such brief notice during this time of morning. Mr. Responsible... My face heats in shame as I mutely nod and slip my shoes on.

Like a chastened child, I meekly follow Eric into the elevator. The ride is quiet as we study the floor display. Even though I'm pissed by his comments, I make a note to call Roger when I get a chance.

The doors open to the level of the underground garage reserved for the Steele family's vehicles. Roger has four including a Black Badge Rolls-Royce Cullinan, the most gorgeous SUV ever crafted, and the powerful and sexy Aston Martin DB7 Vantage. Several other cars of all colors, brands, and models line up along the wall. Four motorcycles cluster in another area.

We make our way to Roger's Rolls-Royce Corniche,

already positioned to face the exit. No time to waste. Every detail well thought out. Eric opens the back door for me. I slip onto the buttery soft leather. He places my attaché on the floor by my feet. As he shuts the door, I thank him.

A faint hint of Roger's cologne lingers in the air. It wraps me in a comfortable, familiar embrace. I lean back against the seat and let it cradle my head. My eyes close as I take a deep inhale the combination of the leather scent and Roger mingle pleasantly.

"We'll take the fastest route and arrive at the property in ten minutes, mademoiselle," Eric states once he settles in the driver's seat. "Would you prefer the partition up or down? I can also diffuse some lavender or lemon in the air to relax you before your meeting."

I sit up and open my eyes to meet his gaze in the rearview mirror.

"Perfect. Please put it up and lavender would be lovely, *merci*," I respond with a smile.

Eric nods and the partition rises soundlessly. As the soft scent of lavender wafts through the air, the vehicle's filtration system removes the last vestiges of Roger's cologne.

I rest again as the dull ache in my head increases. Thankfully, the tinted windows lessen the sunlight filtering through the windows, the quiet interior, and the soft seat recreate the cocoon of the bed. I drift off to a dreamless catnap.

"Mademoiselle Beaulieu? Mademoiselle? We're here."

A gentle tap on my shoulder rouses me as the sound of Eric's voice reaches my ears. Momentarily disoriented, I glance around confused. When my eyes land on his face, he smiles encouragingly.

"We're here, Mademoiselle Beaulieu."

He steps back and offers his hand to me. I take it gratefully as I slip my Birkin on the bend of my elbow and pick up my attaché.

"*Merci beaucoup*, Eric," I reply. "What time is it?"

He glances at his watch, a sleek Cartier Tank in gold with a black alligator-skin band.

"It's just 9:59, mademoiselle. But don't worry. At Monsieur Steele's request, I sent a text message to the assistant to inform her you're here."

Again, my face flushes. Then I remember I didn't send the text message to Roger. *Merde...*

"You're the best, Eric. Enjoy your day," I tell him as I hurry to the front door of the majestic apartment building.

"Oh no, mademoiselle, I will wait for you—"

"*Merci*, but that's all right. I can get a ride with a colleague," I interject thinking there's no need for him to wait for so long.

"My apologies, Mademoiselle Beaulieu," he shakes his head. "Monsieur Steele asked me to drive you around today. I'll send a text message to you, and you can reply when you're ready."

I nod and thank him, again. On the way up into the lobby, I deftly apply lipstick and mascara. Blair would tease me about my modeling quick-change skills, I laugh to myself. Once inside, I spot the Design Team. They wave me over and I join them.

"I apologize for my tardiness—"

"No worries, Leonie, you're right on time," Clinton the design director on the project tells me with a kind smile.

"Ah, *oui*. But to be early is to be on time; to be on time is to be late; to be late is unthinkable," I respond with a grin.

They laugh, and Clinton says he'll add that nugget to his

list of adages. I notice Delia just stares at me, her expression unreadable. Unfortunately, Clinton chose her to join this project. So I've seen more of her than before. I smile, not wanting her to sense my disdain. Roger may be an ass, but he's my ass. And I don't share.

"On that note, let's review some specifications for this renovation," Clinton says, looking at each of us.

This is one of my favorite buildings in Paris. Near to my duplex and Lola's penthouse in the *seizième*, I pass it frequently. This arrondissement is renowned for the ornate nineteenth-century buildings, wide avenues, prestigious schools, museums, and spacious parks. French high society has flocked here for their places of residence for years. The *seizième* is comparable to the luxurious Kensington and Chelsea neighborhoods in London. French popular culture has coined the phrase *le 16e* as association with great wealth.

I share some of my insight with the team. They're impressed with my knowledge of the history and culture. Others contribute their thoughts so we have a lively discussion.

"Excellent observations. Now we'll go to some common areas, sample flats, and the courtyard," Clinton starts. "Be sure to note the original details, fixtures, and elements that we can preserve or recreate. STEELE wants to keep the property as true to the original as possible. As you know that's their trademark with historical buildings."

We pull out our tablets and prepare to make sketches and notes. Then Clinton tells us to partner up for the walk-through. When we return to the office, we'll meet in the conference room and discuss our findings and initial recommendations.

Brandon Eliot, an architect I've had lunch with a few

times strides over to me. He's a handsome man in his early forties. I smile at him as he gets closer. His arctic blue eyes brighten.

"You intrigued me with your knowledge of the building. I have some ideas that you could help me flesh out. Would you like to do the walk-through together?" He asks as he runs his fingers through his wavy, sandy blond hair.

"That would be great, Brandon," I respond returning his smile.

We head off to examine the inner courtyard to get a feel for the exterior and what elements we may incorporate in the interior areas.

"I've always loved the style of the nineteenth century," Brandon says as he covers his eyes with his hand to gaze up at the facade. "The detail is incredible."

"Yes, *La Belle Époque* is my favorite..."

Brandon and I chat amiably as we go from one section of the property to the next. We're so absorbed in our conversation and tasks, the two hours pass by quickly. We rejoin the group in the main salon of the ground floor.

Delia peers at us, shifting her gaze between Brandon and me. I look at her pointedly, daring her to insinuate something happened between us. She must sense that I'm not in any mood for her shit today. So instead of making a snide comment, she turns away.

"We'll meet in the conference room in thirty minutes that should be enough time for everyone to return to the office," Clinton says.

"Also, we're ordering lunch in, so please send you order by text message to my mobile," the assistant tells us. "I sent the menu to you already."

My stomach rumbles at the mention of food. I didn't

have time to eat breakfast or grab one of Anita's protein bars. I pull out my mobile to scan the menu and to send Eric a text to let him know I'm ready.

"Would you like to share a cab back?" Brandon asks.

I forgot about him beside me, so focused on getting something to eat. I glance over at him and shake my head.

"I have a ride. Would you like a lift?" I ask.

Brandon nods and smiles as he responds, "That would be great, thanks."

We leave the building. Eric is right where I left him. I wave and he opens the back door.

"Eric, Brandon Eliot is a colleague who'll ride back to the office with me," I tell him as I slide onto the seat.

Eric nods, and Brandon thanks him as he joins me.

"Nice car. A design marvel of its own," Brandon says, admiring the handmade luxury vehicle.

I feel awkward telling him it's Roger's car when he's the president, so I just smile.

Now that I'm still, I realize I haven't heard from Roger. I unlock my mobile to double-check for a message or missed call. Nothing. He's probably still angry I behaved "like a little girl." I get irritated with him all over again.

"—compile our notes and come up with some ideas. Your extensive travel really is an asset."

I glance at Brandon and tuck my mobile back into my handbag. Focus, Leonie! Remember... prove Roger wrong!

"That sounds good, Brandon. Let's compare what we jotted down before we get to the office," I answer as I remove my tablet from my attaché.

"Excellent," Brandon says opening his crossbody bag to retrieve his device.

We spend the next fifteen minutes on an outline. When

we arrive, Brandon doesn't wait for Eric to open the door. Instead, he hops out and offers his hand to me.

"*Merci,*" I smile, then turn to Eric, "Thank you so much! Enjoy your day, Eric."

"Of course, Mademoiselle. Have a good day," he responds, then gets back into the driver's seat without a word to or glance at Brandon.

We stroll inside the building. The lobby is bustling with activity. So we hurry to the elevator bank for the STEELE floors. Other companies have their offices in The Tower. Just as we arrive at the elevators for the top floors, one opens and we duck inside. Brandon tells a joke about move slow, you blow, and I laugh heartily.

Other members of the team enter the conference room shortly after us. Clinton stands at the head of the table with the whiteboard behind him. He lists headers for tasks with slots for names to handle the duties. When the last person settles at the table, the assistant shuts the door and Clinton clears his throat.

"Now, we'll get to business of expectations, budget, organizing activities, and creating the project schedule. As you know management set occupancy for six months from today…"

We dive right in. A slideshow presentation takes us through the history of the building from construction to remodeling. We review the schematics and other construction details. Then get into the parameters for the job.

It's thrilling.

The assistant steps out and returns with our lunch orders. The delivery person helps her to set up the credenza where we'll pick up our food. My nose doesn't appreciate the varied smells as they blend in the air. I take a sip of water and try to concentrate on the discussion.

"Everything is ready," she tells us.

While several colleagues head to the credenza, I hang back. The smell is overpowering. When Brandon sits down with his egg salad sandwich, saliva fills my mouth. In a panic, I jump up from the table as I cover my mouth. I rush out of the room to the hallway that leads to the ladies' room.

"Leonie! Hey, are you all right?"

I can't risk answering Brandon for fear I'll retch all over the place. Instead, I increase my pace. He catches up to me just as I stumble from a wave of dizziness.

"Hold on, I'll help—"

"Leonie!"

A powerful arm grips my waist and hauls me against a hard body. The sudden movement proves too much for my resistance. With a surprising burst of energy, I push away from him and rush into the bathroom.

I barely make it to the first stall. My entire body shudders as spasms rock me. I feel hot and cold. On a moan, I heave into the toilet bowl. My empty stomach emits nothing but the water I drank. I moan pitifully.

"Baby, it'll be okay. Just breath, baby."

Finally, my mind registers it wasn't Brandon who held me. It was Roger. How did he know, I wonder? I don't have time to ask since another wave hits me. It's too much. I sob.

"Françoise! Call the medic to the ladies' room on the twentieth floor!"

I try to wave my hand to stop Roger from calling for the doctor. But I feel too weak. I wonder if I caught a bug in Mozambique.

At last, my body stills. I sit back on my heels and wipe my mouth with toilet tissue. How embarrassing, I think and groan.

"Can you stand?" Roger asks softly, stroking my hair.

I nod, and he lifts me up. He leads me to the sinks. He fills a disposable cup with cool water, then hands it to me.

Shakily, I put it to my lips and rinse my mouth out. Roger's gray eyes search my face intently. I blush from the scrutiny, knowing I must look a fright. I duck my head and bend to rinse my face off. The water cools my heated skin.

Roger rubs my back in circles, easing the tension in my body. I glance at him in the mirror. He looks worried and starts to speak, but the door opens.

"Monsieur Steele, what's happening?"

The doctor hastens to my side when he sees my reflection in the mirror.

"Mademoiselle, tell me what happened," he says.

"I'm fine. I just… I haven't eaten yet. That's all," I respond, straightening my clothes and brushing my hand over my hair.

"Leonie…" Roger starts.

I glare at him. But before I can speak, the doctor cuts in.

"Monsieur Steele, please be so kind as to wait for us outside"—he raises his hand to stop Roger's response—"She is a patient and I must respect her privacy."

Roger looks flabbergasted. But the doctor holds firm and shakes his head. Then points to the door. Roger looks to me. But I offer no consolation. He leaves without a word.

"Now, tell me what happened," the doctor says.

I tell him about not eating and the smells upsetting me. He takes an assessment of my vitals, including blood pressure and temperature. I mention my thoughts of a bug, and he nods.

Finding nothing untoward, he tells me to go home, have a light meal, and rest. Should my symptoms worsen, I'm to go to hospital for a full checkup. I thank him and we leave the bathroom.

Roger, Brandon, and Clinton stand just outside the door. They turn in unison when they hear it open. I offer a wan smile. Roger curses and strides over to me.

"I'm taking you to the hospital," he declares. "You don't look good."

I roll my eyes and sigh, "Gee thanks. Just what every woman likes to hear…"

The doctor coughs to cover his chuckle. Then responds, "Monsieur Steele, Mademoiselle Beaulieu should be fine with a light meal and some rest at home. I told her to go to hospital if her symptoms worsen."

Turning to me, he pats my arm and wishes me good health. I thank him again and he leaves with Françoise, who also wishes me a speedy recovery.

"Yes, Leonie, you should go home. Don't concern yourself with the project right now," Clinton says, concerned.

"I'll keep you up-to-date. Don't worry," Brandon adds with a smile.

Roger gives him the once over. But doesn't respond. Down, caveman…

"Leonie, are you all right?"

We turn towards the voice. Delia stands there with an expression of concern on her face.

I don't buy it.

"*Oui, merci,*" I respond.

Roger puts his hand on my lower back and guides me past them. He nods at Clinton, who inclines his head slightly.

When we're out of their line of sight, Roger pulls me close and kisses my temple, brushing his nose against my hair. He takes a deep inhale and sighs.

"You scared the shit out of me when I saw you run past the conference room I was in for a meeting.

Françoise took your things upstairs. Let's go home, Kitten."

As soon as we arrive in his bedroom, Roger leads me to the bathroom where he carefully strips me and wraps me in my robe.

"Are you okay to freshen up while I fix you something?" he asks, touching his fingertips to my cheek in a caress. "I'll bring a tray for you to eat in bed, okay?"

I close my eyes as I nuzzle against his hand and nod.

Roger sighs and kisses my lips before he backs out. His stormy gaze never leaves mine until he turns to walk out of the door with a nod.

When he returns, I'm snuggled under the covers wearing one of his t-shirts. He sets the tray on the bench at the foot.

"Do you want to eat a little something or at least drink a bit of ginger tea to settle your stomach?" He asks.

"*Oui, merci,*" I respond as I sit up.

Roger fluffs the pillows behind me. Then places the tray over my legs. He waits for me to take a sip of the tea before he sits facing me.

"I'm sorry, Leo—"

"Forgive me, Roger—"

We speak at the same time. I giggle, and he chuckles when we talk over ourselves again.

"You first," he says.

I take another few sips of tea; the ginger eases my nausea. The scent of Roger's cologne and the softness of his worn cotton t-shirt comfort me.

"Forgive me, *Mon Cœur*. I was a brat, and you didn't deserve it. I love you," I say, overcome with emotion.

"Baby!" Roger exclaims as a tear rolls down my cheek.

He moves the tray to the bench and sits next to me as he pulls me onto his lap.

I snuggle against him, inhaling deeply.

"I love you too, Leonie. So much. I don't want to control you," he says, then adds. "Well... Aside from in bed."

My shoulders shake as my tears turn into snorts of laughter. Only Roger, the love of my life and sometime control freak.

ROGER

$\mathcal{T}$he nightmare from two weeks ago of Leonie sick is a distant memory as I sit on the sofa in my penthouse's primary bedroom watching her rush around. It's the morning of her graduation ceremony. In fact, it's an hour and fifteen minutes before the commencement starts. And as always, Leonie is late getting ready.

I learned my lesson the morning she took ill. Instead of reminding her over and over, I told her when I came in ten minutes ago we need to leave in twenty minutes. Well...

"Roger! Where's my makeup case?!" She storms in from the bathroom wearing a Lola's Coterie sheer silk, flesh-toned bra and thong set.

Fuck...

My dick comes to life at the sight of her. My eyes wander languorously from her toenails painted white to her shapely, long legs over her belly to the swell of her hips. I tilt my head as I stare at her chest.

Is it my imagination or do her breasts damn near spill from the bra cups? The nipples more prominent? Her tits appear more lush than before, or is it the push-up bra, I muse as I lick my lips.

"Ow, fuck!" I exclaim as I rub the side of my head.

"Stop ogling me! I asked you a question, Roger!" She bellows as she prepares to launch another missile at my head.

I peer around me and spot her hairbrush on the floor by my feet. I didn't even see it coming. She has spot-on aim. Damn.

"Was that really necessary, Leonie?" I ask petulantly.

Her eyes widen. Then narrow to shoot amber flames in my direction. If I could combust, I would from the heat of her glare.

She flings her arms up in disgust. Then goes on a tirade, screeching French obscenities as she stomps off to the bathroom.

My dick jumps at the sight of her round ass jiggling with each one of her steps. I glance at my watch, debating whether we have time to temper her poor attitude with a quick fuck or not. Not, I realize when I note we now have less than an hour and fifteen minutes to the start of the ceremony. I rise from the sofa and sigh.

"Leonie, I don't care if you get pissed. But I will not let you be late to your graduation, babe," I tell her as I stand in the doorway to the dressing room.

She stormed in here after a fruitless search in the bathroom didn't reveal her missing makeup case. She's now dressed in a strapless white jumpsuit and skin-tone strappy sandals. Her hair cascades down her back in silky waves. It's gotten longer these past six months as it now reaches her waist.

I want to grip it in my fist and fuck her really hard. Use it as leverage to bend her body to my will. I run my hand over my burgeoning bulge that aches to drive deep inside of my Kitty's tight, wet heat.

She spies my action and growls at me. Even lifting the corner of her lip to flash her incisor.

Damn if it doesn't turn me on more. But I can't help a chuckle. My *Lion* is fierce today. And I have just the thing to tame her. I slip my hand in my trousers pocket and run my thumb over the velvet box.

"Besides, you're glowing, Kitten. You don't need any makeup. Let's go," I add a with a touch of command.

Leonie glances up and gives me the once over. Then nods to herself as though she's decided to not argue with me.

"Fine, let's go," she says as she sweeps past me like a queen.

I shake my head and chuckle some more.

"I heard that!" She snarls.

I duck as I come out of the bathroom, not wanting another ding to my head. Fortunately, Leonie stalks out of the bedroom door with her cap and gown in her hand.

I notice her mobile still plugged into the charger sitting on the nightstand by her side of our bed. I shake my head as I snag it. Then follow her out of the door.

"Congratulations, Mademoiselle Beaulieu!" Eric exclaims as Leonie and I step off of the elevator to the Steele family private garage. "I wish you much success!"

Leonie no longer a temperamental lioness beams at Eric.

"*Merci beaucoup*, Eric! How kind of you!" She says as she gives him a big hug.

He inclines his head as he reddens from her attention. He can't meet my eyes knowing how possessive I am of Leonie. But I know he's happily married with two sons. If he were not…

Leonie slips inside of my Black Badge Rolls-Royce Cullinan as Eric holds the back door open. I help her inside. Then walk around to the other door. We're picking up her parents on the way to the school. So we need the additional third row.

For now, I sit beside Leonie. She smiles at me and takes my hand.

"Thank you too, *Mon Cœur*," she says. "I didn't mean to bite your head off."

I lean in to whisper in her ear, "Later, you'll have my other head down your throat. So don't fret."

She snorts and slaps me on the chest.

"You Steele men are cretins without a doubt!"

Not sure what she means—but not caring either—I bring her hand to my lips and kiss her palm. Then slide them to her inner wrist where I kiss it softly.

She whimpers and strokes my face with her fingertips.

"I love you, Roger, so much," she whispers. "You've supported me and believed in me. Even when I argued with you. The completion of my degree would have been a lot harder and taken more time without you. You pushed me and made me realize I could do better if I just focused more. *Merci, Mon Cœur*."

Fuck… I have to look away as my eyes fill with tears. Damn, this woman gets to me. I close my eyes and lean back against the headrest.

Leonie gives me a moment to collect myself. She just strokes my face gently.

I inhale deeply and turn to face her. I cup her face in my hands and slant my mouth over hers. She opens up to me. My tongue slides into her mouth to draw hers to mine. She moans as the passion of our kiss increases. Sparks zip from our dancing tongues to my heart.

So caught up in our love, we don't notice the SUV stopped until Eric's door opens and closes. He hops out to get the door for Josy and Guy, who stand in front of their mansion.

I pull back and kiss the tip of Leonie's nose. Then move to the rear bench. Leonie's mother will sit in the bucket seat I vacated. Her father will sit in the passenger seat up front with Eric.

"*Mon Trésor!*" Her father bellows as he gets in the SUV. "We are so proud of you, Leonie!"

"*Oui, Ma Chérie! Félicitation pour ton passage!*" Josy says, hugging Leonie when she settles in her seat.

Leonie tears up, and I pass my handkerchief to her. She smiles gratefully and dabs her eyes.

Quietly she responds, "*Merci, Maman et Papa.*"

"Bonjour, Roger!" Josy says with a bright smile so like her daughter's as she shifts in her seat to face me. "Thank you for picking us up."

"Bonjour, Josy. No worries," I respond. "Leonie would have it no other way."

"Yes thank you, Roger. Good to see you," Guy adds, glancing over his shoulder at me.

I nod and answer, "You're welcome and good to see you too, Guy."

The rest of the ride Leonie shares stories about some of her memorable times at the Paris American Academy. She's so happy, we listen attentively.

We pull up to the drop off area with ten minutes to spare. Leonie hops out and blows kisses to us as she follows the other graduates to their section of the auditorium. I watch her rush off, slipping her gown on and straightening her cap on her head. Once she's through their entry, I turn to her parents.

Josy smiles at me warmly. Then loops her arm through mine and Guy's. We make our way through the crowd to the section Leonie reserved for her family. Already seated in two rows are my parents, Sebastian, Lola, Malcolm, Harris, Haley, Luc, Blair, Billie, Patrick, Starr, Lucien, Joel, and Hettie. They wave us over, and we sit just as the faculty walk onto the stage.

The New York City crew and Starr, Billie, and Patrick flew in last night on Sebastian's and Patrick's private jets. My parents are staying in their penthouse at The STEELE Tower Paris. Sebastian and Lola claimed dibs on the one below theirs. While the others, except for the Paris locals, stay at STEELE Place Vendôme where we'll have dinner after the graduation finishes.

I scan the crowd of students for Leonie. With everyone in caps, it's impossible to find her. So I settle back in my seat and listen to the presentations. I feel a poke on my arm from behind.

Lola grins at me like the Cheshire Cat. I glance to her left to Sebastian who's purposefully ignoring my stare as he studies the graduation program. My gaze moves back to Lola and I smile at her. But shake my head and turn around to focus on the stage when she starts to speak.

She huffs and mutters how I'm no fun.

I hold back a chuckle. No need to encourage her. Besides, I don't want to miss a thing.

My mother who sits beside me leans in to whisper to me.

"When are you going to introduce us to Leonie's parents?" She asks, then sits back and arches her eyebrow at me.

Duh! In my haste, I forgot to make any introductions. I mouth an apology to her and turn to Josy and Guy.

"Please forgive me. I was so busy focused on the ceremony I forgot to introduce you to my family and friends," I whisper.

Josy pats my arm and Guy nods.

As quietly as possible, I share everyone's names and relationships to me. Josy is especially happy to meet Shelley and vice versa. Guy and Morgan appear equally pleased. Good.

Everyone else makes Josy and Guy welcome. Now that I've made everyone acquainted, we continue to listen to the ceremony.

A little over an hour in, the president steps to the podium to announce the student speakers. He explains how the faculty selects one based on their academic grade point average and the other selected by the graduates.

"For the first time in the history of Paris American Academy, the student with the highest grade point average and the student voted upon by their peers is the same individual."

He pauses as a hush falls over the crowd. He glances out at the students, then continues.

"Please join me in congratulating this year's valedictorian... Mademoiselle... Leonie Beaulieu!"

The crowd erupts in applause. The students jump to their feet and clap for Leonie.

Everyone around me goes wild with whistles, hoots, and clapping. I'm so stunned I don't move until my mother grabs my arm to force me to my feet.

My mind reels when I see my woman sashay across the stage. She owns this platform just as she does the fashion catwalks all over the world. Leonie waves and the cheers increase in volume. Once she reaches the president, she hugs him and he proudly holds her hand up in the air in victory.

Flashes from mobiles and cameras capture the moment.

Leonie shines like a megastar. I'm so proud of her achievements. Career switch to study in a different field. Balancing modeling while completing studies for her bachelor's degree. Mentor to young girls and teens. The addition of her part-time junior designer position to the mix. With all of her hard work, she deserves her honors.

I join with whoops and clap louder than anyone else. That's my woman!

Leonie stands before the podium and motions for silence. The auditorium quiets. She glances around those seated until she finds us in the crowd. We wave and blow kisses. She bows her head, overwhelmed.

Then she straightens her spine and recites her speech from memory. Just as she shared stories with us in the Cullinan, she shares some now. Her words of farewell to her classmates and faculty inspire all. Her speech enraptures everyone in the audience.

At the end, she thanks her parents, Luc, and Lola. All four are in tears when she finishes her praise for them. Leonie focuses her gaze on me and my heart skips a beat. Our eyes lock.

"Also, I thank the love of my life. His support and belief in me was unceasing. Even when faced with my fierce lioness."

The audience laughs, and Leonie smiles as she continues.

"Without him, my completion of my degree would have been a lot harder and taken more time. He pushed me and made me realize I could do better if I just focused more. You are so dear to me, Roger. *Merci, Mon Cœur. Merci pour toujours.*"

I rise from my seat and in a clear voice heard throughout the auditorium I respond, "*Je t'aimerai pour toujours,* Leonie Beaulieu."

She holds her fist to her heart, brings it to her lips, and kisses it. Then releases it towards me. I catch her love and kiss with my fist and bring it to my lips and to my heart. She bows to the audience and strides off of the stage.

Exhilarated, I take my seat. Her father shakes my hand and her mother kisses my cheeks. Lola hugs my neck while my mother kisses my cheek. My father also shakes my hand, and Luc claps me on the back. Everyone is excited about Leonie's pronouncement.

We settle down and listen to the students' names as they're called to receive their degrees. Once again, the crowd cheers loudly for Leonie. Our section is the most rambunctious. She waves again, bursting with joy.

As soon as the president calls an end to the ceremony, we make a beeline for the reception area. When we arrive, Leonie is waiting for us by the door. I hurry over and sweep her off her feet. She holds my face between her hands and kisses me silly.

We only come up for air when we hear the wolf whistles. Leonie throws her head back and laughs. The sound makes my heart swell with satisfaction.

Lola tugs on my arm to let Leonie down. Reluctantly, I set her on her feet. She's surrounded by our families and friends offering their congratulations and well wishes. I stand aside and bask in her glow. Her eyes meet mine and she winks at me. I chuckle as I return one to her.

After a while, we leave the reception and go to the restaurant at STEELE Place Vendôme. It's one in Lucien's stable, so he prepared all of Leonie's favorite dishes and desserts. As we enjoy after-dinner drinks in the private room, Leonie calls for everyone's attention. We turn expectantly towards her as she stands before us.

"Thank you, everyone for celebrating my big day with

me. It marks a new page in my life. So, I want you to be the first to know my plans."

She pauses and smiles around the table before she continues.

"As of now, I plan to work full-time at STEELE Paris as a newly promoted project designer. I will model only for Lola's Coterie and for the global cosmetics company."

We offer more congratulations as we toast her, and Leonie beams.

I notice her expression pinches for a moment. But she seems to shake it off. I gulp down the rest of my Jackson Special Blend Scotch and set the snifter on the table. Then stand and take Leonie by the hand.

She follows me to the center of the room.

I bring her hand to my lips and kiss it. Then drop to one knee as I pull the little navy blue velvet box out of my trousers pocket. I take a deep breath and open my mouth.

"Leonie!"

Lola's scream makes me falter. I swing my head around to look at Lola. She's ashen with wide eyes and pointing at Leonie. I turn back around and stop breathing.

There's a red stain blooming on the white of Leonie's jumpsuit. Her eyes follow my stare. Then widen when she notices the blood.

What the fuck?!

I must have spoken out loud because Leonie drags her frightened eyes to mine. She whispers my name as she touches her stomach and reaches for me. Then she faints in my arms.

All hell breaks loose as screams resound around the room, chairs crash to the stone floor, and Guy shouts. Above it all, I hear a high-pitched wailing.

It's not until my father and Sebastian try to lift Leonie

from my arms do I realize the sound is coming from me. The wail turns into a growl as I cradle Leonie with one arm and use the other to push them away from my mate.

She moans from the jostling, and I freeze.

Josy kneels before me and gently takes her treasure from my arms. She rocks Leonie's limp body against her bosom for what seems like an eternity. But in reality is only ten minutes, as long as it takes for the ambulance to arrive.

The medics bustle in and within moments have Leonie strapped to the gurney, wheeling her out of the room. I rush behind them, focused on her pale face. Every so often she winces in pain and moans.

Before they let me into the ambulance, they ask if I'm her husband. I tell them her fiancé. One tells me family only and I almost punch him in the throat. Guy steps up and demands my entry or he'll sue them for endangering his daughter's life with their delay over semantics.

I nod gratefully to Guy and hop on board. I sit in a corner while the medic sees to Leonie. I answer his questions to the best of my ability. I send a prayer for her well-being as my eyes never leave her face.

She moans what sounds like my name and I call out to her, I'm here. I yell for them to go faster. But the medic ignores me as he calls in to the hospital, issuing details in code I don't understand. He's also speaking in French, and my mind is far beyond the capability to translate right now.

Only moments later we stop, and the doors open. I jump out of the way as nurses and doctors take over. I rush after them as they wheel Leonie inside the hospital's emergency room. I hear my name called. But I don't stop. I have to stay with her.

At the end of the corridor, we arrive at swinging double doors. A nurse steps in front of me and puts her hands up to stop me from going any further. I glare at her and try to get past. I won't hit a woman. But I will move her aside.

"Monsieur, you cannot come into the OR! Please come with me," she insists.

I glance behind her, debating my chances of getting around her smaller frame when a hand on my shoulder holds me in place. I whirl around with my fists at the ready to strike.

It's Sebastian, with Malcolm and Harris beside him. They shake their heads and I snarl at them.

"I need to know what the fuck is going on!" I shout, spinning around to the operating room.

"Stop it right now, Roger! You're not helping the situation. Leonie needs their full attention and not you going crazy."

At the mention of my love's name, my knees buckle and I collapse to the ground. On my hands and knees, I punch the ground. But Malcolm pulls my arm back before my fist can connect and I break my hand on the hard, unforgiving tile.

I drop my head and sob.

My brothers lift me up like a rag doll and half carry, half walk me to the waiting room. I drop into a chair and lower my head into my hands. I can't think of or see anything but the bright red bloodstain on Leonie's white clothes.

What the fuck happened? Was it the food? Did she cut herself somehow?

I shake my head, unable to wrap my brain around what's going on. This is a nightmare I cannot wake up from.

"Roger, honey?"

I can't look up at my mother or I'll break down. I shake my head and cover my face, my cheeks aflame.

Understanding I cannot speak at the moment, my

mother sits beside me and rubs my back soothingly. Haley sits on my other side and strokes my hair.

After a while, the room comes into focus slowly. Softs cries from Josy and Lola filter through first as Blair tries to console them. Followed by the murmurings of my father, brothers, and Lucien. Guy's footsteps as he paces back and forth in the middle of the room. Luc on the phone speaking in French urgently.

Billie, Patrick, and Starr enter the room with trays of coffee and tea. Joel and Hettie help to pass them out. When Hettie offers a coffee to me, I shake my head. My mother and Haley also decline.

How the hell did we get to this? One minute Leonie's sharing her future plans, and I'm about to ask her to share her future with me. The next minute, we're sitting in the waiting room of a hospital with Leonie in an operating room.

What the absolute fuck is happening?!

Abruptly, I stand. I can't sit around and not have any answers. She's been in there for an over an hour! Somebody is going to tell me something right now.

"Roger!" My mother cries as I storm to the door.

Suddenly the door opens.

A doctor in surgical scrubs walks into the waiting room and removes his cap. His expressionless eyes scan the area, observing one anxious face after the other.

He takes a deep breath and says, "Monsieur et Madame Beaulieu…"

* * *

Roger & Leonie's Story Continues: *Stoke My Desires*

Stoke my
DESIRES

ROGER & LEONIE PART II

Charmaine Louise Shelton

I dedicate this novel to those who never give up on true love and each other.

Fulfill Your Desires.

xoxo
Charmaine Louise

ABOUT STOKE MY DESIRES
ROGER & LEONIE PART II

The tempestuous, fiery love affair of Roger The Responsible and Supermodel-cum-Interior designer Leonie The Lion continues to spark in part two of their billionaire romance story.

With his Pretty Kitty back in his life finally, Roger expects days of peace and nights of passion. But life holds many surprises, including unwelcome interest by another. Leonie draws on the strength of her feline namesake to save their reignited romance time and again.

Love tested, legal troubles, hospital emergencies... Who said watching paint dry is boring?

Join this white-hot pair as their turbulent romance takes them to villas set in the hillsides of Beverly Hills and Capri, above the azure waters of the Mediterranean in Cannes, opulent Parisian manoirs, and high-in-the-clouds

Manhattan penthouses in this electrifying romantic suspense Sexy Fantasy.

Their love story is a standalone second chance romance trilogy in the series. Get a glimpse of their dynamism in other books.

Anthem: "Secret" Madonna
https://www.youtube.com/watch?v=EPHUZenprKc

Playlist:
https://www.youtube.com/playlist?list=
PLXwYvn0e218Bx18MlEj1svXS-8-NachjU

Visit CharmaineLouiseBooks.com

LEONIE

"*J* am so very proud of you, Leonie. You've accomplished your dream, babe. You did it and everyone will celebrate with you tomorrow. I love you so much."

"*Merci, Mon Cœur, je t'aime aussi.*"

Roger's words from earlier this evening linger in my mind as I lie here wrapped in his powerful arms. The heat of his body still consumes me after we made soul-stirring love for hours. I bask in the glow of our lovemaking and in his praise. Both mean the world to me.

I snuggle deeper into his embrace and smile to myself as even in his sleep Roger tightens his grip to hold me possessively, never wanting to let me go. He murmurs my name and rubs his cheek against my hair with a sigh of contentment.

My mind turns back to how far we have come from almost two years ago.

. . .

THE MEETING my best friend Lola Lewis had to expand her lingerie company Lola's Coterie with STEELE International, Inc. set off a chain reaction for her and for me. She met the love of her life, Sebastian Steele. I met his younger brother, Roger.

I giggle to myself as I think back to his initial reaction when he walked into the wrong conference room and came upon my half-naked voluptuous body. To prepare for the fashion show portion of Lola's presentation, the models, glam squad, and I were using the room. Roger caught more than an eyeful as I stood before him in a thin, silky thong that covered my bare mons and nothing else.

His mouth gaped and his gray eyes popped out of his head comically. An impressive bulge grew to punch against the zipper of his bespoke trousers.

"They're only breasts, *chéri!*" I teased him as I cupped them in my hands for emphasis. "No need to look so stunned!"

Transfixed in a daze, he licked his lips. Then beat a hasty retreat when someone cleared their throat.

During the fashion show, Roger sat in the correct conference room with an unblinking intense stare. His expression never changed as scantily clad models strutted past him—me, *The Lion* included. His gorgeous eyes tracked our moves. But he didn't show interest or displeasure. He was a hard read.

Boy, was I wrong...

Who knew my being the spokesmodel and sashaying my way through the fashion show would result in an unexpected two-month-long relationship?

Our insta-attraction sparked further when Roger blocked other suitors from me at LEVELS New York. Lola surprised me with her purchase of seven-day All Access membership passes for us to experience the flagship of the three luxury BDSM and dance club—Paris and London have locations, too. Global and Local All Access Membership or Dine & Dance Membership options for the über-wealthy and high-profile people who prefer discretion.

On a night I ventured alone, Roger absconded me. We moved from the Peepshow banquette to one of the private suites. Our tryst turned into an evening of sharing our lives and goals. A release of our souls to the other. I'd never felt so connected to a man as I did with Roger.

We ended my week in New York City bound for Paris on his Gulfstream 650 and bound at the hip.

While in the city—where funnily enough we're both based—our relationship continued to flourish. Roger guest lectured one of my classes at Paris American Academy. It was a natural fit as he's the President of STEELE's Residential Properties Division, and I was completing my interior design bachelor's degree. Of course Dalia Shaw, another student, flirted shamelessly with Roger. Later that night, he and I role-played naughty schoolgirl punished by her professor at LEVELS Paris.

Despite the good times, Roger's control-freak ways drove a wedge between us as he constantly nitpicked my coursework ethic as too lax. When he publicly harangued me, then had a fight with my seat mate Antonio Vasquez at our end-of-the-semester reception, marked the beginning of the end.

Roger apologized to me. He paid for Antonio's medical costs and gave him a sum of money in recompense. In addition, Roger had STEELE Paris' Human Resources team set up an annual paid internship program for two students awarded in perpetuity.

Happy to move on, our relationship progressed until we

had the horrible blowup. The last argument that led to the end of our short-lived relationship. Sadly, the immediate electricity of what I thought was our *coup de foudre* fizzled.

A shudder runs through me as I recall how the numbness of despair hooked its tentacles into my heart. Then ripped it out when Roger so callously told me he wanted "a serious-minded partner and not a wayward woman who cannot stay focused for over five minutes."

As I made my way from the pleasure we had just shared in the surf at Palmilla Beach to the luxury villa beside STEELE Cabo San Lucas, I could barely keep the tears from falling. It made my pain even worse when Roger refused to relent as he pinned me with his stoic stare. That damnable intense expression he gets when he's being pigheaded. So, I left.

Three weeks later, my tender heart cut anew when at the Grand Prix after party in Monte Carlo I saw Roger cozy up with Verónica Casal. The Spanish supermodel had her claws in him, and he didn't appear to mind at all.

Despite me being with Giovanni Mattei, the anguish was genuine. After the Cabo fiasco, I couldn't help but return to the arms of my on-again-off-again paramour. I needed some way to soothe the pain in my heart.

Gio and I fell back into our agreed upon relationship: to the public we were the hot, passionate couple; in private, our amorous encounters never reached intimate penetration. So once again, I put up with his seeking full release with others as long as I was not a witness to his rendezvous.

Yet, it was not enough.

Eight months later, Roger insisted upon speaking to me. Until then, I ignored his phone calls and text messages. Finally he reached me while I was visiting Lola at Sebastian's penthouse duplex in The STEELE Tower. The clan occupies the top floors of the mixed-used property where their company's headquarters are on Fifty-seventh Street and Fifth Avenue—Billionaires' Row. I was in New York to help Lola with her wedding plans.

Roger was adamant to make amends.

"Please Leonie. For the sake of Lola and Sebastian, let's set our situation aside. Put their minds at ease about how we'll behave at their wedding. I promise I will not bother you. Okay?"

I agreed. The mind-blowing kiss he gave me to seal our agreement reignited my desire for my love.

Ever the fighter—Roger trains as a boxer—he and Gio came to blows at Lola's Coterie Dubai's opening night party just two months later. And a week before the wedding...

After which, Roger left a heart-wrenching voicemail asking me to forgive him and to tell him what to do to make things right with us. I couldn't resist him.

I can never resist him.

FORTUNATELY, that was then, and this is now.

Roger and I realize we need each other and respect each of our ways: Roger exacting and me more carefree. We truly are *un coup de foudre*—a second chance version. So we've learned to adapt to one another. But also to take on some of the other's qualities. Roger loosened up and doesn't have to stick to a regimented way. I focus more on the tasks at hand and not flit around. We make our relationship work.

And it does.

Over the last six months we've been back together, Roger and I have grown and our relationship has matured. We get it and each other. At last.

* * *

"ROGER! WHERE'S MY MAKEUP CASE?!"

I yell as I storm in from the bathroom wearing a Lola's Coterie sheer silk, flesh-toned bra and thong set.

It's hours later and I'm trying to get dressed for my graduation ceremony. Nothing is going right so far: I forgot to set the alarm; my toe decided to jam itself against the cabinet when I kicked it closed; cramps battling my insides. Now my makeup is missing...

Merde!

Roger of course is all cool and collected, fully dressed as he sits on the sofa in his primary bedroom. Meanwhile, I'm running around like a madwoman.

He has the absolute audacity to eye me from my toes up my legs over my belly to my hips. Then he tilts his head as he stares at my breasts, transfixed again. This fool is eye fucking me!

I let him have it.

"Ow, fuck!"

He exclaims as he rubs the side of his head.

"Stop ogling me! I asked you a question, Roger!" I bellow as I raise my comb to take aim at his stupid head since my hairbrush wasn't enough to knock some sense into him.

Can't he see how stressed I am??

I nearly blow a gasket when he asks if it was necessary to ding him upside the head. I refuse to answer. Instead, I pivot on my heels and storm into the bathroom as I mutter obscenities in French

No sign of my makeup case, I head to the dressing room. At least my strapless white jumpsuit and skin-tone strappy sandals go on without a hitch. I let my mahogany hair loose from the topknot to cascade down my back in silky waves to my ass.

D'accord!

"Leonie, I don't care if you get pissed. But I will not let you be late to your graduation, babe," Roger says.

I turn around to find him standing in the doorway to the dressing room. Damn is he sexy... all six feet, three inches of him.

Roger Steele could be a male supermodel. His sultry gray eyes and ebony hair slightly long, cut to skim his ears and neck along with the angular cheekbones and cleft chin of his clean-shaven face. The olive skin tone doesn't completely hide the shadow of hair beneath the surface.

But at this moment, he makes the mistake of running his hand over his burgeoning bulge. Does he think of anything besides sex?!

I growl at him as I lift the corner of my lip to flash my incisor. *The Lion* is not pleased with her mate.

He chuckles, not at all bothered by my histrionics.

"Besides, you're glowing, Kitten. You don't need any makeup. Let's go," he commands.

I glance up and study him. I decide he's not fucking with me. So I nod and not argue with him. My golden caramel-colored skin is flawless thanks to genetics, clean eating, and regular exercise. My mother is Tunisian and my father Parisian. They taught me at an early age to treat my body well.

"Fine, let's go," I respond as I sweep past him.

Roger shakes his head and chuckles some more.

"I heard that!" I snarl as I stalk out of the bedroom door with my cap and gown in my hand.

We take the family's private elevator at The STEELE Tower Paris to the garage. Similar to the New York City

Tower, it's mixed-use with commercial and residential space plus the largest mall in Paris. Being in the *quinzième* with spectacular views of the Seine and of the Eiffel Tower adds to its appeal. Location. Location. Location.

Roger's driver Eric Vogler has the Black Badge Rolls-Royce Cullinan ready. We'll pick up my parents Guy and Josy Beaulieu from my family's ancestral home *Le Beaulieu Manoir* in the wealthiest neighborhood of the *seizième*. Eric offers me congratulations and I thank him with a hug.

Once settled in the plushy SUV, I relax. Then smile at Roger and take his hand as he sits beside me.

"Thank you too, *Mon Cœur*," I say. "I didn't mean to bite your head off."

He leans in to whisper in my ear, "Later, you'll have my other head down your throat. So don't fret."

I snort and slap him on the chest, "You Steele men are cretins without a doubt!"

He brings my hand to his lips and kisses my palm. Then slides them to my inner wrist where he kisses it softly.

I whimper and stroke his face with my fingertips.

"I love you, Roger, so much," I whisper. "You've supported me and believed in me. Even when I argued with you. The completion of my degree would have been a lot harder and taken more time without you. You pushed me and made me realize I could do better if I just focused more. *Merci, Mon Cœur*."

Roger takes a moment to collect himself from the effects of my words. I truly love this man more than he can ever imagine.

He kisses me with such passion that we don't realize we've arrived at my parents' home until they get into the SUV. Now it's my turn to feel overwhelmed as they praise me. I can only whisper my thanks. Roger gives his handkerchief to me to dab the tears from my eyes. My heart bursts with joy surrounded by my loved ones.

We arrive at Paris American Academy. I rush to join the other graduates, slipping into my gown and placing my cap on my head. My nerves have my stomach in knots. I feel queasy, but ignore it.

The excitement is palpable as I make my way to the side of the stage. I peek out to spot my crew. I'm so excited everyone came to celebrate with me.

Lola and Sebastian along with Roger's parents Morgan and Shelley, his second oldest brother Malcolm, Harris and Haley fraternal twins and the youngest flew in from New York City. Plus Blair Thomas and Billie Chandler Lola's personal assistants-cum-close friends, Starr Knight who became another close friend after we attended her fitness retreats came on Patrick Rockett's private jet—Billie's Scottish billionaire beau. The Paris locals include Luc Montaigne Lola and my billionaire mentor and Blair's not-admitted *Le Renard Argenté*, Lucien Jackson, Roger's cousin, and Joel Bailey and Hettie Fuchs, Roger's close friends.

Boy, will this surprise them, especially Roger…

"For the first time in the history of Paris American Academy, the student with the highest grade point average and the student voted upon by their peers is the same individual."

The Academy's president pauses as a hush falls over the crowd. He glances out at the students, then continues.

"Please join me in congratulating this year's valedictorian… Mademoiselle… Leonie Beaulieu!"

The crowd erupts in applause.

As I sashay onto the stage, I wave and smile at the audience thrilled they're delighted for me. It took more time than usual since I maintained my modeling career full-time. And I didn't focus as I much as I could have...

The president and I hug, then he raises our hands in victory. Yes, this is a tremendous success for me. I deliver my valedictory of anecdotes and inspiring stories. It's well received. I end in thanks to my parents, Lola and Luc, and Roger.

"Also, I thank the love of my life. His support and belief in me was unceasing. Even when faced with my fierce lioness."

The audience laughs, and I smile as I continue.

"Without him, my completion of my degree would have been a lot harder and taken more time. He pushed me and made me realize I could do better if I just focused more. You are so dear to me, Roger. *Merci, Mon Cœur. Merci pour toujours.*"

I'm ecstatic when Roger rises and responds, *"Je t'aimerai pour toujours,* Leonie Beaulieu."

My happiness reaches its peak as I blow a kiss to him and he catches it.

Once the ceremony ends, the graduates and faculty go to the reception area to await the guests. I take a spot by the door to get an unobstructed view of my family and friends. Roger hurries over and sweeps me off my feet. I cradle his face between her hands and kiss him fervently.

Wolf whistles draw us apart, to which I throw my head back and laugh.

Roger puts me down reluctantly when Lola wants to hug me. It's a glorious moment as everyone shares their congratulations and well wishes.

I glance around for Roger and see him standing to the side, watching me intently. My amber eyes meet his gray orbs, and I wink. He chuckles as he returns one to me.

The reception is lovely. But we're ready to go to the restaurant at STEELE Place Vendôme. Lucien—*The Sexy Chef*—runs the restaurant along with several other businesses that Jackson Corporation partners with STEELE. As a surprise, he prepared all of my favorite dishes and desserts. While we enjoy after-dinner drinks in the private room, I call for everyone's attention. They turn expectantly towards me as I stand at the table.

"Thank you, everyone for celebrating my big day with me. It marks a new page in my life. So, I want you to be the first to know my plans."

I pause and smile at everyone gathered before I continue.

"As of now, I plan to work full time at STEELE Paris as a newly promoted project designer. I will model only for Lola's Coterie and for the global cosmetics company."

They offer more congratulations as they toast me, and I beam.

A sharp pain zings my belly. It's enough to make me cringe. But I ignore it, not wanting to ruin the moment.

Roger distracts me when he stands and takes me by the hand to lead me to the center of the room.

I smile at him as he brings my hand to his lips and kisses it.

My vision blurs just as Roger drops to one knee. The pain is excruciating. Bile rises in my throat as a warm sensation seeps from my core.

"Leonie!" Lola screams.

Roger swings his head towards Lola, who's pointing at me. Then he turns to me.

Confused, I glance down as my eyes follow their stares. A red stain blooms on the white of my jumpsuit. My eyes widen in fright when I notice the blood—the source of the warmth and pain.

"What the fuck?!" Roger yells.

I drag my eyes to his as I touch my belly, stricken with another zing and reach for him, feeling faint.

"Roger—"

My vision goes black as I fall into his arms.

ROGER

"*M*onsieur et Madame Beaulieu..."

Those words from two days ago continue to haunt me along with visions of Leonie pale and soaked with blood and of her lying limp in my arms.

I choke back a sob as I hold her small hand in my larger one, stroking the back of it with my thumb gently.

"Baby, please... Please don't leave me... I love you so much..."

My sentence trails off when a knock on the door to her private suite cuts me off. I shift in my chair beside Leonie's hospital bed to glance towards the sharp rap. Then call for the person to enter. Doctor Pierre Berger walks in briskly, exuding the confidence of being the best in his field.

And the best is what he is as Luc pulled rank as the major benefactor of the hospital.

After we learned the cause of Leonie's affliction, he demanded the top OB-GYN attend to her. Not just of the hospital, but of all the country. As the multibillionaire CEO and Chairman of the Board of his family's multigenerational, global banking empire Banque Montaigne, he used his considerable influence to procure Dr. Berger. Since this is the top hospital in Paris, Dr. Berger has his affiliation with it and serves as their OB-GYN department director and a practicing doctor.

Yeah... OB-GYN...

Leonie's affliction is actually a pregnancy. Dr. Berger estimates she's eight weeks pregnant... With my child.

WHEN THE EMERGENCY room doctor entered the waiting room, Guy and Josy responded eagerly to know the status of their beloved *Trésor*. He introduced himself as Leonie's attending physician and ushered them from the room for privacy. But they held back and told him I could take part in the conversation as her fiancé. I was thankful for their recognition and hurried behind them.

Lola's soft cries intensified in alarm as I left. My heart beat in my chest wildly.

The ER doctor led us to a separate room where he gestured for us to sit.

"Mademoiselle Beaulieu is in stable condition now," he pauses to gaze at each of us before he continues. "We put her under heavy sedation to help her body to heal itself more efficiently."

Josy's mournful wail made the hairs on the back of my neck rise. Guy pulled her into his arms as he rubbed her back. But kept his obsidian eyes riveted on the doctor.

Despair caused an anguished cry to escape my lips. But I also watched him, hoping for some words to reassure us.

He sensed our need for more, the doctor continued.

"Are you aware of her medical situation?" He asked with his gaze on me.

Taken aback, I stammered no.

Guy's eyes raked over me for any sign of guile.

My face reddened, torn between anger he would think negatively of me and in embarrassment I didn't know something was wrong with my woman.

The doctor nodded.

"I see. Mademoiselle Beaulieu may not have known either, as it is in the early stages. It's quite—"

"Early stages of what, man?? Get it out already!"

I exploded, not able to take another second as my mind went into overdrive on "early stages" of the worse diseases imaginable.

The doctor had the decency to appear chastened and rushed on in his explanation.

"She is pregnant. Congratu—"

"What the hell??"

"*Que voulez-vous dire?!*"

"*Quoi?! Mon Dieu!*"

Leonie's parents and I shouted in unison. Then peppered the doctor with questions of how. He turned to me and gestured as if to say ask him, not me.

Guy and Josy turned to me.

My mind blanked. I stood and paced. Then stopped and ran my hands through my hair.

A smile spread across my face. This was just what I wished for as Leonie and I strolled through the grounds at *Le Beaulieu Manoir*. I envisioned her playing with our children on her family's ancestral lands. My heart soared then, but plummeted when I took in the anxious expressions on Josy's and Guy's faces.

Right... Blood... Fainting... Under heavy sedation...

Fuck me!

I dropped back into my chair and shook my head. I

recalled Guy's words to me during dinner the first night I met Josy and him.

"Leonie is a special gift of her mother and mine. Madame Beaulieu and I tried for many years to conceive. Many painful miscarriages and the resulting agony finally gave fruit to our magnifique petite fille. After she was born, we could not have any more children. She means everything to us."

Yeah... Fuck me.

"You are the father, *oui?*"

The withering look I gave the doctor made him sit back in his chair as though I physically punched him in the chest.

If my mobile hadn't rung, I would have done it. I kept him pinned with my stormy gray glare as I barked, "Steele."

"Rog... Roger... Pl... Please tell me Leonie is okaaay..."

Lola's distressed plea pulled me back from the brink. I had to get my shit together and take control of this situation. I gave my head a firm shake to clear the disorder.

"Yes, don't worry, Lola. We'll be in shortly."

Her sigh of relief filled me with determination to get back on track. I sat forward and asked the doctor about the well-being of my woman and my child.

He confirmed they were both stable and would require follow-up with an OB-GYN. I asked the cause of the bleeding. The doctor told us bleeding was common in the early stages of pregnancies, and it appears as though sexual activity led to repeated impact with her cervix.

My stomach dropped as I recalled the hours of lovemaking we made the night before. Being well-endowed with ten inches and wide girth, Leonie often told me I reached the end of her channel. The sensation of pain morphed into pleasure for her as I stretched her tight pussy to accommodate my cock.

This was my fault. Damn.

Guilt seared my soul. Leonie and our child were in danger because of me. Fuck.

Josy reached over and squeezed my hand, drawing my attention to her.

"It is not your fault, Roger. Do not take the blame. Leonie is young and strong—"

Josy choked back a sob, more than likely at the memory of her suffering. Guy soothed her, then looked at me.

"Roger, Josy is correct. You are not at fault," he starts. Then says as much to Josy as to me, "Decades have passed since our experience. Medicine and technology have improved. The best medical team will care for our *Trésor*. I promise we will get through this with a positive outcome."

Since only one or two people could see her at a time in the ICU, we decided Josy and Guy would go first. I returned to the waiting room to fill the others in on the details.

No sooner had I opened the door than everyone spoke at once asking about Leonie. My heart swelled at their love and concern. Guy was right, we'd make it together.

* * *

"BONJOUR MONSIEUR STEELE," Dr. Berger says as he crosses the room to shake my hand.

I rise to greet him, but continue to hold Leonie's hand. I'm not letting her go for even a moment. My mother could barely persuade me to shower and change.

"Doctor Berger, good morning," I respond, noticing the rest of his team as they file in behind him. I nod in greeting. Then return to my seat, scanning Leonie's face for a reaction.

I realize she's still under heavy sedation, but I know she

can hear. I squeeze her hand to let her know I'm not going anywhere.

"We have good news."

My head jerks up when I hear Dr. Berger's statement.

"From what the tests show, Mademoiselle Beaulieu and your baby are progressing positively. We will wake her from under sedation now."

"Thank you, Doctor Berger! I'm sure her parent will want to be present. They just stepped outside for some fresh air. I'll call them now," I respond as I pull my mobile from my jeans pocket excitedly.

The doctor speaks with his team while we wait for Josy and Guy to arrive. Shortly, they burst through the door, their elation palpable. Josy hurries to my side and takes my hand, smiling up at me. Guy stands beside her and greets the doctor.

The anesthesiologist steps forward and administers the drug through the IV. Guy and I watch him intently—no mistakes allowed.

Josy joins us as we expel a collective sigh of relief when Leonie's eyelids flutter and she licks her lips. I say a silent prayer of thanks.

The doctor and a nurse tend to her while we stand to the side. I hate the lack of control I have over the situation. I feel responsible and useless. Only able to wait for others to take care of my responsibilities. My eyes drift to Leonie's still flat belly beneath the covers.

Wow. My baby is inside of her, growing stronger every day. I'm in awe of Leonie. She and our child will want for nothing. I will use every ounce of my power to protect and to provide for them. Mine!

My mobile vibrates. A quick glance at the screen shows

it's my mother. While still keeping my eyes trained on Leonie's face, I back from the bed slightly to answer.

"Roger! Honey! We're in the waiting room. Sebastian saw the doctor and his team walk by! What's happening?"

No one returned to the US. Instead, we commandeered the waiting room, turning it into our base. Once again, Luc used his sway to arrange cots and comfortable chairs, tables and power strips, and a catered food area. They gave us access to the staff locker room facilities—although I use the bathroom in Leonie's suite. The locker room is too far for me, even if it is only one floor below us.

"Leonie and our baby are fine, Mom," I respond. "The anesthesiologist is waking her up now."

The joyous scream from Lola is deafening. My mother has the call on speaker so all in the waiting room could hear. The sound carried over my phone despite not being on speaker. The doctor and everyone in the suite peer at me, and I shrug. Then disconnect the call after I promise to call them when she awakens.

"Rrr... Rog... Roger?"

ROGER

"*P*regnant? I'm pregnant? Are you sure? This makes little sense... You must be mistaken..."

Leonie's voice trails off as she tries to make sense of what Dr. Berger tells her.

She's been awake for an hour and started asking what happened as soon as she realized she was in the hospital. But the doctor thought it best to allow Leonie time to adjust from the sedation reversal before answering her questions. Her parents and I agreed.

Instead, the doctor monitored her vitals, and the nurses helped her to use the bathroom and to shower. I had to hold back a possessive growl when Leonie's gown dipped dangerously low, almost revealing her full breast. It was bad enough the outlines of her plump nipples poked against the thin material.

Even half out of it, Leonie glanced at me and with a shake of her head reached to adjust the negligible garment.

I preferred to care for her, particularly the bathing part. But I let it go for now. I don't want to jar her or cause any discomfort. However, I sent a text message to Lola to request some more suitable loungewear delivered from her lingerie boutique pronto.

Dr. Berger gave the all clear for Leonie to eat. So, Lucien called her favorite restaurant of his and ordered a variety of dishes for her. The tantalizing aroma of lobster bisque, consommé, steak frites, and roast chicken with boiled vegetables filled the room. I haven't had a decent meal in two days, so whatever she doesn't eat, I'll finish!

Now, both of us—rather all three of us sated—Dr. Berger smiles at Leonie.

"*Oui*, Mademoiselle Beaulieu. You are most definitely pregnant. I estimate eight weeks, in fact."

Leonie's gorgeous amber eyes widen, and she peeks at me from beneath her long eyelashes.

"But I'm on birth control. I... I didn't do this on purpose. I'm sorry," she whispers as tears glisten in her eyes.

I reel from her words. My mind tries to find answers.

On purpose? Why the hell would I think she got pregnant on purpose? I may be a multibillionaire. But Leonie comes from a wealthy Parisian family that dates back to the eighteenth century and the royal court. Plus, she's a multimillionaire on her own from her modeling career.

Could it be she doesn't want a baby? Or she doesn't want a baby with me??

Fuck!

I draw on my ability to control, to reign in my emotions.

"Sorry?? What are you sorry about, Leonie?"

"Please allow me to address your birth control," Dr. Berger intercedes. "Birth control is not infallible. Medications like antibiotics or not taking the birth control at the same time consistently or other factors can impede its effectiveness."

Leonie nods, still stricken.

"When did your last menses occur?" He asks.

She thinks for a moment as she leans back against the pillows.

"It ended before Roger and I went to the South of France two months ago," Leonie responds.

"Well, that aligns with the tests. Now, I must inform you of your options. Should you wish to not move forward with your preg—"

"*Mais bien sûr!*" Leonie roars like a lioness protective of her cub as she places her hand on her belly.

"Leonie please!" I growl, unable to contain my caveman instincts to protect what's mine.

We shout at the same time and stare at each other. I take a second to realize she wants to have my baby. Thank fuck!

"Oh Roger, you do want to have a baby with me!" She cries, relieved.

* * *

I BUNDLE her onto my lap and bury my face in her silky hair. I take a deep inhale of her scent, the classic sultry perfume Dior's Pure Poison's blend of florals with amber and musk fills my nostrils. Mine!

Quietly, the door of the suite clicks closed. Dr. Berger left us for privacy.

Leonie's tears dampen the front of my long-sleeved t-shirt. I rock her in my arms and croon words of love and forever. They rumble from my chest to hers; the calming vibration eases the tension as Leonie melts against me.

"Of course I want to have a baby with you, my precious love. We are having our baby and any others. You are mine, Leonie Beaulieu, as are your children. All mine to love, cherish, and protect forever. You have nothing to be sorry for, sweetheart."

She nods, but my wet shirt muffles her response since she pressed her mouth against it.

I ease back and cradle her face in one of my hands as the other continues to hold her in my firm embrace.

"I love you so much, Roger. But I'm scared... The bleeding, that's not normal... My... My mother's—"

I cover her lips with my fingertips and shake my head.

"We will not speak of the past, only of our future. Your father and I promise we will provide the best medical and technology available. Luc found Dr. Berger, and he is the absolute top in the field of OB-GYN in all of France. This hospital scores the highest rating; Luc is the major benefactor. All you need to do is relax and enjoy your pregnancy. You maintain the support of our families and friends."

I pull back to stare at her intensely, "Do you understand?"

Leonie acknowledges my Alpha male in control and responds yes. As she peers up at me, Leonie's amber eyes glow with the fire inside of her stoked once again. My *Lion* is back.

* * *

"OH, Lola, don't cry, *Chérie*! We're fine."

Leonie smiles and pats her belly lovingly to reassure her best friend as they sit on our bed under a cashmere throw.

"Don't worry, *mon amie!*"

Dr. Berger discharged Leonie earlier this morning with orders for a month of activity restriction, no stress, and to monitor for cramps or excessive bleeding after sexual activity.

I could barely look the doctor in the eye when he mentioned the sex part. Fuck me if my big dick didn't hurt my baby, or rather babies... We may just have to pause on the lovemaking...

The news of my cock hitting her cervix caused the bleeding surprised Leonie—not the best when a woman is in the early stages of pregnancy. She peeked at me to gauge my reaction.

Since I already knew, I maintained a neutral face. No need for me to freak her out, even if I was still recovering from the news.

I stared at the doctor to avoid her questioning gaze. So, she returned her attention to Dr. Berger's commentary. Inwardly, I sighed with relief. The plan is to avoid that conversation as much as possible.

Now, we're home in our penthouse. As soon as my head was on straight, I had all of Leonie's pertinent belongings moved here. A closet company reconfigured two of the guest rooms to accommodate her vast wardrobe.

How many handbags, shoes, and little black dresses can one woman own?? Sure she's a model who's given tons of clothes and stuff, but damn.

Most of Leonie's toiletries and such were already in our bathroom. When she's up to it, we can go to her duplex to get her personal items. For the time being, I had her photo albums put in the family room. Then set up another room as her studio for painting and sketching. Since she needs to cut back on activities, I arranged for the start date of her full-time position as a project designer delayed until further notice. So I made an office for her from another room.

The floor-through penthouse below the one my siblings use just became available. My parents agreed to move into that unit so I could expand mine into a triplex with their current floor. My hope is the project will preoccupy Leonie, and she won't be pissed I delayed her job at STEELE. Besides, we need room for our growing family.

The thought makes me smile. But even though I told Leonie not to think of the past, I can't help visions of her mother's experience from lurking in the back of my mind. I pray we don't go through the same hellish struggle.

"I know, but you scared the absolute shit out of me, Leonie!"

Lola's exclamation brings me back to the bedroom.

"The blood stood so bright against the stark white..." Lola trails off as she shudders and hugs herself, tears shimmering in her hazel eyes.

"Babe, Leonie and the baby are fine. Don't stress her out," Sebastian says as he stands beside Lola and rubs her back to soothe his wife.

The platinum wedding band glints on his ring finger.

Which reminds me, I didn't have the chance to complete my proposal to Leonie. She hasn't mentioned me being on one knee at the restaurant. So I wonder if she remembers. Nor did she respond one way or the other when the hospital staff referred to me as her fiancé.

Regardless, tonight I plan to rectify the situation. Tomorrow will not dawn without Leonie wearing my ring. My woman, my baby, my ring—mine.

"Sebastian is right, Lola! Only happy thoughts," my mother adds from the sofa by the window as she wraps her arm around Josy's shoulders.

Josy nods and says, "*Oui, chérie!* This is a time of joy and celebration!"

Our fathers agree and decree only the best care for Leonie and their grandchild.

"*Absolument!*" Luc concurs.

Almost everyone surrounds Leonie. She sits like a queen holding court as though in her private chambers in Versailles. Our bedroom may not be as ornate. But we added a sofa and some chairs to the existing loveseat and bench to accommodate her visitors. The spacious room provides ample footage.

Vases filled with flagrant flowers sit on almost every surface here and throughout our penthouse from Malcolm, Harris, Haley, Lucien, Blair, Joel, and Hettie. Before they flew back to the US, Starr, Billie, and Patrick dropped by with more bouquets and well wishes.

We kept the media from finding out since we were in a private room at the restaurant. Other patrons could not see who the medics rushed from the establishment. The restaurant and hospital staffs, bound by solid nondisclosure agreements, cannot disclose anything.

Our lives are private and will remain so. The less fodder given to the media, the better. As with most old money families, the Steeles and Beaulieus like media coverage to further our business gains, but prefer intimate aspects to remain private.

"Yes, we will celebrate our blessing and ensure the best care for mommy and baby."

I declare as I place my hand on top of Leonie's resting on her belly and smile affectionately.

"*Oui, Mon Cœur*," Leonie purrs as she cups my face.

"But first…"

I lower to one knee beside the bed as I remove the little navy blue velvet box out of my jeans pocket. Then open it as I take a deep breath and pray nothing interrupts me this time.

With Leonie's left hand held in my grasp, I say the words that have burned on my tongue for months.

"Leonie Beaulieu, I love you with all of my heart, body, and soul. You mean more to me than anything in this world. I want us to spend the rest of eternity together. Marry me, my love."

Leonie sits stunned. Then tears pop out of the corners of her gorgeous amber eyes as she chokes back a sob.

The twenty-five carat Asscher cut diamond ring set in platinum is a sight to behold. So I expect her shock. The exquisite beauty has as much fire in it as our spark-filled relationship.

The ring is a family heirloom given to one of my paternal great-great-grandmothers as a gift to commemorate the birth of an heir. I chose it from the family's collection for that very reason and explain its provenance to Leonie as I place the impressive ring on her finger.

"*Oh, Mon Chéri, c'est exquis, merci...*" She murmurs in awe.

"Oh, don't you just love the Steele men and how they just expect you'll say yes without waiting to put their ring on it!"

Lola's remark makes everyone laugh as she hugs her best friend.

"There can be no other answer, babe!" Sebastian chuckles, not embarrassed by his alpha tendencies.

"Definitely not!" I add before I kiss Leonie silly.

"Let her get some air already!" Haley exclaims as she pushes me out of the way to hug Leonie. "Congratulations, sister! Now I have two to balance the four beasts... Um, I mean brothers!"

"Whatever, baby girl," Malcolm jabs as he leans in to hug Leonie, too. "Now, we have two more busybodies to watch after!"

"Yeah, youngin, respect your elders!" Harris adds despite being only a few minutes older than his fraternal twin. "Welcome to the family officially, Leonie!"

"Yes, welcome, sister!" Sebastian adds as he moves our siblings out of the way to hug Leonie. "And welcome to you, our Little One!"

Leonie laughs as he pats her belly.

"Thank you so much!" She says smiling as she glances around the room at our loved ones.

When her gaze returns to mine, I grin with my eyes full of love.

LEONIE

"**W**hoop, whoop! Don't hate! We've got the best rings ever!"

Roger has been insistent I rest and relax. So for almost two weeks, he has only allowed me to move about the penthouse. No lifting, no carrying, no sudden moves, no sex...

He sensed I was about to lose it and booked my favorite spa to cater to my every need. To make sure no one disturbed me, he reserved the spa exclusively for Lola, Blair, Hettie, and me.

Lola's gleeful outburst bounces off the walls, overpowering the peaceful music playing in the tranquility room of the spa. I can't help but laugh as she bounces and shimmies in the plush suede chair. She waves her left hand causing not only her engagement ring to sparkle, but her hand harness, too. Both have ginormous diamonds that glitter in the light.

I gaze adoringly at my gigantic ring and smile like the Cheshire Cat. Not one to boast, but... Gotdamn!

I recall Elizabeth Taylor's response when Princess Margaret proclaimed the actress' Krupp Diamond ring, she dubbed My Baby, as "very vulgar;" "Yes, ain't it great?"

Well, my ring is like it, only eight carats smaller than the famous one Princess Margaret hated on.

I tell Lola the story, and we titter as we do our happy dance. The Elizabeth who was famous for her astounding jewelry collection is her icon and inspired her to create Lola's Coterie. So it overjoyed her when Sebastian gave her an engagement ring, a tad bit smaller and in the same emerald cut as her idol's Ice Skating Rink ring. Another Steele heirloom piece.

"Your rings are beyond stunning," Blair sighs as she holds my hand in hers to gaze upon the sparkler. "What woman wouldn't want a flawless rock on her finger? I mean, you're both will zillionaires. Who would expect any less?"

Hettie laughs and quips, "Right! Give me vulgar any day of the week, month, year, princess! Now go sip some haterade from a golden, jewel-encrusted chalice, honey!"

Our laughter turns into snorts and guffaws until tears roll down our reddened cheeks.

After I catch my breath, I turn to Hettie.

"You and Joel have been dating for a few years now and living together. Do you want to get married?"

Joel met Roger at a business function some years ago. Outside of his family, Joel is Roger's closest friend. In the time they've known each other, Joel began a relationship with Hettie. They too met because of business. He's an investor in real estate, and she's an attorney who specializes in commercial property law. They share a half-through flat in The STEELE Tower Paris a few floors below Roger and me.

Hettie stares at the bubbling, layered-stone fountain in the center of the room. The hypnotic sound of the splashing water captivates her while she ponders my question.

For a moment, I sense I struck upon a sensitive topic and wish I hadn't asked. Hettie and I have been friends for only a few months after Roger introduced us at dinner with Joel. Since then, Hettie and I have gone shopping and had lunch a few times. Perhaps it's too soon for personal probing. But I'm so used to sharing relationship details with my other girlfriends, that I didn't think twice about asking Hettie.

"We have. He claims we 'have a good thing going... As it is. No signs of marriage on our horizon. I'm way too young to commit for the rest of my life.'"

She sighs and glances at the rest of us. Then continues.

"I, on the other hand, would like to get married and start a family before I turn thirty-three in two years. Hell, Joel acts like he's in his twenties. He'll be thirty-six in a few months!"

We nod encouragingly and offer her words of support.

"If Sebastian *Alpha Playboy* Steele can settle down, Joel can too! Just give him some time," Lola says.

I smile and add, "Billie's adage 'why pay for the cow if you can get the milk for free?' Might give you a hint of what to do to encourage Joel to put a ring on it... Move out or at least not be as readily available to him. Give him reason to miss you, if you know what I mean."

Blair claps and bobs her head repeatedly.

"Exactly! I found the more attention I paid to Luc and the more I made myself accessible, the less he responded to me. It's a man's nature to chase and conquer, you know..."

Although not as forthcoming with their relationship, Lola and I surmise Luc and Blair are a steady if not committed couple. Luc being the refined *duc* never discusses his intimate relationships with us. Blair has taken on his trait and keeps mum, too.

We also know Luc's concern with their age difference. He's seventeen years older than Blair. Despite being in his early fifties, the super sexy *Renard Argenté* continues to turn heads. His deep blue eyes glitter like sapphires. Black hair with some gray sprinkled in it adds to his distinguished appearance. His body remains fit with regular workouts and healthy eating. The nickname Lola and I gave to Luc goes beyond appropriate for the attractive, fifty-one-year-old man.

It's only heightened Blair interest in Luc. She's not at all put off by his age. Obviously, she learned her lesson and cut back on the shameless flirting she did before they dated.

Hettie ponders our words, then sits up straight, throwing her shoulders back.

"You're right! Joel was a lot more attentive before I moved in with him. He always popped around my flat with pastries for breakfast or a bottle of wine and popcorn for a night of Netflix. Funny enough, my sub-tenant just finished their lease and moved out last week. I haven't had a chance to let it. It's a sign!"

She throws her head back and laughs.

"Just as I believe in *un coupe de foudre,* I believe in signs and all point to you getting your ring sooner than you thought!" I giggle.

"Go, girl!" Lola whoops.

"Yay you!" Blair adds, giving Hettie a high five.

We chat some more while we finish a light lunch of salads and citrus-infused water the staff brought us after our last treatment.

"Pardon me, mesdames, but are you ready for your next sessions?"

The general manager's question cuts into our conversation.

We've had body polishes, waxing, aromatherapy, reflexology, and massages. Now it's time for manicures and pedicures. Dutifully, we troop behind our aestheticians to yet another room.

I peek at My Baby engagement ring as I place my hand on My Baby belly and smile. I'm thankful for a man who loves me and who's not afraid to commit to me and to our child. My smile widens when my "vulgar" ring blings as the wall sconces catch it in their light.

"I SWEAR, Leonie, you're glowing and I don't think it's from the facial. Hot Momma Alert!"

Hettie laughs as she wets her finger and sizzles it against her hip.

"*Merci!* I do feel a whole lot better now," I respond, my tinkling laughter joining hers.

"Yeah, you gave us a major scare. But we'll only talk about positive things! 'Positive vibes,' as Starr says!" Lola chimes in.

Blair turns to Lola, "And what about you, missy? When are you popping out a mini Sebastian?"

Lola amber eyes widen and she puts her hands up to ward off Blair's questions and shakes her raven-haired head vehemently.

"Bite your tongue, Blair! I hadn't planned on a relationship and look what happened! I'm thankful, yes. But Sebastian and I are nowhere near being ready for kids. For now, Lola's Coterie is my baby and STEELE is his!"

We laugh at her dramatic reaction.

"So, bestie, you don't want to be pregnant at the same time as me? How much fun—"

"Don't you dare put the whammy on me, Leonie Beaulieu! I mean it! Stop laughing at me!" Lola screeches.

The rest of us laugh so hard, we nearly fall out of our chairs as we wait for our nails to dry. Lola glares at each of us before she cracks up at her hysteria.

My mobile vibrates in my robe pocket, interrupting our taunts. Roger insisted I keep it near so he could easily reach me. I know he's putting on a brave face for me. But he's just as concerned as I about my mother's experience. Neither of us wants to face such pain. So I didn't argue about his request.

"Ciao, *Mon Chéri!*" I answer in a chirpy voice. No need to add to his worry.

He breathes a sigh of relief before he responds, "Ciao, my love. How are you doing? Are the sessions okay? The general manager assured me the treatments are safe for pregnant women. According to the schedule she sent to me, you should almost be done. Are your nails dry? Should I have Eric bring the car around to pick you up now? He's just—"

"*Mon Cœur*, take a breath! We're fine! Don't worry," I say to stop his drilling. "Yes, we're drying our nails. But I'm not ready to leave just yet. I'll call you ten minutes before. Okay, *Mon Chéri?*"

Roger sits in silence for a second, then agrees.

"Aw, he's so concerned. How sweet!" Lola says as I put the mobile back in my pocket. "Roger *The Responsible!*"

"*Oui*, so responsible, he delayed my start date at STEELE for the 'unforeseeable future' without asking me..." I grumble with a frown. "Then tells me he has a project to keep me busy once I feel up to it... Morgan and Shelley are moving into the penthouse below the one you and Sebastian are in. We're going to take over their old one. I get to manage the combination of the two penthouses into a triplex..."

Lola fidgets and avoids my eyes.

"What? Spit it out, Lola Steele!" I demand, sensing my best friend knows something she isn't sharing with me.

She defers her answer in favor of adjusting her topknot to get it just so...

"Spill it now, Lola..." I repeat, pinning her with my most fierce glare.

She snaps to attention and mumbles under her breath.

"What? You know we can't hear you, Lola!" I exclaim as I lose patience with her stall tactics.

"Okay... Okay already! Baz mentioned Roger being adamant to push back your start date when you were under sedation. I agreed it was a good idea."

She raises her hand to stop me as I interrupt.

"You do not understand how frazzled Roger was... He wouldn't let anyone take you out of his arms... He tried to bogart a nurse to get into the emergency room... He was inconsolable... Morgan and Shelley were so concerned. But Roger regained control as soon as the ER doctor explained you were pregnant and the bleeding was normal."

Lola lets me absorb her words. Then she continues.

"Remember, he's the one out of all the siblings who's the most in control—the most straight and narrow. He had zero control over your and your baby's wellbeing. He got his shit together pronto, though. So cut him some slack, sweetie."

Tears well in my eyes. I had no idea. Roger has said

nothing, and I'm sure he told everyone not to mention it. He keeps saying he only wants me to be happy and to have a healthy stress-free pregnancy. I cannot ask for anything more.

However, I can do something for him...

ROGER

"Why hello there, Monsieur Steele."

Leonie's seductive purr draws my attention away from the paperwork I have in front of me. My eyes nearly fall out of my head when I gaze up to find her leaning against the doorframe of my home office. Her voluptuous body on display for my hungry eyes.

Barely there red stretch-tulle embroidered with flowers and satin trim for a bra and matching panties set peeks out from beneath a red satin floor-length robe. The plump nipples of her fuller breasts poke against the lace like succulent dark berries, begging for my mouth to engulf them.

Leonie's belly may still be flat. But her hips flare, and my hands itch to clutch them as I pound into her tight, wet pussy.

Her long, shapely legs ending in fuck-me mules are the perfect length to wrap around my neck...

Fuck!

My cock grows along my thigh as it hardens inside of my gray sweatpants. Thankfully, the soft material allows for stretch. However, the crewneck collar of my black t-shirt feels like it's choking me. The temperature in the room increases, and my skin heats.

I shake my head to clear the instant lust that shoots through every fiber in my being for my mate.

No, calm down, boy. I can't harm her and our baby again.

She saunters into the room, exaggerating the sway of her hips, then stands before my desk akimbo. I have to grip the edge until my knuckles turn white. It's the only thing I can do to keep from jumping up and throwing her over my shoulder to carry her off to our bedroom and ravish her.

Damn! Two weeks and no Leonie, and I'm at my breaking point.

Get it together Steele... Your woman and your child first, caveman.

"*Amoureux*, I want to thank you for treating my girls and me to a wonderful spa day. They pampered me and drained all tension. Except for one," she purrs as she trails her long red fingernail over her shimmery caramel-colored skin. My ring on her finger sets sparks off in the light.

I gulp when she pinches her right nipple between her fingertips and mewls. Her amber eyes narrow to slits as she whimpers from the pain in the pleasure. My dick jumps.

Breathlessly she says, "I know you're busy catching up with work. But I wanted to let you know just how thankful I am for your thoughtfulness, *Amoureux*..."

Leonie's voice trails off as she sashays around my desk and squeezes between it and my chair. Then slides the paperwork off to the side before she plops her lush ass on top. My eyes trail up her thighs, riveted to the wet patch on her panties. The scent of her arousal wafts up to fill my nostrils and stokes my inner caveman desires.

Fuck. Me.

"You don't mind, do you, *Amoureux?*" She asks with hooded eyes as she uses the tip of her nail to lift my chin.

My stormy gray orbs meet her golden amber gaze. I'm fucking captured by her spell. Captured.

"*Oui ou non?*"

She whispers in my ear as her long nail scrapes along the cleft in my chin. Her warm breath combined with the rasping sound as her nail goes across my five o'clock shadow is the last straw. I shudder from the effort to keep my hands gripping the armrests of my chair and not her ass. I ache to scoop her up and ram my fat, long cock inside of her wet, tight pussy.

Again, I shake my head.

That's what caused her to bleed, jerk! No!

"No, Leonie. I mean yes... I do mind," I say as I stand.

Before I can stride away, she wraps her legs around my waist and pulls me back in place.

"Roger, you do not understand how my hormones are raging... I need you. I need you inside of me, *Amoureux... S'il vous pla"t.*"

Trapped, I cannot resist her siren's call. But I must try...

"Leonie, my love, are you sure? I'm afraid to harm you and our ba—"

She cuts off my words as she covers my mouth with hers. The intensity of the passion in her kiss blows my mind. It obliterates all fear. I give in. But I will not lose control.

To temper my rampant desire, I take the reins. I cup her face in my hands as I tilt it to just the right angle and tangle my tongue with hers. She tastes like the iced lemon ginger tea she's started drinking instead of her Réserve Jean de Lillet Blanc.

Her soft purrs as I dominate her lioness make pre-cum bead on the tip of my dick.

As though Leonie is telepathic, her small hand slides over my rock-hard, six-pack abs to slip under my waistband and encircle my throbbing cock. The girth won't allow her fingers to touch. But the long, pressured strokes she applies more than make up for any shortcomings.

I groan into her mouth when she pinches the leaking slit. My entire body poised for release. Not yet.

My hands travel over her full mounds to heft their extra weight. More than a handful, and my hands are sizable. Perfectly mouthwateringly plump.

When I tweak her nipples at the same time, she growls and arches her back. Yes, her buds have become sensitive because of her pregnancy. I roll the distended tips between my fingers. Leonie moans as she scoots forward to the edge of the desk, tugging my cock free of my sweatpants.

It bounces against my abs just below my navel. Losing her warm hand amplified by the cool air.

Leonie stops our entwining tongues and peers at me from beneath her long eyelashes.

"*Amoureux*, I ache for you," she pleads with hooded amber orbs.

I tease her pussy seam through the soaked stretch-tulle as I watch her face to witness her in the throes of ecstasy. Her eyes close.

"Open your eyes, Pretty Kitty. I want to see your pleasure mount," I command.

She complies and leans back on her hands as she widens her thighs to give me better access.

I slip two thick digits beneath her slick panties and coat them with her essence for a natural lubricant. Once they're fully covered and Leonie writhes on the desk begging for more, I slide them inside of her pussy. The gentle strokes brush against her G-spot, and she cries out in bliss.

"Oooh, Roger... So good... So good," she pants.

"I know, Kitten. I'm going to make it so good for you, I promise," I croon.

My fingers move inside of her wet warmth. Then I scissor them to prepare her pussy for my cock. She rocks against the base of my palm, soaking it with her juices as an orgasm steamrolls towards her. I speed up my pace, alternating the rhythm, then admonish Leonie when her eyelids shutter. She jerks her head, and her gaze return to mine.

"Good girl, Kitten," I praise her as I pinch her engorged clit. "Cum for me."

Leonie breaks beautifully for me. Her body quivers as a sheen of sweat glistens on her skin, and she keens in untamed pleasure.

My wild cat purrs as I continue to stroke her pussy, bringing her down from her climax gently. Her soft cries drive me to the edge again.

I rein it in and kiss her passionately.

She wraps her hand around my dick and scoots almost off of the desk to line her pussy up with my bulbous head slippery with pre-cum.

When the tip enters her wet, warm channel, we both groan. Thirteen days, seventeen hours, thirty-eight minutes, and we're finally as one again.

The sensation as I stretch her with my girth makes me hiss. Then growl when she contracts the muscles of her inner walls. Her greedy pussy pulls me in deeper, almost to my base.

Fuuuck!

I gather the strength to withdraw before I hit her cervix. I remain ever mindful—Roger *The Responsible* Steele...

"Mmm mmm... *Non*," Leonie whines, saddened by the unexpected loss of contact.

I ease back in as I pluck her breasts out of the bra to rest atop the soft cups. Her fully aroused nipples beckon to me. I lick one of the tips. Then suckle it into my mouth, surrounding it with heat as her pussy gushes around my dick.

"Ooooo... Oh!" Leonie coos, then cries out as I nip her sweet bud.

My hips flex to drive short and long strokes of my cock at a leisurely pace. The pace ensures she feels the velvety steel texture and every inch of my pulsating dick as it grazes her inner walls. I shift the angle to dive deeper. But avoid the delicate entrance to her womb.

We lose ourselves in the sensuous dance of the ages. A sexual thrall overtakes us as we reach an unchartered level of cloud nine simultaneously.

A spine-tingling sensation shoots through my body and jets out my dick as I spew more of my seed inside of Leonie. The amount so copious I could impregnate her all over again if it were a possibility.

"Rogeerrr! *Mon Dieu!*" She screams, my name falling from her lips repeatedly as I take us over the edge.

"Take it... Take all of me... Fuuuckkk!" I bellow as I throw my head back and roar my release, my body shuddering from the force.

I collapse back into my chair with Leonie straddling my hips, still bound together.

The sound of our heavy pants and the smell of our carnal sex permeate the room. I close my eyes to revel in our blissful connection as I stroke Leonie's back. She nuzzles her face into my neck and sighs. Neither of us is inclined to move. So we rest.

. . .

"I KNOW when you made me pregnant."

My hand pauses with the fork of jerk chicken and steamed vegetables halfway to mouth. I glance at Leonie across the table in the dining room.

After we soaked in the bathtub, we heated up two Anita Green's delicious and healthy prepared meals. Leonie's no cook, and I don't have the inclination to waste time in the kitchen. So we either go out to eat, order in, or eat the meals.

Anita is Norman Green's—my boxing trainer and STEELE business partner—wife. Along with being a highly followed yoga instructor with a flourishing practice, Anita recently finished culinary school at Le Cordon Bleu. Then started a meal plan delivery service.

Norman is a former world heavyweight champion for nine years straight. When I met him at STEELE Las Vegas after his last bout in the ring, I offered him the opportunity to open chains of branded gyms through our Entertainment Properties Division. One for underprivileged youth and another as exclusive elite training facilities for the über-wealthy and star athletes. He accepted and took me on as his first private client.

Norman added Anita's customized plans to the paid offerings of the elite facilities and complimentary healthy snacks to the youth. She also took over the food services in both chains. They rank as the most popular couple in the fitness world.

I have to put the tasty morsel back on my plate and sit back to stare at Leonie.

"How do you know?" I ask.

A beatific smile spreads across her glowing face—Anita

designed a meal plan specifically for the nourishment of a mother and growing child as Leonie's meals.

"It was during the night we spent in Cannes," she says triumphantly as she rubs her belly.

I cock my head and think back on that unforgettable night of passion.

"Oh, baby... You feel so fucking good... So hot and wet..." I grunt with pleasure.

Leonie writhes beneath me with her wrists bound to the headboard above her. She pulls against the silk restraints fruitlessly as her fists clench and unclench. I can tell she needs more.

I move one hand from her hip to place my thumb in her slack mouth. Without hesitation, she suckles it eagerly. Once it's sopping wet, I pull it from her mouth with a pop and sit back on my haunches. Still connected, I lift Leonie up to settle her on top of my muscular thighs.

In this position, I have better access to her luscious body. My lips trail down the length of her elegant neck to wrap around one of her pebbled nipples. At the same time, I pull her round ass cheek aside to expose her puckered hole. Then press the pad of my wet thumb against her back entrance. The painful pleasure makes her tighten the muscles in her pussy and ass. I grunt from the force on my throbbing cock.

I plunder her bottom hole with my well lubricated thumb and use my powerful thighs to pump my dick up into her greedy little pussy.

"Aaahhh!" Leonie screams.

Her back bows, and she keens as each thrust hits the end of her channel. I can feel her pussy walls flutter as an orgasm peaks. She rides me fervently to reach her impending climax.

"Fuuuck... Leoonnieee!" I roar as her release triggers mine with a blinding jolt down my spine to my balls and out the tip of my dick.

Inside of her, my shaft swells impossibly larger, bumping into her cervix before hot ropes of my seed bathe her womb. Another wave crests over us as we continue to pound our bodies driven by the innate need to mate. Our frenzy desire to sate our carnal needs.

When the last drop of my life-giving essence flows from my body to Leonie's, we fall to the bed. No longer having the strength to maintain our position. Fully drained, we lie on the bed in a state of bliss.

"I love you, Leonie Beaulieu," I murmur in a voice thick with emotion as I brush my lips against her temple.

She lifts her head from my sweat-soaked chest where my heart beats in sync with hers to gaze into my eyes. I nuzzle my cheek into her palm as she strokes my face and rubs her thumb across my lower lip.

"I love you, Roger Steele." She says in a voice hoarse from her screams of mind-blowing pleasure.

I kiss her fingertip and cradle her head back against my heart before we fall asleep.

"Huh, you think? Well, it was most definitely intense. Damn," I respond as I shift in my chair to reposition my enlarging cock. "I guess you can say my most caveman-like moment."

I tease as I squat beside Leonie and cover her belly with my large hand.

"Mine!" I state possessively as I kiss first her lips, then my baby. "How are you, Lil Cub?"

Leonie giggles and runs her fingers through my collar-length ebony hair. She massages my scalp and sighs.

I glance up at her. Then straighten when I see her amber eyes glisten with tears.

"What, baby? What's the matter? Does something hurt?" I ask, holding back the panic.

Leonie shakes her head, her waist-length mahogany hair falls over her face like a wavy curtain. I brush it back and cup her chin to force her gaze to mine.

"Tell me," I command.

She takes a deep shuddering breath, closes her eyes, then reopens them to respond.

"I… I want everything to be okay…. And not worry you or anyone else…"

My heart aches. I pull Leonie from her chair and cradle her on my lap as I re-take my seat.

"Hush, baby. It's all right. You and our baby are fine. You're not worrying anyone and especially not me," I murmur.

She tilts her tear-soaked face to gaze into my eyes, studying me.

"If anything should happen, Roger, promise me you will take care of our baby."

What the everlasting fuck?!

No way am I going to allow that to pass.

"Leonie, understand me clearly. If for any reason I have to choose between you and this baby or any other, I choose you always. You mean everything to me. We can try for another baby, or we can adopt a baby in need of a wonderful home. But you… You are irreplaceable, my love. Call me selfish. But I will not live without you, Leonie."

She speaks. But I cut her off with a firm shake of my head. I don't give a damn how harsh it may sound. But it's the damn truth.

"No! This is nonnegotiable. And we will not speak of such things ever again. Do you understand?"

Leonie nods, still sad.

"Words, Leonie. I will have your words," I demand.

She takes some time to consider.

I feel her body stiffen, and she sits up tall. The surrounding energy vibrates anew. Then Leonie stares me straight in the eye with a fiercely determined expression.

"*Oui*, Roger. You are right, *Mon Cœur*. We will move forward from this moment on with only positive thoughts and words of love. You are the most responsible person I know"—she smiles brightly as she strokes my cheek—"But we will share the responsibility of our blessing together. I don't want you to think you have to be strong for both of us. I will not neglect your needs either."

Tears blur my vision as my heart soars with so much love for this woman of mine. She gets me like no one else. I couldn't have asked for a better woman. I chide myself when I recall the awful words I said to her when we had the horrible argument in Cabo San Lucas. The one that pushed her past her limits and drove her out of my arms.

"Leonie, you were 'clear' with me on the jet. Now let me be clear with you. I want a serious-minded partner and not a wayward woman who cannot stay focused for over five minutes. You consistently flit around and avoid your studies. Coming up with excuse after lame excuse. You want people to respect you. But you cannot respect yourself."

I give a silent prayer of thanks she forgave me and we understand one another better. I shake my head to banish the offensive words—'only positive thoughts!' Now here we are engaged to be married with a growing family.

"Well, since you decided to delay my start at STEELE... I may as well start the penthouse makeover project and not remain idle any longer," Leonie says, drawing me from my musings.

I kiss her arched eyebrow, and she giggles as she swats me away.

"Seriously, Roger! You caveman! From now on, we

discuss things as a couple before we make decisions," she admonishes me. "But, *Mon Chéri*, you are correct again. I'm not quite up to a hectic schedule."

Leonie pauses and stares at me with skittish eyes.

"Not that I'm flitting around or making any excuses! *Non*! I want the position!" She cries with her hand over her heart as a vow.

I throw my head back and laugh uproariously. Yeah, Leonie and I are on the same wavelength!

How can it get any better?!

LEONIE

$\mathcal{I}$ keep telling myself I told Roger not to worry, and we'd only have positive thoughts going forward. But I'm still nervous to hear what Dr. Berger will say after he examines me this morning. It's been just over a month since my graduation celebratory dinner.

My stomach still knots whenever I think about what happened. I can't help it.

Just like now as I stand in the all white, Carrara marble and glass walk-in shower. The temperate water sluices all over my body from the multiple jets. Even though it's big enough to hold four and the calming scent of lavender wafts around me, I feel claustrophobic.

I lean my forehead against one of the glass walls and close my eyes. My lips move in a silent prayer: the safety of our baby like a mantra. I finish with deep breaths like Starr taught me during our last Skype yoga session.

She designed a prenatal program with guidance from Dr. Berger and told him she would act as my doula during delivery. We meet six days a week for an hour. The sessions include asanas, pranayama, meditation, and yoga *nidra*. The yogic breathing I've done in other classes. But I never tried yogic sleep.

Starr insisted it would relieve stress by placing me in a sleep state during which she would guide me in mediation. The first time we tried yoga *nidra*, I didn't only "reach a deep level of relaxation." But fell asleep, then woke myself with my loud snoring!

I smile as I think of my health and wellbeing focused friend. The worry lifts—just a little...

"What's so funny, Kitten?"

A shiver runs through me despite the warm water as Roger's huge hands slide along my flanks and hips to cover my belly. My belly that's no longer flat as a washboard. Our baby has made itself known by pushing my tummy out to make room.

I place my smaller hands over his and melt into his loving embrace. His strength seeps into every cell of my body to center me better than all the eight limbs of yoga combined.

"I'm thinking of Starr and how I snored during my yoga *nidra* session," I respond with a giggle.

Roger chuckles as his lips drag along the side of my neck, leaving a trail of open-mouth kisses. At the sensitive juncture of my neck and shoulder, he sucks the skin into his mouth. The pulls intensify, guaranteeing a mark.

My mate never lets a day go by without claiming me. I moan and press my ass against his thick shaft, eliciting a grunt from him.

"Naughty, Pretty Kitty," he rumbles in my ear. "You want your little pussy stretched before the doctor examines you?"

I mewl and rub against him some more. That's exactly what my body craves.

His deep chuckle reverberates through me. In response, my core pulsates as my juices flow in anticipation of Roger's massive dick filling it.

He shifts to the side. The sound of wet skin on skin smacking echoes in the shower.

I gasp from the shock of Roger spanking my ass.

"Oh no, Pretty Kitty. You will not have my cock interfering with your examination. But you will have a spanking for your untimely desires," he croons with his lips pressed against the shell of my ear.

I dance on the tile. But Roger's firm grip around my waist prevents me from slipping. He may punish me. But he would not endanger our baby or me.

My pussy swells and my clit becomes engorged from the arousal building within me. My juices slip from my core to coat my inner thighs.

Merde! I. Want. My. Mate. Now.

As though sensing the peak of my arousal, Roger drops to his knees behind me and grips my hips. He tilts my pelvis to angle my dripping pussy lips to his mouth. A long swipe of his tongue along my seam drives me to my toes as I slap my palms against the steam-slicked glass wall.

Roger's eager feasting of my sweet pussy exemplifies his hunger to the point of greed. The slurping sounds blend with his guttural growls and groans of satisfaction to reverberate around us. His fingers tighten on my hips to lock me in place when my body quivers with the start of an explosive orgasm.

When his tongue wraps around my clit and his thumb breaches my puckered hole, I lose all control. My head falls back and I yowl. The sound slices through the air.

"Oh. Oh. Oh. Aaaaaahhh!!"

The intensity of the onslaught of many waves cresting

one after the other dragged on by Roger's continued banquet brings me to my knees.

Roger, not sated fully, guides me to all fours with my ass high to the shower floor, never moving his mouth from my wrung-out pussy.

Another climax takes me and I drop my forehead to the cool marble as a strangled cry falls from my slack mouth. My pants come quickly and I close my eyes, unable to take anymore.

"Roger, please…"

In response, his passionate growl vibrates through my pussy.

"Aaahhh…"

Not until Roger licks the last drop from my thighs does he pull me onto his lap. He cradles my heavy head against his powerful chest. The hypnotic beat of his heart along with his soft murmurs of love fill my ears as I drift into a blissful state of orgasm overload.

"BONJOUR, Mademoiselle Beaulieu and Monsieur Steele. Please have a seat in the east parlor and a nurse will be with you shortly."

I thank Dr. Berger's cordial receptionist as I return her welcoming smile.

His office inhabits the ground floor of his grand personal townhouse with a separate entrance for patients. The receptionist sits at an ornate desk in the foyer. One of the front salons serves as the waiting room. While the other salon has two secretaries seated at desks with guest chairs in front of them. Wooden file cabinets line the wall behind them.

Roger and I admire the fine architectural details and rich

decor befitting of the impressive mansion as we make our way to the salon.

Another couple sits on one loveseat and glances our way as we enter the room. Recognition fills their eyes when they see me.

Roger and I haven't released a statement regarding our engagement yet. We decided to wait until I met with the doctor again. Roger didn't want the media, bloggers, and gossips going crazy like they did when Sebastian and Lola announced their engagement. The media already dubbed Sebastian, Malcolm, Roger, and Harris as the STEELE Quaternity—the most sought-after of the world's eligible billionaires.

Toss in my popularity as an internationally known supermodel, and it would increase tenfold. All it takes is one person to see us and wham! Broadcast news! I agreed I wasn't ready for the added stress.

Now, Roger nods in greeting, and I smile. Might as well get used to people's reactions, I muse. My pregnancy will show soon enough, and my engagement ring isn't exactly subtle. Besides, I want the entire world to know Roger is mine! He's not the only possessive one in our relationship.

With his hand on the small of my back, Roger guides me towards a seating area furthest away from the couple. As we pass them, the man gawks at me openly. Undoubtedly envisioning my sexy *Sports Illustrated Swimsuit Issue* covers and my seductive Lola's Coterie billboards. Roger glares at him, and the man shifts his gaze immediately.

Inwardly, I shake my head and roll my eyes. Staring at me while seated next to his woman...

"Fucker! He keeps it up, and I'll rip his eyeballs out," Roger growls as we sit.

I cover my mouth when a snort of laughter pops out. Roger side eyes me, and I turn away to stifle more snorts.

"You like that fucker staring at you, or are you laughing at me, Pretty Kitty?"

Instantly, I cease all laughter at Roger's Alpha tone. I curse when my pussy clenches with need.

"Plus jamais, Mon Cœur," I purr.

Roger grunts. Then sits back with his legs spread. He holds my hand on his muscular thigh. The caveman dominates the space and claims his mate in full view of an interloper.

I flip through a pregnancy magazine on my lap with one hand. To distract Roger from glaring at the man, I show him some articles as we wait for the nurse.

When she arrives, we follow her to an examination room that could pass for a bedroom except for the table with stirrups attached in the middle of the floor. Once she leaves with instructions for me to put the gown on with the opening in the front and no underwear, I slip out of my silk wrap dress, lingerie, and strappy sandals.

Roger shifts in his seat, and I glance at him over my shoulder as I shake my ass to give him a show.

"Leonie…" He warns.

I giggle and sit on the edge of the table. As I look around the room, I notice the medical equipment artfully hidden in plain sight. My nerves come back, and I take a deep inhale. A knock on the door precedes my exhale.

Roger glances at me, and I nod.

"Come in," he calls.

Dr. Berger and the nurse smile as they walk in.

"Bonjour, Mademoiselle Beaulieu and Monsieur Steele. How are you doing?" He asks.

All eyes turn to me, and silently I repeat my mantra for the safety of our baby before I respond.

"Much better, Dr. Berger. We've followed your precepts, and the low-level prenatal yoga sessions have helped to lessen my stress."

He nods, then continues, "Any cramping or bleeding?"

Roger squirms.

"*Non*, none at all, doctor," I answer confidently and smile at Roger.

He returns my smile and sits up, reassured.

"*Très bon!* Let's do your examination first. Then your ultrasound," Dr. Berger states.

The checkup proves all is indeed much better.

Relief fills me. Next, the scan. I'm excited to see our Lil Cub!

The cool gel on my belly makes me shiver, and Roger who now stands beside me squeezes my hand in his to support me. Without glancing away from the screen, I smile in acknowledgment.

The images before me make no sense at all. So I wait for Dr. Berger to say something in explanation.

He leans forward to peer at the monitor more closely. Then sits back with a frown as he shakes his head. He reaches out to turn a knob for the volume.

The sound of an irregular heartbeat fills the quiet room.

My world collapses. Every negative thought races through my mind. The awful experiences my parents faced come to the forefront. All positivity vanishes in a puff of smoke. Pouf...

Merde!

Unconsciously, my grip tightens on Roger's hand to the point of pain as I hasten to sit up. The wand slips off my belly and my gown falls open. I don't give a damn.

"What? What's wrong? Why does its heart sound funny? *Mon Dieu!*"

I cry in French, unable to think in English.

My eyes fill with tears, and I feel as though the walls are closing in on me. Panicked, I swing my gaze from Dr. Berger to the nurse to Roger and back to the doctor.

"Tell me!" I demand.

"What the fuck?! Answer her!" Roger bellows.

Dr. Berger raises his hands, palms out in compliance as he shakes his head.

"*Non, non!* You misunderstand! Nothing is wrong! You're fine! Your babies are fine!" He exclaims as his words tumble from his mouth.

The room falls silent again as we stare at the doctor. Then Roger and I yell at the same time.

"*Qu'est-ce que tu viens de me dire?!*"

"Babies?!"

ROGER

"*O*h, *Mon Trésor*! You're glowing! How beautiful you look!"

Leonie's mother exclaims as she hugs her treasured daughter to her bosom tightly. Tears glisten in her eyes. But Josy doesn't allow them to fall. Her soft amber eyes so like Leonie's shut as she squeezes her even more. Her lips move as though in silent prayer.

Guy beams at his wife and only child as he stands next to them in the foyer at *Le Beaulieu Manoir*.

His brawny six-foot-four-inch frame towers over the mother and daughter pair. He's a foot taller than petite Josy. Even with Leonie in sky-high heels, he has two inches on her.

"Oui, *Mon Trésor*, absolutely spectacular!" He agrees, grinning broadly.

Guy's voice booms around the grand entryway of their palatial French Rococo mansion. Set on twenty acres on the outskirts of Paris in Neuilly-Auteuil-Passy, their ancestral home is one of the finest in the wealthy neighborhood. And

Guy is the epitome of the Alpha male of the estate, with his finely tailored clothes that underscore his fit physique and statuesque frame.

Leonie gets her height and wavy, mahogany hair from her father and the lush curves and eyes from her mother. Personality wise, she's a combination of Guy's bold confidence and Josy's elegance and warmth.

I wonder who our twins will favor. The Beaulieu leonine amber eyes and aristocratic demeanor. Or the Steele signature gray eyes and dominant tendencies. They'll definitely match the height on both sides, even if Josy is the smallest of us all. However, as long as our babies are healthy, it doesn't matter.

"And you, Roger. Good to see you, son!"

Guy claps me on the back and draws my attention to the room.

Since Leonie and I became engaged, he's taken to calling me son. He explained he's thrilled with his daughter, but a son is a welcome addition to their small family.

I'm thankful he's accepted me. Not one to fear anything or anyone, Guy's frank warning when we first met makes him one to acknowledge as better to have as a friend than as a foe:

He leans forward. His obsidian eyes bore into mine.

"Do not fuck my daughter over or you will pay the price."

I train as a boxer and can hold my own. However, Guy is a force to take into consideration. He may be in his early sixties, but he's studied jujutsu for decades. He's just as comfortable in the French salons as in the back alleys. It's best for all parties involved, we're on solid footing.

"Good to see you, too, Guy! You look well," I respond heartily.

He nods and gestures toward the all-glass solarium that

overlooks the rear rose garden. Our regular spot for the Sunday brunches we've enjoyed over the last several months. We pass the now familiar salons on our way. I spot new items Josy must have added from Beaulieu Enterprises, SAS's ever-changing stock of high-quality antiques, antiquities, and fabrics.

Over the centuries, the Beaulieu's continued to grow their merchant business. Now, Guy as the *président* has expanded it into a multibillion-dollar enterprise.

While Sebastian was in Paris after his honeymoon, we met with Guy and his team to discuss partnership opportunities. They impressed Sebastian. He made the alliance between STEELE International, Inc. and Beaulieu Enterprises, SAS his first big deal since being named the new CEO by our father. Morgan, who took part int the meetings via video conference, gave his approval.

Their company is privately owned and Leonie is the heir apparent. After our engagement, Guy expressed his wish for me to take on the helm with Leonie when he retires. Leonie made it clear she is not interested in running the day-to-day responsibilities as she wants to focus on her interior design career.

We agreed we would incorporate Beaulieu within the STEELE organization. But Leonie will maintain majority control with our children, taking on the company at the appropriate time. The Beaulieu company will continue to pass on to the next generation as it has for centuries.

The future addition pleases Sebastian and my father. Morgan and Guy admire one another as equals. It's the perfect solution for both companies and families.

Leonie and I arrived early to spend some time with Guy and Josy before my clan joins us for brunch. They're ideal in-laws—no hovering, no forcing themselves into our lives, no judgment. Even with their concern for Leonie and the babies, neither Guy nor Josy force their way in our relationship. Although I wouldn't mind at all.

"Tell us about Dr. Berger's assessment of your wellbeing, *Mon Trésor*," Guy says as we settle on sofas near the wall of glass.

The view of the manicured park-like grounds with the stables, tennis court, and swimming pool with cabana is peaceful. A pleasant respite from the bustling city. No wonder Leonie raves about her happy childhood. Who wouldn't with such a lovely place to grow up?

"Oh, *Papa*! All is good!" Leonie exclaims clapping her hands as her amber eyes glow and her cheeks blush. "But we want to wait until we gather everyone before sharing any details."

She turns to smile at me and takes my hand in hers.

I nod at her lovingly and respond, "Yes, Leonie is doing very well! Dr. Berger is pleased with her progress."

"*Bien, bien!!*" Guy slaps his muscular thighs with both hands. Then wraps an arm around Josy to hug her close.

She closes her eyes with a contented sigh and leans into his massive chest.

My smile widens as I take in their joy.

Leonie kisses my cheek, and I place my hand on her belly as its outline presses against her buttery soft, black leather shirt dress.

We spend half an hour chatting about everything from Josy's latest recipes and philanthropic endeavors to Leonie's yoga escapades with Starr.

"And Roger joined one of my sessions… You know, since Sebastian takes classes with Starr. You should have seen how Roger tried to analyze each asana. Starr was very patient with him. While I threatened to ban him from future sessions!" Leonie tells them.

"Now, don't tease Roger, Leonie! That's not nice," Josy admonishes, then continues. "You know how very serious he is!"

Her laughter tinkles around us—light and high. Only in her early fifties, she keeps a youthful quality. Another trait I'm sure Leonie will inherit from her.

"Roger, practicing yoga will help with your boxing. The focus and breathing will enhance your technique," Guy adds.

"Yes, I can see those benefits. Despite what Leonie says, I will join one or two of her sessions"—I put my fingertip to her lips when she protests—"But I won't interfere. Starr is an acclaimed teacher who I trust implicitly."

"Fine!" Leonie huffs.

The chime of the doorbell pauses our conversation.

Since they give the staff the weekend off, Guy goes to the entry and returns with my parents, Sebastian, Lola, Malcolm, Harris, Haley, Luc, and Blair. Our cousin and Lucien's older brother Lachlan, the President of Liquor at Jackson Corporation, is in town from his home base in Aberdeen, Scotland. He has business at their Paris offices this week. He follows Haley into the solarium.

"Leonie, honey! You look marvelous!" My mother Shelley gushes as she pulls Leonie into an embrace.

"Indeed! Nice and healthy, young lady!" Morgan adds with a warm smile sparking his platinum eyes.

The rest of the clan offers more hugs and words of well wishes.

"Leonie, it's so good to see you well," Lachlan says as he double kisses her cheeks.

This sly fucker. Lachlan always uses his Cary Grant

movie-star looks to woo women. I growl low in my throat, and he laughs, draping his arm around Leonie's shoulders.

"Calm down, Papa Caveman! I'm off the market!" Lachlan winks.

A stricken sound behind him makes us turn.

Haley stands staring at Lachlan. Her gray eyes widen behind her glasses. Scarlet flushes her cheeks as she turns away quickly.

Lachlan's usual Alpha Dom bravado falters as he watches her stalk towards the sideboard. She takes a flute filled with a Mimosa and gulps half of it.

I clear my throat, then cock my head at Lachlan when he faces me again.

He averts his gaze and gives Leonie's shoulders a last squeeze before he steps away.

I glance up and my eyes meet Sebastian's as he stands stoically.

"*Mon Cœur?* Are you ready?"

Leonie stares up at me with her hand on my chest.

Whatever the fuck is up with Lach and Haley, if anything, will have to wait until after Leonie and I share our glorious news.

"Yes, my love. You want to tell them?" I ask.

Leonie shakes her head and pats my chest, "*Non*, you."

I wrap my arm around her waist and kiss the top of her head. Then linger as I inhale her scent mixed with the blend of florals with amber and musk of her perfume. Divine.

"Everyone, please take a flute to toast our fantastic news," I say, glancing at each face around us.

Lola claps and whoops as she heads to the sideboard. The others follow. I pick up two glasses of Leonie's new favorite drink, iced lemon ginger tea, and hand one to her.

A hush falls over the room as everyone gazes at us raptly.

I loop my arm back around Leonie's waist and raise my glass in the air.

"Leonie and I are expecting…"

I pause for effect while Leonie giggles.

"Bro, if you don't spill it, I'll hack into the doctor's medical records right here, right now!" Harris threatens as he whips out his latest innovative gadget.

Haley pulls her mobile from her handbag and poises her fingers over the screen as she glares at me.

I don't doubt one of our two tech wizzes will do just that if I don't finish fast enough.

"All right! All right!" I laugh.

I lift my glass high and shout, "Identical twins!!"

An uproar of boisterous cries of surprise and glee mixed with claps, feet stomping, and sharp whistles fill the solarium. Everyone speaks at once as they go wild with glee.

They sweep Leonie from my arms by either Josy and Shelley or Lola, Haley, and Blair. Her joyful laughter makes my heart leap. They surround her as they rub her belly and kiss her face.

"Damn, bro! Twins??"

"Congrats, man! Hot damn!"

"Well done, son, well done!"

"*Félicitations, fils!*"

"Holy cow! The caveman made his claim without a doubt!"

"Excellent, Roger! *Bon travail!*"

"Tag! You're next, Baz!!"

The most incredible sensations flow through me, igniting every fiber of my being with an electric charge. I chuckle when I think of how Leonie calls our love affair *un coupe de foudre*. How apropos!

"Well, Roger, honey, you and Leonie certainly have your

work cut out for you! Wedding plans, penthouse makeover, delivery! Josy and I volunteer to assist with all!"

I throw my head back and laugh uproariously.

"Of course, Mom! I've heard through the grapevine about your military strategies and tactics..."

Now it's Shelley's turn to laugh loudly. She wipes the corners of her eyes before she responds.

"I have no doubt! I take full responsibility!"

"*Oui!* So much to get done! But first, we eat!" Josy adds.

Leonie nods enthusiastically as she pats her belly and points to her mouth.

"Time to feed the babies!" She exclaims.

Everyone laughs and heads to the delicious dishes arranged on the buffet. The tantalizing aroma of savory and sweet foods fills the air. Josy blends traditional Tunisian and French fare of meats, vegetables, and baked goods. Our mouths water in anticipation.

Lucien, who's joined us at some brunches, claims he's going to use her recipes for his restaurants and eateries.

Josy quipped how he might as well since Leonie refuses to learn them as is the family's way to pass the recipes down through the generations.

Today's lively conversation is a perfect match to the festive atmosphere. Everyone is excited Leonie and I decided to find out the babies' sex at the eighteen-week scan.

"We have enough to get done without worrying about what colors to use," Leonie laughs.

"We need more girls!" Haley declares. "We have more than enough testosterone and overinflated egos to last a lifetime!"

Neither Sebastian nor I miss the wince Lachlan makes at her declaration. Once again my eldest brother and I share a a glance. Lachlan is his best friend. So I'm sure Baz will get the truth out of him.

Haley will prove to be harder to crack since she insists we stay out of her love life. I must admit it has to be hard to have four older brothers who intimidate any guy she dates. Not to mention no one is good enough for our father's princess. Only our mother sympathizes with Haley.

Oh, well... Too bad, Baby Sis.

"How much time do we have to prep for this wedding?" Lola snickers.

Sebastian gave her little time. He refused to wait. I don't blame him one bit.

"You are lucky I allowed you any time, Lola," Sebastian says in his Alpha Dom voice with his eyebrow cocked.

I chuckle to myself when Lola lowers her gaze as her face flushes with heat, and she squirms in her seat.

Every man at this table is an Alpha male. Some have the extra Dom characteristic. So no one bats an eye at Sebastian and Lola's D/s exchange. Hell, my brothers and I peg our parents as having a D/s marriage!

The women we love are all independent, smart, feisty, and bring something to the table other than their good looks. Some may be subs, some not. A need drives each male to provide the utmost pleasure to their mate. However, all play is consensual between adults who respect one another and their limits.

Leonie is not a sub and I'm not a Dom. But I dominate her in the bedroom. And she loves it!

A small hand glides along my inner thigh beneath the linen-covered table. Fingertips dance across my crotch. Then give a squeeze to the burgeoning bulge.

I have to take a sip of my iced tea to hide my unexpected groan.

Meanwhile, Leonie captivates all with her tales of yoga, my "zealous attentiveness," and her changing eating habits, including a desire for salty things. At which point, she tweaks my cock in emphasis.

Fuck. Me.

Yeah, this morning, she made an almighty meal of my dick. Just thinking about her decadent feast makes me swell. I have to adjust my lengthening cock surreptitiously to lessen the pinch of the zipper teeth on my trousers.

"*Oui, oui!* Roger has mastered my needs. He expects them before they even form in my mind!" Leonie says, laughing at her private pun.

"So when is the wedding date?!" Shelley demands.

"Well… Honestly, I'm ready to marry Roger right now. But I've always dreamed of a fairy-tale wedding. I want time to create it and to cherish every moment from idea to honeymoon." Leonie whispers.

I cup her chin in my hand and turn her head to bring our eyes on a level. Then I kiss her lips gently.

"Whatever you want, my love, it is yours. Just leave the honeymoon to me. For all intents and purposes, you are mine. My ring, my babies, my woman. Mine." I respond.

Tears well in her eyes. A reminder of how her "hormones rage inside" of her as she reminds me daily.

"However, I have my limits. I will not wait more than a few months," I add.

She leans her forehead against mine and inhales deeply as we share breaths for a moment.

"Fine. Four months… I need four months from today. Enough time to plan our wedding extravaganza, redo the penthouse into a triplex, and prepare a gorgeous nursery for our bundles of joy."

Leonie sits back to stare me in the eye directly. Her amber eyes ablaze.

"D'accord?"

"Oui, Mon Amour, d'accord! I promise you will have your fairy-tale wedding no matter what."

"Well, thank goodness! I can do four months! Josy?" Shelley says, clapping her hands.

"Oui! Oui! Four months is fantastic! *Mon Trésor* will have the wedding of her dreams!" Josy responds jubilantly.

"Well then, a toast to four months!" Guy stands at the head of the table and raises his crystal flute.

"To four months!"

The chorus rings around the solarium.

Leonie smiles at me with such a profound expression of love on her face.

My heart bangs against my chest. I will do all I can to ensure the love of my life always has that look permanently etched on her gorgeous face.

My lips find hers and my hand rests on her belly bump.

All. Mine!

ROGER

"Tell me how Leonie is doing?"

My Vibram Fivefingers-clad feet pound the roof-top track of Norman Green's Elite Training Facility. The Champ and I run around the course as part of my cardio for this morning's training session.

It's a clear sunny day. So they withdrew the retractable glass roof into its casing. The sounds of the city drift up the six stories and remind us we're still in the heart of Paris' bustling business district. The location proves the ideal spot to attract high-powered titans of finance, real estate, media, and other industries. The waiting list for membership stands at four months long.

I lift my face to the sky, enjoying the sun on my olive-toned skin. Sweat glistens on my face and neck even as the wind whips around us. The moisture-wicking fabric of my shirt and training pants keeps my body dry. Which is a good thing since Norman has me doing a balls-busting workout. And the run is the warm-up...

Now he's asking questions. Sure he cares about Leonie's

wellbeing. But it's also a test of my endurance. Can I talk comfortably while running laps? Or does the effort cost me my breath? I give Norman the side eye.

"Look, Steele, I want to know how she's doing, seriously! You had Anita and me worried! Talk to me, man," he says sincerely, holding his hands up as he runs beside me.

That's one reason members clamor to train with him. He gets in it with you. A man who doesn't just talk the talk. He works out right along with you. All in.

"Thanks, man. I appreciate your concern. Leonie is doing really well. In fact"—I pivot to jog backwards—"Call me Big Poppa... We're having identical twins!"

Norman's firm jaw drops, and he stops short in surprise.

I jog in a circle, throwing my hands in the air. I'm a true player. Take dat. Take dat!

Identical twins!

Every time I think about them, a big goofy grin spreads across my face. Leonie just laughs and shakes her head whenever she catches me spacing out, smiling to myself. She's dubbed me Big Poppa after her favorite rapper, The Notorious B.I.G.

"Shut up, Steele! You got it like that, man? Damn!" Norman chuckles as he shakes his head.

He and Anita have a little girl named Antonia—a combination of their names. He's the only one of my friends who has children. So, he's become my source for firsthand experience.

"As I said, call me Big Poppa!" I toss over my shoulder as I return to our run.

Norman catches up to me with ease.

"Congratulations, Big Poppa! They say twins run in the family. But man, I tell you... Double the after-midnight feedings, diapers, crying. But oh so worth it," he says as he slaps me on the back.

We settle into our run for another lap. Then head inside for some footwork training followed by the heavy and speed bags. I notice an improvement on my focus in my speed bag work from my new yoga practice.

Even though I told Leonie I would join her sessions, I only come in during the mediation or yoga *nidra* portions. Instead, Starr teaches me separately based on my needs assessment. She found I would benefit from Ashtanga, as it requires strength and stamina with the added memorization of the sequence element. It appeals to my intense nature.

"Anita had your and Leonie's meals for the week delivered to your penthouse. She wants you to know she added more of the jerk chicken Leonie enjoyed," Norman tells me as we walk to the locker room after our session ends.

"Great. Leonie will be ecstatic. Give Anita my thanks," I respond. "Too bad you can't join the guys and me tonight at the lounge. Lachlan has a new blend we're testing."

"Yeah, I know. It sounds like a good time. But Anita and I have plans for date night, dinner and the ballet, I can't break."

I nod, understanding I wouldn't change my plans with Leonie either.

"Next time," I say as we shake, and I clap him on the shoulder before we head into the locker room.

"Count on it. Ballet or bros?" Norman says.

"Bros!" We reply in unison.

Our deep chuckles bounce off the travertine-tile walls as we stride to the showers.

· · ·

"Now this is my latest creation. No one but the craft team has tasted it. You, my brothers, will be the first beyond the walls of Jackson Corporation to experience this exquisite blend of—"

"Give us a damn snifter already!" Joel interrupts Lachlan's razzle-dazzle speech.

"Here, here!" Lucien adds as he picks a Baccarat crystal snifter off of the tasting table.

We're in one of the glass-enclosed tasting rooms at Jackson Smoke&Scotch the new lounge Lucien opened five months ago. In the Place Vendôme/St. Honoré area on Rue Saint-Honoré, it quickly became the spot to see and be seen for old society, fashionistas, and celebrities. *The Sexy Chef* has a way with food and drink as much as with women.

Tonight is no exception. He's invited a few ladies to what was supposed to be our Guys' Night Out. Sure, the three women are beautiful and dressed provocatively. But none can compare to my Pretty Kitty. Who I left at home lying on our bed in a silk negligee writing in the baby journal I gave to her.

Leonie's fuller breasts overflow the lace cups as her succulent nipples poked through. She left her mahogany hair hanging down to her the curve of her ass, partially covering one eye. My very own Jessica Rabbit.

Without even trying, Leonie is irresistibly sensual. Not like the brunette who just touched my chest. Uh, no…

"Pardon me," I say as I step away to pick up a snifter.

Just as I pass her, she grips my forearm to stop me.

"Aren't you Roger Steele? As in the STEELE Quaternity of billionaire brothers?" She asks, her little pink tongue flicking over her overly inflated lower lip.

I stare at her hand on my arm, then back at her with my eyebrow cocked.

She titters and squeezes.

Where did Lucien find this one? Damn.

The press release went out two days ago announcing the engagement, wedding date, and congratulations on the expected birth. The news spread like wildfire. The Internet blew up. Bloggers sent into writing frenzies. Trending social media hashtags #TheLionCaught, #SteeleScoopedII dominate feeds.

Guests who attended Sebastian and Lola's wedding call my mother for invites. My office and Leonie's modeling agency flooded with calls for interviews. Two Steele bachelors off of the market in eight months prove fodder for the media and society alike.

However, this woman missed the memo…

"Yes, I am Roger Steele"—she preens and bites her lip—"And no, I am not interested, as my gorgeous fiancée is at our home waiting for me. So again, pardon me."

I extricate my limb from her grip and stride to the tasting table without a glance back. That should answer her question and prevent any further advances. One can hope I muse as I take a hefty gulp of Lachlan's self-proclaimed best damn Scotch ever…

"That hottie was all over you, bro," Joel says as he appears at my elbow.

I glance at him as I cradle my snifter of what actually is an excellent blend. Lachlan wasn't being a blowhard after all. The taste of chocolate and dried fruit mix well together. The trademark bite drags along the back or the throat before settling with a warmth in the stomach. Tasty.

"No thanks. I've got an all-natural hottie at home. In fact, I'm not staying much longer. I planned on a Guys' Night Out. Not a meat market where I'm on the hook," I reply as I glance at my Vacheron Constantin Patrimony Traditionnelle.

Joel chuckles as he takes a sip of his Scotch, eyeing the red head across from us.

I pin him with my intense stare.

"What the fuck, man?" I demand.

Joel doesn't look away from the woman as he responds absently, "What?"

"Well, let's think about it, shall we... Hettie Fuchs... Your girlfriend. Sounds familiar?" I deadpan.

Now his attention drifts away from the redhead. Joel's arctic blue eyes flash as he glares at the wall. He snorts and finishes his Scotch in one long swallow.

Oh, boy. This can't be good, I muse.

"Oh, you mean Miss I'm Moving Back Into My Apartment Out Of The Blue??" He growls scowling into the empty snifter.

Nope. Not good at all.

"What the hell did you do, Joel?" I ask, positive he had to do something to make Hettie leave after they've lived together for so long.

"How do you suppose it's my fault, Roger?" He says snidely.

I sigh and glance at my watch again. Enough of this shit. I belong home snuggled up with my woman, not being harassed by a stranger and arguing with a friend. Give me a damned break already.

"Well first, Hettie committed herself to you. So she wouldn't just up and leave. Second, did it occur to you she may want more than what you're offering, Mr. I'm Way Too Young To Commit?"

I throw his words back at him from the first time we were in this very lounge talking about our relationships. I also realize I'm thinking from a female's perspective. Leonie is rubbing off on me...

Joel looks uncomfortable as he loosens the Prince Albert knot of his silk necktie. He stiffens, and I glance up to see the redhead sidling over to us with a seductive smirk on her face.

"Hi, would you like some help with that?" She purrs, batting her long eyelashes at Joel as she reaches for the tail end of his tie.

He jerks backwards as though burned and shakes his head vigorously.

"No!" He collects himself and softens his response. "No, thank you. Actually, I have a girlfriend."

"Well, I don't see her here," she presses on. "And you seem tense, sweetie."

Her hand slips up his tie as she flicks her long fingernail on his exposed throat.

Joel catches her wrist and removes her hand. Then he cocks his eyebrow and responds, "No. Thank. You."

Damn, is it the Scotch or what? These women are super aggressive tonight. I turn my back to refill our snifters as I shake my head in disbelief.

Fortunately, the red head takes the hint and moves on to where Lucien and Lachlan stand chatting with the other two women.

I watch Lachlan and wonder if Sebastian got any details from him about Haley. Lachlan senses my intense stare and glances in my direction. I give him the I-see-you chin bob and sip my Scotch.

Slowly, he returns my nod. Undoubtedly knowing what I'm thinking.

Not blood cousins. Rather, our mothers have been best friends since they met in New York as young women before either married their billionaire husbands. As a result, the Steeles and Jacksons grew into a tight family unit, and the children consider themselves cousins.

Close or no; blood or no. I'll kick Lachlan's ass if he fucks with my baby sister. I'm sure Sebastian made that clear to him before he returned to New York City.

"You're right, bro. I fucked up with Hettie."

Joel's confession brings my focus back to him.

"What happened?" I ask, concerned for both of my friends.

He sighs and tells me how she asked him flat out if he planned to have the cow for free. He had to explain that one to me. It made sense and reminded me of Leonie's hesitancy to move in with me and Lola's back and forth with Sebastian. Somehow, I realize they're behind this one. I keep that theory to myself and let Joel continue.

"I miss her. I mean badly. But I can't just go crawling back. You know what I mean?" Joel asks, looking like a lost puppy.

I clap my hand on his shoulder and squeeze it.

"Man, take my advice. Go get your woman and put a ring on it already!"

I gesture towards Lachlan and Lucien. Then to the two of us.

"What would you rather... Women who only want you for your name and wealth? Wasting time on those who don't give a fuck about you the man? Or a woman who's been with you for years and loves you for you? And all she wants is your commitment to her as she's given hers to you. Doing things your way all this time... Come on, man, it gets old. Trust me!"

Joel takes a moment to consider my speech. Then nods his head.

"You're right. This last month showed me I had a good thing with Hettie, but it could be great. Well... I guess they'll be hashtags about us next."

He laughs and touches his snifter to mine in a toast.

I join in his laughter and finish my Scotch.

"And on that note, I have a sexy as fuck fiancée curled up in my bed. Gotta fly!"

Joel chuckles and places his snifter next to mine on the tasting table.

"Right with you! I have to send a text message to my shopper to ask the manager of Harry Winston to open real quick for me. Then I'm dragging Hettie back to my cave where she belongs. This time with my ring on her finger!"

Our boisterous laughter fills the room. The others turn to gawk at us, and we salute them.

Then waltz out the door whistling *Going to the Chapel of Love* between chuckles.

I CAPTURE the image of Leonie curled under the covers on my side of the bed with her head resting on my pillow when I return to our penthouse. Her wavy hair fans across the silk pillowcase. The contrast of the mahogany and the cream frames her beautiful face. One boob popped out of her negligee, enticing me with its pebbled tip. But I let her rest as she appears so peaceful.

Instead, I stride into my dressing room and swap my bespoke three-piece suit and custom shirt for a pair of navy silk pajama bottoms. After I brush my teeth and wash my face, I return to stand at our bedside.

Leonie is so gorgeous. A natural, effortless beauty who takes my breath away. I glance down at the profile of her baby bump and my smile widens. MILF Alert! I'm a lucky so and so.

I open the little navy velvet box and set it on the night-stand. The two large pear-shaped diamonds and the pavé diamonds in the platinum band of the *toi et moi* ring sparkle in the lamp's glow. Leonie left one on for me. The identical, flawless stones will act as a reminder of our twins every time she sees it, I think as I place it on her right ring finger.

Leonie sighs and murmurs my name in her sleep as she unconsciously closes her fist on her new ring.

How symbolic, I think as I kiss her forehead softly. Then slip under the covers behind her. I spoon my body around hers with one hand on her belly and the other on her breast. Happily, I join her in a peaceful slumber.

LEONIE

"*How* ow are Blair and you doing, Luc? Long distance can put a strain on a relationship."

I mask my burst of laughter with a cough at Roger's out-of-the-blue question. Ever since he played counselor for Joel and Hettie, he's offering advice like the Love Doctor!

In reality, Roger did well with our friends.

Joel proposed to Hettie a week ago, and she's in seventh heaven. She was more blown away by his unexpected popping of the question when he showed up at her flat late at night, than she was with the flawless twenty-carat, cushion-cut diamond!

Hettie did a FaceTime call with me the next morning from the bathroom while Joel was still asleep in bed. She couldn't contain her excitement any longer. She had to tell me and show her stunning Harry Winston ring right away.

Later at lunch, Hettie shared more details about his proposal from the doorman announcing she had a visitor to Joel dropping to one knee when she opened the door to them not making it to her bedroom.

I covered my ears and responded TMI—too much information!

They chose a date six months from now. Like me, Hettie desires the wedding of her dreams and Joel is more than willing to do what she wants. He's just happy she's decided to spend more time at his flat. Hettie told him she was only moving a few of her items back in. She plans to stay the majority of the time in her flat.

"I told Joel, 'you only have the cow part-time!' He groused about it. But I stood firm."

Now, Roger, Luc, and I are on board Roger's Gulfstream G650 headed to LAX. Since Dr. Berger cleared me for work, Lola and I decided I would get in some photo shoots before The Twins took over my body. The photographer can PhotoShop my babies bump without taking away the integrity of the images.

My role as her exclusive spokesmodel will continue throughout my pregnancy. As previously planned, I'll do appearances at Lola's Coterie boutiques and at the high-end retailers that carry her collections. Interviews—print, television, radio, online—will run according to the media schedule.

Once The Twins grow larger, I won't model the lingerie and loungewear anymore. The evening wear collection won't fit my new frame either. So over the next few weeks, I'll pose for the camera. In the words of my modeling godmother, Rupaul: I better work! Shantay, shantay, shantay!

Roger insists I'm a MILF and still every man's sexy fantasy.

I don't disagree. A pregnant woman is a beautiful reminder of the power of nature and the strength of a woman.

Besides, I don't have any issues with my body. I embrace my curves—full C-cup breasts, slim waist, grip-worthy hips, round ass, and all. My healthy eating and exercise habits won't change. So, the only weight will come from The Twins as Dr. Berger recommends.

I intend to rock my fitted dresses, skin-tight leather pants, and bikinis. Plus, strut in my stilettos. Just add my name to the list of Hot Mamas: Hilaria Baldwin, Blake Lively, Ciara, Jennifer Lopez, and more!

Lola says she has a surprise for me. She refused to give one hint even though she knows the anticipation drives me crazy. Never mind, I'll know soon enough. Well, in another eight hours...

But the expression on Luc's handsome face proves the entertainment on this flight increased tenfold!

Luc is of the upper echelons of society. A man with a genteel upbringing and impeccable manners who does not discuss his private affairs. Period. Lola and I tease him mercilessly. But Luc remains mum.

Roger sprang the question on him just as he took a sip of his Chateau Lafite Rothschild. Luc sputters dribbling the pricey potable down his clean-shaven cleft chin. The crimson shade of his face matches the wine's hue. Luc's denim blue eyes widen, aghast at such an intimate question.

Even though he's known Roger for almost two years, he's known Lola and me far longer and doesn't share with us. So his shock is real.

And laughable. Cue the popcorn!

We started eating dinner a moment ago with casual conversation. Now, I sit back to enjoy the show.

"Hey, are you okay?" Roger asks as he passes a linen napkin to Luc over the formally set dining table.

Despite being thousands of feet in the air, we dine on

fine porcelain dishes with sterling silver flatware and crystal stemware. The delicious six-course meal prepared by one of Lucien's restaurants, then delivered to the private jet for the flight attendants to serve.

Luc dabs his full lips as his eyes flick between Roger and me.

My amber eyes dance with mirth as Luc struggles to regain control of his emotions. Poor Luc, I've never seen him so flustered. He must be serious about Blair.

"Roger, while I appreciate your concern for my... personal affairs, I prefer to keep them private," Luc responds finally as he pins Roger with an intense stare.

Not chastened, Roger continues.

"I understand and respect your preference. I merely ask because a friend of mine inquired as to Blair's romantic availability..."

Luc's jaw drops, and he blinks rapidly as he absorbs Roger's newest remarks.

Merde...

I wonder if he's serious until I feel a nudge to my thigh beneath the table. I stop myself from reacting and reach for my iced lemon green tea.

"Well, that is not for me to say. Now is it?" Luc rejoins.

Roger nods agreeably as he removes his mobile from the breast pocket of his suit jacket. His fingers fly across the screen.

"What are you doing?" Luc asks sharply as he leans across the table, eyeing the device like a snake.

Roger doesn't bother to glance up, just continues to type.

"Oh. Sending Blair's number to my friend so he can ask her on a date while we're in Beverly Hills. You see, he met her at one of Lola's Coterie's openings. He's in town at the same time as us. But based in New York... like Blair. No need to worry about long-distance romance. Huh?"

Luc loses all of his aristocratic cool as he snatches Roger's mobile from his hands.

"Now wait a minute! You cannot just give out Blair's number to some random man!" He huffs.

Roger feints aggrievement as he sits back in his chair openmouthed. He says not a word as Luc rages on about his boorish behavior. Then he pauses and narrows his eyes at Roger.

To his credit, he doesn't alter his facial features under Luc's arctic glare.

"You're fucking with me, Steele..."

Roger throws his head back and howls with laughter. Then smirks at me as he waggles his fingers in a vee.

"Two for two!"

* * *

THE EXHILARATING sensation that rushes through my veins when the flashes flicker, the photographer calls for angles, and the music blares reminds me why I love to model. The glitz and glamour of it all thrills me!

"Darling, tilt your face towards the light for me!"

The opulent Beverly Hills Mediterranean-inspired estate that was the backdrop for the iconic movie *The Godfather* serves as my plush playground. I'm lying on a chaise beside the sparkling swimming pool, surrounded by three arched pavilions.

The latest set for Lola's Coterie Beverly Hills is in a vibrant fuchsia hue that complements my caramel-colored skin. The lustrous stretch-silk satin trimmed with coral lace is the buttery soft material for the bra, briefs, and suspender belt. The matching robe flows from my shoulders to puddle on the grass beneath the chaise.

My hair cascades down my back in shiny waves with a fuchsia bow tied like a headband. The makeup artist kept the look fresh and dewy.

I'm channeling Old Hollywood Glam—portraying the wife of a movie studio mogul. Instead of a male model playing the role, Lola insists Roger do it. At first he was hesitant. But Sebastian and Luc goad him on. While the marketing team explains how a campaign featuring us would drive sales, being we're the trending couple.

The camera loves his devastatingly handsome visage. After a bit of direction, he picks up the poses and cues from the photographer easily.

Roger grins at me as I tilt my face to the light. The direction of which aligns my mouth with his crotch as he stands over me.

The photographer wants sizzling… Well, he's getting it in an abundance. And I'm not complaining… Yum!

I lick my lips and wink at him seductively. I swear his cock twitches in his white swimming briefs. The outline of his length and the curve of his tip apparent in the tight material.

"Great, Roger, flex those rock-hard abs and thick thighs of yours!" Calls the photographer.

Roger bites his lip to keep from chuckling. But he does as requested.

When he mouths MILF, I can't help but crack up. Doubling over the chaise, snorting in a very non-MILF way. I cackle so much, my breath catches. So, I hold my belly, falling back onto the chaise.

The makeup and hair teams rush over to fix my face from the tears and bow I dislodged.

Roger swats them away as he checks on me. When he deems I'm fine, he motions for them to proceed. He stands on guard behind them with his arms crossed over his powerful chest; the biceps flexing. He's a sexy Roman gladiator.

"Leonie! What's gotten into you?" Lola admonishes.

"Him!" I snort as I point to Roger, then to my babies bump.

Everyone on the set joins in my laughter.

Roger smirks like right, I made them babies.

After the pool scene and more shots in different lingerie, we move to the stone terrace for the evening wear collection. These dresses are Lola's most recent addition—a take on the lingerie as gowns befitting Hollywood award shows' and premiers' red carpets.

The sparkly peach sequin-covered georgette gown is drama overload. Wispy feather-embellished sleeves tickle midway down my arms. Designed in an elegant wrap silhouette with ties to adjust the fit. Then falls to a floor-sweeping train that trails behind me as I sashay towards the fountain. My long, toned legs, lengthened by the cream-colored strappy sandals, show with each stride. The gown reminiscent of a silver screen siren's luxurious dressing gown.

I smile at Roger as I near him, standing in a custom tuxedo beside the fountain. His eyes shimmer liquid silver in the sun as his lips curve into an alluring smile.

Roman gladiator turned James Bond heartthrob.

I slip my hand into his outstretched palm.

"Why hello there, Monsieur Steele."

Roger smirks and leans down to murmur in my ear, "Hello there, Pretty Kitty. I have something for you."

He reaches behind him to the fountain's rim for a large, flat velvet box. Then holds it aloft.

I press the crystal closure and gasp when I see a suite of rich, pure yellow and white diamonds glowing against the black suede. My eyes fly to Roger's.

He smirks as he pulls the necklace out and drapes it around my neck. Next he closes the bracelets around my wrists and slips the ring on my right index finger—I never take off my toi et moi ring. He holds his hand out with the dangling drop earrings for me to put them in place. Then he slides the comb in my hair. With a satisfied nod, he steps back to admire his gifts.

"*Merci, Mon Cœur*," I purr as I rub my lips across his, wrapping my arms around his neck.

Roger's hands rest on the curve of my ass as he pulls me close. His thick cock presses into my belly.

"Hold it! Don't move!"

The photographer shouts as his camera clicks in rapid succession. Capturing our classic embrace.

"HONEY, you are lit up like the Christmas tree at Rockefeller Center!"

Billie teases me since I refused to take off my new baubles.

"Ho, ho, ho! Well call me Santa!" Roger chuckles as he kisses my radiant hand.

"Thank you, Santa Baby," I purr.

"See… That's what got you preggie in the first place!" Lola exclaims.

"Oh, don't tease them. They're so cute!" Starr chimes in, her dimples flashing as she smiles.

We're gathered at the steak restaurant in STEELE Rodeo

Drive for dinner on our last night. Billie flew in from Las Vegas for the week and Starr joined us. Blair sits leaning into Luc, who's been super attentive the whole trip.

"They're my rockstar yoga couple!" Starr adds.

We met with her every morning for in-person sessions at her Starr Light Fitness & Wellness Beverly Hills. I miss her live energy and hands-on adjustments. What a treat!

She's promised to fly over next month and stay for a week. She knows Anita from the yoga world. They have plans to catch up while Starr is in Paris. She's going to ask Anita to partner with her on my sessions. Since my pregnancy is progressing, Starr wants a teacher in the room with me. Roger and I think it's a great idea.

"Okay. Besides, it'll help with the authenticity of the new maternity lingerie collection... Surprise!"

Lola's announcement catches me off guard, just as she hoped.

"What do you mean?" I ask, excitement bubbling up at the thought I'll still be able to model and not just talk.

Lola claps her hands and shimmies in her seat. Her hazel eyes shine.

"I want you to collaborate with me on a sexy maternity lingerie and loungewear collection! We can design the pieces together as you go through the stages. Plus shoot campaigns with you and Roger all along!"

She pauses and gazes at me steadily. Suddenly serious,

"As long as Dr. Berger gives his approval. We will not overtax you," Lola adds.

It's my turn to clap and shimmy in my seat.

"How exciting! I already have some ideas! Like a bra with removable cups to allow The Twins to feed—"

"Hey! That's enough!" Roger cuts me off, growling at the mention of my breasts in front of other men.

"Cue the scene—Caveman Roger drags Leonie by the ponytail back to his den..." Lola jokes.

"And you are next, Lola," Dom Sebastian interjects.

Luc turns to Blair and asks, "Do you have anything to add, Blair?"

She blushes bright red from her hairline to her ample bosom.

"No, Sir!"

Billie chokes on her glass of Marcassin Estate Chardonnay. Then stares gobsmacked at Blair.

Lola's shocked eyes snap to mine, and we burst out laughing.

Le Renard Argenté is Dom Luc! Who would have thought? I guess their relationship is definitely doing well after all. Long distance be damned...

LEONIE

"*T*he bright lights of Las Vegas always give me a thrill! I love the partying, dining, and the cheers when people hit it big... The baccarat table is calling my name, baby!"

Starr exclaims leaning closer to the window, her excitement palpable.

"It never gets old for me. Even after years of living here. I love Vegas!" Billie adds as she peers out of her window. Her Savannah, Georgia accent still prevalent. Forever a Southern Belle.

We finished the last business in Beverly Hills and now jet to Sin City for Lola's Coterie Las Vegas. The campaign for the latest collection exclusive to the boutique needs to get done earlier than expected. Thanks to The Twins!

Billie and Starr flew with Roger and me aboard his G650 private jet. Luc opted to fly with Blair on Sebastian's plane. As much as Luc wants to spend time with Blair, I'm sure he's equally happy to avoid any further intimate questions from Roger...

I glance out of my window to take in the view of the world-famous Las Vegas Strip. Starr is right. The neon lights stand in stark relief to the darkness of the night desert beyond. As the jet flies into McCarran International Airport, the lights are like beacons luring travelers to the revelry of the "What Happens in Vegas, Stays in Vegas" city.

Only since the boutique opened, have I spent as much time here. Monte Carlo and Macau are my choices for gambling. Yet, just as others, I'm drawn to Vegas.

"We'll definitely hit the tables after dinner," Roger says as he squeezes my hand resting on his lap.

I turn away from the sparkling vision and smile at him as I scan his handsome face.

He hasn't shaved. So the five o'clock shadow adds to his sex appeal. The photographer for the Vegas shoot wants Roger to have an edgier appearance. This time the scene is the Alpha playboy meets the seductive showgirl.

"Your refusal to add points to our Mile High Club earns you no orgasms for the rest of tonight, Pretty Kitty..." he murmurs in my ear huskily.

I shiver from his warm breath tickling my skin and the subsequent jolt of electricity that zings my pussy. But no way was I going to have sex while Starr and Billie were on board. Even if the bedroom is at the back of the jet with plenty of space between us. Uh, no.

Soon we're headed to STEELE Las Vegas in Roger's Black Badge Rolls-Royce Cullinan, driven by Eric, who accompanied us on the trip. Starr and Billie ride in one driven by a STEELE chauffeur. The two five-diamond resort and casino properties in the middle of the action on the Strip are magnificent. Each soaring tower features the signature STEELE gray glass. They shimmer from the neon lights' reflection on their surfaces.

The valet opens the doors on the passenger side while Eric opens the other for us. Roger takes my hand just as Starr and Billie hop out of their SUV. We stride through the ornate, but tasteful main lobby towards the private reception foyer for the twelve Bridge Penthouses.

They're designed to attract high rollers and the über-wealthy clientele. The penthouses act as a bridge to connect the two properties with the mall between them from the ground level to the third floor. Roger and I will stay in his penthouse that's on one of the top six floors. While Billie and Starr share another; Sebastian and Lola in theirs, and Luc and Blair in a fourth.

As we pass through the lobby, various staff members greet Roger by name. A few of the woman watch the girls and me.

I smirk and run the fingers of my left hand through my hair. Their eyes bulge out of their sockets when they spy My Baby. Yeah, sweeties... He's very much mine.

Cameras flash to our left, and we turn to the source. What appears to be a soon-to-be-bride and her gaggle of girlfriends recognize us. No doubt the images will show up on Instagram shortly.

Used to the commotion my presence causes, I smile and wink. Roger keeps his typical intense stare straight ahead, even increasing his speed.

"No respect," he huffs.

I giggle and rest my hand on his forearm to soothe him.

We reach the etched-glass, double-doors for the doorman to allow us entry to the separate foyer of the Bridge Penthouses. Beyond are three reception and two concierge desks, four sitting areas, and a bank of three private elevators, each accesses two of the Bridge Penthouses in this tower.

"Hey, we just arrived. I can't wait to hit the casino floor!" Lola says as she shimmies, her hazel eyes lighting up like the Strip.

"Where are Luc and Blair?" I ask, glancing around the expansive room.

"Their penthouse is in the other tower. Billie and Starr are in one here," Sebastian responds.

Hmmmmm, *Le Renard Argenté* prefers privacy so much so, he and Blair are not in sight of the rest of our party…

Lola must think the same, because she titters as she shakes her head.

The receptionist brings card keys to Billie and Starr. Roger and Sebastian's penthouses have entry plates coded to their palm prints. So we have no need for keys.

The porters take our bags via the service elevator as we ride up in the guest ones for each of our penthouses. We agree to meet in the foyer in an hour.

"Finally, alone! You think you can avoid me much longer, Pretty Kitty?"

Roger's deep baritone wraps around me as much as his arms as he pulls my back to his front. He bends his knees so his thick length nestles against my ass.

"*Non, Amoureux, jamais,*" I purr as I grind against him.

Roger slips his hand under the hem of my bohemian, red floral and geometric motif silk-crepon mini dress. The dainty, flouncy ruffles of the tiered skirt pose no barrier to his wandering fingers. His other hand slips the bow out of the slim ties at the neckline to cup one of my heavy breasts. The slightly fitted bodice shirred along the bosom provides room for him to explore.

"Aaahhh, *Amoureux…*" I moan as he flicks my sensitive nipple with his fingertip.

When two of his thick digits breach my pussy folds, I groan and increase my grinding on his dick with my ass.

Roger's arousal mimics mine for some forbidden pleasure.

The last time we were in the throes of ecstasy on an elevator, Lola and Sebastian caught us. My leg wound around Roger's hip and his hand cupping my pussy. Our mouths connected with our tongues dueling for control.

Merde...

"So tight... So wet... So sweet..." Roger says as he withdraws his fingers to suck them clean in his mouth.

The sound of his slurps intensifies my desire for him to finish what he started.

"Roger," I whine, arching my back.

He tweaks my nipple as my breast fills his hand even more. Then returns to his fingers fucking my dripping core.

The juices slide down my inner thighs, and I ache for release. The pressure builds as I ride his fingers, humping my mons against his palm to reach my climax.

WHAP... WHAP... WHAP

"Aaarghhh!" I snarl as Roger spanks my swollen pussy lips. The last strike hits my engorged clit, and I jerk, half ready to cum and half ready to run. "Owww!"

"What did I tell you only an hour ago, Pretty Kitty?" He growls.

"No... orgasms... for... the... rest... of... tonight, Pretty Kitty," he repeats in my ear huskily.

Each word marked by a swat to emphasize his horrid statement.

Fuuuck!

The doors ping as they open onto the foyer of the penthouse. Unsatisfied and aroused achingly, I sag against Roger as he leads us through the doors.

"No fair!" I cry. "You can't possibly expect us to make love on a plane with other people on board, Roger! Now I have to suffer?!"

He chuckles darkly and strides to one wall of windows. I trail behind him like a petulant child, causing him to tug me along by the hand to keep up.

Once again, he stands behind me and holds me in his powerful embrace. I sigh at the feel of being in my man's arms and at the sight of the Strip shining brightly all around us.

We stand in silence for a moment, absorbed in our separate thoughts. Roger kisses the top of my head and reminds me it's time to get ready for dinner and fun at the casino.

"Well, Mr. Steele, if I cannot cum, neither can you!"

I quip as I sashay ahead of him to the bedroom. Then squeal when he swats my ass.

"We shall see, Little Kitty. We shall see," he chuckles again.

* * *

THE FOUR DAYS in Las Vegas lead to our New York City leg of the whirlwind Pre-The Twins Modeling and Marketing Push for Lola's Coterie. No pun!

We'll spend the next five days in the city. Then go out to the Steele Southampton Village waterfront family compound for the remaining four.

Billie stayed in Vegas while we flew a red-eye flight plan to arrive this morning. Today, Roger and Starr insist I rest. I don't disagree. A break is very much needed as I notice my stamina decreasing because of the activity.

At fifteen weeks, my body adjusts to the horny hormones, needing naps, and growth spurt of my belly. I feel as though it was just a minor bump only yesterday. A woman's ability to adapt is amazing!

"Remember to breathe with intention, Leonie. Inhale to reach; exhale to return. Your breath will guide you through the postures."

Starr's melodic voice guides me through our session.

Roger surprised me with a custom yoga studio in our penthouse. Starr helped him to fill it with every yoga-related item imaginable. Mats thick enough to protect my knees; straps to extend my reach as my belly grows; wool blankets to keep me warm during Savasana. Not to mention the candles, meditation pillows, and a *Puja* space.

I love it!

We finish the opening sequence and move on to the standing asanas. As we flow through each pose, I allow my mind to focus on the movement and my breathing. Starr is right. The breath sets the way.

"Hi, ready for me?" Roger asks as he joins us for yoga *nidra*.

Starr smiles and nods to the mat, bolsters, and blanket she set up for him next to my space.

"*Bien* sûr, *Mon Cœur*," I reply, holding my hand out to him.

Roger smiles at us and takes my hand as he lowers himself to a cross-legged position with ease. Once seated, he kisses my cheek. Then turns to Starr expectantly.

"Namaste, Enlightened One," he says, placing his palms together at his heart center and bowing his head to her.

"Namaste, Sassy Student," she says as she returns the gesture.

We laugh good-naturedly.

Starr helps us to get into comfortable positions as we lie supine on the mats. She places the bolsters under our knees and necks. Then, like babies, she swaddles us in the blankets, ensuring we're covered fully. Before she steps away, she places lavender-scented pillows over our eyes. Starr dims the lights and allows the candles to glow around the studio.

Her soothing voice guides us through the session from consciousness to a state of semi-consciousness. The mental countdowns and memories she asks us to invoke keep us from falling into a slumber. Not like my first few sessions where my snores woke me!

The forty-five minutes pass blissfully. The sound of chimes brings us back to full awareness. We recall how far we could count and the recollections from the past. It's amazing how my practice has improved.

Fully rested with the equivalent of three hours' sleep, I feel rejuvenated. Roger and I head to our bedroom while Starr goes to her guest suite on the other side of the penthouse. We insisted she stay with us since we have more than enough space since it's a floor-through property.

Situated high above the Manhattan streets, it's on the fifty-second floor of The Steele Tower skyscraper. Through the gray-tinted, floor-to-ceiling windows, the city stretches out with unobstructed views. The prime location at the southwest corner of Fifty-seventh Street and Fifth Avenue is in the heart of Billionaires' Row.

Central Park to the north, the Hudson River to the west, the East River opposite, and the rest of Manhattan to the south from Midtown to Battery Park. On a beautiful, cloudless day like this morning, the vista draws you to gaze out of the windows for hours.

But not this morning. Roger and I have plans to shop the baby boutiques and lunch at La Goulue It's my favorite restaurant in New York. I'm ordering the *Moules sauce*

Poulette or *le Pavé de saumon aux lentils.* I'm so excited to have time to go while we're here. Mmm mmm mmm!

Roger and I decided to pick up unique items for The Twins in each city. While in Beverly Hills, we found some cute clothes and toys including two giant cuddly bears Roger had to get. They took up more space than the humans on the jet!

After a quick shower, I change into a fiery tonal-orange and white patterned mini dress cut in a classic shift silhouette. The button-fastening tabs at the sides and sleeves adjust the fit and coverage. Perfect for my growing babies bump.

I pair it with beige with black tip Chanel ballet flats, a woven Bottega Veneta Cabat handbag, and classic Versace shades. In New York, so I have to rep The Notorious B.I.G. with the vintage black and with gold accents sunglasses. My hair has grown so much, I pile it atop my head in a messy bun.

Roger opts for a navy v-neck cashmere sweater, dark denim jeans that stress his firm ass and luscious bulge perfectly, and black Gucci loafers. He shaved his stubble showing his cleft chin and left his tousled hair to air dry. His dove gray eyes covered by the silver metal and pale blue lenses of his Tom Ford aviators.

Sexy Big Poppa! Rawr!

"The contractors sent an update for the renovations. Did you have time to read their email?" He asks as Eric drives us to the first boutique.

"*Oui*, I saw it. But haven't answered since I'm waiting for my latest AutoCAD files to come back from the graphics team. What did you think of their estimated timeline for completion?" I respond, flipping through my emails for their message.

"Okay, but not good enough. We need them to cut off three weeks," Roger starts. "Two need to be for the decorating to complete and a week for us to settle back in. We will not wait until seven days before your due date. We need to be ready early."

I smile to myself. As he mentioned, it's not unusual for twins to arrive at thirty-six weeks. Roger's been reading books on twins and babies in general. He's gotten into the habit of spouting off facts and details. He's read more than me!

"What's so funny?" He asks, cocking his eyebrow at me.

"You've become quite the expert... Roger *The Responsible* Steele!" I tease.

He smirks and shakes his head.

Eric stops the car on Madison Avenue and we hop out of the Rolls-Royce Corniche. A friend who owns a textile company recommended the boutique. She supplies the fabrics for their clothes and nursery items.

"Hello, please let me know if you need any help," says the shopgirl pleasantly.

"*Merci*," I respond while Roger nods.

We stroll through the section for newborns, and the sweetest onesie catches my eye. It's made of super soft cotton and has a cartoon lion on the chest.

"Roger! Look at this! It's so adorable!" I exclaim.

He grins and holds a yellow one up to my bosom.

"We should have one made for you, Mama Lion," he laughs. "Then I can tuck all of you in bed like triplets!"

Our loud snickers cause the other patrons to glance at us and smile.

I notice one woman who appears to be shopping alone glimpsing at Roger every so often. I shake my head—thirsty girl. But when she accidentally brushes up against him as she passes, I growl.

"Back off!"

She jumps and scampers away. She doesn't dare to look at me.

Mama Lion doesn't play with her mate!

Roger chuckles and kisses my lips softly.

"Now who's the possessive one? Hmmm?" He teases.

I roll my eyes at him for repeating the words I told him last week. The caveman snarled at a guy who asked to pose with me for a selfie as Roger and I strolled along Rodeo Drive.

"Whatever. Blame the hormones!" I retort.

"THESE SHOTS ARE INCREDIBLE!" Lola says as she peers over the photographer's shoulder.

We're in Dubai, the last stop on the five-city global trip. Luc returned to Paris after New York for meetings. The rest of us spent three of the seven days allotted to the United Arab Emirates' boutiques in Abu Dhabi.

I suggested we contrast the city's sea of desert with the turquoise waters of Dubai, The Empty Quarter Desert in Abu Dhabi serves as the first backdrop. The Bedouin noblemen see the world's largest sand desert as a vast ocean to travel across on their journeys.

We paid homage to their history with a twist. I portrayed a desert princess who captivated a desert traveler, Roger. Our steamy affair took place over the course of three nights in a lavish tent.

Lola outdid herself with the collection exclusive to her Lola's Coterie Abu Dhabi boutique. The vibrant colors, sumptuous materials, and sophisticated lines make for extraordinary pieces. Of course I requested a few sets of the lingerie and loungewear for our maternity line collaboration.

We've been sketching like mad since Lola told me about it. Our goal to maintain the sex appeal with pre- and postnatal functionality has our creativity with the materials and cuts keyed up. So far, the designs realize what we want to project. Roger concurs.

The six-hundred-foot megayacht we're using for the Dubai photoshoot is lavish and belongs to one of the royal family members. The impressive boat parallels the view. Spread out beyond the dazzling water with glittering ripples that reach across to the shore is the city's varied skyline.

Architectural marvels grow out of the surrounding desert. The contrast of the modern glass towers—some in unusual shapes—to the nature around it is remarkable. It provides the perfect scenery for the Dubai boutique's collection.

Lola incorporated the gorgeous blues and greens of the water with the earth tones of the sand for the color palette. Glittery Swarovski crystals embellish the bras, panties, slips, and evening wear pieces to mirror the glass structures.

This time Roger and I play the roles of dashing billionaire mogul and paparazzi-hounded celebrity. Our holiday is fraught with dodging photographers with high-powered lenses while on our megayacht to being chased through the streets after a night out. Not much different from reality...

"*Oui!* It's as though we're experiencing our everyday lives!" I giggle as I look over his other shoulder at the photos.

Roger grunts and adds, "Right. Well, if it gets as extreme as this storyline, you're getting security."

I open my mouth to respond. But Sebastian cuts in, holding up his hand to stop me.

"I agree with Roger completely. You are carrying the next generation of Steeles. And as the eldest of this line, it is my responsibility to protect everyone. Period."

Now I know how Lola must feel when Sebastian enacts his Alpha Dom. He's so commanding, I'm about to say, yes Sir!

I turn to Lola and she shrugs. Outnumbered and understanding their concern, I nod in agreement.

"Words, Pretty Kitty. I will have your words," Roger demands.

"*Oui*," I answer.

Roger and Sebastian reply excellent in unison, and Lola smiles as she wraps her arm around my waist.

"Get used to it, Hot Mama. There's nothing that will stop these cavemen from taking care of their loved ones."

Now I know how Haley feels with four older brothers. *Merde...*

* * *

WHEN THE CAMPAIGN IS COMPLETE, Lola and I round out this city's trip with marketing efforts. We host private viewing parties for the city's VIPs and dinners at STEELE Dubai. We take part in interviews with local fashion magazines and lifestyle television shows. Social media takeovers increase followers for the business and our personal accounts. The results satisfy the public relations and marketing teams.

Thankfully, we're on our way back to Paris. Roger and I sleep in the bedroom of his private jet while Starr stretches out on the sofa converted into an additional bed. Sebastian, Lola, and Blair head to New York City on his jet.

It exhausts everyone after the month of non-stop travel. But it was well worth it. The early shots are incredible as predicted. The sales team expects great numbers in revenue and an increase in brand awareness.

They hinted at Roger being a regular in the campaigns to keep the momentum up. He didn't comment. Although his response to a male model partnering with me was to huff a negative on that suggestion.

The next campaigns will be for the maternity collection. So, I would prefer my sexy fiancé to another man. We'll see—

"Stop thinking so hard, babe. Shall I ease your tension?"

Roger's husky voice along with his rock-hard cock poking my bottom as we spoon on the bed pulls me from my musings.

My body tingles in response. My nipples tighten painfully. My core throbs with desire.

Oh, well... Points added to the Mile High Club cumming up!

ROGER

"*H*ey, babe! Are you ready, yet? We needed to get going fifteen minutes ago!"

I call to Leonie, who's running late as usual. But not today!

It's been three weeks since we returned from the Lola's Coterie boutiques trip. I cannot believe how time passed so quickly. Nor how much Leonie's body has changed.

She's noticeably pregnant from the front and side with her belly poking out. Now, I can rest my hand on top and cradle her belly underneath. Her breasts are deliciously plump. Just thinking about suckling her tips makes me hard.

Every morning and night after we shower, I massage warm oil all over her belly and breasts to keep the skin soft and pliable. Then rub her back, legs—especially her calves and ankles—and feet to soothe the cramps and to prevent swelling. The sounds of Leonie's contented purrs as she writhes with pleasure on the massage table add to my desire for her.

MILF Alert for damn sure!

"Leonie! If you do not come out of that dressing room in five seconds, I will carry you out of here, to the car, and to Dr. Berger's office wrapped in a robe!"

Yeah, we're almost late for the big reveal. Are The Twins boys or girls?

Hopefully, we'll get to his office before they're eighteen years old and not eighteen weeks.

I run my hands through my hair and sigh. I make my mind up. I cannot wait any longer. As I storm towards the door of her dressing room, it opens.

Leonie walks out looking afuckingmazing.

Her ass-length hair parted in the middle cascades down her back in silky mahogany waves. The soft black cashmere mini dress skims her long legs mid thigh. While a fashionable take on cowboy boots in black leather reach below her knees. Her black suede shoulder bag and glamour girl shades finish her chic outfit.

The babies bump sticks out as a reminder she's pregnant and not *The Lion* megamodel prowling down the catwalk.

My mouth gapes.

She tucks a lock of hair behind her ear and giggles at my reaction.

"Roger, you boost my ego! I couldn't find anything that fit!" Leonie exclaims as she pats her belly.

So far she hasn't gone shopping. Instead opting to make do with items from her vast wardrobe. Every day, designers send maternity clothing or pieces that can work with her new figure. Leonie combines them with her existing wardrobe and always looks stunning.

"Babe, you are hot as hell! Go shopping with Hettie or Anita or both. But right now... We're out of here!"

I grab her hand and rush from the room.

Fortunately, Eric has my Aston Martin DB7 Vantage

pulled up. I help Leonie into the passenger's seat. Then race around to the driver's side as I thank him.

"Of course, Monsieur Steele. Best of luck!" He responds with a goofy grin.

Even reticent Eric is eager to hear the news.

I grin back and jump in the car. I need to something to keep me sane, so I opted to drive us to the appointment. A glance at my platinum Rolex Cosmograph Daytona confirms we have fifteen minutes to make a twenty-minute ride.

"Call Dr. Berger's office," I request to the built-in phone system.

"Dr. Berger's office."

"Good morning, this is Mr. Steele. Please inform the doctor Mademoiselle Beaulieu and I are on our way and will arrive five minutes late. Thank you." I say.

Leonie has the grace to appear sheepish.

But I don't make a big deal out of it. She's adjusting well and doesn't need a lecture. I simply accept her tardiness as par for the course.

"It's all right, Caramel BonBon. We'll get there soon enough," I say as I squeeze her thigh.

She brings my hand to her lips and kisses it softly. Then rubs her cheek against it, purring like a kitten.

"Yeah, yeah, yeah… I love you, too," I laugh.

We make our way through the bustling Parisian streets. I park in one of the two spaces Dr. Berger has reserved for patients. Then hop out to help Leonie from the low seat. Despite being pregnant, she loves to ride around in my "James Bond sexy spy car."

"Ready, babe?" I ask her, knowing she's nervous and pretending she's not to keep me sane.

"*Absolument!*" Leonie says with a brilliant smile that lights my heart.

We make our way through the double doors of the townhouse. The receptionist assures us Dr. Berger understands our delay and will be right with us. Just as we settle on a sofa, his nurse calls to us.

Once inside the examination room, Leonie changes. But this time she doesn't offer the flirtatious shimmy.

"Babe, it's going to be fantastic knowing their sex," I say as I rub her belly, then jerk away in surprise when I feel movement.

"Did you feel that?! Was that a kick?" I ask Leonie excitedly.

She glances up at me with wide amber eyes. She's just as shocked as me.

"Holy shit! That's incredible! The experts say when you're nervous, it can give the baby a jolt of energy," I continue babbling in amazement.

"Oh, Roger! I can't believe it!" She responds with tears in her eyes now. "I can't wait to see them!"

A knock at the door interrupts our First Moment. Dr. Berger enters with the nurse and asks Leonie about her wellbeing. Following her examination, he preps her for the ultrasound.

Leonie grasps my hand as her eyes remain riveted to the screen. Smiling this time when she hears their heartbeats fill the quiet room. A tear slips down her cheek.

I bend over and kiss it away. Then nuzzle her cheek with my nose, inhaling her sultry perfume.

"Roger! Look! Look at them!" She exclaims as she points at the screen.

Two tiny faces appear. One with a thumb in their mouth

and the other holding the umbilical cord. Their eyes are closed tight as though sleeping peacefully.

It's surreal that I made them from my seed jetting into Leonie's womb. My babies. Mine!

Obviously Dr. Berger learned from the last visit not to incite hysteria with frowns and shakes of his head. This time, he smiles broadly at us when he announces The Twins' sex.

"Congratulations! Two healthy boys!"

"Fuck yeah!" I shout to the heavens as I punch the air with my fist not being squeezed by Leonie.

"Are you sure? Everything is in place?" She asks anxiously.

Dr. Berger smiles and moves the wand over her belly slowly. He points to the monitor to show us exactly how certain he is in his pronouncement.

I beam as the proof appears without a doubt. Call me Big Poppa!

After the doctor and nurse leave, I pull Leonie into my arms. I bury my face in her hair as she wraps her arms around my neck. She presses her face against my chest while we take a moment to absorb the incredible news.

"Thank you, my love. You've made me the happiest man in the world. You and our baby boys are healthy. I love you so very much."

I murmur as tears fill my eyes now.

"Merci, Mon Cœur, je t'aime aussi," Leonie whispers as she holds me tighter. "Our little family."

* * *

"TELL US, *Mon Trésor!* Don't keep us in suspense any longer!"

Josy blurts out as Leonie and I walk into the Petite Salon at Apicius, the Michelin starred restaurant.

We're having dinner with both sets of in-laws. My parents flew in yesterday afternoon, eager to hear in person the sex of The Twins. Everyone wanted to come to the doctor. But we decided to have dinner instead for the big announcement.

Leonie chose Apicius for its modern French cuisine. She favors the light, elegant and inventive dishes and teases the traditional bourgeois dishes fit with her father's ideals.

I love the architecture of the nineteenth century former residence turned hotel. The outdoor dining in the courtyard is enjoyable in the heart of Paris.

We selected the Petite Salon for its privacy instead of the Dining Room. No need to worry about people overhearing over conversation. Leonie and I want to keep the details of our babies under wraps for as long as possible. The media is already going wild with bump sightings.

"Oh, *Maman*! It's such wonderful news!" Leonie exclaims as they hug and double kiss.

"Shelley, *Maman Aussi*! I'm so glad you and *Papa* Steele came!" She continues as she hugs her second mother.

I smile whenever I hear Leonie refer to my parents as hers. They welcome the terms of endearment. My mother even teared up when Leonie asked if she could call her by *Maman Aussi*.

"Glad to hear it's good news, *fils*!" Guy says as he claps me on the shoulder in greeting. "You appear pleased."

I chuckle and nod as I return his greeting, "Very pleased indeed, *Papa* Beaulieu!"

"Josy's right. No need to draw it out, son," my father Morgan adds when we embrace.

I help Leonie into her chair. Then I sit beside her, taking her hand in mine and kissing the back of it.

She glances up to smile and nod for me to tell the news.

I turn to our loved ones gathered and grin broadly.

"Leonie and I are expecting twin... Drum roll... boys!"

My father rises from his seat and lifts Leonie to her feet. He kisses her cheek as he holds her hands.

"Well done, daughter! Congratulations!"

Leonie beams as she squeezes his hands. Her amber eyes dance with delight as she glows with pure happiness.

"*Merci beaucoup!* You'll be a grand-père to twin boys soon!"

We share more words of good cheer all around. The room is full of our laughter and predictions of their birth date. I remind them about the earlier expectation of twins, and they poke fun at me for being so responsible with my research.

Leonie pulls out her iPad to FaceTime Lola and Sebastian. Then adds on the rest of the clan. I put the iPad on the middle of the table so they can see all of us.

"Well??? What are The Twins?" Lola demands.

"Boys!!" Leonie cries. "See for yourselves!"

Dutifully, I pass out copies of images from the ultrasound to those gathered. While Leonie holds up one for the FaceTime group.

"Holy cow! You can see their faces and everything!" Harris exclaims peering closely from his iPhone.

Haley claps and adds, "They're absolutely incredible! Roger, they look like you!"

We laugh at the folly of her comment since they don't have true distinguishable traits yet.

"Fantastic, bro! We see what you made," Malcolm says, giving me a virtual high five.

"Mini Steeles in the oven!" Sebastian laughs, then glances between Leonie and me. "In all seriousness, we're so happy for you both. Congratulations, Mommy and Daddy!"

Leonie and I thank them all.

Once it's quieted down, I turn to Leonie.

"My love, this is a day I want you to always remember"— I take a flat black leather case out of the breast pocket of my suit jacket—"this is for you."

Leonie peeks up at me, then presses the sapphire-studded closure. She kisses my lips and murmurs thank you against them.

I remove the platinum necklace and place it around her neck. The three large, pear-shaped sapphires styled like her *toi et moi* ring settle against her heart. The intense, velvety, deep royal blue colored stones are the rarest and most valu-able—just like the three males in her life.

"Oh, Roger, this is beautiful. *Merci, Mon Cœur,*" Leonie says as she fingers the sapphires sliding along the chain. "All three of my boys close to my heart."

Tears fill her eyes as she cups my face and kisses me. Then she wraps her arms around me to bury her face against my neck.

I rub her back soothingly as I murmur words of ever-lasting love.

"The heavenly blue of sapphires signifies the epitome of celestial hope and faith. Believed to bring divine insight, prosperity, and safe keeping according to the ancient and medieval world."

Guy's worldly knowledge sums up the reasons I selected sapphires besides their blue color represent males tradition-ally. Everyone comments on his words and the gift's beauty.

As planned, the wait staff enter with bottles of Taittinger Comtes de Champagne Blanc de Blancs. Under normal circumstances, it's Leonie's favorite thanks to James Bond in *Casino Royale*. But tonight they bring her iced lemon green tea in a flute.

Her laughter bubbles like the champagne when she spies her cocktail.

"*À votre santé!*" She says standing with her hand on her babies bump as she leans into my side.

"Cheers!" We follow, raising our crystal flutes in the air with hers, including everyone on FaceTime.

Lola has meetings in Paris. So she and Haley arrange to come together to see Leonie "live and direct." Harris tells us he'll create the best baby monitoring system ever with all the high-tech bells and whistles available. We chat some more. Then end the video call to eat.

"Yummy for my tummy!" Leonie says after swallowing a bite of her herb-crusted chicken and closing her eyes.

When her little pink tongue pokes out to lick leaked juice from the corner of her mouth, my dick twitches. I shift in my seat to adjust my suddenly tight trousers. We haven't had sex in two days since she's tired from the pregnancy and working on the penthouse renovation. It's nice to spoon at night and all. But damn if she doesn't keep me on the edge...

"Now you can plan the nurseries' color schemes. You should pick up on the blue in your sapphires."

Josy's mention of nurseries distracts me from my carnal needs.

"What a wonderful idea!" Shelley adds, clapping her hands. "You'll need one for each home. Paris for you, Josy, and me. Monte Carlo for your penthouse and Roger's villa. Positano for Villa Sogno. Manhattan for you and me and Steele Southampton—"

"Oh, Shelley, you have the child's head spinning! She

need not think about all the homes now. The Twins won't travel for a bit anyway," Morgan admonishes her, chuckling as he places his finger against her lips.

She laughs and nips his fingers. His nostrils flare as his dove gray eyes darken.

Talk about live and direct…

My parents are a hot as hell couple. They may be in their mid-sixties and mid-fifties, but Dom Morgan and sub Shelley don't let age stop their love affair.

That's how Leonie and I will be. Forever committed to each other.

ROGER

"— *S*cheduled a bunch of appointments. She's a sergeant, I tell you!"

Leonie's laughter draws me out of my musings. When I frown, she rolls her eyes and repeats herself.

"Your mother Shelley scheduled a bunch of appointments for our wedding planning for this week. She's a sergeant who kept everyone on point with Lola and Sebastian's nuptials. My mother is proving to be just as bad!"

I join in her laughter as I recall Sebastian throwing his hands up in surrender. They only allowed him to plan the honeymoon and to select our formal attire. And that was only after he put his foot down and wouldn't budge. He didn't mind not having much say in any other part of the planning for his wedding...

I'm of the same mindset. Let them have their fun. But I decide on my fun with my new bride. Period.

"Well, remember, I get to plan our honeymoon. You must block two months after The Twins turn 3 months old and can travel," I say.

"That's around six months after we get married," Leonie pouts, then rubs her fuller belly. "Thanks so much, Little Cubs!"

I laugh and kiss both sides of her belly.

"Now look what you've done. You've upset your *Maman's* honeymoon timing."

Leonie tsks at The Twins. Then reaches for her mobile as it vibrates beside our bed. She shakes her head when she sees the name on the screen and sighs resignedly.

"Bonjour, Maman Aussie…"

Leonie shifts on the bed to sit up. Ready for the day's marching orders.

I help her to fluff the pillows behind her back. Then head to the bathroom. Time to start my day.

"THE PROJECTIONS' estimates are above the recommended budget we provided last week. We must regroup with the contractors, finance, and marketing to generate an alternative plan…"

The weekly update meeting seems longer than usual. I keep glancing at my mobile for the time rather than being obvious, flicking my French cuff back to view the face of my Vacheron Constantin watch.

Leonie's words and discontent swirl in my mind. They overshadow the team's progress reports as it works to find a solution.

She's right that she has a lot to work on with our wedding plans, her hectic modeling schedule, renovations for our penthouse makeover project, and helping my mother with their new space. Not to mention her pregnancy. She insists on doing everything herself. It's ludicrous.

"—what are your thoughts... Roger? Roger, would you prefer we renegotiate the terms?"

I stop rubbing my top lip to glance up and find all eyes on me. Their questioning looks leads me to conclude they expect an answer. I will not bullshit them. I didn't hear a dam thing they said. I shift my gaze to the presentation screen. That's not the last slide I saw.

"I apologize. Would you go back to the slide on with comparison charts and go from there?"

They nod and proceed.

This time I pay attention for the rest of the meeting. Not a good look for the President of Residential Properties Division to ignore his team's work.

Fortunately, the meeting ends in another thirty minutes. My assistant of five years Françoise Faucher smiles as I return to my offices. She's in her mid-fifties and commands respect from everyone. In fact, she's one of the company's best employees. I value her as an integral part of my team.

"Mademoiselle Beaulieu called for you—"

"Is she all right?? You should have told me right away—"

I trail off as I rush to turn the knob on my door and pull out my mobile, propriety forgotten. Fuck!

"Are you okay??" I ask anxiously when Leonie answers on the third ring.

"*Oui, oui!* Nothing is wrong. I asked Françoise not to worry you since I knew you were in your weekly meeting."

I sag into my desk chair and run my hand through my hair as I lean my head back. I'm too wound up with worry. My mind clicks on the solution... We need a break. Now.

Babymoon floats to the surface of my muddled brain like a life preserver floats on the ocean to save a drowning man. That's the solution!

"Babe," I say, cutting into Leonie's sentence about food selection and paint colors. "Get you passport and be ready to go in an hour. I'll pick you up then."

Stunned silence.

"Babe, I've gotta call the pilot. We need a break. Be ready."

Leonie sputters, then agrees hesitantly.

"Whatever *Maman Aussi, Maman* Josy, the penthouse contractors, the wedding vendors, Lola's damn Coterie or the cosmetics company want from you, can wait until we get back next week. We'll return in time for your appointment with Dr. Berger. *D'accord?*"

"*Oui, oui! D'accord!!*" Leonie exclaims.

I hear her clapping and singing to The Twins how they're going on holiday with *Papa.*

That's what I want. The fun loving, easygoing Leonie who laughs and shimmies her happy dance.

Especially when said shimmy gets my cock hard as nails...

* * *

"Oh, Roger! *C'est fantastique! Merci, Mon Cœur!*"

Leonie says as she bounces on her seat in the Mercedes-Benz G-Wagen when Lucien's lavish hillside Villa dei Fiori in Capri appears around the bend in the driveway.

Her much fuller breasts bounce right along with her, nearly spilling from the scoop-neck of the long-sleeved top. Leonie's black lace cups runneth over deliciously.

Yup very wise decision.

"It's good to see you so exuberant, my love," I respond, flicking her prominent nipple with my finger.

"Bad boy!" She giggles as she swats my hand away and peers through the windshield. "It's pink!"

The salmon-colored stucco exterior with white trim around the windows, columns, and roof lines blend beautifully with the lush greenery and stunning sea views from all sides. The sea-edge gardens, bountiful with camellias, magnolias, and palm trees prove as captivating as the impressive views of Mount Vesuvius, the Peninsula of Sorrento, the entire Gulf of Naples, and Anacapri. Its private swimming pool set in the grass of the side garden and its exclusive sea access with a second plunge pool below makes it a unique property.

Lucien bought it a few years back while studying with a chef on the isle. If it can make Leonie this excited, I'll buy it from him at whatever cost!

"Yeah, babe. It's the most luxurious and historical villa in Capri. I knew you'd appreciate its design," I respond, grinning at her.

We stop in front, and the staff greets us and helps us to get settled in. Leonie, the gracious lady of the manoir, receives them with aplomb. As awed by her beauty as she is of the villa, they hurry to assist her, especially when they notice her babies bump.

"*Oh guarda il bambino! Bella ragazza!*" They exclaim.

Leonie giggles with glee. Then responds, "*Grazie mille! Ragazzi gemelli!*"

Fluent in English, Italian, German, Spanish, and of course French, Leonie easily converses with them. As do I since Italian is the third language I know besides French and English. Often we'll role-play scenes from a *Fish Called Wanda*. Just thinking about Leonie screaming my name with sexy Spanish phrases makes me want to carry her off behind one of the flowering shrubs. Instead, I wrap my arm around Leonie's waist and we head inside.

I've been here before and know to choose the sumptuous gold and red suite. It's on the second floor with expansive views of the Sorrentine peninsula and beyond. An anteroom and separate bath round out the large space.

"I love it!" Leonie declares when we enter. "My, my, my... The bed is massive..."

She sashays over to it with her maxi skirt swirling round her long legs. Then she sits down with her arms spread wide. With a wink, she beckons me to her.

"Kindly leave our bags. We're fine, *grazie*," I say, only moving my gaze from the siren for a moment.

"*Sì, Signor Steele*," the two porters respond.

The soft click of the door closing behind them is my signal.

I saunter over to Leonie, pushing the sleeves of my linen sweater to my elbows. I've got work to do. Without breaking our intense gazes, I kneel before my lover and cup her face. I tilt it to the perfect angle, then slant my mouth over her plump lips.

Leonie's mewls and purrs when I deepen the kiss harken me with a primal call. She's been so busy, her energy has been lower. Now she's recharged and I'm going to fill her socket.

"Open for me, Pretty Kitty. I need more room," I tell her as I rub the palms of my hands along her inner thighs.

She complies with a coy smile. Slowly, she spreads her legs to accommodate my broad shoulders. Then lifts her heels to elongate her limbs. With the tips of her fingers, she gathers her skirt to reveal she's sans panties.

A deep passionate growl falls from my mouth. I slip my

arms under her thighs, spread her wider, and cradle her ass. Pulling Leonie to the edge of the bed, I dive into her moist pussy. A deep inhale of her tantalizing feminine scent lengthens my dick.

I nuzzle my nose against her folds, bumping against her swollen clit. When she wiggles her ass to move closer to my mouth, I spank her butt cheek.

"Be still or I'll bind you to the bed and edge you for the next two hours," I threaten with a growl.

Leonie whimpers.

I know she misses our lovemaking as much as I do. So I intend to make it last and well worth the time we missed connected as one.

Her sweet essence flows. My tongue laves and sucks at the juncture of her thigh and pussy, folds. I hold back on her clit and probing her channel until her body lets me know she's at the point of explosion.

Leonie writhes and whines as I increase my ministrations. One hand grips my hair, pulling the long strands from their roots to lock my mouth to her pussy.

"Roger, *Amoureux*, please…" she pants, tossing her head side to side.

Her pussy walls flutter when at last I fill her channel with my tongue. I lap up her juices, not wanting to miss a drop of her sweetness.

"Aahh… Aaahh… Roger… please!" Leonie cries. "Please… let me cum!"

I drape her legs over my shoulders. Then lift her ass off the bed, repositioning the tilt of her pelvis to allow me more access. My powerful arms and core hold her aloft easily. My thigh muscles tighten to stabilize my position.

Leonie uses one hand to balance and the other to continue her grip on my hair.

I coat my thumb with the juices on her upper thigh. Then my tongue prods the textured tissue on her upper pussy wall while my thumb thrusts into her bottom hole.

Leonie wails like a teakettle on full steam. She tosses her head back and bucks against my mouth and thumb. Her hand slips on the silk bedding. But I hold her higher as I rise to my feet and slide her along the top of the mattress. Never moving my mouth or thumb.

"Rogeeerrr... Ooohh, Rogeerrr!" She wails as her body continues to convulse.

My cock presses to the point of pain against the zipper of my jeans. With Leonie positioned on her side, I free my aching weeping dick and settle behind her. She bends her leg at a ninety-degree angle and reaches for me greedily.

Happily, I oblige my siren.

"Fuuuck!!"

My eyes close and my breath catches as I sink deep within her pussy and her walls clamp on my cock.

"So fucking good, Kitten... Fuuuck. Me..." I growl as Leonie quivers around me.

I grip her hip with one hand and wrap the other around her body to hold her throat. Locked together, I rock in and out of her pussy, grunting like a feral animal.

Leonie meets each thrust with one of her own as she undulates her hips. She tenses when her orgasm nears and clenches my cock in a vise-like grip.

"Uh. Uh. Uh. Uh."

Her grunts echo mine as we ride each other over the edge.

"Cum for me, Pretty Kitty!" I command.

Her strangled cries of rhapsody push me to the brink. My spine tingles as my cock expands and pulsates to jet my seed within my mate.

"Fuuuck… Yeeesssss!!" I bellow.

White spots dance before my eyes and my mind blanks. Working by instinct alone, my hips continue to pump my dick into Leonie until the last drop of my copious jizz coats her pussy walls.

As I collapse to the bed, I lift my arm around her waist and pull her to me. Still fully dressed and connected at our cores, we fall into a sated slumber.

* * *

"ROGER, THIS IS DIVINE," Leonie says as she floats in the mosaic tile lined swimming pool overlooking the Bay of Naples. "This was your best idea ever!"

I chuckle and slide my hands along her flanks as I bury my face in her neck, breathing in her heavenly scent.

"Mmm mmm. My 'best idea ever'… Really, babe?" I say, then nip the delicate shell of her ear.

She giggles and swats me away.

Reluctantly, I let her go and watch as she takes long, leisurely strokes to the other end of the pool. Her mahogany hair fans out behind her like a mermaid. The sun glistens on her toasted caramel-colored skin like diamonds on golden topaz. I'm entranced by her natural beauty.

"It's so tranquil. I never want to leave!" Leonie pouts as she peers past the palm trees to the sea beyond.

I make a mental note to send a text message to Lucien with an offer—what Leonie wants, Leonie gets, and more. Then dive under the water to swim below the surface. I pop up next to her and she splashes me. When she tries to scamper away, I catch her by the hips and hold on tight.

"Not so fast, Kitten," I growl.

Leonie twists her hips until she rubs her round ass against my crotch, activating my cock instantly.

I return her grinds with my own. Then trail the fingers of one hand around her hip to cup her red string bikini-clad mons.

"Mine!"

"*Oui*, only you *Amoureux*," Leonie purrs seductively as she continues her dick-awakening grind.

"You got that right!" I respond and push my thick digit inside of her tight pussy.

I flex and curl it, then add another to bring Leonie to a quick climax to prepare her for me. As she pants leaning heavily into me, I let loose my hard cock. Leonie braces herself against the rim of the pool as I slide home.

Fuck me. She feels so damn good. Words to describe the sensation escape me. So I don't bother to think on it. I just let our bodies do their thing to bring us a vision-stealing, mind-blowing orgasm at the same time.

I slip out of her warm heat and hold her close to my chest. The beats of our hearts matching in rhythm.

"I want us to stay..." Leonie whispers sleepily.

Now, lying in bed for the night, I think about how I'd like to stay, too. But tomorrow our week-long getaway ends. Back to business. But with revisions.

My Responsible side won't allow Leonie to drive herself crazy. She'll get an assistant for basic tasks and work with a wedding planner. Well, that is, if my mother will allow someone else to take over.

As the head of STEELE International, Inc.'s STEELE Foundation that builds and manages attractive, affordable housing for urban, lower-income families, Shelley grew accustomed to throwing elaborate galas and events. She's the family's go-to party planner. I'm sure Lola can convince Leonie it's best to leave Shelley to her task like Lola did with her wedding.

For the modeling, she's completed the bulk of her assignments. That whirlwind five-city trip exhausted me. So I know Leonie felt it, even days after we returned. That's done along with this year's campaigns for the cosmetics company.

As for the design side of her life, that will take some convincing. She's excited about the Lola's Coterie maternity lingerie collection. She stays up sketching pieces and talking with Lola at all times of the night since she's based in New York City now. They act like they're both still in Paris chatting instead of five hours apart.

The renovations for our penthouse and my parents' dominate most Leonie's time. I'm going to check on someone at STEELE who can manage the projects for her. Leonie will still have the final say. But she need not saddle herself with the day-to-day aspects, just the bigger parts.

Especially now that Shelley put the nurseries into Leonie's head. It's crazy to think we need that many—nine. Give me a break. That will take more convincing...

"Mon Cœur, what are you thinking about? Your body is all tense."

The connection Leonie and I share astounds me. No matter what or where, we sense the other's thoughts and emotions. Tonight is no different.

"How we can keep this blissful feeling going after we leave tomorrow," I respond and kiss the side of her neck.

"Bof! Who says we're leaving?" She huffs with her Gallic shrug.

I zerbet her neck and she bursts into a fit of giggles.

We spend the rest of the night making lasting memories of our first holiday at Villa dei Fiori. Then a nod to those to come.

LEONIE

"*I*'m walking towards the elevators. I'll call you ba—Oh!"

As I'm jostled from behind, my Chloé Silverado bag falls off of my shoulder. Followed by my mobile clattering to the floor. I place one hand protectively on my babies bump while the other reaches out to slap the wall beside me.

Merde!

"Mademoiselle? Mademoiselle! Are you okay?"

I lift my eyes to the voice. A man holds my arm and gazes at me with concern. I peer over my shoulder to see Delia Shaw standing behind me.

Did she just push me??

Just as I open my mouth to ask just that, she speaks.

"Oh, Leonie. I'm so sorry! I didn't see you."

She pauses to glance pointedly at my belly. Then scans my body from the tips of my Manolo's to my high ponytail with a smirk.

"Although... I shouldn't have missed you! You're very

pregnant. Much bigger than before," she continues. "My bad. Are you all right?"

My mouth drops open at her audacity as my face flames. Is she serious with me right now??

"Wow! How does Roger, I mean *Mr. Steele*, feel about your... change? Oh, never mind. There's the elevator. Some of us need to work for a living. Not all of us are engaged to the boss. Nice seeing you, Leonie. Tootles."

With amber eyes blazing hot enough to set Delia ablaze, I watch the curvy brunette saunter to the open elevator. Then pivot and waggle her fingers at me as the doors close.

What the everlasting fuck was that all about?!

That brazen floozy... heifer... shrew!!

Delia. Fucking. Shaw.

I haven't seen my American former classmate and colleague in over four months, and I'm glad of it. She's been a pain in my ass for far too long. Today proves no exception. The gall!

First, Delia flirts blatantly with Roger when he guest lectured one of my classes at Paris American Academy. Then she accuses me of scoring the internship at STEELE Paris since I was "dating the president." Although in reality, I was at human resources for my *third* interview as a part-time junior designer on the Interior Design Team.

She and Antonio Vasquez—my former seat mate and, unbeknownst to me, interested suitor—were selected as the inaugural PAA interns at STEELE. An internship Roger had to create to make up for his gaffe of fighting Antonio at the PAA end-of-the-semester reception.

Roger, the possessive caveman, thought Antonio and I were kissing and punched him in the face. To make amends, Roger provided compensation for Antonio's medical costs and a generous sum of money in recompense. In addition, he had the STEELE human resources team put together an annual paid internship program for two students awarded in perpetuity.

Unfortunately, human resources and management chose Antonio and Delia. Antonio with the Technical Design Team since he's a computer wiz and specializes in AutoCAD software. They placed Delia on the Interior Design Team with me.

Despite working together, I successfully avoided both of them since I was part-time. Only the occasional interaction at team activities with limited conversation. Sure, they tried to play nice and invited me to lunch often. I declined. I trust neither of them, particularly Delia.

Roger told me about her incident in his office. She appeared unannounced and unexpected; her behavior just short of stripping and jumping his bones. Delia could bypass the stone wall of Françoise, his assistant, since she was at lunch.

Fortunately, she returned and promptly censured Delia for inappropriately entering the president's offices and trying to seduce him. Then Françoise escorted her to security and human resources like a rebellious student sent to the principal's office for correction.

How Delia accessed the executive floor in the first place is still a mystery. The security team found her STEELE ID programmed to include the twentieth floor. They assumed it was a fluke when it one of their staff originally set it since they control the computer software for all IDs. Sneaky hussy...

"Here, mademoiselle, let me help you sit down."

Drawn out of my ruminations, I turn to him as he hands my mobile to me.

"Mademoiselle Beaulieu! What happened?"

Françoise appears and bustles the man out of her way. She clutches my arms. Then she stares into my eyes before she glances at my belly to assess me carefully.

"What did you do?!" She demands of the man who helped me, her icy blue eyes glare at him with contempt.

Two security members approach and take the man by the arms.

"Oh! Wait, *non, non!*" I start as I lift my hand to stop them. "You misunderstand, he helped me."

Everyone turns to me and I notice other passersby have gathered. Some hold their mobiles out for photos and video.

Merde!

This is not what I need right now. Delia already made me to feel like a blimp. I don't need this scene splashed across the Internet. No fodder for the media.

"I'm fine. Really," I say as I straighten and take my mobile from the man. "*Merci beaucoup, Monsieur.*"

He nods and hastens away without a backwards glance once the guards let him loose.

"Shall we inform Monsieur Steele?" The taller security member asks of Françoise.

She turns to me and I shake my head. She declines their offer and leads me to the private elevator for the executive floor. Meanwhile, the guards disperse the crowd.

I pause at the elevator and look at Françoise, "*Merci* to you, too. But I need to go to the other elevator bank. I'm meeting with a few designers about the penthouses renovation projects."

Françoise nods, "*Oui*, I will have them set up in Monsieur Steele's private conference room. He's not in at the moment, and it would displease him if I let you out of my sight."

She raises her elegant brow and tilts her head. The woman is formidable. I give in without an argument.

She presses her ID to the plate and the doors open. Once inside, she types in a code on the keypad for the twentieth floor. The other floors don't have the feature.

"Hmm, that's new," I muse aloud.

"*Oui*, after Monsieur's unsavory visitor, Ms. Shaw, he had security add this feature as double verification," she responds with an expression of disdain on her face.

Smart move…

We exit the elevator and walk to the conference room. I smile at the receptionists and other staff members as we pass them along the way. Once inside, Françoise offers me tea or water. I accept a glass of water gratefully. Then return my disrupted call and assure my agent all is well.

Françoise uses one telephone to arrange the meeting relocation. When she finishes, Françoise glances at me expectantly.

"If you don't mind, please tell me what happened. Monsieur Steele will want to know details."

Of course, she would keep him abreast. I don't mind as she has my best interests in mind.

"The infamous Ms. Shaw jostled me from behind. Apparently, she didn't see me. Oh, but that was despite me being 'very pregnant' and 'much bigger than before' she told me…" I respond with a smirk.

Françoise's eyes widen before she collects herself to maintain her professional demeanor. But she can't help herself either.

"That Delia Shaw is a true troublemaker. I will let Monsieur Steele know immediately," she replies.

I shake my head and let her know I will speak with him later. I don't want to interrupt his off-site meeting. She agrees and we chat about my pregnancy progress and wedding plans while we wait for the designers.

When Clinton, his assistant, Brandon Eliot, and another designer arrive, Françoise excuses herself.

Before my hospital scare, I worked with Clinton as the design director on a new STEELE residential project, and Brandon was one architect. The other designer is a woman I haven't met before. Perhaps they hired her after I, or rather Roger, put an indefinite hold on my position.

When he suggested I restructure my time to preserve my energy, I agreed with him. The renovations for our penthouse and his parents' take up most of my focus. My passion is design and the reason I switched from my highly successful modeling career of eighteen years. But I realize I can't do it all alone. Especially such extensive projects. Someone else from STEELE can manage them for me based on my ideas, and I'll make the final decisions.

The same is true of our wedding plans. My mother and Shelley were more than thrilled to take over. General Josy and Sergeant Steele to the rescue! They told me I will merely show up and chose from three options at the most—no stress for *Petite Maman*.

The bigger items, like my dresses, will wait until my body shows what it will look like closer to the date. I have sketches of exquisite gowns from Monsieur Valentino on standby. Lola, Haley, Blair, Billie, and Starr are in cahoots with their dresses as matron of honor and bridesmaids. Roger, his brothers, Lucien, and Luc will wear bespoke tuxedos.

The location was the easiest to decide—*Le Beaulieu Manoir*. The majestic home and picturesque grounds will serve as the backdrop to my fairy-tale wedding. My father was beyond pleased Roger and I chose my ancestral home for our momentous occasion. I'm super excited!

I told Roger I would schedule interviews for assistants vetted by Françoise. So far, she hasn't found suitable candidates. I'm not in a rush with everything else taken care of for now.

"Leonie! So good to see you!" Clinton says as he shakes my hand and double kisses my cheeks.

"How lovely you look!" Brandon adds, his arctic blue eyes glow.

The assistant and new designer nod in agreement and smile.

Well, at least they don't think I'm unappealing...

Clinton makes the introductions. Then we get down to business.

I was happy for an opportunity to work with him and Brandon again. So I suggested them to Roger, and he agreed they would do a superb job. Although he was hesitant about Brandon being a part of the team. He's a handsome man in his early forties and was a regular lunch mate of mine. Roger felt Brandon involved himself too much when I became ill at the office.

Oh boy, Possessive Alpha Male Alert.

The meeting goes well as expected. Their ideas blend seamlessly with mine. Plus, they offer alternatives I had not considered. We set a date for them to tour the penthouses. Then end with more congratulations and well wishes.

That checked off my to do list, I thank Françoise and make my way back to Eric who waited to drive me to another baby boutique. The highlight of my day!

ROGER

*D*amn. I'm running late for my meeting with the Interior Design Team. Although I have to say, the sweet taste of Leonie still lingering on my tongue was well worth being tardy. The greedy Kitten, I chuckle to myself.

Surreptitiously, I adjust my cock that decided to awaken at the thought of Leonie's delectable pussy that I left wrecked and passed out in orgasmic bliss on our bed. The jacket of my pinstripe Ermenegildo Zegna three-piece suit covers the bulge and hides my groin as I shift it.

"Oh, Mr. Steele!"

I glance over my shoulder mid-stride to my private elevator. Fuck. It's that intern from before—Delia Shaw. Since our last encounter, I reviewed her file hoping to uncover a reason to end her internship. Unfortunately, I found none.

"I am not available," I answer as I quicken my pace.

Undeterred, she speeds up and reaches me just as I place my ID on the plate.

"Yes, Sir. I understand. Just a question on the new

project in the sixth arrondissement? If I may ride up with you to the meeting..."

I sigh and gesture for her to enter the open doors. Then press the button for the nineteenth floor. I fold my arms defensively over my massive chest and nod for her to speak.

She lowers her gaze to the floor as her creamy complexion blushes a rosy hue. The contrast to her brunette hair makes it more noticeable.

Delia is a curvy, sensual woman. Her straight hair falls down her back like a curtain made of silk. Fringed with long lashes, her moss green bedroom eyes can captivate a man easily. The Cupid's bow of her full upper lip begs for a kiss.

I take in the rest of her. The emerald green fitted suit jacket nips her tiny waist to flare at the swell of her hips. The tops of her tits peek out from beneath a flesh-toned lace camisole, high and firm. She's petite. But her shapely calves end in sky-high, fuck-me heels to add length and height. Although she still stands a good six inches shorter than my six feet, three inches.

"Mr. Steele?"

Her Demi Moore-like husky voice brings my focus back to her face.

A flicker of desire appears in Delia's eyes.

But when I blink, it's gone. Perhaps I was mistaken. I nod again, and she continues.

"Well, I reviewed the AutoCAD renditions and found—"

The elevator lights blink on and off.

I shift my gaze up to the ceiling. They appear normal. I look down at her and she appears distressed.

"It's fine, the power must have had a surge. Go on," I encourage her.

She rubs the back of her neck as she stretches it to the side to release tension.

"Well, uh…"

The lights go out completely and the elevator jolts to a stop.

I fall back against the wall and hear a thud.

"Fuck!" I grumble.

What the hell happened?!

The interior of the elevator is so dark that I can't see my hand in front of my face. Groping along the wall, I feel for the panel. My fingers find the emergency call button, but it doesn't activate. None of the buttons work. Damn!

"Aahh…"

The painful cries from the other side of the elevator stop my mutterings. Right, Delia.

"Are you all right?" I call out.

More pitiful moans fill the air of the noticeably warmer space. Not wanting to step on her, I inch closer to the sounds with my hands outstretched. The tip of my Oxford shoe bumps against soft flesh.

Another moan comes from Delia.

"My apologies. Are you standing or on the floor?" I ask, not moving forward to avoid hurting her.

Delia doesn't answer.

"Hey. Did you hit your head on the wall or something?"

This time I reach out and make contact with her body. The feel of it is soft and heavy. I jerk back, realizing it's her breast.

Fuck!

"Excuse me! I didn't mean to touch you inappropriately. I can't see—"

The full weight of her body falls into mine as the elevator drops several feet. With one hand, I grab a hold of what must be her waist to keep her from dropping to the floor. The other hand I reach out for the wall to gain purchase. Delia wraps her arms around my neck. The elevator cuts off again.

Disoriented, I continue to hold her. She presses her pillowy breasts against my chest. The hold around my neck tightens.

"I... I... I'm claustrophobic..." Delia wails, the sound of her voice muffled by my shirt and tie.

Gently, I pat her back to soothe her. This is not good at all. The elevator is going haywire, and she's scared. Great. Just fucking fantastic!

"Okay, it's okay. The building operations team will take of it," I offer as consolation.

Her fingers climb up into my hair, gripping it. Then musing it up as she pulls her hands away. They slide down my shoulders to my tie. She jerks on it as she falls backwards.

The movement throws me off balance, and we tumble to the floor. The sound of material ripping fills the elevator as her knee bends. I land half on top of her and half on the floor. My left hand takes the brunt of my fall as I try to avoid crushing her with my weight. It twists as it hits the floor at an awkward angle.

"FUCK!" I bellow from the pain.

"Ooomph!"

Delia lands on her ass with her legs around my waist. She still grips my tie in her fist and my shirt with her other hand.

I scramble backwards like a crab away from her as I clutch my hand to my chest. It throbs like crazy. The pain shoots up my arm in endless waves. I'm on my ass with my knees bent and my back against the wall.

Suddenly, the lights turn on and the doors open.

The difference from pitch black to bright white is blinding. I squeeze my eyes shut and stars dance before my eyelids. My head falls back against the wall.

"*Mon Dieu!*"

"Hey! What happened?!"

"Are you okay?"

"Isn't that Mr. Steele the President of the Residential Properties Division?"

"Yeah. Who's he with, though?"

I open my eyes. Once they adjust, the first thing I see is a red-faced Delia lying unconscious on her back, legs splayed out, skirt and camisole torn, hair disheveled. One shoe on her foot, the button on her jacket hanging by a thread.

What the fuck?!

My head swings to the crowd at the elevator doors. Security, maintenance, and members of the Interior Design Team stare at us. Some look aghast, others angry, all curious at the spectacle before them.

"Oohh..."

Delia's soft cries amplified by the now silence spectators.

Shocked, I realize my tie and shirt also tore and my hair tangles about my head.

What could only be minutes stretch on with everyone frozen in place.

The sound of heels clicking on the tile rapidly precedes Françoise. She surveys the sight, then moves past the gawkers. She doesn't enter the elevator. Rather, she galvanizes the security team to disperse the crowd and the maintenance crew to keep the doors from closing.

She punches a number on her mobile, and in a low voice she speaks in French. Satisfied, Françoise glances at Delia, then back to me.

"Monsieur Steele, is your hand hurt?"

I gather my wits and rise from the floor. I slide up the

wall and get my feet underneath me to stand. My wrist feels like it's broken for sure. The pain is intense and unrelenting.

"Yes, I land—"

She holds up her hand for me to stop speaking.

"Nothing else, Monsieur Steele," she responds. "Mr. Perry is on his way."

I close my mouth and nod.

Françoise has summoned the STEELE Paris General Counsel?

Fuck. Me. It's worse than I thought.

My head clears immediately.

"Ms. Shaw? Can you hear me?" Françoise asks as she now turns her attention to Delia still without entering the elevator.

I glance at Delia, and my mind goes over the events. I did nothing to harm her. She looks like I have assaulted her.

FUCK ME!

LEONIE

$\mathcal{M}$y poor baby has been beside himself for over a week after the fiasco with that conniving Delia Fucking Shaw…

Instantly, I knew something was wrong with him when he walked through the door. The sling may have been the obvious clue, but it wasn't the only one.

I was off center for over three hours. I couldn't put my finger on it. But I knew something was wrong. Call it my maternal instinct or the crazy connection that Roger and I share. It wasn't good.

"ROGER?" I ask. "Roger! What happened to you?!"

The water slides down my body as I rise from the bathtub. Careful to hold on to the sides, I place my feet on the slip-proof mat at the bottom firmly. I pay no heed to my body's reaction to its mate. My hardening nipples and the heat pooling in my lower belly go ignored after one look at Roger's tired face.

He leans against his vanity, but moves to help me one-handed step out of the bathtub. His gray eyes are hollow and dark circles visible below speak to his troubled countenance. Wordlessly, he wraps a warm bath sheet around me as I step into my terry slippers.

"Mon Cœur, please speak to me!" I implore, his silence too much to bear.

Roger nods, "First dry off. I want you to sit on the bed."

I protest. But he cuts me off with his fingertips to my lips, and he shakes his head.

With a sigh, I comply.

Once dried, Roger hands my floral silk Lola's Coterie kimono to me. He holds one side up to ease my arm's entry into the sleeve. Then takes my hand and leads me to our bed. He settles me on the bed with the pillows behind my back, toes off his shoes, and sits beside me.

I watch him as he leans his head against the pillows and closes his eyes. He winces as he adjusts the sling across his dress shirt. I notice his suit vest and jacket draped on the sofa. I take his hand into mine and stroke his cheek. I need to be closer to him. So I curl into his side and put his arm around me. I place my hand on his chest and wait until he's ready to speak.

Roger is home, and he's in one piece. So, I can be patient.

A few minutes pass and I wonder if he's fallen asleep. His breathing has evened out, and he's more relaxed than before. I lift my head to peek at him, and he opens his beautiful gray eyes. I scoot up and cover his lips with mine, hungry for my mate.

He opens his mouth to my probing tongue. I lick at his tongue, aching to taste him. On a groan, he grips the back of my head, fisting my long hair, and tilts me to an angle better suited for him to deepen our kiss.

Fiery desire ignites throughout my soul, flickering over my flesh with a flame set on high to make me combust. The urge to be one with Roger won't be denied. I know he needs me, too.

Right now.

I lift to my knees and around my expanded belly, fumble with his belt and the zipper of his trousers. He grunts when I free his turgid length. It grows ever larger in my hand. Impatient, I bring his bulbous tip to my already wet seam and lower down onto his dick, massive even though it's not fully erect.

"Fuuuck Leonieee..." Roger groans as his hand grips my hip.

He's so big I have to lean forward to position my pussy to take his entire length. I Rest my arms on his shoulders with my palms flat on the headboard. Then rock back and forth and circle my hips to get him inside of me. My juices flow and ease the slippery way.

I throw my head back when my ass lands on his muscular thighs bunched up with sexual tension. The feeling of warm wetness makes me cry out as Roger's mouth engulfs my puckered nipple as he latches on to it.

He suckles strongly, pulling on the sensitive bud and nipping at it. The sounds of his lapping and the combination of pleasure and pain drive me crazy.

I speed up my movements and ride Roger in wild abandon. I sense his need and it spurs me on. My mate is in pain and he needs me to comfort him, to take it away.

"Aaahh... Roger... Roger... Mmmmmm... Amoureux..." I cry as an orgasm rips through me.

"Fuck!" He grunts as my pussy walls clench around his cock.

He digs his heels into the mattress for leverage and wraps his arm around my back to grip my opposite hip. As he slides below me, Roger jacks his hips up to pound up into me.

I squeal in delight and tighten my thighs to lock him to me. My fingers twine in his hair at the nape, and I tug hard.

He responds with a bite to the side of my neck at the juncture with my shoulder. His mark.

I yowl and ride him harder as another climax hits me.

Roger is all grunts and growls. A feral beast in the throes of mating. His soul focus on satisfying our needs.

With his one arm around me, he lifts us up and shifts our position. I hang from his neck with my upper back pressed against the headboard and my legs wrapped around his hips, ankles locked at his tight ass. He kneels and pistons into me with a snarl.

Sweat coats his forehead and his hair hangs in his eyes, still squeezed shut as though fighting off an internal foe. Only our connection keeps him grounded.

The sensation of his enormous dick swelling and throbbing serve as my only warning before Roger throws his head back and roars his release. His hot seed shoots into my pussy, filling me, then spilling from my core.

I'm triggered by his intense climax and scream his name as another orgasm carries me to another level of ecstasy. On its own accord, my pussy convulses to pull out every drop. My mind drifts and my body goes limp. The last things I hear before sweet slumber collects me are Roger's words of his everlasting love for me and me only. Incoherently I mumble I love you. Then surrender.

* * *

LATER THAT NIGHT, he told me about the second unprovoked incident he had with Delia.

Trapped in an inoperable, pitch-black elevator for twenty minutes with her crying claustrophobia and him trying to help her. Only for the doors to open and the scene depicts one of an unwanted advancement witnessed by several STEELE staff members was unbelievable.

Once again, Françoise saved the day with her fast thinking. Preempting any negative talk with the General Counsel taking control of the situation and calling the medics was smart.

They were both taken to hospital. But not before the human resources team took photos of both. Roger treated for a badly sprained wrist that requires him to wear the sling for two weeks. Delia had a mild concussion sustained when she hit her head on the elevator wall.

As a precaution, Albert along with HR video recorded statements from both for the record. Roger gave a full account. Delia said she was frightened and nothing out of sorts occurred between them. She took a few days off to recover. Today was her first day back...

The building operations and security teams cannot account for the malfunctioning of Roger's private elevator. Albert had multiple systems-check tests run by the internal maintenance crew and by two external companies. They added all reports submitted to the file.

Done and time to move on.

Now I wait for Roger at LEVELS Paris. I sent a hand-written invitation and a mask to him via Eric. Roger had a late meeting and Eric was bringing him home. Instead, he'll bring him here. It's Masquerade Night. Perfect for anonymity and a change of pace.

LEVELS Paris in the 7th Arrondissement Palais-Bourbon Le Faubourg inhabits the former Parisian home of a pampered courtesan to a French king. The magnificent *maison* on a tree-lined street sits behind duplicates of the original double carriage doors and features a spacious interior courtyard. They host grand soirees during the warm-weather months under the stars and strings of fairy lights.

The layout—the same as the other two locations—spreads across seven levels. The main entry foyer has two sides with two greeter stations for access to Dine & Dance levels and BDSM levels; 7th Sky Lounge, as with each club, the Sky Lounge offers a view of a nearby landmark for Paris a stunning view of the Eiffel Tower resplendent in lights at night, a bar, restaurant by day dance club by night, a coverable pool that's open for the summer, and a glass-retractable roof; 6th and 5th multilevel dance club with two bars and a lounge for food and drinks; 4th Level 4 Restaurant and bar open for breakfast, lunch, and dinner; 3rd has twelve private suites for members to continue their pleasure apart from the BDSM levels; 2nd Peepshow for BDSM with seating alcoves, main stage, performance rooms, and a bar that serves non-alcoholic mocktails; below ground the Cellar BDSM dungeon with mocktails bar. The Dine/Dance members only have access to the party levels—Sky Lounge, Dance Club, and Level 4 Restaurant.

With it in my native city and its stunning architecture make LEVELS Paris my favorite of the three.

Roger doesn't want others to recognize me. So, we only go when members wear masks and play in the Cellar or act as voyeurs at Peepshow. At other times, we sneak in through the employee entrance and go straight to our private suite.

Tonight I'm in our suite. I had the Level 4 Restaurant set a decadent dinner of his favorite dishes—lobster bisque, steak frites, and a green salad. I'll be his dessert with straw-berries, warm chocolate sauce, and fresh whipped cream. Yum!

The click of the door lock disengaging makes my heart flutter. He's here!

Roger strides in, looking more tantalizing than dinner. Behind the black mask, his dove gray eyes twinkle with mischief when he spies me sitting at the table. I'm naked except for a red mask and pussy bow around my neck. His full lips curve into a sensual smile as his gaze travels over my exposed body.

He slips his hand into his trouser pocket and cocks his head to the side. His intense stare pebbles my nipples and makes my pussy drip juices onto the leather seat. The increasing bulge of his dick adds fuel to my burning flame.

"*Bonsoir Monsieur Steele,*" I purr as I rise to my full height of five feet, ten inches.

Roger watches me with hooded eyes sashay over to him. The sway of my hips tracked by his piercing gaze. I use all of *The Lion*'s grace and seduction to entrance him.

All thoughts of my being an undesirable blimp fade away each time Roger looks at me with unbridled desire.

That trollop won't take my man's or my happiness away from us.

Tonight, I plan to rock his world.

* * *

ROGER

It surprised me when Eric handed to me an envelope with Leonie's calligraphy-style handwriting on the front of it. The scent of her sultry perfume, Dior's Pure Poison, wafts around me as I sit in the backseat of my Cullinan. I close my eyes as I bring the envelope to my nose and inhale deeply to allow the scent of my mate to fill me, washing away the day's stress.

It's been a hell of a week.

From the crazy elevator ride to the shock of seeing Delia sprawled out to Albert's cover-your-ass plan. He encouraged me to go back to work as usual. So I did just that with meetings, being seen around the offices, events, and so on. Behave no different from prior to the encounter. Present the unflappable presence of their leader, a president of STEELE International, Inc. Be a Steele.

Then Delia returns from her sick time off today.

I had a meeting on the nineteenth floor, and she was a part of the team present. I was the polite head of the division—nothing more, nothing less.

Tension rose in the room as those gathered waited for something to happen or to words spoken. But I gave them no inkling of the irritation that ran through me at the sight of her.

Delia wore her hair in a severe bun. Her gaunt face on full display with dark smudges under her tired eyes. Her underdog demeanor and demure choice of clothing so opposite to her flirtatious self stood out. She whispered a hello to my greeting, but avoided any further engagement.

Later, Françoise, who attended the meeting purposefully, told me to be careful as she sensed Delia was up to no good.

I agreed and met with Albert before I returned to my offices. We connect with Sebastian to keep him in the loop via video conference. I tell them about the meeting along with Delia's appearance and behavior.

They thought it best to keep away from her and the team she's on. Her internship is over at the end of the month. Only four weeks and Delia Shaw leaves for good.

When I open the decadent envelope to find Leonie's invitation to LEVELS Paris, I knew I was in for a treat. I just didn't know it would be to this extent.

Leonie *The Lion* became every man's fantasy from the moment she simultaneously graced the covers of *GQ*, *Sports Illustrated Swimsuit*, and *Maxim* years ago. She's even hotter today. Her pregnancy enhances her beauty: glowing caramel skin, mouthwatering melons, and grip-worthy hips. No doubt my woman surpasses all.

My cock thickens and lengthens as she sashays her way to me with feline majesty. The purr of her greeting sends a zing down my spine straight to my balls. They fill with the need to claim and mate her.

I run the tip of my tongue over my bottom lip and stroke my growing cock with my unbound hand.

"Here, Kitty, Kitty, Kitty," I growl to Leonie.

She sucks the corner of her plump lip between her teeth as her amber eyes narrow. With ease, she drops to her hands and knees and keeps her ass high as she prowls towards me. Her hungry gaze never leaves mine.

Fuuuck. Me.

When she reaches where I stand salivating over her and not the delicious smelling dinner, Leonie nuzzles her cheek against my trousers leg as purrs rumble in the back of her throat. The bow around her long, slender neck adds to her pussy cat persona.

Leonie nudges my hand from my dick to rub her nose and open mouth against the front of my trousers.

A groan falls from my lips, then a hiss when she nips my weeping tip through the material. My head falls back as I close my eyes to enhance the sensations of her play.

With her teeth, she undoes my belt and zipper. She buries her nose, mouth, and chin inside of my pants, showering my cock with kisses through my black silk boxer briefs. A long lick makes my dick jump.

Fuck this sling!

I pull my arm from the contraption and release my aching cock. My other hand grips her ponytail and wraps it around my fist to use as a handle to guide her head.

Leonie's muffled hums vibrate along my length as she

takes all of me down her throat. Her gag reflex kicks in, and I groan.

"Yesss! Take every inch. Take... it... all..." I growl, thrusting my hips as I hold her head in place.

She drags her long fingernails up my inner thigh. Tendrils of desire swirl on my flesh. Leonie reaches into my trousers, then cups my sac and massages my tight balls. When her fingernails dig into the sensitive skin, I howl.

I lock her head in position with my grip and fuck her face like a madman.

"You're mine. Your mouth, your pussy, your ass, your heart. Only... mine..."

As my spine-tingling climax rushes headlong, my thighs shake and my eyes roll back.

No thoughts of Delia lying on an elevator floor as though sexually assaulted by me in front of STEELE staff. No concerns for negative aftereffects.

Nothing but a state of sheer euphoria surrounds Leonie and me.

The power of my release—not only physical, but mental—knocks my legs from underneath me. My cock falls from Leonie's mouth with a pop, and she moans from the loss. I land on my ass and cradle her in my lap, burying my face in her hair.

Once again surrounded by her scent calming and centering me as I let it all go.

"I will love you always, Leonie," I murmur.

"*Oh Mon Cœur, je t'aimerai aussi pour toujours,*" she whispers hoarsely as she wraps me in her warm embrace.

Before I follow Leonie into a stress-free slumber, I carry her to our bed. I slip her under the covers. Then strip and crawl in behind her, pulling her back to my front.

At last, I surrender to the peace.

LEONIE

"*O*MG! May I have your autograph?!"
"Can we take a selfie with you??"
"Even pregnant, you look ahmaaazing!!"

I laugh and do as requested of three young fans with British accents who cluster around the table of the outdoor café. They pepper me with questions about diet and exercise, skin tips, and fashion advice for an upcoming date night.

Their attention doesn't bother me since I enjoy sharing my time with girls and teens.

Twice a month I go to the center to meet with my mentees. It's a passion of mine I've done for over ten years now. My mentees trust me and find the center a safe space to open up. Even those I've mentored before often come back to meet with me and to talk to the new girls. It's so good to watch them grow up.

Besides their concerns about life and the state of the world, we discuss their goals and what they want to do after they graduate from school. Just as important, they share their thoughts on body image and stereotypical misperceptions about women.

As someone who has worked hard my entire career to dispel models as dumb; only clothes hangers; only good enough to stand there and pose prettily, not think, I can relate. I've encouraged my peers to do the same.

My mentees and I also have fun doing makeovers and spa days. Several times a year, they attend my photoshoots and fashion shows. Several photographers and designers have joined our sessions and become mentors.

Today's fans breeze in and out. But I make an effort to leave them with a positive impression and positive memories. I wave as they go about their day, giggling at their mobiles. Undoubtedly posting to their social media accounts.

"You're good, girl."

"I'd say!"

Anita, Hettie, and I are having lunch at the historic Café de la Paix in Le Grand Hotel. We're on a break from our shopping spree. Our last stop was Galeries Lafayette across the street. So we popped over here for some of the café's tasty fare.

I finally followed Roger's advice to buy some clothes. At twenty-three weeks, The Twins have grown and so has my belly. No longer a bump, it's more of a mini beach ball! We just had our third appointment with Dr. Berger yesterday. All is well, and we scheduled appointments with him every two weeks.

"Oh, I love talking with young girls and teens! Their perspective on life intrigues me. I learn from them as much as they learn from me," I respond.

"Would you have preferred girls instead of your twin

boys?" Hettie asks. "You have such great handbags, clothes, and shoes! Your daughter would be lucky."

Anita nods in agreement, her jet black curls bob around her heart-shaped face.

"Yeah, like Diana Ross and Tracee Ellis Ross. She always wears her mother's fabulous clothes and looks fantastic!"

I shake my head as I rub my belly.

"No, I'm thankful for my boys. Perhaps in the future we'll have a girl. But all I care about is having healthy babies and a successful delivery."

We pause in our conversation as the server takes our order.

"I agree. When I found out I was pregnant, all I wanted was a healthy baby. We didn't learn the baby's sex in advance," Anita starts, then continues. "Norman wanted a boy—you know all testosterone. Not that it disappointed him when Antonia was born. He's a softie when it comes to his baby girl!"

We laugh at the thought of the former world heavy-weight champion nine years straight—eight by knockout—playing with a toddler. Anita entertains us with stories of tea parties where Norman wears pink feather boas and floppy hats and combs dolls' hair and dresses them up.

"The men he knocked out would pass out all over again this time laughing if they got a glimpse of him now!" Anita giggles.

Her words make me think of my little family. I envision Roger and our sons at *Le Beaulieu Manoir*. As they play hide and seek amongst the clusters of ancient trees. Ride ponies and a horse along the scenic trails. Dive in the waves on the private beach in front of the Steele Southampton Village family compound. Wonderful, I smile.

"What about you, Hettie? Do you and Joel want children?" Anita asks after the server places our dishes in front of us.

Hettie nearly chokes on her sip of Chardonnay as her sepia brown eyes bulge and her face flushes scarlet red.

Anita and I burst out laughing, and I start to snort. Other patrons glance at us and smile at our silliness.

"Ha. Ha. Listen, I just got the man to put a ring on it after dating for three years. I don't want to give him a coronary by mentioning little ones!" Hettie says, clutching her chest dramatically.

We laugh some more. Then dive into our food.

I'm so hungry these days. And horny. And moody. Good grief!

Roger teases me mercilessly or fucks my brains out until I can't take another orgasm or runs in the opposite direction, ducking for cover.

My yoga sessions with Anita keep me grounded and somewhat sane. She and Starr coordinated my new program. With all the yoga flows and now pre-natal Pilates, my flexibility and core strength including my pelvic floor have increased. They agree the workouts will help with delivery. I'll take it!

"Joel mentioned you and Roger are going to London for a Lola's Coterie meeting. How is she doing? Is the maternity collection going well?" Hettie asks.

I nod and pull out my mobile to show them some of my sketches. Lola has prototypes to show me. Since Sebastian has business at STEELE London, Roger and I plan to meet them next week.

I'm excited to see my best friend in person. It's been forever...

After six years of living in Paris and working together, life has put us on separate continents. Now instead of hanging out at each other's penthouse with bottles of Lola's favorite Dom Pérignon Rosé Vintage 2005 or my Réserve Jean de Lillet Blanc, we FaceTime at all hours. She drinks the Dom P. while I sip iced lemon ginger tea in a Baccarat flute.

Another good thing is we've fallen in madly in love with brothers. So we'll always be close. Our families have expanded exponentially. We went from only children to two to being a part of the Steele clan of five siblings. Our children will be blood relatives. It's so incredible how life unfolds!

But I am thankful for Hettie and Anita. They're my new crew. We must go on one of Starr's international fitness retreats with the entire gang, including Billie and Blair. It'll be an epic Girls' Getaway!

My mobile chimes with a text message. I pick it up to find it's from Roger.

Hi, babe. How's it going? Did you get some agreeable things?

I text back: *Hi, all's good. We're at Café de la Paix. I picked out a few things. The stores will deliver them. We're not done, yet.*

Good! Anything I might enjoy? ;)

Naughty Boy! I will see you later xoxoxo

Bisou Bisou

When I glance up, Anita and Hettie are smirking at me. I shrug my shoulders and put my mobile back on the table.

"Don't hate!" I retort.

They snicker and roll their eyes.

We finish our meal and head to the Cullinan. Even though both women have cars and drivers, Roger insisted I ride with Eric.

"I'm not putting you and our Twins in the hands of any other driver. Would you rather I take you?"

I giggle to myself at Roger's overprotectiveness as Eric

helps me into the SUV and ensures I buckle up. Hettie and Anita hop in on the other side. Then we're off to Rue de Rivoli.

I make a note to stop by Lola's Coterie Paris to pick up some new pieces for Roger to enjoy...

LEONIE

"*H*ere, let me see."

Roger reaches across the armrests to triple check my seatbelt fits securely, yet comfortably over my mini-beachball belly. After readjusting the buckle, he sits back in his leather chair, still eyeing my seatbelt. Satisfied, he nods and mumbles to himself about that should do it as he clips his seatbelt together.

We settled on board his gleaming charcoal gray Sikorsky S-92 Executive Helicopter bound for London. The one hour thirty-five minutes will pass quickly aboard the $17 million plus luxury aircraft. The decked-out interior features platinum silk wall treatments, charcoal gray carpet, dove gray leather seats, ebony wood tables, and steel accents. The color scheme is like the STEELE corporate offices in New York City.

I stroke his cheek and smile adoringly at my responsible love.

"*Merci, Mon Cœur*. You're so good to us."

Roger takes my hand and kisses my fingertips. He entwines our fingers as he rests our hands on my armrest.

The flight attendant steps into the main cabin to let us know the pilots are ready for departure. Roger informs her we're all set. She smiles before she disappears through the ebony wood door that separates the crew's area from ours.

Roger turns to me with his intense gray-eyed stare.

"Let me know if you feel in any way out of sorts."

I squeeze his hand and nod to reassure him.

The flight is as comfortable as ever, with the attendant serving us plenty of water to stay hydrated and my new favorite snack of honey graham crackers. I spend the time reviewing my notes for my meeting with Lola, Luc, and the creative and marketing teams for Lola's Coterie.

She wants to surprise me with the prototypes from the sketches we did together. The process has been exciting, choosing the color palette, going to the fabric houses, and thinking up ways to keep the sexy along with the functionality. I can't wait to see and try the pieces!

I glance over at Roger and admire the strong profile of his handsome face. He's let his five o'clock stubble grow in and he looks delicious. Except I miss being able to lick the cleft in his chin. He'll more than likely shave tomorrow morning, though.

"Are you peeping at me, Pretty Kitty?"

I giggle at being cold busted. Roger was so engrossed in his laptop I didn't think he noticed me studying him.

He rises to stretch. Then squats down in front of me with his hands on either side of my belly.

"Hello there, my babies. Your *Papa* can't wait to hold you in my arms for real," he croons as he rubs his thumbs along the sides of my belly.

His touch sends a thrill through me. Not the I want to

fuck you until we pass out. But the you made these babies and are my mate.

I run my fingers through his hair, dragging my nails along his scalp.

Roger shivers. Then places two kisses on my belly.

When his gaze lifts to mine, the gray orbs darken with desire. As he stands, he leans on my armrests and slants his full mouth over mine. Our tongues dance as they tangle. He dominates the kiss and ends it with a bite to my lower lip as he tugs it when he rises to his full height, towering over me.

My hungry eyes stay glued to his and spark with intense need.

Roger chuckles darkly and sits back in his seat, shaking his head as he buckles up.

"Not now, Pretty Kitty. Not now."

He picks his laptop up and goes back to work.

I whimper and pout.

But he shakes his head and presses his index finger against his lips to shush me.

Merde!

With a huff, I snatch my laptop out of the side compartment and open it. Two can play this game. But I up the ante.

Feigning warmth, I fan myself and unbutton more of my pink Oxford maternity shirt to reveal the ruby red silk balconette bra. The lace trim designed to cover the nipples barely, reveal my aroused brown buds.

I pluck an ice cube from my glass of water and rub it along the back of my neck. With my hair piled atop my head, my long neck shows the trail of melted water. Once the ice reaches the side, I put it to my lips and suck on it with my eyes closed. A moan of pure bliss from the cool relief slips out.

The commotion of metal hitting metal and a growl draw

my attention to Roger. In a blur, he's out of his seat, kneeling before me, and tugging the bra cups down. My much larger breasts spill out, and he latches onto my nipple with a growl.

My head lolls back against the seat as I enjoy the sensation of him suckling the sensitive bud. He alternates between them as he massages my heavy breasts. The ache in more core intensifies with each pull, sending a jolt to my engorged clit.

Roger's hands drop to the button on my maternity boyfriend jeans and rips it open along with the zipper. His thick digit slips inside my soaking pussy, then withdraws to have two others join it. He curls them to rub my G-spot, and I levitate off my seat.

"Oooh, fuuuck…." I groan, followed by a hiss when he pinches my clit.

With my hips lifted, Roger pulls my jeans down enough for him to duck his head between my thighs as they rest on his shoulders. He presses for the seat to recline, and he scoots my ass to the edge. As I lean back, he hunkers down to his premium on-board meal.

I lose myself in the sensations of his firm tongue sweeping my pussy walls, collecting my nectar. Roger laves and nips at my lower lips when his fingers return to my core. I'm so enthralled, I heft the weight of my breasts and tweak my nipples, tossing my head side to side.

My eyes pop open when the tip of his massive dick breaches my folds and drives into my pussy with one thrust. I'm so wet, he glides right in.

Roger allows my body to adjust to his girth. He lowers his head to my breasts, swatting my hands out of the way with one hand. The other slides in position against my ass to lock me in place.

As he moves, I match his thrusts pound for pound. I bite my bottom lip to keep my screams of ecstasy from erupting throughout the cabin. No need for the flight crew to hear my pleasure.

Roger buries his face in my neck to stifle his own grunts and groans as he continues to ride me like a wild stallion. His body tenses, and he sucks in a breath as his dick expands within me. His long middle finger slips into my bottom hole, and it's the catalyst to make us explode together.

Our bodies tremble as he slows his pace to bring our scattered pieces back together from the ether. The beat of our hearts and our labored breaths decrease. Roger holds me tightly until we rejoin the world, whole once again.

"Naughty, Pretty Kitty," he murmurs gruffly in my ear.

We watch as he pulls out of my pussy slowly. His dick slick and glistening from our combined arousal. He groans deep in his throat when he slips from my well-used pussy.

It's so fucking hot, I no longer need to pretend.

Roger kisses me, and goes to the water closet. He returns with his pleasure pole tucked away and his clothes neat. But his face is flushed and his eyes glow. He wipes me clean with a warm washcloth and helps me to redress.

The flight attendant announces we'll land in fifteen minutes.

"Right on time..." Roger says as he waggles his eyebrows.

"Mmmhhhmmm..." I murmur, stifling a yawn.

Roger laughs, "You brought it on yourself, Sleepy Head!"

I FEEL REINVIGORATED and ready for my meeting when we land on top of STEELE London's Tower.

Roger takes my hand to help me disembark, and with

Eric we make our way to the entry for the stairs to the elevator. Even though he's going to Sebastian's office, Roger rides down with us to the lobby. Then walks me to one of the Sebastian's cars his driver left for Eric.

I slip inside the back of the sleek, gunmetal gray Mercedes-Maybach S 650 Sedan. Roger leans in and buckles me in. I laugh.

"Thank you, *Papa*. Now go to work! Tell *Oncle* Baz hi."

"Have a good meeting and tell everyone I said hello"—he chuckles and gives me a kiss, then continues—"I'll see you at *Oncle* Baz and *Tante* Lola's later."

He shuts the door and raps on the roof to signal Eric he can drive me to Lola's Coterie London.

Roger and I wave even though a tint covers the windows. I watch until he's out of sight before I settle in the cushy leather seat. I've gone from one cocoon of luxury to another.

While we drive to Bond Street, I return emails and text messages.

Françoise found three candidates for me to interview as personal assistants. I skim through their resumes. Then I ask her to schedule them for next week. I need someone who's organized and companionable. So if Françoise likes these three enough to send to me, they must have the rest of the skills to handle the tasks.

The design team for the penthouses sent updates and revised plans. They're on track to meet Roger's timeline. We'll move in with my parents while the construction takes place. The *Manoir*'s massive size affords plenty of space. Next week we're set to move into the East Wing with the entire section to ourselves. So again, I'm set.

My mother and Shelley have also eased my workload tremendously. They're like a well-oiled machine: vendors selected, invitations sent, menu and caked arranged. I answer a few of their questions and make some requests. Simple. All is good on that front, too.

We pull up in front of the boutique and Eric helps me to get out. Then he walks me to the door. As he holds it open, I thank him and stroll inside.

"Certainly, Mademoiselle Beaulieu. I'll be right outside," he responds.

Stylish, sexy shopgirls assist fashionable, gorgeous women and men. The boutique invites patrons to relax in an atmosphere of splendor and entices them to indulge their inner sexpot or to gift their lover with pieces.

They recognize me and wave as I pass through to the elevator to take me to Lola's office on the top floor with the atelier and business staff offices. When I step off the elevator, I skim the large white space for my best friend.

She's at a large table in the center with Luc, Blair, others, and Billie's face on a monitor via video conference. The table has portfolios on it and two racks of cloth-covered bags line up next to it. Lola's talking, but stops and claps her hands when she spies me. She rushes over with her hazel eyes shining and a huge grin on her face.

"Hot Mama! How gorgeous you look, Leonie!"—she exclaims as she hugs me and bends down to greet her nephews—"Hello to you, too! My have you grown, Little Ones!"

I rub my belly and laugh.

Luc and Blair stride over and embrace me, too.

"Leonie, you're glowing, *chérie!*" Luc adds as his sapphire blue eyes take me in from head to toe. He nods his approval and gives way to Blair.

She double kisses my cheeks and smiles as she holds me by the arms to get a good look at me.

"I agree. Pregnancy has made you even hotter, honey!"

We laugh and head to the table. Billie waves and blows kisses, motioning to my belly. I greet the other familiar faces, and we start the meeting. The creative team starts with an overview of the inspiration, thought process, and initial designs.

I glance at Lola, and she's beaming at me, bursting to show the prototypes. I'm as eager to see them, and though I appreciate the team's efforts, I want them to get on with it already!

They must read my mind because one assistant brings a rack forward.

We gather around as they unveil the pieces one by one. Jewel-toned lace, silk, and satin bras, thongs, briefs, slips, and kimonos appear. A kaleidoscope of colors and textures blend beautifully before us.

I suggested the theme of precious stones and their colors since babies are a gift and come in a variety of skin tones. Soft materials to lie against sensitive skin. Easily removable cups for breastfeeding and built-in pockets for leak-proof pads serve as examples of functionality. While the cuts and structure amp up the sensuousness of a woman's pre- and post-natal body.

The collection impresses everyone and lives up to the Lola's Coterie brand. I'll take some pieces to try. Once Lola and I give final approval for the collection, it will go into full production.

The marketing team presents next. They share ideas for the campaign, the tagline, media focus, and timetable. They want to continue with Roger and me since the last round of campaigns scored the highest engagement and sales this year.

I smile to myself as I think of Roger's reaction. He'll

grumble, but won't have any other male near me and his sons. So, I tell the team it's a good idea.

They're pleased and finish their deck.

The meeting rounds out with open discussion for feedback and ideas. Lola and I thank everyone for their skilled work, and we adjourn the meeting. Billie signs off with a promise to come to Paris next month.

Lola loops her arm through mine, and we go to her office with Luc and Blair.

"So, how are you doing? Does your progress please Dr. Berger?" Lola asks before the glass door can shut.

I smile at my best friend and reassure them all is well. They take turns touching my belly when one of The Twins moves, followed by the other.

Luc tries to cover the sadness in his eyes. Almost eight years ago, he tragically lost his wife Carole during the birth of his son and only heir Lucas, who also didn't survive.

I squeeze Luc's hand, and he nods at me gratefully.

Blair places her hand on his arm, and Luc glances down at her with a smile. He pats her hand and shakes off the sadness. Clapping, he turns back to me.

"I have a surprise for you!"

He gestures to the sofa and table where a beautifully wrapped box sits.

I smile and take his arm as he leads me to sit. Like a child at Christmas, I rip into the paper and pull the top off. Nestled amongst tissue paper is the complete collection of *Winnie the Pooh*—the first editions. My eyes fill with tears as I read his touching note.

Luc offers his handkerchief to me and puts his arm around my shoulders.

After I gather myself, I thank him and promise to read to The Twins every night.

We spend the next couple of hours catching up before we leave. Luc and Blair have a gala to attend. Lola and I drive to her home with Eric—not even Sebastian's driver is good enough for Roger...

We arrive at their palatial estate in the ultraexclusive Kensington Palace Gardens. Like The STEELE Tower in New York City is on Billionaires' Row, their West London home is on Billionaires' Boulevard. Lola tells me the mansion has at least forty rooms over five floors—including the attic.

"Yeah, and my first time here, we christened each room over the three days we stayed!" She giggles.

"Well... the Steele men certainly don't lack stamina!" I add joining in her laughter.

We burst into guffaws that turn into a fit of snorts. I nearly pee on myself. We laugh even harder when I tell Lola. By the time Eric opens the doors, tears roll down our cheeks, and our faces flush bright red.

Lola loops her arm through mine and we walk up the steps, still in tears from our jokes.

The ornate wooden door opens to reveal Roger and Sebastian. They take one look at us and panic.

"What the fuck happened?!"

"Who the hell bothered you?!"

I look at Lola, and we crack up.

Roger and Sebastian exchange glances, shake their heads, and bring us inside.

"Okay, private jokes... Got it," Sebastian smirks.

"Come on, Giggles..." Roger adds as he takes me by the waist.

I burrow my heated face in his side to muffle my snorts.

We walk past elegantly decorated rooms filled with sunshine streaming through the floor-to-ceiling windows.

Priceless antiques blend with modern art against a muted palette of pewter, platinum, and cream with marble floors covered in handwoven Aubusson rugs. We pause in front of an elaborate, double-story twin staircase.

"Come, we'll take the elevator to your suite so you can change. After, I'll go to mine," Lola says as she takes my arm again.

I glance at Roger and note he and Sebastian wear sweatpants and long-sleeved t-shirts with soccer slides. Nice and comfy for our slumber party. I'll do the same. I give Roger a kiss on the cheek and go with Lola.

We turn to an alcove with a door. While Roger and Sebastian go beyond the stairs towards the back of the home. Lola presses for the third floor, and she fills me in on the layout.

Once the elevator opens, she leads me down the hall to the end where a set of double doors stand ajar. She pushes them to show the first room. It's large with a sitting area before a fireplace, desk by one wall, and two chairs on the opposite for reading. It's well-appointed and welcoming.

We step through to the bedroom. It features an oversized four-poster bed with antique furnishings. Lola points out the marble bathroom and separate dressing rooms. The maid unpacked my bags and placed my clothing and toiletries in both.

I turn to Lola and smile.

"This is a gorgeous home, *Chérie*! I can see the touches you've made already," I say as I point to her favorite prints on the wall above the fireplace.

She smiles back and adds how Sebastian said the house needed a woman's touch to make it a home. Lola hugs me and goes to their suite on the second floor. We'll meet on the first floor by the elevator in fifteen minutes.

I return to the bathroom to take a quick shower. After I change into a white tank top and matching pink cashmere kimono and lounge pants with slippers, I ride the elevator to the main floor. Lola is already there, sitting on the steps.

She points at her wrist exaggeratedly as she shakes her head.

"Yeah, yeah, yeah.. I move slower these days, you know," I answer pointing to my belly.

"Sure, whatever you say!" Lola laughs. "You've never been an on-time person, Leonie... Pregnant or not!"

I help her up, and we head in the same direction as the boys. The delicious aroma of Indian food fills the air and grows stronger as we near what must be the kitchen.

Lola pushes a door open and my mouth waters. Not only from the table laden with dishes. But from the sight of Roger and Sebastian shirtless flexing their arms and chests à la Arnold Schwarzenegger.

They're super fit from boxing and MMA training, respectively. So one isn't better than the other. Even five years older than Roger, Sebastian is hot as hell. No disrespect to my bestie. But it's the truth!

Lola and I stand by the door unbeknownst to them. We listen to them debate the benefits of their preferred disciplines very seriously. It's a glimpse into them as children— super competitive, unmoving in their beliefs, ridiculous.

When they notice us finally, they don their shirts and agree to disagree.

"Give us a break! Mine is bigger than yours. Blah, blah, blah!" I tell them as I make my way to the table—*Maman* is hungry.

Lola laughs, "Right, you big babies! Sit down and eat!"

Their egos mollified, Roger and Sebastian join us at the table. We fill our plates with vegetable samosas, tandoori chicken, vegetable biryani, dal makhani, and paratha. It's a full-on smorgasbord. And I'm in heaven.

"How did the prototypes come out?" Roger asks between bites.

I take a sip of my iced lemon green tea—Lola had a fresh batch ready for me—before I answer.

"*Fantastique*! Even better than I imagined them! The details, the sumptuous materials. They're as sexy as the regular collections."

"Yes! Leonie's designs capture the needs of the moms with the allure for the dads," Lola adds waggling her eyebrows at Roger.

We laugh and I assure him he'll experience the pieces firsthand. Lola had them packed up for me to take back to Paris when we leave in two days.

"How were your meetings?" I ask Roger and Sebastian.

They fill us in as we finish dinner.

Afterwards, we stretch out in the entertainment room to watch a movie on the big screen and chill. I miss the easy camaraderie and fun Lola and I have together. It's so good to have days to catch up. No need to go anywhere. Just hang out all weekend like old times.

The new times are wonderful, too, I think to myself as I snuggle against Roger between his legs on a double chaise. He holds me tighter, twining our legs, and kisses my head. I glance over at Lola and Sebastian cuddled up similarly. He's whispering in her ear as she fidgets, locked in his embrace.

I nod. Yup, even better.

ROGER

"**What** the fuck?? You've gotta be fucking kidding me!!"

I bellow as I lose control completely. Responsible Roger takes a back seat in the face of this absolute bullshit.

The papers flutter in the air as I throw them at the conference table in my office. Security escorted a man who insisted upon speaking with me personally up to the executive floor. He bypassed Françoise to hand a manila envelope to me. Then he left in a hurry five minutes ago.

Curious, I opened it and withdrew a sheaf of papers. One glance at the heading and I lost it.

Delia Shaw, Plaintiff,
>   vs. Roger Steele, Co-defendant
>   STEELE International, Inc. Co-defendant
>   Petition
>   Civil Claim

Unfuckingbelieveable!

After I read enough of the document to make my blood boil, I fume and pace my office. Thoughts of how the hell did this spin out of control swirl in my mind. Delia Fucking Shaw!

A knock on my door stops me. I pivot to snarl at the invader. But it dies on my lips.

"Roger?"

Leonie stands in the doorway with her hand on her belly protectively as she eyes me cautiously.

"Fuck!" I throw my head back and roar at the ceiling.

I run my hands through my hair and tug. I cannot believe that conniving woman dropped a bomb on my life just as it's going so well.

Fuck. Me.

Small hands placed on the middle of my back tenderly and over my heart calm me instantly. Leonie presses her hands towards each other and leans into my side to still me. I drop my hands from my head and wrap them around her, letting her comforting presence seep into my every cell.

I take deep inhales and slow exhales as Starr taught me to settle my soul. Only, I know this is way beyond the scope of pranayama.

Another knock and I groan into Leonie's hair.

She pats my back and turns to the door, angling herself between me and the outsider. My *Lion* protects me now.

"Oui?" She asks brusquely.

I glance over her head to see Albert. They've never met. I squeeze her once more, then stand tall. Time for Roger *The Responsible* to take over.

"Bonjour, Mademoiselle Beaulieu. I am Albert Perry, STEELE's General Coun—"

"Ah, *oui, oui.* Forgive my bluntness. *Enchanté,* Monsieur Perry," she interrupts as she extends her hand to him.

"Albert, please," he responds, shaking her hand. "Now, what has happened, Roger?"

He turns to me, and I gesture to the sofa and club chairs for them to sit. I gather the lawsuit petition and civil claim from the conference table. Then hand them to Albert as I take a seat beside Leonie on the sofa.

She takes my hand in hers and squeezes as she flicks her concerned amber gaze between Albert and me. After a few minutes of silence while Albert reads, she shifts to face me.

"Please Roger, tell me what's in those papers?"

I bow my head, pissed and ashamed.

I have to tell the woman I love, will marry in a month, and carries my sons another woman accuses me of sexual assault and harassment—the elevator and office encounters combined. Said woman feared for her safety since I attacked Antonio Vasquez at the Paris American Academy end-of-the-semester reception. She wanted to wait until after her internship ended in case I retaliated and fired her, a blemish on her career. The whole thing is surreal.

Leonie sits for a moment, quietly searching my face after I tell her.

Fuck! If she doubts me, I'm truly fucked. Not with the legal ramifications, but with her lack of trust in me and in us. I'd never cheat on Leonie, ever. Period. She's my every-thing and has to know it.

"Leonie—"

"Roger, we need to make some moves right away. I will have Françoise get Morgan and Sebastian on the line imme-diately."

Albert rises and strides to the door.

The whole time he spoke, my eyes never left Leonie's. I put every bit of emotion into mine to convey my love for her and my unquestionable faithfulness.

She closes her eyes. Her breasts rise and fall with a deep, even breath. She holds it a moment and exhales as she reopens her eyes. A fire burns within them and ignites that spark we share. Leonie grips my hands and with fierce determination tells me we will get through these nasty accusations and come out more powerful and united than before.

Tears burn at the backs of my eyes. She is an incredible woman. I am forever humbled by her.

Albert returns and I close my eyes to gather myself. Leonie squeezes my hands and sits forward to face him.

"Let us sit at the conference table. Françoise will have them on video conference shortly," he says, taking the petition and claim with him.

She enters and hands Albert a sealed file. Then leaves with a nod of support to Leonie and me.

I help Leonie stand, and we join Albert. The screen fills with my father and eldest brother, the former and current CEOs of STEELE. Shame floods me once again. But with Leonie unshakeable beside me, I know we'll get through this. Not to mention the fact I'm innocent.

"Give it to me straight, Shaw," my father demands, the original Alpha Dom in full effect.

Sebastian nods as he runs his thumb over his lower lip. He's in profound-thinking mode.

Albert recounts the petition and monetary damages. Then he reviews the cover-your-ass file he created with human resources. My father and brother listen and wait for him to lay it all out. Their questions for him and for me hold no judgment. Neither is unfamiliar with inane cases brought against them. It goes with being multibillionaires and people wanting money.

They agree with Albert there's no basis for a case. But we

must go through the motions. They want assurance the damages to STEELE and to me are minimal.

Albert will put together his best team and handle the situation quickly and efficiently. He doesn't expect any obstacles to clearing my name.

We end the impromptu meeting with plans to regroup tomorrow after Albert briefs his team.

Once he leaves my office for his own, Morgan and Sebastian encourage me to go home and rest with Leonie. But return to work in the morning. They reiterate: present the unflappable presence of their leader, a president of STEELE International, Inc. Be a Steele. Business as usual.

Morgan shifts his attention to Leonie.

"Now, young lady, do not allow this ridiculous claim to upset you in any way. You have yourself to see to and Baby Steeles to nurture. If at any time you need to speak with someone, call me or *Maman Aussi*. Do you understand?"—he pauses for her words of confirmation before he continues— "My son is innocent. The two of you will carry on as usual."

Sebastian agrees and says he'll have Lola call Leonie once he thinks we're settled at home.

Leonie and I thank them and end the video conference.

"I am so sorry, my love. Are you okay with everything?" I ask, cupping her face so I can stare into her eyes directly.

With no hesitation, Leonie places her palms on the sides of my face and pulls me down to kiss her. I cover her mouth with mine and devour her with a kiss so passionate, her toes must curl. She whimpers in response and wraps her arms around my neck, clinging to me.

We kiss until we need to catch our breath. I lean my forehead against hers with my eyes still closed, breathing our mingled air.

"Only you, Leonie. I have never loved nor wanted a

woman the way I need you. You are my life. Only you, my love," I murmur, my voice thick with emotion.

"Oh, Roger, I love you more than you'll ever know. I trust you and have no doubt of your innocence, *Mon Cœur*," she whispers in response. "Let's go home. I need you inside of me. I need to be one with you."

My soul soars at her words.

LEONIE

"*Merci beaucoup*, Nanny Grace! These are so lovely!"

I hold one of the two hand-crocheted, navy blue cashmere blankets up and admire the fine stitchwork of the intricate design. The center panel has an entwined B and S for Beaulieu and Steele, surrounded by a twelve-inch border of swirls and whorls. The matching beanies and booties complete the sets. They're the perfect addition to the nursery in the East Wing of *Le Beaulieu Manoir*.

Because of the hullabaloo caused by that woman who shall not be named, I forewent an assistant in favor of a nanny. I can handle the work of my everyday life now that the other aspects are taken care of by my helpful wedding planning *Mamans* and design team. Plus, the maternity collection is in production and doesn't require as much of my attention as before. I sketch new pieces, but nothing too time-consuming.

A nanny is a better addition to our household. Françoise

found the agency the überwealthy and celebrities use to hire their nannies, nurses, and governesses. Their training is top-notch in everything from changing a diaper to language lessons to disarming a would-be kidnapper. Although Roger has a security detail at the ready...

Grace Hart presented as the best candidate. Besides being appropriately trained and smart. She fits in with my personality, has the stamina to handle twin boys, and is a widowed, early forties, mature woman. Not a trollop and has zero interest in my man.

Roger warmed to her just as I did. My mother and Shelley met with Grace, too. They grilled her in their demand for only the best for their grandsons. My father and Morgan ran separate extensive background checks on the agency and on her. All are suitably pleased.

Yesterday, Roger and I completed our move into the East Wing. We'll stay here for the next two months or so while our penthouse reconstruction completes. We took over my former bedroom suite.

The rest of the wing comprises several bedrooms and bathrooms, kitchenette with eating area, library, art studio, media room, and living room. In essence, it's a house within a house and was all mine before I bought my duplex. It's where I stay when I visit my parents. The maids maintain it. So it only required the arrangement of our personal items and clothing.

Now I'm decorating one of the nine nurseries Shelley and my mother insist we need. The number may seem like overkill or an extravagance. But they want The Twins to have the comforts of familiarity in whichever home they're in. After I thought about it, I agree. And hell, why not?

Roger and I combined two of the other bedrooms into one as their nursery to afford plenty of space. They finished the construction last week with the cream, aqua blue, and platinum palette in place. Sunlight streams through the windows and the balcony doors. We had hidden blackout shades added to keep the light from disrupting their sleep. Or causing them to wake up before Roger and I do!

Rather than purchasing all new furnishings, we opted to combine items from both families to fill their room. Shelley gave us the matching cribs she had made for Harris and Haley—acknowledgment of them being the first set of twins. The cribs made from mahogany wood stand on Sheraton legs, have carved head- and footboards, and feature sides cut in one-dimensional shapes of the legs. Musical mobiles with new colorful animals hang above each in the same style. They're simply stunning.

Once our penthouse renovation completes, we'll move the cribs to The Twins' nursery there. We want the gifts to be their main beds. We'll replace them with bassinets we found in the attic here that are being refinished.

The rocking chair and ottoman used by one of my paternal relatives sits near the window. It is mahogany, too. We reupholstered the pieces in pewter suede with a cream silk pillow. Then had a reproduction made for Roger to sit on. One would never guess they're from different time periods.

The rest of the furnishings, including the dressers, changing table, and storage selected to complement the chairs. They blend seamlessly.

Harris made good on his promise and created state-of-the-art baby monitors for each nursery. He installed the set here last week while he was in Paris on business. He will do the others when the rooms are ready. I told him he should market them. The Steeles and their money-making ideas.

The nursery is near the suite of rooms Roger and I share.

While Nanny Grace's room will be down the hall. For now, she's staying in her flat until The Twins are born. Then she'll also have a room at the penthouse.

Although Grace will have rooms at each of our residences, she'll only stay until Roger gets home or when we go out. She will travel with us, too. But we plan to be hands-on parents who have the help of a nanny. We'll raise our children, thank you very much.

"You're so welcome! My hobbies have been crocheting and knitting since I was a little girl. I stitched these up in no time."

I turn my gaze from the soft, cuddly blanket to smile at Grace. The twinkle in her eyes shows her love of her craft and sincerity.

"The Twins thank you, too!" I respond.

"They are lovely indeed, Nanny," My mother adds as she admires the beanies. "You did a beautiful job."

Shelley walks over from where she was putting the bedding in the linen closet to peer over Josy's shoulder.

"I agree, very nice and thoughtful of you. They're heirloom quality," she nods.

She and Morgan flew over with Sebastian and Lola last night. They came to help us get adjusted and to check on the status of the legal claim. The men are at STEELE Paris meeting with Albert and his team, then finishing the workday. We're meeting them for dinner later.

"Hhhmmm. Have you ever considered using your skills for fashion?"

I make a face at Lola.

"Don't you even think about wrangling my babies' nanny away from them, Lola Steele!"

She laughs and puts her hands up, palms forward in surrender.

"Just asking, *Maman Lionne!*"—she peeks over her shoulder at Grace and winks—"Crochet would make an intricate trim or cups in my new collection."

I throw a ball at her, and she catches it laughing. Wagging my finger at her, I continue.

"Last warning…"

"Okay, okay! Just teasing. I'd never poach your nanny. She's the one I liked the most for The Twins, remember." Lola says as she puts the ball in the antique toy chest.

Working as a team, we finish organizing the nursery faster than expected. We take a survey of all drawers, closets, bathroom cabinets and agree it's ready for The Twins. Then head to the solarium for lunch. Nanny Grace joins the staff to eat before she goes home.

"*Mon Trésor*, I am so proud of you! Next month you get married and just over two months and you'll have our grandsons!" My mother says as she clasps my hands in hers and kisses my cheek.

I tear up, and she gives me a hug. When I sit back, Shelley reaches over and pulls me into her embrace.

"Oh, hugfest time!" Lola says as she wraps her arms around both of us and beckons to my mother for her to join in.

My tears stop and I squeeze them each in turn.

"*Merci, merci, merci! Je vous aime tous!*"

* * *

"How did you make out with nursery number one?"

I glance up at a smirking Roger and laugh. Right!

"It's even more beautiful than I imagined it would be from the sketches and in my mind!" I respond with a laugh. "One down, only eight more to go!"

"Uh... make that nine! *Tante* Lola and *Oncle* Baz need one in New York, too," Lola says.

"Right next to our own?" Sebastian asks pointedly with his eyebrow raised and a glance to Lola's flat stomach.

She swats at him and rolls her eyes with a huff.

Everyone laughs at their antics. It's a known fact Lola is resistant to having a baby so soon after they married. Even though it's been a year...

We're having dinner at Guy Savoy the three Michelin star restaurant famous for its mixture of true luxury and ultimate simplicity in both decor and dishes. In the chic *sixième* Île-de-France region of Paris.

Mr. Valentino sent an assortment of dresses that would fit my growing belly. Tonight I wore a pink mini dress. I fell in love with the off-the-shoulder neckline trimmed with a scalloped ruffle. It's such a pretty, feminine touch—especially with all the testosterone floating through me. The body is unencumbered and flows away below. The sky-high strappy sandals add length to my legs and makes me feel glamorous and sexy.

Roger smiled appreciatively when I walked up to him waiting at the bar with my father, Morgan, and Sebastian. It sent a thrill through me at the desire in his gray eyes.

Now he squeezes my thigh under the table as he smiles at me again.

"My baby can have as many nurseries as she wants," he winks.

His lighthearted mood makes me hope the meeting with the legal team went better than expected.

We weren't so optimistic since the tabloids somehow got wind of the story. From the grocery store checkout racks to the Internet gossip sites and social media, word spread rapidly. A photo of Roger scowling at some random time splashed across the covers alongside a shot of Delia looking terrified. They even dragged up a photo of me yelling at Roger to stop fighting Antonio. Nothing of substance, pure sensationalism to add fuel to the fire.

Even as we walked through the dining room, I noticed a few people turn to gaze as we passed them by. Some with open curiosity, others skeptically. These types of patrons are used to scandal. But the world being the way it is with the MeToo movement, everyone questions the truth. Except in this case, Roger is innocent. I'm glad he doesn't notice. No need to ruin our evening.

Damn that she who shall not be named!

I grin at Roger and kiss his lips.

"Merci, Mon Cœur..."

The conversation turns to our wedding, teasing Roger about the late honeymoon, and life. It's fun and lively with no one giving any thought to the legal situation. We enjoy a regular family dinner.

"Pardon me while I go to the restroom before we leave," I say as I push back from the table.

Roger rises to help me and Lola says she'll go, too.

We giggle like two schoolgirls going to the bathroom on break as we make our way through the tables. While in my stall, I hear two women enter the room chatting. At first I don't pay them any attention. But the words rapist and Steele catch my attention.

Merde!

I hasten to fix my clothing and open the door.

Lola also rushes out with a look of anger directed at the pair. The petite spitfire has always been my protector from unwanted attention at clubs with guys trying to get to handsy. So her blazing hazel eyes and fierceness don't shock me.

"How dare you?!" She demands. "You have no clue what you are speaking. Yet you have the audacity to judge an innocent man?!"

"Right! My fiancé is not guilty of any wrongdoing!" I add resting my left hand protectively on my belly as I pin them with an icy glare.

The women blink and widen their eyes in surprise at our vehemence. They flick their gazes from Lola to me to my very pregnant belly with my enormous engagement ring shining in the light. Speechless, they flee the restroom.

I reach for the counter, light-headed suddenly.

Lola grabs me, and we slip to the floor. I bury my face in my hands and weep. I've held in the stress of the entire ordeal and get myself busy with the move, the nursery, the design work. But hearing their nasty comments out loud is too much for me to bear. I just can't take it anymore.

"Hush, Leonie. Don't let them upset you. They don't know what they're talking about. Roger is innocent and the truth will come out. I know it has to be hard and you being pregnant makes it tougher to handle. But know you have the support of our family. We love you and Roger very much and won't allow anything to hurt either of you."

Her words soothe me. But I don't have the energy to get up just yet. So we sit a while longer.

The door bursts open and Roger and Sebastian rush inside. Roger drops to his knees before us and clutches my arms with an expression of panic. Sebastian pulls out his mobile and makes a call.

"What happened? Are you all right?" Roger asks, scanning me from head to toe.

I nod, and Lola responds.

"She's fine. These two wo—"

I put my hand up to stop her from speaking. I don't want

to upset Roger and ruin our evening. But she shakes her head forcefully.

"No, Leonie. He needs to know."

She turns to Roger and continues to tell him about the encounter.

I watch dismayed as his face reddens and his eyes darken. I can feel the anger coming off of him in waves. It reminds me of his initial reaction at his office upon receiving the paperwork. I hate it and my heart aches for him.

I place my hand on his cheek. But it takes a moment for him to register my touch. Slowly, he turns his gaze to me. I see such anguish in the depths of his eyes it hurts my soul. This is so unfair.

"Come. Let us go back to the *Manoir*," Sebastian says authoritatively as he lifts Lola to her feet, then me.

Roger hangs his head and takes a deep breath before he stands too. Sebastian claps his shoulder and pulls him close to whisper in his ear. The words have the effect of making Roger stand tall and straighten his jacket.

He nods and claps Sebastian on his shoulder in return. Then faces Lola and me.

"Lola, thank you for supporting us and for helping Leonie. My love, I am so sorry I put you in a position to experience such behavior. I do not want you to get upset, and we will call Dr. Berger to meet us at the *Manoir*. Sebastian is right. Let us go now."

"It's all right, *Mon Cœur*. However, you are not to blame. Once we reveal the truth, we can all rest."

We nod solemnly and leave the restroom.

I avoid making eye contact with anyone as we bypass the dining room to head to the entrance. I'm not sure what I'll do if I see those women gawking at us.

My mother and Shelley have anxious expressions on their faces. While my father and Morgan are in a serious discussion. When they see us approach, they bustle my mother and Shelley out the doors. We follow and get into the cars.

It's silent except for Roger's conversation with Dr. Berger. He agrees to meet us right away. Satisfied, Roger strokes my cheek, then my belly. I rest my hand on top of his. We ride the rest of the way, each in their thoughts.

"Leonie, you go change and wait for the doctor in your rooms—"

I start to protest my father's directive once we're in the foyer of the *Manoir*. But he lifts his hand to stop me.

"Do not argue with me, Leonie. Your wellbeing is of the utmost and I will not allow you to suffer. We will change and wait in the East Wing's living room. If he says you and The Twins are fine, then you may join us."

I glance up at Roger for his opinion, and he nods.

"I agree with your father, Leonie. It is best for us to hear Dr. Berger's assessment."

With a sigh, I nod, and Roger leads me to the elevator. I want to argue I'm not a child. But I know it concerns everyone, and they want nothing to happen to me or to The Twins. So I give in.

Roger helps me to undress and kisses the top of my head once he has me settled on the bed with a cashmere blanket tucked around my legs. He goes into his dressing room and emerges in sweatpants and a long-sleeved t-shirt. Just as he sits beside me and holds my hand, there's a knock at the outer door.

"Come in," he calls.

Dr. Berger and our parents enter the bedroom.

"*Bonsoir, Mademoiselle Beaulieu,*" Dr. Berger says as he

strides to the bed. "Let's get your vitals and see how you feel."

He checks me and finds my blood pressure elevated slightly. So he recommends I rest for the rest of the night in bed.

I ask if I can join everyone in the living room and sit on the chaise. Roger sits forward to object. But Dr. Berger gives in when I offer my most pleading puppy eyes.

"She'll be fine as long as she relaxes and keeps her legs up," he says with a smile.

I smile and thank him. Then kiss Roger on the cheek as I lean into his side.

Our parents nod and walk out with the doctor. Both *Mamans* cast worried glances over their shoulders at me. But I give them the thumbs up and swing around to get up. They nod and smile.

"Are you sure, my love?" Roger asks after the outer door closes. "I don't want you to feel compelled to put on a brave face. I realize that's what you've been doing, and I ask that you be honest with me."

I hang my head this time. Then peer up at him through my eyelashes before I respond.

"You're right. I just didn't want to upset you. You have enough to worry about without me adding my concerns to them."

Roger shakes his head and cups my face, lifting my chin to bring our eyes in line.

"You are my number one priority, Leonie. I am the one to take care of you. I appreciate you wanting to protect me. But no one could protect me from myself if something happens to you. Promise me you will keep nothing from me," Roger responds.

I nod.

But he cocks his head and raises his eyebrow.

"Words, Pretty Kitty. I will have your words," he demands.

"*Oui*," I answer.

"*Bien*," he says as he kisses my lips.

I sigh with contentment and melt into his loving embrace.

We'll be just fine.

ROGER

"*B*ro, this shit is fucking insane! I almost knocked the teeth out of some paparazzo on our way in."

I look up to see my second oldest brother Malcolm striding into my office, followed by Harris. Sebastian is in a meeting in his offices down the hall.

He, Lola, and my parents have been here for the last two weeks to support Leonie and me. Malcolm, Harris, and Haley arrived this morning. They'll work from their offices here, too. However, Haley will work remotely from the *Manoir*. She wants to stay close to her sisters.

I'm thankful for their love and support. It's typical of the Steele clan to drop it all to rally behind one of us. This time, it's me.

Fuck!

It's been a nightmare. More negative media coverage. More comments from "sources close to" blah blah blah. More absolute bullshit.

Malcolm's experience isn't the worse of it. I had to implement the security detail for Leonie when a reporter harassed her after leaving a baby boutique with our mothers. Eric had to intervene and knocked the reporter to the ground for pushing her in his eagerness to get a shot of her in distress.

I lost my shit and had the reporter arrested and threatened to destroy the newspaper if any photos surfaced.

Now Leonie avoids going anywhere but to the penthouses to check on their status or for her prenatal visits every two weeks. I insist she only leave the *Manoir* with her full detail present. She's being honest with me and hasn't had another fainting episode. Thank God!

Guy hired additional security for the *Manoir* since some paparazzi scaled the wall to get photos of us on the grounds and in the mansion. Fucking drones circle overhead at all times of the day and the night. Federico Fellini said it best in his interview with *Time*: "Paparazzo... suggests to me a buzzing insect, hovering, darting, stinging." How apropos. It's an invasion of the worse kind.

The team includes foot patrols with giant guard dogs trained to attack on command. We reinstated the guardhouse at the front gate instead of just the intercom; a man approves entry. Harris worked with the security company to update the surveillance system and the control room. It's twenty-four-hour, seven-days-a-week coverage.

I even upped the ante at STEELE Paris. Obviously to no avail based on Malcolm's encounter. Before I respond to him, I call the vice president of security to update him and to request additional precautions. When I ring off, I nod at my brothers and go to the drinks cabinet for some waters.

"It's a pain in the ass. These fuckers are like sharks with one drop of blood in the vast ocean," I say as I toss them bottles.

We stretch out on the sofa and club chairs while I fill

them in on the latest developments. Just listening to myself makes me angry. I still can't get over the fact that my woman, sons, and family are being treated like they're criminals. If the media would only focus on me, fine. But to include them is merciless. Particularly since Leonie is visibly pregnant. They don't give a fuck.

It makes me wonder what's happening with Delia Shaw. I truly doubt she's receiving this treatment since her legal team has gone out of their way to make her appear as innocent as a newborn baby...

She's doing the press junket with interviews on talk shows and with magazines and newspapers in Paris and in the United States. It's global coverage since we're both American and the encounters took place in France. Because the legal claim involves STEELE International, Inc. and a Steele makes it sensational. The media can't get enough of it. I heard they offered her a book deal for millions of dollars.

Fuck. Me.

The atmosphere at STEELE Paris varies with each new headline. Some days it's quiet and on others there's a buzz in the air—the tension palpable. Of course it gets hushed when I come around. Human resources noted an increase in the number of time off requests or "concerns with managers." Full investigations prove no validity to the claims. It's just a domino effect.

But as they have advised me, I continue with business as usual and move ahead. Françoise has been a rockstar. She's shut down the executive floor except for upper-level management who have offices here. No one gets to me without her approval first. I made a note to increase her salary and send her on a two-week, all-paid trip to anywhere in the world. She deserves my thanks and more.

The ringing of my mobile interrupts Harris' comments. It's Leonie's ringtone. I stride to my desk to retrieve it. Every time she calls, I brace myself for some new shit. I take a deep breath to avoid stressing her out with my concerns and answer.

"Hi, babe. What's up?" I ask as evenly as possible.

I physically sag when I hear the tinkle of her laughter as she's saying something to Haley in the background. No crisis, after all.

"Ciao! You didn't tell me Haley and Blair were coming! I'm so happy to see my girls! They said Malcolm and Harris are with you?" Leonie says.

"Yes, they're here, and they wanted to surprise you. Surprise!" I laugh, a genuine one.

Leonie claps and I can envision her shaking her hips and dancing around as she does her shimmy—just a little slower...

"It's wonderful! Plus, Hettie is here, and Joel is joining us for dinner. Ow... And Luc, too! Okay, okay, Blair!" She adds laughing.

Obviously Luc and Blair are still going strong. I'm sure she came to support her friend. But the added benefit of being with her lover must rank just as high.

I shake my head as I think back on Luc's expression when I asked him about the two of them. I chuckle, thinking how I ruffled the unflappable French aristocrat.

"Well, gotta fly! *Je t'aime beaucoup!*" Leonie exclaims as she ends the call on a laugh.

"It's good to see you smiling, bro."

My gaze shifts from my mobile I was staring at with I'm sure must have been a goofy grin to Malcolm.

He smiles just as wide and tips his water bottle to me in salute.

I return his gesture and amble over to talk some more with my brothers.

The cure to the blues: family and friends.

ROGER

"*R*ight, that sounds doable. What about the portion where—"

As I swivel in my desk chair, my gaze goes beyond the glass wall and door of my office to the outer office and the floor beyond. The sight of my father, Sebastian, and Albert striding with purpose to my offices breaks my concentration on the conference call.

Fuck.

"Listen, I must get back to you.... Right, sounds good," I say to the vice president on the new build in Manila.

Françoise glances at me from her desk on the other side of my door, then back at the trio. She stands to greet them, more than likely to offer them coffee.

From the solemn expressions on their faces, I'm sure we require a more potent brew. I take a cleansing breath and brace myself as I round the desk to open the door.

My father's gray eyes are stormy as he pins me with an intense stare. He never breaks eye contact until he passes me and heads to the conference table. He doesn't speak a word until everyone takes a seat.

"Roger, they set the date for a preliminary investigation conducted by a pretrial judge for a month from now. Since she filed the petition with a civil claim, the magistrate may proceed with the investigation. Albert confirms it is a routine part of the judicial process."

Morgan delivers the news with aplomb. But I don't have the same self-confidence.

This shit is so fucked up.

"Albert also said they didn't have enough for a case to move forward," I snap.

I can't keep the snark out of my voice as I stand abruptly and pace.

"What the fuck?! I did nothing to that lying witch! She damn well knows it true! This shit is all about money! That slimeball Antonio got paid. Now, she wants some…"

While I rant and rave, Sebastian rises and goes to my desk. He presses the buttons to lock my office door and to darken the glass. No need for anyone to see me lose it. That will only add fuel to this fucked-up situation.

They allow me to run out of steam.

I drop into my desk chair and swivel to face the Paris streets. My thoughts turn to Leonie. How will she take this fresh development? She's thirty weeks along now and doesn't need the stress of a pretrial investigation. I know she believes me. But it must be a strain for her. We promised to be honest, so I have no choice but to tell her.

I lift my gaze to the heavens and send a silent prayer for her and The Twins' wellbeing, strength, and guidance. Along with another cleansing breath, my head clears. I return to the table with renewed confidence. I'm determined to get through this and to come out stronger as Leonie said weeks ago.

"Father, Albert, forgive my rude behavior. I appreciate all that you're doing for me."—I lean forward and lock my intense stare on Albert—"Tell me, what do we do?"

We spend the next two hours speaking first as our group, then Albert's team joins us. Françoise orders lunch for everyone delivered so as not to disrupt our discussion. She also clears my schedule for the rest of the day and tomorrow. As always, she proves to be indispensable.

Albert summarizes the procedure for the criminal felony charge. Since an inquisitorial system serves as the basis of the French criminal procedure, the pretrial judge takes an active role in investigating the facts of the case. Therefore, the judge may investigate any violations related to the application and proceed to further inquiry people who may have involvement as witnesses or who may have evidence.

The proceedings conducted in writing or made into a written record immediately afterwards. If the pretrial judge determines the case should go to prosecution, they will refer it to the district court of appeal for prosecution rather than directly to the court.

Albert leaves it at that stage with acknowledgement of the case going to felony court if they determine prosecution. He says he's optimistic it won't proceed as far as a full trial. His team agrees.

I turn to my father for his opinion.

"I trust Perry. We will move forward with his recommendations, posthaste. The sooner we get beyond this bullshit, the better for you and for STEELE. Understood?"

"Yes. I agree and will proceed as planned," I reply.

Sebastian asks a few questions, then concurs.

After we review next steps, Albert and his team leave to handle their side of the case.

"I'm going to the *Manoir*. With all the 'leaks' and 'sources,' Leonie needs to hear this from me as soon as possible," I tell my father and Sebastian. "It may also be an opportune time for her to get away for a few days with her girls. Not just a spa day. I can fly Starr and Billie over, too."

"She may insist on staying here and not leaving your side. But it's worth a try. I'll ask Lola to encourage her," Sebastian says.

Morgan nods, "It would de her good. However, the wedding is in ten days. What are your plans?"

Fuck! Me!

I totally forgot, being all caught up in this bullshit. The last thing I want is for this scandal to overshadow Leonie's fairy-tale wedding and our memories.

The media is already going crazy. This pretrial will make them worse. Forget blood in the water—it'll be an all-out feeding frenzy. They'll use any excuse to tarnish whatever comes in contact with me.

I won't let them ruin our wedding day. I'm taking control.

My father and Sebastian agree it would be best to postpone until after this entire thing concludes. With the pretrial in a month, I can't imagine the proceedings taking more than a month. So on the upside, we can marry shortly after The Twins are born and be closer to our honeymoon time.

Yeah... I'll keep trying to convince myself it's a logical, necessary course of action and will go over smoothly.

This is going to piss Leonie off.

. . .

"Wнат?!?!"

As expected...

"You cannot be serious, Roger?!" Leonie shouts.

She was quiet and understanding—braver than I expected—when I told her about the pretrial. She reminded me she has unwavering trust in me and knows we'll prove my innocence.

The wedding postponement... Not... calm... at... all.

Leonie turns into a ferocious feline and rises from the sofa quickly, considering her belly has grown a lot. When I try to help her, she slaps my hands away and stands on her own, albeit awkwardly.

Her amber eyes flash; the gold specks explode like sparklers.

Note to self: do not twist *The Lion*'s tail... Damn.

It is the most withering glare I've ever seen in my nearly thirty-three years. If I were a weak man, my balls would shrivel up and my dick disintegrate.

Instead, I stand to my full six feet, three inches, and crowd her space.

A lethal lion never backs down, especially when cornered. And Leonie is no exception. She lifts her chin and continues to glare at me in defiance of my dominance. Her own blazing through.

Fuck me if my cock doesn't twitch.

Okay, *Queen of the Jungle*...

I growl deep in my chest; the rumble vibrates out of me. My eyes darken to slate in an instant. My wolf is ready for you.

"Don't you even try it, Roger Steele!" Leonie snarls, widening her stance like a cage fighter. "You want to give in to that sneaky trollop? Let her take more of our joy? Well, I say *non*!"

She folds her arms under her bountiful breasts. The action causes them to sit up even higher, pushing against the thin material of her silk tank top.

My gaze drops to the tops of her mounds. They've doubled in size and are more than a mouthful.

The nipples poke through the lace of her Lola's Coterie maternity bra and beg for me to draw them between my lips. Her breasts have gotten sensitive again. Dr. Berger says it's because of her body preparing for milk production.

Well... Let me get some chocolate chip cookies.

Unconsciously, I run my tongue over my salivating mouth.

"No you do not, you beast! How can you stare at my tits at a time like this?!" She screeches.

Slowly, my eyes glide up her body as though touching every bit of her exposed skin. Her chest is flushed red and her jaw set. Those luscious lips pout and her eyes bore into mine.

When she notices my hooded expression, her body reacts instantly. Her chest rises and falls. No longer from her anger. But from her burning desire. Her nostrils flare, and her eyes match mine, full of lust. Leonie can't resist our magnetic pull no more than I can avoid it.

I refuse to answer her with words. I let my body speak for me to hers. Each likes what the other offers. The whiplash change in mood elevates the erotic tension swirling around us like electricity in the air.

My fingertip retraces the path taken by my eyes in reverse. I tweak her nipple, and Leonie moans as her arms drop away, opening her body to me. My *Lion* bows before her Alpha mate.

"Pretty Kitty, you say you trust me. That you know I do

what is best for us. Yet you fight my decision to postpone our wedding day," I growl in her ear.

My other hand reaches around to give her ass three rapid spanks. Leonie mewls closing her eyes as she rises to her toes gripping the lapels of my suit jacket.

"It was not a simple decision to make. But it is for the best. With the media frenzy this pretrial will cause, I will allow no one to ruin your fairy-tale wedding and to tarnish the memories of our cherished day," I continue as I drag my lips down the column of her neck to suck on the juncture at her shoulder.

Leonie purrs, then hisses when I increase the pull to leave my mark on her smooth skin.

"Once this scandal is behind us, I promise we will celebrate our nuptials immediately"—I say with the whisper-soft touch of my lips to her throat—"And go on our honeymoon as planned."

I cup her ass then squeeze it as I press my rock-hard dick against her soft, curvy hip.

"You will be all mine sooner than you think, Mrs. Roger Steele... Mine!"

Leonie yelps when I sweep her off her feet with ease to carry her bridal style to our bed. She burrows her face into my neck as she wraps her arms around it.

"It's just so unfair, *Mon Cœur*. Why must we suffer while that lying cow parades around garnering sympathy and painting you as some giant monster? I hate it," Leonie says miserably.

My heart sinks. She's been on the damned Internet again. I try to tell her it won't do any good for her peace of mind if she keeps reading the tabloids and gossip sites. I won't address it. Instead, I kiss the top of her head.

I know what's best to remedy this situation, too...

.   .   .

"*Oooh... Oh, mon Dieu! Tu as.... Tu as raison! Ooohhh,*" Leonie screams.

Her body trembles from her third successive climax after I kept her on the edge for the last thirty minutes—one for each ten. Sweat coats her flushed skin. Her chest heaves and her eyes flutter close with exhaustion as she sags against the pile of pillows.

"It pleases me you finally see I am correct. Now, it is my turn, Pretty Kitty," I murmur as I wipe my soaked mouth against her quivering inner thigh.

I extricate her fingers from my hair and sit back on my haunches as I survey my handiwork.

Leonie is absolutely gorgeous splayed before me. Her glowing face is serene with satiety. The enlarged nipples taut from my eager suckling—proof of my goal to drink her soon-to-be-ready milk. The fullness of her belly nurturing my sons amps my ego. Her long, toned legs so powerful from all the yoga sessions felt like a vice around my head when she came.

I lift one of her feet and massage the arch with my thumb, then rub the other.

My cock jumps at the sound of her contented purrs and the sight of her wiggling hips. I stroke my aching length as I lift to my knees between her legs. Unable to resist, I lave her swollen nipples with one stroke of my tongue.

Leonie writhes beneath me, and my dick thumps her belly. She moans and grips it, stroking from base to tip, smearing the pre-cum over the bulbous head. She repeats the motions, increasing the pressure and speed as I buck in her hand.

The tingle in my spine zings my heavy balls. I close my

eyes and thrust my hips repeatedly, chasing my climax. My ass, eight-pack abs, and muscular thighs tighten as my release nears.

Blinded by the intensity, I bury my face in the hollow between her breasts. Then groan as copious amounts of my cum spurt onto Leonie's belly. I roll onto my back, spent.

With a seductive purr, she rubs the viscous essence onto her round stomach and ample breasts. Then staring at me with her feline eyes aglow, Leonie licks her fingers clean one by one and releases them with a pop.

It's the hottest thing I've ever seen.

MINE!

LEONIE

"*O*h, Leonie! Cheer up! Think how much nicer your wedding will be once this shit is over! You don't want to reminisce and have a cloud of negativity shrouding your big day, do you?"

I glance over at Lola and raise my eyebrow.

"Hey! I'm not taking sides. But Roger *The Responsible* is right," she adds. "That's the best solution. Now you can wear your choice of gowns without a big ole belly bump!"

She balls up her Hermès beach blanket and puts it under her tunic. Then grabs mine and includes it to make her pseudo-bump larger.

I roll my eyes and walk faster towards the chaise lounges. But can't help laughing when she waddles past me, pretending to walk down the aisle.

"I hate you, Lola Steele!" I call after her.

She puts her hands on her lower back and exaggerates her movements even more than before. Her snorts of laughter trail behind her.

"Some best friend, huh?"

I shift my gaze from Lola to Starr, who loops her arm through mine. Despite her attempt to maintain a serious expression, her sorrel-brown eyes twinkle with mirth. When Lola sumo squats to sit on her chaise and the towels fall to the sand, Starr bursts out laughing. Her dimples deepen in her angelic face.

Although she's acting the devil now...

"Oh, don't tease her—so badly," Billie chimes in as she cracks up.

Haley nods, "Well, you know Roger, he'll do what he thinks is best no matter what. However... I most definitely agree with his decision. For once, one of my overbearing older brothers is correct."

Hettie, Anita, and Bair stand firm with my Alpha male fiancé, too.

At first, the level of my upset was incredible, and it disheartened me Roger decided unilaterally that we would miss our day. I mean, ten days before the ceremony and boom! They announce the pretrial date. Talk about bad timing.

It pissed me off. But I changed my mind, albeit grudgingly. Roger's wily ways in the bedroom softened the blow —damn, he's a fantastic lover! After I awoke from my multiple-orgasm-induced slumber, my mind cleared.

Reality set in. No, I don't want to look back on our wedding day and have the stigma of a criminal investigation of sexual assault and harassment overshadowing our union. It's taken us over two years to get this far. A few more months won't make a significant difference.

Although I know I'll appear phenomenal in my gowns now or then. Big ole belly bump and all!

I also know Roger arranged this Girls' Getaway to make up for the delay. It's so incredible how we went from only

Lola and me to Blair and Billie, then Starr, and now Hettie and Anita. He knows how close I am to my crew and the comfort they provide me. Not to mention the laughs, like Lola's hijinks...

"Ha, ha, ha, Loser Girl!" I say as I lower myself down onto the chaise next to hers.

"Remember to engage your pelvic floor, Leonie," says Anita.

I nod and do a few Kegel's before I put my legs up. Roger appreciates the newfound strength of my inner muscles. His groans of rapture are a source of inspiration when I just don't feel I can take another squat. I giggle to myself and do two extra squeezes.

At thirty-one weeks, Dr. Berger told me during my last visit the prenatal yoga and Pilates sessions were beneficial. The backaches and circulation improved with the movement and stretching. Even my balance is better. I sleep well when I mediate before I go to bed to ease my brain activity and any tension from the day. Seven months and counting. I can't wait to hold my babies in my arms and not just in my belly.

"I can't believe I've never been here before after all these years of living in France. It's spectacular!"

Hettie's exclamation brings me back from my musings.

Roger didn't want me to go too far—no more than an hour's flight time from Paris. So my father suggested the seaside resort town of Arcachon on the southwest coast of France, known as the *Côte D'Argent* or the Silver Coast. Off the Atlantic Ocean, the luxury spot is south of Bordeaux's Haut Medoc vineyards and famous for its delicious oysters and seafood. Unfortunately, being pregnant, I can't partake in either...

But the stunning unspoiled sandy beaches, like the one

we're on, still make the getaway worthwhile. The magnificent villa we rented sits on the seafront and is only a brief ride to this beach.

Roger insisted Eric and a STEELE driver along with my security detail escort us. They drove from Paris in our and Sebastian's Cullinans ahead of the girls and me. Then met us at the heliport. Roger refuses to take any chances with The Twins and my safety.

We arrived last night and just chilled at the villa. It's a marvelous architectural piece of history. The slate tile roof and stone facade with pale blue trim are ornate. With three floors and a large parcel of land on the seafront, it's a sizable property. Each of us has a suite of rooms with private baths.

After changing into Lola's Coterie loungewear, we met in the eat-in kitchen for a simple dinner prepared by the chef. She made several platters of freshly caught seafood, herb chicken, and roasted vegetables. We ate the tasty dishes buffet style around the table.

Later we stretched out in the media room and watched a movie while we stuffed ourselves with the variety of pastries the chef made from scratch. The girls enjoyed aperitifs, and I had my iced lemon ginger tea. We spent more time chatting than we did watching the latest chick flick. The drama in our lives proved more entertaining than the anything the characters faced!

This morning we headed to the beach. I chose a baby pink gingham pattern bandeau bikini with a fluttery ruffle on the top. It's so cute and feminine. The girls teased that if I didn't turn to the side or face them, they would never know I had a giant beachball for a stomach. Nice compliment... I guess.

Once settled on my chaise, I put a pillow behind my back and Blair helps me to put another one under my knees.

Then I sit back and take in the view of the white sandy beach and deep blue-green Atlantic Ocean. The air is crisp with the saltwater scent as seagulls call out to each other. The sun is warm on my skin. Its warmth is a luxurious sensation after being in clothes for so long. I tilt my head back against the chaise and close my eyes as I absorb my surroundings.

Peace and serenity.

"Great idea! Let's have a five-minute meditation session," Anita says when she spies my hands formed in a mudra on my thighs.

"Yes! Wonderful way to embrace all of this natural beauty," Starr adds.

I open my eyes to find everyone gathered around, settling on to the two chaises on either side of me. I smile and make room for Anita to sit at the foot of my chaise. We face each other cross-legged.

She leads us through a guided meditation that reflects on our connection with nature. Her melodic voice enchants us as we're led on the mind-body-surroundings journey. She ends with a chant and namaste.

When I reopen my eyes, my thoughts are clear and I feel lighter. So far, so good.

"Tomorrow morning we should come down and do a flow class on the beach. I'd love to start my day with a sunrise session," Billie suggests.

Starr nods, "I have a new sequence I'd love to share with you. Leonie, I can modify it for you. Although I must say, your strength shows in your movements. You can probably teach it!"

I laugh and thank her for her words of encouragement, but decline.

"I'm not ready for prime time! I'll leave the teaching to you and Anita, *merci!*"

"Well, I'm all for morning yoga tomorrow. But right now, I'm getting in that glistening water!" Haley announces as she stands and takes off her Missoni tunic.

"Me, too! I can't wait to dive in," Hettie adds as she takes off her Norma Kamali sarong-style midiskirt. "I won't say last one in is a rotten egg because you smell nice, Leonie!"

Everyone laughs, agreeing I would be the last one in the water. I must admit I'm not my usual quick moving self these days. Lola helps me to my feet and links her arm through mine as we walk to the water's edge en masse.

My security team keeps a distance. But stay near since the beach is busy with other visitors, vendors with trinkets, and waitstaff. They're discreet in swim trunks and t-shirts. Only their clear earpieces hint at their purpose.

I acknowledge them with a slight nod.

When we reach the water, the girls dive and jump in. I waddle... I mean wade right behind them as I giggle thinking about Lola's antics. The buoyancy makes me feel even lighter than the mediation session.

"The water is perfect! I'm so glad your father recom-mended Arcachon. Who knew France had Caribbean-style beaches!" Blair says as she floats over to me.

"We used to come often when I was younger. A simple trip my parents enjoyed since you get the beaches, the wine region, sailing lakes, and pine forests. The variety of activi-ties kept us busy. The visits increased my interest in archi-tecture with the historic homes of Ville d'Hiver," I respond, smiling at the memories.

Yeah, Roger is right. I want to look back on our wedding with a smile like I'm reminiscing now. It's just the fact she who shall not be named interfered with our plans.

C'est la vie.

"I know it's early. But I can really go for some more of those oysters. They were delish last night!" Anita says. "They made me miss Norman!"

She adds with a wink.

Unfortunately, I couldn't partake of the aphrodisiac. Although Roger put it on me so good before I left, I'll be fine for the next four days!

"Why are you grinning like the Cheshire Cat?" Billie asks as she raises her elegantly arched eyebrow.

I laugh out loud at being so busted.

"Oh, let me guess… That fine ass man of yours and oysters?" Billie says grinning.

"Maybe, maybe not!" I respond, then duck away, feeling my face flame from the carnal thoughts of Roger's lovemaking.

"That's a definite maybe!!" Yells Billie at my retreating form.

The others giggle and taunt me.

We spend the rest of the time enjoying the sun, sand, and surf for a relaxing day at the beach. When we return, I check in on the penthouses then take a nap while the girls go about their business. Lola, Blair, and Billie get in some work for the boutiques. Starr and Anita record Instagram videos for their thousands of followers for a crossover challenge. Haley geeks out on her computer where she's working on some top-secret project she's cagey about when asked. Hettie works on some cases for her clients. We're Independent Women who work hard and play harder!

"LEAD the way to the baccarat table, *merci!*"

Starr replies when the general manager for the Casino

D'Arcachon greets us and asks for our favorite games. Her eyes twinkle in glee as she claps her hands in anticipation of a night of gaming.

We decided to glam it up big time tonight in all red outfits. Starr wears a cutout crystal-embellished crepe mini dress that reveals a sparkly sequin and crystal-embellished bra cup. Lola flaunts her toned legs in a smock exaggerated pussy-bow hammered silk mini dress with ruffled shoulders and elasticized cuffs on the breezy sleeves. Haley goes for the sparkle with a crystal and paillette-embellished tulle mini dress. Blair picks a new piece from Lola's Coterie evening wear collection, a contoured lace-up satin mini dress with contrasting lace-up detail and underwire cups. Billie's elegant outfit of a strapless filigree-like appliqué crystal-embellished mini dress. Hettie goes for a 90s style in a slinky, open-back chain-mail mini dress. Anita does a take on the classic tuxedo with a crystal-embellished satin-trimmed halter-neck mini dress. I rocked my babies bump in a stretchy, one-sleeve ruched mini dress with an asymmetric skirt detailed and adjustable drawstrings on the shoulder and hem. We're all flowy hair, tan skin, and high strappy heels!

"*Absolument mademoiselles!* Please follow me," he says with a chuckle at her enthusiasm.

We walk through the 19th-century Château Deganne, where the casino is located. The impressive Neo-Renaissance-style mansion on the edge of the beach harkens to the grand times the area experienced. It's elegance similar to the Casino de Monte-Carlo reminds me of a James Bond from the time.

"I'm going to try my hand at blackjack," Hettie announces when we pass the table.

Anita nods, "Oh, me, too! I love pushing as far as possible without going over twenty-one."

Blair and Billie join them as the rest of us set up at the baccarat table.

A crowd gathers around our table to cheer Starr on her winning streak. Our laughter rings out above the excited din of the rooms.

"This is such a blast! Who would have thought this little gem of a town would have a casino?" Haley giggles as she picks up her winnings from another bet. "This may become a regular spot for me!"

Lola and I nod in agreement.

"STEELE should open a property here or take over this casino. I'm sure Malcolm would take it to the next level," Lola whispers so only Haley and I can hear.

Starr, too absorbed in the game, doesn't pay us any attention. Her laughter when she wins yet another round makes us laugh, too.

"Girls, I'm on a roll! You better put your money down and get in on this streak!" She turns to us and says with a wink.

"Hey, I'm all in on this one!" I answer, putting my chips on the table. "What's the saying, 'Mama needs a new pair of shoes,' right?"

They laugh as I rub my belly in emphasis.

"*Oui, mademoiselle*. But your shoes seem more than good to me."

I glance over my shoulder, then tilt my head back to meet the eyes of the stranger. He's around Roger's height, handsome with aqua blue eyes, and a smooth baritone voice. His smile widens when our gazes meet.

Is he flirting with me?

Uh, *non*...

468

"*Merci, monsieur.* How kind of you. My fiancé would agree," I say as I rub my belly with my left hand, the giant stone shooting sparks in the light.

The stranger glances down and nods slightly.

"Lucky man, your fiancé," he replies. "Well, I shall leave you to enjoy your evening."

He bows and strides away just as my security detail moves into position behind him, ready to handle the situation.

Lola bursts out laughing, "Okay MILF Alert! Roger better be careful!"

Starr, who paused her game to face the stranger, nods in agreement.

"He needed to go. I don't want any bad vibes around my game!"

We crack up and get back to baccarat.

After a late dinner at the casino, we call it and head to the SUVs. The night is full of wins and losses, but all fun.

* * *

"Hey, why aren't you guys dressed yet?" I ask as I walk into the villa's living room to find the girls lounging about.

"Oh, don't you look lovely!" Lola says sitting up. "Can you do me a favor and hand me my tote from the foyer?"

I frown and cock my head questioningly.

Lola raises her hand to stop me from speaking.

"Come on, Leonie. You're already standing, and it's just around the corner. Please?!" She says with puppy eyes.

I roll mine and about-face, grumbling to myself.

It's our last night and we're supposed to go out to dinner at this great restaurant the house butler recommended. Now these girls haven't even dressed. We're going to be later than expected—considering I'm ten minutes late as it is...

I wanted to look extra nice since it's the night of my wedding had we been able to have it. It's also the one-year anniversary of Roger and I being back together. They know I was feeling down today, and now they're puttering around in pajamas!

Meanwhile, I'm all glammed up in a white stretchy, pointelle-knit halter neck mididress with a subtle diamond pattern. It's designed with a flattering ribbed waist and gold buttons along the arms for a little flair. I took care with my hair flowing in silky waves past my butt and a little makeup with shiny nude lip gloss. The white looks fantastic against my sun-kissed caramel complexion.

I guess I'll just change and hang out with the gang eating ice cream out of the tub...

"Hello, Kitten."

My eyes jerk up from the floor and land on Roger, who's standing in the middle of the foyer. I gasp and put my hand to my heart, shocked by his unexpected appearance. The emotions—and hormones—swirl through me. Tears fill my eyes.

"Oh, sweetheart, don't cry. I wanted to surprise you. I know today is technically our wedding day and our anniversary. How could I leave you alone at a time like this?" Roger says as he pulls me into his powerful embrace.

"I love you, Leonie, so much. I promise all will turn out well, my love," he croons against my hair.

I loop my arms under his and over his shoulders to hold him closer as the sobs rake over me.

He lifts my chin and kisses the trail of tears, then my lips.

At once, I'm engulfed in the flame of our intense love. The heat of our passion ignites the stoked embers.

Roger deepens the kiss and heat races through every cell of my body. He feels it, too, and groans against my lips.

"I miss you, too, Kitten," he starts, then pulls away gently. "But we have reservations for dinner first."

He presses his forehead against mine.

"Okay," I sigh softly. "Let me just rinse my face."

When I return to the foyer, Roger kisses my hand and leads me out the door.

The Girls' Getaway just got even better!

ROGER

"*O*kay, Steele, get with it now or I'll kick your sorry ass all around this ring. We don't have time for bullshit, man!"

Norman just landed his second blow to my flank, and I never saw it coming.

Fuck! That shit hurt for real.

He's not joking at all.

I'm grateful he didn't hit me in the head with that hammer fist of his. I shake my head and bounce on the balls of my feet for a few seconds to get my mind back in the game.

Another week passed, and we're two weeks away from the start of the pretrial investigation. In preparation, Albert's been grilling me and with the legal team he's been going over every possible scenario and angle to clear my name and STEELE. They're still confident of a positive outcome. We just have to get through the process.

Sebastian and Lola returned to the United States two days ago. Sebastian has some business in Chicago, and Lola plans to visit her Beverly Hills and Las Vegas boutiques. They'll return in a week or so.

Malcolm flew to Greece to look at some private island options for a new resort. Harris and Haley are still in Paris, working from their offices at STEELE or at *Le Beaulieu Manoir*.

My father and mother left the *Manoir* to move into their penthouse yesterday. They won't return to New York City until after the pretrial ends. Morgan says it's best to show a united front.

In the meantime, they're pleased with Leonie's designs and decor choices. Shelley is super excited about the completed nursery. She's beside herself in anticipation of "little babies puttering about again." Morgan is just as enthused with the continuation of the Steele family line.

Our penthouse is ready, too. But Leonie isn't ready to move back in as of yet. The media hanging around STEELE Paris would keep her trapped inside. I agree it's best to stay at the *Manoir* until after this complete fiasco is over and done. That way she can stroll outdoors or relax in the gardens. No need for her to stress out over getting some fresh air and direct sunlight.

It thrills Guy and Josy we're staying. Even though it's not for the happiest reason. It was Guy's idea to wait, and I thanked him for their hospitality. He merely laughed and told me we're family and that's what families do. Besides, the East Wing affords so much space and distance from his and Josy's wing.

Most nights we have dinner together and whoever is in Paris will come over for Josy's now famous Sunday brunch. Lucien has become a regular, too. He and Josy spend a lot of time in the kitchen making dishes from her family's recipes. Tonight we're going to the opening of his latest restaurant where he's debuting some of their pairings.

"Are you with me, Steele, or what?"

Norman's voice and the sound of his fists hitting each other bring me back to his training facility. He's staring at me like I'm nuts for getting distracted while in the ring with him. And he's right.

I shake my head once more and punch my fists together, signaling I'm back.

"Good! Now, let's get at it!" Norman responds.

We spar for another hour. Then follow up with a few laps in the heated pool and a dip in the ice bath. After a shower, I'm ready to start my day.

"BONJOUR MONSIEUR STEELE," Françoise says as I pass her desk.

"Bonjour, how are you?" I respond.

Her expression stops me cold. She looks crestfallen.

"What's the matter?" I ask.

Françoise picks up a paper from her desk and stands, indicating my office.

I nod and gesture for her to go ahead of me. This can't be good. I hope she's not resigning. She's an asset I can't afford to lose, especially now.

Once I close the door behind me, Françoise hands the paper to me. I skim the words, then have to resist crumbling the summons in my fist.

Fuck!

The pretrial judge called her as a witness. Ordered to appear and to offer evidence, Françoise has no other choice but to do so. I wonder if they summoned others, and if so, what they'll say. It was pretty damning when the doors to the elevator opened and they saw Delia sprawled out with me next to her.

I shake my head, pissed already, and the day only started.

"Thank you for letting me know, Françoise. I don't want you upset. We'll get through this," I start. "Do you mind if I call Albert? He needs to be aware of the pretrial judge's actions."

Françoise nods, "Of course. Also, the vice president of security and the head of building operations told me they received summonses, too. They said to let them know what you need them to do. We don't know of anyone else being summoned."

I thank her and call Albert. He and his team ask for Françoise and the others to meet him in his conference room in ten minutes. I'm to stay in my office.

Next I call my father and Sebastian on three-way. They're not surprised, as we expected they would order some STEELE staff to take part in the investigation. We talk some more, then ring off.

I have meetings all day and will not allow myself to get distracted from the tasks at hand. I can't sit around and wonder what will happen, who will say what, how did this come about. No. I'm a Steele and Roger *The Responsible* Steele to boot. I have work to do, and I'll do it. Period. End of.

My mobile vibrates and I see Leonie's beautiful smile as I pull it from my trousers pocket.

"Hello, gorgeous. Can't get enough of me?" I tease.

Leonie's laughter lifts my spirits. It tinkles over the line straight to my heart, pushing the negativity out of my mind.

"Oh, you! Ha, ha! Actually... I wanted to remind you we're having dinner tonight at Lucien's new place. He just changed the time to seven instead of eight so we can go to the VIP cocktail hour," she says.

"Sounds good. I have a late meeting, so I'll meet you there," I respond. "You can ride with your parents, right?"

"*Oui*, no need for you to come out here to go back to the restaurant. I'll be fine riding with them," Leonie says. "My mother is super excited! She can't stop talking about it. Oh… Listen, I have to go. She's calling for me. I love you, *Mon Cœur*."

We end the call, and I get to work.

"—DON'T know what to think. He's always been a stand-up type of guy. Plus, he's engaged to that hot as fuck super-model. Why the hell would he want the intern?"

"Who knows? She's a desirable piece of ass. Always down to go for drinks after work. It's fucked up either way."

"Yeah. I'd say—"

The two male employees enter and leave the restroom, unaware I'm in a stall. Their comments must be like what others must say. It's interesting to hear their unfiltered thoughts. It's a good thing they said nothing disrespectful about Leonie, I muse.

After I left my last meeting, I stopped in here since my next appointment is on this floor with the design team Delia was a part of. No need to go to my office. I'm glad I didn't.

Now let's see how the team reacts. I'm curious to know if any of them received notification from the judge. I doubt they'd say, and I'm not asking. The last thing I need is for someone to complain I harassed them, too…

I make my way to the conference room. As I pass offices and cubicles, I get the district sensation of being watched. I shrug it off and keep my head held high. I'm not guilty, and I'm no wuss.

"Good afternoon, Mr. Steele."

I turn to the right and see a young woman smiling at me. Oh, brother. Here we go...

"Good afternoon," I answer as I keep it moving.

"Oh, sir?"

Her question stops me, and I glance back at her.

She hurries over, and in a clear voice for all in the vicinity to hear, she speaks.

"Mr. Steele, I want you to know the majority of us believe in you and hope you are successful in getting past this ridiculous accusation. I've been an employee at STEELE for over six years, and never once have you or anyone else behaved inappropriately. We support you, Mr. Steele!"

I blink, taken aback by her decree. Then look around us at the other staff members who nod in agreement or who simply stare. She's right, more of them are on my side than not. Their loyalty warms my heart.

I return my gaze to her and nod.

"Thank you. I appreciate your support." I say sincerely.

"You're welcome, Mr. Steele," she smiles and nods before she returns to her desk.

I acknowledge the rest of the staff, then I continue to the conference room. My step lighter than before.

"*TOUTES NOS FÉLICITATIONS, JOSY ET LUCIEN!*"

"Cheers!"

"Congratulations! Well done!"

We toast Josy and Lucien after we gather for the VIP cocktail hour.

The red carpet was full of media and guests. Leonie and I could run the gauntlet without any major disturbances. She looks sensational in an Azzedine Aläia black jersey, jump-suit with a sleek high neck, long sleeves, and body-hugging fit. Her embellished black sandals lengthen her mile-long legs and add sparkle to the ensemble. Her hair flows behind her like a cape, adding to her superwoman appearance.

"I'm so glad *Maman* found someone to carry on the tradition of our Tunisian family's cooking. I certainly couldn't do it!" Leonie laughs as she raises her glass of iced mint tea to Lucien in salute.

He raises his flute of champagne.

"And I thank you for allowing me to adopt your mother as my second *Maman!*"

We laugh at their banter and continue with the round of toasts.

After a while, we take our seats and the rest of the guests join us.

The aroma tantalizes and makes our mouths water. The food as we expected is scrumptious, rich in flavor with exotic seasonings. The blend of French and Tunisian tradi-tional dishes round out the menu. Satisfied sounds fill the air as much as the din of conversation and laughter.

"How was your day, *Mon Cœur?*" Leonie asks between bites.

"It was good. A couple of surprises. But all is good. Let's enjoy our dinner and I'll tell you later," I respond.

Leonie eyes me skeptically.

"It was fine! No bad news." I say. "I promise, Caramel Bonbon."

She nods and turns to Luc, who whispers something in her ear. They laugh and get back to eating.

Josy's delicious double-chocolate soufflés are a hit for

the desert. No one can resist the tasty treats. Including Leonie, who gets a dollop of fresh cream on the corner of her mouth. Without hesitating, I kiss it off and kiss her lips when she laughs.

Her amber eyes glitter in the low light, just like her namesake feline. Her beauty captivates me. I'm not a wuss. But Leonie makes me weak.

As if reading my thoughts, she turns to me and winks.

LEONIE

My Adonis is a piece of art that rivals Michelangelo's sculpture of David. One chiseled arm thrown over his face to block the morning sun coming through the windows. Its rays of light slant across his powerful chest and eight-pack abs, highlighting the happy trail of dark hair. Even lying flaccid and against his thigh, his massive dick with its bulbous head, veins, and heavy balls makes my mouth water. His thick thighs and muscular calves stretch out beneath the silk sheet.

I satisfy myself by sketching his sleeping form. So peaceful and at rest. No concerns for the pretrial investigation to worry him in his slumber.

One more week and it starts. I know he's stressed by it. But keeping high spirits to avoid me worrying. I've resolved myself to the fact we can only do what we can and not allow a negative thought to disturb us. Roger is innocent. That's my focus.

For now, I'll take advantage of his rest to capture his beauty.

The five o'clock shadow along with his mussed, collar-length hair emphasize his sex appeal. His sensuous full lips and long eyelashes make any woman jealous. Balanced out by his sculpted cheeks and jaw add a decidedly masculine edge to his features. No mistaking Roger is anything but all man.

My charcoal pencil flies across the sketch pad. I want to note as many details as possible before he awakes. I plan to make a painting as a gift to him for our wedding. We can hang it in our bedroom. My eyes only—mine!

I'm so distracted by my task of getting the draping of the sheet just right, I don't notice him lift his arm and open his eyes. That is until in one swift move he swoops over and zerbets my neck. I swat at him with the pad to no avail.

When his no longer flaccid dick bumps against my belly, I know I won't finish my sketch today. I drop the pad to the floor and give in to his ministrations with a sigh of contentment.

"Good morning, Pretty Kitty," he murmurs, his lips tickling my sensitive skin. "What were you doing?"

His sudden nip to my neck makes me squeal in pain and pleasure.

Merde!

"Ahhh... Nothing," I moan.

"Wrong answer, Pretty Kitty!" Roger says.

He begins to zerbet and tickle me.

I laugh and try to fight him off fruitlessly. He's relentless. I surrender and let him have his way with me.

The zerbets turn to open-mouth kisses and the poking fingers begin to prod my core. I'm already wet for him. My sexual needs have increased once again. I could complain. But why, when it's so worth it?

"Is this all for me, Pretty Kitty?" He asks, slipping two of his long digits deep inside of my pussy. "Have you been thinking about me all this time?"

I gasp when he flicks my engorged clit, then pinches it.

His baritone voice thrums in my ear, "Answer me, Pretty Kitty."

Without hesitation, I answer yes. My reward, Roger begins to finger fuck me in earnest, driving his fingers in and out. Each thrust brushes my G-spot and I lift my hips for more friction. My orgasm is within reach. I just need—

"*Non! Non!*" I wail when Roger removes his fingers and sits back on his haunches.

He tilts his head and stares at me as he puts his drenched fingers to my lips. He raises his eyebrow in silent demand.

Immediately, my little pink tongue darts out to lick each finger. I moan at the sweet taste and musky scent of my pussy juices. Once they're clean, I suck on them one by one, challenging Roger with an intense, seductive stare of my own.

He reacts by stroking his swollen cock with his other hand, rubbing the pre-cum over the tip.

"You want something to suck, Pretty Kitty?" He growls, squinting at me with darkened slate-gray eyes.

I nod and murmur yes around his fingers.

He pulls them free with a pop. Then stands on our bed holding the trellis canopy as he looks down at me.

I rise to my knees, then sit back on my heels with my palms on my thighs. His throbbing dick at level with my mouth.

Roger nods and taps my lips with his tip until I open up. He glides to the back of my throat. Then withdraws. Lazily, he repeats the movement as he watches my reaction. When I moan for more, he increases his pace and proceeds to fuck my throat.

I take every inch and beg for more with moans that vibrate along his length.

Roger throws his head back and roars his release.

Thick jets of his cum shoot down my throat, straight to my stomach. So turned on by his climax, I stroke my clit and drive my fingers into my sopping wet pussy as I seek my release. His last thrusts culminate in an orgasm that rips down my tingling spine and makes my toes curl. I get off as much from my climax as I do from causing him to explode. Roger's dick falls from my mouth as I wail in wild abandon.

He drops to his knees and kisses me passionately. Our tongues seek the other out and tangle as the kiss deepens.

Still recovering from my mind-shattering orgasm, my body trembles and I whimper.

Roger cups the back of my head with one hand and my ass with the other, locking me in place. We kiss until our lips swell and we fall apart, panting for breath.

He smiles at me and brushes a lock of damp hair out of my eyes.

"Good morning, my love," he murmurs as he strokes my cheek, his gray eyes full of love.

I close mine and lean into his magical touch.

"Leonie, you're doing well, and The Twins are growing at the appropriate rate. They'll gain more weight each week from now until your delivery."

I'm too busy watching our boys blink to pay attention to Dr. Berger. Their activity seen on the monitor beats whatever he's saying. I chance a glance at Roger and see him grinning from ear to ear at his sons. I squeeze his hand and he smiles down at me and kisses my forehead.

"You're in your thirty-third week or eighth month. So I

want you to get your rest, move slower to avoid clumsiness, and continue your pranayama to help with shortness of breath. Do you have questions for me?" Dr. Berger asks, glancing between Roger and me.

"No."

"*Non.*"

We answer in unison and everyone laughs.

"All right, then. I'll see you in two weeks. Just monitor yourself and call me should you have any concerns," Dr. Berger finishes before he and the nurse leave the room.

Then he turns at the door.

"I'll leave some pamphlets for you with the receptionist. They offer significant information on breastfeeding and ways to connect with your babies before they're born," he adds.

Roger and I thank him, and they leave.

"Well, *Maman*, only a few more weeks to go! Are you ready?" Roger asks as he helps me get down from the examination table.

Once I'm on my feet, I cup his face and smile.

"I am so ready! *Et toi, Papa?*" I ask.

He grins again and responds, "Absofuckinglutely! It's time I hold them after you've had them for so long!"

We laugh, and I get dressed. With my sizable belly, it's all about Diane von Furstenberg silk wrap dresses and Lanvin wedge heels—classic and chic.

On our way out, we pick up the pamphlets. We settle in our new Rolls-Royce Phantom Extended. Roger custom ordered it since I had difficulty getting in and out of the too high Cullinan and too low DB7 Vantage. I felt like Goldilocks trying different automobiles until I found one that fit!

I skim through the pamphlets and stop at the one on

naming your baby. We hadn't discussed names yet. At first I was nervous thinking about my mother's experiences. But now that I'm so close, it's time we decided on names for The Twins.

I hand the pamphlet to Roger and watch for his reaction.

His eyes widen as he reads the title. Then he shifts in his seat to look me directly in the eye.

"Are you sure?" He asks with a hopeful expression on his handsome face.

"Absofuckinglutely!" I mimic his earlier word choice.

He kisses me and flips through the pamphlet.

"What do you have in mind?" Roger questions as he holds my hand in his reassuring grip.

I take a moment to think about it. I'm the last of my Beaulieu family line. I'm sure my father had hoped for a son to carry on the name. After their difficulty in conceiving, then not being able to have more children, it left him with a girl. When Roger and I marry I intend to take his name. So Beaulieu will drop from my name, too.

An idea forms.

"I'd like their middle names to be Beaulieu. A symbolic way to carry on my family's name," I respond.

Roger tilts his head in thought. Then he focuses his intense stare on me for what seems like forever.

"That's a wonderful way to honor your father and to keep your family's name going," he says smiling.

Relief rushes over me, and I relax back into the cushy leather seat.

"What about first names?" He asks. "I was thinking something French would remind them of their heritage. They'll have the Steele name, so it would be respectful to have a name from your family, even beyond Beaulieu."

Tears blur my vision—damn hormones—at his suggestion. Roger is an Alpha male who's confident in himself so much he doesn't have the need to force his dominance in the naming of our sons.

"Aw, babe, I didn't mean to upset you. Don't cry," he croons as he leans over the armrest to cup my face. "Think about it. We can speak with your parents for their input. Okay, my love?"

I can only nod, too caught up in the emotions of seeing my babies so lively and being so close to term.

Roger's soothing voice murmurs words of love all the way back to the *Manoir*.

"I LOVE the idea of Beaulieu as their middle names. But you could name them Beau and Lieu, too!"

My mother cracks up at her own joke, and I join in.

We are so similar as we sit next to each other on the sofa in the living room in our East Wing. My parents spend more time here, so I don't have to walk so far to get to the bedroom should I need a nap.

We just finished lunch and shared the latest ultrasound images and our ideas for The Twins' names.

"*Mais non*," my father responds with a grimace. "Not at all."

He mutters about the destruction of our family's name and shakes his head.

"Do you want them to have the same first letter or similarities of some sort?" Shelley asks as she holds a set of images. "They are too cute!"

I cock my head to the side as I ponder the question. Deep in thought, I bite the corner of my lower lip. Then I shake my head.

"Not necessarily. I don't want them to get confused.

They need their own identities, too. That's what the pamphlet mentions on twins," I respond, handing the pamphlet to Shelley.

"Guy, do you have family members you'd like to honor?" Morgan asks as he glances over her shoulder at the pamphlet.

We talk some more about the names. Different ones pop up along with their meanings. Guy means wide. Leonie means brave as a lion. My parents named me that since they said I looked like a lioness with a head full of mahogany hair when I was born and because I was so brave to make it to full term. Beaulieu means lovely place. So meanings are important to us.

I rack my mind thinking of the best names. Inspiration hits when my gaze meets Roger's intense gray eyes.

"Rodolphe *et* Gaspard!" I shout.

Everyone turns to me, surprised by my outburst. Then they laugh.

"Oookay... And why those names?" Roger asks between chuckles.

"Well, we should include you in some way, as should I since they come from us. So, Rodolphe means famous wolf; I call you *Mon Loup*, my wolf. And Gaspard means—"

"A treasure bearer, *Mon Trésor!*" My father claps his hands and rises to hug me. "So thoughtful, Leonie!"

"Rodolphe Beaulieu Steele and Gaspard Beaulieu Steele!" Roger declares as he kneels before me and kisses my belly.

As if in response, two kicks or punches poke me, and Roger laughs when he feels them, too.

"You like your names, my sons?" He asks, stroking my belly on both sides.

They respond with more movement as I laugh. Dr. Berger wasn't kidding when he mentioned strong fetal movement at this stage of my pregnancy. They feel like David Beckham going for the winning goal during the World Cup Finals!

Roger peers up at me with such a heartfelt smile, I feel it in my very soul.

"Thank you, my love," he says in earnest. *"Merci beaucoup."*

ROGER

"*R*oger! Why did you sexually assault Delia Shaw?"

"No means no!"

"Roger Steele! *Honte à toi!*"

"Leonie! How can you marry a monster?"

"Leonie! This way!"

Fuck!

This is a damn media circus combined with a protest that's beyond fucked up. And this is only day one...

Albert and his legal team take the lead up the steps of the pretrial courthouse. Their mood is no nonsense and all business. They set the tone for us.

Sebastian and I flank Leonie, holding her arms as we move through the crowd held back by our security detail and the police. I feel her stiffen at the insults and accusations thrown at us. However, she keeps her head high and her back straight. My woman is no shrinking violet who simpers in the face of opposition. She's a fierce *Lion*.

The rest of our family and friends follow us. All Steeles; Guy and Josy; Lachlan and Lucien Jackson; Luc; Joel and Hettie; Blair, Billie, and Starr; Norman and Anita came out in a full force of support. Françoise, along with several other STEELE staff members join us in solidarity. Their presence is as much a comfort for me as it is for Leonie.

No one speaks while we proceed to the courtroom. The halls are full of people who turn in our direction as we pass. Our pace doesn't slow. We want to get in and settled quickly.

A flash goes off to our left. Followed by more as the media within the building take notice of our group.

More catcalls fill the already tense air.

Leonie squeezes my hand to reassure me when I bristle at a particularly offensive comment.

These people have zero knowledge of facts. Yet they judge and condemn me. The state of the world today assumes the man is guilty automatically. Some may be. But I am not. The immediate castigation angers me. I'm more determined to prove my innocence just to shut them the fuck up.

Finally, we reach the doors to the courtroom. More police officers stand guard to maintain control and to prevent overcrowding. They allow us to pass with nods.

Upon entering, the first person we see is Antonio Vasquez standing behind the claimant's table. He glares at me and places a supportive hand on Delia Shaw's shoulder. She shifts in her seat to glance at him. Then faces us when he indicates with the tilt of his chin our entrance.

For a brief moment, the real Delia shines through with a

sneer directed at Leonie. The fleeting expression reveals her cocksure attitude and devious intent. In a blink, it's gone, replaced by a chaste, eyes downcast countenance. Then she widens her eyes and covers her mouth on a sob before she turns away slowly. Antonio pats her shoulder comfortingly and whispers in her ear.

If I hadn't seen her glare at Leonie, Delia's performance would have been believable—and the Academy Award for Best Actress goes to...

Sebastian huffs in response to Delia's dramatic behavior.

I agree, but remain silent, as does Leonie.

After I help her into her seat on the bench between her parents and mine, I join Albert and the legal team at the defendant's table. Not once do I glance at the other side. Instead, I maintain a neutral expression and face forward.

Game on.

At the call to order, the din of voices quiets and everyone stands. When the judge enters the courtroom, the solemnity of the situation hits me in the chest like a Mack truck.

Inwardly I curse the day I fought Antonio Fucking Velasquez. That slip in my control led to the creation of the damn internship program and subsequently to his and Delia's hiring as the first interns. A moment of weakness becomes a period of hell. Not just for me, but for my loved ones.

I have to force myself not to glance over my shoulder at Leonie and all who gather behind me. I know they believe in my innocence. Nonetheless, the embarrassment to my family and to our multigenerational multibillion-dollar company makes for a hard pill to swallow.

The proceedings start with an opening statement presented by Judge Favre as a summary of the claim and the parties involved. The magistrate outlines the timeline for the proceedings. He plans to convene eight times after today on alternating days over the next month. Today will give both sides the opportunity to make opening statements. With the investigation set to begin next week.

Delia's legal team presents their opening statement. They drone on to paint me as a sex maniac who preyed on Ms. Shaw—an innocent, trusting university student who earned her position as an intern. Her only mistake was being in the division run by a monster...

Her appearance would support her claim of purity with a navy blue conservative skirt suit, severe bun, and no makeup. Her curves no longer on display and her vivacious personality hidden behind a sorrowful persona.

It's hard to get a read on the judge. He sits stoically on his bench. Periodically during the claimant's statement, his eyes flick to me with an analytical stare. It's as though he can reach deep within me to find every bad thing I've done since childhood.

Damn. And I thought I had an intense gaze.

However, I don't flinch or change my facial expression. I know how to play the game, and I will not lose my control. Judge Favre can't pique me.

Rather than listening to their lies and get my blood pressure up, I focus on how my family and friends will celebrate the end of this farce. I envision us at the penthouse drinking Taittinger, then having dinner catered by Lucien with Josy's dishes and double-chocolate soufflés. I'd love to go to back to Capri and stay at our new villa—Lucien drove a hard bargain, but no price is too high for Leonie. However, in four weeks' time, she'll be too close to her expected delivery date to travel.

The thought of my sons increases my determination to

finish this quickly. I don't want a blemish around their birth, no more than around our wedding. With Leonie at thirty-four weeks, she's close. Dr. Berger mentioned twins can arrive earlier than expected.

I tried to convince Leonie to stay home and not stress herself out being in the courtroom. But to no avail. She insisted her presence would make a difference: pregnant fiancée supports me despite the nasty accusations. Plus, she's famous and will have her supporters, too.

Her followers on social media constantly send direct messages and leave comments of encouragement. It's incredible the power of social media and the influence of those popular on it. Albert agrees it's a good idea for her to be present. As does everyone else.

Her parents' concerns mimic mine in that we don't want her to stress out. Leonie promised me she wouldn't overexert herself, and if she felt tired, she would return to the *Manoir*. Her health and our babies outweigh "appearances."

Albert rising from his seat cuts into my thoughts.

He presents our statement in a succinct, factual manner. Unlike the claimant's attorney, Albert completes his opening remarks in less than fifteen minutes. Even the judge seems to appreciate the brevity of Albert's words as Judge Favre's face relaxes a fraction.

He thanks both sides for their opening statements. Then he reminds everyone we will re-convene next week. He rises from his bench and exits the courtroom as we stand.

We wait until Albert and his team gather their paper-work before we leave. I walk past Delia. I refuse to pay her any attention. And it's obvious she's the type that lives for attention.

Leonie kisses me on the lips in full view of everyone.

The sound of cameras clicking fill the room. She knows how to play the game, too.

We make our way back out to the waiting cars. Sebastian and I flank Leonie again as we move through the crowd. More insults and questions come at us from all directions. I squeeze Leonie's hand, and she nods slightly in acknowledgement. Sebastian mutters, "Assholes."

At last we get inside the four Mercedes-Benz Sprinters and pull away from the courthouse in formation. Albert suggested we lease the souped-up vans instead of driving our personal vehicles since strangers would view the license plates. We certainly don't want stalkers finding our homes. The damn drones and paparazzi are bad enough. We take a roundabout way back to the *Manoir* to avoid being followed.

I'm relieved today was a relatively short time. I reach for Leonie's hand and bring it to my mouth to kiss her fingertips gently. She smiles and takes off her glamour girl shades. Her amber eyes are tired. I curse to myself. She does not need this bullshit!

As if sensing my thoughts, Leonie offers a smile and strokes my cheek.

"Don't worry, *Mon Cœur*. We're all right"—she rubs her other hand across her belly—"No need to look so grave!"

"Leonie, next week you need to stay home—"

"*Non! Non!* I will not let you face that trollop's shit without me by your side! We are in this together, Roger Steele! I mean it!" She roars with her amber eyes flashing sparks, no longer weary.

The Lion will not back down.

"Fine, but you have to promise me truly you will not stay if you need to rest. If not, I will lock you in our bedroom…" I respond.

But Leonie only laughs at my threat, knowing it's an

empty one. Although I would tie her to our bed with only enough length to get to the bathroom.

"Good luck with keeping Leonie away, Roger!" Lola laughs from the back row. "Her maternal instincts are on high right about now!"

Everyone joins in her laughter, including me. She speaks the truth.

We wait until we reach the *Manoir* and sit in the living room before we discuss the investigation. Albert gives his feedback along with his team. They pulled a report on the judge and found him to be stern and only interested in facts, not emotions. The statement made by Delia's legal team was full of emotion. While Albert's was all facts. He says it's a score for us.

My father and I ask more questions. But there's not much to go on at this point. The real action will occur next week. Albert suggests we enjoy the weekend, rest, and return ready for the tough part. He and the team leave, declining an offer to join us for an early dinner. Françoise also leaves and offers words of encouragement before they go.

The rest of the group heads to the dining hall—the larger eating area that harkens back to *Le Manoir Beaulieu*'s days of entertaining royalty in the larger space. The staff serves the meal prepared by their chef. Josy cooks on the weekends when she gives them the days off.

We dine on the scrumptious dishes and wines from their ancient cellar. No one discusses the proceedings. We opt to have a normal conversation with Harris teasing Haley about some mysterious project she's working on, and Hettie recounting Joel's time at their cake tasting with his allergic reaction to almond paste. Norman regales us with stories from his most renown matches, and Anita tells how he's a softy for their daughter Antonia. It amounts to a good time with loved ones.

* * *

"NOTHING BEATS a stroll through the Bois de Boulogne on a sunny day," Leonie sighs.

We entered the park from a side gate of *Le Beaulieu Manoir* not detected from within the park. The *Manoir* is on the westernmost part of the outskirts of Paris in Neuilly-Auteuil-Passy. It's a majestic property with manicured park-like grounds, stables, tennis court, swimming pool and cabana, and a palatial mansion. They built the hamlet between the thirteenth and seventeenth centuries. Later, during the reign of Louis XV, it became a fashionable country retreat for French elites. The Beaulieu's twenty acres of land border Bois de Boulogne with parts of the acreage awarded to their ancestors by the monarch.

"It's a beautiful day. But not as lovely as you," I respond.

Leonie rolls her eyes at my sappy remark, and I laugh.

"Okay, okay! So, I'm not a poet. You've gotta give me some points for trying!" I add with a smirk.

She kisses my cheek and rests her head on my shoulder as we stop at the pond.

Children float sail boats on its surface while actual row boats glide by. The tranquil scene offers a respite to the bustling Paris streets.

Unconsciously, Leonie rubs her babies bump.

I can tell she's thinking about Rodolphe and Gaspard. I move behind her and place my hands on top of hers as I lean my cheek against the crown of her head.

We stand in silence as we watch the children play and listen to their squeals of laughter. Their joy in the simple act of their boats skimming the water reminds me to just let go and allow the tide to take me.

Today, I can enjoy the ease of being with my love and taking time to connect with her and our sons. A simple stroll on a sunny day is just what I need.

LEONIE

"$\mathcal{L}$eonie, you have a noticeable increase in your blood pressure. It's not from your pregnancy, as you have no other signs. It's stress related. How are you holding up with the investigation?"

I lower my gaze, upset with myself for letting the pretrial stress me out after I promised Roger I wouldn't. It's just been more than I expected, with the constant taunts and barrage of questions. And that's before we even get inside the courtroom where the real inquisition takes place.

Roger had to be in court this morning.

At this stage, it's super important I keep my prenatal appointments. So Lola came with me. I avoid her eyes when Dr. Berger announces my blood pressure and voices his concerns.

I just get so pissed seeing that fake ass hussy pretending to be so innocent! How can she cause all of this drama when there are women who actually face sexual predators and the women don't get an opportunity to be heard? Or they're not believed. It's not right on any level.

Sure, people have said I wasn't there, so how can I know for sure. Well, I wasn't there. But I know Roger. Yeah, that's what they all say… My response remains the same: I believe him and I trust him.

Delia, not at all.

She's flirted with him from the start in class and at his office. Then tried to castigate me for being Roger's girlfriend. All along she wanted him, and my relationship with him rankled her.

That nasty sneer she threw at me on day one in the courtroom was hardly the first time she hated on me because of Roger. Delia did the same thing when we were at human resources. She had the nerve to insinuate they hired me because of Roger.

Pathetic witch.

Now she's using the courtroom as her stage to play out this obsession across France and the United States. All because Roger doesn't want her.

It's just confounding how they ended up on the elevator together. No one can figure out what happened with the elevator controls no more than they could her ID badge accessing the executive floor.

That puzzle piece keeps me up at night. If only we can solve those issues, we would be in a better place.

So, yes, my blood pressure is elevated because of stress. Whose wouldn't be??

"—Leonie… Leonie?"

A tap to my shoulder disperses the turmoil swirling in my mind. I glance up at Dr. Berger, the nurse, and Lola. They're watching me expectantly.

"*Excusez-moi*. Please repeat your question," I say.

"For your health and the wellbeing of The Twins, you

must not return to the courthouse," Dr. Berger says with finality.

I deflate and burst into tears. The emotions are overwhelming. I cover my face as the tears stream down my flushed cheeks.

Why? Why is this happening? Why now?

I HATE THAT HUSSY!

"I'M FINE, *Maman* and *Maman Aussi*. Really I am," I say as I lie in my bed at *Le Manoir*.

Lola insisted I return right after the prenatal visit. She sent text messages to my mother and Shelley. They left the courtroom and met us at the front door. The three of them promptly escorted me to my bedroom. Then they undressed me, put a nightgown on me, and tucked me in bed with pillows fluffed behind my back and legs.

"How's Roger? Did he see you leave?" I ask concerned their departure upset him.

My mother shakes her head, her ebony curly bob sways.

"*Non*. He didn't notice, and we didn't tell him. Only Your father, Morgan, and Sebastian know you're here."

Shelley takes my hand and nods.

"Don't worry about Roger. We need you to focus on yourself, Rodolphe, and Gaspard. High blood pressure is not good for any of you, especially so close to term," she says with concern in her chocolate brown eyes.

I nod and stroke my belly as I lean back against the abundance of pillows. My body calls for me to sleep. I let my eyelids drift close.

"HOW LONG HAS SHE BEEN ASLEEP?"

"It's been two-and-a-half hours. It exhausts the poor baby. Come, let's go to the living room so as not to disturb her rest."

"But is she all right??"

I shift my position towards the voices. They sound like Roger and Shelley. His voice laced with apprehension. I force my eyes open so he doesn't worry.

They're headed to the bedroom door.

"Roger," I call out softly.

He pivots and rushes to my side.

"Baby, how do you feel?" He asks as he sits on the bed and takes my hands in his firm grip.

I promised him I wouldn't lie. I glance away sadly because I am tired and I need a break. My mind wants to be strong for him, for us. But my body wins, and it demands I rest. No wonder I slept for so long.

Merde!

"Hey, it's okay, my love"—he cups my face to bring my gaze back to him—"You, Rodolphe, and Gaspard need to take it easy."

I nod as tears fill my eyes.

"I told you once before, and I will repeat it again. You mean everything to me. You are irreplaceable, my love. Call me selfish. But I will not live without you, Leonie. And if you keep going on stressed and your blood pressure continues to elevate... I do not want to think of what can happen. I cannot lose you, ever."

Roger finishes his sentence in a husky whisper, his voice clogged with unshed tears. He leans his forehead against mine and closes his eyes as he squeezes my hands.

We sit in silence, absorbing one another's breath and gathering strength from our love.

"*Je t'aime aussi, Mon Amour,*" I whisper.

Roger sits back enough to look within the depths of my eyes. As he searches for any hint of me going against his wishes, I ease his fears.

"I promise I will stay here and rest. I won't return to the courtroom until it's time for the judge's determination," I say as I hold my hand up to stop him from interrupting me.

"I will be there on that day only. I will not leave you to face his decision without me," I finish.

Roger considers what I said. Then he nods.

"Fine. But you will use the rear entrance to avoid the craziness at the front. And no matter what he decides, you promise to stay calm?"

I nod.

"Words, Leonie. I will have your words," Roger demands.

Without hesitation, I respond.

"*Oui*, Roger. I promise, *Mon Cœur*."

"Good," he says, kissing my fingertips.

* * *

"YOUR NUMBERS HAVE IMPROVED EXPONENTIALLY, Mademoiselle Beaulieu! Monsieur Steele will be very pleased."

I smile at Nanny Grace.

As part of the deal of me staying at home, Roger insisted I have a nurse. I wasn't up for interviewing potential candidates. But then I remembered: Nanny Grace is a trained nurse.

She agreed to start earlier than the birth of Rodolphe and Gaspard. She comes over in the morning and stays until the evening. Throughout the day, Grace checks my vitals and records them in a log. Then she forwards them to Roger.

It gives him peace of mind. So I don't argue. He has enough to deal with the investigation and maintaining STEELE business as usual.

The company receives backlash in the media constantly. It's as though they can't wait to destroy the man and the company before they have any proof of wrongdoing. It's all based on speculation.

Being privately owned, it doesn't impact them as severely. They pull on their deep roots and impeccable reputation developed over generations to overcome the image the media attempts to create.

Their marketing and public relations departments began campaigns to thwart any negativity. They highlight STEELE Foundation's work to build and manage attractive, affordable housing for urban, lower-income families led by Shelley. Their other philanthropic activities reinforce the company's connection with the community. Multiple interviews with prominent individuals and businesses fill the networks and publications on both continents daily.

As a result, STEELE hasn't lost partnerships. Some may have held off until after the decision. But contracts that were pre existing continue.

So if Roger isn't at the courthouse, he's at the office. Norman keeps him training to avoid him burning out and losing focus. "Don't lose your head, Steele!" Norman tells him. Roger still joins me for some of my mediation and yoga nidra sessions with Anita in my studio at the *Manoir*. All the disciplines blend to keep his mind and body at optimal performance.

I remind Roger how he insists I stay healthy, then he has to do the same.

"Yes, it will thrill him, Grace," I respond, just as pleased.

It's just the two of us here today. Everyone is at the courthouse. I told both sets of our parents to stand by Roger since I can't be there. Their presence is the closest I can get to supporting him at the moment.

"So what would you like to do now?" Nanny Grace asks as she puts away her log.

I consider my options: paint Roger's portrait, sketch more designs for the Lola's Coterie maternity line, or crochet another pair of booties—Nanny Grace taught me.

For years I've had such a busy schedule traveling all over the world for photo shoots and commercials, my interior design schoolwork, and events. I'm not used to being so still!

In the end, I opt to paint. While Roger isn't here, I can get more of it done without fear of him seeing it. He's forever surprising me with gifts, I want to do the same for him.

"I'm going to my art studio until it's time for lunch. Would you come and get me then? Once I start painting, I lose track of time," I answer.

Nanny Grace agrees and says she'll be in the library.

We part ways at the door to my sitting room.

Once in the art studio, I turn on my Seductress playlist for inspiration. The sensual songs combined with Roger's enticing form on the canvas and sketch pad get me going in no time.

The door chime cuts into my playlist—Harris outfitted it so I wouldn't miss a knock when I play music loud.

I glance at my mobile and notice three hours passed.

Wow!

The painting is nearly complete. Roger's likeness is unmistakable. My eyes roam over his beautiful body. I lick my lips as my gaze lands on his massive dick. So lifelike, I want to lick it all over. Yum!

Not wanting anyone to see him, I re-cover it with the tarp and call out for Nanny Grace to enter.

"It's time for lunch, Mademoiselle," she says.

Then she raises her eyebrow when she sees me stretching my neck.

"Have you been sitting still this whole time?" She asks.

"*Non*, I've moved around and did some stretches and leg pumps," I respond.

She nods and we leave the studio for the kitchenette's eating area.

My stomach growls as we near the tantalizing aromas of grilled wild-caught salmon and roasted vegetables. Dr. Berger wants me to eat salmon twice a week to increase my omega-3 fatty acid intake. The fish oils help with early development and postpartum depression. So I'm all for it.

After we eat, we head outdoors for a walk through the grounds as exercise. We stop by the stables and feed the horses some apples. I can't wait to see The Twins riding on the trails like I did as a child. They'll keep their ponies here and can have lessons. Maybe they'll take up polo.

Nanny Grace and I return to the main house. Along the way, I point out some memories from my childhood to her. She laughs at my clipping all the roses to make the biggest bouquet ever for my mother on Mother's Day. Instead of getting angry I botched her prized rose bushes, my mother smothered me in kisses and hugs.

That's what I want with my children. Wonderful memories full of love and happiness. And I will be damned if I allow she who shall not named to ruin it!

I make up my mind to be extra careful over the next week and a half so I can be in tip-top shape to face that cow in the courtroom.

I can't wait to tell her, "Bye, Bitch!"

ROGER

"All rise... This court is now in session. The Honorable Judge Favre presiding. When each witness goes to the stand. Please state your name for the court."

Another day of testimonies by witnesses. Who knew so they would call many people before the judge for an incident that occurred between two individuals over less than twenty minutes in the dark?!

It's been weeks, and it drags on and on. Delia's legal team has a flair for dramatics as much as she does. They take hours to interview people. Drawing out answers. Recross examinations take place. Requests for additional time to review evidence. It's ridiculous.

It's also apparent they're in it for the money. Part of her petition involves monetary damages, including her legal fees covered by STEELE and me. It's obvious her attorneys plan to rack up billable hours, no matter how absurd they appear in the process. The circus extends beyond the frenetic scene outside to within the courtroom.

Although it feels more like the nine rings of Dante Alighieri's *Inferno* than the three rings under The Big Top of Ringling Bros. and Barnum & Bailey Circus...

The judge has to ask his questions. It takes time. But at least he's concise and the ringmaster.

Albert also stays within a reasonable amount of time. He's extremely thorough and puts doubt in any attempt by her team to paint me as a sexual deviant.

We've called character witnesses to support my defense. Business associates, leaders from nonprofit organizations, and STEELE staff have willingly come forward to dispute any claim of me being an aggressive predator. My reputation in business and in my personal life is impeccable.

Judge Favre interviews them, and his line of questioning is unbiased. Yet one can tell it's going in my favor. Delia's team is failing to provide suitable evidence for a prosecution determination.

Now it's time for the two of us to take the stand for questioning. It's the last step in the process before the judge announces his decision.

Albert and my legal team are confident it will be a positive outcome. I certainly hope so.

Leonie has been a real trooper. She's kept her promise to stay at the *Manoir* and rest. And it shows. Once again she's radiant and relaxed. It's as though a light switch flipped on within her. No longer are the golden flecks in her amber eyes flashing in warning. They're bright with happiness.

Next week she'll be thirty-six weeks. I can hardly believe it. Although her much larger belly proves she's close to the end of her pregnancy.

I'm pissed I missed her last prenatal visit with Dr. Berger. Thankfully, Lola went with her and heard his concerns about Leonie's blood pressure. If I had noticed my mother and Josy left the courtroom, I would have left too. I wouldn't have given a damn what the judge or Albert said.

The doctor's words scared Leonie more than anything I've said. So she's taken it to heart and keeps calm. Nanny Grace sends accounts of Leonie's vitals to me daily. The proof of her following doctor's orders keeps me sane. One less worry in my overcrowded mind.

Thoughts of getting back to Leonie, hearing about her day, and feeling my sons' movement make these long as fuck hours in the courtroom bearable.

When this is over, I swear we're taking a long vacation.

"ALL RISE... This court is now in session. The Honorable Judge Favre presiding. When each witness goes to the stand. Please state your name for the court."

Once the judge takes his seat after a break in the proceedings, he announces the witness testimony of Delia.

I ensure I plaster my most impassive expression on my face. No matter what she says or does, I will remain apathetic. My mantra of "I am innocent" runs on repeat in my mind. I take a cleansing breath and settle myself.

Delia, of course, came just as prepared as me.

Today she wears a somber charcoal gray skirt suit with a boxy fit and a crisp white shirt, black stockings, and basic black heels. Her brunette hair pulled up in a French twist draws attention to the trepidation in her eyes. Little to no makeup on her face. A simple pair of pearl studs adorn her ear lobes.

All she's missing is a book, and she'd look like a mousy elementary-school librarian.

Give me a fucking break. I nearly break form and snort in derision.

When Delia reaches the witness stand, she faces the bailiff and states her name softly with her eyes downcast.

He asks her to repeat her name louder, and she does a fraction.

I want to roll my eyes.

Delia takes the oath to tell the truth, then takes her seat. Her eyes scan the crowded courtroom. When her gaze lands on me, she flinches and sits back in the chair. Her gaze lowers to her lap where she wrings her hands anxiously.

"Are you all right, Ms. Shaw?" Judge Favre asks as he stares down at her from his bench.

She glances up from beneath her eyelashes and nods her head.

"Kindly speak your response, Ms. Shaw," the judge requests.

Delia responds yes, and he turns to his paperwork.

Great... Here we go.

"Mademoiselle Shaw, kindly tell us how it came about you were with Monsieur Steele on his private elevator?" Judge Favre inquires.

Once again she flinches, this time at my name, and darts her eyes in my direction.

"I... I was going..." Delia's voice trails off as she falters.

The judge peers down at her. Then tells her to take her time.

She responds how she's nervous, and the judge encourages her to take her time. She nods, then takes a moment before she continues in a somewhat stronger tone.

"I was on my way to the weekly Interior Design Team meeting. That morning, I... I had just found a discrepancy in the AutoCAD renditions for the new project in the sixth arrondissement," Delia starts.

She pauses to take a sip of water.

"They had the potential to ruin the structure of the building—"

Just like her legal team, Delia drones on about the computer-generated drawings instead of getting to the point. She takes what seems like forever to answer Judge Favre's question.

"—when I saw Mr. Steele in the lobby. I caught up with him, and he invited me onto his private elevator."

Delia shivers and sips more water.

That lying, scheming…

Like hell I "invited" her onto my private elevator! I tried to avoid her. Even going so far as to say I wasn't available!

Albert's hand opens and closes on his yellow legal pad atop our table.

Fuck!

It's his signal I need to check my control. I must have reacted in some way to Delia's blatant lies.

With a deep breath, I resettle myself and repeat my mantra.

Inhale, I am.

Exhale, innocent.

Pause.

Inhale, I am.

Exhale, innocent.

Pause.

"What exactly did Monsieur Steele say to you as an invitation?" Judge Favre asks after he takes notes.

Delia nods.

"He said, 'You can ride me. I mean ride with me… on my private elevator.' His words exactly, Your Honor," she responds, then glances down at her hands.

Murmurs fill the room as the crowd of spectators,

media, and protestors react to her words. Or rather, my false ones.

I cannot believe her bullshit is going to fly! More fucking lies! And she's under oath!

Albert doesn't lose his cool. He merely makes a note on his pad. Then continues to listen to the inquisition.

The judge also writes on his pad. He maintains a neutral expression the entire time. He sets his pen down and returns his gaze to Delia.

"Mademoiselle Shaw, kindly tell us what occurred once you were on Monsieur Steele's private elevator," Judge Favre inquires.

Delia swallows visibly. Then she reaches for the water pitcher to refill her glass. As she does so, her hand shakes, and water sloshes onto the railing around the witness stand. She emits a soft cry and searches around for something to wipe up the spill.

The judge calls for a five-minute recess and indicates the bailiff to get paper towels. He returns and helps Delia to clean up.

She's all "I'm so sorry" and "I'm just so nervous" that I want to dump the whole pitcher over her head.

Give me a fucking break already!

We resume, and Delia recounts the encounter. Or rather, her version that's full of more damning lies.

"Mr. Steele followed me onto his private elevator. I could feel his breath on the back of my head, he was so close... Before I could speak, he stared at me from my head to my toes. I felt as though he were undressing me... It reminded me of the time I was in his office—"

Delia shivers and clutches her arms.

"I felt uncomfortable. But you see, I was an intern, and this was my chance to prove myself worthy of a full-time position! So I just ignored his creepy stare and told him about the AutoCAD renditions. Suddenly the lights went out! I thought he did it on purpose, so I backed away from him. When the lights came back on, he was closer to me..."

Again she trails off and glances down at her hands, now pale in a death grip. She stops speaking.

"Ms. Shaw, do you need a moment?" Judge Favre asks.

Delia shakes her head and wipes her nose as she sniffles. When she raises her head, her eyes have tears in them.

What the fuck?!

"Judge Favre, Your Honor?" Her lead attorney calls out.

The judge glances at him.

"Judge Favre, my client is under duress. The events traumatized her when they happened and continue to plague her with nightmares. As you can see, she's shaken. We would like to request a recess for an hour, Your Honor," her attorney requests.

The judge turns to Delia and asks, "Ms. Shaw, do you require some time before we proceed?"

She nods tearfully, then answers verbally when he cocks his head.

"The court will resume in one hour," Judge Favre proclaims.

"ALL RISE... This court is now in session. The Honorable Judge Favre presiding. When each witness goes to the stand. Please state your name for the court."

Delia takes the stand again, and the bailiff reminds her she's still under oath.

Like that does any damn good...

"Mademoiselle Shaw, the question again is that you

kindly tell us what occurred once you were on Monsieur Steele's private elevator," Judge Favre reminds her.

Delia takes a deep breath and sits taller. Then she turns and points at me.

"Roger Steele tried to rape me."

Fuck the rings, all hell springs loose.

The room explodes in a melee of shouts from the protestors calling me a rapist to the clicks of photographers' cameras to the spectators' shocked gasps. The commotion draws the attention of the police stationed outside of the courtroom.

They rush in from all doors and take command as Judge Favre and the bailiff shout for order in the court. More officers enter and start to remove protestors, the loudest and most violent in the crowd. My security detail stands at the gallery railing to prevent anyone from harming my family and me.

I glance at Delia.

For a second, our eyes meet. The hateful glare she throws at me sends chills through my body.

This bitch is out for revenge. She doesn't give a damn what lies she tells or who she hurts in the process.

In a blink of an eye, the expression disappears from her face. Then she brings her hands up to hide behind them.

My resolve for proving my innocence hardens further.

Albert tells me to remain seated and not to look at Delia or her legal team. He stands beside me on alert.

Half an hour later, the courtroom gallery clears of everyone except for the people present to support Delia and me.

Judge Favre calls for the proceedings to continue with Delia expounding upon her accusation. He asks her to recount what happened and not for her conclusion. He explains the difference to her, and she continues.

Delia puts a negative spin on every action that took place:

The lights come back on; I'm on top of her.

I reach out to help her; I groped her breast.

I try to prevent her from falling when the elevator plummets; I slammed her against the wall and made her hit her head.

She holds onto my neck; she scratched me to make me let go of her.

I try to comfort her since she claims to be claustrophobic by patting her back; I tore her camisole to feel her up.

She fingers my hair and pulls it; she fought me off and yanked my hair out.

She falls backwards yanking my tie and pulling me off balance to fall with her; I pushed her to the floor and ripped her stockings and skirt in a frenzy to fuck her.

I use my left hand to brace my fall and sprain it; she used a self-defense move to bend my wrist backwards.

I scramble away from her; She kneed me in the balls to stop me from raping her.

She's sprawled out on the floor of the elevator; the impact of the blow I inflicted when I slammed her head on the wall caused her to suffer a concussion and lose consciousness.

Then her legal team jumps in with "evidence" collected at the hospital: my hair and pieces of my skin beneath her fingernails; one of my shirt buttons in her hand; bruising on her inner thighs consistent with force used by a knee to separate her legs.

By the time Delia's testimony and her attorney's questioning conclude, I doubt my damn myself.

Shit, did it happen that way for real?

Hell to the fuck no!

Again, Delia has it in for me, and she's going to the extreme.

It's my word against hers since the cameras failed along with the functioning of the elevator. Besides, it was dark. They're not programmed with night vision capabilities.

I can't believe this bullshit.

My face heats. My armpits tingle. My head pounds with an instant headache caused by the tension that racks every cell in my body.

This is beyond fucked up.

Despite it all, I maintain my stoic expression. I've trained my sense of control for years, and I rely on every lesson to keep my shit together. I cannot crack.

Judge Favre asks Albert if he wants to question Delia. He does.

"Ms. Shaw, would you like a moment before we begin?" Albert asks her while he sits at our table. "Perhaps a sip of your water?"

Taken aback by his kind offers, Delia's eyes widen and she glances at her legal team.

I don't follow her gaze. Rather, I look straight ahead.

"Uh... No... Er... Thank you," she responds, eyeing him warily.

"Fine. Ms. Shaw, I do not wish for you to relive the encounter. But I do wish for you to clarify some comments you made," Albert says.

Then he turns to the judge, "Your Honor, I would like to hand this deposition transcript to Ms. Shaw."

The judge allows Albert to approach the witness. She takes the document, and he points to a page.

I realize it's from the cover-your-ass file Albert insisted we create immediately following the incident.

He swiftly and summarily refutes all of her statements with her own words. He plays the video testimony from both Delia and me as further evidence of the encounter. By the time he's through, Delia's face is the one that's red.

Albert thanks her for her time and returns to his chair.

Thank fuck!

Judge Favre calls for a thirty-minute recess and exits the courtroom.

Upon his return, the judge calls me to the witness stand.

I state my name and take my oath in a clear voice.

Once I'm seated, Judge Favre peers down at me. Then he asks me to recount the encounter from Delia approaching me in the lobby to the elevator doors re-opening. I answer honestly and succinctly. My tone remains even and strong.

I do not waiver. Not even after her attorney attempts to draw my anger by insinuating I wanted Delia because I was no longer attracted to Leonie because of her pregnant state. I nearly laughed as I recalled we had incredible sex right before the nightmare with Delia occurred!

Albert however was having none of it. He demands Delia's attorney censured for his obtuse line of questioning.

Judge Favre agreed.

Of course. Leonie could be pregnant with sextuplets and any man would still want her.

When Delia's attorney finishes his questions, Albert begins.

Once again, he quickly points out errors in Delia's testimony through answers I provide in response to his questions. He makes an exceptional case for my defense and ends in less than fifteen minutes.

Judge Favre calls for closing arguments.

Delia's attorney speaks first, and he lasts as long as his opening remarks. Then Albert presents a summation on par with his Harvard Law School Juris Doctor degree—superb.

Judge Favre announces he will make his determination at our last session in two days' time. Then he adjourns court for the day.

I take a cleansing breath and repeat my mantra.

Inhale, I am.

Exhale, innocent.

Pause.

Inhale, I am.

Exhale, innocent.

Pause.

Thankful to head home to Leonie and my sons at last.

LEONIE

*R*oger tosses and turns all night.

I tried to persuade him to stay in bed with me. But he didn't want to disturb my sleep. Well... I guess he doesn't realize I can't sleep if he can't.

Instead, from our bed, I watch him on the sofa. His long limbs are not at all comfortable as he flips from one side to the other. At one point, his blanket falls off. I wait a moment to see if he will reach for it. But he doesn't. So I pick it up and drape it back over his sleeping form.

I sit on the chair and watch him for a while. I must have dozed off because I awake in bed, and Roger isn't on the sofa. With a groan from the pain in my achy back, I get up and follow the sound of water to the bathroom.

Roger stands at the vanity, shaving his face. I lean on the doorjamb and watch my man. When he nicks his chin for the second time, I go to him.

"Hey, babe. I didn't know you were awake. It's early, you need to go back to sleep"—he raises his hand to stop me from speaking—"And the chair is no place for you to get your rest."

He quirks his eyebrow at me, and I roll my eyes.

"Nor is the sofa for you, Monsieur Steele. You have a big day today. You need your rest, too."

I take the razor from his hand and push him away from the sink. I squeeze between him and the counter.

Roger lifts me and settles me on top of it.

"Now, allow me, Monsieur Steele," I say as I shave his face.

Roger closes his eyes and rests his hands on either side of my hips.

Silently, with a steady hand, I remove the morning's stubble from his cheeks and chin. Careful not to nick him, I rinse the razor and apply fresh shaving cream each time. When I shave all the hair, I put a warm wet cloth over his face. Then pat it.

Roger rinses the rest of the cream off his face and kisses me on the tip of my nose.

"*Merci beaucoup,* Kitten," he says with a smile, his gray eyes shine like liquid platinum in his gorgeous face.

I cup his chin and pull his lips to mine. *Non*, a peck on the nose will not do. No, sir!

Roger covers my mouth with his and takes control of the kiss as he angles my head just so. Our tongues dance, and I moan in appreciation.

"What do you want, Pretty Kitty?" He asks huskily.

"You, Roger, I want you, *Amoureux*," I purr, tilting my neck to give him better access as he kisses from my ear to my collarbone.

"Mmmmmm… Then you shall have me, Pretty Kitty," he growls.

Roger grips my hips and moves my ass closer to the

edge. He slides his hands up my thighs, taking my silk negligee with him. He lowers his mouth to my puckered nipple and suckles it until I writhe on the counter.

He chuckles against my skin.

"Eager are you?"

I huff and put my fingers in his hair to pull his mouth back to my sensitive bud. Then I groan when he nips it into his wet mouth.

"Yeeesss," I hiss as I drop my head back and lean on my other hand.

Roger continues to lavish attention on my breasts.

My pussy clenches on air with each tug. I need more! I sit forward and cup his heavy balls in the palm of my hand, kneading them.

He growls and thrusts his hips in sync with my motions. Roger loosens the tie on his black silk pajamas, and they slip down his hips to the floor. He takes the base of his dick in hand and shifts me forward until he impales me with his massive shaft.

We groan in unison as he enters me. Then take a few breaths as my pussy stretches to accommodate his girth.

Our rhythm is slow and deep. We allow our bodies to connect and speak for us. Only our moans fill the air along with the scent of our lovemaking.

Roger's cock swells, and I squeeze my inner muscles to draw out his release. With a shout he cums, and I follow right behind with a strangled cry.

"I love you, Leonie," he murmurs against my neck.

I shiver and bury my face in his hair.

"I'M READY!"

This is the fastest I have ever gotten ready in my nearly

thirty-three years of life. Today is the determination day, and I refuse to be late! I will be by Roger's side to face that trollop once and for all.

I even went to see Dr. Berger yesterday to provide proof to Roger that I listened and stayed calm. My vitals and the stage of my pregnancy impressed both. At thirty-six weeks or nine months, The Twins have dropped and my waddle has increased.

And I'm going to waddle my ass to that courthouse and strike a fierce pose for that bitch.

Maman Lionne is ready for you!

My parents turn in surprise at my sudden arrival.

To accommodate my larger belly, I opted for a three-quarter-sleeved knit mididress in gray—the color of Roger's eyes—and a patterned silk Hermès Giant Scarf over my shoulders. A pair of gray Lanvin wedge heels and my hair in a sleek low ponytail round out my outfit. I pull my glamour girl Tom Ford shades from my Himalayan Birkin and head for the front door.

"Now, Leonie, you must promise to let us know if you get upset," my father says once we're in the Sprinter.

"*Oui, Mon Trésor*, no matter what happens, you must remain calm!" My mother adds. "The Twins are close to term. *Oui?*"

I agree and smile brightly at them.

No need to mention how my lower back has been bothering me since Roger and I made love earlier. He was gentle. So, I'm sure it's nothing to worry about.

Eric drives us around the back of the courthouse. Roger is right, the crowd stays in the front. He left an hour ago with everyone else to serve as a distraction. He didn't want the crowd's jostling and catcalls to bother me.

My security detail scans the area before we exit the

Sprinter. Once they give the all clear, we climb out of the van. My father holds my arm as they escort us up the flight of steps. The police officers at the doors allow us entry.

A few people stand about the hallways as we cross through to the courtroom. But it appears the majority are inside or on the streets since it's the last day of the investigation. Everyone wants a front-row seat.

Whispers follow us. But I keep my head held high. There's no way I'm letting them get me upset, especially before I can get to Roger.

We keep as brisk a pace as we can considering my new runway walk...

Finally, we arrive at the doors. The guards open them and we step through.

My eyes go directly to Roger's table. He faces forward with his back ramrod straight.

The change in the crowd's murmurs at my appearance and the whispers of my name make him shift in his chair.

Our eyes lock. Everything and everyone fades to the background. Only Roger matters now.

I smile at him, and he smiles back.

Antonio also turns to look my way. I give him a withering stare, and he shrinks.

Asshole.

I spot Delia next.

She sits at the claimant's table attempting to look prim in a navy dress and bun.

Yeah, right, honey. I know you.

Delia must sense my stare. She glances over her shoulder, and our eyes connect. Hers widen at the sight of me since I hadn't been here in almost two weeks.

Rumors swirled that I left Roger; I gave birth and left Paris; Roger dumped me... Utter garbage. I wouldn't doubt it if she and her legal team started the lies. From the bit Roger shares with me about the investigation or I glean from Lola, Delia lied through her teeth during her testimony.

Non, hussy! I'm here and not going anywhere!

"Leonie, come sit here, sweetheart."

I shift my gaze from the liar to Shelley.

"*Merci, Maman Aussi*," I answer as I double kiss her cheeks in greeting.

In my periphery, I notice Delia frown and face forward.

Good!

As I take my seat between my parents and Morgan and Shelley, I wave at our family and friends. Lola, Sebastian and the rest of the Steele clan, the Jacksons, Joel and Hettie, Norman and Anita, Luc, Blair, Billie, and Starr, and Françoise and some STEELE employees gather in support.

Moments later, the bailiff calls the court to order, and the judge enters the room.

My stomach flips with worry. I close my eyes and send a silent prayer for Roger and STEELE cleared of these false claims.

Delia just wants attention and money. None of what she said holds an ounce of truth.

I glare at the back of her head. Then shift my focus to the judge.

He's unreadable. His eyes scan the crowd as he waits for silence. Once the gallery is quiet, he gazes at Delia, who squirms, then at Roger, who sits tall.

My mother and father take my hands in theirs and squeeze.

I don't realize how tense I am until I startle at their touch. My eyes stay riveted on Judge Favre as he reads his summation of the case.

He's so slow.

Mentally, I push him to read faster. Just give us the answer already!

"Because of the testimony provided by both the plaintiff and the defendant, the evidence brought forth, and of my careful deliberation, I determine Roger Steele and STEELE International, Inc. should—"

"AAAH… *MON DIEU!!*"

* * *

Roger & Leonie's Story Continues: *Justify My Desires*

Justify my

DESIRES

ROGER & LEONIE PART III

Charmaine Louise Shelton

I dedicate this novel to those who would love a life of happiness, good times with family, and fantastic sex with your most treasured one!

Fulfill Your Desires.

xoxo
Charmaine Louise

ABOUT JUSTIFY MY DESIRES
ROGER & LEONIE PART III

The smoldering love affair of Roger The Responsible and Leonie The Lion concludes with their struggle to make lightning strike a third time for their happily ever after in their second chance billionaire romance story.

The loving duo may be heading down the aisle in a winter wonderland wedding with their adorable twins, but will the shadow of Roger's legal woes follow them?

Come along for their steamy holiday romance as they travel to Verbier for a sizzling Merry Christmas & New Year, personal fireworks in Southampton for Labor Day, Capri for yachting, Paris for home sweet home, and wherever their rendezvous take them!

Their love story is a standalone second chance romance trilogy in the series. Get a glimpse of their dynamism in other books.

Anthem: "Justify My Love" Madonna
https://www.youtube.com/watch?v=Np_Y740aReI

Playlist:
https://www.youtube.com/playlist?list=
PLXwYvn0e218CZOKMieHtBQ3QRL3xlxMA8

Visit CharmaineLouiseBooks.com

ROGER

"*ecause of the testimony provided by both the plaintiff and the defendant, the evidence brought forth, and of my careful deliberation, I determine Roger Steele and STEELE International, Inc. should—*"

"AAAH... MON DIEU!!"

"*Qu'est-ce que—*"

"*Oh, Mon Trésor!!*"

"Leonie!! What's wrong?!"

"ROGEEERRR!!!"

My fiancée Leonie Beaulieu's ferocious roar of my name snaps me back to the Parisian hospital's bustling operating room and out of the hell of the pretrial courtroom.

What an emotionally charged day...

From making love to Leonie so intense it felt as though our souls blended to the rollercoaster ride of the courtroom right before the pretrial judge's determination on the prosecution of the case and now she's in labor.

Damn.

WHOMEVER SAID money is the root to all evil wins the gold medal.

Delia Fucking Shaw wanted more than my billions. She had her sights set on the ultimate prize... Roger Steele of the media-dubbed STEELE Quaternity.

They consider my three brothers—Sebastian, Malcolm, Harris—and I the most sought-after of the world's eligible billionaires. Although not a part of the group, Haley, our youngest sibling and the fraternal twin to Harris, has a multibillionaire status that attracts men to her like bees to honey. Not that we allow just anyone access to our baby sis —no fucking way!

I should have known Delia was up to more than simple flirting with the professor when I guest lectured one of my then girlfriend Leonie's classes at the Paris American Academy.

As my family's multigenerational multibillion-dollar company STEELE International, Inc.'s President of Residential Properties Division, Leonie thought I would impart some of my knowledge on her classmates. She was in her last year for her interior design bachelor's degree.

Wanting to help her make a good impression on her professor, I agreed.

Leonie has always had an eye for design. The combination of being the world-renowned megamodel *The Lion* for almost nineteen years and as the daughter of an old, wealthy Parisian merchant family that travels seeking antiques, antiquities, and fabrics instilled in her a love for the aesthetics. Transitioning into interior design has been her dream for years. And in any way I could help her, I promised I would.

Unfortunately, it came at a price.

During the class, Delia flirted with me, and Antonio Velasquez flirted with Leonie. I gave him the look of death, and he backed off. Or so I thought...

The dick didn't learn his lesson then. So I had to teach him at their end-of-the-semester reception when I caught him kissing my girlfriend—MINE!

My training with a former heavyweight boxing champion primed me to knock Velasquez on his ass and then some.

Which led to restitution as a vast sum of money for him and a STEELE internship program with the Paris American Academy for two of their students in perpetuity. Unluckily, the first two recipients turned out to be none other than Delia and Velasquez. Pain in my ass number one and pain in my ass number two—initially in either order.

Now, Delia takes the top spot.

Although I'm sure she would have preferred the bottom position with her writhing beneath me... Billions and a ten-inch cock.

Despite my best efforts to elude her unwanted attention, she managed to get at me twice.

The first with an unannounced and unapproved visit to my offices on the executive floor of STEELE Paris. My take-no-shit personal assistant, Françoise Faucher, thwarted Delia's double entendre comments and advancement. Françoise made it her personal mission to escort the intern from my offices to security for the reprogramming of her ID card access and to human resources for a refresher in protocol with the president.

The proverbial nail in the coffin came in the form of

Delia insisting I speak with her on my way to the Interior Design Team's weekly meeting, at which she was a participant.

Against my better judgement, I allowed her to ride up to the conference room on my private elevator with me. Said elevator oddly malfunctioned, and we were stuck together in the dark for twenty minutes—no cameras, no help, nothing but the two of us. No one knows how the hell my elevator went on the fritz.

Delia's interpretation of the events on the elevator differs so greatly from mine. She filed a legal petition. A petition against me for sexual assault and harassment and against STEELE International, Inc. as co-defendant with a civil claim for none other than... a vast sum of money.

Meanwhile, for the last eleven weeks, the love of my life has had to cope with the stress of this bullshit while pregnant with our twin boys. Already struggling with the fear of her mother's experiences with multiple miscarriages before giving birth to Leonie and her parents' subsequent inability to ever have children again compounded by Delia Fucking Shaw.

So instead of having her water break under normal circumstances at her family's ancestral estate *Le Beaulieu Manoir*—where we're staying to avoid the rabid media and stalkers—it happened in the fucking pretrial courtroom. Surrounded by protestors, onlookers, Velasquez, and Delia, Leonie screamed in anguish from the contractions and the ensuing gush of amniotic fluid protecting The Twins.

Pandemonium broke out.

I gave zero fucks about Judge Favre's pronouncement. My baby was in pain, and I would be damned if I didn't go to her.

Without approval from the judge or STEELE General

Counsel Albert Perry, who's representing me and the company, I rushed to Leonie's side.

The expression of fear and hurt on her beautiful face struck me in the gut like a sledgehammer. Her pitiful cries galvanized me.

My eldest brother Sebastian and I carried her between us while my other brothers, our male friends, and security detail cleared a path for us. With Lola Steele—Leonie's best friend and Sebastian's wife—leading the way, we exited out the back of the courthouse. Then we hurried into one of the Mercedes-Benz Sprinters I leased to transport everyone during the pretrial.

Starr Knight—Leonie's friend, yoga teacher, and doula— called her OB-GYN Dr. Pierre Berger. Starr confirmed he was on his way to the hospital as the five of us sped off. My trusted driver Eric Vogler maneuvered the crazy Parisian traffic to get us to the hospital in record time. Thankfully, Starr kept Leonie relatively calm during the ride.

Luc Montaigne—Leonie's mentor and friend and the multibillionaire CEO and Chairman of the Board of his family's multigenerational, global banking empire Banque Montaigne—once again used his considerable influence as the major benefactor of the hospital to garner approval for a custom suite. This after he procured Dr. Berger as her doctor.

When we found out Leonie was pregnant, Luc demanded the top OB-GYN attend to her. Not just of the hospital, but of all France. Since this is the most esteemed hospital in Paris, Dr. Berger has his affiliation with it and serves as their OB-GYN department director and a practicing physician.

No sooner had the nurses settled Leonie in her suite did Dr. Berger arrive with his team. An anesthesiologist, two pediatricians—one for each Twin—two labor and delivery nurses, an OB tech, and a nursery nurse followed him into Leonie's suite.

They went to work in prepping her for the first stage of pregnancy, pre-labor. Dr. Berger explained in twin pregnancies, it can take up to thirteen hours for her body to be ready for the actual delivery. He expected the first Twin within two hours after and the second Twin less than twenty minutes later.

Leonie was a lot less fearful now that she was in the hospital's safety and under the doctor's care. She may have been better prepared, but still in the throes of labor as she experienced acute contractions.

Her golden caramel complexion flushed rosy from the sensations overtaking her body. Her feline amber eyes glowered at my wolfish gray ones, while French curses spilled from her lush lips. Her ass-long mahogany waves once pulled in a sleek ponytail, now in one thick braid thanks to Starr.

She and Lola fussed over Leonie as Sebastian and I hovered around her bed. Soon the rest of our family and friends arrived from the courthouse. Leonie's mother Josy and my mother Shelley hurried to her side, hustling Sebastian and me right out of their way. Haley joined them at the foot of Leonie's bed as she massaged her feet and calves to comfort her.

Surrounded by the most important women in her life, Leonie braved the pre-labor stage for just over twelve hours. Now, the ferocious Lion is loose...

"ROGEEERRR!!!"

"Oh, mon Dieu!!! Aidez moi!!!"

She squeezes the fuck out of my hand.

I wince from the bite of pain, but persevere. If she has to go through contractions and all, I won't wuss out and will remain by her side.

At this stage, besides the medical team, Starr is the only person with us in the operating room. Dr. Berger moved Leonie from her suite to here since twins can have complications during delivery. He wants to ensure all equipment and support are available with no delay.

Thank fuck since I would lose my shit if something happens to Leonie or to our babies. My thoughts drift back to the conversation we had early in her pregnancy before we knew we were expecting twins.

"Leonie, understand me clearly. If for any reason I have to choose between you and this baby or any other, I choose you always. You mean everything to me. We can try for another baby, or we can adopt a baby in need of a wonderful home. But you... You are irreplaceable, my love. Call me selfish. But I will not live without you, Leonie."

She speaks. But I cut her off with a firm shake of my head. I don't give a damn how harsh it may sound. But it's the damn truth.

"No! This is nonnegotiable. And we will not speak of such things ever again. Do you understand?"

Leonie nods, still sad.

"Words, Leonie. I will have your words," I demand.

She takes some time to consider.

I feel her body stiffen, and she sits up tall. The surrounding energy vibrates anew. Then Leonie stares me straight in the eye with a fiercely determined expression.

"Oui, Roger. You are right, Mon Cœur. We will move forward from this moment on with only positive thoughts and words of love. You are the most responsible person I know"—she smiles

brightly as she strokes my cheek—"But we will share the respon-
sibility of our blessing together. I don't want you to think you
have to be strong for both of us. I will not neglect your needs
either."

So, God forbid, anything goes wrong, I set my mind. But
I push the negative thoughts out and return Leonie's bone-
crushing squeeze of my hand with a much gentler version
to hers as I stroke her reddened cheek.

"Yes, my love? You're so brave and strong. We are so
lucky to have you—"

"BULLSHIIITTT!!!"

Leonie snarls and swats my thumb from her face. The
golden flecks in her eyes flash dangerously as she glares
at me.

An unceasing slew of French curse words follow a
particularly painful contraction.

Starr turns her head. But not before I glimpse the smile
on her face. Her dimples deepen as her sorrel-brown eyes
dance with mirth.

Even Dr. Berger coughs to hide his laugh.

I glance around the room, and others avoid my gaze.
Suddenly everyone has an important task...

"Oooh... How much more?" Leonie huffs huskily. *"Mon
DIEU!!!"*

Dr. Berger peers between Leonie's legs—the caveman in
me wants to carve his eyeballs out with a flint knife—to
check.

"One more push, Leonie. You can do it. He's almost
here," the doctor states, back to business. "Now!"

With what must be a Herculean effort, Leonie delivers
our first Twin. Their piercing cries mingle in the tense air
of the operating room.

Rodolphe Beaulieu Steele enters our world.

My eldest son. Named for me. Leonie nicknamed me *Mon Loup*, my wolf. His name translates to famous wolf.

Tears fill my eyes at the sight of mother and son.

My protective instincts kick in. I follow his pediatrician —Dr. Constance Taylor recommended by Dr. Berger—as she carries my son off to the side in order to care for him. I split my gaze between her actions and Leonie, who's being comforted by Starr. I confirm she's fine, then turn my full attention to Rodolphe.

"How is he?" I ask as I watch possessively over the doctor's shoulder while she tends to him.

She smiles at me and responds, "He's in excellent health! All ten fingers and toes! He weighs 5.2 pounds. An acceptable size for a twin. Congratulations, Mr. Steele!"

Relief washes over me. Then anxiety sweeps in when she places a freshly cleaned Rodolphe in my arms. When I look at her in a panic, Dr. Taylor smiles encouragingly.

I glance down at his red face. He may be tiny, but the weight of responsibility hits me in that moment. This is one of my sons, the fruit of my loins. I am his father. His safekeeping ranks as my utmost priority along with his soon-to-be-born brother and their mother.

"Roger? What's taking so long? Is he okay?"

Leonie's soft voice filled with concern calls me back to the operating room.

"He's perfect, my love. See for yourself," I respond as I stride over to her and place Rodolphe on her chest.

Leonie's face lights up with such love and joy when she stares at our son. Tears stream down her cheeks. Her fingers tentatively touch his soft jet-black hair, and his eyes open slowly.

Gray eyes and black hair. The Steele family traits continue.

Leonie peers up at me and smiles.

"*Mon Loup*," she whispers.

I bury my face in her damp hair and cry.

"FUUUCK... YOU!!!"

Stage three begins...

Rodolphe sleeps in a warm hospital crib while his younger brother is being born. And his father is being cursed out by his mother.

I learned my lesson the last time. Instead of speaking sappy words, I go for the Alpha male route.

"Leonie. You will push when Dr. Berger says and not a moment before. Do you understand—"

I didn't even see it coming.

Leonie slaps the shit out of me.

"Don't you dare pull that dominant bullshit on me right now, ROGER STEELE!!!"

She bellows, eyes shooting golden fire.

Struck speechless, I can only stare at the wild Lion before me. The tame and loving new mother of ten minutes ago disappears in a puff of smoke.

Yeah, fuck me...

THIRTY MINUTES LATER, a fatigued, not ferocious, Leonie rests in her suite's bed with our sons in skin-to-skin contact against their mother's body as she breastfeeds them.

The sight is so poignant; I have to capture it with a few photos by my mobile. The clicking attracts her attention, and she lifts her weary gaze to mine.

"Hi, baby. I love you so much," I breathe. "Do you need anything?"

Leonie shakes her head and pats the bed beside her.

I sit and brush my fingertips across her cheek.

She closes her eyes and nuzzles against my palm; a soft purr slips past her lips.

"*Non, merci, Mon Cœur, je t'aime aussi,*" she whispers, followed by a yawn. "Only you and our sons."

Gaspard Beaulieu Steele, my second son. Named for Leonie. Her parents nicknamed her *Mon Trésor*, and we name our son treasure bearer. His gray eyes and jet-black hair mark him as a Steele. A perfect baby who weighs a healthy five pounds with all ten fingers and toes.

A beautiful fiancée and identical twin sons. My heart swells. My family.

MINE!

LEONIE

"*T*he next generation of Steeles is born! May they carry on our clan name and STEELE and Beaulieu forever!"

Declares Morgan Steele as he holds his day-old grandsons proudly.

"*Oui, Mon Trésor* extends her family's line with males, one for Beaulieu and one for STEELE!" My father Guy adds proudly as he plucks Gaspard from Morgan's arm.

The two titans refer to the alliance forged between STEELE International, Inc. and Beaulieu Enterprises, SAS by Sebastian as CEO of STEELE and my father as Président of Beaulieu. Morgan approved it since the deal was Sebastian's first major one after taking over from his father.

My family's company is privately owned, and I am the heir apparent. After my engagement, my father expressed his wish for Roger to take on the helm with me when he retires. I made it clear I was not interested in running the day-to-day responsibilities as I prefer to focus on my interior design career.

We agreed we would incorporate Beaulieu within the STEELE organization. But I will maintain majority control, with our children taking on the company at the appropriate time. The Beaulieu company will continue to pass on to the next generation as it has for centuries.

The future addition pleases everyone. It's the perfect solution for both companies and families.

Now my sons are but a day old and their *grand-pères* reaffirm the partnership and The Twins' future roles.

I shake my head and smile.

Roger slips his hand in mine and dips his head to kiss my lips.

"Let them have their fun, my love. You've made them so thrilled," he murmurs.

"And you? Have I made you happy, *Mon Cœur?*" I ask softly as I lean into him, seeking his warmth and strength.

Roger straightens and cups my chin. His signature intense gray-eyed stare pins me in place.

"Absolutely. With no doubt. Once you bear my name, as our sons already do, you will make my life complete, Leonie," he responds in a voice thick with emotion.

I whimper and bury my face in his neck as I sob.

So much has happened so quickly, I feel overwhelmed. From the highs of graduating from the Paris American Academy, learning I'm pregnant, and becoming engaged after a tumultuous on-again-off-again relationship. Then the lows of being apart from Roger, the scandalous false allegations of she who shall not be named, and the as yet announced determination.

Throw in the hormones raging through my body, and I can't control my emotions.

Merde...

"Oh, sweetheart..."

Roger's comforting murmurs of love and support boost my spirit. He's my rock.

"Let's give them some privacy—"

My best friend's suggestion reminds me I'm surrounded by my loved ones. My babies are healthy. My true love is by my side. I have a lot to be thankful for.

With fresh resolve, I face my family and friends.

"*Non, non,* stay. Don't mind my blubbering," I say as I dab my face with Roger's handkerchief. "You do not understand just how much I love and appreciate you. It's been a trying time. But new life brings great joy."

My mother comes over to the bed and clasps our hands before she kisses them. I see my amber eyes reflected in hers, set in the same oval-shaped face. Her fawn-colored complexion deeper than my caramel skin tone due to the combination of her Tunisian ancestry and my father's Parisian pedigree.

The power of genetics to pass traits from parent to child amazes me. Just as illustrated in The Twins and the Steeles. I smile at her.

"*Mon Trésor,* never make excuses for your emotions! Your body is going through a lot"—she turns to Shelley and gestures for her to join us—"I may have had only one baby, but I know how you're feeling. Shelley, who's had five, will agree."

Roger's mother, or my *Maman Aussi* as I call Shelley, smirks and strokes my cheek.

"Yes! And you thought you had some choice words for Roger. Well, let me tell you, I laid Morgan out each and every time!"

The room fills with our laughter, Morgan's chuckles loudest of us all.

It's even more funny since Roger swears our fathers are Alpha Doms and our mothers are subs. The visual of the men being in a submissive circumstance cracks me up.

"I agree! Norman may have been the champ in the ring. But I won by a TKO when he dared to utter one word while I was in labor," Anita says from the sofa.

Norman feigns the impact of a crushing blow and collapses against the armrest. The same king of the boxing ring who plays dress up and has a tea party with his toddler daughter.

Again, the tough guys are always the softies at heart.

"—YOUR *Maman* is resting now, Rodolphe. You and your brother wore her out coming into this world, you know... Yes, I know. You're tired too... Tell me all about it, *mon fils.*"

The low drone of Roger's words enters my dreams.

It's later in the evening and our family and friends have gone home. The quiet of the room makes it easier for his voice to carry.

I awake to find him pacing the floor with a small bundle bouncing in his arms. For a few minutes, I watch transfixed by the sight of my six-foot, three-inch, powerfully built Alpha male negotiating with our eldest newborn son.

Rodolphe responds with low-pitched whining, just as engaged in the conversation as his *Papa*.

My gaze leaves them to find Gaspard still tucked in his crib, covered in a soft, white cashmere blanket and matching beanie. They're a gift from his *Oncle* Luc. Gaspard sleeps peacefully. So I return my attention to my man and other son.

"—Do you know how much I love you and your brother?

545

A whole lot, Rodolphe. The two of you are an unexpected joy. The thought of having children anytime soon never occurred to me. But your *Maman* stole my heart the moment I heard her melodic laughter outside of my offices. She says it's *un coupe de foudre*. I have to agree it was love at first sight. It took us a while. But here we are and here you and Gaspard are, too. I will do all in my power to protect and care for your *Maman*, Gaspard, and you…"

Roger's voice cracks, and I realize he's holding back tears.

I'm not the only one on an emotionally charged ride. He needs me, too.

"*Mon Cœur,*" I call to him softly.

Roger stops walking and lifts his gaze from our son's face to mine. In the low light, his eyes sparkle with unshed tears.

My heart clenches.

"Come," I say, opening my arms to welcome both of them.

Roger sits beside me, and I lean forward to kiss his lips. Then place my forehead against his.

Rustling from the crib draws our attention to Gaspard. Our other bundle must sense he's missing family time as his movements escalate to cries.

I take Rodolphe, and Roger rises to bring our Treasure Bearer to me. Time for The Twins to drink from the golden chalice.

Roger watches us with such love in his weary gray eyes. He told me he still can't believe we're parents and have healthy identical twin boys. The day he found out about my pregnancy—when I was rushed to the hospital—was like a bolt of lightning to his heart, again.

He understood then the importance of providing a safe and happy home for us—his own little family, one he created from his heart and loins. Without saying it, he alluded to the pretrial needing to complete posthaste in his and STEELE's favor so we could move forward with our new life together.

Nothing and no one would come between us. We would be an impenetrable unit powerful enough to withstand any assault—she who shall not be named included.

I wholeheartedly agree with the love of my life. We will get through this nasty pretrial and have the life set for us even before we knew one another.

Our *coup de foudre* proves it, I smile to myself as I watch Roger stare at our sons and me.

Once they're fed, changed, and tucked in their cribs, Roger takes off his robe and returns to the bed.

With the custom suite, we could bring in a larger sized hospital-style bed that could accommodate both of us. Why should Roger cramp his large frame in a convertible chair? Many thanks to Luc!

"Your words were so sweet, *Chéri*," I tell Roger as I snuggle against his shoulder.

He wraps his arm around me and pulls me closer as he kisses the top of my head.

"I didn't mean to wake you," he responds quietly.

I lean back and cup his face in my hand. His clean-shaven face now with more than a five o'clock shadow is weary, too.

"Hey, we made them together. We care for them togeth-er," I tell Roger. "You've been just as stressed, if not more... So you need a break, too."

I rest my head again and continue.

"*Maman Aussi* told me the secret is to get sleep when they

sleep. Sooo, *bonne nuit mon amour et fais de beaux rêves,*" I say as my eyelids close.

Roger chuckles and murmurs his love for me, too.

The rhythmic beat of his heart lulls me into a peaceful sleep where I dream of our return to *Le Beaulieu Manoir* tomorrow.

ROGER

"*Fortunately, Judge Favre made an exception for Leonie going into labor and allowed a medical recess. However, he called for the court to return to session tomorrow morning. He requires your presence.*"

Albert's words play on repeat in my mind since his call yesterday afternoon.

The delight of my sons' births hours before dims from the shadow of these bullshit allegations. I didn't mention the call to Leonie, just to my father and Sebastian.

I will not allow the news to lessen Leonie's joy of her new motherhood no more than I allowed the pretrial to overshadow our wedding day. I can't postpone my return to the courtroom like I did our ceremony. But I chose not to discuss it then.

Now, I have to tell Leonie where I'm going.

Although I'm sure she's been thinking about it. I've caught her peeking at me with a wistful expression before she can cover it up with an overly bright smile or avert her gaze.

It's not as though we can completely ignore the situation. Fuck the elephant in the room. It's a ginormous blue whale.

I take a last glance at my reflection in the bathroom mirror. I shaved after two days and my collar-length hair is well-kempt. But the angles of my face emphasize the shadows beneath my dull eyes.

It's not that I've given up. Rather, I'm tired of the shit and want to enjoy my new family without wondering if I'll get to see them beyond a partition in some French jail.

Albert and the legal team remain confident. They were certain it wouldn't go to pretrial too…

But as Leonie says, stay positive and no negative thoughts!

With a deep breath, I resettle myself and repeat my mantra.

Inhale, I am.

Exhale, innocent.

Pause.

Inhale, I am.

Exhale, innocent.

Pause.

As I open the bathroom door, I hear Leonie's giggles as she coos at one of our sons.

But her smile fades when she glances up to see me in one of my bespoke three-piece suits, custom dress shirt, silk tie, and Oxfords. Gone from the room is her laughter, just like my long-sleeved t-shirt, joggers, and soccer slides.

We stare at each other in silence for a moment before we speak at once.

"Where are you going—"

"Judge Favre called court—"

Leonie nods as her shoulders slump. Tears fill her eyes, and she glances away, biting her lower lip.

"Baby, remember only positive thoughts," I say as I turn her face back to mine. "The judge will make the determination. No matter what he says, know that I am innocent of any wrongdoing."

She whimpers and closes her eyes.

I brush the tears from her cheeks and kiss her lips gently.

Leonie sobs. But wraps her arms around my neck to pull me closer as she deepens our kiss. Her passion ignites a fire within each of us. The heat that always simmers between us roars to life, engulfing us.

I tilt her head to take control.

A knock on the door brings us back.

"I love you and our sons, Kitten," I tell her gruffly before I kiss Rodolphe and Gaspard on their foreheads.

Their baby smell fills my nostrils, and I close my eyes to inhale it deeply.

Inhale, I am.

Exhale, innocent.

Pause.

Inhale, I am.

Exhale, innocent.

Pause.

Fucking déjà vu.

Hecklers and protestors scream false accusations and obscenities as I make my way to the courthouse doors. Once inside of the courtroom, I notice Delia who sits prim and proper, dressed like a mousy elementary-school librarian. Velasquez sits behind her in the gallery, smirking at me.

Everyone except for Josy and Starr return with me in a show of support. Lola wanted to stay at the hospital. But Leonie insisted her best friend go with me since Dr. Berger hasn't discharged her from the hospital yet. My parents, Guy, siblings, Jackson cousins, Luc, Blair, Billie, Joel and Hettie, Norman and Anita, Françoise and other STEELE employees sit in the gallery on my side.

"All rise... This court is now in session. The Honorable Judge Favre presiding."

Good. Let's get this over with already.

I say a silent prayer as I rise and watch Judge Favre enter the room.

He sits stoically on his bench. Then his eyes scan the courtroom before they flick to me with his analytical stare.

"I understand Mademoiselle Beaulieu is in good health?" The judge asks without preamble.

"Yes, Your Honor, thank you," I respond, surprised by his unexpected question.

"*Très bien*," he nods formally. "We shall begin."

Judge Favre leafs through the papers in front of him and scans the documents. Then he summarizes the claim and the parties involved, similar to his opening statement. When he pauses, a hush descends on the crowded room.

In my periphery, I notice Delia stare at me long enough that her attorney nudges her and whispers in her ear. With a shrug of her shoulder, she faces forward again.

Judge Favre raises his eyebrow and turns a blistering stare on Delia as he speaks.

"Because of the testimony provided by both the plaintiff and the defendant, the evidence brought forth, and of my careful deliberation, I determine Roger Steele and STEELE International, Inc. should not face prosecution and the claim dismissed with prejudice. I shall make these proceedings into a written record immediately afterwards. Court is adjourned."

Pandemonium breaks out again in the form of Delia Shaw.

"What?! No!! Roger Steele tried to—"

Bam bam bam!

"Silence!!"

Judge Favre's command stuns Delia. She gapes at him as he pins her with a glacial gaze.

"You will control your client and her outbursts or face a fine, Counselor," he says in a chilling tone.

Delia's lead attorney sputters as his eyes bounce from the judge to her. Then he nods and offers his apologies. One of his associates bustles Delia out of the courtroom, followed by Velasquez, who scowls at me as he passes by.

Good fucking riddance to bad fucking rubbish! I'm free of this bullshit!

The din of the courtroom increases once the group exits out the side door.

"Excellent outcome!" Albert says as he shakes my hand. "I will finish with the paperwork now."

I shake his hand and clap his back as I nod, "Thank you, Albert! Well done!"

Albert smiles, and I thank the legal team before I turn to my family and friends.

"Congratulations, Roger!"

"Hell yeah! It's over!"

"You're innocent, big brother! The world will know, I promise!" Haley declares as she hugs me tightly.

Everyone whoops and claps as they share their glee.

I smile and answer on autopilot. While my mind swirls with emotions of relief, thanks, and elation. It's all behind us now. We can move forward unencumbered by the malicious accusations and the vicious commentary.

My thoughts move to Leonie, Rodolphe, and Gaspard. It's time I get back to my little family.

"—HEARD anything, yet? I'm worried sick—"

Leonie stops speaking when she sees me standing in the suite's doorway. Her eyes widen and her mouth forms a perfect O before she claps her hands over it.

"Hello, my love," I say gruffly as I step into the room. "It's over."

Leonie gasps and closes her eyes as she falls back against the pillows. Her body shudders as her sobs increase in her hands.

I rush to her side and pull her into my arms, kissing her face as I murmur words of love.

The click of the door's lock draws my attention back to the room. Josy and Starr left. When I walked in, I glanced at them barely. My sole focus was Leonie.

Now, as I hold her in my embrace, I look around to see Rodolphe and Gaspard asleep in their hospital cribs. Swaddled, they lie quietly. My sons.

No longer do I have to worry about not being with them and their mother. We're free to make our family official. I won't wait long to claim Leonie as my wife.

ROGER

"*T*his chalet hasn't sold yet. It's the largest with five stories, twelve bedrooms, sixteen bathrooms, four fireplaces, an oversized ski room, and the usual entertainment rooms including a sixteen-person cinema room, game room, gym, and wine-tasting cellar. The indoor-outdoor heated pool pavilion with spa is an added bonus. Staff quarters are above the six-vehicle garage."

I barely hear the project manager rattling off the details of the luxury chalet. The spectacular view of Verbier and the Swiss Alps through the floor-to-ceiling windows capture my attention.

After a month of being with Leonie, Rodolphe, and Gaspard—we only left the *Manoir* to attend Joel and Hettie's wedding—I couldn't put off the final walk-through of STEELE's latest Swiss project.

The STEELE Verbier Hotel & Resort had its grand opening during last year's ski season. We planned the Residential Properties Division's completion of the by-application-only compound of ten state-of-the-art chalets and private clubhouse to take occupancy for this year's season.

Verbs, as the in-the-know jet-set call it, is a town in the Swiss Alps. A part of the Valais canton in the southwest of Switzerland, France borders Verbier to the west with Italy to the south. It's the most exclusive ski destination in the world.

It's the winter version of Monaco, with the difference being people who go to Monaco want to watch or be watched. Whereas Verbier has an understated style where wealth is glamorous, stylish and tasteful. People are here for the reasons one goes to a ski resort—the superb skiing. Not to mention the phenomenal bars and restaurants; the après-ski is perfect for party lovers. Verbier is a glamorous winter playground.

The luxury chalets occupy the area south of the Médran lift. They're slightly away from town along Rue de Médran, where the extra space means they are rarely overlooked and have a private, exclusive vibe. The residential compound is opposite to the STEELE Verbier that's closer to the heart of the village square. The concept is for the STEELE Verbier Chalets to access the resort for its five-star amenities. The most important include the luxury thermal bath spa and the three Jackson Corporation restaurants headed by our cousin Lucien *The Sexy Chef* as he's known by his millions of followers.

I'm surprised this chalet is still on the market. The decor is modern Alpine chic with traditional materials of timber and stone complemented by the high-quality fixtures and fittings and custom furniture. Combined with the view, it's an incredible property.

"Well, damn. Maybe I'll buy it."

I glance over at Malcolm and raise my eyebrow questioningly.

"Why not? We all ski and could use a place here to hang out," he adds with a shrug.

At only two years apart, he's Sebastian's doppelgänger: same six feet, four inches in height; gray eyes; black hair; clean shaven or 5 o'clock shadow covers a firm jaw. As kids, Malcolm strove for his own identity, hating being in Baz's shadow. Fortunately, they grew past their teenage angst to develop a close relationship.

We're all close. And close enough to hang out together regularly. We even spend lots of time with our parents going on vacations, the holidays, birthdays. What can I say? The Steeles enjoy each other's company.

An idea hits me. I'll buy the chalet and gift it to Leonie for Christmas. She loves to ski, and winter is her favorite season.

We can have our wedding at *Le Beaulieu Manoir* as planned two days before Christmas Eve. The next day we come to Verbier to celebrate the holiday and New Year's Eve with our families, then our honeymoon alone. We didn't want to travel too much with The Twins since they will be with us. Perfect!

"I'll buy it. It'll be my Christmas gift to Leonie. Plus, we can all come here after the wedding for the holiday. Afterwards, Leonie and I wills stay with The Twins for our honeymoon," I say with finality.

Malcolm cocks his head to consider my pronouncement. Then he nods.

"Sounds good to me, bro," he responds. "Leonie will love it. Man, what a way to celebrate, new babies, new wife, new beginning. I'm happy for you, brother."

I smile at my second oldest sibling. We're only a year apart, so he's never lorded over me with an age difference. Harris and Haley get ribbed the most for being the youngest, especially Haley for being the only girl. Her declaration that we're not her father never gets old.

"Thanks. Sebastian, me... Now it's your turn..." I say waggling my eyebrows.

I'm on a roll with my love matches—Luc and Blair, now Malcolm and Starr. He thinks no one's aware of his feelings for the beauty. But he made it clear at Baz and Lola's wedding Starr was on his radar. Neither has said much recently. But oh well. That ends now.

"How's Starr by the way?" I ask.

Malcolm dodges the answer with a conference call he claims he has to take. Then hightails it out of the chalet with a promise to meet me for dinner later.

The project manager hides his laugh with a cough.

I turn to him and nod.

"Let's get this deal closed now. I'll need a copy of the promotional video emailed to me pronto," I tell him.

Yeah, Leonie is going to love it. She jokes about hanging out with the glitterati—as though she's not a part of that clique—when she's at her penthouse in Monte Carlo. Here she'll rub elbows with British and Danish royalty and others of the jet-set who prefer Verbier to Gstaad and Zermatt as their ski destination.

What's also great about it is the family friendly atmosphere. Not only the royals holiday with their children. But other high-net wealth clans hit the slopes with their toddlers and teens.

Rodolphe and Gaspard will join them. I can't wait to watch my sons zip down the trails and toboggan in the winter, then hike and swim in the summer. This will be another great vacation spot for us to make memories.

The ringing of my mobile breaks into my reverie. A smile big enough to split my face breaks out. I excuse myself from the project manager and move closer to the wall of windows.

"Hey babe. What's happening?" I answer. "I was just thinking about you and The Twins."

Leonie's laughter warms my heart as I stare at the snowy vista.

"You better be Monsieur Steele! Who else should occupy your mind?" She responds.

I chuckle and shake my head. Feisty as ever.

My father was right when after the pretrial he told me:

"You go to Leonie and your sons. Important bonding occurs in the early days with newborns. Plus, your fiancée needs you."

The past four weeks will forever remain etched in my memory. Each milestone from The Twins lifting their heads on their own to watching me more intently than I watch anyone to cooing and smiling.

And Leonie... Well, her tits blew up several cup sizes, and I have the privilege as the breast masseuse to care for them. She started on a postnatal routine designed by Starr and Anita. Leonie is determined to get her pre-Twins figure back before our wedding. She declared:

"Well, now that they're born, I want to look fabulous in my gowns and wherever you're taking us on our honeymoon!"

"No one but you, Chocolate Bonbon. Who might compare to you, my love?" I murmur.

Leonie laughs again. The seductive, husky sound makes my cock throb.

We haven't fucked since the morning she went into

labor. My fist has been pretty busy in the shower each morning, beating my morning wood. I don't bother Leonie about it. Hell, she has enough to handle. Besides, she came up with the crazy idea to wait until our wedding night to make love again.

And like a wuss, I agreed. Fuck!

"Absolutely no one," she purrs. "I miss you, *Amoureux*."

Yup, another twitch.

"What are you going to do about it?" I taunt.

Leonie purrs, "Are you alone?"

I pivot to face the project manager, who's busying himself on the other side of the great room.

"I'll meet you back at your office at the hotel to complete that paperwork," I tell him hurriedly.

Shit, if Leonie wants me by myself, it must be for an NSFW reason. My dick lengthens down my thigh in anticipation. Yeah, buddy!

With a nod, he leaves, and I jog up the stairs to one bedroom.

"Are you there, *Amoureux*?" Leonie asks.

I damn near throw myself onto the bed, kicking the paper booties off I changed into when we entered the mudroom.

"Yes!" I respond as I lean back against the pillows and adjust my thick girth.

"Mmm mmm *bon*… Call me back on FaceTime. I want to see you naked, *Amoureux*…"

Leonie's lusty growl ignites my passion as I race to strip at her command.

Without hesitation, I pull the black cashmere turtleneck over my head and toss it to the floor. The pile grows until I'm free of my trousers, silk boxer briefs, and even my damned socks. Not one thing will hinder the satisfaction Leonie is about to bestow upon me.

When she answers the FaceTime video call, she's a delight to my eyes. I can just make out her plump brown nipples and now DD-cup breasts beneath a semi-sheer gold dressing gown. Her ass-length mahogany mane cascades around her shoulders and down her back in shiny waves. The gold flecks in her amber eyes dance in the candlelight.

My baby set the scene with our bedroom darkened except for candles placed around our bed where she sits on her heels in the middle. The sultry sound of *"Je T'aime,... Moi Non Plus"* by Jane Birkin and Serge Gainsbourg plays in the background.

Fuck me! I wish I were between Leonie's hips coming right now!

I growl in frustration and throw my head back against the pillows of the big empty bed.

"Oh, *Chéri*, don't despair. I've got you," she coos. "Open your eyes and look at me. I want to make up for all the time we've missed. If only for a moment..."

The temptress seduces me. Caught in her thrall, I obey.

"Take you dick in your hand. Pretend as though it's mine. See let me show you, *Amoureux*" she says.

My mouth drops open when she takes one of our sex toys, a custom replica of my ten-inch dick in her hand. It's crafted from a mold and mimics every vein and ridge along its length. Leonie's long fingers cannot circle its girth as she strokes it from the base to the tip.

I glance from the pseudo-cock down to the real deal. It lays heavy along my six-pack abs to above my navel. The bulbous tip glistens with a bead of pre-cum. I use the natural lubricant to coat the head and slide my fist to the base.

My hooded eyes watch Leonie as she continues to stroke the toy. Typically, we use it for double penetration of one of her holes while I pound another—toy to ass, cock to pussy; cock to throat, toy to pussy; or any combination. Now she uses it for our long-distance tryst.

"That's it, *Amoureux*," she purrs. "Pinch your tip for me just... like... this..."

I follow suit and grunt as my balls draw up. Damn, I want my dick buried deep within her wet pussy, feeling her inner walls milk every drop from it. Fuck!

Leonie guides me for a few more minutes as my groans fill the air.

Then my eyes pop out of my head.

She opens her dressing gown only enough to show the curve of her ample tits. While she watches me from beneath her long eyelashes, she slides the toy between her mounds. Then with the sides of her arms she pushes her breasts around it as she leans forward biting her full bottom lip. When her little pink tongue darts out to poke the slit at the tip of the toy, I lose it.

FUCK. ME.

On a roar, I vigorously pump my cock and thrust my hips up with my muscular thighs spread wide, heavy balls hanging between them. I don't stop until ropes of my creamy cum shoot all over my bare chest, pecs, and abs tight with tension. I throw my head back as I squeeze my eyes shut and yell Leonie's name. The vision of my girth stretching her throat appears in my mind.

The intensity of my release ricochets through my body. My heated skin tingles. Spots appear behind my closed eyelids. The weight of my head too much as the lightheaded sensation takes over. My curled toes relax as I allow myself to recover.

"Feel better, *Mon Cœur?*"

Leonie's voice is low and throaty. The same as after she's swallowed me whole.

An entranced, lopsided grin spreads across my face as I nod like a bobblehead. My temptress has me under her spell.

LEONIE

"*H*ow excited are you to get married and to become my sister officially? I mean, we've been best friends and the closest we've ever had to flesh and blood siblings for over eight years. But now on paper! Woo—"

"You mean my sister, too, Lola!"

I smile at Lola and Haley, my future sisters-in-law.

Lola and I share a special bond forged from the first day I met her. I remember Luc insisted I meet a new lingerie designer, and I thought, *mon Dieu*, really?

At twenty-five, I was at the height of my modeling career with well-established designers pleading with my agents to book me to open and close for their shows. Global cosmetics companies clamoring for me to represent them with exclusive, multimillion-dollar, multiyear contracts. The face of *The Lion* graced hundreds of billboards and magazine covers.

So, an up-and-coming designer like Lola was far from my radar. Luckily for her, Luc knew me through mutual acquaintances and insisted that I meet with Lola. I chuckle to myself as I remember how persistent Luc was for me to give her a chance to discuss me being the spokesmodel for Lola's Coterie. The very handsome and sexy nobleman—or *Le Renard Argenté,* the Silver Fox Lola and I nicknamed Luc —can be very persuasive. How could I say, no? But really, I knew that if he said she was worth it, she must be special.

Now who would guess we'd go from a relationship just as strong as sisters to marrying brothers making us true sisters-in-law!

Haley. Well, the first time Roger and I dated Haley, and I didn't spend any time together. The brief love affair of two months was fast-paced and all-consuming. It didn't allow for time with others except for a business trip Roger accompanied me to Las Vegas for the opening of a Lola's Coterie boutique.

My relationship with Haley developed over planning Lola's wedding since Haley was a bridesmaid and I was the maid of honor. Even though Roger and I weren't together at that point, Haley and I bonded, especially during another business trip cum Girls' Get Away to Los Angeles.

Over the past fifteen months since Roger and I reunited, Haley and I have grown closer. She's become as much a part of our girls' crew as Billie, Blair, and Starr. From our trip to Buenguerra Island off the coast of Mozambique to her support during the pretrial when she came and stayed at the Manoir to being at my side with the pregnancy.

Between Lola and Haley, I won't ever lack a sibling I can rely on and love.

"Mes chères sœurs... My dear sisters, there's more than enough of me to share!" I tease, laughing. "No need to squabble, little ones!"

Sure, I'm only a year older than Lola and two more than

Haley, but I rib them anyway regarding them being younger.

"Little ones, my butt!" Haley retorts with a roll of her gray eyes behind her glasses. "Don't even try it. I don't need another big brother slash sister..."

We crack up as the door to the private room in my fashion designer friend Elie Saab's Parisian atelier opens.

"So much joy, my love!"

My gaze shifts to the voice, and I smile at my friend.

"Elie! How good to see you, *mon ami!*" I exclaim as I rise to greet him.

Throughout my modeling career, I opened and closed his runway shows and was the feature model in many of his campaigns. Over time, our business relationship developed into one of close friends. Often I spend time with him, his wife Claudine, and their three sons at their home in Lebanon.

For Lola's wedding, the bridesmaids and I wore Elie Saab custom creations. Since he has a studio in Paris and is my good friend, he made my gown specifically for me matching Lola and Baz's color palette. It's a dreamy strapless column of silk organza layers in various shades of the orange and fuchsia hues.

Haley's design is a halter-top column dress and follows the same layers as mine. Billie and Blair's were similar in fashion and feel, accentuating their curvy assets.

Now, it's my turn for my wedding gowns!

"Congratulations on your sons! Claudine sends her love and a gift from all of us," Elie responds as we embrace.

One of his assistants steps forward and hands a large gift-wrapped box to me. The giant navy blue velvet bow drapes over the matte platinum paper.

I smile and thank her, then open the gift and gasp.

It's an extraordinary jewel-encrusted copper box. The handcrafted piece has a hinged lid that opens to a ruby-red velvet-lined interior. A removable tray lifts out to reveal another compartment. A parchment with The Twins' names and date of birth written in a beautiful calligraphy script rests on the bottom. It's the most exquisite gift we've received.

"It's a keepsake box for you to put your most treasured memories of your sons. It's over a hundred years old and a rare piece made by Lebanese artisans," Elie says.

Tears fill my eyes as I thank him for such a thoughtful gift. He knows my family's history as merchants and my innate love for the aesthetics. What a perfect way to commemorate The Twins' milestones, especially Gaspard, whose name means treasure bearer!

"Oh, Elie! How lovely!" My mother adds as she hugs him.

She's joined me on some of my trips to visit him and his family. They've become close, too.

I introduce him to Shelley, and he greets Lola and Haley, remarking on how good it is to see them again. Then we get down to the business of my gowns.

This is my second fitting and the first with the actual dresses. So I clap my hands and do my happy shimmy dance with Lola when another assistant rolls two garment racks into the room with the haute couture pieces hanging from them.

We incorporated my Christmas wedding palette of cranberry, burnished gold, champagne, and ivory into the colors of my gowns. Touches of platinum will add shimmer and match Roger's gorgeous eyes. The fiery and cool colors symbolize all the blazing levels of our white-hot romance.

Roger, our fathers, and the groomsmen will wear white-tie attire to go along with our ultra-formal evening wedding. So debonair!

The first garment rack has my reception and party dresses on it. For the reception, it's a one-shouldered, backless mermaid gown made of tiny platinum elongated beads stitched onto silk. A double fan shape forms the neckline at my shoulder and rises to one side of my jaw line. The body-hugging silhouette clings to my waist and hips, then drapes around my knees to the floor in front. The back of the gown has three bands of the beaded material crossing from one shoulder down to the other side, exposing my back to end in a vee just above my ass. The mermaid tail flows from the vee to trail on the floor in a sweep length.

Here's to the endless hours of working out with Starr and Anita! Even Norman gave me conditioning lessons.

The party dress is not so much a dress, but a bodysuit with an open-front skirt attached to a two-inch gold metal band. Sheer champagne tulle netting covered with intricate gold filigree makes up the bodysuit that features a deep-vee halter top with an open back framed by two strips of the material. The gold metal belt holds the skirt up with a large appliqué at the side of my waist. The skirt made of more sheer tulle with veins of gold sequins embroidered on it flows from my waist to pool in a train behind me. My legs left bare save for the gold double ankle strap sandals on my feet.

Talk about *Goldfinger*! The outfit inspired by the sexy femmes fatales in James Bond movies—my favorite delectable secret agent.

The second garment rack holds my wedding gown and veil.

To pay homage to my family's height of success as

members of Louis XV's courtiers and when he awarded some acreage for *Le Beaulieu Manoir* to add to its existing land, Elie designed a ball gown of the era. With its wide silhouette and gold and platinum detailing, the ball gown embraces the Rococo style, which is highly ornamental and popularized in France, then spread to Central Europe.

The intricate bodice features an illusion neckline of sheer tulle that finishes in long sleeves with shimmery platinum embroidery covering the netting. Then it has a sweetheart dip at my bosom. Gold lace covers the gown from the dip to below my waist before the lace mingles with more of the shimmery platinum embroidery over sheer champagne tulle. Underneath the sheer tulle is a champagne silk chiffon skirt with layers upon layers of crinoline beneath to emphasize the wide silhouette.

From behind, the illusion material continues until it meets the gold lace midway down my back. The silk chiffon skirt flows to the floor in a circular train behind me to a chapel length with the sheer tulle a few inches beyond.

The pièce de résistance is my exceptional veil. It comprises two parts. An elbow-length blusher that will remain over my face until Roger lifts it during the ceremony. Then, for the most regal entrance and exit fit for *The Lion*, I had to have a cathedral-length veil.

The blusher ends in a raw edge of the sheer champagne tulle that has the shimmery platinum embroidery covering the netting to frame my face. The cathedral portion also has the embroidery throughout its length. It falls elegantly from a cap of elaborate platinum appliqués that starts at the crown of my head. The artisans stitched diamonds from my family's heirlooms collection throughout the cap to add to its luster.

The entire ensemble is absolutely breathtaking.

I try on each gown, and the seamstresses make adjust-ments. They used my pre-The-Twins form with room for my much more ample bust line to make the muslin test garment to check for the fit. Again thankful for my hard work and dedication to getting the babies weight off in time, the seamstresses have minor changes to make.

"You go, Girl! Peep you rocking your *The Lion* hot bod just as fierce as ever!" Lola whoops as she high fives with me as I stand in the party dress. "Your legs look phenomenal!"

Playfully I give a Moulin Rouge-worthy kick, and everyone laughs.

"Roger is going to lose it when he sees you!" Haley adds, giggling. "We may not get to see you on the dance floor!"

Elie claps his hands, and all eyes turn to him.

"Ladies, now is the time for Leonie to don her ball gown!" He exclaims.

Cheers and claps fill the air as I step off the fitting plat-form and sashay to the dressing room.

When I emerge, everyone sits in silence. I glance from one face to the next. Each makes my emotions run high.

My mother is the first to sniffle, then sob. Elie hands a handkerchief to her and pats her shoulder. Soon we're all bawling like Rodolphe and Gaspard before I feed them. The assistants rush about handing out tissues to dry our eyes. The seamstresses fuss over my gown and drape it with a silk smock to keep my tears from splattering on its beautiful surface.

"*Oh, Mon Trésor… Comme tu es belle dans ta robe de mariée!*" My mother says through her tears.

I brush a tear from my cheek and reply, "*Merci, Maman.* I feel beautiful."

"Roger will be so pleased, Leonie," Shelley whispers as she dabs her eyes. "You look amazing, sweetheart."

I nod my thanks, too overcome with emotions to respond verbally. The thought of Roger chastising me with his Alpha-male demand for my words makes me smile. My heart leaps knowing we'll marry next month!

While I changed into my regular clothes, Lola and Haley went to their dressing rooms to put on their matron of honor and bridesmaid dresses. They come out and we clap in delight.

Both of their dresses have a rich cranberry base with different details. Lola's dress has an off the shoulder sweetheart neckline with a bodice encrusted with gold and champagne shimmery beading. The embroidered skirt flares from her narrow waist, cinched with a gold belt to widen at her hips down to the floor. The silhouette similar to my ball gown harkens to the Rococo period.

Haley's strapless dress has layers of silk chiffon with a neckline of a confectioner's sugar swirl of the silk. An intricate appliqué of gold, champagne, and touches of cranberry attaches at her waist and crosses her body from one hip up to cover the opposite breast. The skirt mimics mine, too.

"The two of you are divine!" I squeal, clapping my hands and beaming. "I cannot believe what a fantastic job Elie did just from our conversations! *Merci! Merci!*"

"Thank you, my friend! We had video conferences with Billie and Blair for their fittings. The seamstresses enjoyed their trips to Las Vegas and New York City, taking private jets and staying at STEELE hotels!" Elie responds. "We'll do the final fittings here two days before the wedding. All will be spectacular, I promise!"

My mother and Shelley chat with Elie while Lola and Haley change.

Meanwhile, my mind whirls with happy thoughts.

I'm so excited everything is going to plan from the decorations to the food and drink—thanks to my mother and Lucien—to the musicians and the DJ. Roger spared no expense to bring my fairy-tale wedding to fruition. That's my man... *Roger The Responsible*. And I cannot wait to make him mine all MINE!

ROGER

"Cut it out, Harris! Pass the cranberry sauce to me already!"

Haley growls, frustrated with her twin's antics as he teases her relentlessly. Her gray eyes flash like a stroke of lightning as she glares at him.

"Harris Steele! That is enough, young man. Stop taunting your sister and give her the platter at once," our father commands in full-on Alpha Dom mode.

Immediately Harris complies—albeit grudgingly, with a smirk on his face—and hands Haley's favorite Thanksgiving side dish to her.

"Jerk," she mutters under her breath as she snatches it from him.

He in turn mimics her response wordlessly lest our father hear his new gibe. I hide my laugh with a cough and shake my head at Harris. He smirks until our father pins him with a steely stare.

Then I can't help myself, and I laugh out loud.

Leonie peers at me questioningly, and I shrug as I continue to chuckle.

Those two will never stop. It's their usual behavior at any of our family gatherings. When we were younger, Haley would sometimes leave the dining room in tears. Our parents would chastise Harris and send him to his room.

I was always the one to go after her and offer comfort. Yeah, the responsible one.

Now it's our first Thanksgiving as a family with Leonie, Rodolphe, Gaspard, Guy, and Josy. Even Luc joins us. My gaze travels around the dining room table of my parents' new penthouse on the twenty-eighth floor at The STEELE Tower Paris designed by Leonie. Everyone smiles and appears peaceful. The atmosphere is one of gratefulness and happiness.

The pretrial judge declared me innocent; The Twins at two months are our new bundles of joy; I'll marry the love of my life in a few weeks. All is right in the Steele-Beaulieu World.

"Leonie, you did such an incredible job with the redesign of our penthouse!" My mother declares as she raises her glass of Chateau Lafite Rothschild. *"Merci ma fille aussi!"*

"Well done, Leonie!"

"It's marvelous!"

"Cheers!"

Leonie preens.

I lean over and kiss her temple. Then inhale her classic sultry perfume, Dior's Pure Poison. She tells me it makes her feel powerful, like a woman who commands attention. The blend of florals with amber and musk is the perfect balance of femininity and masculinity. My cock twitches.

"It was an honor. Thank you for entrusting me with your home," she responds humbly.

Luc shifts in his seat to face her and asks, "When do you expect to return to your new career, *chérie*? We know how important interior design is to you."

Leonie glances at me, then turns to Luc.

"Roger and I haven't spoken about it yet. But I was thinking once Rodolphe and Gaspard reach six months, I could return to STEELE's Interior Design Team part-time as a project designer."

She glances at me from beneath her eyelashes and smiles.

I return her smile and kiss her hand.

"Whatever you want, my love. We have Nanny Grace to help us. Plus, you can even design a nursery for The Twins next to your office if you want to keep them close," I say.

The adoring smile that brightens Leonie's face makes my heart swell with love.

"Oh, *merci, Mon Cœur!*" She squeals as she pulls my mouth to hers and plants a toe-curling kiss on my lips.

We get ribbed for the PDA. But we're in France, so *c'est la vie*!

"Well, that means you have to make time for your Lola's Coterie campaigns, too! And we need to work on more designs for the pre- and post-natal collections. They've been a colossal hit!"

Leonie and I separate so she can answer her best friend.

"*Oui, oui! Absolument!* I cannot wait. I have some new sketches for you, *Chérie*," Leonie says giggling as I continue to plant kisses on her cheek.

Fuck, I love this woman! I cannot wait until our wedding night so I can ravage her until she can't move a single muscle—well, aside from her pussy walls...

"*Très bon!* That's splendid news," Luc says. "Excellent idea, Roger. Leonie, you should consider a specialization in interior design for children. What I've seen of three of the... What is it? Nine? Nurseries for The Twins, they're incredibly well done. You could design nurseries, playrooms, bedrooms—"

"Ooh, and playhouses that match the families' mansions!" Haley adds. "I've read they're extremely popular with chichi parents."

I have to give it to Luc; his thoughts are never far from revenue-generating ideas. Haley, the nerd, more than likely read about the mini mansions during one of her many Internet searches.

"That's an area STEELE International doesn't cover. The focus has always been on the main properties and amenities. Perhaps you'd like to lead your own division?"

My intense stare meets Sebastian's.

With a nod to me he adds, "If Roger is game, we can set it in motion as a subset of his division."

"That would add another offering to our clients, and we would include it in future projects. Another revenue stream," Morgan adds, ever the CEO even while retired.

Leonie looks at me, her amber eyes glow with excitement.

I pretend to consider the idea with a scowl on my face. But I can't hold it and start to chuckle.

"How can I deny my love anything? Not to mention the CEO and Steele Patriarch... Thanks, Luc, for an excellent idea!" I proclaim as I raise my glass of Chateau Lafite Rothschild. "Here's to Leonie's new division!"

"Hear, hear!"

"*Félicitations!*"

"Cheers!"

Leonie claps her hands and does that shimmy with her

hips that makes my cock come to life. She turns to me with a grin and kisses me silly again.

This will never get old.

"How did you like Thanksgiving dinner, Josy?" Shelley asks as we sip Rémy Martin digestifs in the library.

Josy gestures to my mother with her Baccarat snifter, "It was delicious, *merci!* Guy and I spent Thanksgiving with Lola at her Parisian penthouse on many occasions. She would cook a delectable multi-course meal. Luc would bring scrumptious pastries, and I would bring my double-chocolate soufflés for dessert."

She turns to Leonie and quirks her elegantly arched eyebrow at her daughter.

"Leonie, however, brought the wine since she doesn't cook despite my best efforts to teach her our Tunisian family's recipes."

Lola scoffs, "That's a wasted effort, *Maman* Josy! I've told you so for years!"

Leonie's golden caramel cheeks flush red, and she shakes her head.

"Don't tease her, *Mon Amour*. She takes after her Beaulieu side with her love for beautiful things," Guy responds as he winks at Leonie.

Daddy's Little Girl blows him a kiss in thanks.

"Well speaking of food, Nanny Grace just sent a text to me. The Twins are ringing their dinner bell! So pardon me," Leonie says.

I rise with her, but she pushes me back to my seat gently.

"Stay, *Chéri*, Nanny will help me," Leonie says as she smiles lovingly at me while she runs her fingers through my hair, massaging my scalp.

577

Malcolm claps his hands, and we glance at him in surprise.

"Do bring my nephews back. I haven't spent enough time with them," he says. "I don't want them to forget their favorite uncle!"

Sebastian sputters on his sip of cognac.

"Hell no! I'm their favorite uncle. So bring them to me!" He exclaims.

Harris and Luc join in, all proclaiming their place in The Twins' lives.

Leonie laughs, and her eyes twinkle.

"Simmer down, boys! You're all their favorite!"

I chuckle as she leaves the library.

"Well, don't get me started on their favorite aunt!" Lola adds.

"Yeah... Me!" Haley cuts in, lifting her snifter in salute.

Everyone laughs good-naturedly.

"Since Leonie is out of earshot, I'll tell you some stories about her as a child," Josy says gleefully.

We listen and laugh some more until Leonie returns with The Twins.

I go to Nanny Grace and take Gaspard from her arms with a word of thanks. Then I kiss his rosy cheeks as he coos happily.

"That's it. Hand him over, bro," Malcolm hustles over and plucks Gaspard from my arms just as Sebastian scoops Rodolphe from Leonie.

I roll my eyes at my siblings and shake my head.

"Hey, you could have your own, you know..." I rib them.

Baz smirks and inclines his head towards Lola.

"Yeah, no need to tell me. Have that conversation with your sister-in-law," he retorts.

Lola gives me the stink eye, and I opt to not comment. Instead, I cock my head at Malcolm.

"So what's your excuse, lover boy? How're things with—"

"You mean the sexy AF yoga teacher? Because if you're not interested, I'll step in without hesitation!" Harris says.

A growl comes from Alpha Dom Malcolm as he glares at our youngest brother.

Harris snickers and pulls out his mobile, typing on the screen.

"Oh, hi Starr... Yes, Happy Thanksgiving to you, too... I wanted to wish you a wonderful holiday and ask how the new surveillance system is going... Mmm... Right... Okay, great! I'm looking forward to the retreat, too. Thanks for inviting me... See you soon."

Silence descends on the library, making the sound of Malcolm's ragged breathing loud.

10... 9... 8...

"You. Little. SHIT!" Malcolm explodes.

I reach for Gaspard. But Malcolm pulls away and turns his glare on me.

"I know what I'm doing with a baby! Lest you forget, I used to wipe the snot from your nose," he snaps before he pins Harris with another heated stare.

"You'll pay for that when you least expect it, little brother. And lest you forget, I'm. Not. Haley," he snarls.

Harris' smirk falters since he knows Malcolm is *The Enforcer* amongst us. Damn. I feel right sorry for the jokester.

"Ha! Good! Get 'em for me too, Malcolm!" Haley shouts, punching the air in victory.

Malcolm winks at her and responds with a dark chuckle, "Will do, Baby Girl, will do."

"One day you'll learn, little bro," Sebastian laughs. Then

leans over to Gaspard and adds, "Just ignore your *Oncle* Malcolm's foul mouth..."

Now Malcolm looks chagrined and glances at Leonie.

"Sorry, sis. It won't happen again," he promises.

Leonie's laughter morphs into snorts as tears fill her eyes. She shakes her head and waves her hands in front of her flushed face.

"No worries, *mon frère*! They don't understand words yet, just emotions," she tells Malcolm as she pats his shoulder. "But, Harris, boy oh boy, I feel bad for you!"

LATER WE GO UP to our redesigned triplex penthouse to give everyone a tour.

Leonie did another excellent job with combining my parents' former penthouse below my duplex to create one large home for our growing family. It's on the top three floors, thirty through thirty-two.

Located in the Front de Seine district of Beaugrenelle in the *quinzième*, the property, like The STEELE Tower New York, is mixed-use with commercial and residential space plus the largest mall in Paris. The views of the Seine and of the Eiffel Tower are incredible, especially now at night when the spectacular light display flits across the monumental iron structure.

We decided to move into our new home when we return from our honeymoon. While we're gone, Josy agreed to oversee the move. Until then, Leonie, The Twins, and I will remain in Leonie's East Wing at *Le Beaulieu Manoir*.

The spacious wing is more like a house within a house. We took over her former bedroom suite and the nursery Leonie designed for The Twins. The rest of the wing comprises several bedrooms and bathrooms, kitchenette with eating area, library, art studio, media room, and living room.

It was all hers before she bought her duplex. It's where she stayed when she visited her parents. The maids maintain it. So it only required the arrangement of our personal items and clothing.

"Nicely done, Leonie," Luc says when we return to the main living room on the first floor. *"La Tour Eiffel* resembles a sparkling Christmas tree!"

"My favorite room is your Pilates and yoga studio," Lola gushes. "I need one! Then I can get a good workout at home."

Sebastian snorts and whispers in her ear.

Lola blushes scarlet red, but her hazel eyes spark with desire. Playfully, she swipes at Baz. He chuckles, wrapping his arms around her waist and pulling her back to his front. He places his hands possessively on her lower belly as he nuzzles her neck.

Leonie slips her hand into mine and smiles up at me knowingly.

Yeah, it won't be long before Baz and Lola have their own bundle of joy.

LEONIE

"*G*uess what today is, *mes beaux fils*? ... What did you say? ... *Absolument*! Your *Maman* and *Papa* become husband and wife forever and ever... And the two of you have starring roles!"

At three months old, The Twins are more active and react to sounds. The singsong of my voice attracts their attention as they lie on their tummies in front of me on the bed.

Gaspard lifts his head and laughs out loud. Drool spills from his Cupid's bow lips. Rodolphe rolls over onto his back and turns in the sound's direction. Wide gray eyes fringed with thick ebony lashes so like his father's sparkle as he studies me intently. Their serious personalities so similar.

I reach to pick him up, and he lifts his arms. It's amazing how quickly they develop.

"I know! I can't wait either!" I tell him as I nuzzle his tummy through his onesie.

His ah-goo vocalizations make me laugh with him.

I nestle Rodolphe in the crook of my knee as I sit cross-legged and lift Gaspard in the air to nuzzle him, too.

He squirms and laughs some more. It's delightful music to my ears. His carefree personality, so like mine.

"You agree, *Mon Petit Amour?*" I ask, giggling.

My mobile buzzes with "Big Poppa," Roger's ringtone. When we found out we were having twins, I dubbed Roger Big Poppa after my favorite rapper, The Notorious B.I.G.

"Speak of him, and he shall appear," I say sagely as I scoop my mobile from the pillow beside me.

No sooner than I press to accept the call, Roger's deep baritone filters through the speaker.

"Good morning, my love. Are you ready to become Mrs. Roger Steele?" He asks.

I close my eyes and take a deep inhale.

My mind wanders back over the last sixteen months we've been back together and then the twelve months prior. For over two years, it's been a roller coaster ride of highs and lows.

The best parts being our *coupe de foudre* when we met during the Lola's Coterie meeting with STEELE International, Inc. in New York City; reconciling after Lola and Sebastian's wedding in Dubai; our trip to the South of France where I became pregnant in Cannes; the birth of our Twins and our subsequent engagement here in Paris.

The struggles of our opposite personalities, with Roger being so intense and inflexible and me being more apt to go with the flow—sometimes too much so. The time we were apart was like a dull blade in my heart, constantly twisting and causing me sheer agony. To learn Roger felt the same made the ache less severe. We realized we need each other and will adjust to make our relationship work. The turmoil only made our love for one another stronger.

In the end, our initial love-at-first-sight passion proved justified.

So, am I ready to become Mrs. Roger Steele?

HELL. YEAH!

I exhale, then open my eyes and tell the love of my life just those words.

Roger guffaws. I hear Joel cracking up and Harris whooping in the background.

Oops… Did I roar it?

My cheeks heat, but I don't give a damn. I'll shout it from the top of *La Tour Eiffel* with a bullhorn proudly! By the end of this fairy-tale day, I'll be MRS. ROGER STEELE!

"IT WAS a good idea to keep the boys busy at STEELE Place Vendôme overnight and until the ceremony this evening. Tradition is important, *Mon Trésor*."

I nod and smile at my mother as we sit in the living room of the East Wing at *Le Beaulieu Manoir*.

Roger had it transformed into a mini spa so my girls and I could get pampered before the wedding. He arranged for my favorite day spa in Paris to set up multiple stations and rooms for our treatments.

My mother and I have facials done in an area separated by an antique, hand-painted Chinese partition. While Lola, Shelley, Haley, Starr, Blair, Billie, Anita, and Hettie have five-star massages, scrubs, and waxings. We'll all end up together in the manicure and pedicure chairs.

We started the day with a vigorous yoga flow led by Anita, followed by meditation with Starr. So this is a much-needed respite. So relaxing and rejuvenating!

"*Oui, Maman*, I agree. We don't want any bad vibes on

our wedding day!" I giggle. "We only want good times for sure!"

The aesthetician tsks when my giggles turn to snorts, causing her application of cream to miss its mark. Which in turn makes me laugh even harder. I can't help the giddy feelings swirling through me. I'm just so ecstatic!

"What's so funny, love bunny?"

Billie's silly question evokes more snorts to the point I have to sit up from the table and fan my heated face. The cucumbers roll off my eyes and plop onto my lap.

"Ha! She's hysterical! Leonie is losing it, folks!" Lola says, bouncing on her feet and clapping her hands.

Everyone laughs, even the aestheticians, albeit discreetly.

Again, I don't care. Call me mad because I'm crazy in love with Roger Steele!

Shelley walks over and plucks the cucumbers from my lap and says, "Oh, let her be. It wasn't so long ago you were in the same position, Mrs. Sebastian Steele."

Then with a wink, she adds, "Although I can understand why... My sons are fine catches!"

She glances at Starr, and her smile broadens.

Starr, however, bites her lower lip and suddenly finds interest in the nail polish selection.

Shelley snickers and helps me from the table.

"I remember how nervous I was before I walked down the aisle to Joel," Hettie starts. "It terrified me he'd get cold feet and duck out of the church!"

We laugh, and I think about how I encouraged Hettie to move out of the flat she shared with Joel and back into hers. The separation gave Joel a reason to pursue her. It worked, and after a Guys' Night Out, he bought her an incredible diamond engagement ring from Harry Winston at Roger's urging.

I too benefitted from the spontaneous shopping.

Roger bought me an extraordinary *toi et moi* ring. Two large pear-shaped diamonds with a platinum band set in pavé diamonds. The identical, flawless stones act as a reminder of our identical twins every time I see it on my right ring finger.

I gaze down at it now. My heart warms with love for my man and my babies.

"Up and at 'em! We've got a schedule to maintain," my mother says as she slips off her table and joins the others at the mani/pedi chairs.

Lola and I glance at each other and bust out laughing. We thought Shelley was a sergeant with Lola's wedding. Well... my mother is just as bad!

As our nails finish drying, one servant enters the living room-cum-spa with a beautifully wrapped box in her hands.

Throughout the day Roger sent gifts to me. A painting of a golden lioness with two cubs trailing behind her as they amble through the grasses of the African savanna. A red suede bound book filled with love letters he'd written to me, but never sent while we were apart. A themed playlist of love songs he curated. Each precious and heartfelt.

I thank the servant. Then I lift the top—of course Roger The Responsible thought to make the gift easy to open after I had my nails done. Inside is a flat blue velvet box. I press the sapphire cabochon closure, and the lid lifts to reveal an exquisite suite of diamonds set in clusters of pear-shaped stones in various sizes: a pair of earrings; a bib necklace; a bracelet. They glitter as the light bounces off their flawless surfaces. Simply dazzling.

"Whoa! Someone pass my shades to me, stat!" Exclaims Blair as she shields her eyes from the brilliance of the diamonds.

Haley claps and adds, "My brother knows how to treat a lady!"

Indeed, he does. I smile to myself as tears of absolute joy fill my eyes. Sure, the jewelry is phenomenal. But it's the entire package—a man who loves me and our sons and with whom I'll spend the rest of my life.

It doesn't get any better than that.

"Shelley, *chérie*, you are right. Your sons are fine catches!" My mother says.

We head to the solarium in the East Wing that faces the Bois de Boulogne for the bridesmaids' luncheon. To go along with the spa theme, the menu comprises green salads, grilled herb-crusted salmon, roast chicken, and citrus-infused water. We prefer to eat light before putting on our gowns. Besides, I've waddled enough during my pregnancy. No need to waddle down the aisle...

I giggle at the thought.

"There she goes, again," Lola says gleefully as she twirls her finger in a circle by her temple. "Looney Tunes alert!"

"How cute are they?!"

"OMG! Hey, Little Fellas!"

Rodolphe and Gaspard look like two Christmas angels in their cranberry velvet onesies with gold bib fronts dotted with Swarovski crystal buttons. Their cleft chins bob as their eyes light up dancing from the face of one adoring woman to another gathered around them.

I smooth their silky ebony hair with the hairbrush, and it gleams. My boys are gorgeous like their father.

Even though Nanny Grace is on hand, between The Twins' *grand-mères* they were bathed and dressed in moments. Now they're ready for their official debut.

Roger and I chose to keep them out of the media. The Steeles, like many old wealthy families, prefer to stay out of the limelight except for business purposes. Being that I'm a world-renowned supermodel, I can't help but be front and center. However, our children are private to us and will remain out of the media as much as possible.

The wedding is a family affair, even if we have three hundred guests in attendance. It's not public per se. Photographers and videographers have followed Roger and me separately all day and captured images of The Twins. But again, the images are for our private albums.

I smiled when I glimpsed some photos of Rodolphe and Gaspard. They could easily model just as their father did with me for the last Lola's Coterie collections we shot in Beverly Hills, Las Vegas, New York City, Abu Dhabi, and Dubai.

Lola insists they join me in the upcoming campaigns with their faces not appearing on camera. More authentic to the post-natal vibe, she claims. I told her Roger and I would let her know. She convinced Roger with the others; we'll see if she's successful with his sons.

"Leonie, it's time for you to get dressed, my friend."

I turn to the doorway of bedroom we converted into a dressing room for me.

Elie strides inside with his two assistants and several dressers ready to help the girls and me get into our gowns.

My heart skips a beat as I realize it's almost time to say I do to the man I love.

As I STARE out the window past the pristine snow-covered grounds to the forest beyond, I reflect on my childhood here in my ancestral home. With the next generation of

Steeles and Beaulieus sleeping peacefully beside me in their bassinets, I imagine them running and playing on the lawns or riding their horses on the trails. The Twins will grow up and explore just as their ancestors and I did before them.

However, they'll have the added benefit of growing up in New York City and spending time at other Steele family properties around the world. Roger and I decided we'll globe-trot while The Twins are young, at least until they're of school age.

We want them to experience different cultures and lifestyles. See the off-beat places and the conventional destinations. It's the traveler in my DNA.

A soft knock on the door brings my attention back to the room. I peer over my shoulder to find my father smiling at me with tears in his eyes.

"How beautiful you are, *Mon Trésor*"—his voice hitches and he clears it before he continues—"So regal and stunning... My baby girl."

Tears threaten to spill from my eyes. But he raises his hand and shakes his head.

"No crying. Only laughter and joy!" He proclaims.

I nod and suck in a shaky breath as I bow my head to gather myself.

A moment later, my mother and Shelley enter the room to pick up The Twins. They'll enter the Beaulieu Chapel in the arms of their *grand-mères*. Bundled in their snowsuits, they'll stay nice and warm on the drive over.

I give them hugs and wave as my mother and Shelley go through the door.

"Your turn, *Mon Trésor*," my father says as he drapes the custom cape over my shoulders carefully.

The dresser plans to add my veils once I arrive at the

Chapel. We didn't want the delicate piece to sustain any damage before I walk down the aisle.

I place my hand on my father's arm, and we make our way through the house to the ornate horse-drawn coach out front. The gold leaf and cranberry lacquer glimmer in the glow from the fairy lights strung on the palatial French Rococo mansion and throughout the estate's twenty acres.

A footman helps me up the step, and I settle on the soft leather seat.

My father joins me and beams.

"My little princess on her way to her prince," he says, his voice gruff with emotion.

I nod, too overwhelmed to speak aloud. I take the time of the short ride along the path to our family's Chapel to practice my deep breathing, hoping to calm my racing heart.

The surrounding land and the facade of the Chapel also have strings of fairy lights. The sound of a harpist with the angelic voices of a choir singing Christmas carols fills the air. The atmosphere is heavenly.

Once I alight from the coach, I pause to take it all in. My pulse races again as my face threatens to split from the smile that breaks out. I glance up at my father and he's grinning, too.

Then the wedding planner spies us, and she ushers us into a side room. The dressers remove the cape and rearrange my gown. They place the diamond-encrusted cap of the cathedral-length veil on my head before they add the blusher.

Lola walks in and adjusts my train and the veil over my gown.

I peer into the full-length mirror. Then smile at the sparkles that bounce off my opulent gown, my head from the cap and my ears, décolletage, and wrist from the suite

Roger gifted me. I feel like a princess bride and I'm more than ready to marry my prince.

Lola dabs her eyes and air kisses near my cheeks before she leaves the room to line up behind the rest of the bridal party. The pairs formed by Luc and Blair, Malcolm and Starr, Haley and Lucien, and Harris and Billie.

My father holds out his arm, and we follow Lola to the wrought-iron gates at the entry to the Chapel's primary room. My breath catches at the sight of my fairy-tale wedding come true.

Thousands of fairy lights twine with the dark greens leaves and red berries of holly around the gates, the columns, and up the walls to the ceiling bathing the Chapel in a soft, golden glow. An abundance of wreaths and flowers ranging in hue from deep cranberry and burgundy to champagne and ivory fills the Chapel. The sweet, hot spiciness of cinnamon mixed with the floral scents waft through the air. The space is at once elegant and festive.

The bridal party turns to me and everyone smiles as they murmur praises. Then the music changes for the start of the procession. The Trans-Siberian Orchestra perform their "Christmas Canon." The strains of the violins swirl around me and the sweet voices of the boys bring tears to my eyes as the Chapel fills with the sounds.

When the last verse ends and the instruments continue to play, my father walks me down the aisle—the most important runway of my life—to my prince, my love, my Roger.

ROGER

"*Well* my friend, this time tomorrow you'll be a happily married man and join the likes of Sebastian, Norman, and me in the bliss of wedlock. Here's to you and your beautiful bride-to-be!"

Joel raises his Baccarat crystal snifter in a toast.

The glint of the amber liquid reminds me of Leonie's twinkling eyes after I've wrung multiple orgasms from her sweet, juicy pussy, and we—

"Damn, man! Get a grip on yourself with that goofy ass smile on your face!"

Along with Joel and Norman, my brothers, Luc, Lachlan, Lucien, and Laurent guffaw.

The tantalizing image of a sated Leonie spread before me dissipates as Norman's bellow and their resulting laughter resound around the room.

I heave a disappointed sigh at the loss and refocus on my bachelor party or Bro Bonding, as Laurent calls it. The youngest Jackson is their company's director of cigars and a rebellious playboy who loves to party. He's game for any opportunity to drink and have fun.

We're at Jackson Smoke&Scotch Lounge Paris—what's quickly become my favorite spot to unwind with my boys as we partake of their top-shelf Scotch offerings. I rarely smoke their fine Cuban cigars, but tonight is a special occasion.

I take a long draw on it and settle back in my leather club chair. The tasting notes of the spicy, earthy, and woody flavors linger on my palate. They blend well with the smoky, dark berries flavor of the Jackson Reserve Scotch. Its trademark bite drags along the back of my tasting.

Much like my delectable and tantalizing Leonie. As Pam Grier says in *Foxy Brown,* "the darker the berry, the sweeter the fruit, honey." And Leonie is all that, and then some...

The thought makes my mind drift, again.

The lounge is near where we're staying at STEELE Place Vendôme while Leonie and her girls stay at the *Manoir.*

Leonie and her traditions. First no more sex until our wedding night. Then I couldn't see her before the ceremony, which meant no wrapping my larger frame around her lush curves in an attempt at relief for my aching balls last night...

Fuuuck.

"Who would have thought from one meeting over two years ago would bring us to two Steele men capturing the hearts of my mentees and friends?"—Luc shakes his head and his navy blue eyes sparkle with mischief—"Roger, *oui.* But Sebastian... mmm mmm. A surprise!"

Malcolm, Harris, Lachlan, and I chuckle remembering how jealous Baz was of the Silver Fox's relationship with Lola.

Luc may be in his early fifties. But as Leonie and Lola pegged his nickname, he can go toe-to-toe with any of us for a woman's affection. Hell, he may even win! An Alpha Dom at six feet, four inches with salt and pepper hair, a clean-shaven face that highlights the cleft in his chin. He could pass for a movie star. Not to mention being a billion-aire duke, the last of his noble line.

We laugh some more when Baz bristles.

Only after he put his ring on Lola did he loosen up a smidgen on Luc. Obviously, it's still a touchy topic…

"Ha! Just fucking with you, Steele," he chuckles. "I trust you and your brother will do well by Lola and Leonie. That is, if you know what is best for you."

He pauses to pin both of us with a don't-fuck-with-them stare, then raises his glass for a toast.

"*À la tienne, mes amis!*" He proclaims with a smirk.

I laugh and raise my snifter high, knowing I will forever cherish Leonie, the one and only love of my life.

* * *

ENCHANTING.

That's the only word to describe the sight of my precious love walking down the aisle towards me as the Trans-Siberian Orchestra performs her favorite Christmas song. With the Chapel alight with tiny lights and covered in flowers as the background, she looks like a dream. An unforgettable fantasy.

It takes all of my well-known self-discipline to anchor my feet to the Chapel's stone floor to prevent myself from rushing to Leonie and sweeping her into my arms. I want to carry her and our cubs away to my den.

"Slow down, bro. She's yours forever."

Sebastian, as the eldest who's always felt responsible for his younger siblings, must sense my caveman need to claim my mate. Right. Now. Plus, his being an Alpha Dom makes him very familiar with my need to mark what is mine. He chuckles and pats me on the shoulder.

I relax a bit and watch enthralled by my princess bride floating towards me on an ethereal carpet of fragrant white rose, camellia, and gardenia petals.

Through Leonie's veil, I can see her brilliant smile rivals the diamonds in her ears and on chest. Our eyes lock, and the grin that spreads from one ear to the other threatens to split my face; my cheeks hurt.

Slowly, I pull my gaze from Leonie to travel down her body, taking in the opulence of her regal gown.

The demure neckline can't hide the voluptuousness of her full breasts. The rounded tops peek above the sweetheart shape, held back by sheer material. More sheer material with shimmery silver lace covers her toned arms to her wrists where her diamond bracelet glitters. Her narrow waist appears smaller than before she gave birth to The Twins. The slimness enhanced by the flare of the skirt from her hips to the floor.

Leonie's presence captivates not only me, but our guests. Locked in an awed silence, their eyes follow her down the aisle.

Guy pins me with an intense stare before he answers firmly, he and Josy give this woman to be married to this man. Then he turns to his *Trésor* and embraces her.

I remember his words when I first met him.

He leans forward. His obsidian eyes bore into mine.

"Do not fuck my daughter over or you will pay the price."

He rivets me in place for a full minute.

Now, he extends his hand to me, and we shake as he nods his acceptance of me as Leonie's husband.

First Luc, then her father. The men in her life are protective of her, but not as much as me. I will keep her and our children safe from harm, and they will want for nothing. They are mine.

At last I have Leonie's hands in mine as we listen to the officiant, then recite our vows of everlasting love. Leonie tears up, as do I when we each say I do.

But a squeal soon replaces the tears when Sebastian presses the clasp on the blue velvet jewelry case.

Leonie sparkled before, but the enormous diamonds of the custom hand harness and her eternity band make our guests find their voices as they exclaim over the jewelry. I took a page out of Sebastian's book with a twist. I designed it to take her *toi et moi* ring symbolism to another level, including myself with our sons.

The chain of diamonds connects to her eternity band on her middle finger by three pear-shaped diamonds in a row that rest atop her hand attached to a diamond triple bracelet. Her engagement ring sits on her ring finger. The harness is removable. So she can wear her band and ring together.

I slip the entire piece on her and Leonie gasps along with her bridesmaids. Her feline eyes fly to mine, and I cock my head as I raise my eyebrow. Marked as mine for all to see.

She lifts her hand to admire the harness. Sparks fly from the flawless diamonds, even more blinding than her suite.

A ripple goes through the Chapel as the guests whisper about the magnificent piece.

Leonie winks and says, "My turn to claim you, Monsieur Steele!"

The gathering laughs and I join in.

Smiling, she places my classic platinum band on my finger. She holds my gaze and adds, *"Pour toujours, Mon Amour."*

The officiant pronounces us husband and wife.

My heart bursts with joy. Ecstatic to complete our bond after twenty-nine long months. This can only be the bliss Joel talked about. I rejoice at joining Sebastian and him.

With a smirk, I lift Leonie's veil then lift her in my arms to kiss Mrs. Roger Steele until she's breathless.

The guests stand, clap, and whoop.

I growl and end the kiss with little nips to her swollen lips; she purrs. Damn. We may not make it to the reception as strung tight as I am right now from the caress of Leonie's luscious body against mine.

With a Herculean effort, I step back.

Leonie whimpers, and my cock twitches.

Fuck. Me.

I take a deep breath to clear my head and send a silent prayer that no one notices the enormous bulge in my tuxedo pants.

Lola places Leonie's bouquet in her hand and straightens her long veil and the hem of her gown as we turn to our guests.

My gaze zooms in on our sons, who are just as much a part of our nuptials as Leonie and me. I grin when I see my mother holding Rodolphe and Josy—my new mother-in-law, so cool to say it at last—cradling Gaspard.

My sons are adorable as fuck in their bespoke formal onesies designed to match the wedding colors. Might as well get them used to dressing in the finest garments men of means can purchase.

So attentive at three months, they move their heads to take in the world around them, attracted to the sounds and lights. I swear Rodolphe's eyes widen in recognition of me when I pluck him from my mother's arms. I laugh and snuggle him close to my chest.

A small hand rubbing my lower back, then circling around my waist draws my attention to Leonie who holds Gaspard in the crook of her arm. She beams up at me with a radiant smile, and I kiss her full lips.

I grasp her hand in mine, and as a family, we stroll down the aisle to the cheers of our guests.

"You're all mine, now, Madame Roger Steele," I tell her as soon as we pass the wrought-iron gates at the entrance to the Chapel's primary space.

Leonie giggles and tugs my hand as she leads me to a separate room.

Once inside, she wraps her arm around my neck and pulls my mouth to hers. This time, she kisses me silly, and I groan into her mouth. Our tongues tangle as she deepens our fiery connection.

"And you are all mine, Monsieur Roger Steele. Never forget it!" She commands as she presses her forehead to mine.

We stand in our own little family bubble until a knock at the door interrupts us.

I call out to come in, and Sebastian followed by Lola and the rest of the bridal party barge in.

"Yeah, yeah, yeah... Time for pictures in this Winter Wonderland Chapel, Love Birds!" Lola calls out. "The guests head back to the *Manoir's Grand Hall*. The wedding planner said to hang out in here until they're all gone."

Starr laughs, "Lola, you are no good!"

I notice Malcolm stands close to Starr with his front inches from her back. His focus remains on her the entire time we're in the room.

He might as well admit something's up with the two of them. They can't keep mum forever...

I glance at Luc to see him and Blair in a tête-à-tête near a corner. She giggles and covers her mouth with her hand after he whispers something in her ear. Her face flushes a rosy pink while he smirks down at her.

What's it about weddings?

Hell, I know I couldn't take another moment without Leonie at Sebastian and Lola's nuptials. It's hard to evade love when it swirls around you. The very atmosphere charged with the electricity of two people deeply in love.

I chuckle at myself, waxing poetic.

"What's so funny, *Mon Cœur*?" Leonie asks, staring up at me while she bounces Gaspard on her hip.

I bend over and kiss the tip of her nose, then whisper, "Love is in the air…"

She follows my line of sight and takes in first Luc and Blair, then Malcolm and Starr—now facing one another, lost in their own world.

Leonie turns back to me and whispers, "Who do you think is next?"

I consider, then waggle my eyebrows.

"Double ceremony?"

Leonie cracks up, drawing everyone's attention to us.

Fortunately, the wedding planner enters and ushers us into the primary space. Hairstylists and makeup artists touch up the girls' before we pose for the cameras.

The Twins steal the show. The photographers and videographers came prepared with colorful fuzzy balls suspended from sticks to keep Rodolphe and Gaspard looking toward the cameras. They reach for them and track the balls as an assistant moves them through the air. Pros just like their *Maman*!

Since Leonie avoided me like the plague all day, a photographer and a videographer captured the guys and me in candid and posed shots. The girls did the same. So we spend little time on the group photos.

When we exit the Chapel, I laugh at the golden coach led by four horses with a driver and two footmen waiting to take us back to the mansion. Their liveries just as formal as my white-tie attire, harkens to days of the centuries past.

The beauty of the snow-covered lawns and twinkling trees remind me of being inside of a snow globe for a wintry fairy-tale. The stars glitter in the ink-black sky and the air is crisp. Sound muffled by the falling snow. It's fantastical.

Once settled in the coach, I lean over to Leonie and ask, "How's your fairy-tale wedding so far, my love?"

Her smile shines brighter than the stars and millions of tiny lights. I warm in its luminosity.

"Unbelievable! Better than I ever imagined! *Merci, Mon Cœur*," she responds breathlessly. "But nothing will compare to the consummation of our marriage…"

Forget twitching. My cock lengthens down my leg in anticipation of a warmth even better than Leonie's smile.

I smirk and respond, "What are you waiting for?"

Leonie's laughter rings out. Then she replies, "Soon *Amoureux*, soon."

ROGER

"*L*adies and gentlemen, presenting Mr. and Mrs. Roger Steele and their sons Master Rodolphe Beaulieu Steele and Master Gaspard Beaulieu Steele!"

Leonie glances up at me. Another of Cupid's arrows hits its mark and dings me in the heart. She lifts her stunning face up for a kiss. Without hesitancy, I indulge my wife—I can refuse her nothing. Our guests rise to cheer as we enter the *Grand Hall* through the screens passage.

The room is resplendent in our wedding colors of cranberry, gold, champagne, and ivory. Each table feature towers of flowers as centerpieces with cranberry and champagne colored crystal glasses, ivory plates, and gold napkins and tablecloths. Even the silver utensils have gold accents.

They covered the walls in silk drapery the color of champagne with swathes of cranberry. Christmas wreaths hang vertically in groups of four. They didn't miss the magnificent chandeliers and three-story-high ceiling either.

Garlands of flowers, golden glass balls, bows, and tiny lights twine overhead.

As we pass the ornate stone hearth, I glance up at the elaborate overmantel with stone carvings on top of which the Beaulieu coat of arms and heraldic mottoes adorn the space. Even there, miniature topiaries mimic the table centerpieces and tiny lights make them glow. The fireplace is large enough to walk in and stand inside. But tonight, a roaring fire fills the grate.

Leonie smiles and nods at our guests as we make our way to the other end of the *Grand Hall* to the dais where the high table waits for us. Flanking it just below sit two tables for our bridal party on one side and for our parents with their closest friends on the other. My Uncle Connor and Aunt Lucie Jackson—parents of Lachlan, Lydie, Lucien, and Laurent—join them as the women have been best friends since before either married their billionaires.

Just beyond the dais, Nanny Grace and another nanny wait in one of the private rooms. She's a temporary helper for Nanny Grace while Leonie and I enjoy our reception. We trust the temp since she's from the same agency as Nanny Grace that the überwealthy and celebrities use to hire staff for their children, including nannies, nurses, and governesses.

However, Harris set up one of his high-tech video monitoring systems so we can check in on The Twins right from our table. Our parents have one at their table, too.

Mine to protect and all.

Before Leonie and I sit, we place The Twins with their grandmothers so we can have our first dance, and they can watch.

Leonie wanted to surprise me with the song, so I don't know what to expect as I pull her into my embrace on the dance floor. But as the opening strains of "La Vie en Rose" by Édith Piaf play, I glance up at the minstrel's gallery to see Céline Dion with a full band.

The talented songstress smiles and launches into the first verse, singing in Leonie's native tongue. Since I'm fluent in French, my eyes well with tears when Céline sings about the woman belonging to the man and he takes her into his arms to whisper words of love.

I hold Leonie even tighter and do just that.

"*Je t'aime tellement mon amour... Pour toujours...* Never leave me again..." my voice breaks, and I bury my face in her hair.

Leonie gasps and wraps her arms tighter around my neck as she melts into me. Her body trembles as she too sobs, knowing how far we've come and the heartache we had to endure.

It all ends tonight. We're on a fresh path with no obstacles.

I cradle her face in my palms as I swipe her tears with my thumbs. Then I vow to her she will only see life in pink from this day forth. She nods vehemently and mouths I love you. I cock my eyebrow in return.

"Words, Pretty Kitty. I will have your words," I say.

"*Oui, oui,*" she answers.

"*Bien,*" I respond as I kiss her quivering lips.

Leonie sighs with contentment and melts into my embrace.

I also relax, knowing my woman loves me as much as I love her. Till the end of time.

When Céline finishes "La Vie en Rose," Leonie blows kisses and I bow to her. She offers us the best of everything in our lives together. Then she continues with her serenade.

Our parents join us on the dance floor with The Twins.

Happily, we scoop them into our arms and dance some more. Leonie partners with her father and I dance with my mother while my father twirls Josy into his arms. We continue until everyone dances as a pair while Céline performs more love songs and even her glorious renditions of Christmas carols. Then we return to our seats for Guy's welcome to the guests.

Between courses of our meal, Leonie excuses herself to feed The Twins. I rise to help. But she waves me back to my seat.

I'm chatting with Guy when his face lights up with a wide smile. A glance over my shoulder reveals a radiant Leonie in a shimmery platinum curve-hugging gown. My jaw drops at her beauty.

Leonie entered not from behind me where she left the room, rather from the screens passage. All heads turn as she sashays across the floor. The gown dazzles. But it's the sway of her hips that has me mesmerized.

She stops before the dais and lifts a microphone to her lips.

"Roger, you are the love I've always wished for. Each day with you is the best day of my life. As exceptional as our wedding day is, I know that every tomorrow will be even more divine"—she takes a crystal flute of Taittinger Comtes de Champagne Blanc de Blancs from a server and raises it high—"To you *Mon Cœur*."

I rise and lift my flute without breaking eye contact.

Her little pink tongue slips out to skim across her lower lip before she sips. The glass hides her smirk barely as her heated eyes narrow.

My nostrils flare, and I dip my head to acknowledge her flirtatious act. Little does she realize if she keeps it up, I'm going to snatch her from the room and pound into her until she's hoarse from screams of intense passion.

Leonie spies my smirk and bites her plump lip as she shifts on her feet, more than likely feeling the same ache as me.

Yeah, Mrs. Steele... You're playing with a horny as fuck Alpha male.

Sebastian joins her on the floor and double kisses her cheeks after he takes the mic from her. She returns to my side, and I pull her into a tight embrace. She giggles when I tell her to be very careful. Then we listen to our family and friends regale us with fond memories and best wishes.

We cut the cake and toss Leonie's bouquet and garter. Funny enough, Starr catches the flowers, and Malcolm—despite Harris making a grab for it; he'll never learn—scoops the garter mid-air. We whoop and holler when Malcolm dips Starr and captures her mouth in a mind-blowing kiss. He brings her back on her feet, and she peers at him dazedly while he grins. They leave the dance floor with her tucked against his side and her head on his shoulder.

Check.

Leonie tells me she'll be right back, and I watch her and Lola slip through the crowd chatting with guests as they go.

"You finally got your girl, bro."

I glance to my left and see Sebastian chuckling. His gray eyes shine with mirth.

"About fucking time, I'd say!" Lucien adds. "If I had to watch you looking all pitiful another night at LEVELS Paris, I was going to revoke your Global All Access membership!"

I grimace at the reminder of the many nights I spent at his and Malcolm's BDSM/dance club.

Lucien came up with the idea since he figured the club

would fill the void for safe, uninhibited sexual activities amongst the world's wealthiest and most influential people. They convinced Sebastian a global, luxury, members-only entertainment venue focused on hedonism would add to STEELE's bottom line. Baz, the net-net guy, saw the potential and gave them the green light.

Before Leonie, I would satisfy my sexual needs at LEVELS New York, London, or Paris. When we were together, we used the club frequently. However, during our time apart, I'd go, but never found solace with another woman. Instead, I'd just join the voyeurs and take pleasure in others' sexual satisfaction.

We haven't been in months. So I make a mental note to go once we're back from our honeymoon.

The wedding planner approaches to let me know they're ready for my surprise gift to Leonie. Just in time as I see her waltz back into the room.

This outfit change has her in a gold sheer vee-neck body suit with patterns of gold sequins and a matching open-front, floor-length skirt. Her long, toned legs go on for miles and end in fuck-me strappy heels.

I grin wolfishly and hold my hand out to her. Then I kiss her palm and twirl her to put her back to my front while I wrap my arms around her waist. We face a projector screen previously hidden behind the drapery. When the lights dim, the room goes silent.

A panoramic view of the snow-covered Swiss Alps fills the screen. The camera pans to Verbier Village, then to the exterior of the chalet I purchased for Leonie. The video continues to show me as I stand by the great room's massive fireplace.

"Hello, my love. We must be married, and you are all

mine forever. I promised you the world and will begin with this chalet in Verbier as one of my wedding gifts to you. Tomorrow, after I fully claim you during our wedding night, we'll fly to Verbier with our families to celebrate Christmas and New Year's. Then, we'll boot them all out, except for our adorable sons of course, and enjoy our honeymoon. Two months of your favorite season, winter, and your favorite pastime, skiing. I love you with all my heart, Mrs. Roger Steele. Now, bid those fine guests adieu. It's time for us to say good night!"

The video pans to a mountain slope with golden rocks forming the words I LOVE YOU, MRS. ROGER STEELE on the snow.

Leonie whirls around and throws her arms around my neck as she jumps into my arms. She plants kisses all over my face as she squeals in delight.

Leonie

I've never been so nervous in my life to get on a stage and stand before a crowd in skimpy lingerie. But my heart races since I'm as fuck right now.

It's Masquerade Night at LEVELS Paris and as my surprise to Roger, I booked the primary stage at Peepshow on the second level.

The seating alcoves are full of members in various stages of dress and sex. The mini-stages have demonstrations taking place. While others booked the performance rooms booked solid. Couples mingle at the bar that serves non-alcoholic mocktails or sit and watch the hedonistic displays before them.

He pinned me with an intense stare when he our driver

Eric pulled up to the rear entrance. But I handed him a black leather half mask and donned a full one coated in gold and jewels. No one will recognize us.

It's been forever since we came, and I miss the thrill of the sex club. I'm not a sub and Roger isn't a Dom. We're into voyeurism, bondage, and plenty of toys. We well use all LEVELS Paris and all the other locations have to offer.

But me being on the primary stage in front of a crowd is a first.

For this little surprise, I had to persuade Malcolm and Lucien to help me. Initially they were adamant they would never let me get on stage without Roger knowing in advance. Once I told them I wouldn't strip completely and showed them my lingerie, they gave in. They arranged a Masquerade Night to take place the same night as my wedding with the insistence I wear a full mask.

Now it's showtime!

When the sounds of "Justify My Love" by Madonna start, my body automatically responds as it's used to the start of fashion shows with music. It's on.

I saunter onto the stage and the spotlight flicks on to reveal me in a floor-trailing red silk kimono. My mahogany mane is flowing down my back to below my ass. Roger doesn't want me to cut it since he likes to fist it when he takes me savagely from behind. I shiver at the memories as my pussy clenches.

The good thing is the spotlight is so bright, I can't make out the crowd. I only know where I left Roger standing and focus on the area.

Billie told me about a world-famous Las Vegas burlesque performer who offers private lessons via Skype. She helped me to choreograph my routine. When I performed it for her yesterday, she gave me a standing ovation.

I move to the music sensuously and disrobe one piece of specially designed Lola's Coterie lingerie at a time. The gold body sheen glows in the light and stresses my every curve and toned muscle.

The crowd quiets as they watch me perform, and the music grows louder.

I lose myself in the seductive rhythm and dance only for Roger. My hands become his as I cup and caress my heavy breasts, then pinch the turgid nipples through the lace. Turning from the crowd, I shimmy my hips as I bend at the waist to grab my ankles. My swollen, wet folds remain hidden behind the tiny briefs—I don't want Roger to have a coronary.

At the end, I widen my stance and slide to the floor in a straddle split. Then I press my torso flat to the floor as my hands reach in Roger's direction. The spotlight turns off.

The wild cries of the crowd bounce off the walls. I giggle giddily and rise. Hands grab me by the waist and hoist me in the air. I land over a shoulder in one swift movement.

Roger!

Wordlessly, he stalks off the stage and out the double doors straight to the elevator.

I hold on to his waist and squeeze my thighs together. The ache to have his ten-inch dick inside of me threatens to consume me in a fiery explosion. I whimper in sheer agony.

We exit the elevator and pad down the hallway to our private corner suite on the third level. Once inside, Roger deftly sits on the bed and places me across his lap, face down with one leg over mine.

WHAP... WHAP... WHAP... WHAP... WHAP

I jerk and yowl as Roger uses the palm of his hand to spank my ass. Each sharp blow hits my ass cheeks in rapid succession. I squirm to avoid the slaps. But Roger holds me firmly across his thick muscular thighs. The muscles bunch beneath me as the punishing blows continue.

WHAP... WHAP... WHAP... WHAP... WHAP

He adds in my upper thighs and the juncture under my ass where it meets my thighs.

Merde!

"Rrr... Roggerrr..." I wail, twisting as much as I can in his iron grip. "Whaaat... Pl—"

WHAP... WHAP... WHAP... WHAP... WHAP

The pain morphs into pleasure as my pussy contracts and my juices flow done my thighs to soak into his tuxedo pants. My squirms change into thrusts as I lift my hips to meet his palm. I mewl wantonly.

WHAP... WHAP... WHAP... WHAP... WHAP

"MINE! MINE! MINE! MINE! MINE!"

Roger's possessive growls make my nipples pebble into points, and my core vibrates with the need for his enormous girth to fill it.

I don't have long to wait.

He flips me to my hands and knees on the bed and stands behind me. The sound of his zipper opening makes me shudder.

YES! YES! YES! YES! YES!

Roger grips my hip with one hand and slides the other under my torso to wrap his fingers around my throat. The possessive hold renders me immobile.

I feel his bulbous tip touch my pussy opening. Then wham!

With one quick thrust of his hips, he plows deep inside until his balls hit my swollen clit and his pelvis smacks my redden ass. The force pushes me up the bed, but he tightens his grip. Then pounds into me with grunts and growls like a feral beast.

I keen and arch my back as my greedy pussy sucks him in deeper. I'm soaked and ready for penetration. My inner walls ripple as he pistons in and out. Each stroke more wild and out of control than the last.

A giggle bubbles past my kips.

Leonie *The Lion* once again causes Roger *The Responsible* to lose control!

Four quick spanks to my ass cheeks have me screaming.

"You think it is funny for me to see you in front of hundreds of men naked, Little Kitty?!" He growls as he increases his spine-jarring pumps.

I shake my head as I moan loudly.

"Words!" He commands.

I jolt forward from the impact of his pelvis and immediately respond, "*Non!* It was for yoouuu!"

Roger grunts in response. Then slides his hand from my hip to tweak my sensitive clit.

I scream as another orgasm crashes over me.

Roger is still hard and unrelenting in his claiming of me.

My eyes close and I twist the bedding in my fists as I give in to his dominance. He's all Alpha male and my lion bows before his wolf.

As if sensing acquiescence, I feel Roger's dick swells and pulsates. One last brutal thrust signals his impending release. Hot jets of his cum coat my pussy, burrowing deep to my cervix.

Roger lets off a bellowing roar that reverberates around us.

It triggers another orgasm for me, and I cry out in wild abandon.

"YEEESSS!!!"

· · ·

ROGER

I stroke Leonie's soft, damp cheek as we lie in bed tangled in the sheets after hours of consummating our marriage. Without a doubt, we have fulfilled the requirement many times over.

She sighs in contentment as she snuggles her warm, naked body closer against my side. One of her long legs thrown over my thighs; Leonie's left hand sparkles in the moonlight with my rings on my chest. My arm loops under her to lock her in place with my hand on her rounded hip.

Undoubtedly Leonie's ass and pussy will be extremely sore for the next day or so. It's been three months since we last made love. And I haven't punished her since…

As much as I appreciate Leonie's surprise, I cannot abide others seeing her, even if she left on a skimpy lace bra and tiny as fuck panties. Nothing can contain her ample curves, and I know every man at Peepshow had a hard-on just looking at what is mine all MINE.

Not gonna fly!

Yes, I'm possessive by nature. But the caveman roared to the forefront and snatched his mate off the stage—albeit after he witnessed the entire cock-hardening performance —and claimed her fully.

Now my love sleeps wrapped in my embrace, and I can join her in a peaceful slumber.

LEONIE

"Good morning at last, Mr. and Mrs. Roger Steele! So nice of you to join us…"

The cabin explodes with a ruckus of wolf whistles, stomps, and laughter as Roger and I board one of STEELE's Gulfstream G700 private jets.

It's not quite my fault we had them waiting on the tarmac at Le Bourget Airport for twenty minutes. Blame it on the steamy shower sex scene we enacted before we left LEVELS Paris. Fortunately, we didn't have to take more time to get dressed since I had overnight bags packed with our clothes already at the suite.

Since Roger kept our honeymoon destination a secret, I picked simple outfits to keep us comfy during our travels. For him I chose a red vee-neck cashmere sweater, black cashmere joggers, and Adidas sneakers. I opted for a red oversized cashmere cardigan with black leggings and Loewe sneakers. Our mothers dressed The Twins in elf onesies. We have to stay true to our Merry Christmas theme after all!

As for the rest of our trip, Roger assured me he arranged

for appropriate attire and belongings. Now that he revealed where we're going, I'm just bummed I didn't have a chance to buy new ski gear and sexy looks for après-ski.

"Leonie, I'm surprised you were on time to your wedding!"

Lola cracks up at her clever remark.

Sure, I'm just as famous for being perpetually late. But this time it's not my fault. Although I won't admit to why we're late. No need for the details, no matter how entertaining and juicy…

"Leave the newlyweds alone," Morgan says as he chuckles. "We added a buffer to the flight plan. So, we have plenty of time to spare."

Roger and I thank him and head for Rodolphe and Gaspard. Haley and Starr hold them playing with colorful rings on their laps. They're seated on the sofa near the center of the large jet.

"Hmmm interesting," Roger murmurs in my ear as he nods towards Starr.

I thought I was the only one amazed to see her on board. She and Malcolm must be coming out. They're worse than Roger and me!

"*Bonjour, mes beaux fils*," I coo, lifting Rodolphe from Starr. "And to you too, *mon amie*. Nice to see you spending Christmas with us."

My eyebrows waggle as I purse my lips.

Starr unsuccessfully attempts to hold in a laugh. Her dimples deepen as a flush reddens her chestnut complexion.

"Well, the more the merrier. Right, Malcolm?" Roger adds as he scoops Gaspard in his arms.

Malcolm who sits at the table across from the sofa huffs.

Roger and I take the fifth living area behind them. We settle The Twins in their car seats, one next to each of us at the dining table. Then, sit back and enjoy the luxury of a custom-built seventy-five-million-dollar aircraft.

The ultra-plush G700 easily accommodates both our families and staff. The spacious interior boasts the tallest, widest, and longest cabin of all private jets. Its size suits the Steele men and my father whose large frames range from six feet, one inches to six feet, four inches.

I stretch my own long legs in front of me with a sigh.

Roger reaches across the table to grasp my hand and smiles. With his left sleeve pushed up his forearm, the sunlight coming through the panoramic oval window makes the platinum of his wedding band and Cartier Love bracelet gleam.

The bracelet was one of my wedding gifts to him. There will be no mistaking Roger is mine, even if he removes his band to box. It's my Back-Off-Bs message to all those women who still eye him after we announced our engagement. He's not the only possessive one in our relationship...

Funny enough, Roger gave me the Love bracelet diamond-paved in platinum for similar reasons!

We stare at one another and smile as only couples who are in tune can communicate without even speaking. Smiles that say, we made it, my love.

"WE WENT on a huge shopping spree for you! Roger gave us his AMEX Centurion Card. He asked us to get everything you'll need for a fabulous winter honeymoon—ski gear, après-ski, clubbing, even bikinis! Moncler, Bogner, Fusalp, only the most upscale for his blushing bride. Plus an entire wardrobe to leave here. Girl! We went all out!"

Haley's breathless by the time she finishes rattling off the clothes she and Lola picked out for me.

"Yeah, and Shelley and Josy bought everything for The Twins, too!" Lola adds. "We didn't leave the Little Pumpkins out."

Haley, Lola, Starr, and I are in the primary bedroom of my new Verbier chalet. I named her *Chalet de la Joie* since the home will bring us such joy to spend family holidays here.

As soon as we arrived and walked into the great room with its magnificent Christmas tree, my mother declared we'd spend every Christmas and New Year's here. "One big happy family," Shelley clapped in agreement.

Roger glanced at me and raised his eyebrows questioningly.

With a whoop, I gave my consent. Why wouldn't I want to surround myself with loved ones and The Twins have beautiful memories of their times here?

I peppered his face with hundreds of kisses until he couldn't hold me up from laughing too hard.

He gave us the grand tour. My face hurt from grinning so hard. I'm giddy with glee!

Now my girls and I stand in my dressing room with a custom closet filled to the brim. Lingerie, party dresses, Moon Boot snow boots, sky-high heels, ski suits, jeans—for a clotheshorse like me, this is absolute heaven.

"*Merci! Merci!*" I exclaim clapping while Lola and I do our happy shimmy dance. "I love it all! *Fantastique!*"

The rest of our bunch migrated to different areas of the chalet. Roger took the guys to the garage to check out the new snow toys he ordered. Our parents chose babysitting duties, or as they say, "important bonding time with their grandsons." So Nanny Grace acclimated herself with her suite of rooms above the garage.

We'll meet back up for an early dinner at home with a

meal prepared by one of the chefs from STEELE Verbier. Roger left it to me to hire a permanent chef once I sampled a few dishes they'll make for us in the coming weeks. Yummy!

"How did your burlesque show go? I'm surprised Roger didn't lock you away in a tower for the rest of your life!" Haley quips.

Starr laughs and adds, "I know, right?! When Malcolm told me, I was like oh, boy..."

All heads spin to her. Realizing her mistake too late, Starr tries to backtrack. But we zoom in on her flub and demand answers on their relationship situation.

Too juicy for words!

Afterwards, the girls go to their suites, and I head to The Twins' suite through their dressing room passage connected to our primary bedroom. I find them fast asleep cuddled up in their cribs. I kiss my bundles of joy then chat with my parents and in-laws, still on duty in the nursery's anteroom.

My mobile beeps with a text message from Roger asking where I'm at in the massive house. Moments later, he strides into the room with his hair disheveled from the beanie and his olive-toned cheeks reddened by the icy mountain air. His dove gray eyes dance.

This is the most carefree I've seen him in a while. My heart swells with love for my husband.

He's had so much to deal with these past few months because of the pretrial that hussy caused. Then compounded by his concern for me having a healthy pregnancy with my mother's experience of multiple miscarriages scaring both of us. I say a silent prayer of thanks we made it over all hurdles.

"Hey, babe. How're my sons?" Roger asks as he bends

over to kiss my lips. "Did you like your things? Are you all settled?"

I don't want him to get ramped up. So, I grab the sides of his face and pull him back to me for a full kiss to stop his rapid-fire questioning.

Roger sighs and opens up to my prodding tongue. I continue until he groans softly.

"All is good, *Mon Cœur*," I breathe against his full lips. "All is good."

* * *

"Ha! Can't keep up, slowpoke?"

Roger shouts as he schusses past me on the black diamond piste, his Rossignol skis silent on the fresh powder.

The sunlight makes him shimmer as he zooms by in a black iridescent-effect Moncler Grenoble jacket with his eyes covered by orange Anon googles and matching helmet. Roger's long, muscular legs covered by black salopettes help him carve through the snow. He moves with ease and grace down the expert slope.

It's Christmas Eve morning and we're out en masse for an early morning run. The entire Steele clan and Beaulieus make our way from the top of the mountain piste to the base lodge. It's a popular time to come out, so other skiers bob and weave around us.

I've skied my entire life, so I catch up to Roger quickly.

He turns his head briefly to grin at me and blow a kiss before he zips ahead, his laughter trailing behind him.

"Last one down!" Malcolm yells as he, too, races towards the finish.

Another fine male specimen in his white and green

Bogner ski suit. He bobs his head covered by a green helmet and mirrored googles over his eyes.

I laugh and tuck to bullet my way down the piste. My movements unrestricted by my new Bogner neon green stretch-ponte ski suit.

My outfit makes me feel like a racer, with black and white stripes on the upper arms and white strips along the outside of the legs. But the white KASK helmet with its silver eyes shield reminds me of an astronaut. Either way, I'm fast and overtake the others.

"That was incredible!" Starr exclaims when she reaches me.

One by one, everyone arrives. Our ski butlers help us remove our equipment and hand us our heated après-ski hats, sunglasses, and footwear.

Starr loops arms with me, and we follow the group inside for a hearty breakfast on the deck kept warm by heat lamps. As we walk through the great room of the lodge, I wave at friends who happen to be on holiday in Verbier, too. It's a popular destination for the low-key of the chichi crowd.

I stop to chat with a photographer I've worked with for years while Starr continues on. I don't realize how long I've been until a hand on my lower back and the press of a large body against mine draws my attention.

"Pardon. My wife's family requests her presence for breakfast," Roger says gruffly.

I make the introductions, and he leads me away to the deck, satisfied the photographer wasn't making a move on me. I tease Roger, and he zerbets my cheek.

"So sorry to keep everyone waiting! Let's eat!" I say when we arrive at the table laden with delicious food and steaming beverages.

"So what's the plan for the rest of the day?" Harris asks as he piles his plate high with eggs, bacon, sausages, and toast.

We turn to Roger and he claps his hands like a group excursions guide. The thought of *National Lampoon's European Vacation* comes to mind. Just don't let private, sexy videos of Roger and me get out, I giggle to myself!

"Yes, my darling wife, we will have loads of fun! We'll go for another run, then return to the chalet. Shower and change to stroll through the village with The Twins. Take in the sights and do gift buying for those who are always last minute..."

Roger raises an eyebrow at Harris, who shrugs.

"That may be true. However, I always have the best presents. This year, you'll get coal in your stocking if you keep it up, big bro," he retorts as he takes another giant bite of his food.

Everyone laughs and digs in.

"It's just so beautiful here! Usually, we go to Courchevel in France or Gstaad in Switzerland. What made STEELE open a ski resort here instead of somewhere else?" I ask Roger as we meander through Verbier Village.

He peers into the clear pane of the double stroller to check The Twins who ah-goo at the sights and sounds of the town's bustling Christmas market.

The cloves and spices of mulled wine mix with baked goods like bredele, semi-sweet cakes, pretzels, and macarons to scent the crisp air. Carolers dressed in costumes stroll through the aisles singing cheerfully and ringing bells. Vendors fill their stalls with handcrafted music boxes and toys, knit sweaters, scarves, and gloves, and candles and ornaments.

The festive atmosphere fills me with such joy!

"We have a resort in Gstaad. But wanted another one in a less congested location and less trafficked by tourists. Verbier has been popular with the jet set since the fifties but remains low-key with only those in the know spending time here. It also has the best off-piste trails, so more expert skiers choose Verbier. The après-ski partying is just as attractive as the slopes."

I grin up at Roger as I squeeze his arm.

"What?" He asks.

"You're just so passionate about STEELE," I respond.

He bends down to whisper in my ear, "Not as passionate as I am about getting you on the faux-fur blanket in front of our fireplace and making you beg to cum. It's the only spot we haven't christened in our bedroom."

My pussy clenches at the thought of Roger pounding into me from behind as our sweaty bodies bond in front of a roaring fire. Or me on my knees while he fucks my face; my nipples pebble and my juices drip between my thighs as sweat drips down my spine from the heat of the fire at my back.

Merde! I'm ready to go back home now...

Roger must sense my desire as he chuckles.

"But you will have to wait, Pretty Kitty, until our babies get their fill of the Christmas market," he says.

I pout and sigh dramatically.

"Oh, I will make it worth your wait. Don't you worry your pretty little head about it," Roger adds with a smirk, then kisses my lips.

"Get a room already!"

We glance up to see Sebastian and Lola striding towards

us. Baz's hands filled with shopping bags brimming with presents. Lola beams at us, then squats in front of the stroller.

"Ciao, Little Pumpkins. How are you enjoying the Christmas market?" She asks The Twins in fluent French. "I know! It's something else... If you're good, Santa Claus will have lots of gifts for you!"

Roger gives Sebastian a look to say it won't be much longer. Baz grins and nods in agreement. Lola oblivious to their exchange finishes her conversation.

I smile knowingly. Yeah, my BFF's mind is changing definitely.

"Where's everyone else?"

Malcolm and Starr appear with him similarly laden with bags. Starr replaces Lola as she chats with Rodolphe and Gaspard.

Roger and Sebastian laugh out loud.

"To keep with French tradition, we'll open two presents each on Christmas Eve and the rest tomorrow," my father announces as he stands in front of the beautifully decorated eighteen-foot tree.

It even dwarfs him, and his brawny frame stands at six feet, four inches, still physically fit for a man in his sixties. He's studied jujutsu for decades and maintains a healthy lifestyle.

After returning from the market, we added our new gifts to the already vast number beneath and around the tree's base. The colorful boxes of all shapes and sizes fill the space.

We're gathered in the great room with a blazing fire in the sizable stone hearth. Mariah Carey's "All I Want for Christmas Is You" plays in the background from my favorite

Christmas playlist. The classic songs of Nat King Cole, Johnny Mathis, Céline Dion, Gladys Knight and the Pips, Frank Sinatra, and of course the Trans-Siberian Orchestra never get old.

The chef prepared steaming mugs of delicious hot chocolate and mulled wine for us to enjoy with the tasty morsels we bought. I asked her to make Roger's favorite Christmas treat—gingerbread cake with butter rum toffee sauce and fresh whipped cream.

When he saw it, he whispered how he intended to drizzle the warm, sticky sauce over my naked body and lick each delectable inch clean slowly. Then fill my pussy to the brim with the cream and eat it out.

Merde... I started to ooze my own cream right then and there.

Harris jumps up and rubs his hands together.

"Excellent idea, *Papa* Guy! I'll start with a gift for you," he says with a wide grin. "We give the best gifts first, you know!"

We spend the next hour exchanging presents and enjoying the goodies. I saved the painting I made of Roger for our return. I had it hung in our bedroom for our eyes only.

Instead, with Roger being an aficionado and collector of fine watches, I give him the Assouline coffee-table book on Rolex and a watch. The hand-bound tome in a handsome presentation case offers a selection of the watchmaker's most exceptional timepieces in its history. He'll find it to be an interesting read.

Sebastian—another avid collector—told me about the rare Cosmograph Daytona Paul Newman "John Player Special" in eighteen-carat yellow gold going to auction. Its stunning black and gold livery makes it distinctive and eye-catching, just like my man. My bid of $1.54 million won. Without a doubt, I had to swoop it up for him!

"Leonie, babe, this is incredible... There are only ten known pieces in the world... *Merci, Mon Amour*," Roger says awestruck.

"The way you're ogling that watch makes me jealous!" I tease, laughing. "Should I worry, *Mon Cœur?*"

He smirks and says, "Well, she is an exquisite golden and black beauty, Caramel Bonbon..."

I giggle and swat his hands away as he reaches for my waist.

Undeterred Roger plucks me from the sofa and spins me around as he kisses me silly.

"Rest assured, no one and nothing compares to you, Mrs. Roger Steele."

I giggle and respond, "You had me worried for a minute there, Monsieur Steele!"

"Never," Roger replies gruffly. "Forever you."

Wolf whistles and applause fill the room. Even The Twins ah-goo from our mothers' laps.

Roger puts me on my feet, and we bow and curtsey to the enthusiastic crowd.

The chef announces dinner, and we troop to the dining room. She prepared another award-winning menu waitstaff from one of the STEELE Verbier restaurants serve.

In keeping with the French tradition of le *Réveillon de Noël* for the Christmas meal, the dishes include Beluga caviar, foie gras, oysters, lobster, scallops, fresh truffles, roast goose, venison, and cheeses. We end with the paramount French Christmas dessert *la bûche de Noël*—the Yule log. All the while, a selection of wines and champagne please our palates.

We move to the cinema room to watch *It's a Wonderful*

Life, Roger's favorite Christmas movie and a Steele clan tradition to watch it the night before. I adore the ringing of the bells and always add a new one to my tree every year.

Roger and I take a detour to feed Rodolphe and Gaspard in one of the nearby rooms. My new uniform of a comfy cardigan keeps it simple for me to feed The Twins. Roger also enjoys the easy access when he wants a little taste.

Once Roger helps me to get situated, he sits on the chair opposite with his elbows on his knees and his hands clasped in front of him. He shakes his head and smiles, then lifts his luminous gray eyes to me.

"What?" I ask as I shift Gaspard slightly. He gurgles, and I smile at him while I stroke his chubby cheek.

When Roger doesn't respond, I glance over at him and ask again with my eyebrow arched questioningly.

"When I heard the melodic sound of your laughter, then saw your naked boobs two-and-a-half years ago, I never would have thought I'd see my sons feeding from them," he responds, shaking his head. "Damn, Leonie, can you believe how far we've come? It's amazing truly, babe."

I ponder his words, then shake my head, too. He's right. It hasn't been so long a period. Yet here we are, parents and married. Our blended families—my parents, Lola, the Steeles—enjoying time together during the holidays. It is amazing.

Never would I have imagined a meeting would end in marriages for my best friend and me. Particularly to brothers!

"I agree. And I'm so very thankful for it all"—I stare into his eyes intently—"How about you? Are you happy, *Mon Cœur*? Truly?"

Rodolphe chimes in with a loud laugh and waves his arms. His brother picks up on the sound and joins in.

Roger and I look at each other and crack up until tears roll down our reddened cheeks. I try to catch my breath, but with two babies it proves a challenge. He helps me by lifting Gaspard into his arms as he chuckles some more.

"Well, my sons took the words right out of my mouth!" Roger starts as he bends over to kiss me, "My love, I am beyond happy truly!"

My heart swells with joy.

LEONIE

"ey. What are you doing up so early?"

Lola glances at me over her shoulder. She's curled up on a settee in the windowed walkway that connects the chef's kitchen and butler's pantry with a cluster of rooms. An oversized cashmere throw bundled around her, engulfs her petite body.

The sad expression on her face makes me pause.

"What's wrong?!" I ask urgently as I sit beside her hurriedly. "Why are you out here and not upstairs with Sebastian? Did something happen?"

My mind races with possibilities: she and Sebastian argued; she misses her parents, who died in a horrific car accident when she was a teenager; something happened with Lola's Coterie. The most important things in her life jump to the forefront of my guesses.

She sighs and wipes a hand over her heart-shaped face. With a smile, she shakes her head. The glossy raven tresses move about her head. "Sebastian and I—"

"I'll kick his ass! I don't care if he's Roger's brother! What did he do to you?!" I demand thinking how I warned him not to hurt my BFF when they first started dating.

Lola giggles and holds up her hands to stop me.

"No. It's not what you guess," she says. "He wants to have a baby for a while now. At first he only hinted at it, later mentioned it outright. Now, being around The Twins and seeing how happy you and Roger are and how you're making the family thing work, Baz brought it up again last night. I couldn't fall sleep. I stayed up thinking long after he fell asleep. So I came down here for some chamomile tea."

She twirls a strand of hair around her fingers. Her gaze goes back out the floor-to-ceiling windows and to the beauty of the snow-covered Swiss Alps beyond. Puffs of snow fall from a leaden sky.

It's Christmas morning and a picturesque wintry day. My best friend should enjoy a cuddle with her hubby instead of sitting down here all alone. I wait for her to continue.

Moments later, Lola shifts on the settee to face me.

"I do want children, and I know we can make it work, too," she starts. Again she looks away. "But I'm scared about them losing one of us like I lost my parents at seventeen. It's really so hard…"

Lola's voice cracks and tears fill her hazel eyes as her lower lip trembles.

I scoot closer and pull her into an embrace. The maternal instincts in me make my rock Lola and hum softly as I rub her back soothingly. I cannot imagine how she felt that night when the police came to her family's apartment on Manhattan's Upper East Side. Only a few hours before, she'd wished her parents a good time at dinner with their out-of-town friends.

Merde.

Lola gives me a squeeze before she sits up, drying her eyes with the back of her hand. She takes a deep cleansing breath like Starr taught us. On the exhale, Lola nods as though coming to a decision.

Again, I wait for her to speak, knowing my friend so well and how she likes to think things through uninterrupted.

"I can't not live because of a what may happen. I want what you and Roger have just as much as Sebastian. Hell, probably even more"—she chuckles and clasps my hands in hers—"What do you think? Am I being silly?"

I squeeze her hands and shake my head.

"Absolutely not! You had a traumatic experience that's not so easily overcome. Luc and I helped you and being around my parents did, too. But it still had to be hard"—I squeeze her hands again and continue—"But now, you have a man who loves you madly and an even bigger family with the entire Steele clan. You have the support of many loved ones. 'Live. Live. Live' as Auntie Mame says!"

Lola giggles at my reference to one of my favorite movies about the eccentric, carefree socialite who let nothing or anyone make her change course—much like me.

"There you are!"

"We've been looking all over for the two of you!"

Roger and Sebastian stride down the hallway, their long legs make quick work of the distance between us. Baz cocks his head to the side and narrows his eyes when he notices Lola's tear-stained face.

"What's wrong, baby? What happened? Are you sick?" He asks rapidly as he rushes to kneel before her.

I study his stricken face and determine he's more than the right partner for Lola as he's proven over the years. His love for her is limitless. I pat his shoulder and squeeze it. He glances at me, puzzled.

"Take her upstairs. Despite how nice it is for us to have some BFF alone time, I'm positive Lola would rather be with you than in this walkway with me," I say grinning.

Baz nods and scoops Lola in a bride-like hold. She wraps her arms around his neck as she nuzzles against him. Roger claps him on the back as they pass.

Once they're out of earshot, he turns to me and asks, "What happened?"

I pat the settee next to me and cover us with the throw. As I lean my head on his broad shoulder and he puts his arm around me, I recount Lola's concern and my response.

Roger agrees they're ready. Suddenly he laughs at how he bested his eldest brother for once.

He pulls me tighter to his side and lifts me onto his lap as we watch the snow continue to blanket the surrounding landscape. It's so beautiful and evokes a sense of calm.

Moments later, the sun breaks through the overcast gray and turns the sky fiery with shades of orange, gold, and blue. The clouds disperse for a glorious Christmas Day.

"How are you feeling now?" I whisper to Lola.

We, along with Haley and Starr, finished a few runs and kick back on chaises at the base lodge deck sipping hot cocoa.

Roger and his brothers went off-piste on Chassoure, as the locals call it, or Tortin to everyone else. It's one of the most challenging runs in Verbier and well-known in the ski world. The terrain and the level of difficulty concerned me. But he assured me they would take precautions with a trail guide, and each of them set with high-tech tracking devices and satellite phones.

In fact, all of us wear the gadgets and carry the mobiles whenever we're on the mountain slopes.

Still, I told Roger I'm not looking to become a widowed, single mother!

He promised me they'd be perfectly safe and would meet us back at the chalet later. After a scorching, knee-jellifying kiss, he slapped me on the ass and marched out the door. The carnal caveman...

But damn if my pussy didn't clench and heat permeate my core as my nipples hardened to points. Yeah, I can't wait for my virile Alpha male to get back home.

Our parents met up with friends who happened to be on holiday here, too. While The Twins stay with Nanny Grace.

All of which left time for a much-needed Girls' Day Out of good friends, laughter, and plain ole silliness!

Now a humongous smile breaks out on Lola's face, and her eyes glitter more than the sun-kissed snow. She claps and shimmies before she shares their conversation. When she tells me Sebastian's reaction, I cover my ears and sing loudly. TMI!

"What's going on?" Starr leans forward from her chaise to ask.

Lola hesitates for only a moment. Smiling, she launches into the details once again. Afterwards, she stares pointedly at Starr and Haley.

"So, who's next? Hmmm? Lachlan... Malcolm... Do not consider for one second we haven't noticed signs and sexual tension between you guys!" Lola says, waggling her perfectly shaped eyebrows. "Don't even try to deny it."

"Yeah! Sparks were zipping amongst you at my wedding

from the rehearsal dinner through the reception," I add, daring them to dispute the obvious.

Shy Haley flushes crimson while always-remain-balanced Starr gets flustered.

Lola and I rag on them some more, but all in good fun. We make a bet on who will come back next Christmas with whom. Included in the lineup are Luc and Blair and Billie and Patrick Rockett—her Scottish billionaire boyfriend and the CEO of STEELE International, Inc.'s biggest competitor Rockett Construction Company. Both couples showed their affection for one another openly during my nuptials.

"Well, Starr's already in this year and Malcolm is not one to bring women around at all," Lola says. "In over two years, I've never seen him with anyone seriously. But you had him disconcerted the morning after my wedding."

I agree with Lola in over the year Roger and I have been back together, I've only seen him occasionally with a sub at LEVELS New York or Paris. However, I don't mention that part to Starr. It's not as though they were dating at the time or even together as far as Roger and I can figure out. Both of them have been pretty mum about their situations.

"I know. But I'm not sure if I'm ready to get involved with anyone, and I've been putting him off for quite some time now," Starr admits. With a sigh, she tells us more.

We offer her words of advice and encouragement.

She's fast become a part of our inner circle since Lola met her at Starr's first international fitness retreat on Fijian Laucala Island. As the founder of Starr Light Fitness & Wellness Beverly Hills, she wanted to extend her yoga and meditation classes beyond Cali.

Lola raved about her experience and how cool Starr is as an instructor and friend. Later, she introduced her to Malcolm as he's the president of STEELE's Entertainment

Properties Division, Malcolm oversees their casinos, hotels, and resorts. A partnership with STEELE gave her the access she wanted.

However, Malcolm wants more access, too...

"And you, miss?" I ask.

"Right... What's your story, morning glory?" Lola chimes in as we turn to Haley.

Normally she would push her glasses up her nose, but she's taken to wearing contact lenses recently. She says it's better for her peripheral vision. So instead, she pushes her mirrored Ray-Ban Aviators to rest better on the bridge. I think it's more of a nervous tell.

I also know not one of Haley's big brothers would appreciate Lachlan getting involved with their baby sister. Particularly Sebastian since he and Lachlan are best friends and Baz knows he's an Alpha Dom. Roger told me the idea of his little sister being a sub to Lachlan makes him want to knock him out.

Even though they refer to the Jackson siblings as their cousins, there's no blood relationship—only their mothers being BFFs for decades. So technically, the boys should stay out of it—if an it exists truly.

Lola and I think they'd make a cute couple—shy, curvy Haley and movie-star-looks, dominating Lachlan.

Roger and Baz would have conniptions if they even though Lola and I had a smidgen of interest in their cousin. I laugh out loud at the thought. Lachlan is as sexy as them, but Roger is it for me!

"What's so funny, Leonie?" Haley asks self-consciously.

I wave my hand and respond, "Thinking about your overbearing brothers. Better you than me!"

Haley shakes her head and purses her lips. She fills us in on her latest escapades with Cary Grant lookalike Lachlan.

"Speak of the devils... Look who shows up now. I thought they were meeting us at the chalet," Lola says, nodding towards the entrance.

As Haley finishes, and we were ready to dive deep with an analysis and strategic plan, the boys walk out onto the deck.

Every woman's head turns to gawk at them—young and old alike. I growl, feeling more possessive than my caveman. Back off, I want to snarl. Mine!

Yet, who can blame them?

As soon as Roger spots us, he smiles brightly and leads them our way. From his broad shoulders to his tapered waist and powerful thighs, he's the epitome of masculine beauty. He takes his Moncler Grenoble black skull cap off and runs his long fingers through his thick, collar-length ebony hair. His usually clean-shaven face covered by stubble he says keeps his cheeks and cleft chin warm while he skis.

To me, it adds to his sensuality. Mmmmmm.

Sebastian, Malcolm, and Harris don't differ from him at all. Baz and Malcolm could easily pass for twins being of the same stature and looks. Harris, who may be the shortest at six feet, one inch, is still cut from the same ultramasculine cloth as his elder brothers.

They're like a pack of Alpha males whose high testosterone levels call to every women's womb with an aching need to be pounded and filled by them. Funny enough, even some men glance their way in awe of their commanding presence.

The STEELE Quaternity live and in full effect.

In pairs, shoulder-to-shoulder, the boys glance neither left nor right as they stride past several tables and chaises to reach us.

All of us but Haley salivate at the sight of them. She

groans and throws her head back against her chaise in annoyance at the interruption of her relationship advice session.

"Give me a fucking break already," she mutters.

Yup, and there goes our Girls' Day Out!

ROGER

"*F*uck me, bro! How the hell are you sitting here all relaxed sipping Scotch while your sexy AF, new bride shakes her thing in a swishy mini dress on that center pedestal?"

Harris' disbelief at my outwardly stoic behavior makes me laugh.

In actuality an inferno burns within me, licking along my spine to my fill balls. A smirk curves my lips as I take another sip of the Jackson Reserve Scotch the fire in its bite matches the fire in my loins. Yeah, I appear at ease. However, I'm enjoying the show Leonie is putting on more than Harris can ever imagine.

We're at Farm Club Verbier, the dance and nightclub famous since the early 70s. It's maintained its popularity for decades, symbolized by its glamorous vibe and great reputation. It's like the Studio 54 of Verbier—if the walls could talk...

And with the way Leonie is doing her signature shimmy —laughing with her arms thrown overhead, wriggling her curvy body while her hips sway to the beat—everyone is talking. The 20s flapper-style mini dress hugs her in all the right places as it rises to the tops of her toned thighs. Layers of white swishy beaded and sequined fringing atop white sheer chiffon glimmer on the dance floor.

The catch is Leonie wears my engagement ring, wedding band, and hand harness. The sizable jewels sparkle more than her dress. No one can miss she's taken. And by a man with the means to give her the world on a platinum platter.

So nah, I'm not worried in the least. Hence my relaxed stance as I partake of a fine Scotch.

"Leonie is dancing for me, little brother," I answer to put his mind at ease. "Watch closely."

No sooner do the words slip off my tongue than Leonie lifts her heated feline gaze to where I stand by our booth in the VIP section. When our gazes connect, a curl touches the corners of her full lips as she inclines her head slightly. Seconds later, she spins to put her back to me and jiggles her round ass. The plunging, glittery vee cut of the dress acts as a flashing pointer to the bullseye.

I accept the invitation, and with a nod to Harris, I go to claim my mate. Now everyone will see the man to whom she belongs. I lick my lips in anticipation of her lush curves against my hardness as my cock thickens and lengthens along my thigh inside of the black leather pants.

Harris' hearty chuckle follows me out onto the dance floor.

As I make my way through the throng of partiers, a small hand on my forearm slows me.

"Hi handsome," a buxom redhead murmurs in my ear. "Dance with me."

She presses her surgically enhanced tits against my side as she grinds her pelvis into my hip.

Uh, no.

As I shake my head and lift my left hand to show my wedding band, I extricate myself from her clutches. Just in time because over her head, I get a glimpse of *The Lion* stalking towards us. The dancers part like gazelles darting from the African Savanna's apex predator.

The expression on Leonie's face is deadly, more so than her namesake.

Oh shit.

Unfortunately, the redhead doesn't take the hint or chooses to ignore my ring because she loops her arms around my neck. She melds her body to my front.

"Wow! Oh my... Is that big ole thing all for little ole me?" She coos, gyrating her narrow hips.

Without delay, I pull back and grip her arms to unyoke myself. Leonie finishes the removal by grasping the woman by the waist and moving her aside.

I swear I can pick up a growl come from Leonie, but the sound of the music makes it hard to determine it clearly. However, she glares at the redhead with such ferocity the unlucky woman hastens away quickly, peeping over her shoulder to check she's not being chased by *The Lion*.

Leonie watches the redhead until she blends in with the dancers. Then she tosses her glossy mane and rounds on me with an arched eyebrow and pursed lips.

My cock twitches at her possessiveness.

I grip Leonie's hips and crush her against me as I bend my knees to grind my engorged dick up against her clit.

The momentum forces Leonie's hands around my neck to maintain her balance in the five-inch fuck-me heels. Her pillowy tits press against my pecs; the pointed nipples poke through my thin cotton shirt.

We're eye to eye and chest to chest, connected intimately

at our pelvises. I want Leonie to know just how much I want her and only her. No one else will ever do for me again.

Her nostrils flare as she scents the pheromones emanating from her mate. Slowly she traces the tip of her little pink tongue across her upper lip, then sucks her plump lower lip into her mouth.

I lose it and capture Leonie's mouth with mine.

Immediately her lips part, and my tongue surges inside to tangle with hers. I suck and nip at it until she whimpers and grips my shoulders to remain upright on wobbly legs. The savage kiss leaves her breathless as I plant open-mouthed kisses on the column of her slim neck.

She tilts her head to the side to give me better access.

Once I reach the sensitive juncture of Leonie's neck and shoulder, I suck a bit of the flesh into my mouth. Not until I'm satisfied my mark remains, I worry the skin.

Leonie cries out softly and squirms in my passionate embrace. My cock jumps from the pressure. She feels it and moans with her head thrown back. Her ample tits push towards my face.

I ache to bury my face between them and ram my swollen cock into her tight pussy. But settle with lifting her leg up to drape around my hip. With a tilt to my pelvis, I angle my bulge against her pussy lips through her thong when the hem of her mini dress rises higher.

We groan at the erotic contact and grind against one another steadily. When Leonie moans and shudders in my arms, I know she's reached her climax.

My mouth leaves her neck and I slant it over hers. My hips continue to move, but then still when Leonie slips her hand between us and unzips my fly. When I try to pull back, she winds her leg around the back of my thigh, locking me in place. A slight shift, and I'm balls deep inside of her warm, wet pussy.

Fuck. Me. Now.

With the lights dim and caught in the press of the party-goers, no one notices I'm fucking Leonie in the middle of the dance floor. I pound up into her repeatedly as both hands grip her firm ass, my fingers dig into her flesh beneath her mini dress. More marks for my mate.

The pressure mounts and my spine tingles with a frisson of electricity. A few more thrusts, and I jam my dick farther up her pussy, striking her cervix. My body stiffens and my thighs quiver as my release runs through my body from my heavy balls, through my dick, and out the bulbous tip.

Leonie's pussy walls flutter up and down my shaft, milking every drop of my cum deep into her womb. I cover her mouth with mine to muffle our cries of ecstasy as our bodies continue to pulse.

As I withdraw, my seed spills down the insides of her thighs. I collect some of it on my fingers and bring them to her mouth.

With a wanton gaze, she parts her lips for me to place my coated digits on her tongue. Purring contentedly, she laps them clean. I continue to swab her thighs with my fingers, and she licks them anew until not a bit remains.

Leonie lowers her cheek onto my shoulder as we sway to the seductive, throbbing beat of our racing hearts. The rhythm proves better than any music ever played.

And here's to another carnal story for the walls of Farm Club Verbier: Roger Steele took his new bride Leonie Steele higher than the Matterhorn in an explosion of fiery passion.

* * *

"Dude, you need to open a LEVELS Verbier. Ski in, ski out style! A little action on the slopes and in the playrooms."

Harris says as we take shots of Oval Vodka at Public Verbier, the swanky spot and counterpart to Public London.

We hit all the hot spots leading up to New Year's Eve since we'll celebrate it at the chalet.

Leonie prefers to ring in the New Year as she would like the rest of the year to be—good times with family and friends at home for dinner and a party. It's a tradition for her and the Beaulieus. She gave me Christmas, so she can have her way.

Damn, look at me, a considerate hubby.

"You know, that's not a bad idea," Sebastian adds, slamming his glass down with a smile next to the Swarovski crystal bottle of vodka. "Of all the clubs we've partied at, none can compare to LEVELS. Bring the heat to the Alps!"

"Yeah, spoken like a true Alpha Dom," I chuckle.

Baz's laughter rings out.

He's been in an exceptional mood since we found Leonie and Lola in the walkway the other morning. I imagine getting his way adds to his happiness.

Good for them! I'm in favor of a family. Especially with a certified banger wife like Leonie. And Lola is no exception, the sexy petite firecracker.

"I can see that being a profitable possibility. Surprising how a tech geek can think beyond code," Malcolm ribs Harris good-naturedly.

He and Haley founded the subsidiary STEELE Technology and Cyber Security and jointly run it as co-heads. We tease the Dynamic Duo often for being nerds. But they're smart as hell and keep STEELE, other businesses, and high-net worth individuals up to date with their systems and well protected.

Yet, he's still an Alpha male, who like the rest of his brothers seeks release within the LEVELS clubs. Haley, not so much. We'll be damned if some schmo ties our baby sister to a St. Andrew's Cross and canes her ass.

Malcolm continues thoughtfully, "We can take over one property near the hotel and close by the other clubs for accessibility. I'll run it by Lucien tomorrow, thanks."

They fist bump, and we down another round of shots.

Our server appears with an assortment of finger foods including Russian pancakes with Beluga caviar, marinated mushrooms, and cheddar olives. The leggy blonde bends over the table to reach for Malcolm's plate, nearly spilling her ample tits out her top.

He ignores her and carries on his conversation with Baz.

She lingers to throw a meaningful glance Harris' way, and he winks at her with a smirk. Taking his response as an invitation, she sidles up next to him to ask if he needs anything else.

A sly smile crosses his face, and he beckons her close. As he whispers in her ear, a crimson flush spreads across from the tops of her breasts to her cheeks. When she stands, she bites her lower lip and nods before she walks away. The exaggerated sway of her hips makes her skirt flutter around her thighs.

"Obviously you're doing all right without the play-rooms," I tell him, smirking.

Harris sits back and plants his feet wide on the floor, spreading his arms along the back of the booth.

With a smug expression he responds, "You could say so. I'll have some not so little action tonight."

Malcolm lifts his shot glass in a toast, "Here's to ski in and ski out, my brothers!"

"Hear, hear!"

"Abso-fucking-lutely!"

"You can say that again, bro!"

We raise our glasses and toss back the vodka shots.

Hands slide up my back, and slender arms wrap around me, pulling me into an embrace. The sultry scent of Dior's Pure Poison wafts in the air.

Leonie.

"Oh *Amoureux*, come dance with me," she purrs seductively in my ear.

I grin at our new code phrase for fucking. My cock pulsates knowing I'll be balls deep within her always ready for me pussy. I turn to my brothers and bid them a good night.

Time for my action to start.

LEONIE

*W*hat a way to end the year with my legs thrown over Roger's broad shoulders and his head between my trembling thighs. He laps from my back hole past my pussy lips to my sensitive clit.

"Aaaahhh… Fuck… ah…"

A gasp falls from my slack mouth when Roger nips my nubbin. He worries the distended tip with his teeth and the flat of his tongue to draw another toe-curling climax from the depths of my being.

I arc off the bed, screaming his name, clamping my legs against the sides of his tousled ebony head. My hands push and pull at the long strands, undecided to accept the pleasure or the pain.

It's been hours of lovemaking with only moments of rest between bouts.

Roger insists upon completing a marathon representing each month we've been back together before midnight New Year's Day. Every opportunity he gets, he seeks to achieve his goal. With a total of seventeen months, that's a hell of a of fucking in a few days...

The sex-driven man chuckles darkly against my pussy lips as he kisses them. After he readjusts his grip on my ass, Roger spreads me wider and presses my body back onto the tangled sheets.

Now my most private places are super-exposed to his onslaught. I try to squirm, but to no avail.

"No getting away from me this morning, Pretty Kitty," he hums against my seam. "I will have my fill of my succulent, pink pussy."

The vibrations roll through my core; my wrecked pussy weeps.

"*Merde... Tu te sens si bien, Amoureux... Aaahhh... S'il te pla" t...*" I wail as my inner walls clench then spasm with another massive orgasm. No longer able to think clearly, I lapse into my native tongue to tell my lover how good he feels and to plead for relief.

Roger responds to me in fluent French to deny my request and continues his ministrations.

His molten-platinum eyes stare intently as I writhe and shake my head from side to side. His tongue flicks lazily over my swollen clit.

Unable to look away from him, I watch helplessly as Roger settles deeper between my legs. His wide shoulders push my achy thighs further apart.

"Give me one more, Pretty Kitty," he growls before he spears me with his tongue.

Rapid strokes to my G-spot send me over the edge once again. I yowl as another wave of pleasure swallows me.

"Good girl," Roger croons as he slides over my sweat-soaked body, trailing open-mouthed kisses on the heated flesh.

I shiver and mumble incoherently, too spent for any other response.

However, my mind snaps to when Roger's plunges his ginormous dick past my soaked folds to plunder my dripping pussy.

Each powerful thrust rocks the bed and shifts me upwards

"Hold on to the headboard," he growls. "And keep your knees separated, thighs on the bed."

Straightening out over the length of me, Roger widens his legs and rises to his toes with his hands on either side of my head.

Locked in place, I can only take the force of the impact. My breasts bounce with each powerful thrust. The intense pleasure like nothing I've ever known. I cry out repeatedly and beg for more, harder, deeper.

Roger with precision focus gives me exactly what I crave. His grunts and groans as savage as his brutal pummeling.

"Whose is it? Who do you belong to?" He demands.

My pussy contracts around his thick length in response to his caveman possessiveness. I mewl and toss my head, tilting my hips to take him deeper.

"FUUUCK!" Roger roars. "MINE… MINE… MINE!"

He slams home each word battering my wet heat, triggering another orgasm for me as I follow his.

"ROGEEERRR!" I keen.

"Say it!" He rumbles in my ear, the weight of his much larger body pressing me into the mattress as we remain tied in our erotic embrace.

"*Tout à toi, Mon Amour…*" I murmur, twining our limbs before bliss envelops me.

* * *

"Good thing each of the bedrooms are soundproof," Roger says, smirking. "Or else everyone would know how well I pleasure you, Pretty Kitty."

I awake in a state of sheer euphoria. Languidly, I stretch my sore limbs as I blink at my demanding lover.

Roger kisses the peaks of my nipples, then leans on his elbow. He traces patterns on my skin while he stares back at me.

"How very true, and I thank you for your inimitable foresight," I reply cheekily, my voice low and throaty from screams of ecstasy.

I hiss when Roger pinches my nipples. He arches his eyebrow and cocks his head in response.

Merde.

When I refuse to give in, he straddles me and tickles me nonstop.

Laughter bubbles up, then snorts as I squirm to keep the upper hand. I toss my head to deny him again and again.

My Alpha male has none of it. Roger ups the ante with zerbets wherever his lips reach.

The combination proves too much, and my resistance crumbles. Hands raised up; I call a truce. But a truce is not enough. Roger wants it all as he does with our lovemaking. Relentlessly he tickles me until I give in fully.

"Fine! Fine! I apologize for being snarky!" I shout breathlessly.

Roger nuzzles my neck and rolls onto his back, pulling me along with him. He rubs my flanks to soothe me as my body calms.

"Bully," I mutter against his muscular chest, only to get swatted on my ass.

Roger laughs as I yelp.

"*BONJOUR, MES BEAUX FILS*," I coo as I walk into their nursery through their dressing room passage.

Nanny Grace lifts her head from dressing Rodolphe to glance my way and smiles brightly.

"*Bonjour*, Madame Steele," she greets me.

"*Bonjour* to you, too! It's a glorious day, *non?*"

We chat for a bit as we get The Twins ready.

Roger wants to go to the village for breakfast at one of the quaint restaurants. Followed by a stroll while we shop. He wants some family time with only the four of us before the year ends.

A knock on the door calls my attention from bundling Gaspard in his navy blue Moncler snowsuit. I pop the hood on his head as I call for the person to come in.

"Bonjour! How are my darling nephews?" Haley asks.

She swoops Rodolphe from Nanny Grace and cuddles him to her chest. Then she strides over to me and kisses Gaspard on his chubby cheek, the only part not covered.

"Where are you going?" Haley asks as she bounces Rodolphe, who laughs. "Bouncy, bouncy, baby!"

Everyone's enthralled by The Twins, I laugh to myself.

"Into the village for some family time."

Roger's booming voice makes us turn around. He greets Nanny Grace and takes Rodolphe from Haley.

A disheartened expression crosses her lovely face. She nods and heads for the door.

I glance at Roger. He rolls his eyes, but shrugs, albeit reluctantly.

"Hey! Why don't you come with us? We can have breakfast and see what's going on," I ask Haley.

She declines. But I know it's only because she doesn't want to intrude.

No such thing. We're family and families make time for one another. Besides, she and Harris are the only ones unattached. Well... Harris had some dalliances. But those don't count.

In the end, we climb into one of the Mercedes-Benz G-Wagen and head to Place Centrale. We drop the SUV with the STEELE Verbier valet, then walk along the main street checking out the options.

The delicious scent of cinnamon and nutmeg escapes the warm confines of a restaurant as a couple with a toddler exit. They smile at us, and the husband holds the door. We thank him and ask if the restaurant is kid friendly. They laugh—understanding some patrons prefer a peaceful meal —and nod.

The Twins fully fed and fast asleep in their carriers won't disturb anyone. Even if they wake, they're not likely to make noise. They're new things are to stare at their surroundings and to vocalize.

Roger slips his beanie off, and his hair falls around his stubble-covered cheeks. The light streaming through the oversized windows makes his eyes sparkle as he smiles at the hostesses.

They nearly swoon.

Haley and I glance at each other, then roll our eyes. A baby in his hand and two women with him don't deter women. Good grief.

One of them seats us and grins at Roger the entire time. Shortly after we settle The Twins, a server takes our orders.

"So, you're the new DILF on the scene?" I tease Roger.

Haley cracks up, and we come up with jokes about hot

dads until he growls at us. Which only adds to our humor. We laugh louder.

"Haley?"

We turn to find a handsome Scotsman towering over her chair. His emerald green eyes darken when she smiles at him. She introduces us to him as Callum Graham—a duke she met while attending Harvard Business School.

He explains he was just leaving since his friend never showed up because of a hangover.

Haley looks to Roger, and he offers Callum to join us. He accepts happily.

While we make room for him, I peep how his eyes never leave Haley. Then I notice how Roger's eyes never leave Callum. *The Responsible One*'s signature intense stare on full alert. Undoubtedly he'll arrange a comprehensive background check. Not even a duke is good enough for their baby sister.

I giggle, and Roger glances at me. With a shake of my head, I busy myself with adjusting my linen napkin.

We enjoy a tasty breakfast during which Callum regales us with royal tales. The Twins wake to gaze around themselves ah-gooing at the sights and sounds.

After the meal ends, Callum asks Haley to go for a stroll around the village. She agrees and they leave us with a promise by Callum to return her to the chalet.

"The four of us at last!" Roger huffs as we bundle The Twins in their gear.

I laugh, "Everyone will leave in two days and you'll have us all to yourself for two months!"

Roger leans down to kiss my lips, then responds, "Exactly how I want it, my love."

. . .

"WHAT DID you and Sebastian get up to today?"

Lola, Haley, Starr, and I stretch out in the chalet's spa sauna before our deep-tissue massages start. Ninety-minute of pure decadence.

As a treat, Malcolm arranged for a Girls' Spa Day with masseuses and aestheticians from the hotel's facility to pamper us prior to our New Year's Eve dinner and party. He said we were good girls and deserved special goodies.

Haley and I rolled our eyes at the "good girls" part. But Lola and Starr grinned from ear-to-ear. I knew Lola was a sub, yet Starr...

Whatever the situation, I appreciate the treats. Between Roger's marathon lovemaking and the rigors of skiing, tobogganing, and ice skating, my muscles need a rubdown.

I lift my hands to consider my mani/pedi color as I wait for Lola's response—a matte silver would do nicely with my jewelry. I'll never get over the exceptional pieces!

"Oh, a little bit of this and a little bit of that," she hedges.

Starr shakes her head, causing long, curly tendrils to escape her messy topknot. As she tucks them back in to the Scünci, she laughs.

"What kind of evasive answer is that?" She asks. "What exactly does that entail?"

Lola giggles and waggles her eyebrows.

"Well, if you'd prefer all the details... Sebastian bound my arms and legs to the four bedposts with red silk cords—"

"Uh, no, thank you!"

"TMI!"

"Girl! Not all of those details! Please!"

Lola's giggles turn into snorts as she doubles over, cracking up. Her eyes twinkle with mischief when she lifts her gaze.

"Okay, okay! I mean, you did ask for it!" She starts. "After a morning of multiple orgasms, we went ice skating. Boy, when I tell you my legs were wobbly—"

Haley throws a towel at Lola's head and she ducks, laughing hysterically.

"Lola!! I do not care to hear of my brother's sex life!" Haley shouts. "And that goes for the two of you, too. Not interested in the least."

Starr and I exchange looks, then throw towels at her. Lola grabs the one Haley threw and tosses it back at her. We end up laughing and exchanging our tales for the day, minus the sex scenes. From the broad smile on Starr's face, I conclude Malcolm put it on her real good!

A gentle knock on the sauna's door draws our attention. A masseuse reminds us it's time, so we troop out to rinse off.

Aside from the sauna and showers, the spa accommodates a steam room, plunge pools for hot and cold therapies, a tranquility lounge, and four of each manicure stations, pedicure chairs, and treatment rooms. We settle in the rooms for our sessions.

The rejuvenating massages put us in even higher spirits when we reemerge. They added a body polish treatment, so our skin glows and feels like satin. The warm oil soothed my achy body and added to the softness.

The aestheticians help us into the pedicure chairs first. We gab some more while they set to our feet and hands. The start of a new year excites everyone. We're ready to leave all the drama behind and to begin anew!

BEFORE THE FULL-LENGTH MIRROR, I take a final spin in my 70s disco era style white chiffon party dress. The white and blue sequins glisten from the plunging vee neckline to the nipped-in waist to the hem at the top of my thighs. I love how the voluminous bracelet sleeves showcase my wedding jewelry. I paired it with shiny silver leather high platform chunky heels with straps around my toes and ankles to round out the 70s glam.

My hair cascades down my back in waves, skimming the middle of my ass. The glow from our spa day remains, so I leave my face bare except for glossy lips and extra mascara on my eyelashes.

The party girl is ready!

A wolf whistle cuts through the air.

I pivot to find Roger leaning against the doorframe. He's debonair in a black tuxedo with a black dress shirt open at the neck. His patent leather shoes gleam as much as his jet-black hair. His hooded gaze takes me in from the tips of my toes to the top of my head, lingering around my hips and décolletage.

He licks his lower lip and peers at me through his thick lashes.

"*Bonne soirée, Mon Amour,*" he croons.

I bite my lower lip as I smile. My body thrums from the sound of his seductive purr. Will we make it out of the dressing room, I wonder.

Merde...

"We're missing one," he says as he strides towards me.

I cock my head in question.

A devilish grin spreads across Roger's gorgeous face. His nostrils flare.

Continuing to walk forward, he drives me back against the mirror. A quick kiss, and he spins me around as he places my hands on the glass with his on top, twining our fingers. His nose runs along the side of my neck, eliciting shivers down my spine and sparks in my pussy.

Boxed in by the press of his massive frame against my smaller one, I melt into his embrace.

"One last fuck before Midnight. Or did you forget, Pretty Kitty?" He growls.

That answers my questions. *Merde.*

Roger slips hips hand beneath my mini dress to cup my mons. His middle finger strokes the crotch of my silk thong.

My pussy juices flow and moisten the material.

Roger purrs in my ear as he plunges his finger inside my core. He grinds his hips forward, wedging his thick dick between my ass cheeks, driving me to my tiptoes with each thrust.

My forehead drops to the mirror's steamy surface, hot from my pants.

The sound of his zipper is music to my ears. I delight in it and relish the first pistoning stroke.

Roger doesn't delay my satisfaction. He grunts as he slams into me, and I squeal.

He's rough and fast. We grunt and groan with the effort. The raw, primal fucking brings us to climax quickly. Copious ropes of his cum shoot deep within my pulsating, dripping pussy.

"Happy Early New Year, Baby."

Roger chuckles darkly as he withdraws and watches me slump against the mirror, breathless and spent.

"So, who's the bonnie Scotsman with Haley?"

Starr appears at my elbow and nods towards the other side of the wine cellar.

I glance at Starr before I turn to the cuddled-up couple.

She looks fantastic in a slinky metallic lamé brown and

gold wrap-effect mini dress. Her long, toned legs end in brown sky-high sandals with gold serpentine metal straps wrapped around her ankles. The long curls of her chocolate-colored hair frame her heart-shaped face, the dimples pop with her giggle. She reminds me of Christie Doll, Barbie's friend.

"Well, don't you look fabulous, darling!" I tell Starr.

"Why thank you! We're hot babes, huh?" She laughs.

"Very hot indeed."

Starr and I startle at the unexpected gruff voice of Malcolm. He chuckles and strokes the five o'clock stubble on his chin. His eyes rove up and down Starr as she shifts from one foot to the other.

All righty then…

I laugh and pat his shoulder as I make a fast exit, their erotic energy too hot for me to handle.

We're enjoying pre-dinner cocktails with our families and friends, including some we met up with on holiday. The bartender and sommelier for STEELE Verbier crafted a selection of drinks and wines for our dinner and party.

I head over to my parents, who chat with a couple I recognize from their social club. A pair whose son would like to have me on his arm.

"*Bonsoir*, welcome. It's good to see you," I greet them with a smile politely.

"Congratulations on your marriage, my dear," the wife responds. "And your beautiful sons. Your mother showed us their photos."

"Thank you very much."

I glance up to Roger, smiling warmly as he extends his hand to the couple and places the other on the small of my back. I lean into him and rest my head on his shoulder.

"Ah. You did well for yourself, Monsieur Steele. We've

tried unsuccessfully to match our son with Leonie for years!" The husband adds.

My father sputters as he sips his drink. While my mother and the man's wife look aghast.

Roger stiffens, and his fingers slip around to grip my waist, pinning me to his side firmly.

"That's because it always meant Leonie to be mine forever," he replies. "*C'est la vie*! Excuse us."

He nods and draws me away. I smile and wave.

"What the fuck?!" Roger huffs. "He comes into my house as a guest and tells me some bullshit about hooking my wife and the mother of my children up with their son. *Bof*!"

I giggle, and Roger glares down at me.

"I'm wearing off on you! *Bof*!" I explain.

It's in reference to my "arrogant Gallic shrug" as Lola says where I stick out my lower lip; raise my eyebrows and shoulders simultaneously; followed by a patronizing, *Bof*.

Roger leans close and murmurs, "Well, they say couples begin to take on the other's attributes. So like I told him, MINE!"

He swats my ass for emphasis.

I yelp as the butler enters the wine cellar to announce dinner is being served.

Roger returns his hand to my lower back and guides me to the dining room. We chat with others as we make our way upstairs.

Fortunately, the delicious meal goes off as planned with no more graceless comments. Roger keeps our family and guests entertained. His mood much improved after he reminded me it's his seed buried deep within my womb right now, not some sod.

I shiver when I recall Roger's declaration I couldn't wash

his essence from my pussy, only what dripped down my legs. He wanted his mark to remain on me.

Mmmm… *Merde…*

The DJ from Farm Club spins a range of music perfect for everyone.

We party it up in the disco next to the wine cellar. The set up works well with people moving seamlessly from the bar to the dance floor or the banquettes along the walls. A gigantic screen shows scenes of countries around the world celebrating the start of the New Year with Sydney, Australia first.

Roger twirls me, then pulls me close. He buries his nose in my hair as I drape my arms around his neck. We move in sync, letting the stress of the past dissipate with each bump and grind. Finally carefree with no drama!

A piercing whistle blasts, and we turn to see Sebastian on a raised platform with one arm around Lola and the other beckoning to Roger and me. Then he raises his champagne flute.

"Before midnight strikes, I want to congratulate my brother on his new bride and darling Twins, my new sister and nephews. We love you all. Steeles for life!"

Everyone claps and stomps with more wolf whistles.

Roger picks me up and swings me around before dipping me and kissing me silly.

The DJ calls for more champagne with five minutes to go.

Earlier, Harris angled the exterior cameras toward Verbier Village and relayed the footage to the screen. Now, he switches the feed, and the live view appears for the countdown clock and fireworks display.

Nanny Grace emerges through the cluster in the cellar to bring Rodolphe and Gaspard to Roger and me. We thank her and kiss their sleepy faces. Mini noise-canceling head-sets cover their sensitive ears.

Roger hands me a flute from a passing server, then slips his arm around my waist, pulling me close. I smile up at him and whisper I love you. He kisses the tip of my nose and tells me the same.

The lights dim as the countdown begins.

The screen is so large, we might as well be front row in the village.

I'm so ecstatic and say a silent pray of thanks.

We chant the countdown, then cheer as midnight strikes and glittery silver, gold, and white balloons fall from the ceiling.

Roger leans over and whispers in my ear, "Round two begins for month seventeen and seven days…"

ROGER

*I*t's been two weeks of pure bliss at *Chalet de la Joie*. We've had our home to ourselves since our family and friends left after New Year's Day. I love them all, but need some private time with my wife and my sons.

We've spent enough time with others, having lived at *Le Beaulieu Manoir* for six months initially because of the reconstruction of our penthouse duplex into a triplex. Then, by necessity, because of the rabid media and the frenzy behind the pretrial, we stayed through to our wedding day.

Even there, the media pestered us with drones and hanging outside of the front gates. We increased security patrols and upgraded the surveillance systems under Harris' supervision.

After being harassed by a photographer while out shopping for The Twins, I hired a security detail to protect Leonie. The paparazzo didn't give a damn she was pregnant. I promised to destroy him and the rag he worked for. Pain in my ass.

I sent Nanny Grace to stay at the hotel, not wanting

anyone else on the property with us. She'll come as we need her help. We're hands-on parents and can take care of The Twins with ease.

Now, we're alone for six more weeks. No distractions; no work; no news or the Internet. Leonie insisted we give up our mobiles, too. Our family can reach us on the chalet's landline. Otherwise, we're untouchable. Period.

Sebastian and Malcolm volunteered to manage my division in the interim. The same as Malcolm and I did for Baz when he and Lola took a two-month honeymoon yachting to private islands in the South Pacific. He only had two satellite phones. Talk about untouchable…

Hell, I don't blame him in the least, I chuckle to myself.

Leonie stirs in bed next to me. She reaches out for me and murmurs my name.

My heart swells at her wanting me while she's still asleep. I gather her outstretched hand to press a kiss to the knuckles.

She sighs and settles back to sleep.

The sound of one Twin—I hazard a guess it's Gaspard as he's more vocal, like his *Maman*—comes through the baby monitor on the nightstand.

I grab and turn it down before his cries wake Leonie. She needs her sleep since I had her up all night revering her luscious body. It's amazing how flexible she's become with her regular yoga sessions. Pretty Kitty is a sexy contortionist.

On my way to their dressing room passageway, I cover my nakedness with a pair of sweatpants. No need for them to see the family's jewels.

"Good morning, Rodolphe! Good morning, Gaspard!" I greet them.

As expected, my younger son fusses in his crib, waving his arms in frustration. I imagine he's saying, "Feed me!"

"Okay, okay. Breakfast coming right up, boss! Kindly forgive my tardiness," I chuckle as I stride over to check on each of them.

Rodolphe gazes back at me and offers a gummy smile as he lifts his hands up. I collect them for a good morning hug and quick diaper change.

"So what's the plan for today? Shall we go to the village or take a sleigh ride?" I ask as I feed them in their chairs.

Leonie and I thought it best to speak to The Twins in French and English to encourage their multilingualism. And those are just the beginnings of their languages. Both of us are fluent in Italian, and Leonie adds German and Spanish. Since we live in Europe with different countries, it's best to understand as many languages as possible.

"Let's ask *Maman* what she'd like to do, too. She's still asleep. Let's give her a rest for now, yes?"

With his belly filling up, Gaspard laughs around the bottle. Yeah, like Leonie, who also gets hangry. It's intriguing to watch their personalities develop along with the growth.

"Happy now?" I tease.

"*Non.* I reached for you, but the sheets were cold, *Mon Cœur.*"

My cock jumps when I glance over my shoulder to see Leonie leaning against the doorjamb in nothing but my cashmere sweater she ripped off me last night.

She's tall, but it still falls to the tops of her bare thighs—thighs I forever want to nestle between, cock or mouth. Her disheveled hair hangs past her round ass. The memory of the silky strands wrapped around my fist as I bow her back to spank her from behind makes me diamond hard. Her nipples poke into the soft material, standing in bas-relief from my vigorous suckling.

Leonie's full lips pout tantalizingly as she toys with the hem.

"You should have woken me to help you," she says, then pushes off the doorjamb.

The unintended seductive sway of her hips mesmerizes me. I want to grip them as I pull her beneath my body and drive my dick deep inside her warm, wet pussy.

The desire raging through me must reach my face because Leonie smirks.

"I would have fed them," she says, cupping her bountiful breasts. "I'm full."

A growl slips out of my mouth as I lick my lips, "No worries. I'll ease your ache."

Leonie nods her head and tweaks her nipples.

Fuck. Me.

"I'll get their bath ready," she says sashaying into The Twins' en suite bathroom and heisting the hem at her ass up for a peek at her globes.

Cushion for the pushin'.

Another growl, and Leonie shimmies as she raises her arms overhead to slide the long sleeves past her elbows. Her giggle makes my balls tighten.

This woman will be the death of me.

The Twins finish breakfast, and I carry them into the bathroom. Leonie puts my waxed apron on me. We've learned the hard way; The Twins enjoy splashing the water everywhere. Bath time is full of fun with squeaky rubber ducks and bubbles.

And anytime with water is sexy with Leonie.

Once our sons are nice and clean—and Leonie and I are

dry—we carry them into our bedroom. Leonie plays with them on the bed while I shower, then we switch.

When she comes out, I've made the bed, and she kisses me silly in appreciation.

Any man who doesn't help his woman with their children and domestic tasks misses out on their exuberant thanks. I love my sons and will care for them for life, but I love how Leonie thanks me just as much!

We head downstairs for our adult breakfast. Although not a cook, Leonie made certain the chef prepped a variety of meals for us before I threw everyone out.

I felt like Martin Lawrence: "Get to steppin'!" I would have added the jump kick as I held the front door open, but it would have proven too much.

"What should we do today?" Leonie asks as she adds yogurt to her granola.

"How about a sleigh ride? The Twins liked the tinkling of the bells and laughed at the horses," I respond. "It's colder today, but we can bundle up under the blankets."

Leonie agrees it's a good idea.

Gaspard laughs while Rodolphe ah-goos in support of our planned family activity. Leonie's giggle joins The Twins.

"THIS IS SO MUCH FUN! The Twins love it!"

Leonie exclaims as the horses pick up their pace to a trot and the red sleigh with brass bells zips along the snowy trail.

We just left the bustling streets of Verbier Village, and the driver cracked the whip in the air above the horses' rumps. They tossed their heads and neighed in response as they forged ahead.

A light snowfall drifts around us as we cuddle beneath the heavy wool blankets—Leonie insists we use our own and not the ones from the sleigh ride company. With the blanket up against The Twins' faces, she doesn't want one used by countless others on our sons. I agree wholeheartedly.

The breathtaking scenery of the Swiss Alps depicts the awesomeness of nature. Majestic snowcapped mountains rise skyward to incredible heights. The sheer beauty of the pristine peaks makes my heart soar.

"I love it, too!" I respond, laughing as the wind whips around us.

Slipping my arm around Leonie's waist, I snuggle her closer to my side, and she leans her head on my shoulder. The Twins bounce on our laps, thrilled with the action.

Yup, this is the idyllic family life for me!

LEONIE

"*H*appy One Month Anniversary, *Mon Cœur*. I love you from the depths of my soul."

I raise my flute of Taittinger Comtes de Champagne Blanc de Blancs—my favorite thanks to James Bond in *Casino Royale*—to toast Roger.

We're sitting in a private dining room at STEELE Verbier's STEAKhouse restaurant run by Lucien through one of their many Jackson Corporation partnerships. A reservation at the three Michelin star restaurant is the most sought-after in this part of Switzerland.

Lucien created a special menu of Roger's favorite foods, including lobster bisque and steak frites. Then he sent it to the chef to prepare. The sommelier paired the dishes with the most choice wines. I planned it shortly after we arrived, determined Roger would have a scrumptious meal for our celebration.

It pays to be the owner's wife!

Time flies by within a blink of an eye. One minute we're

engaged and the next we're celebrating our first month as a married couple. I'm beyond blissed-out.

Roger's such an attentive, caring, and loving husband. Many a morning he wakes up early to feed The Twins and to get them ready for our day so I can rest. He says I carried them for thirty-six weeks, so he can share the load now. Or he'll pretend to be a masseuse who offers happy endings in the chalet's spa. All much to my delight.

But most of all, he's my one true heart. No man has ever loved me the way Roger does. Or put me above all else. Our time apart almost ended me. But our time together makes me whole. Thankfully, our *coupe de foudre* proves its determination to be long lasting.

"Happy One Month Anniversary, baby. I love you more than you can ever imagine," Roger replies with a broad grin.

His eyes sparkle in the light put forth by hundreds of candles positioned throughout the room. Their warmth heightens the scent of his Tom Ford Noir cologne—a heady, sensual blend of Bulgarian rose, clary sage, and patchouli.

For tonight, Roger shaved his temporary beard, so his cleft chin looks lickable. I like the sexy five o'clock shadow, but I prefer the velvety smoothness of his skin. The cut of his bespoke three-piece charcoal gray suit with a custom white dress shirt opened at the neck emphasize his muscular physique. The width of his shoulders, the column of his throat, and the thickness of his thighs call out to me.

My man looks as tasty as our dinner. I can't wait for the decadent dessert I have planned back home...

"You're in for a delightful treat," I say, beaming. "A much-deserved one, or is it two?"

Roger smirks and drags his fingertip around the rim of his flute while pinning me with his intense stare.

"And what must I do to receive the second treat, Mrs. Steele?" He asks huskily, eyes hooded.

I bite my lower lip between the front teeth as my gaze darts between his thick finger and his luscious smug mouth.

Merde... I was supposed to be the seductive one.

"Be a good little boy, of course," I purr.

"As you know, Mrs. Steele, nothing is 'little' about me nor am I a 'boy.' A robust man is more like it," Roger starts. "However, I am very, very good. *Ne suis-je pas*, Pretty Kitty?"

Indeed, he is more than very, very good, I think as my core clenches and leaks juices into the silk of my thong. My body concurs with his assessment wholeheartedly.

Roger's nostrils flare, and he chuckles alluringly.

Yeah, he took the power back... And I happily hand the reins to him. Ride me till I sweat, baby!

"Monsieur et Madame Steele."

We glance up to find the servers hovering at the room's door with our first course in their hands.

As I smile in thanks, beneath the linen-covered table, a silken touch glides up my calf along my inner thigh. My eyes fly to Roger, who chats with his server regarding the dish.

An insistent push to my leg makes me widen my knees to allow Roger's toes access to my upper thigh. His long leg makes it easy for him to tease my mons.

He thanks the servers, and they leave us alone once again. Then turns to me with his hand outstretched, palm up.

"Give me your thong," Roger commands.

Immediately, I comply and rise from my chair. I saunter to his side, slip my hands beneath my mini dress, and shimmy my thong down. Then I lean forward to give him an unobstructed view of my heavy boobs while I step out of the thong and place it in his hand.

Roger brings the damp scrap of material to his nose to inhale deeply, then puts them in his suit jacket pocket. He smacks my ass when I pivot to return to my chair and chuckles when I yelp.

"Fuck your ass is delicious," he says.

I give it an extra shake before easing into my chair while I maintain eye contact with him. The expression of an undisguised desire on Roger's face adds another tick in my power of seduction column. Gotcha!

Automatically, I part my thighs when the touch of Roger's big toe glides up my calf.

"Wider," he demands, prodding my upper leg.

I oblige and am rewarded with pressure to my throbbing clit. Sliding down in my seat, I open my legs even more, wantonly offering my pussy to Roger's propping digit.

"Eat," he commands.

Is this man mad?

How the hell can I eat when he's toying with my sensitive clit and stroking my pussy lips? Better yet, how can he sit there all cool, calm, and collected polishing off his lobster bisque while his toe gets soaked by my wetness?

GRRR!

"What was that?" he asks nonchalantly.

I mutter nothing and tuck into my soup as best as I'm able. When my hips begin to move to match his rhythm, Roger tsks and removes his big toe.

My eyes narrow as I shoot golden daggers at him.

"Patience," he states.

The servers return to remove the soup tureens and replace them with the next course.

But does Roger stop?

No! He keeps up his ministrations despite me being on the edge of an orgasm. Whenever he senses I'm close to exploding, he backs away with a smirk.

I hope to take advantage of his distraction. So I shift in the seat to angle my pussy for better penetration.

Roger swings his intense stare to me.

"Something not to your liking, Mrs. Steele?" He asks with a raised eyebrow.

The servers panic and ask if the food meets my expectations or do I prefer another dish.

I blush, embarrassed they believe it's somehow their fault. I assure them the meal is superb and smile until they leave. Then, I glare at Roger; he smirks.

"Argh! You're being a beast!" I declare.

"So behave," he responds. "I will give you pleasure. Do not attempt to force it."

I mutter how he's the one behaving unfairly. It's our anniversary, for goodness' sake! How can he taunt me?

Roger chuckles. Then he crooks his finger at me.

I scowl and shake my head no. Now I'll behave like a petulant child. I let my hair fall in a curtain to cover my face and tuck into my food.

"Here, Pretty Kitty, Kitty," he croons. "Let me make it better."

My ears perk up, and I cock my head. Hmmm... That's more like it. With a peppier attitude, I rise hurriedly and sashay over to Roger's side.

"There, there, now. Tell me where it aches," he says gruffly.

I point to my pussy and whimper as I shift from foot to foot. The ache unbearable.

"Let me see," he purrs as he lifts the hem of my mini dress. "Show me."

I widen my stance and point to my bare swollen lower lips. My arousal amped up by the possibility of us being caught by the waitstaff.

"Aaawww. My sweet little pussy needs a release?" He asks, stroking my folds with the tip of his finger.

I mewl and rock my hips as I grasp his strong shoulders.

WHAP. WHAP. WHAP.

Sharp slaps strike my pussy, and I squeal from the unexpected pain on my sensitive flesh.

"What did I tell you, Pretty Kitty?" Roger demands as he narrows his darkened eyes at me.

I mumble a response, and he spanks my ass.

"Words, Pretty Kitty. I will have your words," Roger commands.

"You... You will give me pleasure..." I whine.

"Exactly," he responds. "Will you behave, or will you remain unsatisfied on our anniversary night?"

"*Oui! Oui!!* I'll behave, *Amoureux!*" I cry without hesitation.

Roger nods and drapes my leg over his shoulder. He buries his face between my thighs and gorges on my dripping pussy. His fingers dig into the fleshiest parts of my ass to lock me in place, also preventing me from humping his mouth.

His grunts of pleasure intensify as my body ramps up for a mind-blowing orgasm. Roger tightens his hold as his feast continues. Then presses his thumb against my bottom hole. The tight rings of muscle give way, and his thumb plunges inside, twisting and thrusting,

My pussy flutters as my legs quiver. Fuck! This is going to be massive...

Not giving a damn who hears, I throw my head back and

roar Roger's name as wave after glorious wave crashes over me. My body jolts from the white heat he built.

Roger doesn't let up, drawing two additional orgasms from my shook pussy. He ignores my cries of no more to relish in the aftereffects of my release. Gently, he laps at my swollen folds to eat every drop of my juices.

He hums in delight.

I fold over his shoulder and sob.

Fuck! That was indescribable.

"Better?" Roger purrs as he kisses my clit and inner thighs.

I jump, much too delicate for even the slightest touch.

Roger chuckles, and the warm air makes me shiver and my nipples pebble to painful points. He settles me on his lap and strokes my back soothingly.

"So, do I deserve my second treat, Mrs. Steele?"

LEONIE

"*Bonjour, Maman et Papa!* It's so good to see you! How are you doing? Is all well?"

Even though we decided no outside connections, I have an urge to reach out to my parents. It's been weeks since we last spoke. I need to make sure they're all right. So I sent a text message earlier to let them know I'd FaceTime and wanted to get both of them.

"*Bonjour, Mon Trésor!*" My father booms, then continues in French. "You look so happy! Roger must treat you well."

"Leonie! We miss you, honey!" My mother exclaims.

The smiles on their faces warm my heart.

"Oh, I miss you, too... We're wonderful!" I respond. "Wow, The Twins are excited to call you, too."

I angle my iPad to show them in their chairs waving their arms and ah-gooing attracted to our cheerful cries. Granted, their joy also comes from full tummies. My greedy little monsters.

"Aaww. We're glad to hear from you, too," my mother

laughs as she wiggles her fingers at The Twins. "Oh, my! They've grown so much, Leonie!"

We chat some more about their new milestones at five-months old. They crack up over peek-a-boo and hide and seek, watching Roger pop in and out of their view with delight. Another new favorite is playing with their toys. We've noticed they prefer to grab the more colorful toys like their shiny cherry red rings. Their chubby cheeks match the hue of their toys and widen with their smiles.

My parents ask after Roger, and I tell them he's terrific. In fact, he's in the gym working out via Skype with Norman.

"So tell me. Is everything okay? I just had a sense to check in on you," I ask as a worried sensation hovers around the edge of my thoughts.

They exchange glances and communicate as only couples who have been together for years can. My father gives a slight shake to his head, then smiles at me.

"*Mon Trésor*, you focus on your new husband and babies. Enjoy your honeymoon. It's time for you to relax and bond," he says.

I glance at my mother, and she smiles quickly as she nods in agreement.

"Listen to your father, *Mon Cœur*. He knows best," she adds. "Now tell me, which chef did you select? I'm partial to the third one. She has knowledge of various cuisines good for entertaining. Plus, she shared her secrets for the perfect Gateau St. Honoré with me."

I laugh when my mother's eyes widen. She's a pastry aficionado. So anyone who can impress her with their skills goes to the top of my list.

"Well, in that case, *Maman*, she's the winner!" I declare.

"Shall I tell her, or would you prefer to let her know? She

gave me her mobile so we can chat now and then," she replies clapping her hands.

Sometimes I feel terrible I hate to cook and didn't learn our Tunisian family's recipes passed down through the generations. I took after my father's Parisian side with travel and the love of beautiful things. So I tell my mother she can share the good news with the chef. Not quite my substitute, rather someone my mother can offer her knowledge to as she did with Lucien.

Perhaps they'll open another restaurant together in Verbier like they did in Paris! I make a note to ask Malcolm and Lucien when Roger and I return home.

We catch up on other happenings before we end our video call with a promise to connect next week.

I feel better. But I still get a sense they're holding something back from me.

Seemingly it's not my parents. I ignore the tons of text messages highlighted on the banner for my Messages app and shoot a quick text to Lola.

Hey! How's everything? I miss you!

Immediately, the three dots appear as Lola types her response.

OMG! I was just thinking about you!! :D

All good, I hope!

LOL Yes! I miss you, too :(We're in Paris this week. Baz has some things to take care of. Hey! Aren't you supposed to not have your mobile???

I know! But I have a weird sense and want to check in. My parents are well, but evasive. So I wanted to ask you...

A minute passes, and Lola hasn't typed. Huh. I wonder if she's busy or dodging my question like my parents did.

Helloooo...

She's taking forever. *Merde*. Finally, the dots show up on my screen.

Sorry about that. Baz just came in and you know how he kisses me breathless when he

Errrr! TMI Lola!

;D Look, I've gotta fly! TTYL Kiss my Little Pumpkins XOXOXOXO.

Well, perhaps I'm going crazy, I mutter to myself.

The sound of clangs draws me from my musings. Rodolphe discovered slamming his rings onto the tray in front of him makes a loud noise. Gaspard follows suit. Soon the room is full of cymbal sounds.

I giggle and join in, clapping my hands and singing. The Twins go wild. Soon my thoughts drift from concern to bonding with my sons like my father suggested.

Whatever may brew, it will take care of itself for now.

"WHAT HAVE you been up to, babe?"

With The Twins napping after their orchestral performance wore them out, I sat in the window seat of our bedroom to sketch. Some ideas for playrooms come to mind as The Twins grow and become more active. The peacefulness of the pristine scenery clears my head to let the images form.

I glance at the door to spot Roger striding in, oozing sex appeal without even trying.

A warm flush from his boxing session covers his cheeks —he's kept the stubble to a minimum for me—and his eyes shine like liquid platinum. The long-sleeved t-shirt clings to his powerful chest and biceps while the gray sweatpants hang low on his narrow hips. His flaccid dick runs down the length of his thigh; its head outlined through the material.

My man is hung, honey! Yum.

Roger runs his fingers through his hair. It's grown longer since we've been here. The glossy ebony waves frame his chiseled face.

I can never get enough of looking at him. He's like a Renaissance masterpiece sculpture come to life.

"Hey there, handsome," I purr. "Yearning for you."

He grins as he heads towards me and bends down to kiss my proffered lips.

"Mmmmmm chocolaty," he says, smacking his lips together.

I nod at the cup of cocoa on the side table.

Roger takes a sip, then kisses me again.

"Tasty, Caramel Bonbon," he says. "Shall we discover what other decadent uses the whipped cream has for us?"

Roger hums as he places a dollop on my lips and licks it off.

"*Absolument, Amoureux,*" I purr, sucking his finger clean.

Children's playrooms give way to adult fun in a flash of fiery heat. The blast sizzles enough to melt the glaciers of the Swiss Alps.

Roger removes the cashmere blanket from my lap and folds it neatly as his intense gaze heats my skin. His deliberate delay makes me want more. Right. Now. He snickers as he senses my instant need for his carnal touch.

"Anxious, Pretty Kitty?" He asks as his eyes spark brightly with desire. "Patience, my dear wife. Know I will always satisfy your every need, when you need it most."

I watch his tight ass muscles flex beneath his sweats as he strolls over to place the blanket on the foot of our bed. The power of his ass and thighs when he pistons inside of me drives me insane with pleasure. My pussy walls clench on air just thinking about the pounding Roger gives to it.

Merde…

When he turns, he catches me staring at his lower half, and he chuckles darkly. With a glint in his eyes, he stands still. One hand grips the back of his shirt and yanks it over his head, then pulls the sleeves off to reveal his thick biceps. They bunch and flex along with his eight-pack abs when he tosses the garment to the side.

Roger glides his fingertips down the chiseled chest of his beautifully ripped torso, slowly reaching for the drawstring of his sweatpants. A tug, and the waistband loosens to show the mouthwatering v-cuts of his Adonis belt.

I lick my lips and swallow hard.

A smirk appears on his face. He bends at the waist, never taking his wolfish eyes off of me as he pushes the pants down his thick, muscular thighs and calves. Then he steps out of the sweats to stand to his impressive height of six feet, three inches. His giant dick—in all its ten-inch glory—stands tall and proud to reach above his navel while his sac hangs heavy below.

Did I say my man looks like a Renaissance masterpiece sculpture come to life, or what?

HOT DIGGITY DAYUMMM!

Sizzling doesn't describe Roger. But he has me burning up inside.

My face heats with a flush to my cheeks and chest. Pricks to my underarms tingle as my nipples harden to points. My chest rises and falls with an increase in my breath, just shy of panting with my mouth hanging open and my tongue lolling out the side. My pussy weeps at the sight of his splendid form, knowing the power of his dick will stretch and fill it to the maximum capacity.

I ache for his dominant possession.

Roger cocks his head to the side to survey my wanton

reaction. Lazily, his fist strokes his turgid length. He's back to that slow burn.

The anticipation builds until I want to scream as I press my thighs together for some semblance of relief.

Then an idea strikes... Meet him where he stands...

With a smirk of my own, I pin him with my predatory feline stare as I rise from the window seat. Ever so slowly, I slide my fingers in the waistband of my leggings, bend at the waist, and shimmy my hips to slide the clingy material down my long legs. Then fold them neatly before I put them on the seat behind me.

I glance over my shoulder as I start to unbutton my cardigan. Letting it fall down one shoulder, then the other until it slips to the floor in a heap. The tips of my hair brush my bare ass cheeks, and I shiver. Folding in half, I slip my thong off, ensuring my most private parts show.

Roger isn't the only one with enticing bits.

He growls and rushes me.

"You want to poke the bear, Pretty Kitty?" He rumbles in my ear as he pins my back to his front with his knees bent to align our centers. "Because I can poke back with something much larger."

He punctuates each word with a thrust of his hips, poking the crack of my ass.

I moan with indescribable need.

"Well, then... What are you waiting for?" I ask cheekily.

Roger's lips curl into a grin against my neck as his grip tightens on my upper arms. He starts a slow, circular grind of his hips. One hand glides down my arm to slip around my hip to land on my lower belly, pressing me in place.

His erotic dance enthralls me, and my head lolls onto his broad shoulder.

Roger takes advantage to the access to suck the flesh of

my neck into his fiery mouth. Like a caveman, he marks his mate. Then growls and licks the sensitive area to soothe the delicious bite of pain.

I groan and press back against his thick dick.

More, my mind shouts.

Roger kicks my feet apart to open me to his probing fingers as they glide along my belly to my damp folds. Two fingers plunge inside my pussy, stretching me as they flex and curl to stroke the rough textured mound just inside. The palm of his hand grinds against my mons, adding more pressure to my throbbing, aching clit.

I mewl and ride his hand as he fucks me with his talented fingers.

"Uh... Uh... Uh... Uh..." I moan, closing my eyes tightly to give in to the carnal sensations my lover inflicts upon me.

My orgasm rocks me on my feet as I cry out in wild abandon, bucking against Roger's hand.

He continues to finger fuck me. Then he takes his claim on my body even further when with his other hand, he cups my heavy breast and pinches my beaded nipple.

"Aaaahhh... *Amoureux*!!" I wail, writhing in his firm embrace. "*S'il te plait*... I need you inside of me!"

Roger rumbles in my ear, "Ready for the larger poke now, Pretty Kitty?"

I plead again, and he satisfies my desire by forcefully thrusting his massive dick deep in my dripping pussy with one demanding stroke, driving me to my toes with an anguished wail.

The sound of his balls slapping at my ass mingled with the sounds of our grunts and groans fill the room.

Roger adjusts his grip on my hip and urges me forward to rest my hands on the window seat. The muscles in front of his thighs strike the back of mine. I revel in his primitive mounting of me!

His punishing strokes continue as he wrings climax after climax from my quivering pussy. Roger is a demanding lover who seeks to draw out my pleasure before he seeks his own.

"Rogeeerrr... Oooh... Oooh... No more... Please!" I wail as another orgasm replaces the snowflakes outside the window with dazzling stars before my eyes.

"Yes? Your teasing is over, Naughty Kitty?" He growls, still jackhammering through my earth-shattering release.

"*Oui, oui!*" I cry pitifully, no longer able to take another mind-blowing climax. "*Je promets!*"

"You promise, do you? Remember who's in control in our bedroom, Naughty Kitty," Roger rumbles in my ear as he increases his steady rhythm.

My head drops to my chest, and I give in to my Alpha male's dominance. He knows exactly what I need and when I need it. My caveman, my husband, my lover.

Roger's pummeling picks up as his massive dick grows impossibly larger and harder inside of my pussy. His release is near.

I tighten my inner muscles and clamp down on his cock with a groan. I'm rewarded with three successive smacks to my ass—again I tried to take control—and a roar from Roger as his dick pulses and pumps his hot, thick seed deep within my greedy pussy.

"Yaaassssss!!!!" I scream, undulating my hips as his release triggers another one of mine.

My hand slaps the window seat, and I toss my head back. So. Fucking. Good.

Roger's legs shake, and he huffs as he collapses against me. His powerful arm braces him from crushing me with his sizable weight. The other arm winds around my waist, locking us together.

He nuzzles my neck as his sultry breath sends goose-bumps along my sweat-soaked, feverish skin.

"We forgot the whipped cream. Naughty Kitty, you distracted me with your wily ways," Roger chuckles against my neck.

"Well, *Amoureux*, there's always round two…" I taunt.

Roger nips my shoulder and shakes his head.

"You will never learn will you, Naughty, Naughty Kitty?" He laughs.

I giggle and turn my head to meld our lips in a passionate kiss.

Non, I never will, and he loves it.

ROGER

"*T*his is just so incredible. Words cannot describe it. *Merci, Mon Cœur.*"

Leonie whispers in awe of the impressive Corbassière Glacier.

The panorama from the glacier to the majestic Grand Combin mountain massif is breathtaking to say the least. The snow-covered terrain glistens from the rays of the sun as it rises for the day. The backdrop of the inky sky morphing to varying shades of pink, orange, and gold makes it all seem surreal.

The location is easily accessible since it's in the same Valais Canton as Verbier. The concierge at the hotel arranged our sunrise visit via helicopter with a guide to top off our honeymoon.

I want to give Leonie one more unforgettable experience before we head back to the real world tomorrow morning. And this surpasses all my expectations.

Leonie isn't the only one entranced by the beauty of nature. I'm rendered speechless.

We stand with her back to my front, my arms wind around to hold her firmly to my body. I rest my chin on the top of her hood-covered head.

She places her mittened hands over mine and leans into my embrace.

No more words pass between us as we're captivated by the stunning sunrise. The next ten minutes provide a kaleidoscopic display of naturally colored lights. Their dazzling glow demands no competition from any sound.

When the last traces of the night disappear in the face of the rising sun, I give Leonie a squeeze.

"Let's take a selfie, baby. I want you to have a keepsake," I tell her.

She nods, and we shift so the glacier and the mountain are behind our backs. The view is further depicted in the reflections on our silver mirrored ski goggles. Oversized to protect our eyes from the intense glare, they emphasize the enormity of the scenery.

The guide comes over and takes more photos for us. Then he points out some sights. By the time we're ready to leave, Leonie has more than enough keepsakes.

Once on board the helicopter, the guide continues to explain highlights along the way we couldn't see in the pre-dawn. With the sun up, the view is more impactful.

Leonie swings her head from one side of the helicopter to the other, not wanting to miss a thing. Her enthusiasm is contagious. Neither of us can believe how awesome are the sights.

When we arrive on the edge of the village, Leonie and I thank the crew before we head to the G-Wagen. The concierge also arranged for the hotel's restaurant that serves breakfast to open early for Leonie and me.

"How did you like the glacier, baby?" I ask as I drive the short distance.

Not surprisingly, the streets bustle with early risers eager to hit the ski slopes for the fresh powder.

"Oh, Roger! It was amazing! I've seen nothing like it before," Leonie exclaims as she claps her hands.

I lean over and kiss her lips. Fuck! I want to devour her.

She giggles at my growl of longing.

"Where are we headed?"—Leonie's amber eyes widen when she spots STEELE Verbier—"You're taking me to the hotel to ravage me??"

I bust out laughing. Not a bad idea. One that should have occurred to me. Instead of sitting in a restaurant, I could dine on Leonie in the palatial Matterhorn Suite and take her to heights unknown.

My guffaws die out as I consider the possibility.

"Dial STEELE Verbier concierge," I voice command the SUV's mobile system.

Leonie's mouth drops, and I chuckle.

"You asked for it, Pretty Kitty," I smirk. "We were having an early breakfast at the hotel's restaurant only. But since you insist…"

Leonie squirms in the plush leather seat as she bites her lower lip.

"I do," she breathes huskily.

My cock throbs.

"Dial Nanny Grace…"

HOURS after we end our honeymoon with an unforgettable bang—more like five or six—I stare at my wife and sons on board my Gulfstream G650 headed back to Paris. We flew out of Verbier on my Sikorsky S-92 Executive Helicopter to

Geneva, then switched to the jet for the seventy-five-minute flight.

They're my precious cargo I vow to love, care for, and protect with my life. I will allow no one to bring them harm or heartache. Leonie is a fierce *Lion*, but I'm a feral wolf whose pack is his top priority. Don't fuck with me.

Especially after the bullshit ordeal with Delia Shaw. The stress caused Leonie to go into labor early. We made it through with healthy, beautiful sons. But no repeat of outside interference to my family.

Leonie must sense my intense stare and glances over at me. She tilts her head to the side and arches her eyebrow in question to the scowl on my face.

"Nothing, babe," I respond. "Just thinking about the real world popping our bubble after eight, well nine if we include the holidays, weeks off the grid."

Leonie's laugh lights the cabin as she throws her head back in glee.

"If you consider being in a multimillion-dollar, ginormous chalet in a bustling Swiss ski village 'off the grid.' Roger, you crack me up!" She whoops.

I roll my eyes.

"Semantics. You know what I mean, smart aleck," I retort. "You do realize what happens to sassy pants? Do you not, Pretty Kitty?"

Leonie glances at the door that separates us from the flight crew where Nanny Grace also sits.

It's closed and soundproof. No one will enter our section of the jet once the Do Not Disturb light turns on.

Her gaze returns to mine and she juts her chin out in defiance.

"*Non*, I do not 'realize what happens to sassy pants,'

Monsieur Steele," Leonie states using her fingers for air quotes.

Slowly I rise to my full height of six feet, three inches, and stalk over to her.

Leonie's eyes track my movement as she licks her lips. Once I near, she glances at The Twins asleep in their seats.

"Well, you better be quiet so as not to wake them," I say as I indicate their peaceful sleepy forms with a nod.

Leonie shivers and her amber eyes darken as her pupils dilate, driven by lust.

"Well, I guess so," she replies.

"Ah, still so cheeky are you now, Pretty Kitty?" I ask with a smirk. "Hmmm. Let us see how much your cheeks appreciate your mouth."

Abruptly, I lift her to her feet and crush her body to mine as I slant my lips over hers in a scorching kiss.

Leonie's moan morphs into a squeal when I smack that ass, alternating cheeks several times through the thin material of her leggings. She squirms in my arms.

But I hold her firm, not breaking our kiss. A nip to her plump bottom lip, and I pull her to the bedroom at the back of the jet. She whimpers and trails behind me, easily keeping pace with my long strides.

I urge Leonie through the door ahead of me, then leave it open so we can hear The Twins should they awaken.

She peeks at me over her shoulder and watches as I walk past her to sit on the bed with my feet planted wide.

"Strip," I demand.

A flush blooms on Leonie's cheeks, and I smirk thinking how it will soon appear on her ass. Through my jeans, I stroke my cock, lengthening in anticipation.

She unbuttons her cardigan and lets it slip off her shoulders, then shimmies out of her leggings and thong. Her ample tits jiggle with her movements and almost spill over the tops of the bra cups.

When she stands, Leonie runs her hands over her breasts and moans when she pinches the nipples through the lace. She unhooks the front clasp, and the bra slides down her arms to the puddle of clothes at her feet.

Splendidly naked before me, I lean back on my hands and marvel at her beauty. I'm reminded of our first encounter when I walked in on Leonie topless in the conference room at STEELE New York. Her plump brown nipples were just as succulent.

My cock strains against the zipper of my jeans. I shift my hips for some relief.

Leonie smirks as her gaze lands on my impressive bulge.

"Come," I command.

She swallows when I pat my thighs. Her curvy hips sway as she sashays to stand before me.

I grip them and pull her forward to press my open mouth against her bare mons. A deep inhale fills my nostrils with the succulent aroma of her arousal. My tongue darts out to prod her seam, laving her juices in one slow swipe.

"Ohhh, Roger," Leonie moans as she grips my shoulders, widening her stance.

I swat her ass, relishing in the jiggle the spank evokes. Then I drape her torso over my thighs. Her hip rests against my engorged cock.

She wiggles. But I hold her in place with one hand clasping hers on her lower back and one leg over hers.

Whap. Whap. Whap. Whap.

My palm connects with her round cheeks—left, right, left, crease of her ass and thigh, right, left.

The steady rhythm has Leonie dancing on my lap. With each spank, she gasps.

A brilliant crimson bloom spreads with the heat. Her cries become mewls as her heady arousal fills the bedroom.

"Now do you realize what happens to sassy pants, Pretty Kitty?" I purr in her ear. "Or do you need a further reminder?"

Leonie shakes her head, and the curtain of her mahogany waves undulates.

WHAP. WHAP. WHAP.

Another quick volley to her cheeks—left, right, left, crease of her ass and thigh, right, left—reminds her to use her voice.

"*Nnooon... Non...* I mean *OUI!*" She cries as she slumps over my thighs in surrender.

I purr against her neck as my middle finger slips between her ass cheeks. A swipe from her puckered hole to her soaked seam makes Leonie judder with a strangled cry.

Slowly I pump my thick digit in and out of her slick pussy, adding another pointer finger as my thumb presses her swollen clit. All the while I purr, nuzzling her damp neck.

The flutter of her pussy walls vibrates along my fingers, announcing the arrival of her release.

"Cum for me, Pretty Kitty. Cum undone for me," I command in a voice rough with desire.

Leonie's pussy contracts as my pumps increase in tempo, plunging deeper within her dripping core. A strangled scream falls from her slack mouth. She arches her back like a cat and grinds her pelvis into my thigh, adding pressure to my thumb on her clit.

"Give it to me, now!" I growl.

Leonie stiffens, then wails as her entire body ignites from the erotic energy coursing through every cell of her being.

Soothingly, I pet her and croon in her ear as she returns from a state of sheer euphoria. When she stretches languidly in my arms, I nip her ear.

"My turn."

In one swift move, I rise, place Leonie on her hands and knees at the edge of the bed, and tear open my jeans. My painfully swollen cock bobs free and hits my abs, the bulbous tip an angry red and shiny with pre-cum.

I grip the base with one hand and Leonie's hip with the other before I ram home.

"Fuuuck... You feel so good," I groan balls deep within her warm, silken pussy.

Leonie keens. She digs her nails into the bedding as she drops her head, panting. My long and lean strokes grow wild, and she slides forward.

I grip the top of her shoulder to hold her in place, leaning my torso over hers as our lower bodies slap against the other. My heavy balls hit her clit with each strike.

We buck and grunt.

Leonie cries out from another orgasm.

I'm relentless and demand two more from her before I give in to my own spine-tingling release with a roar.

We collapse onto the bed in a sweaty heap, still intimately connected. Moments later Leonie peers at me over her shoulder, her feline eyes glow.

"*Amoureux*... I change my mind. I need a further reminder after all..." she purrs as she wiggles her hips.

LEONIE

*M*y body still thrums from our lovemaking as we ride in the private elevator up to our newly renovated triplex penthouse. I cannot wait to move in to our family home officially.

My mother assured me all is ready and my big surprise for Roger hangs in our bedroom still covered by the tarp. I didn't want the movers and the installation crew to see Roger's nude body.

It's for my eyes only—mine!

It's just the four of us tonight. Tomorrow, Nanny Grace will move into her suite of rooms on the first floor. Although Grace will have rooms at each of our residences, she'll only stay until Roger gets home or when we go out. But we plan to be hands-on parents who have the help of a nanny.

The porters took the service elevator to bring our luggage to the service entrance of our penthouse. So when the elevator doors open to the foyer and Roger sets The

Twins down in their car seats beside the front door, I glance at him.

He grins and swoops me from my feet in a bride hold against his powerful chest. Then he places his hand on the plate to unlock the door before carrying me inside.

"Welcome home, my love," Roger says.

The open expression of emotion on his face makes my heart soar.

I clasp his cheeks and pull his mouth to mine. The electricity that roars between us is undeniable. We will never be apart again. Over and over we justify our love.

Ga-ga-gas from the foyer remind us of our little ones, and our passionate kiss ends in laughter. Lovers, yes. But parenthood calls.

Roger places me on my feet, kisses my lips, and brings our sons inside.

"Welcome home to you, too, Rodolphe and Gaspard!" I tell them.

Smiles widen their chubby cheeks and drool slips down their chins. Roger and I exchange glances and laugh some more.

"Yes, my sons, welcome home," he chuckles.

We make quick work of settling them in their nursery. I'm eager to show Roger his wedding present. He must sense my excitement and asks what I'm up to. I giggle and pull him from the room.

We race holding hands to our suite of rooms, laughing along the way. Our mood is light and carefree. Once we pass the lounge, I pause at the double doors to the bedroom and en suite bathroom.

"I have a surprise for you, *Mon Cœur*. Close your eyes," I tell him.

Roger grins and rubs his hands together, "In the bedroom? Give it to me, baby!"

I lead him inside and position him at the foot of our massive, four-poster canopy bed. As I move away, he grabs for me, but I swat his hands.

"Behave! Or I won't give your wedding present to you, naughty boy!" I reprimand.

"We've had this conversation before, babe," he says, motioning towards his sizable crotch and thrusting his hips.

"You are impossible, Roger Steele! Give me a minute," I laugh as I remove the tarp and stand back at his side. "Surprise!"

Roger opens his eyes, and they widen when he sees the life-sized painting of his nude body as he sleeps. My eyes follow his as they roam over his beautiful form. His likeness is unmistakable and lifelike.

So peaceful and at rest. No concerns worry him in his slumber.

One chiseled arm thrown over his face to block the morning sun coming through the windows. Its rays of light slant across his powerful chest and eight-pack abs, high-lighting the happy trail of dark hair. Even lying flaccid and against his thigh, his massive dick with its bulbous head, veins, and heavy balls makes my mouth water. His thick thighs and muscular calves stretch out beneath the silk sheet.

The five o'clock shadow along with his mussed, collar-length hair emphasize his sex appeal. His sensuous full lips and long eyelashes make any woman jealous. Balanced out by his sculpted cheeks and jaw add a decidedly masculine edge to his features. No mistaking Roger is anything but all man.

I captured his beauty. My Adonis.

"Leonie, this is magnificent, thank you," he murmurs in awe. "When did you paint me? Where are we? Wait a minute who hung it?"

I cover my mouth and giggle. Roger *The Responsible* on full alert.

"First, it remained covered by a tarp I sealed around the frame. So no one but me has ever seen you in all of your glory!

"I'm so happy that you like it. It was eight months ago at *Le Beaulieu Manoir*. A moment in time while you were so peaceful and undisturbed... Before the pretrial began."

My voice trails off at the unwanted memory. But I let go of the negativity and offer Roger my most seductive smile.

"So, how are you going to thank me, Monsieur Steele?" I purr, gazing at him from beneath my eyelashes. "This portrait always makes me so hot and achy for you."

Roger bites his lip and lowers his head before he charges and tosses me onto our bed. He pounces and thanks me repeatedly.

* * *

"*Joyeux Anniversaire!*"

"Happy Birthday!"

My parents, the Steeles, and Luc celebrate The Twins' six-month birthday the day after we return from Verbier.

We're gathered around the dining room table with Rodolphe and Gaspard sitting in their high chairs. They're bedazzled by the flickering candles on the identical cakes before them.

As everyone sings, The Twins bounce and wave their arms in amusement. Each has one little tooth that gleams in the light. All the drooling and tears led to their first tooth. Every day, they surprise us with their growth.

I still can't believe it's been half a year already.

Roger and I bend over to blow out the candles. When we lean in to kiss their chubby cheeks, Gaspard says, "Dada, dada!"

My eyes fly to Roger, who looks stunned.

"Dada, dada."

We look over to Rodolphe, and he waves his arms, repeating the words.

Roger has tears in his eyes as he lifts first Gaspard, then Rodolphe into his arms. He kisses their cheeks and holds them close.

I wrap my arms around the three of them. Roger buries his face in my hair. It's an unexpected, momentous occasion that overwhelms us.

The room is silent save The Twins and their baby sounds.

"Well, Dada, don't get all sappy on us!"

Roger and I lift our heads as Harris laughs.

"I'm ready for some cake, bro!"

Everyone laughs at the jokester.

While Roger continues to hold The Twins and chats with Sebastian, Lola helps me cut the Gateau St. Honoré cakes. With the recipe tips the chef shared, my mother made them. The Twins' birthday gave her the perfect excuse to try the recent version.

I glance up to see her nervously watching Lola and I cut into the flaky confections. My mother looks relieved after Harris takes a bite and raves about the delicious factor being off the charts.

She smiles at me, and I hug her, whispering congratulations and my thanks for such thoughtful goodies. I take a bite of my piece and swoon from the delicious flavor. Harris is right!

We spend the next half an hour opening presents. With The Twins' development in mind, the gifts include stacking toys with different-sized rings and multi-colored cubes; cars, trains, and balls that roll, light up, and make music to encourage crawling; roly-poly toys; sturdy toys that encourage pulling up to standing; to keep them entertained, colorful board books.

The Dynamic Duo give them some gadgets claiming one is never too young for technology.

Luc bought them their first stock portfolios. The men were more impressed and had a lengthy discussion about their growth potential.

Afterwards, we go to the cinema room with aperitifs.

Haley surprises us with a compilation movie of our first family Christmas and New Year's. No one even realized she was taking footage while we were together. Some scenes from us skiing, the angle straight on as though we were still on the piste; making s'mores at the outside firepit; The Twins first snowfall; the New Year's Eve fireworks in the village.

She has it set to some of my favorite Christmas songs, including "Christmas Canon" and Andrea Bocelli and Céline Dion's "The Prayer."

I give her an enormous hug as tears well in my eyes.

Haley impresses everyone, and we request copies. Always prepared, she handed out artfully packaged copies to each of us.

Later, as Roger wraps around me with my back to his front in bed, I think about how tomorrow we'll return to reality. Roger has a full schedule of meetings set up at STEELE and site visits already. I plan to finish my sketches and proposal on my new division for Sebastian. Then present them to him, Roger, and Morgan at the end of the week.

I sigh and snuggle closer to the warmth and solidness of Roger. The strength he exudes is more than enough to sustain us both. I smile when I correct myself, the four of us.

Yes, I'm an Independent Woman. But I value all that my Alpha male provides. So with him, I have no doubt we can emerge from our bubble and face the real world head on—

"Stop thinking, my love. Sleep. I've got you," Roger whispers.

ROGER

"What the fuck?! I thought this bullshit was over already! What do you mean another lawsuit?!"

My mind blows through the roof at STEELE Paris. I am so pissed my body vibrates.

Today is my first day back. When Sebastian mentioned we had meetings this morning, I presumed they were project status updates. I found it odd he insisted I wasn't late—not that I am late to a meeting, ever.

My angry eyes move from one face to the next at the conference table in my suite of offices. My father and my siblings along with Albert Perry STEELE Paris' General Counsel stare back at me.

"Roger, it is understandable it upsets you. Sit back down. We have mush to discuss," my father states.

I run my hands through my hair, tugging at the roots to ground myself.

"Leonie. She has to be here. I promised her I wouldn't

keep anything from here again," the words tumble from my mouth as I reach into my trousers pocket for my mobile.

No way can I speak. She'd hear anger in my voice and question me. Questions for which I do not have answers.

Hey, I need you to come to my offices now.

A moment passes, and my mobile rings. I have no choice but to accept.

"What happened?" Leonie asks without preamble.

I sigh, then respond, "We're having a meeting about some unexpected developments. You need to be here. Just come now. Please."

Dropping into my seat, I toss my mobile onto the table's shiny wooden surface. I watch it slide until it rests against a leather pen holder.

"She's on her way," I say unnecessarily since they picked up my side of the conversation. "We'll continue once she arrives."

I swivel my chair to face the wall of floor-to-ceiling windows. The city stretches out before me with unobstructed views from the twentieth floor. The Seine below with the Eiffel Tower in the distance serve as the notable landmarks in the area. On a clear, sunny day like this morning, the panoramas are riveting.

Today, not so much.

My mind is in turmoil. Thoughts bounce around as I try to wrap my brain around this news.

FUCK!

No one speaks loudly; inaudible murmurs and the shuffling of papers fill the void.

"What happened?"

Leonie burst into the room. Her amber eyes glow as her gaze seeks me out.

When we connect, she rushes forward. Concern covers

her beautiful face. I did not want her to worry so soon after we return. Now this.

I stand to meet her, and she implores me again. Instead of responding, I gesture to the chairs and we sit.

Leonie looks around the table expectantly. Morgan nods at Albert.

"Delia Shaw filed a lawsuit in New York City against STEELE International and Roger. The allegations differ slightly from those in the previous claims. The Paris legal team has been working with the New York general counsel for the past few weeks—"

"Few weeks?" I explode. "Why am I hearing about it now and not when it started?"

Morgan holds up his hand for silence.

"You were on your honeymoon. I left you to enjoy time with your new wife and sons. The baseless claim did not need your attention," he starts. "Allow Albert to finish. He will explain."

I glare at Sebastian and spit out, "I should have been told."

Leonie takes my hand in hers and shakes her head.

"Roger, our anger is not for our family. They did what they thought was best," she pauses, then continues as she rubs her thumb over my hand. "I agree. That woman inflicted enough pain. We deserved to enjoy our honeymoon. Please, *Mon Cœur*."

Leonie's heartfelt plea and her soothing presence refocuses me.

I cup her face and stare into her eyes deeply.

"Okay, my love. Okay," I comply.

The smile she rewards me with could light the Eiffel Tower more brilliantly than any extravagant light show. She turns her head and kisses my fingertips.

I beam at her, then nod at those gathered.

"Give me the net net. This ends now."

"Now there's the Roger *The Responsible* we all know and love," Sebastian smirks. "And for the record, I voted to tell you, that is after Lola threatened to deny me the pleasures of—"

Haley throws her hands up and screams at the ceiling, "I've had enough of my brothers' sex lives already!"

The tension in the room dissipates after shy Haley erupts. Everyone laughs, including me. As always, my family has my back. I'm sure I would have done the same for them.

Our father clears his throat, and Albert continues.

Leonie and I learn Delia Fucking Shaw has been extremely busy these past seven months. The shit starter left France shortly after the pretrial ended to return to the United States. But instead of going home to West Bumfuck, she went to New York City.

In an attempt to divulge STEELE information, Delia applied for a position at Rockett Construction Company.

Sebastian says he received an urgent call from Patrick. His head of human resources flagged Delia's resume as a former STEELE employee. Immediately he brought her application to Patrick's attention. He recognized her name from Billie mentioning the trouble she was causing me and the company—not to mention how she wanted to strangle Delia for upsetting Leonie.

Patrick and Baz devised a scheme for Delia to interview with him under the pretense he wanted information on their top competitor from the source directly. She agreed to the videotaping, and he captured her disclosing confidential plans. Hell, she even flirted with him and offered to tell him more over dinner.

From one multibillionaire to another...

Patrick turned her down for the position and the offer.

Delia does not know STEELE and Rockett are on better terms since Billie started dating Patrick. So he gave the footage to us—and signed an ironclad nondisclosure agreement. Now we have an ace in the hole.

Not one to give up easily, Delia sold her story to some gossip rag, and a bottom-of-the-barrel book publisher had a ghostwriter fabricate her tragic tale. Some low-level legal firm accepted her case with more bullshit claims. She has a smear campaign leading up to her book tour, including appearances on less than stellar talk shows.

My personal assistant Françoise video conferences the STEELE New York legal team on the big screen. They provide an update and answer the questions Leonie and I ask. The judge scheduled a meeting with the teams in two weeks. However, the general counsel assures us the case won't make it to court. The fact the French pretrial judge threw out the case adds to our favor. Their confidence puts us at ease.

Next the global head of communications joins us with her New York lead via video conference as her Paris lead enters my office. They discuss protocols to handle the media—they're already circling like vultures—and next steps. They drafted a press release for our review and scheduled some good-feeling stories to run for STEELE and me.

I'm a proponent for community improvement and volunteer through STEELE Foundation regularly. My mother runs our family's foundation that builds and manages attractive, affordable housing for urban, lower-income families. The name is a play on the house foundation, being strong and supportive like steel. So it's not a tough sell for our philanthropic efforts.

The communications team forwards a list of interviews and events they encourage Leonie and me to take part in together. They want to present a united front and highlight our newlywed status and family life.

Leonie agrees immediately and offers valuable suggestions. Her experience being in the world's spotlight as a megamodel makes her accustomed to handling all kinds of media coverage with ease. She impresses everyone with her knowledge.

After further discussion, the communications team signs off.

The room grows quiet as everyone absorbs what we discussed. I know my mind is mulling it over, so I don't doubt they're cogitating it. too.

My father turns to me and scans my face. Then his gaze falls on Leonie. He makes a decisive nod before he speaks.

"Roger, do not stew over these latest developments. We defeated that woman's baseless claims once. These circumstances do not differ," he says before shifting back to her.

Morgan continues, "Leonie, you settle my son and provide support for hum. However, you must take care of yourself, too. We cannot allow you to stress over this nonsense, again. The Twins need their mother healthy and happy."

"We are a family and as such everyone takes on the mantle of tending to each other's needs. Everyone here, your parents, Shelley, and Lola stand as one," he concludes, as he spreads his arms wide to indicate all, including those not around us.

"*Merci, Papa* Steele, family is extremely important to me, and I appreciate your kind words," Leonie says, her voice thick with emotion before she clears her throat and a fierce look brightens her eyes. "I agree with you completely. She who shall not be named will not hurt our family again."

"Hear, hear!"

"Well said!"

"Absolutely agree!"

"Oh, she'll get what's coming to her. I guarantee."

Every head spins towards Haley. The determined expression on her face belies her shy nature. Rarely does she speak so adamantly. She's the most soft-spoken one of us all.

Haley meets our surprised gazes with a steely glint to her gray eyes.

"If that is all, I have work to do," she says, then rises when our father confirms we're done. "Roger and Leonie, no need to worry."

A nod and she's out the door.

"Well, all righty then... Was Haley enigmatic or what?" Harris laughs, pushing back from the table. "Leave it to me to solve the mystery of my twin. Leonie, Roger, I'm here for the next week or so. Holla at your boy."

I chuckle as Harris salutes and about-faces before following in his twin's footsteps.

"Thanks, everyone"—I squeeze Leonie's hand and smile at her. Then glance around the table at our family—"We appreciate your support. And I'm not mad you left us to enjoy our honeymoon. This news would have put a damper on it without a doubt."

Sebastian smirks, knowing the fun had during two months of uninterrupted time with a new bride. He nods and claps his hands.

"Well, now that's over... We have a company to run, revenue to generate, profits to increase. You know the really important matters," he says. "Leonie, my lovely sister, we must bid you adieu. It's time for business updates since Romeo has been otherwise engaged."

She laughs, then rises to salute the STEELE CEO à la Harris.

"Yes, Sir!"

Baz busts out laughing when he spies my reaction to "Sir." The Alpha Dom finds it hilarious my wife referred to him by the title.

Leonie winks as she leans over to kiss me.

"Oops... Did I say something wrong?" She purrs against my lips, audible to me only. "See you later, *Amoureux...*"

My cock jumps.

LEONIE

"*W*hy, Monsieur Steele, don't you look scrumptious? My own James Bond oozing sexiness in a bespoke tuxedo. Rawr..."

The sight of my man oh so debonair makes me wet my lace thong.

We're heading to a charity gala for the girls and teens center I mentor at twice a month. It's a passion of mine I've done for over eleven years now. My mentees trust me and find the center a safe space to open up. Even those I've mentored before often come back to meet with me and to talk to the new girls. It's so good to watch them grow up.

Besides their concerns about life and the state of the world, we discuss their goals and what they want to do after they graduate from school. Just as important, they share their thoughts on body image and stereotypical misperceptions about women.

As someone who has worked hard my entire career to dispel models as dumb; only clothes hangers; only good enough to stand there and pose prettily, not think, I can relate. I've encouraged my peers to do the same.

My mentees and I also have fun doing makeovers and spa days. Several times a year, they attend my photoshoots and fashion shows. Several photographers and designers have joined our sessions and become mentors.

This is the first year I didn't chair the gala committee because of my wedding. However, Roger and I donated the use of the rooftop ballroom at STEELE Montaigne. Funny enough, the city named the street for Luc's family.

In the *huitième* arrondissement the five-star hotel has extraordinary views of the Champs-Élysées, Arc de Triomphe, and the Place de la Concorde, not to mention the Seine. At night, with the lights of Paris shining brightly, will prove a spectacular venue for the gala.

But nothing compares to the sight before me of sexy Roger Steele in his tux. Yum.

He chuckles and adjusts the sleeves over his cuffs. The platinum and diamond cuff links glint in the light—along with his wedding band.

Mine!

"Pleased with my appearance, Mrs. Steele?" He asks in a husky voice with his eyebrow raised.

I step into his personal space. The air between us charges with erotic energy. Immediate tightness in my nipples and pussy makes me lightheaded with desire.

Skimming my hands over the lapels of his jacket, up his muscular chest to wrap around his neck makes my fingertips tingle.

"*Absolument, Amoureux,*" I purr, my lips brush against the sensitive shell of his ear.

The sensation of Roger's sizable frame shuddering with need resonates through my smaller body. He grips my hips possessively and grinds his burgeoning erection against my mons. Pressure to my clit sends a zing down my legs to curl my toes in the sky-high strappy sandals.

"You are even more delectable in this sexy as fuck gown, Mrs. Steele," he murmurs against the side of my neck. His warm breath and seductive growl cause goosebumps to surface on my heated skin.

When Roger cups my ass, I purr in contentment as I melt into his embrace.

The crotch-high slit in the floor-length, silver silk-satin gown allows me to wrap my long leg around Roger's hip. I rise onto the ball of my standing foot to align our centers.

Simultaneous growls fall from our mouths as Roger ups the ante by bending his knees to prod from below. The increase in contact rocks my mind.

"Do you want something from me, Mrs. Steele?" He murmurs between hot, open-mouthed kisses to my collarbone and the tops of my breasts along the sweetheart neckline.

"Make me cum," I respond breathlessly in need of release from his massive dick.

Roger chuckles, squeezes my ass, and unhooks my leg.

"Duly noted, Mrs. Steele," he says as he holds my hips to steady me.

The sudden loss of his solid body and heat leaves me on wobbly legs. Like a newborn foal, my footing is unstable.

I clutch his wide shoulders and scowl.

"We can't be late, slowpoke," he teases me for my time flaw. "They expect the gala hostess on the red carpet as scheduled."

My lips form a pout, and Roger nips at them as he murmurs, "Be a good girl, and I will make it up to you, Pretty Kitty."

With a pat to my ass, he strides to the wall of drawers.

"Oh, so I See, Monsieur Ste—"

My words stop at this new sight dangling from Roger's hands: a diamond necklace crafted like a zipper. The Van Cleef & Arpels Zip necklace stuns me speechless.

Roger smirks as he lays the couture zipper with filigree lacework and sumptuous tassels around my neck. The cool platinum heats as the zipper dips into my décolletage, the diamonds on the tassels tickle the delicate skin.

"You were saying, Mrs. Steele?" Roger prompts as he toys with the tassels, setting the zipper to just the right closure. The tips of his fingers brush against my skin.

My nipples pucker from his touch.

He chuckles and returns to the drawer. When he stands before me, he opens his left hand, gesturing towards my ears.

Quickly, I remove the antique diamond and sapphire chandelier earrings and place them in his outstretched palm.

Roger nods and opens his right hand. Light sparks as a pair of matching diamond tassels shimmer.

With an eagerness a woman who receives such magnificent jewels can muster, I nearly snatch the baubles from his hand. Set in my ears, I grin from ear to ear as I swing my head from side to side, loving the feel of the tassels tickling my jaw.

"*Merci, Mon Cœur!*" I exclaim as I kiss his luscious lips curled into a smile. "You're so good to me!"

"Yes, and you will be even better for me later in your diamonds only, Pretty Kitty," Roger growls into my kisses.

I purr in delight.

. . .

"Roger! This way!"

"*The Lion*! Here, here!"

No sooner do we step out of our Rolls-Royce Phantom Extended at the STEELE Montaigne, then the photographers go wild. Their flashes put spots before our eyes.

Roger tightens his grip on my hand, the only sign of the tension in his body. He's bracing for their questions. The smile on his face as he pulls me into his side to pose for their cameras gives no clue.

My modeling instincts kick in. A tilt to my head, the angle of my hips, a purposeful kick of my bare leg with my wedding jewelry on my upper thigh. Not to mention the dazzling smile made blinding by the diamonds framing my face.

The photogs go wild.

Gotcha!

I rule this land, not some wannabe trollop seeking her fortune at the expense of others. *The Lion* is ferocious. Don't fuck with my family or me.

A subtle squeeze to my hip, and Roger encourages us to continue down the gauntlet of the red carpet as the STEELE Paris communications lead joins us. When we near the center, another roar from the crowd harkens Lola and Sebastian.

Roger and I watch as they play to the cameras.

Lola looks radiant in a black strapless Swarovski crystal-embellished gown with a slit as high as mine. The red silk lining of her gown draws the photogs like a bull by a matador. Rubies adorn her ears, neck, and fingers. Baz—as dashing as my Roger—smirks with his hand possessively on her waist as the flashes go into overdrive.

The center's public relations manager approaches Roger and me with a request for an on-carpet interview with an

American magazine. He confers with the STEELE lead, and they decide she will shut down the interview should it go left with questions about she who shall not be named.

"Ready?" I ask Roger, stroking his back as I gaze up at him.

"Yes, my love," he responds, then brushes his lips over mine.

The female reporter and her male photographer eagerly watch us approach. She begins the questions directed at me regarding my involvement with the center—basic. Then she swings her gaze to Roger and her eyes gleam.

"Mr. Steele, how supportive are you of your wife's endeavors with young women?" She asks.

Roger smiles down at me before he responds with praise and admiration.

"What are your thoughts on women having the right to say no?" She asks glaring at him.

"Thank you for your questions," the STEELE Paris communications lead cuts in as she opens her arm to separate us from the interviewer. She moves us away.

"Oh, so no answer, Mr. Steele?" The magazine writer persists. "Don't women have—"

"Women have every right to say no. And men have every right to not fall victim to someone who falsely accuses them under the guise of sexual assault. That tactic does a disservice to women, and men, who have been victims of actual sexual assault. Not fabrications for monetary gain. Thank you for your questions."

Roger's response silences the woman, and her photographer nods in agreement.

Sebastian and Lola stand behind us, along with Luc and Blair—who Roger and I hadn't seen arrive. The interviewer glances at them and back to us. Daunted by their show of support, she turns away without further comment.

"Well said, bro," Sebastian says when we move away from the row of media reps. "You handled the situation perfectly."

The STEELE Paris communications lead agrees and tells us she will contact the magazine publisher to follow up on the piece. She takes us along the line to media reps she vetted in advance. Fortunately, we don't encounter another ridiculous question.

We pose for more photos in front of the step and repeat highlighting the event sponsors including STEELE International, Inc., Lola's Coterie, Banque Montaigne, Jackson Corporation, Elie Saab, Van Cleef & Arpels, and other high-profile companies.

Lola and I joke about our leg-baring gowns while Roger and Sebastian chuckle. The photogs eat it up.

"Hey, Hot Mama! I love your necklace!" Lola exclaims. "It's beyond gorgeous!"

I run my fingers over the handcrafted piece and grin.

"My latest present from my husband," I respond.

"I'm glad you like it. Monsieur Steele commissioned it especially for you, Madame."

Lola and I turn to the alluring French voice to find the President and CEO of Van Cleef & Arpels smiling at me.

His cornflower blue eyes shine.

"In fact, Madame Steele, we would love to discuss a spokesmodel opportunity with you," he continues. "It would honor us to have *The Lion* represent our Maison."

I smile at him as I extend my hand, "The honor would be all mine, Monsieur."

"My office will reach out to your agent next week," he

replies then turns to smile at Lola. "Madame Steele, the Maison's Flowers look lovely on you."

She grins and touches her fingers to her ears as she thanks him. "Roses are my favorites."

A palm on the small of my back draws my attention to Roger, who also extends his hand to the head of the jewelry house. They chat along with Baz before we make our way to the cocktail hour with signature libations crafted by Lachlan using the Jackson portfolio. *The Sexy Chef* Lucien created the tantalizing hors d'oeuvres.

"The decorations are fantastic! I love how they incorporated the rubies and diamonds theme," Blair says.

She dazzles in the Van Cleef & Arpels Snowflake Collarette with earrings that match the pendant. Her red mikado-piqué strapless mermaid gown skims her curves and sweeps the floor in the back. With her chestnut brown hair swept up, her wide cerulean blue eyes stand out in her heart-shaped face.

"*Oui*, Leonie, tonight's gala is spectacular, even better than last year. Are you ready to host?" Luc asks.

I smile at *Le Renard Argenté*. Lola and I are so happy he's found a partner in Blair. Who would have thought he'd give in to her flirtations?

"So are you saying this year is better since I was less involved?" I tease.

Luc chuckles and his sapphire blue eyes shine.

"Of course not, *chérie*. You are an essential part of this center and have helped to involve many others, including me. Few would be here tonight, or any in the last few years, had you not been a mentee to the young women," he responds.

His words make me proud of the impact I've accomplished with the center. Luc is correct it wasn't widely known when I started and their donations were not as abundant. What I care about the most are the girls and teens who keep coming back and being certain they have a facility with staff worthy of them.

"How kind of you! *Oui*. I'm excited and cannot wait to get started," I say. "We have a great surprise for the young ladies."

For the rest of the cocktail hour, we mingle and place bids on the silent auction.

Normally, I would offer a date night with me or a chance to have backstage passes at one of my fashion shows. The high numbers would generate incredible donations for the center.

This year, to avoid Roger going buck wild, my offer is a mock cover shoot with a famous fashion photographer, designer clothes, and a glam squad makeover. The pictures compiled in a portfolio as a unique coffee-table book.

As Roger and I stroll past the displays, we check out the other offers. The week aboard a vintage steam yacht in the Mediterranean Sea catches my attention. Its design fascinates me. I place a significant bid since it would make for a fun getaway.

I notice a pair of prints for offer. Intrigued by the tableau of a spring day in Bois de Boulogne, I take a closer look. The artistry is superb. But it's the sponsor that offers them that makes my eyes widen.

Mattei Art Galleries!

Of course. My ex-paramour Giovanni Mattei supports the center—at my request—and provides a piece from his collection for the gala every year.

Gio is a wealthy nobleman from an Italian aristocratic family dating back to the Middle Ages. And was nowhere near being ready to settle down when we dated for a few years. The billion-dollar playboy, who races cars professionally to boot, attracts women with no effort. They throw themselves at him—one reason I ended our affair. He believes he's *God's Gift* truly.

I glance around. But it's a pointless endeavor since the alcove with the auction doesn't allow a view of the primary room. Nonetheless, I don't want Roger to spot them. He'd likely rip Gio's head off. They do not get along. At all.

"Mon Cœur, let's take our seats at the table," I say as I all but tug Roger out of the alcove and surreptitiously shift my gaze about us.

We make it without incident to the dining area. The view is spectacular with three of the walls comprising floor-to-ceiling windows that lead out to an enormous terrace. Paris stretches out before us with the beauty of its lights aglow.

"This is lovely, Leonie!" Lola exclaims as I settle in my chair beside her. "Who's the event planner? I'd like to use them."

We chat through dinner with Roger and Sebastian and Luc and Blair, along with Lucien and Lachlan and their dates. The meal as expected tastes divine. We congratulate Lucien on another delectable menu.

Before they serve dessert, the head of the center and public relations manager come to our table. They escort me to the stage for my welcome speech and the presentations.

I quip to Lucien to save a dessert for me. The chocolate torte with mocha ice cream sounds irresistible.

As I make my way through the tables—stopping to chat with guests—a hand on my arm stops me. I glance over my shoulder into the warm chocolate brown eyes of Gio.

From the table next to me he stands to his full height of six feet, three inches. His muscular frame emphasizes his commanding presence. With a charming smile, he runs his fingers through his collar-length, curly brown hair.

"*Ciao bellissima. Come stai?*" He asks, double kissing my cheeks with an enormous hand on my waist.

Too taken aback to speak, I stare at him with my lips parted. I'm not sure how I'm doing.

Fortunately, the head of the center interrupts to usher me along to the stage.

I'm shook at seeing him so unexpectedly. But by no means sense any desire for him. Roger claims my heart completely. With that thought in mind, I take the stage and deliver my impassioned speech and appeal for donations.

The guests show their appreciation with a record-breaking total of €750,000. The silent auction generates an additional €250,000. The young women share their gratitude with touching speeches and a video montage of the past year's activities and highlights.

At the end of the presentations, Roger joins me on the stage for the last speech.

I watch him approach and marvel at his sex appeal. *Non,* Gio's name may mean *God's Gift,* but Roger is my heart. No comparison and no competition. At all.

He slips his arm around my waist, possessively pulling me into his side as he thanks the guests for their generosity. Then he adds on behalf of STEELE International, Inc. he presents a check to match the total €1 million raised.

The guests applaud with a standing ovation as the head of the center accepts the check and the photographers capture the moment.

I beam at Roger, completely off guard by his gift.

The Zip necklace and earrings are beyond. But the money to support the young women's center tops it.

As we step off the stage, Roger bends down to murmur in my ear.

"Do not think I did not see that slimy dick kiss you, Pretty Kitty. You wear my rings. You bore my sons and will give me more. You are mine. I am not concerned. However, you will atone for his actions in only your diamonds when we return home. *Tu me comprends?*"

Merde...

ROGER

"*W*ell, that's a fucking relief!"
I say as I slap my palms on the conference table in my office and jump to my feet.

The chair slides backwards and spins at the force. The bang of it colliding with another piece of furniture doesn't faze me in the least bit. I'm in a state of impenetrable euphoria.

The New York City judge threw out the case after two months of talks.

Hell. Yeah.

Leonie leaps into my arms, wrapping her legs around my waist, and grabs my face, planting kisses all over it between words of joy and gratitude.

I cup her round ass and hold her tight to my chest. Our hearts beat wildly with excitement. Six months of marriage and this will never get old.

"Excellent work! Now we can put that woman behind us permanently," my father proclaims at the other end of the table to Albert and the New York legal team present via video conference.

Sebastian slaps me on the back and says, "Absolutely. Keep that bullshit in the past. However, we'll continue to monitor her activities. We can never be too sure with the likes of that conniving woman."

"I'm already on it. My top guy in surveillance at STEELE Cyber Security and I have the situation well in hand," Haley adds with a confident nod.

Harris also nods and returns his gaze to his tablet. His focus had been on it all along.

What is the Dynamic Duo up to now? I wonder.

"That's fantastic news!" Malcolm says as he bro hugs me. "She's one annoying ass broad. Don't even look at the rearview mirror when you zoom past that one. Leave her in the dust."

Everyone laughs when he shudders in revulsion.

"This calls for a celebratory dinner tonight!" Leonie exclaims as she claps her hands and shimmies her shapely hips. "Let's go to Alléno Paris au Pavillon Ledoyen."

"Great idea. Invite Françoise, Luc, Blair, and Lucien. I want to thank my entire support team," I respond, then turn to Albert as I extend my hand. "You and your lead must come, too. Your team did a stellar job."

We shake with claps to the backs, and he agrees.

Leonie makes the call to her friend, who's the chef of the seventh-century restaurant.

Set in the *huitième* arrondissement amongst the gardens of the Champs-Élysées, the three Michelin star eatery is a favorite of ours. Besides the quality dishes, we love the architecture and design, not to mention the views.

Leonie confirms the reservation for the upstairs private

dining room that still boasts some original features. Then calls everyone not present.

I pop my head out of my door to ask Françoise to join us now for a champagne toast—who cares if it's only three in the afternoon—and dinner at eight.

"Monsieur Steele, I am so happy for you. That woman deserves to punishment for her incessant lies," Françoise says as she enters the room.

"That is the absolute truth!" Malcolm *The Enforcer* adds as he rubs his hands together. His eyes gleam devilishly with his smirk.

Once again we laugh at his comment.

Baz pops the bottle of Dom Pérignon Vintage 2002 and pours the elixir in Lalique Crystal flutes. Haley hands them out, then takes hers as my father raises his glass in a toast.

"To the power of family unity. The Steele clan forever!"

Amen to that, I muse as I lift the flute to my lips and squeeze Leonie's waist.

LEONIE and I arrive early at the restaurant—unbelievable for Ms. Tardy—and sit at the bar for a drink. The mixologist recognizes us and waves while he makes our preferred cocktails.

When he brings the drinks to us, we chat for a moment. Then he's off to work his craft for other patrons.

"*Mon Cœur*, I am so thrilled for you and STEELE," Leonie says as she lifts her Kir Royale. "Here's to a fresh start so rightly deserved!"

I raise my Rocks Glass of Jackson Reserve Scotch on ice and stare intently into her eyes, the same color as the liquid. I'd much rather wrap my lips around her clit than around the tumbler's rim. But when I tried to ravage her earlier, she promised me later.

"I'll make it worth your wait, Amoureux. I promise you," Leonie purred as she stroked my thick length when I crept up behind her in the shower.

Now, watching her little pink tongue lick the edge of the crystal flute, I regret not pressing the issue.

Sensing my thoughts, the wily seductress winks at me as she sips the champagne and Chambord Liqueur cocktail. Her thumb and index finger glide up and down the stem when she sets the flute on the bar top. Leonie glances at me sideways beneath her full eyelashes and smiles.

"What's on your mind, Monsieur Steele?" She purrs softly.

Without hesitation, I lean towards her, place my lips against the shell of her ear, and murmur, "Your swollen clit lapped by my tongue. I know you are wet for me, Pretty Kitty. I can scent your arousal since we left the shower."

I nip her earlobe, then lick the sensitive flesh when she jumps. A dark chuckle falls from my lips as I sit back in my chair.

"Well, well, well, don't let us interrupt your love affair."

Leonie and I tear our eyes away from the other and glance up to find Lola and Baz smirking at us.

"I mean, we only came here to celebrate with you, Roger. But if you'd rather take your party to LEVELS Paris... Well, let me get my collar," Lola continues deadpan.

Baz chuckles and whispers in Lola's ear as he tucks her into his side. Her reddening cheeks and giggles prove whatever he said was encouraging and well received.

"Honey! I'm so glad it all ended as we knew it would!" My mother gushes as she hugs me and kisses my face. "And Leonie, sweetheart, what a relief for you!"

They double kiss and embrace.

When the rest of the group arrives, we head upstairs to the private dining room. The waitstaff have more flutes of Dom Pérignon Vintage 2002 and bottles in ice baths ready to pour. They also have trays of Beluga caviar on toast points and foie gras on toasted brioche to complement the champagne.

The waitstaff leave us to enjoy ourselves and only return to serve our food or to replenish our drinks.

Alone in the separate room, not encumbered by other diners, we relax and unwind. The atmosphere is jovial as we chitchat and laugh.

Harris cracks jokes, and Lucien quips how he's insulted we didn't choose one of his eateries for the impromptu party. Josy concurs with Lucien, and we laugh some more.

At the end of our meal, the chef enters. He greets Leonie with double kisses and grins when he spies Lucien, who nods in acknowledgment. We thank the chef for accommodating us on such brief notice and for the delicious meal, particularly since he included some of my favorite dishes.

As we part, my mother hugs me tightly and whispers how glad she is it's over. Then my father—followed by Guy —claps me on the shoulder and shakes my hand.

Leonie and I bid everyone good night and slip into my Aston Martin DB7 Vantage. She mimics the purr of the engine as she glides her thumb and index finger along my cock through my trousers. It's quick to swell along my thigh.

When she tweaks the tip, I growl.

"You are playing with fire, Pretty Kitty. If you keep this up, we will not make it home before I take you," I rumble.

Leonie leans over and coos in my ear. Her warm breath

and the brush of her full tits and pointed nipples against my arm further ignite my desire.

I pull into a space on a side street and cut the engine. The power seat slides back and reclines.

"Here, Kitty, Kitty, Kitty," I tell her as I pat my muscular thighs.

Leonie's amber eyes glow in the dim light from a lamppost on the corner. She lifts her midi skirt over her long, toned legs to straddle me.

Although Aston Martin did not design the interior of the sports car for fucking in the driver's seat, we intend to make it work.

I grip Leonie's hips and lower her exposed, wet pussy—she's no longer allowed to wear panties with dresses and skirts—onto my crotch. We groan as she undulates her hips, rubbing her slick folds against my hard cock.

"Oh, *Amoureux*, I want you deep inside of me now," she mewls, biting her plump lower lip.

"You will have my thick dick how and when I say," I respond with a growl. "First, you will ride my fingers—"

Eagerly Leonie rises onto her knees, her back brushing the roof of the car, to give me access.

"But, you will not cum until I say."

She whimpers in frustration, then moans when two of my thick fingers plunge inside of her pussy. Leonie's breathing increases to pants as I drive my fingers in and out of her slippery channel. The flutters of her inner walls foreshadow her orgasm.

I withdraw and she growls until my fingers press against her upper lips, demanding entrance for her to lick them clean.

"Mmmmmm," Leonie hums as she delights in the taste of her sweet pussy juices.

The vibration on my fingers and her moans of pleasure make my cock jump.

"Unzip my pants and take out my dick," I command.

Leonie scrambles to move her hands from my shoulders to my fly while my fingers remain in her hot, wet mouth.

My head falls back against the seat with a thump when her fingers wrap around my achy cock. As she spreads the pre-cum over the fat head, a groan falls from my parted lips. When Leonie rises to her knees again and strokes her wet folds with my sensitive tip, my hips jerk up as my hands tighten on her waist to pin her in place.

She gasps when I slam into her pussy in one long thrust. Leonie recovers posthaste and grinds her pelvis into mine.

Our erotic connection scorches us.

I grasp her buttocks in my generous hands to hold and to steady her. Then piston my hips to slam my cock to the very end of her channel. Through the vee-neck of her silk blouse, I latch onto her turgid nipple covered by sheer mesh.

She rides me as my brutal thrusts rock her to her core. Each time she's close to her climax, I slow the pace and depth of my strokes. I wet her tits from my suckling and laving. She's ready to break beautifully for me.

I pull her ass cheeks apart and press my thumb against her back hole. The rings of muscle give way as she babbles incoherently. The sensation of her pussy walls clenching through the thin membrane that separates it from her back hole precedes her plea for release.

"Come undone for me, Pretty Kitty," I command in a voice rough with desire.

Her entire body tenses. My fingers nearly break when her pussy walls clamp down on them. A keen starts from her toes to rise to her slack mouth.

As it fills the car with the guttural sound, simultaneously a jolt runs up the backs of my legs and down my spine to meet at the base as my heavy balls fill.

A roar rips from my mouth as I jackhammer into Leonie, chasing my climax. Three plundering thrusts, and my hot seed spews from my pulsating cock to fill her wrecked pussy.

I possess Leonie fully.

And she possesses me.

LEONIE

"*Oh mes beaux fils*, you like your New York City nursery? ... Really? Is that so? ... Well, your *Papa* had to go downstairs to his offices for loads of meetings."

At ten months old, I adore their jibber-jabber as they speak actual words, and their new thing of blowing kisses makes me laugh. Roger got a kick out of them when we escorted him to the Steele family private elevator.

We're in The STEELE Tower's luxury, modern, gray-tinted glass fifty-seven story mixed-use skyscraper on the southwest corner of Fifty-Seventh Street and Fifth Avenue. The area known worldwide as Billionaires' Row.

The residential portion of The Tower runs from the thirtieth through the fifty-seventh floors. Our penthouse on the fifty-second floor is one of the Steele residences. Morgan and Shelley occupy the top two floors with the penthouse duplex. Sebastian and Lola live below in their duplex. Malcolm, Harris, and Haley live in penthouses on the fifty-third, fifty-first, and fiftieth floors, respectively.

The elevator Roger rode down to the executive offices

on the twenty-ninth floor links the Steele penthouses to the floors occupied by their divisions.

We came to the city for work at the STEELE headquarters on the nineteenth through twenty-ninth floors of The Tower. Other businesses take up the eight through the eighteenth floors with a luxury retail mall on the street level through the seventh floor. Lola's Coterie has a prime spot as one of the anchor stores.

We'll be in town for the next three weeks leading up to Labor Day weekend.

Roger's tasks include some potential residential sites, visits to current construction projects, and overall meetings. He also has to attend the quarterly board meeting.

Morgan has the role of Chairman Emeritus since he retired, making Sebastian Chairman. Malcolm moved up to First Vice President, replacing Baz as Roger moved to Second Vice President. Harris and Haley serve as members.

I also have a full schedule of meetings with the Residential Properties Division's Interior Design Team and the Entertainment Properties Division's Amenities Team. We're set to review plans for my newly created STEELE Children and Young Adults Division to incorporate for residential nurseries, bedrooms, playrooms, and playhouses and for hospitality kids clubs and play areas. As the head of the division, I report to Roger and Malcolm, respectively.

While I'm in town, I'll take care of some Lola's Coterie business. We scheduled some photo shoots and marketing activities. Plus, I have the latest designs for the pre- and postnatal collections.

Our hectic schedules called for Nanny Grace to join us for the next couple of weeks.

We'll take one of the company's Sikorsky helicopters out to Steele Southampton Village before Labor Day weekend for the annual party. Shelley and Morgan use it as a fundraiser for STEELE Foundation. The family's magnificent beachfront compound comprising a massive main mansion and three smaller—but no less impressive —mansions.

Roger explained they purchased the adjacent properties over the decades. The elder siblings occupy the three smaller homes while the twins stay in separate wings of the main house. All the residences share the similar style of weathered shingles on the exterior and beach-chic interiors.

He told me I could redo our home, however I preferred. But I told him not this summer since I have a lot on my agenda.

My parents and Luc will fly over to join us for the weekend festivities. Billie and Blair are already in town working with Lola. While Starr plans to come in from Beverly Hills. Baz even invited Patrick—although he's still skeptical...

I love how well our families and friends blend seamlessly.

Tonight, however, Roger and I have plans for LEVELS New York. It's been forever since we last played at one of the clubs. And I cannot wait!

"YOU ARE DRIPPING, Pretty Kitty. Obviously you take pleasure in watching others in the throes of passion, little voyeur. Tell me. What do you want? Do you want me to fuck my pussy until you lie boneless beneath me? Or do you want me to plunder your dirty little hole while I spank that luscious ass?"

I can only widen my hooded eyes and moan in response.

Roger stuck three of his thick fingers coated with my arousal inside of my mouth.

I do my best to lick them clean while I balance reverse cowgirl on his lap, enjoying the view before me as much as my taste.

We arrived at LEVELS New York forty-five minutes ago. After we selected the black enamel bracelets reserved for voyeurs, we entered Peepshow on the 2nd level—my absolute favorite spot with the multilevel dance club next. Both allow me to get my groove on.

To avoid unwanted interactions amongst club participants, the system requires partnered subs to wear collars given to them by their Dom; partnered Doms wear gold bracelets; available subs wear red; available Doms wear white; voyeurs wear black.

All LEVELS locations mandate consensual interactions.

They enforce strict protocols members, their guests, and applicants must follow. From nondisclosure agreements to no-names given unless provided by the person to super tight ongoing background checks and other security measures.

Besides being luxurious and catering to the elite, LEVELS clubs provide safe, judgement-free zones where all sexy fantasies can come true.

Right now, my sexy fantasy is to just cum!

My teasing husband has kept me on edge the entire time we've been in this darkened alcove, not to mention on the ride over. His fingers toyed with my puckered nipples and swollen clit as my Lola's Coterie Swarovski crystal-embellished black sheer tulle chemise and matching sheer stretch-tulle thong mesmerized him.

This time we didn't wear masks—although Roger will never let me walk around stark naked...

And boy is he right. The sight of the carnality all around us makes my pussy juices drip down the crease of my ass to puddle on his massive bulge covered by his black leather pants.

The Peepshow atmosphere is all about bacchanalia with the melodic thrum of sensual music and the moans and groans of men and women as the backdrop to intense sexual play. Some show off their punishment or bondage skills on the demonstration platforms, while others fill the seating alcoves in various stages of intercourse. The air is heavy with the scent of perfume, cologne, and sex.

I grind down on Roger's dick, seeking enough friction to rub my aching clit. My mouth works his fingers like cherry-flavored Popsicles. It's my way of pleading for a reward.

"Words, Pretty Kitty. I will have your words," he demands.

I gasp when he plucks his fingers from my swollen lips. Then glance at him over my shoulder, swinging the curtain of my hair out of my line of sight.

"*S'il te plait, Amoureux*," I plead. "Fuck me with your big dick, please!"

A smirk spreads across Roger's handsome face. In one yank, he tears my thong from my body. The crotch pinches my wet folds, and I yelp.

He rasps in my ear, "Poor, Pretty Kitty. I will make it all better."

Roger grips my hips and lifts me in the air. My fuck-me mules slip from my feet and clatter to the tile floor. He steadies me on the banquette with my feet on either side of his hips. Then he places my hands on the tops of his sturdy thighs.

My bare pussy and bottom hole sit within tongue distance to his face.

Merde!

One long, sinful swipe from the top hole through my slit to my clit, and my knees turn to jelly. Roger wraps his powerful arms around my thighs and delves into his feast.

That skillful tongue of his makes my body quiver in ecstasy. My cries of passion mingle with those of the other members surrounding us.

I ride Roger's face. Then freeze when my pussy clenches and my toes curl from my orgasm as it rips through my body. My back bows, and I scream his name as wave after wave washes over me to the point of lightheadedness.

The pounding of my back against polished wood wakes me from my carnal stupor. I open my eyes to Roger's blackened, focused stare.

My gaze skitters away from the intensity of his eyes to take in my milieu.

We're in one of Peepshow's performance rooms with the curtains drawn over the viewing window. I'm naked and bound by my arms to a St. Andrew's Cross.

Roger holds under my thighs to cup my ass. His forceful thrusts drive me into the cross repeatedly. His grunts and groans fill the room.

Fully awake, my moans join his passionate growls.

"Uh. Uh. Uh. Uh."

I follow each pistoning stroke with a strangled cry as my head tosses side to side and my fingers ball into fists.

"Tell me… Is this how you want my big dick to fuck you… Pretty Kitty?" Roger demands, without faltering in his rhythm.

"YEEESSS…" I scream, then hiss when he shifts the angle, and his tip hits my G-spot.

Electricity races along the surface of my heated skin. I

squeeze my eyes shut to revel in the sensations bombarding me.

The scent of our sex floats around us. Wet suctioning sounds as my pussy captures and releases the thick invasion of Roger's ribbed and veiny cock. The smooth texture of the wood against my sweaty back. His firm grip bordering on painful, sure to leave his mark.

Once again, I'm on sensory overload.

"Take it... Take every single inch, Pretty Kitty," Roger demands.

I mewl because it feels so fucking good. I just can't take anymore.

Roger clutches my chin to tilt my face back down. When our eyes meet, he growls, "Cum on my cock. Cum for me now!"

My body fractures and floats away.

"Hi, my love. How do you feel?"

My eyes flutter open to find Roger peering down at me as we lie in the bed.

No longer driven by lust, his gray eyes return to their liquid platinum state. His tender look caresses me more deeply than his fingers skimming my cheek.

"I love you, Mrs. Steele," Roger murmurs before his lips meet mine in a sweet kiss.

When his mouth slides to my neck, I whisper, "I love you, too, Monsieur Steele."

LEONIE

"*I* love the different shades of ocean blues around the Hamptons. Mixed with the warm tones of caramel and orange and a base of eggshell white, it's the perfect palette for a beachfront home."

Roger smirks, "Really? Well, you told me you're not interested in redecorating our home at the compound. So, what's with 'the perfect palette'?"

I nudge his side with my elbow and roll my eyes.

"Just a comment, smarty pants," I respond. "Is that all right with you?"

"*Just* saying…" He quips. "You declined the opportunity, babe."

We along with The Twins, Nanny Grace, Sebastian, Lola, and Blair are on board the STEELE Sikorsky helicopter heading to the Southampton Village Heliport. Billie will fly in with Patrick on his helicopter later this afternoon and stay at his beachfront property.

Already at the beachfront compound are Morgan, Shelley, Malcolm, Starr, and Harris. Haley and her "we're just friends" Callum also left early. They're prepping for tonight's sunset dinner on the beach—a traditional New England Clambake. And I cannot wait, yum!

My parents and Luc should have landed by now at the private airport for the Hamptons. They flew in on Luc's new Gulfstream G700. He heard how much we enjoyed our flights for Verbier in the STEELE jet, so he ordered one even though he has a plush G650. This trip his excuse to try his new toy. I teased he's a spoiled *duc*!

"Bro, it's been eight months. You haven't learned, yet?" Sebastian chuckles. "Sometimes you have to not say a word!"

"Yeah. Happy wife, happy life and all that," Lola says, glancing up from her laptop.

Then she turns to The Twins in their car seats and adds, "Learn that lesson now, Little Pumpkins, and you'll be all right."

Rodolphe waves his car in the air while Gaspard claps and says, "Dada, Dada!"

"Yeah, Dada," I laugh and point to Roger as I clap.

Everyone joins in, and The Twins' laughter is the sweetest of all.

Malcolm, Harris, and Haley meet us at the heliport with two Black Badge Rolls-Royce Cullinans and a Suburban. The guys load up the Suburban with our luggage while Lola and Blair hop into the back of Malcolm's SUV.

Nanny Grace and I secure The Twins in the middle row of the SUV Haley drove. Then Nanny Grace slips onto the third row, and I sit between The Twins.

When Roger opens the driver's door, Haley crosses her arms over her chest and cocks her head to the side, peering up at him.

"Oh, so you think you're just going to bogart my ride, Big Brother?" She asks.

Roger pinches her cheeks and grins.

"You're so cute when you're annoyed, Baby Sister," he says wiggling her face. "I love you with all my heart. But I will drive any vehicle with my wife and sons in it."

Reluctantly, Haley relinquishing the SUV to her brother. But not without giving him the stink eye as she walks around to climb into the passenger seat.

"Don't feel bad, *Chérie*," I tell her. "Roger does the same thing to me. He refuses to let me drive The Twins anywhere. Either he drives or Eric. *C'est la vie.*"

Haley nods, then says, "Only because of my nephews did I give in to you, Roger…"

He winks at her and starts the engine. His chuckle blends with the purr of the premium engine.

We pull up to the compound's private road. A security guard in a gatehouse triggers the oversized wooden gates set between stone pillars with wrought iron lanterns to swing open. A long driveway of pressed oil and natural stone rolls out before us like the yellow brick road.

We're not in Kansas! This is Southampton luxury living at its finest.

Once past the impressive gates, it's another world. The property rests on ten acres all beachfront. Its incredible surroundings include native trees, grassy areas, and closer to the ocean sandy dunes. The briny scent of the ocean through the open windows fills my lungs. The calls of seagulls ring out.

On either side of the primary driveway, secondary ones appear as we drive along. Malcolm pulls off to one on the right. Roger turns onto one of them to our left and Harris follows.

A shorter driveway ends in a circle before a classic Hamptons-style three-story mansion. Robin egg blue shutters lean against gray weathered shingles. Beneath the windowsills flower boxes filled with white blossoms add to the beauty of the home.

"Here we are," Roger says as he pulls to a stop at the front door behind a golf cart and cuts the engine.

We hop out, and I wrap my arm around his waist as I gaze at the house. Atop the widow's walk, an antique weathervane idly switches direction with the breeze. The top half of the navy blue Dutch door stands open. It's absolutely picturesque.

I glance up at Roger to find him staring at me with a soft smile. His aviator sunglasses reflect mine. He drops his head to kiss me sweetly.

"You're here!"

"Mon Trésor!"

We look to the front door to see Shelley unlatching the bottom and my parents behind her. They wave and walk over to us. We exchange greetings, and The Twins pulled into hugs.

The interior doesn't disappoint. It's a center hall with a double staircase rising along the walls. The cream, pale blue, and dusty yellow hues complement the stone floors. Canvas covered furniture with the accent colors fill the great room. It's comfy and elegant.

But the view of the ocean out of the wall of windows takes my breath away.

Drawn to the endless expanse of the Atlantic Ocean, I walk over to step onto the deck. Out on the private beach, caterers prepare for the clambake. They dug the pit and lined it with large stones and wood. The fragrant scent fills the air.

"Come, let's get settled then meet up with everyone at the main house," Roger says as he bounces Gaspard on his hip.

I nod and follow him back inside.

We spend the next hour getting our personal things in situated. I ordered clothing and essentials for me and The Twins to leave at this home. The staff put everything away before we arrived. After a tour, we follow Shelley's golf cart with ours and we give Nanny Grace the rest of the day off. The Twins will be well taken care of amongst the entire Steele clan.

The day turns into evening, and we go to the beach for a seafood feast with the backdrop of a spectacular sunset. The perfectly steamed clams, lobsters, potatoes, and corn on the cob topped with melted butter and paired with local beer and white wine make for a scrumptious meal. Dessert options include warm blueberry and apple pies with vanilla ice cream. Afterwards, we sit around the bonfire chatting.

Rodolphe and Gaspard sleep in their mesh beach cots, Blair found online. They enjoyed their first taste of seafood. The greedy little monsters wanted more! So with full bellies, they doze during the rest of our beach time.

"Time to go to bed, Mrs. Steele," Roger murmurs against my windblown hair as I sit between his legs and lean my back against his broad chest.

Wrapped in the warm cocoon of Roger and an oversized blanket, I don't want to move. But nod, and we gather The Twins and bid everyone a goodnight.

"Don't forget beach yoga at seven tomorrow morning!" Starr calls out to me, as she sits huddled up with Malcolm.

I give her the thumbs up and place my hand on Roger's back as he walks ahead of me with The Twins asleep in his muscular arms. I carry their cots and bag.

When we get home, we give them a bath before we put them to bed. Then Roger and I take a steamy shower where we make love beneath the steady flow of warm water from the rain shower head. Roger dries me tenderly, and we collapse in the bed, his body spooning mine.

We whisper I love you and fall into a restful slumber.

* * *

"What a gorgeous start to the day! I'm so glad the summer weather continued into September."

"It could stay summer year-round as far as I'm concerned."

The girls and I spread our yoga mats out on the sand at the beach in front of the Shelley and Morgan's house. Originally, Starr wanted us to gather for a sunrise meditation at six-thirty, but after the long night we convinced her to start later—if only by half an hour.

I fold into Child's Pose to release tension and to prepare my mind and body for our session.

After the mediation, Starr undoubtedly has a vigorous flow planned with a dharma talk during Savasana. My consistent Skype sessions with Starr and in-person with Anita over the last two years increased my endurance and ability to handle more advanced asanas. I look forward to today's practice.

"Let us begin. Come to a comfortable sitting position with your palms face up on your knees, fingers in Gyan Mudra. Center your mind..."

Starr takes us from a reflective guided meditation through a sequence of asanas that build up to the challenging peak pose of Scorpion Handstand.

In practicing asanas, the point isn't to twist oneself into a pretzel and the more you can bend, the better. Rather, the focus on the breath and releasing the mind to move the body.

Starr loves to push our ability to focus, and Scorpion Handstand requires lots of it.

I'm beyond grateful for Savasana as we settle onto our backs. With our eyes closed and our minds open, Starr speaks to us about surrender. Despite the purpose of her dharma talk, I can't help but wonder if she surrenders to Malcolm's Alpha Dom as his sub!

Just as we stand to take a dip in the ocean, here they come...

"Rats, did we miss the yoga?" Patrick jokes in his Scottish accent.

It turns out he and Callum know each other, and it surprised them to find the other with us.

Last night at the clambake, Billie teased how she and Haley are into bangers and mash. The visual of the double entendre made her blush and Callum sputter his ale.

"Of course it's over since I left you snoring almost two hours ago!" Billie replies, her Granny Smith apple green eyes sparkling in the bright sunlight.

With her wavy, medium-blonde balayage hair and pecan-colored skin, everyone says she's Tyra's doppelgänger. Billie is curvy like the megamodel, but a petite version at five feet, four inches. Patrick towers over her by eleven inches.

He scoops Billie into his arms and carries her off to the water as she giggles.

"I saw you with your pussy in the air holding the position for me to come over, grab your thighs, and fuck you until you saw stars in the daytime."

A gasp slips past my lips as my pussy clenches and my

nipples pebble beneath my white bandeau bikini. I sway in Roger's sudden embrace as he presses his front into my back with his hands on my lower belly.

He makes his arousal known with his lengthening dick sandwiched between us.

"Can you back up your claim, Monsieur Steele?" I purr.

Roger chuckles, his warm breath tickles my neck. "Absolutely, Pretty Kitty. Come back to our house, and I will show you."

"Bye, guys! See you later!" I tell the others.

THE NEXT FEW days are so relaxing. We do more yoga, lounge around the pool, swim in the ocean, or hang out on the entertainment level of the primary house to bowl, play in the arcade, or watch movies.

It's good to unwind with everyone since it's the first time we've all been together after the judge threw the New York City case out.

Roger's laughter comes easily, and he jokes with his siblings. They along with Patrick and Callum played a rowdy game of touch football on the beach.

Between drooling over the gleaming muscles, the girls and I cheered them on. Our parents, Luc, and The Twins watched from the sidelines.

Patrick and Callum told them American football sucks and isn't even football since the ball stays in the players' hands more often than not. They insisted on a round of rugby—"the real man's sport."

We couldn't care less as long as the guys remained sweaty.

I giggle about it as I tie the strings on the halter-top of

my white silk maxi dress. The soft caress of the material swirls around my body as it falls to the tips of my crystal-embellished gladiator sandals.

"You look like my new bride all over again."

A glance over my shoulder reveals Roger in the doorway of my dressing room.

He's delectable in an untucked white linen button-down shirt with the sleeves rolled midway up his muscular forearms and white linen pants with a pair of white leather slides. The Rolex watch I gave to him for Christmas on his wrist and his wedding band puts a smile on my face.

His sun-kissed skin makes his gray eyes even more translucent. Two-day stubble covers his cheeks and cleft chin. With his hair combed back, his bone structure stands out. Roger can outdo any male supermodel.

Yum!

The corners of my mouth lift in a grin, and I twirl for him. As I stop, my hair swings over my shoulder to cascade past my hip in glossy waves. My eyes shine with love for my man.

"Beautiful," Roger says.

I blush under the intensity of his stare and bow my head. He makes my heart race uncontrollably.

"Come. Let's get to the party," Roger continues. "Later we'll make our own fireworks."

Now, my pussy throbs. We have hours before the party ends.

Merde.

Roger smirks at me knowingly and takes my hand to lead me to the nursery, where we say goodnight to The Twins and Nanny Grace.

A quick ride in the golf cart along a path separate from

the driveway—that's lined with cars waiting to reach the party's valets—and we arrive at Morgan and Shelley's house.

The giant side lawn, aglow by thousands of fairy lights and lanterns, has two sumptuous pavilions, one for dinner and the other for dessert and dancing. Beyond it, on the beach, several bonfires burn. Waitstaff mill about with trays of champagne and wines or hors d'oeuvres. To one side a band plays lively music piped through speakers, also out on the sand.

Guests mingle, sipping drinks in the different areas, all dressed in the theme of the annual STEELE White Party.

It's already bustling since it's the party of the season and everyone wants a ticket for a chance to see and be seen amongst the world's elite. Not to mention raising funds for STEELE Foundation.

As soon as we're spotted, people approach to get a word with Roger or to take a photo with *The Lion*—"I've been a fan forever!" "You're even more stunning in person!"

Automatically, I smile for the cameras and snicker inside. Oh boy...

When they congratulate us on our marriage, Roger's chest puffs up visibly. Every time, he slips his arm around my side right below my braless boob so his fingers brush underneath it and hugs me close. Caveman.

Finally, we spot people we know and make our way to Luc and Blair.

"Hey! I love your dress!" I gush to her.

She has on a goddess dress that falls to the floor. Her cerulean blue eyes stand out against her tanned skin and twinkle when she smiles.

"Thanks, you look phenomenal, too!" Blair responds.

Luc smiles at her. His hand on the back of her neck slides down as he strokes her possessively.

"Hi! You're finally here!"

I turn to see Lola and Baz striding over. A giggle escapes when I notice Lola wears a diamond and platinum choker—at least that's what those unfamiliar with BDSM would think. Tonight she wears one of the collars Sebastian gave to her as his sub.

Okay... So the guys need to prove we're theirs, huh?

We chat for a few minutes, then return to mingle before the waitstaff serves dinner.

I catch sight of Haley and Lachlan talking off to the side. It appears serious, so I don't interrupt them with a greeting.

The Jacksons, who also have a compound nearby, came over for the party. Laurent, the playboy, flirts shamelessly with three female guests. Lydie who seems to have a new boyfriend laughs with some industry titans—she's a killer in the boardroom. Lucien, whose Southampton restaurant caters the event, holds court in the dining pavilion for last-minute preparations.

A quick scan of the crowd reveals my parents in conversation with Connor and Lucie while Morgan and Shelley stand next to them chatting with other guests. The couples make a powerful trio and became fast friends over the past two years.

Roger and I visit a third tent for the silent auction.

Luc offered two weeks at his family's ancestral seat. In his case, it's a magnificent chateau on one hundred acres of park-like grounds and forests once used as royal hunting grounds. Excursions for cooking and wine lessons and tours of the countryside round out the visit.

STEELE went further with a six-week-long trip around the South Pacific. Two-week stays at three five-star hotels and resorts in Fiji, Tahiti, and Hawaii make for a memorable holiday. Plus, use of a STEELE private jet and helicopter to transport the lucky couple. The imagery for the display is so vibrant and romantic, I want to put a bid on it!

The gong rings to announce dinner.

We follow the guests to the dining pavilion and take our seats. The Steele clan disperses across the room, sitting at tables with guests to make everyone feel welcome and included.

Shelley makes her speech, and the emcee keeps the party going through dinner and on to the dessert and dancing. A DJ famous for his skills on the turntables spins popular music that gets the guests on their feet.

The fireworks display from a barge offshore lights up the inky night sky with vivid sparklers, crowns, glitter, and crosettes. We cheer with each round, delighted by the glitziness.

"I have an explosive pistil with your name on it, Pretty Kitty. Shall we?"

For the rest of the night and well into the early morning, Roger makes me oh and ah in erotic, toe-curling delight.

* * *

"I can't believe *Mr. Responsible* let you take The Twins and drive into the village without him."

I bite my lip and raise my eyebrows at Lola's comment.

We're heading back to our Cullinan after a couple of hours shopping on Main Street. Roger and the guys went to play golf. So I took advantage of his absence to prove I can handle driving us around—alone.

"Wait a minute. Do you mean to tell me you did not let Roger know?" She asks incredulously, stopping in the middle of the sidewalk.

I shrug and press the key fob to unlock the doors.

"Leonie! He's going to be so pissed off with you!" Lola says as she buckles Rodolphe in his car seat. "And do not give me that *Bof* shrug!"

I laugh and respond, "Don't worry! We'll return before them. So stop yammering and get in the car already."

Lola shakes her head and steps up to the passenger seat.

Along the way, we chat about our final dinner tonight before we leave in the morning. We spent an extra week after Labor Day because it was just so nice to hang out.

"It's amazing how time flies! I cannot believe The Twins will be one year old in a couple of weeks—"

WHAM!

The SUV veers off the road and crashes head-on into a tree. Lola and I jerk forward as the front end smashes, then bounce back when the airbags deploy. The Twins' cries fill the car along with Lola's pained moans.

My ears ring as my head pounds. I try to turn to see my sons, but can't see, blinded partially by the airbag dust.

Relief sweeps through me when the back doors open. *Dieu merci*, someone helps us.

"Ar— Are... they okay?" I ask. Still unable to move, I lift my restricted gaze to the rearview mirror.

The chilling tendrils of horror close in when two masked faces stare at me and without a sound take Rodolphe and Gaspard from their car seats.

"*Nooooooon*," I yell, now frantic and forcing my body to move despite the pain in my chest and head. "*Ne prends pas mes bébés!!!*"

Unable to think in English, I scream at them to not take my babies.

In my haste and limited eyesight, I misgauge the height and fall out of the SUV. Adrenaline pumps through me, and

I leap to my feet to run after the kidnappers. Screaming, I pound after them, fueled by the cries of The Twins.

As if in a dream, the kidnappers leap into the back of an unmarked white van and peel away. The tires kick up gravel from the side of the road. Black rubber marks trail in their wake. The dust and caustic smell clog my nostrils.

I give chase until they're too far away.

When the van turns a bend in the road, I fall to my knees screaming.

ROGER

"*R*oger! We have to go. NOW!!"
          I freeze in the middle of my swing at Harris' words.

Leonie!

I drop the club and race after him. He's already running to the golf cart. Luc and Callum close in on us.

My mobile rings, and I snatch it out of my pocket, praying it's Leonie. It's Sebastian.

"What the fuck's going on?" He demands, the sound going in and out as though he's running, too.

In the background, Malcolm and Patrick shout questions.

"Harris! What the fuck is going on?!" I yell as I jump into the cart.

Without taking his eyes from the path, he shakes his head and says, "Your Cullinan crashed."

The world tilts.

Leonie!

Frantically, I end Baz's call and dial her mobile. No answer. I dial Nanny Grace.

"Where are Leonie and my sons?" I yell.

She sucks in a shocked breath, then responds, "Mrs. Steele went into the village with her sister-in-law and The Tw—"

I hang up and kick the front panel of the cart with enough force it cracks, and we lurch forward.

FUCK!

From the back bench, I hear Luc speaking about Lola. More than likely he's on with Baz. Sure enough, yelling comes over the line.

I try Leonie's number again, then the SUV's phone. No answer.

Callum's talking to Haley filters into my brain.

"Where?" I ask Harris.

He tells me it's the road from Main Street toward our compound. His app alerted him to the crash along with the STEELE Cyber Security emergency team. First responders are en route to the scene.

"The scene." My nightmare. Bile rises in my throat as my stomach clenches. I pray they're not injured.

When we get to the country club's parking lot, we abandon the cart and race to the Suburban just as Baz, Malcolm, and Patrick jump from their cart. All of them are on their mobiles.

I go for the driver's door, but Harris stops me.

"You're too keyed up, bro," he starts, then continues when I interrupt. "I got this, get in."

By the time we get to the car crash, the police cordoned off the area. Fire engines and ambulances line the road. Cars backed up prevent us from getting any closer.

We leave the SUV and rush to the yellow caution tape.

An officer stops us, but Sebastian and I yell it involves our wives and my sons. When he reaches for his radio and doesn't lift the tape to give us access, I duck under and run to the first ambulance.

My stomach clenches again when I catch sight of the Cullinan's crushed hood. The force of the impact decimated it.

FUCK!

I step up on the back of the ambulance and see Lola on a stretcher.

Her eyes widen when she sees me. Mine widen when I see the bloody gash on her forehead.

"Leonie? The Twins?" I ask.

Lola bursts into tears, and I nearly die.

Baz pulls me out of the way and climbs on board.

Adrenaline pumps through me, and I race to the next ambulance, screaming Leonie's name.

A paramedic pops her head out the back and waves me over.

Inside, Leonie is hysterical. Her wild eyes dart from the police officer's face to the paramedic as she yells in French, *"Ils ont kidnappé mes fils!"*

My heart stops.

The world falls off its axis.

Leonie turns in my direction when she hears my sharp intake of air. Fresh tears roll down her cheeks, and she covers her mouth with shaky hands.

The officer shifts his position to face me.

"Mr. Steele?" He asks.

I can only nod since my mouth is too dry to form words.

"Please come with me, sir" he says.

My eyes never leave Leonie's. In French, she whispers

she's so sorry, and it's all her fault. I open my mouth to speak, but nothing comes out.

The officer takes me to the side of the ambulance as Harris and Sebastian run over.

"We know where they are!!" My brothers yell simultaneously.

Officers come running, and Harris shows them another of his apps.

Two dots blink green on a map with heat signatures of four other individuals in various locations. The coordinates place The Twins near to where we stand. The street view shows a secluded house on a private lane.

Just then my mobile rings with a call from my father.

"A person contacted me with a ransom demand of $10 million," he says without preamble. "Each."

"We've got The Twins via their trackers, and—"

"*Quelle? Veux-tu dire??*"

Leonie stands behind the officers with Lola. They clutch each other. At that moment, I notice the bruising on Leonie's face, too.

I stride over to her and pull her into my arms as Baz embraces Lola.

Leonie peers up at me and asks again, what do I mean.

Tightly holding her, I explain so only she can hear that every member of our family has a tracker in case we get lost or kidnapped. She questions why I didn't tell her about The Twins having them, and I tell her it slipped my mind.

Then Leonie frowns and asks if she has one, too. I nod and tell her I'll explain after we get them home. She whispers it's all her fault again.

Unlike last time, I find my voice and tell her not to think such nonsense. Then kiss her head and nod to the paramedic to take her back inside the ambulance.

Meanwhile, the officers plan an extraction and send a unit to the compound to monitor the communications from the kidnappers.

Sebastian, Harris, and I insist upon accompanying the extraction team.

The officers see we won't let them deny us, so they give in on the condition we remain in the patrol car. No one knows whether the kidnappers have weapons.

We agree.

Luc promises to take care of Leonie and Lola. Since he's known them longer than Baz and I combined, we trust he won't allow any harm to come to them.

Malcolm drives them and Callum back to the compound.

"More people arrived at the house!" Harris exclaims as he monitors his app's feed. "What the fuck?! Haley is there now!!"

Baz and I swing our gazes to the front seat where Harris sits beside the sheriff.

"Whaaat?!?!" We yell at the same time.

Then we tell the sheriff to drive faster.

Shortly thereafter, we arrive at the house. According to the app, The Twins still blink green in the same room with a heat signature next to them. However, ten heat signatures surround three others in another room while four appear in a third one beside The Twins.

The STEELE's security team lead for our compound flags us down.

"Mr. Steele," he says to me. "We have the situation under control. Ms. Steele alerted us to the kidnapping, and we used the tracking app to locate your sons. They're with the team medic. The kidnappers are being held by other members of the team. Come with me, sirs."

Just as he said, we see our team with three men who sit handcuffed in the middle of the floor. One is jabbering on about not being a part of the kidnapping. His voice gives me pause. It's Antonio Velasquez.

What. The. Fuck!

If Delia is behind this, I'm going to finish the psycho bitch once and for all!

Raised voices draw my attention from the asshole Antonio.

Baz, our security lead, and I rush into the next room. Two of our team members stand aside, but at the ready. Delia runs screaming like a banshee with her arms outstretched and long nails ready to claw at Haley.

Surprisingly, Haley stands her ground in a defensive posture. No one is prepared for what happens next.

"You BITCH!"

WHAM!

"You fucked with my brother."

WHAM! WHAM!

"You tried to steal my nephews!"

WHAM! WHAM! WHAM!

"Stay. The. Fuck. Away. From. My. FAMILY!!!"

Haley whales on Delia.

"I've got your number, bitch, and it's all legit. You're going away for the rest of your miserable fucking life," Haley ends in a deadly tone made more terrifying after her shouts and thrashing.

Delia—whose face already shows signs of swelling—stares with one open eye up at Haley. Delia's busted lip trembles as she mumbles how sorry she is for all she's done.

Haley refuses to give in and tells her it's too fucking late.

The officers rush in, and we explain what happened. They proceed to arrest Delia, who starts crying assault.

When they ignore her and read the Miranda warning, she doesn't have the sense to shut the fuck up.

Instead, she slings more baseless claims against me and curses while they take her away.

Bye, bitch!

"Mr. Steele, your sons are safe and sound."

I turn to face the door and see the security medic as noted by the word on the front of his uniform's bullet-proof vest. He and another team member hold Rodolphe and Gaspard, who wear black adult-size t-shirts.

When they see me, they call out Dada and reach their arms out.

Tears fill my eyes, and my breath escapes me at the sight of their reddened faces puffy from crying. Two strides and they're in my arms. I squeeze them so tightly to my chest they squirm and cry some more.

Never in my life have I been so terrified. All sorts of crazy thoughts ran through my head. Nightmarish and ghastly things are done to children, and I would end anyone who would harm what's mine.

Arms enfold me and I open my eyes to see Baz, Harris, and Haley hugging The Twins and me. We're a tight-knit clan, and I feel the love flowing from them to us. Even The Twins calm, hiccups replace their sorrowful sobs.

We take a moment to absorb the intensity of the situation.

Then Baz squeezes us and looks at each of our faces. His, like ours, streaked with tears. But the steely glint in his eyes shows he's back to business. As our eldest sibling, he's always taken on the responsibility of his brothers and sister —no matter our ages.

"Let us go. Haley, call Leonie. Harris, you get Dad on the line. He needs to prep for our arrival"—Baz turns to the security lead—"I want a full briefing with the team, the police, and the FBI. We will meet in my father's office in an hour."

Big brother, CEO, Alpha Dom, all in one takes charge.

I'm grateful, as I can only think of my wife and sons.

When we reach the compound's perimeter fence, armed security members stand spaced in intervals along its full length. At the front gates, two of their armored Suburbans block the entry and dozens more armed members stand around them. We are on full lockdown.

"ROGEEERRR!!!"

Leonie roars as she runs out of the house.

She throws her arms wide, pulling The Twins and me into her embrace. She trembles as sobs rack her body. I murmur words of love and let her know they're fine to soothe her anguish.

Josy and Guy join us, and we hug in a unit as I did with my siblings. The pile on continues when we make room for my mother and father.

I notice the others hovering, not wanting to interrupt. So I give them a nod and suggest we move inside.

We settle in the living room where Leonie and I hold The Twins on our laps. She checks them over one at a time, rubbing her hands over their bodies and holding their faces to look into their eyes. I tell her they're fine since the medic did an examination, and I assessed them on the ride over.

But *Maman Lionne* ignores me.

The silence broken by Malcolm.

"That bitch is going to pay," *The Enforcer* declares. "No way will she get away with this shit. I want answers now!"

Everyone shares his sentiment, and we decide to have the briefing here instead of in the office for more space.

Before they arrive, Leonie and I take The Twins upstairs

to bathe and redress them. The forensics team took their clothes for evidence, thus the t-shirts.

"I'm so sorry, Roger. This is all my fault..." She whispers sadly.

No way am I going to allow Delia to hurt the love of my life... again. It's not Leonie's fault. Delia is a conniving monster who would stoop so low as to kidnap babies to get revenge and money.

"Leonie... No, look at me," I say when she lowers her head as tears slip down her reddened cheeks. The defeat in her lackluster eyes breaks my heart. "Oh baby, listen to me. This is not your fault in any way—"

"I drove without telling you—"

"True, but... *But*," I repeat when she interrupts. I silence her with my finger pressed to her lips. "That does not give Delia the right to crash into you and kidnap The Twins."

I pause to take a deep breath when the horrific thoughts swirl in my mind once more.

"They could have killed you, our sons, and Lola. All for that monster's selfish gain. She's put our family through enough already. Do not give her power over us," I say adamantly.

"Remember when you told me 'we will move forward from this moment on with only positive thoughts and words of love' almost two years ago?" I ask. "Well, you're 'the most responsible person *I* know.' Sweetheart, you would never put our sons in harm's way."

Leonie leans into me, and I wrap her in my comforting embrace. I have more than enough strength for both of us. I vow we will get beyond this nightmare and come out even stronger.

* * *

IT TURNS out Haley is absolutely correct—it is too fucking late for Delia Fucking Shaw.

When the FBI agents question him, Antonio flips immediately.

He admits it was Delia's idea to claim sexual assault and harassment since I gave him a sum of money in recompense for the fight we had at Leonie's Paris American Academy end-of-the-semester reception. Delia was jealous of Leonie and hoped she would leave me because of the accusations. That plus Delia wanting to get money was payback for me rebuffing her advances.

He also admitted to rigging the security feed and my private elevator the day Delia and I got trapped and no one could explain how it happened. As a tech whiz, he found a loophole and manipulated it to their advantage.

Their fake dating relationship became a true one over the last two years. Recently, he realized Delia was only using him for his skills. When she came back with The Twins and two goons she hired in exchange for some ransom money, they argued because Antonio couldn't stand by a kidnapping.

The "number" Haley referenced is a tech video that further proves my innocence she and a STEELE Cyber Security employee found on a camera Antonio didn't know about.

Finally, my name and STEELE get fully cleared because of Antonio's confession and Haley's findings.

Delia Shaw is in the dust, truly, as Malcolm once said!

LEONIE

*T*he cries of seagulls soaring high above the waves of the Mediterranean Sea as they search for breakfast wake me in the early morning.

Roger, The Twins, and I arrived last night aboard the vintage steam yacht for the week I won my bid at the center gala's silent auction. Then we'll celebrate The Twins' birthday at our villa in Capri with the family and stay for a month.

After the kidnapping, we had to remain in Southampton for an additional week. We met with the FBI and local law enforcement to give statements and to press charges.

It was a straightforward investigation since Antonio confessed in order to gain immunity for the first-degree kidnapping felony and aggravated assault with a motor vehicle charge. They accused him for his involvement in the case against Roger and STEELE International. Regardless, he'll still get plenty of time behind bars.

The asshole!

She who shall not be named is another story. With her

accomplishes, they received the highest charges and face life in prison without parole. When she entered the courtroom for their arraignment already in a prison jumpsuit, the defeated expression on her face proved she finally understood the ramifications of her heinous actions.

Roger had to hold his arm around my waist to keep me in my seat.

I wanted to launch myself at her and rip her to fucking pieces with my bare hands. Haley's whipping didn't satisfy my need to destroy she who shall not be named.

But like my mother told me, *"Mon Trésor, it is not for you to handle. The Divine has a way to right every wrong. So trust and let go."*

And that's what I did. I freed myself of the negativity through a soul-searching sunrise meditation, then a swim in the cleansing ocean waters. A new day dawned.

When I returned to shore, Roger was waiting for me. I loved that he gave me the space I needed to come to terms with my role in the kidnapping—or rather me acknowledging I did not have a role—and letting go of any ego-driven guilt.

Wordlessly, Roger held out an oversized beach towel and wrapped it around me when I stepped between his outstretched arms. He rested his chin on top of my head and sighed, content to hold me close. The warmth of his love dried me more than the plush Hermès terrycloth.

I told him how much I love him.

Roger kissed me senseless. My knees buckled from the sensory overload. He picked me up and carried me home. When we arrived, he continued to carry me up the stairs to our bedroom.

I gave my body to him heart and soul as he made passionate love to me. The entire time he drove his massive dick between my slick folds, Roger murmured more words of love and devotion. All the while, I cried and clung to him like a human life preserver rocked by the waves in open water.

Roger completed my cleansing as he bathed my insides with his life essence repeatedly.

I had gone into self-isolation, but Roger refused to leave my side. The only outside contact I had was to scour the Internet for any word or developments outside of what our attorneys and law enforcement told me.

The media worldwide had a field day with the kidnapping, car crash, Antonio's confession, and the subsequent clearing of Roger's name. They dug up all sorts of sources who came forward to depict she who shall not be named as an amoral gold digger. Antonio became her boy toy who she conned into helping her attempt to destroy Roger and STEELE.

Funny how those "sources" weren't around when she started this whole fucking mess.

STEELE's communications team ran with it and provided the media with more positive stories and images of Roger as a devoted family man who's committed to his community. The team highlighted STEELE Foundation's philanthropic activities to show the company wasn't only about generating billions of dollars; it gives back to those in need.

Even Harris and Haley's STEELE Technology and Cyber Security received a boost from the coverage. Companies and high-net worth individuals reached out to them immediately. The Dynamic Duo's client roster increased tenfold.

Roger persuaded me to step away from my laptop and back into the real world to continue my healing.

So after a few days we rejoined our family. More support

gave me additional strength to move forward and to leave the past in the rearview mirror.

When I flinched at the sight of stitches on my BBF's forehead, Lola insisted I let it go.

She didn't blame me for any of it. She said it gave her the chance to see a plastic surgeon about liposuction and a breast reduction.

Sebastian growled, and Lola burst out laughing. She admitted she was teasing him since he loves her curvy, petite body.

In the morning, she sat gingerly on her yoga mat and quipped Baz proved all night just how much he relishes her hourglass figure.

Even though the medic examined The Twins, Roger flew in the top pediatrician of the Tri-state area. The doctor put them through an extensive exam. The results on their bloodwork and other samples came back negative for any and every toxin imaginable.

We had the best child psychologist analyze The Twins. Again, the results we appropriate for their age with no signs of mental or emotional damage from the kidnapping. She assured us they didn't remember any of it and being so young they rebound quickly.

The testing proved our observations of normalcy were spot on. Roger and I were beyond relieved.

However, the psychologist Roger insisted I meet with suggested I revisit the site and drive. At first I balked at the idea. But she encouraged me to keep it in mind and to try when I was ready.

Before we left, I did it. Lola came with me and The Twins to recreate the situation, but more so for support.

We retraced our steps. The first time we passed the crash site on the way to the village, I tensed and broke out in a cold sweat. On the way back, we pulled over and stepped out of Haley's Cullinan to look around.

My heart constricted when we saw the damage to the tree and expressed our thanks we made it out alive.

Roger and Sebastian were waiting for us at the compound's entry gates. Lola hopped into the golf cart with Baz and Roger slid into the passenger seat. He kissed my cheek and told me how proud he was of me. I smiled and cupped his face for a proper kiss.

We took the Mediterranean cruise as a time to recharge before everyone joins us at our Villa dei Fiori in Capri for The Twins' first birthday party next week. The plans have been in place for months. We refuse to let she who shall not be named derail the joy of our sons' celebration!

"If you want something to think about so deeply, ponder how far down your throat my cock reaches as you take every one of the thick ten inches, Pretty Kitty."

I can't help but to giggle.

A few days ago, Roger said the psychologist suggested he treats me as he normally would and not with kid gloves. His interpretation: fuck my brains out as often as possible and then some more...

Two can play this carnal game.

I roll over to face him. Without looking away, I place my palm between his firm pecs and drag my fingernails straight down. The silky texture of his happy trail between eight-pack abs lets me know how close I am to my impressive, mouth-watering prize.

My teeth draw the corner of my bottom lip inwards when I graze his mushroom head.

Roger shudders. His head hits the pillows as he closes his hooded eyes, when I continue to use my nails along his turgid length. It jumps in my hands and hardens further.

I jerk his dick until Roger opens his eyes. My thumb swirls the bead of pre-cum around the swollen tip. More leaks out as I pinch the sides.

He grunts as his hips lift involuntarily and his fists grip the sheets.

"Are you asking me to swallow you whole, *Amoureux?*" I purr, continuing to jerk and release his dick in a leisurely rhythm.

He hisses when I lean over to lap a bead from his shiny tip.

"Mmmmmm, warm and salty," I moan, smacking my lips against him.

Roger growls and buries his hand in my hair, pushing his tip into my mouth. He groans when I open my throat to his invasion.

Let's see how far he goes.

His girth stretches my mouth as my jaw lowers to accommodate his cock. The tip of my tongue swirls around his ridges and veins, then I flatten my tongue to massage underneath.

I get him down far, but not enough. One hand grips the base of his dick while the other kneads his heavy balls. My pussy clenches, jealous my hands and mouth are full. But my core is empty. I moan from the ache.

Roger sucks in air and lifts his hips. His hand tightens to wind my long strands around his fist. He uses the leverage to drive his dick deeper, then to guide my movement.

My swollen lips press against his groin—that silky happy trail now tickles my nose—as he holds me in place. I gag, caught off guard.

"Breathe, Pretty Kitty," Roger growls.

I lift my gaze to his darkened orbs.

"Fuck! You... are... so... damn... sexy..." he punctuates each word with a powerful thrust of his hips.

Roger returns me to my task, seeking to reach further down my throat. His cock pulses, but he's not ready to cum yet. Instead, he pulls out with a pop and groans when he sees a trail of saliva lead from my lips to his rock-hard dick.

"*Merci, Monsieur Steele*," I utter in a raspy voice. "I want some more, *s'il te plait, Amoureux*."

His eyes spark and his nostrils flare when I open my mouth wide to welcome him.

"As you wish, Pretty Kitty," Roger replies as he puts his dick on my waiting tongue.

I amp up my ministrations until he explodes with a roar, shooting his cum deep down my throat as my lips brush his heated skin.

Roger collapses onto the bed heaving and pulls me on top of him. He wraps his arms around my back and nuzzles my neck with his open mouth.

When he catches his breath, he thrums in my ear, "So, good you are to me, Mrs. Steele."

* * *

"I CAN SEE why you the design of this yacht piqued your interest. They did an excellent job with the restoration down to the minute details," Roger says as we stretch out on the deck.

Luxury of a bygone age abounds in its Edwardian elegance and glamour. Built in the early 1900s to amaze and entertain the highest echelons of society, it features a gleaming navy blue hull and a deckhouse. It has exquisite brass fixtures, polished timber, and sumptuous fabrics. Plus four lavish staterooms perfect for rest. It's a rare and original piece of history.

"I knew you'd love it!" I reply as Gaspard and I play patty-cake. "Can't you picture an opulent and formal Edwardian-themed party? I'd come as Gigi and you as Gaston. A chance to dress like my favorite movie!"

Roger laughs, which makes Rodolphe, who sits on the chaise between his father's legs, claps his hands and calls Dada, Dada.

"You'd like a party, too?" He asks as he tickles Rodolphe's tummy. "Who would you come as, my little one?"

I smile at my three boys.

This is just what we needed—family time floating from one secluded spot to the next, basking in the warmth of the Med.

We spend the rest of the week doing just that until we pull up near our Villa dei Fiori in Capri. We'll use the tender to reach the private dock.

As the crew helps us disembark, I turn to face the yacht once more. It floats majestically on the azure blue water as the sun hits its shiny surface.

"I hate to leave. The boat is so gorgeous, and we had such a good time," I sigh. "Do you think the owners will let us rent her again?"

Roger shrugs and raises his eyebrows.

"Hmmm... I don't know. You tell me," he responds as he shakes hands with the crew.

I frown at him and glance at the captain.

"Would you be so kind as to provide me with the owner's contact information, or I can give you mine," I say. "We really enjoyed ourselves. You and your crew treated us so well."

The captain looks at Roger, then back to me.

"Thank you, Madame Steele," he starts before looking once again at Roger.

I frown again. What is going on with these two?

"Roger—"

He starts to chuckle and points at the yacht.

"You tell me since we own her," he says.

"What??" I ask, shocked.

Roger continues, "You loved it. We have a dock, but no boat, so... I bought her for you. The previous owners signed the paperwork this morning."

"Whaaat?!?!" I screech. "Are you serious, Roger?"

As the captain hands binoculars to me, Roger says, "Look at her stern, baby."

The boat now faces away from us to show its rear end. Gigi Capri. The name and hailing port written in the same red color and font of the movie title.

"Whaaaat?!?!?!" I yell as I wrap my arms around Roger's neck, peppering his face with kisses. "When did you do all of this?"

He explains he couldn't help himself since I was so enthralled by it and it's the only one of its kind fully restored left in the world. So he couldn't buy another one.

I press my lips to his ear so only he can hear and say, "So, good you are to *me*, Mr. Steele."

ROGER

The sight of my wife and sons splashing in the pool beneath the brilliant sun with the flowers around them and the Mediterranean Sea in the distance makes me want to ditch the conference call. It pays to be the boss and take off for a month on brief notice, but I still have obligations—this meeting included.

My Business Development Team has four properties they're presenting for approval to upper management after having shared it with the directors. Every year, STEELE Residential Properties expands its portfolio with twelve to twenty projects around the globe. This set has Kuala Lumpur in Malaysia, Buenos Aires in Argentina, Brussels in Belgium, and Sydney in Australia.

And each location requires site visits on my part—planned and unexpected.

Now with my family, I can't imagine just up and going when an emergency arises or staying for weeks on end. Before my time was my business. The drive to succeed at all costs was my top priority, as it is with all of my siblings.

The one of us who has slowed down if a tad bit is Sebastian, and only since he married Lola. She's as work focused as Baz. That's what drew them together—well, along with their palpable sexual attraction.

Leonie didn't become a megamodel on her beauty alone. She puts in the time and dedication—although in her easygoing way. A style that drove me mad and our clashing nearly ended us forever.

Her plate will be full more than before. With Leonie heading a division within STEELE, she must take time to build the new arm from scratch. Not to mention her spokesmodel contracts with Lola's Coterie, the global cosmetics company, and more recently with Van Cleef & Arpels.

Of course we'll share responsibility for The Twins and have support from Nanny Grace. Yeah, I'm the man of the house, but I respect her career goals as much as I respect mine. We'll coordinate our schedules and as Leonie said, *"We'll put date nights, family time, and getaways with The Twins or together on our calendars in pen!"*

"—concludes our presentation. Kindly share your feedback."

Back to business.

"HOW ARE THE PROPERTIES? Did you decide the next two developments?" Sebastian asks later via video conference.

We're in our weekly one-on-one during which I give him status updates, review timelines, and discuss any concerns or feedback. It's part of the strategy he implemented when he took over as CEO from our father, along with spending a week at each of STEELE's offices worldwide. Baz wants to make sure every member of the staff can have a voice and know their leader. The response has been positive.

"All of them have potential for generating revenue. However, the ones in Sydney and Kuala Lumpur would expand STEELE's footprint in that part of the world significantly," I respond.

Sebastian nods and scans his laptop. When he finds what he's searching for, he turns his attention back to me.

"Malcolm is scouting locations in Kuala Lumpur, too. Let's patch him into the call," Baz says.

The three of us discuss the pros and cons of the sites Malcolm found and the feasibility to purchase property around the site my team selected. Combined with the Entertainment Properties, we would add a hotel and restaurants.

"You know, this project could benefit from Leonie's Children and Young Adults Division. Is she free to jump on the call?" Malcolm asks.

I glance out the window and see Leonie in a teeny orange bikini headed this way, a Twin holding each of her hands. A goofy grin spreads across my face. MILF Alert... Damn, I'm a lucky son of a gun!

"Earth to Roger... Come in, Roger," Baz teases. "I take it you see her. Hopefully she's dressed and available."

I tell them to hold on while I call her out the window.

She comes in and sets The Twins in their playpen filled with toys I have in my office to keep them occupied while I'm working.

"Hello gentleman," she says smiling. "How may I help you today?"

They laugh, and we fill her in on the project. We discuss her division's potential role in the development. She gives great recommendations that impress all three of us. Baz gives the green light to move forward on a plan for Kuala Lumpur and Sydney.

"I can't wait to see Lola and Starr! You're still set to arrive in a few days for Thanksgiving, *non?*" Leonie asks.

Baz and Malcolm confirm, and we end the video conference.

"You did an outstanding job off the cuff, babe. I'm so proud of you!" I tell Leonie as I pull her from her seat to my lap.

"Thank you, *Mon Cœur*, I want to make my division as successful as yours!" She responds. "Besides, who knew I'd take part in a STEELE meeting with a bikini on?!"

Her giggle turns into a mewl when I slide one triangular scrap of material to the side and suckle her brown nipple.

"Yeah, who knew?" I chuckle as I nip the tender bud. "Let's put The Twins down for their naps, then return for an in-depth one-on-one…"

* * *

LEONIE and I stand holding The Twins, waving as the second Sikorsky touches down on the helipad at the rear of the villa.

"Look, Rodolphe and Gaspard, Grandaddy and Grandmommy!" I tell them as my parents alight from the back of the helicopter.

The Twins laugh and wave some more.

Sebastian and Lola disembark next, followed by Malcolm and Starr, then Harris and Haley. They wave and troop over.

"Hey, Little Pumpkins! Did you miss your favorite auntie?" Lola asks as Baz scoops Gaspard out of my arms.

"And your very favorite uncle?" He adds giving Malcolm and Harris the side eye with a grin.

We make our way around to the terrace where Guy and Josy sit. They flew in this morning. Everyone exchanges greetings before Leonie and I show the newest arrivals to their sumptuous bedroom suites.

Villa dei Fiori has fast become one of our most cherished homes. It's where we had our babymoon when Leonie was nineteen weeks pregnant and we'd been back together for nine months. She fell in love with Lucien's former home the moment she set eyes on it—another *coup de foudre*. So, I bought it for her.

The salmon-colored stucco exterior with white trim around the windows, columns, and roof lines blend beautifully with the lush greenery and stunning sea views from all sides. The sea-edge gardens, bountiful with camellias, magnolias, and palm trees prove as captivating as the impressive views of Mount Vesuvius, the Peninsula of Sorrento, the entire Gulf of Naples, and Anacapri. Its private swimming pool set in the side garden's grass and its exclusive sea access with a second plunge pool below makes it a unique property.

We plan to spend more time here than the one time in the last year and a half. Guy and Josy and my siblings took advantage and stayed on different occasions. Since my parents have Villa Sogno across the Tyrrhenian Sea in Positano, this is their first visit.

"Oh! This is a stunning villa! I love the gardens with all the fragrant flowers," my mother gushes as we walk to their suite. "I'm surprised Lucien gave it up."

I chuckle and respond, "He drove a hard bargain. But it was worth it to see the smile on Leonie's face when I gave it to her."

My father nods, then adds, "I know the feeling, son. Nothing is better than your wife's happiness. Remember my words well."

As we pass through the villa, I point out the rooms for a mini tour. The antique furnishings, Murano glass fixtures, and unobstructed views charm both of them.

However, they're even more pleased with their enormous corner suite and balcony overlooking the sea. The cobalt blue, champagne, and gold color scheme with crystal chandeliers and wall sconces, silk fabrics, plus a bathroom in floor-to-ceiling travertine slabs make for a lavish set of rooms.

"Very nice indeed," My father says as he takes in the suite.

I leave them to get settled before we have lunch alfresco in the seaside garden. A quick text to Leonie, and I find her with The Twins, Malcolm, Starr, and Haley seated on blankets in the grass near the lunch table.

"How was your flight?" I ask Starr since she traveled the farthest from Beverly Hills.

She smiles and her dimples pop in her lovely face. Malcolm certainly picked a beauty.

It always strikes me as funny how all of Leonie's girlfriends are so attractive, smart, and self-made multimillionaires. Even Blair who comes from a wealthy English family that owns a manufacturing company and Billie whose family are well-to-do Southern politicians. Given their status, neither of them has to be Lola's assistants; they love fashion and didn't want to follow in their families' footsteps.

But most of all, not a gold digger among them and not fazed by the men in their lives being multibillionaires. Well, aside from the gifts we happily bestow upon them…

"It was long and hard, but comfy on Malcolm's jet," Starr responds, winking at him.

He smirks and adds, "Yes, and rather palatable."

Leonie bursts out laughing, then starts to snort uncontrollably.

"What's so funny?"

We glance up to find Baz, Lola, and Harris behind us.

"Oh, just the rigors and demands of travel," Starr deadpans.

Malcolm sits back on his hands, all smug with a cocky grin on his face. The Alpha Dom took his carnal tastes to the skies for fifteen hours.

Sebastian snickers and Lola snorts.

"No comment..." Haley says, rolling her eyes, disgusted as usual with hearing about her brothers' sex lives, even as innuendos.

She glances down at her mobile and smiles. Then types a response at lightning speed. When she raises her head, her cheeks flush and her eyes shine. No longer wearing her glasses makes the dove gray orbs more expressive. Happy Haley, hmmm interesting.

"What's up, Baby Girl?" I ask, knowing the nickname drives her crazy.

Still in la-la land, Haley startles, then responds rushed, "Oh, uh... Callum's over in Sorrento."

When she doesn't continue, I prod her. He wants to take Haley to dinner. So I tell her he can come here if they want. He's more than welcome. They agree, and I arrange for the helicopter to pick him up in an hour.

As it turns out, my brothers and I think he could be an excellent match for our little sister. Callum proved himself during Labor Day weekend as a guy who's worthy of Haley, has his own fortune, and blends well with our family. We couldn't care less he's a Scottish duke. Baz hired his guy to conduct an extensive background check on Callum as soon as we met him while we were in Verbier for Christmas. Nothing in it caused concern.

Haley being with Callum and not with Lachlan sits better with Sebastian and with the rest of us. Baz can't get past his best friend with his younger sister. Baz had been suspicious since we were at Villa Sogno when he proposed to Lola. Then at our Labor Day party, he argued with Lach after he saw him in an intense conversation with Haley. It has strained things with the friends since.

My parents and in-laws appear. We gather around the table for a delicious lunch of flavorful local dishes prepared by the chef and served by the staff with wines from the villa's prized cellar.

The staff fell in love with Leonie the moment they saw her, so we kept them on after we bought the villa. Besides, they're familiar with it, and Lucien told us they're great.

Shortly after we finish eating, Callum touches down. Haley goes to greet him, and some time later they join us for Limoncello Gin Collins on the lawn furniture. Her lips appear swollen, and his eyes gleam.

Mmhmmm.

"How are things with you, Callum?" My father asks as he sips his digestif. "I read in the *Financial Times* renewable energy is on the rise for another year in a row for Scotland."

They get into a discussion on Callum's family's business, Graham Energy, Oil & Gas Company, based in Aberdeen, Scotland. His father still leads the company as CEO, but he's in the process of grooming Callum for the role in five years. His younger brother and sister hold positions, too.

The conversation flows easily with everyone's participation.

We grew up discussing business to prepare for joining our family's legacy. Balanced with volunteer work to help others and not to live as spoiled rich kids instilled in us by our mother, we're a well-rounded group. Again, having partners who are the same just adds more perspectives to the pot.I lean back in my chair and tuck Leonie under my arm, happy to relax with our family.

* * *

"THIS IS FANTASTIC! I agree we should have an opulent Edwardian-themed-*Gigi* party!"

Leonie and I finished giving a tour of the yacht to everyone, and Lola can't wait to plan the soiree.

They do their happy shimmy dance, then continue on to the bow where we'll have cocktails before Thanksgiving dinner begins.

The last few days have been full of swimming at our private beach or in the pool and excursions to the Blue Grotto, Monte Solaro, and Villa di Tiberio. The Blue Grotto thrilled The Twins when their laughter echoed inside of the water-filled cavern.

Leonie wanted to save *Gigi* for last as the highlight and setting for our Thanksgiving dinner as we cruise around Capri for three hours. We time it for cocktails at sunset and dinner by torchlight—electric since we don't want to risk damage to the boat.

We dress in semi-formal attire with the guys in suits and the women in dresses. The Twins wear shirt and shorts one-piece sets with socks that mimic shoes and outdo us all.

Once we're gathered at the bow with drinks in hand, my father leads us in expressing his thanks over the past year. Each of us takes a turn ending with me. I'm already emotional after Leonie's heartfelt words of gratitude for our lives no longer impacted by Delia and Antonio, and most of all for the safety of our sons.

Coming on the end of her touching speech and tears, I hold her close in my arms and address our family.

"Thanks can never express the depth of my feelings for all of you and others who are not present. Your love and support from the start of that fiasco to the joy of our wedding with the addition of my in-laws and the wonderful holidays we shared to the return of our sons mean more than you can imagine. Mom, Dad, all of our lives you raised us to be a close-knit clan. This past year proves you succeeded. I love you all beyond measure."

I lift my glass and proclaim, "Now let us enjoy this Thanksgiving dinner and here's to many, many more!"

"Hear, hear!!"

"Bravo, Roger! We love you, too!!"

"Happy Thanksgiving, everyone!!"

LEONIE

"*Mmm* hmmm... I made the appointment, *Mon Cœur*... Yes, yes, I'll call you right away. *Oui, je t'aime aussi.*"

Ugh...

I end Roger's call, drop my mobile, and rush from our bed to the bathroom, covering my mouth with my hands. I cannot believe I got food poisoning from the seafood dinner we ate last night. The dish must have had tainted shrimp.

Ughhh...

A queasy sensation came over me the moment I smelled it as I took the first bite. Never again will I ignore my senses and proceed to eat something regardless in my life! This is my third trip to the bathroom since I woke up this morning.

At first Roger insisted upon staying with me. But I know he has some important end-of-the-year meetings all day, and I won't cause him to miss any of them.

He relented after I agreed to go to the doctor, even though I told him the food poisoning just has to work its way out of my system. Given enough time, it should go away. But I promised Roger anyway.

Fortunately, Roger called Nanny Grace to come over earlier than usual. She's with The Twins. So I drag about getting showered and dressed. Then call my doctor's office. The next available appointment isn't until one in the afternoon.

Ughhhh…

I head down to the custom chef's kitchen—not that I use it for more than the basics, like boiling water—and fix some hot ginger tea. The smell is soothing and reminds me of the last time I drank copious amounts of iced lemon ginger tea. It was the only thing that kept the nausea at bay when I was pregnant with Rodolphe and Gaspard.

Merde! Mais non… I just had my period, and my birth control shot isn't due anytime soon.

As I stand staring out at the snow blanketing Paris below, my mind drifts to Verbier. Roger and I leave in a couple of weeks to celebrate our first wedding anniversary while The Twins stay with my parents. They'll bring them when they fly in the day before Christmas Eve, along with the rest of our family.

An entire year has passed. I smile as I reminisce about our Winter Wonderland Wedding. Roger made my fairytale dream come true, and every day since. I love him so very much!

Tears fill my eyes and my vision blurs.

Good grief. Get it together, Leonie!

For the moment, my stomach doesn't roil. I munch on a few crackers from the well-stocked pantry, as I go back upstairs to The Twins' five-room suite.

We expanded by making the original nursery with bathroom Rodolphe's bedroom and converting the two rooms next to it into a connecting playroom and a bedroom for Gaspard with his bathroom. At fifteen months, they need their own space. They'll continue to use their suite as they get older. So it's worth the effort.

"*Bonjour, mes beaux fils!*" I call to them as I walk into their playroom. "*Comment vas-tu aujourd'hui?*"

They're understanding French and English and get the gist of me saying good morning and asking how they're doing today.

I greet Nanny Grace, too. We read to them and play developmental games for a couple of hours. Then I give them kisses and go to my home office to check on some projects.

Hilarie Roux, my personal assistant, amazes me with her ability to keep track of all the details and my schedule given we have seven projects my division currently has in the works. But I should not expect any less from her, given Françoise helped to find Hilarie for me. Only the best will get past Roger's assistant!

The reminder alarm goes off on my mobile. I finish up the spreadsheet I'm working on and text Eric. He responds right away that he's in the garage ready for me to arrive. Then I go upstairs to tell The Twins goodbye.

As I ride in the back of the Rolls-Royce Phantom, a text message from Roger pops up. I smile as I read it.

Hey, babe. Eric texted to let me know you're on your way to the doctor (on time, I might add). Call when you find out what's wrong.. I love you.

Oui, Monsieur Steele. I love you more.

Fortunately, the wait isn't long at my doctor's office. The nurse checks my vitals and notes my temperature is slightly higher than normal. She takes my urine sample and leaves the exam room, saying the doctor will be in shortly.

I answer some emails while I wait. Then glance up when the door opens, and the doctor walks in with the nurse.

"Madame Steele, congratulations! You're pregnant!"

I sit on the exam table in shock.

When the doctor suggests I make an appointment with my OB-GYN, I snap to attention. After he assures me there's no mistake, I call Dr. Berger, who just so happens to have an appointment in twenty minutes.

While I put off Roger's texts stating the doctor had an emergency that delayed my appointment, Eric rushes me over. I ask Eric not to tell Roger I left the doctor's office or where we're headed. He understands and agrees with a smile.

Dr. Berger confirms my pregnancy of eighteen weeks, and the ultrasound shows one perfectly healthy baby. He gives me copies of the scan and anti-nausea medicine along with my prenatal pills.

I laugh and say see you next month!

My mobile rings as Eric opens the car door for me —Roger.

"Leonie, what did the doctor say?" He asks worriedly.

Roger still has two more meetings, so I tell him the doctor gave me medicine to stop the queasiness. Since it's the truth—albeit partially—I don't feel bad. When he gets home, I'll tell him everything.

"Hi, baby, how are you feeling now?"

I suppress a giggle at Roger's mention of "baby," and wrap my arms around his neck, flattening my body against his to give him a passionate kiss.

"Wow! That good, huh?" He chuckles and grinds his hips against me. "Well, I know what will make you feel even better, Pretty Kitty."

Putting my palm on his chest, I smile up at Roger, then step away. The gift wrapped with shiny silver paper and tied with a French Rose pink ribbon sits on the coffee table. I turn to Roger and beckon for him to sit down on the sofa.

He cocks his head to the side, but does as I ask.

I tuck my legs beneath me as I sit beside him. With a smile, I hand the box to Roger.

"Merry Early Christmas, *Mon Cœur*," I tell him softly.

Roger's eyebrows draw together as he looks at the gift, then at me. He holds it to his ear and shakes it.

I nudge his shoulder and nod for him to open it. Without him noticing, I slip my mobile from behind me and hit the video record button. I want to capture his reaction.

He removes the ribbon and ties it around my neck in a pussy cat bow. Then chuckles as he murmurs, "Here, Pretty Kitty, Kitty. Here."

Roger's laughter stops when he pushes the tissue paper aside to find the ultrasound scan image. His eyes widen and fly to mine as his mouth hangs open in muted surprise.

I fill the sudden void with, "Remember our night of fireworks during Labor Day weekend, *Mon Cœur*? Well, all those hours of passionate lovemaking resulted in my pregnancy. We're having a baby girl! *Félicitations, Papa!*"

The most beatific smile spreads across Roger's face.

My heart swells with love for my man. Then races when he jumps off the couch with a whoop and scoops me into his arms.

Between kisses, he buries his face in my hair, murmuring words of love.

"And how are you, my love? What did Dr. Berger say?" Roger asks as he holds me aloft with his eyes full of concern.

It reminds me of his words when we first learned of my pregnancy with The Twins and my mother's experiences scared me.

"Leonie, understand me clearly. If for any reason I have to choose between you and this baby or any other, I choose you always. You mean everything to me. We can try for another baby, or we can adopt a baby in need of a wonderful home. But you... You are irreplaceable, my love. Call me selfish. But I will not live without you, Leonie."

I love Roger with all of my heart and can understand his concern. But we're good.

"Our baby and I are perfectly healthy. The nausea comes from morning sickness, nothing more. So, he really gave me the medication along with my prenatal pills," I answer smiling happily. "My regular physician told me I'm pregnant based on the urine test results. Dr. Berger confirmed eighteen weeks. Right around Labor Day. She'll be born mid-May next year!"

Roger places me on my feet and drops to his knees. He lifts the hem of my pink cashmere maxi lounge dress to kiss my belly. His lips move as he whispers to our daughter.

I stroke his silky hair, massaging his scalp as I continue to record him.

"What are you saying to our Baby Girl, *Mon Cœur*?" I ask, expecting sweet words of love and joy.

"I told her I love her and can't wait to hold her in my arms," He responds, then his mouth moves lower to brush against my bare mons and slit. "Then I told her I am going to make love to her *Maman*. Right. Now."

. . .

Roger

Leonie's giggles morph into moans as I grip her round ass cheek with one hand and slip the fingers of my other inside the crotch of her pink lacy briefs.

She's gone all out with the little girl pink.

Fuck, I love my woman!

All day I found it strange Leonie circumvented my text messages and phone calls. Eric was even mum about their whereabouts. If it weren't for my end-of-the-year meetings and me wanting to clear my schedule so we can leave earlier for Verbier, I would have used the tracker app to find her.

Now I know why.

What's crazy is me being so distracted I hadn't noticed the subtle changes in Leonie's body: her nipples a deeper shade of chocolate and more sensitive to my caresses; the swell to her normally flat belly; how brightly her eyes and skin glow. The sudden nausea should have clued both of us in.

My heart races as joy pumps through me. Another baby and so soon! Rodolphe and Gaspard will turn fifteen months in a couple of weeks. They'll be just shy of two years old when Leonie gives birth to our Baby Girl.

I hadn't wanted to mention my desire for more children since Leonie's fearful of her mother's miscarriages and the pain from their losses. Although The Twins satisfy me plenty, I'd love to have a daughter.

And now I will! What a blessing just in time for Christmas! I give a silent prayer.

Then, turn my attention to the task well in hand— fucking Leonie until she's hoarse from screaming my name. Hell... I may even put another baby inside of her womb! That's how hard I'm going to give it to her.

My tongue slides along her moist slit, lapping at her

pussy juices. The enticing scent of her arousal fills my nostrils, and I inhale deeply. Delicious.

Leonie's legs quiver as she tugs on my hair.

The bite of pain caused by her pleasure hardens my cock against the zipper of my trousers painfully. I put her thigh onto my shoulder and lower my grip to hold the other one in place. Then rip her panties off.

Opened up to me, I devour her pussy.

"Rogeeerrr... Ahhh... Ahhh... Fuck!" Leonie cries as she tosses her head back, gripping my hair to ride my face through her orgasm. "Mmmmmm... so good, *Amoureux...*"

I run the flat of my tongue from her puckered back hole past her slick folds to her swollen clit, claiming every drop of her pussy juices. Her clit gets special attention as I flick the tip of my tongue at it, then wrap it around the engorged nub to tug at it.

Leonie convulses and bends over my head as a second orgasm takes ahold of her. She whimpers as she pants through the waves of pleasure. A thud to the floor, and I notice her mobile fell.

I wipe my wet mouth and chin on her inner thigh and rise to my full height, bringing her to stand on jelly knees.

"Off!" I command, as I lift the dress over her head to bare her to me completely.

Leonie scrambles to get her arms and head through the holes and tosses the garment to the floor. She glances up at me in expectation of my next move. She senses I'm in one of my controlling moods.

I shrug out of my jacket, and eagerly she reaches to undo my tie and shirt buttons. Finally, I free my turgid length from the confining trousers, then stroke it as I stare at my woman.

Leonie gracefully drops to her knees and reaches for my cock.

"No," I say, lifting her back up. "I want to feel your tight, soaked pussy wrapped around my dick, Pretty Kitty. Not that hot little mouth of yours. At least not now..."

Leonie shudders as a frisson of erotic energy sweeps through her at my passionate dominance.

I may not be a full Dom, but I am a demanding Alpha male. Leonie's no sub, but she likes for me to control her in our sex lives. And now is no exception. The caveman comes to the forefront.

Her pupils dilate further as I lead her to the sofa. A soft cry comes from her lips when I command her on her knees spread wide and her hands on the back of the sofa. Once in position, Leonie peeks at me from over her shoulder, her long hair skims her ass. With hooded eyes, she scans my body from head to toe, returning to my fat cock gripped in my fist. Slowly, she licks her lips.

And I'm on her.

One sizable hand grips her hip while the other lines my dick with her pussy.

"*Oh! Baise moi! Oooh!*" She screams when I plunge into her tight channel in one unyielding thrust. "Fuuuck! You're... so... big... Ooohhh!"

My hips take on a mind of their own as I drill Leonie into the sofa repeatedly.

Her head lolls forward, and she pants.

"You are mine. Mine to fuck and mine to give me babies. You know that, do you not, Pretty Kitty?" I demand driving up onto my toes to go deeper within Leonie's core.

The angle hits her G-spot to make her wail, and her nails to dig into the silk fabric. Her pussy walls flutter up and down my dick as she writhes against me through another orgasm.

I use her curvy hips as leverage to piston her body back and forth on my cock. Leonie feels so good I close my eyes and hum as my orgasm starts at my toes and runs up the backs of my thighs. The zing at the base of my spine shoots to my heavy balls as they slap against Leonie's clit.

As much as I want to keep going to increase our pleasure, my body demands release.

I glide my fingers along Leonie's spine to place one hand on her neck to lower her torso parallel to the sofa seat, opening up the length of her channel even more.

Leaning over Leonie, I shift my hold around to her throat and growl in her ear, "Tell me how much you get off from my giant dick wrecking your tight pussy, Pretty Kitty."

Leonie mewls as another climax takes over her. She arches her back like a good little pet and takes me deeper.

In a voice hoarse from her screams, Leonie moans, "Too much to express, *Amoureux*!"

With a dark chuckle, I speed up my thrusts as I buck against her. Our sweaty bodies slip and slide as our sensual scent surrounds us.

Leonie's strangled cry from another climax triggers my release.

I wrap my arms around her waist and pound into her as I roar through my mind-blowing orgasm.

"FUUUCK!!!!"

We collapse to the sofa. I'm careful to hold my weight off Leonie and pull her to lie in front of me as my cock slips from her pussy, dripping with our combined essence.

Leonie purrs as we spoon together, and I pull the oversized cashmere throw around us.

"Thank you for my Baby Girl, sweetheart. I love you

both and our sons more than you can imagine," I murmur against her damp hair.

"I love you, too, *Mon Cœur*. So, so very much…" Leonie rasps as she falls asleep.

While her breathing evens out, I think about how so, so very lucky I am to have her as my wife, lover, and mother of my children.

This Christmas will be even more special than the last.

ROGER

"*I*'m so glad we're back, *Mon Cœur*! The village is so enchanting with the snow falling and the Swiss Alps in the background. It seems like we're inside of a snow globe just shaken with the flakes falling all around us gently!"

Leonie exclaims as we drive through Verbier towards our *Chalet de la Joie*.

I glance at her and smile at her excitement. She's been pumping her favorite Christmas songs all week, even through the jet's sound system on the way here.

She turns to me and sings how all she wants for Christmas is me. Her eyes sparkle with golden flecks as she bounces in her seat, clapping her hands in sheer delight.

Since we learned about Leonie's pregnancy, all the signs are obvious to me now. I place my hand on her baby bump —single, now that we're only having a girl—and rub it lovingly. Mine!

Nothing compares to a man knowing he made his mate

pregnant with his seed in her fertile womb. I haven't stopped grinning in weeks.

During a video conference with Malcolm, he asked me why I was all goofy. But I didn't tell him since Leonie and I choose to wait until everyone gathers at the chalet. They're in for a big surprise!

She's twenty weeks along. So Dr. Berger assures us we're in the clear when I insisted upon a follow-up appointment where I was present to hear all the details for myself. What a relief it is for us to know.

My mission to complete all of my work early redoubled. Now we're here three days before our anniversary. One year and two plus babies. We couldn't get any busier even if we tried!

"Roger, I'm starving! Do you think we can stop by that chocolate shop off Place Centrale and get some of those truffles and the delicious hot cocoa? Oh, and some chocolate chip scones?"

I chuckle at Leonie's request. Yup, she's preggie all right.

"Sure, babe, whatever you want," I respond as I flick the signal to turn right for the shop. "But don't you want to eat some actual food, too? The chef stocked the pantry with your favorites and can come by to fix something for you real quick."

Leonie ponders my suggestion, then brightens as she faces me.

"How about we get the chocolate, then she can cook some steaks frites... Or chicken paillard? *Non, non...* French onion soup! Yummy, yummy for my tummy, tummy!" She says rubbing her belly and smacking her lips.

I crack up, and we call the chef to put in Leonie's smorgasbord. Why pick only one when she can have it all?

As Lola once wisely said, *"Happy wife, happy life..."*

* * *

FOLLOWING the directions Leonie left for me, I step out of the bathroom from a shower wrapped in my Loro Piana cashmere robe.

My eyes scan our bedroom. It's lit by dozens of white candles of all shapes and sizes placed around the space. A roaring fire makes it toasty, filling the air with the fragrant scent of pine.

A heated smile crosses my face when I spot Leonie lying on her back naked on top of the large faux-fur blanket before the stone fireplace. Her naked skin glows in the ambient red and orange light.

When she senses my presence, Leonie bows her back and cups her fuller breasts, kneading them and plucking the beaded nipples. Her head thrown back as she moans deep in her throat.

Fuck. Me.

My cock tents the robe, pushing past the opening. Like a divining rod, it seeks out her wet, warm pussy. I shed the robe with a quickness and stalk over to her. My eager dick bobs up and down in agreement.

"*Joyeux Anniversaire, Amoureux,*" Leonie purrs seductively, her eyes at half-mast.

As she licks her plump lower lip, she widens her bent knees. Fully on display for my viewing pleasure, her juicy pussy glistens and her puckered hole winks at me.

I sink down between Leonie's welcoming thighs, placing my hands on her knees. Then I bend over her so her pebbled nipples graze my hard chest.

"Happy Anniversary, Mrs. Steele" I croon against her luscious lips.

Leonie moans when I nip them and nudge my dick at

her already slippery folds. Then we both groan when I sink myself inside her slowly.

I still to allow her body to accommodate my girth and deepen our kiss. Then shift my hips for long and even strokes, going further with each movement.

On a sigh, I trail open-mouthed kisses along Leonie's neck down to her soft mounds. My lips latch onto her sensitized nipple and suckle strongly until she mewls and writhes beneath me, her hand pushing my head closer to her bosom.

My mouth glides across the hollow between her breasts to reach the other turgid nipple. Sucking hard on the bud until she squirms some more.

Leonie cries out and lifts her hips to meet my thrusts as I change to slow, shallow strokes. She wants it fast and deep.

But not tonight. No pounding into her. Tonight I make sweet love to my wife.

I quiet Leonie with a toe-curling kiss as I continue to rock into her hot, wet pussy in a gentle, steady rhythm. Her small hands clutch my thick biceps while her full breasts flatten between us and her pelvis cradles mine. Our legs intertwine to bring us as close as possible intimately.

We continue to lose ourselves in the other as our climaxes build with the heat of our bodies, now warmer than the blazing fire beside us.

Leonie gasps as her pussy clamps on my cock, sending an electric current up my length and through my body, zipping to my limbs. When her walls flutter and she begs for more, I increase my pace to thrust faster and deeper.

"Cum with me, baby! Cum hard with me now!" I thrum in her ear.

Leonie bucks, then tightens all around me as her orgasm overtakes her.

The soft cries make my dick throb and pulse as I unleash a torrent of jizz deep into her womb.

Together we ride out our pleasure with kisses and words of love forever.

Later, after we stoke our desires, Leonie sits between my legs as we soak in the clawfoot tub. We stare out the window that faces the massive snow-covered Swiss peaks. The sound of more Christmas songs plays in the background softly as the fire crackles in the bathroom side of the hearth.

"We should name her Daphne Beaulieu Steele," Leonie says as she runs her fingertips along my forearms around her waist. "Daphne means laurel tree and Beaulieu lovely place, like the trees around *Le Beaulieu Manoir*."

She shifts to glance back at me and quirks her elegantly arched eyebrow.

"What do you think?" She asks.

I squeeze her and kiss her forehead.

"Sounds good to me, my love," I respond. "Feminine and strong as steel, just like her *Maman Lionne*."

Leonie grins and nuzzles into my chest.

"Thank you, *Chéri*," she says, kissing my pecs.

I place a kiss atop her head, and we sit a few moments more before we climb out and go to bed.

Tomorrow we'll celebrate our news with our family.

* * *

"Hey, hey, hey! The gang's all here!! Merry Christmas Eve!"

Leonie and I laugh as Harris makes his way through the front door after Sebastian and Lola, arms laden with gifts. We tease he looks like a young Santa Claus.

He rejoins with, "A sexy AF one, no doubt! And no last-minute presents for me, Roger dear! Let's see if you get coal in your stocking this year…"

Malcolm and Starr enter behind him, and the girls hug while Malcolm and I bro hug.

"Good to see you, man!" I tell him.

"Still looking goofy, bro!" He teases.

Haley walks in looking glum, and I pull her into a bear hug, lifting her off her feet.

Leonie mentioned Haley was going through some relationship issues, so I know I had to cheer my baby sister up posthaste.

"You better have brought your, A game or I'm going to leave you in the powder tomorrow morning for our Christmas Day run!" I tease her. "Don't blame me when your googles get covered in snow!"

Haley rolls her eyes and retorts, "Even on my worse day, I can outrace you, Roger!"

Guy and Josy come in carrying The Twins.

Leonie and I scoop them up and hold them close. These past few days are the longest we've been apart from them. They laugh at our overzealous kisses and pat our faces with their chubby hands.

My parents are the last to enter, and we greet them warmly.

"This tree is even bigger than last year's," my mother says, smiling as she takes a glass of hot mulled wine. "I love the new decorations!"

Everyone makes their way to their suites while Leonie and I tend to The Twins.

"When should we tell them?" She asks once we're in the nursery.

I think about it for a moment as I wrangle Gaspard out of his snowsuit.

"After we eat dinner and exchange gifts. She'll be another present," I respond, tickling him on his tummy when his shirt lifts.

I still can't believe we have another baby on the way and a girl to boot!

Leonie says we should get a dog so The Twins get used to another being in our home that will share our love.

I told her I don't know. But really have two female Bichon Frise puppies I'll give to her and to The Twins as their presents for tonight. The little balls of white fluff stole my heart when the Parisian breeder sent photos and when I met them last week. They came along with my parents and wait with Nanny Grace in her suite of rooms above the garage.

We head back downstairs to the dining room where Josy chats with the chef she favored about tonight's dinner. It's like last year's in honor of the French tradition of le *Réveillon de Noël* for the Christmas meal.

Leonie made requests for some of her favorites since her pregnancy urges dictate her meal choices these days. The chef was more than happy to oblige her and promised to follow Dr. Berger's recommendations for foods.

We relish in each other's company as we dine on fine dishes and excellent wines. The conversation flows easily.

No one notices Leonie drinks iced lemon ginger tea since it's in a crystal glass like everyone else's wine. She smiles secretly at me throughout our dinner.

Once we're gathered in the great room and exchanged our first gifts as our tradition for Christmas Eve, I stand and pull Leonie to her feet with me. The puppies scamper around our feet, playing with a toy.

"Well everyone, Leonie and I have some news to share

with you," I start gazing from one smiling face to the other before my eyes turn to my wife's gorgeous face.

"We're twenty weeks pregnant with a baby girl!!" She announces, grinning like the Cheshire Cat.

Everyone whoops and hollers.

"Congratulations!!"

"*Oh, Mon Dieu!*"

"Awesome news, Roger and Leonie!!"

"*Fantastique, Mon Trésor!*"

When the well-wishing ends, Sebastian clears his throat and stands, too.

"Roger and Leonie, Lola and I are so thrilled for you! Once again you'll make us an aunt and an uncle—the most favorites, of course," he pauses to pull Lola into his side. "And we will make you an aunt and uncle, too. The most favorite is up to the others."

At first everyone smiles and nods. Then the room erupts when we realize what he means.

He and Lola are expecting a baby, too!

"We're twenty weeks, too!" Lola gushes as she rubs her belly covered by an oversized sweater. "Can you believe it, BFF?!"

"Oh, Lola, Sebastian! We're so happy for you, too!!" Leonie exclaims as she hugs her bestie and they start to cry.

Undoubtedly they remember Lola being upset this time last year as she sat in the windowed walkway in the early morning debating having children with Baz then or later.

Now here we are a year later, and we're both expecting. I knew this Christmas was going to be even more special than the last!

The doorbell chimes, and my mother waves me off as she heads to the entryway to answer. Everyone is present, so I'm not sure who it could be.

I glance down at Leonie, and she shrugs her shoulders.

My mother returns to the great room with Lachlan behind her. She glances at Haley questioningly, then at Sebastian worriedly.

Lachlan strides right in and stops in front of Haley, clasping her hands in his. Without his emerald green eyes leaving her dove gray ones, he addresses my father and Baz.

"No disrespect, Uncle Morgan. We're like brothers, Sebastian. But Haley is mine, and I won't go another day without her for anyone."

Silence descends on the great room. Talk about the other shoe drops, rather the third...

* * *

Roger & Leonie's Story Concludes for Now...

Turn the page for the Steele Family, Author's Note, and a Preview of *A Trilogy of Desires Malcolm & Starr Parts I-III*

THE STEELE FAMILY

STEELE INTERNATIONAL, INC

Multigenerational, multibillion-dollar business luxury real estate development and management corporation

Headquarters & Family's Primary Residences:

The STEELE Tower, New York City

A modern, gray-tinted glass fifty-seven story mixed-use skyscraper on southwest corner of Fifty-Seventh Street and Fifth Avenue within Billionaires' Row

Global Offices:

- The United States of America (New York City, New Jersey, Chicago, California, Miami, Las

Vegas)
- The Caribbean (St. Maarten, St. Barth's, St. Lucia)
- The French & Italian Rivieras (Nice, Cannes, Positano, Capri)
- Monaco (Monte Carlo)
- The United Arab Emirates (Abu Dhabi, Dubai)

STEELE FOUNDATION: A STRONG AND SUPPORTIVE HOUSE

Builds and manages attractive, affordable housing for urban, lower-income families

Available for download at **bit.ly/STEELEFamily**

Author's Note

Thank you for reading Parts I-III of Roger and Leonie's sexy, sizzling romance! I hope that you enjoyed the Happy For Now conclusion of their passionate love affair. If so, I'd love to hear your thoughts, please share a review at **http://bit.ly/CLBooksSI3-5Review** and tell your friends.

Wow! *Roger and Leonie's story* gave lots of hints at what's happening with the Steele clan in the Desires Series!

Click below for the answers to one steamy story featuring thrill-seeking couple Alpha Dom Malcolm and Independent Woman Starr in their sizzling trilogy:

A Trilogy of Desires Malcolm & Starr Parts I-III

It's never too late to start the Desires Series at the beginning. So catch up on the family's scorching, toe-curling trysts.

At **CharmaineLouise.com** take the *Four types of lovers. Which are you?* **Quiz** to match your Sexy Fantasy: sub, Voyeur, Dominatrix, or Dominatrix sub Switch.

Follow me on social media including my CLBooks Coterie Fan Club below or on your favorite channels below and subscribe to my newsletter at **bit.ly/CLBooksNewsletter** for a **Free Book**.

Fulfill Your Desires.

xoxo

Charmaine Louise

BB bookbub.com/authors/charmaine-louise-shelton

f facebook.com/CharmaineLouiseBooks

instagram.com/charmainelouisebooks

g goodreads.com/charmainelouisebooks

COMING NEXT: A TRILOGY OF DESIRES MALCOLM & STARR PARTS I-III

1 *8 Years Ago*

STARR — 13, Beverly Hills, CA

"—YEAH, right! What makes that loser nerd think anyone wants to go to her corny birthday party?"

"Right! And with her weird hippie parents, too! What'll she have there? Unicorns and rainbows?!"

"Did you get a glimpse of her face when we told her we'd go? She grinned ear to ear with happiness braces on full blast... SIKE!"

"With a name like Starr, she's not very bright, is she?"

"That's the problem she thinks she's so smart, knows more than the rest of us—"

My mind reels as their voices fade out behind the closing

bathroom door. I hug my knees to my chest while I rock on the toilet's lid. Tears stream down my heated cheeks, blurring my vision.

I don't need to see clearly to know the voices of Sally, Laura, Gail, Connie, and Jessica—the It Girls of Beverly Hills Junior High School. I could envision Sally, their leader tossing her silky blonde hair over her shoulder as she mimed my glasses. Gail, her main sidekick would have fluffed her curly afro to copy my naturally curly hair.

Obviously, I'm not so smart to have fallen for their easy yeses to attend my thirteenth birthday party this weekend. The It Girls at my simple backyard barbecue? Too good to be true.

For a moment I thought their teasing ways were over since we're in the seventh grade now. Who knew they'd carry over their mean-girl antics from fifth and sixth grades to a new school?

Duh!

A drawn-out sigh slips from my lips when I tilt my head back to stare at the ceiling, hoping to stop the flow of my tears. I'm so tired of them being so nasty to me. And for no reason!

Sure, I like to excel in my classes, and I answer the teachers' questions happily—and correctly. But that doesn't make me a nerd. Just interested in my schoolwork.

The whole braces thing is messed up too. I got them this past summer and grew five inches. So along with a mouth full of metal, thick-lensed glasses, and unruly curls, I tower over the other girls in our class.

Gawky much?!

It was bad enough they teased me ruthlessly about my "hippie" parents, clothes, and crystals in elementary school.

So what if my parents changed their names from Jordan

and Belinda to Peace and Sun years before I was even born?! I like my name, Starr Knight. And doggone it, I am bright, and I love my parents—hippies and all!

They're brilliant environmental law attorneys who take on the most challenging cases against big businesses and win billions! The law firm—Knight & Knight LLP—my parents founded years ago after they met at a music festival while at Stanford Law School ranks in the top five of the United States. With offices in LA, Seattle, Denver, Chicago, Houston, New Orleans, Miami, New York City to represent cases in the top environmentally focused cities. They may be hippies, but they're sharks in the courtroom.

And so am I!

After a sniffle, I rise, shake out my vintage, glittery matchstick midi skirt so the layers fall to my Doc Martens' eight-eye, patent leather boots on a whisper. I smooth my off-the-shoulder ruffle top over the white camisole before I grab my well-worn leather crossbody bag.

Loose tendrils of curls fall over my eyes as I bend over. I sweep them back into the big bun at the nape of my neck with a resigned huff as my rose quartz pendant slips along its leather cord. Determined, I straighten my spine and leave the bathroom.

Time to face the music on the school bus ride home.

"Hi, sweetheart, how was school?"

I lift my head from my notebook and smile at my mother. We look exactly alike. Sorrel brown eyes full of love as she peers at me. Smooth chestnut-colored skin glows from healthy eating and regular exercise. Long, curly, dark brown hair pulled up in a topknot. Dimples highlight her sculpted cheekbones when she returns my smile. She's a beautiful woman in her late thirties.

"History class was interesting, and I loved art," I answer

as I stand three inches taller than her petite feet-foot-three-inch frame. "But the crew siked me into believing they were coming to my birthday party."

I raise my hand when she speaks. A scowl settles on her pretty face.

"Hey, no worries. 'Be equally thankful for what you perceive to be good and for what you perceive as bad. It all happens for a reason. Either way, you don't let it disturb your inner peace. Strive for tranquility no matter the outer circumstances.' Right?" I ask, reminding my mother of her favorite yogic piece of advice.

She cups my face and beams at me.

"Absolutely, Starr!" My mother exclaims.

"What's the 'absolutely' for?"

We turn to see my father stride into the room. His baritone voice booms around us.

I get my height from him being six feet, five inches. He's opposite of my mom and me, with his obsidian eyes and pecan-colored skin. Equally fit and health conscious, he exudes power at forty-one. He's renowned for his command of the boardroom or the courtroom if negotiations reach that extent.

"A bit of a misunderstanding about my party. But no worries!" I respond as I give him a hug.

It's nearly dinnertime, and they make a point of being home as a family each night if possible. Otherwise the chef makes a meal for me.

"Well, perhaps your gift will make up for it," my father says as his eyes twinkle. "How about you open it early?"

With a shriek, I grasp the envelope and rip it open. An itinerary for a two-week stay at an ashram in Rishikesh, India, the world capital for studying yoga and meditation rests in my hands.

I never thought my parents heard me rambling about the center for spiritual studies a few months ago when I found it online.

Another of their traits I inherited is their focus on well-being. Whenever I have encounters with the crew, I practice breathing exercises to brush off their meanness. It takes the focus away from them and brings it back to me, keeping me centered and at peace.

I whoop and throw my arms around my father, then my mother. Yup, hippies and all, I'd have them no other way!

MALCOLM — *15, Southampton Village, NY*

"OH SHIT! What the hell is that on your back, Malcolm?! It better not be real, bro!"

My head whips around, my mouth twisted as I glare at my older brother—older than my fifteen by two years barely.

Since we're so close in age, everyone confuses me with him. We share the Steele clan traits of wavy ebony hair and dove gray eyes. Our olive-colored skin tanned further by the bright sun of Southampton Village, where our family's compound spans for a mile along our private beach.

Baz has a few inches on my six-foot-frame, so I have to look up at him.

But I don't look up *to* him. Hell nah!

He's Mister Perfect. The supposed leader of the Steele siblings. A role he's taken upon himself since forever. That's cool for Roger who's fourteen and the fraternal twins Harris and Haley at eleven. They freaking idolize Baz.

Me? Not so much. I refuse to be in Sebastian's shadow. I

make my own way and don't need his interference in my life. My identity is my own. Screw looking alike.

"Oh, screw you, Sebastian! You're not my father! Back off, *bro*!!" I snarl viciously as my nostrils flare and my face reddens.

I storm off from the party we're having on the beach, sick and tired of his crap. I push past the others ranging from my age to twenties.

Of course it's a crowd. Everyone wants to be around the Steeles. Our multibillion-dollar family has deep roots in New York City with our multigenerational luxury real estate development and management company based out of The STEELE Tower.

Even though it's the summer and we're out in the Hamptons for the weekend, each of us interns at the company. Come Monday, we'll be on Fifty-seventh Street and Fifth Avenue in the heart of Billionaires' Row at our respective divisions, learning our family's business from the ground up.

We have our mother to thank for "not being spoiled rich kids who only lounge around the pool all day." Shelley is a native New Yorker who worked as a shopgirl in one of STEELE's retail spaces. She met our father Morgan when he was on a business call to the store. At the time he was President of the Retail Properties Division and our grandfather was the CEO. Now, our Dad is top dog.

Baz assumes he's next in line, so he runs around barking orders at the rest of us.

Well, to hell with that!

I want no parts of STEELE International, Inc. I plan to start my own company for extreme sports lovers like me. Baz can have it all—Favorite Son and future CEO. I'll continue on as the second son; the rebel; the bad boy billionaire playboy of the family. And billions it will be too. Those I make on my own, not handed to me. Thank you very much!

Who the hell does he think he is telling me how to behave and what to do constantly?! He needs to get off my back already, literally.

That's why I got my tattoo. The wings on my back symbolize freedom from family constraints and the flying as I speed along on my bikes. After I won my latest motocross race, I memorialized it forever in ink. The tattoo artist didn't give me any flack since my height and attitude make me appear older than fifteen. Plus, I flirted with her, then backed it up once she completed my tat. She did a damn good job, and I thanked her royally.

So Baz can shut up with his nagging.

I need to feel the wind in my face to cool down. A quick walk to the garage and I'm astride one of my KTMs, ready to hit the dirt trails outside of the ritzy town. Just as I lift my helmet—I may be a rebel who takes risks, but I value my life —a movement to my left catches my attention.

Damn. Belinda Crane.

Belinda *Baz's Girlfriend* Crane, to be exact.

By her expression, she's not thinking of Big Brother right now. Nor does she mistake me for him. Nope. That heat is all for me.

She twirls a strand of her long silky red hair between her delicate fingers as her eyes travel from my boots to my leather-clad muscular thighs and chest to my smirking mouth. When green meets gray, the lust rolls through us in waves.

I may be fifteen, but this isn't my first rodeo, nor will

this be my first ride of this little filly. Poor Baz has no clue. Yeah, height and attitude make all the difference in life.

Belinda sashays over to me, her grip-worthy hips sway, making the strings of her white bikini dance. The round mounds of her tits bounce with each step. Her hooded eyes never leave my face, but my eyes travel the curves of her luscious body. She's a true redhead.

"I love your tattoo, Malcolm... A lot," Belinda says breathlessly as her fingertips skim over my back from shoulder to shoulder, sparks reach through the leather to make my cock jump to attention.

"Do you now, B.?" I smirk.

She nods and licks her full glossy lips.

My eyes dart to them, and I chuckle.

The first time her little pink tongue wrapped around my hardness, I nearly came before she even started blowing me.

I've learned more control since last winter's break. And I plan to use it.

"I'm going for a ride. You wanna cum?" I ask, not missing she picked up on my word choice when her pale cheeks flush bright red.

A quirk of my eyebrow has her nodding and scurrying to hop behind me. The warm, wet folds of her pussy press against my ass.

Yeah, I can't wait to bury my thick ten inches balls deep in her greedy snatch.

The purr of the engine is a precursor to the purrs I'll have Belinda moaning as soon as I get her writhing beneath me.

At times, it's good to be a Steele.

But on my terms.

***

Click the Link Below or visit books2read.com/u/4X6dz6 for Your Copy

A Trilogy of Desires Malcolm & Starr Parts I-III

STEELE International, Inc.
A Billionaires Romance Series Book 7

Capture My Desires Malcolm & Starr Part I

Click on the link below or visit books2read.com/u/bPgG2r
to get your copy.

Capture My Desires Malcolm & Starr Part I

Books in the Series:

Discover My Desires Sebastian & Lola Prequel
(Available Exclusively to Subscribers)

Fulfill My Desires Sebastian & Lola Part I

Heighten My Desires Sebastian & Lola Part II

Ignite My Desires Roger & Leonie Part I

Stoke My Desires Roger & Leonie Part II

Justify My Desires Roger & Leonie Part III

Deepen My Desires Sebastian & Lola Part III

Capture My Desires Malcolm & Starr Part I

Embrace My Desires Malcolm & Starr Part II

Cherish My Desires Malcolm & Starr Part III

A Trilogy of Desires Sebastian & Lola Parts I-III

A Trilogy of Desires Roger & Leonie Parts I-III

A Trilogy of Desires Malcolm & Starr Parts I-III

Series Extras

Series Playlist

WELCOME TO CHARMAINELOUISE — THE SENSUAL LIFESTYLE

GLITZY. GLAMOROUS. STEAMY.

CharmaineLouise New York, Inc. invites you to indulge in *The Sensual Lifestyle* through **CharmaineLouise Books** and **CharmaineLouise Intimates**. CLBrands immerse you in *Sexy Fantasies* with CLBooks contemporary romance novels and give you *Sexy Under Things & Loungewear* with CLIntimates.

Charmaine Louise Shelton the Founder, CEO & Author of CLNY loves all things classic, elegant, feminine, and of course with an erotic edge! Favorite outfit of choice is a cashmere cardigan, leather pencil skirt, and seamed silk stockings with stiletto heels. Sexy Fantasy Type: sub with a dash of Voyeur. When not writing and designing, Charmaine Louise travels and spends time with her Maltese buddies, ZIGGY and Jynger.

CharmaineLouise — *The Sensual Lifestyle*

~ Visit online at **CharmaineLouise.com**

~ Subscribe to **CharmaineLouise Newsletter**

~ Find us on Facebook **@CharmaineLouiseNewYork**

~ Instagram **@CharLouNY**

CharmaineLouise Books *Sexy Fantasies* launched summer 2020. Sizzling, contemporary romance with your soon-to-be favorite Alpha Doms, Powerful Billionaires, and the women they lust after and love for second chances, insta-love, enemies-to-lovers, and more.

Want to chat it up and share your thoughts with other CLBooks Lovers? Read our blog, join our CharmaineLouise Books Coterie Fan Club and follow us on my author pages and social media to be in the know about the book release dates, exclusive content, giveaways, contests, and more!

~ **Purchase your eBook and paperback novels from my Author Page by clicking here!**

~ Read and subscribe to our blog *The World of Sex*

~ Connect on **Amazon Author Page**

~ **Goodreads Author Profile**

~ **BookBub Author Profile**

CharmaineLouise Intimates *Sexy Under Things & Loungewear* debuted in 2003. Inspired by the sensuous sirens and sylph swans of the past and present, the hand crochet cashmere and silk collections are for the sexy: hence, the line names Ginger — Bombshell; Diana — Showstopper; Jackie — Timeless; Lena — Classic. Also known as The Movie-Star from Gilligan's Island; Ms. Ross The Boss; Mrs. Kennedy Onassis; Ms. Horne.

Do you thrive on seduction and being sexy lounging at home? Read our blog and follow us on social media to receive the tips, the latest additions to the collections, private sales, and more!

~ Read and subscribe to our blog *The Art of Seduction*

~ Find us on Facebook **@CharmaineLousieIntimates**

~ Instagram **@CharmaineLouiseIntimates**

Fulfill Your Desires.